What Readers A about *The Gate Se...*

"The farther I read, the more amazed I became at the depth and scope of the book! I read only small portions at a time so that I would not read it superficially. It deserves far better than that. It often brought tears to my eyes."

POULSBO, WASHINGTON

"The only other novel I have read with captive interest in recent years is *In His Steps* by Charles M. Sheldon. I highly recommend your book—as well as Sheldon's. They are both books that move the Spirit to touch the soul."

EDGAR, WISCONSIN

"I long to see that kind of fellowship...I felt as if I were right there among them."

SONORA, CALIFORNIA

"My mom has read your book about ten times...It is her favourite book of all time!"

KELOWNA, BRITISH COLUMBIA

"I laughed, cried, and thanked God for the biblical insights woven through the text and the experiences of the characters."

NEWMARKET, ONTARIO

"I don't know how many times I had to stop reading to blow my nose and dry my eyes. I so identified with your writing. I realized today, when I finished my second reading, that I had to let you know how much the book has meant to me. I wish I'd had it to read twenty years ago. I'm sure it would have given fresh direction to my ministry."

WIARTON, ONTARIO

"Thank you for giving me hope that true Christians really do exist."

GUELPH, ONTARIO

"I became so engrossed in the book that when I awoke at 3:00 A.M. I stayed up reading it. I am now reading it for the second time."

CASINO, NEW SOUTH WALES, AUSTRALIA

"Few books capture my heart, but I soon realized that this book addresses an issue which we have wrestled with for a long time...This story of a group of spiritually hungry and searching individuals parallels our own."

BURLINGTON, ONTARIO

"I read with great pleasure at 33,000 feet on a recent business trip. As if I weren't already at a sufficiently high altitude, I must tell you that your writing lifted me higher still…Not only did you describe an era which seemed idyllic and now sadly lost, but you moved beyond that to describe a people struggling for spiritual purity and dedication. I was informed, moved, challenged, shamed, and inspired. As a fellow author, I greatly admire your gift of writing."

NASHVILLE, TENNESSEE

"Reading the book has, I think, been one way among others that the Holy Spirit has striven to open my eyes and make me more aware of what God would like in my relationship with Him. I was amazed at the things I had never completely grasped before and so thankful for the truth and clarity of them in the book."

FRIONA, TEXAS

"The story is 'atmospheric' and sets the scene well. It's not hard to imagine the characters."

PENARTH, WALES, GREAT BRITAIN

"What a wonderful story! I felt teary eyed at the finish…reflecting on what I had read, wishing for more. The call, the need these people felt was so real and so spiritual. My father felt that call while ploughing a field. He left all behind; his mother and father, his occupation, his entire life. He went where God directed, setting aside his own plans."

GUELPH, ONTARIO

"Once I got started, I had a very difficult time putting it away. I think it's absolutely fantastic, and next to the Bible this has been one of the most meaningful books I have ever read."

SARNIA, ONTARIO

"As president of the Seacoast Missionary Society, it is my intention to purchase more copies and distribute them, as opportunity lends, to the commercial fishermen, military and merchant seamen, and others along the seacoasts of America…Thank you for opening this window to gaze back to simple ways, to a more pure, humble, and biblical Christianity."

ATLANTIC HIGHLANDS, NEW JERSEY

"[The] characters find a living faith through the guidance of the Holy Spirit, and exemplify the simple, joyful life that His indwelling presence produces. In a short time, this book has impacted so many people for good, creating a burning desire to reach out and share our faith with others as effectively as the believers in the book do. The focus is on Christ to the degree that it makes us want to experience Him in a deeper way than ever before…"

SANTA FE, NEW MEXICO

THE
GATE
SELDOM
FOUND

RAYMOND
REID

HARVEST HOUSE PUBLISHERS

EUGENE, OREGON

Scripture quotations are taken from the King James Version of the Bible.

Cover by Koechel Peterson & Associates, Inc., Minneapolis, Minnesota

Map on page 11 by Marie Puddister.

Illustrations by Roger Witmer, St. Jacobs, Ontario; www.rogerwitmer.com

Cover photo of couple © Allen Russell/Index Stock Imagery

Cover photo of gate © Elizabeth Etienne/Index Stock Imagery

Cover photo of tree © RO-MA Stock/Index Stock Imagery

This is a work of fiction. Names, characters, places, and incidents are products of the author's imagination or are used fictitiously. Any resemblance to actual persons, living or dead, or to events or locales, is entirely coincidental.

THE GATE SELDOM FOUND

Copyright © 2004 by Raymond Reid
Published by Harvest House Publishers
Eugene, Oregon 97402
www.harvesthousepublishers.com

Library of Congress Cataloging-in-Publication Data
Reid, Raymond G.
    The gate seldom found / Raymond Reid.
        p. cm.
    ISBN 0-7369-1369-6 (pbk.)
    1. Christian life—Fiction. 2. House churches—Fiction. 3. Guelph (Ont.)—Fiction. 4. Christians—Fiction.
    I. Title.
    PR9199.4.R457G38 2004
    813'.6—dc22   2003020511

Printed in the United States of America.

04 05 06 07 08 09 10 11 / DP-MS / 10 9 8 7 6 5 4 3 2 1

ACKNOWLEDGMENTS

From the beginning my wife, Gretchen, has been a befriender of my dreams. She listened thoughtfully as I talked at length about my hopes and aspirations for the novel, lending her sensitivity, wisdom, and balance. Our children, Darren and Andrea, have always encouraged me to follow my heart. This solidarity and vibrancy within my family provide the secure environment from which I draw strength and inspiration.

In the early stages, Sandra Sabatini was the first to attack the work with red ink. Although she handed me the initial critique with some trepidation, her comments were of tremendous benefit. As we went along, Sandy offered invaluable advice and creative suggestions, enabling me to develop my writing skills and to see what was needed to breathe life and dimension into the characters.

My heartfelt gratitude goes to Edith Smith for her exceptional contribution. It has been a privilege to work with her, and in the process she has become my friend. Edith's childhood afforded her a deep respect and reverence for simple expressions of faith and an inherent sensitivity to the characters' struggles. I am indebted to her for the literary refinement and historical acumen she supplied. Her creative spark, rural wisdom, and eagerness to be clear have produced a much more engaging saga. Indeed, some of the most vivid pastoral images and colourful dialogue flowed from the nib of Edith's pen.

From our first meeting, she embraced the vision that inspired my novel, and together we have celebrated each step on the staircase to its publication. Without Edith's notable gift as a wordsmith, *The Gate Seldom Found* could never have become the book it is today.

Finally, when I assumed the work had reached completion, and indeed after I had self-published the first edition in 2001, a copy found its way onto the desk of Nick Harrison at Harvest House Publishers. In one of our first conversations, Nick assured me that the writing held considerable promise but that "it wasn't quite there yet." But he did not leave me to flounder with those enigmatic words. Instead, he plunged into the text, focusing his impressive editorial skills as he worked through the entire manuscript. Line by line he identified the characters that called out for detailing, the scenes that needed broadening, the story line and transitions that were sketchy. Once again, the novel could crystalize into its final form only as a result of Nick Harrison's commitment and perseverance towards its literary integrity.

Many times throughout the process, I passed the draft manuscript around for critical review. Several of my friends and acquaintances responded to the challenge, offering perspective and enthusiastic support. Unfortunately, I cannot begin to name everyone who extended particular expertise, shared candid opinions, or wrote letters of encouragement. Your powerful letters testifying of its influence in your lives mean more than I can express on this page. I thank each of you for the role you played in bringing to fruition *The Gate Seldom Found*.

CONTENTS

Foreword   9

Map 11

Author's Note 13

1. Spiritual Winter 15

2. Troubling Questions 35

3. Encounter in Berlin 49

4. First Sunday in May 62

5. Frustrations and Firestorms 78

6. Reaching Out in Love 94

7. Dropping Pebbles 111

8. The Epiphany 136

9. The Baptism 160

10. Tear-Shaped Beads of Dew 172

11. Giving Everything to the Poor 192

12. The Inaudible Voice 208

13. Sowing the Seed 232

14. Beholding the Glory 245

15. Locked Out 262

16. Render unto Caesar 280

17. Ancient Affirmation 297

18. Just as I Am 309

19. Second Harvest 327

20. Conscientious Ploughmen 337

21. The Home Visit 361

22. Settlement of Belwood 379

23. Laura's Dilemma 417

24. Casting the Nets 444

25. Flowering of the Fellowship 465

26. Setting God's Table 496

27. Under the Tent 513

28. Struggle in St. Marys 542

29. The Shooting 565

30. Farewell to a Mother in Israel 585

     Epilogue 605

     Notes 617

     Glossary of Historical and Idiomatic Terms 627

FOREWORD

A house constructed from blueprints and elevations remains only a structure, an edifice, until the builder imbues it with individuality. So, too, a novel remains a structure, a literary house of words until the author's imagination infuses it with passion and conflict.

The first impulse of survival is to create a home—whether transient shelter or permanent dwelling. Literature abounds with images of the hearth and home as a place of refuge. In the larger paradigm, "home" embodies the age-old theme of exile, pilgrimage, and return. An ancient greeting often heard was "Peace be to this house."

On completion of the Temple in Jerusalem, King Solomon assured God, "I have surely built Thee an house to dwell in, a settled place for Thee to abide in forever" (1 Kings 8:13). Knowing that God is neither confined nor defined by structures of stone and mortar, Jesus reassured His disciples that He was going to prepare a place for them in His Father's house, the New Jerusalem (John 14:2).

The author of this historical novel, Raymond Reid, is a strong and sympathetic presence, a family man with a gift for listening. Over the past thirty years he has fulfilled a career of building homes. *The Gate Seldom Found,* his first novel, is a house of faith built word by word into an inviting and hospitable space through whose rooms the characters play out their parts in the Christian drama. In the house of the author's mind, the mysteries of God's ways reveal themselves as abundantly merciful. This novel in your hands dramatizes a fragment of humanity inclusive of men and women, transformed and coming home through that wondrous gate opening to our Father's house.

Edith K. Smith, Ph.D.
McMaster University
Hamilton, Ontario, Canada

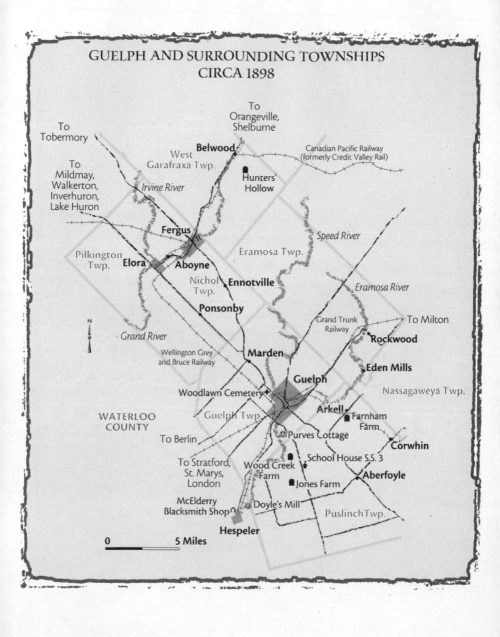

GUELPH AND SURROUNDING TOWNSHIPS
CIRCA 1898

To
Tobermory

To
Mildmay,
Walkerton,
Inverhuron,
Lake Huron

To
Orangeville,
Shelburne

Belwood

West
Garafraxa Twp.

Canadian Pacific Railway
(formerly Credit Valley Rail)

Hunters'
Hollow

Irvine River

Fergus

Speed River

Pilkington
Twp.

Elora

Aboyne

Eramosa Twp.

Nichol
Twp.

Ennotville

Eramosa River

N

Ponsonby

Grand Trunk
Railway

To Milton

Rockwood

Grand River

Wellington Grey
and Bruce Railway

Marden

Eden Mills

Guelph

Nassagaweya Twp.

Woodlawn Cemetery

WATERLOO
COUNTY

Guelph Twp.

Arkell

Farnham
Farm

To Berlin

Purves Cottage

Corwhin

To Stratford,
St. Marys,
London

Wood Creek
Farm

School House S.S. 3

Aberfoyle

Jones Farm

McElderry
Blacksmith Shop

Doyle's Mill

Puslinch Twp.

Hespeler

0   5 Miles

AUTHOR'S NOTE

The story line in *The Gate Seldom Found* is largely fictitious. However, almost all of the characters and events within these pages spring from vivid well-worn stories laid down in my youthful mind by gray-haired elders. These eyewitness accounts of colourful personalities and historical incidents had been preserved in their memories from the end of the nineteenth century. Because names, descriptions, and settings have been imaginatively altered to give the original individuals and their descendants a measure of privacy, any similarity to a specific person or residence is purely coincidental.

Unlike seasoned novelists who devise their plots with meticulous care and fashion their characters months or even years before putting pen to paper, I simply sat down one stormy December morning and began to write. A single sentence, a paragraph, the first page. Line upon line, the words tumbled out, tentatively at first but with growing elucidation and purpose as I traveled back to a world of candlelight and kerosene lamps, of weather predictions by signs in the heavens, and of cures by poultices and plasters.

My characters greeted me for the first time, just as they will you, when they appeared on the page before my eyes. Some stepped forward haltingly and sharpened over time while others leaped off the page, their lives calling out for honest consideration. I often sat at my desk, tears blurring my sight as I entered into the poignant drama and intensity of their choices. But even as my characters confronted, challenged, and chastened me, they also beckoned me into their warm circle of fellowship.

As early as 1906, my grandparents had embraced the simplicity of this time-honoured fellowship of love. My parents, too, became profoundly involved in the house church movement, affording me childhood opportunities to meet and respect the itinerant preachers of whom I write. As a boy I often sat wide-eyed across the breakfast table regaled by anecdotes of these itinerants' rich and memorable experiences. Ultimately their principles of faith settled in my heart as well.

Years passed, and then one evening an engaging conversation with friends sparked the notion of sharing in fictional form the little-known vision of these early itinerants. I felt compelled to nudge open a gate and enable readers to return to an earlier era when simple faith was the touchstone for the people of the novel.

Some readers may be surprised to find footnotes in a work of fiction. However, in the writing of this historical narrative, I realized that some of the truths expressed might be enhanced by allowing readers to see their genesis in the Bible. This decision has been affirmed by the positive responses from readers of the first self-published edition. Some have used the novel as a springboard for discussion groups, while others tell me they value the footnotes for further exploration.

I trust the characters in *The Gate Seldom Found* will find their way into your heart as they have into mine.

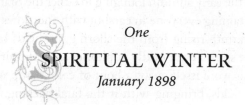

One

SPIRITUAL WINTER
January 1898

It was no day for a funeral—especially Ben Aberlochy's. But blizzard or not, the service would begin at Saint Patrick's in only a matter of hours, and the chores had taken Alistair Stanhope longer than he had reckoned. With his head cast forward, eyebrows caked with snow, the tall angular man raised a frozen mitt to ward off the sharp flakes biting like crystalline mosquitoes into his exposed flesh.

As he floundered through the swirling whiteness in the direction of the farmhouse, Alistair squinted over his shoulder at the stable, already disappearing beneath a chalky shroud.

The storm had given warning of its impending wrath in the ominous double wheel circling the January moon, a sign Alistair had studied with increasing uneasiness for the past three nights. Now all of Wood Creek Farm—the fields, the cedar woods, and the frozen stream—lay struggling under the cloud of seething snow.

Salt tears leaked from Alistair's eyes and froze upon his cheeks, rough with cold, as though nature itself were mocking the ebb and flow of life. That morning over breakfast, he had told Priscilla, "A yoke of oxen couldn't drag me from the fireside into this storm if it were anybody but Ben. It breaks my bones."

It was going to take a long time to make peace with the harsh reality that his friend Ben Aberlochy was gone. Not that Alistair hadn't seen it coming. Indeed, at the age of forty-six, on Ben's last crossing from Bombay to Halifax, he had developed the graveyard cough that had claimed three youthful uncles before him. Responding to ancestral ties at last, and feeling his strength weakening, the old salt had returned to the quiet Canadian settlement of Puslinch, far from the Indian Ocean singing in its sleep.

Ben had spent the early autumn lounging in either the Stanhope kitchen or barnyard, entertaining everyone in earshot with anecdotes of his travels. At first the dry warmth rising from the shorn grain fields had seemed to do him good. His spirits were oddly euphoric, and Alistair's hopes rose. But as the old year wore itself away, a bout of cold, damp weather swept across the frozen fields, bringing with it the fatal hacking. Within days, Ben could only speak in a whisper between coughs, his seafaring tales all told. Still, until the eleventh hour, Alistair had doggedly clung to the illusion that Ben, against all odds, would cheat death and survive into cantankerous old age.

In the first week of the New Year, the hired boy who ran errands for Ben's sister plunged through the hard-crusted drifts from the next concession to inform Alistair that Ben had died on the kitchen couch. "Like I say," repeated the round-eyed urchin as he stood on the Stanhope hearth fumbling with his cap, "'e was racked for a bit, but at the end 'e went real easy. 'is face looked jist like a clock wot stopped and forgot how to go."

That had been three days ago. But now, stumbling forward, Alistair at last reached the refuge of the woodshed that adjoined the farm kitchen, and his stiff fingers pried the door open against the teeth of the raging gale. He kicked a low drift off the threshold before yanking the door shut, his eyes momentarily blinded by the woodshed's blackness.

Alistair hooked the door behind him and began, with unaccountable urgency, to shake the snow off his coat and overalls. His fingers stung as he unhasped his frozen boot buckles and carried his bulky clothes into the warmth of the kitchen. Although it was noonday, a kerosene lamp flickered on the long table, defying the strange darkness in the low-raftered room.

"I left Nell harnessed in her stall," Alistair said as he hooked his coat in the chimney corner to dry, "but it's mean out there. The worst, I reckon, since we took the place over from Pa. That'll be nine years this spring."

His wife, Priscilla, stood over the cookstove, ladling the contents of a black cast iron pot into soup bowls. "No day for a man to go down," she reflected aloud, looking at her husband with compassion.

Alistair assented with a grunt and eased himself into a stiff-backed chair at the head of the table. "Ben deserves better. But it's got to be done."

A moment later Priscilla joined him. After a hasty word of thanks, Alistair reached for a thick crust of bread, his chapped red hands tearing it in two. "Life's tough—in one door and out the other."

The couple swallowed their dinner, neither choosing to mingle words with meat. Finishing his meal in silence, Alistair thrust back his chair and thumped upstairs to pull on his boiled collar and funeral blacks.

Half an hour later, he returned downstairs. Priscilla was adjusting her eiderdown bonnet, facing him from the mirror. "I don't call to mind a north-easter ever sweeping upon us so fast," she pronounced. "Otherwise, I'd have never let Phoebe out the door. We'll need to fetch her from school on our way home." She paused. "Good thing Timothy's safe in town with Aunt Maggie tonight."

Alistair nodded gravely as he opened the door to a chilly gust. "Bundle up good," he admonished. "This wind's so bitter it'll freeze flesh to bone." Then he ploughed through the snow to the barn and brought the horse and cutter to meet Priscilla at the little gate, now drifted over, in front of the house. When she climbed in and settled herself beside him, he tucked the heavy buffalo robe across her lap to cut the biting cold. Again Alistair took the lines and the mare lunged forward into the wind's resistance.

On the way to the church, he judged his place on the road by the stark shapes of familiar trees and rail fences through the blinding storm. The crystallized scarves over their faces forestalled any words, and the couple rode in solemn introspection. Alistair thought back to his childhood and the good times he and Ben had spent together. The two boys had met in the senior second class at the one-room schoolhouse, a mile down the road from Wood Creek Farm. They had been loyal friends ever since they had eyed each other, schoolboy fashion, that first day. A pair of rascals, they had played together, fished together, submitted undauntedly to the teacher's razor strop together, and eventually had gone to barn dances together. But all the common joys the men had known ended Monday when, gasping for the familiar salt air, Ben had lost his battle against galloping consumption.

As the outline of Saint Patrick's emerged through the veil, the horse, through habit, slowed and turned into the churchyard. After tethering Nell in the driving shed with the other snow-encrusted horses, Alistair strapped a plaid blanket around her chest. Linking his arm with Priscilla's, he waded through the drifts to the front doors of Saint Patrick's, where a knot of people huddled as they exchanged greetings in muted tones. Beyond the church-yard fence, a hound could be heard howling as though the storm had been granted the voice of an animal. Alistair brushed the snow off Priscilla's coat before they walked up the centre aisle of the dilapidated old building. As he moved slowly to his place, he gave a solemn nod in the direction of his friends Stephen and Emily McElderry and Bill and Alice Jones. Priscilla slid into the family pew as Alistair walked to the front row. With a glance he acknowledged Mr. Rogers, one of the men on the church board, and his wife, sitting in their prominent place in front of the pulpit.

Alistair shifted uncomfortably on the splintered bench and tried to warm his hands. As his eyes and thoughts drifted to the open pine coffin before him, he was distracted by a commotion from the back of the church. Turning, he saw old Malachi Jackson staggering up the vestibule steps and toward the aisle, his arms swinging in menacing half-circles. An oblong bulge, deep in his coat pocket, betrayed Malachi's source of courage for his only appearance at Saint Patrick's in years. Like a gaunt apparition in a fairy tale, Malachi accosted one of the elders in a voice modulated by years of hard grog. "Get me set down at the front, will you?" he fumed. "There's them as tears a man's friend down before he's cold. They're already sayin' at Crundle's store that Ben was a devil in his day, a woman in every port, y' know. But, Ben…he was a friend o' mine."

Several restraining arms reached out to seize old Malachi and, after confiscating his bottle, planted him roughly inside the door of the rear pew. Nothing daunted, he resumed his tirade with a snort. "'Take heart,' I told Ben on his deathbed, 'you've come home off the high seas to die and you'll stand among the righteous at your latter end, me on your right hand and Sir John A. on your left, see if you don't.' A judgment on all them that thinks otherwise." While the congregation stirred in horrified indignation, Malachi slumped against the kneeler, exhaling a cloud of unholy incense.

Just at that moment Reverend Smithers' black-vested form appeared through the vestry door. He entered the pulpit, and, turning to the Order for the Burial of the Dead, he began to read: "I will take heed to my ways, that I offend not with my tongue." Oblivious to the irony, Alistair stared at the ornate detailing on the corner of the coffin in front of him, the minister's intonations receding in his ears. He tried to concentrate on Reverend Smithers' words, but each time his eyes returned unbidden to the ashen face and lifeless body before him. Alistair clamped his jaw, grief riveted in his gaze, as torn images of his times with Ben flashed through his mind.

Unlike Alistair, a settled, deep-rooted man of the soil, Ben had always been a man of the sea. It was known that in 1815 his ancestors had been numbered among the Aberdeen shipwrights building the *Prince of Waterloo*, and his father's forebears had sailed on its maiden voyage to the colony of Canada. In Ben the blood of a sea-faring race had claimed a son. "Life's a voyage that's homeward bound," he used to say in the whimsical strain of the light-hearted sailor. Without the anchor of wife or children, he had pursued the life of a sea captain and tea merchant. Ben had an ironic edge on his tongue and the hotheaded nature of the Highland Scot. One of his ears, perched slightly higher than the other, gave him a comical, lopsided look, while his tousled red hair and mischievous eyes betrayed the heart and spirit of a boy.

"The sea's a rapscallion of a girl," he had long ago confided to Alistair, "sweet or savage by turns. And if I'm ploughing her waves when she calls me for the last time, I hope they'll hoist me overboard on a starry night and into her arms forever."

Alistair stirred amidst a flood of memories. He recalled the family legend that as an infant at his christening, Ben had reached up and clawed the spectacles off the parson's nose, as if to intimate that the eyes of faith need no second sight. "He'll never comb gray hairs, that one," an old aunt had prophesied at his birth. Alistair blinked, unable to believe her foolish superstition had borne itself out. His Adam's apple threatened to choke him. *When that casket's closed,* he lamented, *I'll never see Ben again...*

He recalled Ben standing, nineteen years ago, in the very place where his body now lay, proud to be the best man when Alistair and Priscilla had been married. The two men shared a bond which even Priscilla's presence as the bride-elect had not altered. As groom and groomsman, they had waited at the communion rail in unspoken camaraderie. Ben had dragged from his memory a cynical old proverb. "Honest men marry soon," he had rasped in Alistair's ear, "wise men, never." He had accompanied this wisdom with a sharp dig to Alistair's ribs. When Reverend Smithers had rebuked him with a stern glance, Ben's features had instantly shaped themselves into an unnatural solemnity even more comical than his original expression. Alistair recalled his own voice, returning from mirth, as he had soberly repeated the words of the marriage vow, "I, Alistair, do take thee, Priscilla, to be my lawful wedded wife..." Ben had ever afterward joked that Alistair, in the nervous throes of the ceremony, had uttered the phrase "my *awful* wedded wife."

Alistair contemplated the sealed lips before him, now silenced forever. Outside, the wind howled and pebbles of hard snow pounded on the windowpanes, penetrating the cracks around the bubbled glass. A gust blew down the chimney, sending a bitter puff of wood smoke over the mourners. Alistair heard muffled sniffles behind him and knew it must be Ben's sister, his only surviving relative. Despite the freezing temperatures outside, Alistair felt a trickle of sweat roll down his back.

He glanced through stinging eyes at the five other men in the front pew, chosen by Ben's sister, along with Alistair, to serve as his pallbearers. Good men, each of them. And yet it took an occasion such as this—the funeral of a comrade—to remind Alistair how little these men really knew each other despite their frequent conversations. On different occasions Alistair had waited and chatted with two or three of these men while their wheels were measured at the wainwright's or their barrels strapped at the cooper's.

Alistair recalled his frustration last week with Sandy MacPherson as the old codger, leaning forward on a wooden grain shovel in one corner of the Aberfoyle mill's grinding room, held a circle of men hostage with his tiresome tales.

Just last Sunday Alistair had spoken to each of these five men. Wilf Clayborn was short of straw in his mow, Jordie Halfpenny and his boys were scheming to cut ice off the creek, the deer were yarding up in Stewart Sheehan's cedar bush. He even recalled hearing that Ethan Danvers was squandering so much time in the hotel that his wife had to use sacks to patch their boys' overalls. But in spite of all the words that had passed between these men, Alistair realized that never in all their conversations had he spoken to a single one of them about anything that touched the core and purpose of life. In one way he called them friends, and yet the truth was, they were barely more than long-familiar acquaintances. Now it seemed as if a conspiratorial silence muffled each man in the face of Ben's death, an event that laid a cold hand on the shoulders of each of them.

As Reverend Smithers droned on, Alistair, for the first time, realized the expanse of the gulf between himself and the others. Searching their tight-lipped profiles, he wondered how they truly felt about Ben's death. He knew that one thing was certain—they'd never talk about it. *Once Ben's sister passes on, there'll be nobody to remark on Ben—the last of the Aberlochy line.* Alistair felt chilled as he turned to stare at his friend's body again.

He was pulled back to the present by Reverend Smithers' sonorous final words: "Forasmuch as it hath pleased Almighty God of His great mercy to take unto Himself the soul of our dear brother here departed, earth to earth, ashes to ashes, dust to dust, in sure and certain hope of the Resurrection…"

On cue, the six pallbearers stood up as the undertaker stepped forward and closed the lid, sealing Ben's image in Alistair's mind. The men flanked the coffin and, lifting together, proceeded slowly down the aisle and out the door to the waiting sleigh. The sharp flakes stung Alistair's face as he helped push the coffin into place, the ornate pine ploughing a trench through the soft snow before coming to rest.

It is only when a man, acting as pallbearer, feels the weight of his friend in death, Alistair reflected, *that the friendship is truly measured.* He straightened his back and moved to one side, wiping his eyes with his cold, damp coat sleeve. "Goodbye, Ben," he whispered as the undertaker set out toward the cemetery. The body, he knew, would be stored in a shed awaiting burial when the ground thawed in the spring. As Alistair watched the casket disappearing into the whiteness of the storm, the sleigh tracks began to drift in before his very eyes, closing behind Ben as certainly as his furrowed wake on the high seas.

The following Wednesday Alistair pulled up his sleigh in front of Crundle's General Store, searching for a padded harness breeching. From the circle of crimson-faced men hunkered around the potbellied stove, old Jordie's nasal whine reminisced aloud. "J'ever hear how 'twas the Aberlochys come to the colonies? 'Twasn't the ship so much as the mule. Seems the dockyards in Aberdeen had a mule for to ferry things to and fro, an obedient old beast, everyone fond of it and all. Well, when the old Aberlochys made to set sail for the New World, they started to load up the *Prince of Waterloo.* You mind how they did, hauling furniture and all, their spinning wheels and barrels and women, and like that. Well siree, didn't the old mule go down on her knees 's if she was a-prayin' to be taken aboard too. Old Aberlochy, I've heard it said, was a soft-hearted old cuss, so he tickles the ass atween her ears and feeds her a pail of bran while she waits, kind of wistful-like. Well, by 'n' by, the old mule finishes the pail, shuts her eyes, heaves one almighty moan, and gives up the ghost."

The storyteller's voice was silenced amid indignant roars and groans from the incredulous listeners. Alistair leaned against the post, his eyes twinkling as he waited for old Jordie to catch his wind.

"The whole shipyard was stunned," resumed Jordie, "and took it as a sign that the *Prince of Waterloo* shouldn't embark. But old Aberlochy—he'd be Ben's grandfather—he says, solemnlike, 'Gimme a knife.' Folks didn't like to inquire what it was he intended. By 'n' by, if he didn't split that donkey open and skin it and hang the hide up to dry in the Scotch mist. When the hide had tightened up a bit and the ship made ready to sail, old Aberlochy picks the hide up with a flourish, and says to it, says he, 'Old girl, you been a faithful thane to the chiefs. A toast to ye now, and a toast when we land in the New World, for there's no way in creation the Aberlochys'll abandon you.' So the clan swigged down a wee dram of Scotch, climbed aboard, hoisted anchor, and heaved ho a-bellerin' *Auld Lang Syne*. And *that's* how the Aberlochys departed the Old Sod. I can just see Ben now, a-graspin' the donkey hide while he wades up to his neck acrost the Jordan." A perverse chuckle ended the tale while knees were slapped in bonhomie all around the blistering stove. Alistair grinned and moved off toward the harness section in the far corner of the store.

As the days following Ben's funeral passed, such stories and remembrances waned throughout the small community of Puslinch Township. But not for Alistair. Throughout the white silence of winter, the memories of Ben often overwhelmed him as he dragged himself to the stable each morning. Heated by bursting pens of cattle and pigs, the pungent cloud of steamy air confronted him like a vague wall when he cracked the door ajar. Once inside he plodded behind the horses standing in their stalls— Nell and the four massive Percherons that did the draft work on the farm. In the past he had always slapped their sleek rumps good-naturedly, but now, often as not, he simply tossed his outer coat onto a peg and began his chores.

Normally Alistair enjoyed the cycle of feeding animals, cleaning stalls, fixing fences, and planting and harvesting crops. The very regularity of the work gave him time to think. But this reassuring rhythm had been shattered. Never again would he see Ben's twisted smile, hear his rollicking guffaw, or listen to his far-fetched yarns. Of late Alistair shoveled out the stalls more abstractedly. The repetitive filling and dumping, filling and dumping of the wheelbarrow made him think about life, about meaning and about the inexplicable desolation he felt.

At one point in Ben's funeral Alistair had leaned forward on the pew, his eyes fastened on Reverend Smithers' face, waiting for something to help him make sense of things. But when no lasting solace had emerged from the minister's liturgy, Alistair had turned to his reverie of Ben for what little comfort he could find there. And the next Sunday had returned to business as usual at Saint Patrick's.

With a resounding bang, Alistair slammed the shovel against the side of the wooden wheelbarrow as he recalled the minister's rousing sermon about the need for more money to construct a new building. "Money, money, money," he muttered. "Why focus on the outward edifice when the inward man is perishing?" Two cats, sunning themselves in the cow stable door, bolted as he grabbed the wheelbarrow handles, charged out through the opening and up a plank to dump the load on top of the steaming manure pile.

As he considered his life as a member of Saint Patrick's, Alistair recalled what it was that pleased him about the Sunday routine: primarily it was meeting the other men on the church steps, where he was able to find out where his neighbour was selling his hogs, who was planting seed flax this year, and which farm was to have the next threshing. His best friends, Bill and Alice Jones and Stephen and Emily McElderry, were there too. He always enjoyed a few words with them. And the very thought of tasting a piece of old Mrs. Halfpenny's fresh strawberry shortcake, which he had been eating at church socials all his life, would make his mouth water. When Alistair honestly analyzed what drew him each Sunday morning, he concluded sadly that it was primarily to see his friends.

On many a Sunday he had sat as a detached spectator in the family pew. In the heat of summer he watched the flies climbing and ever falling backward down the opaque glass of the tall windows. In winter's chill he watched the outline of icicles, piercingly cold, lengthening from the eaves.

Now it occurred to Alistair that he was simply weary of going to church. It seemed to him as if over the past year there had been a hunger for God warming his soul—an unfamiliar yearning he had found difficult to give voice to or even to recognize until Ben's death had jolted him.

Alistair had never thought of himself as a Bible student, but now he often found the Scriptures in his hands. He turned the pages with care, his lips moving silently as he studied each passage, looking for the thing that was missing in his life.

Although the Stanhopes for generations had been married, christened, and buried to the cadences of the prayer book, Alistair found himself drawn instead to the simple story of Jesus. Each day after his noon meal he settled in the rocking chair with his Bible, only to find himself struggling to lay it aside and return to his chores. As he pored over the pages, it was as though an unseen hand were guiding a candle across the text, illuminating particular verses—words that leaped off the page as never before.

As Alistair stepped out of the woodshed and into the sharp afternoon sunshine, he blinked, giving his eyes a moment to adjust. Like a man healed from lifelong blindness, he began to see portions of the ancient writings in a strange new light. This enlightenment, this new way of seeing swelled from a mere pinhole to an expansive admiration for the humble way Jesus had lived and for the profound wisdom of His parables. Hurrying along the snowy track toward the barn, Alistair shook his head, only vaguely aware of the intensity of his growing love for Christ. The New Testament church, he realized, as scales of tradition fell from his eyes, had never been about a building, an organization, or an enterprise which, of late, he believed, Saint Patrick's was fast becoming.

~

One Sunday evening in early February, Alistair trudged to the house after his chores, shed his rank barn clothes, and hung them up to dry on a wooden peg. The aromas of fresh bread and a sirloin roast wafted from the cookstove in the kitchen. Alistair plunked his woolen mittens on top of the warming oven, walked up behind Priscilla, and wrapped his arms around her narrow waist. "Supper smells good, my dear. I'm starving!"

Priscilla smiled and, pressing her back against him, reached over her shoulder to pat his cold, ruddy cheek affectionately. Priscilla's pretty face and creamy complexion were accented by a tiny mole under her right eye. Tonight her long dark hair was gathered at the back in a green silk scarf and hung down almost to her waist.

"You're the sweetest girl in Puslinch Township," Alistair teased as he peered under the pot lids. "Or would be if you kept the turnips out of the carrot pot." He inhaled the steam and turned abruptly to kiss her, catching her cheeks between his fingers.

In mock exasperation she pulled his hands away. "You always say that when I cook a roast. Now go and wash up while I call the children," she ordered. "Everything's ready to put on the table." Priscilla glanced at the splotches on Alistair's wrists. "And scrub—right to the elbows," she added, her dark eyes twinkling as she slid a gravy boat onto the table. "No unwashed man is going to smudge my starched cloth."

"The iron fist in a velvet glove," Alistair noted with a grin, secretly proud of the bedrock convictions his wife concealed under her gracious exterior. *Nobody, including me, is going to railroad Priscilla into anything,* he thought as he walked the length of the kitchen to the granite basin. His tall, lean frame still carried the quick agility of youth, though his growing baldness hinted at his forty-six years. He walked with a slight forward stoop, making him appear as if he were always in a hurry.

After supper he settled into his chair beside the cookstove. Usually he read the *Guelph Daily Herald* for a while, but tonight he couldn't concentrate on the words. He looked around the kitchen, taking pleasure in the way his wife kept their home. Braided mats were scattered on the ochre-painted pine floor. A bullnosed chair rail separated the wainscotting from cheery yellow wallpaper reminiscent of morning sunshine.

Getting up, Alistair retrieved a worn packet from the clock shelf and absently thumbed through the myriad of envelopes, tangible evidence of an erratic correspondence from his friend Ben, scribbled over the years from distant ports of call. Foreign stamps postmarked in Southampton, Le Havre, Gibraltar, Alexandria, and Bombay intimated a footloose sailor who, deep in his heart, had yearned to keep in touch with hearth and home.

As Priscilla wiped down the dry sink, she turned toward Alistair. "I can see you're still missing Ben," she said softly. "Maybe Reverend Smithers could help if you paid him a visit."

"I do miss Ben," Alistair acknowledged. He took a deep breath, carefully untying the string that held the envelopes together as he searched for the right words. "But Ben's not the problem. And I'm definitely not interested in talking to Reverend Smithers again. When I tried last week to put my soul's hunger into words, he couldn't seem to understand. I don't have much faith anymore in the tack he's taking. He's always harping about more money and a new building. You heard him at it this morning."

"That's been on your tongue twice this week," Priscilla retorted. "But you don't get anything for nothing in this world."

"That's right. But my discontent has very little to do with money. It's just a sign of our minister's focus—the outward running of his church. Actually, I'd be happy to contribute a lot more if I felt satisfied. But I'm starving on the inside."

Priscilla was silent, and then she offered, "Maybe the new building'll give us a fresh outlook. Remember how it was when we pasted up this paper in the kitchen? It brightened the whole place."

Alistair's brows drew together. "No," he concluded after a moment. "What goes on in the new building will be the same as in the old one. And if it still won't feed our souls, why build it?"

"You expect too much," Priscilla answered with an edge in her voice. "I can't understand why you're so critical."

"I really wish you could get my drift." Alistair paused, the envelopes clutched in his right hand. "When Bill Jones and I butchered that steer before Christmas, I noticed the four parts of its stomach. Now if I were a steer, I'd have to say that only three compartments of my hunger are being fed. An important part is filled by you and the children. My work around the farm satisfies the physical part, and our friends and social life supplies another. But no matter how many good things I squeeze into the first three parts, I still feel a certain emptiness. Something vital is missing."

Priscilla opened her wicker knitting basket and took out a partially made sweater. At first the yarn resisted the nimble movements of her slender fingers, seeming to unravel itself as though mischief possessed it. She pursed her lips in stony silence.

Alistair tried to read Priscilla's face. "Seems it's only me who feels this way, that something needs to change," he persisted. "I need more answers to the troubling questions of life. What's its purpose? Where am I going? I need to know God for myself. Not all this talk about the building and *its* needs. Why, last fall Ben and I put in the better part of a week painting and puttying up all those old windows. And him coughing his head off…" A hint of bitterness crept into Alistair's voice. "But what did the church ever do for Ben? And where is Ben now?"

Priscilla's knitting slowed as he spoke. She waited for him to finish as she might wait out the tantrum of a child. For a moment she turned over his irritating comments.

"I know there are problems with the church," she finally conceded, "but God will correct them in His own time. It's His church after all." Her face betrayed a slight annoyance at dropping a stitch. "Besides, there's nothing either you or I can do anyway. We should focus on our own private devotions and leave it at that." She loosened the ball of yarn as she started to purl a second row. "It's better if we don't talk about it anymore," she added pointedly. "Let sleeping dogs lie."

Alistair sat motionless, staring at the return addresses in Ben's faded scrawl. In direct challenge to Priscilla's platitudes, his voice rose, unusually strained and tense. "Pa and Ma felt it did them good to go to service every

Sunday. 'Twas the right thing to do. But now, I don't know. 'The right thing to do' seems to be shifting." Alistair's voice took a defiant tone. "It's as if church is coming between me and my Maker." He stretched and clasped his hands behind his head, suddenly reminded of his parents.

Alistair's mother had died when he was eleven, just at the age when a farm boy was starting to shoulder a man's work. His memory of her had dropped back among the textures of childhood: the rough woolen shirts and drawers she had made him wear, the gritty soap and bristly hair brush she kept for him on a nail by the pantry door, and the soft touch of her worn hands as they cupped his cheeks every evening for a goodnight kiss. As he stretched up into a man, her image lay gently on his mind.

Alistair's father had taught him to be honest, both with others and with himself. Alistair's dad had always stood out in the settlement as a highly principled man, whether it was concerning business on the farm or helping his children learn to stand up for what was right. Alistair recalled defending one of the girls at school against malicious taunting and how the boys had jeered and called him a girl too. When he had come home shaken and tense, his dad had put his arm around him and said, "Son, right is right, even if nobody else is doing it, and wrong is wrong even if the whole world is doing it." He never forgot those words or the assurance he had felt looking up into his father's steady blue eyes. Because his dad was his chief example, Alistair learned about life from a man's point of view—working hard, caring for the animals, watching over them like a shepherd, and tending their every need. That was the legacy his dad had passed on to him.

When Priscilla had come as a bride to Wood Creek Farm, it had been Ben who, half in jest and half in earnest, cautioned Alistair: "Remember, man, she's a wife, not an ewe." Ben had hunched himself over the sheep shed threshold, chin propped on his knees, while smoke circles curled up from his pipe as if emphasizing his wise but unsolicited counsel. A hint of ruefulness edged his voice. "Many a man's a fool for a woman, but a wife's her own case. It'll be heavy seas ahead if you don't learn fast…"

Not many weeks had passed before Alistair began to understand the wisdom in the bachelor's words—sheep *were* easier to care for than a wife. He had always been busy, perfecting what he knew and fixing things that needed fixing. But he couldn't fix Priscilla or her problems. Somewhere along the way he had never learned much about loving, only tending.

Alistair picked up the newspaper again. "Some Thursday I'd like to draw in the opinions of Bill and Alice and Stephen and Emily about this," he said. "They're smart young people."

"I suppose you reckon they'll be more receptive to your outlandish notions than me," Priscilla observed curtly.

With the air of a man putting dissension behind him, Alistair tightened his jaw, held his peace, and rustled the newspaper to the livestock auctions on the last page. Although for several months he and Priscilla had opened their kitchen to the two younger couples each Thursday evening— weather permitting—he remained cautious, seeking greater clarity in his own mind before broaching such a tangled subject.

Priscilla reached for another skein of yarn. Alistair's misgivings about the church had stirred up uncomfortable thoughts. She felt needed at Saint Patrick's and liked the responsibility she had been given of overseeing the small choir. The repetitive strokes of the knitting needles soon had her deep in thought, unravelling the strands of her childhood.

Because her harried mother had been unable to spend much time with any of her eleven children, Priscilla had suffered silently from the perceived neglect. In her loneliness she had drawn away from her family. She remembered how she had often retreated to the bedroom which she shared with three older sisters or hid in the branches of an apple tree in the far corner of the orchard. Spending hours alone, she had tried to create her own happy little world in which she was the mistress.

As a young woman she had taken training as a nurse. For a few years, caring for the sick at Guelph General Hospital had given Priscilla a sense of satisfaction. But like most young women, she imagined that having a home and a husband would provide her with a greater sense of self-worth and happiness. She met Alistair when he had come to visit one of her patients, and before long they had fallen in love and married.

In the first year of marriage, their honeymoon faces had reflected the common joy of young newlyweds. But as season turned to season and the farm labours consumed Alistair's strength and attention, Priscilla began to feel neglected again. Even Alistair, she discovered, was incapable of giving everything she longed for. It wasn't that he didn't love her, for she was well aware of his efforts to provide and care for her daily. At times the thought of his abundant provision would make her feel like a spoiled girl and a sense of guilt would sweep over her. But she yearned for something more, her heart aching for reasons she couldn't understand or explain, even to herself.

Priscilla tried to satisfy this empty feeling by constantly hooking rugs, sewing curtains, or planting window pots. When her neighbours down the hollow or across the fields commented approvingly, "Climbing honeysuckle—nobody gets it to bloom like Priscilla," or "Frilled muslin—you'd think she washed and starched 'em every week," she would glow with gratification, but still she felt alone once the day was over.

The private anguish and feelings of rejection she had known as a child grew with her into adult life, darkening her joy like a snow squall in April. But it hadn't been her mother, or even Alistair, who had given her a sense of rejection—it had been herself. For reasons she didn't understand, God's love, of which Reverend Smithers spoke on occasion, seemed vague and unfathomable for her. Like the turmoil Alistair was feeling, Priscilla's uncertainty and lack of peace were breaking down the resistance of her heart. But unaware of God's indispensable stirring, she simply bore what she thought was hers to bear.[1]

She was startled back to the present from her brooding thoughts when she heard thirteen-year-old Phoebe, upstairs in her room, beginning to practice the violin. The music seemed to float down the open staircase like a fragrance. Priscilla had liked music from childhood, but her family could not afford an instrument. So she had learned to sing instead and was now the lead soprano at church. Encouraged by her daughter's desire to play, she had eventually been able to purchase a second-hand instrument for her. To Priscilla, the violin melodies sounded sweet, yet sad. But to Phoebe's older brother, Timothy, the notes were all sour.

"Go outside and play for the tomcat!" she heard him shout from the next room. "The way he yowls at night, he'll understand the noises you're making. Why should I suffer?"

Priscilla pretended not to hear. It was better for them to learn to sort out their own differences. She knew there was no real animosity between the two of them, just the usual sibling ribbing.

Full of mischief, Phoebe was at the age when she loved to torment her brother even though she missed him during the week when he was away at high school in nearby Guelph. When he was gone, she would mope around the house, exclaiming in exasperation that she was at loose ends. Priscilla was careful, on these days, to spend a little extra time with her daughter. She saw a lot of herself in Phoebe's sensitive nature and watched proudly as the young adolescent carried her books and lunch across the pasture fields to S.S. #3, the same one-room school where Alistair had met Ben so long ago.

Hearing a sudden rustle, Priscilla saw Alistair yawn and fold up the newspaper. "Well, I guess we'd better hit the hay," he said. "Tomorrow's Monday, and I have to rouse up early to take Timothy to school."

Priscilla nodded and rose to adjust the dampers on the stove. After turning down the wicks, she blew out the oil lamps and stood for a few moments in the soft darkness, now lit only by the coals glowing from the firebox. The pale light outlined a flannel shirt of Alistair's, hanging by the stove, on which Priscilla had intended to turn the frayed collar and cuffs. She hesitated, and then caught by impulse, she jerked the shirt from the chair knob, bunched it at her throat, and ripped it in two.

"I'll need rags tomorrow," she justified the waste aloud. Then, blinking back tears of frustration, she crammed the torn garment into the drawer below the dry sink and followed Alistair's footsteps up the stairs.

But long after he had hooked his suspenders over the bed post, Alistair continued to perch on the edge of the bed in a shifting patch of moonlight. Priscilla, from deep under the goose-down comforter, saw a triangle of winter-white flesh exposed under the neck strings of his night shirt, and with a pang she perceived him as suddenly vulnerable—but bullheaded.

"Lie *down*," she said, half pleadingly. "You've no idea how cold I am. The storm slats must have been left open."

Alistair lay down beside her, but he didn't turn to her. His silence and abstraction cut her to the heart, like the scraping of a ploughshare over hidden rock in a windswept field.

Thursday afternoon of the following week, Alistair loaded a couple of fattened hogs into a pig crate on the sleigh. He stopped in front of the house and ran to the woodshed door. "I'm off to the Guelph market," his voice rose on the icy chill of the February air. "I'll be gone a good four hours."

Priscilla appeared from her quilting frame, set up in the centre of the parlour. "When you're in town, could you pick up some ginger and molasses? And an eight-ounce bottle of magnesia for my stomach?" Disappearing into the pantry, she returned with a square canister in hand. "There's only a scoop left of the tea Ben brought from Ceylon."

"Sure. Just write it down." Alistair flashed a disarming smile. "You know what my memory's like." Almost as a last minute thought, he added, "I'm going to stop and see Timothy for a few minutes too."

"Good. I'll send along some of the cookies I baked this morning. And please give him and Aunt Maggie a big hug for me."

Two hours later the empty sleigh pulled up in front of a red brick house where Timothy boarded with Aunt Maggie during the week while he attended the Guelph Collegiate Institute only seven blocks away. As Alistair hurried up the front steps, clutching two dozen cookies wrapped in last evening's *Guelph Daily Herald,* he felt a wave of nostalgia. Aunt Maggie, the only living sister of Alistair's mother, had tried hard to fill the void after her sister's death, and over the years she and Alistair had become particularly close. Because of her love and strong resemblance to his mother, Alistair had, from youth, fallen into the habit of visiting her nearly every week.

Alistair pressed the familiar thumb latch, let himself in, and found his way to the kitchen at the rear of the house, where the elderly widow was stirring a handful of raisins into the creamy batter of a vanilla cake.

"My goodness, Alistair," Aunt Maggie exclaimed cheerfully, "it's not nice to sneak up on an old lady who's as deaf as a post." Alistair laughed as she clamped his face between her lean hands, leaving imprints of white flour on his ruddy cheeks.

"Your rheumatiz acting up?" he inquired as she hobbled ahead of him into her airless parlour.

"Something terrible in winter," Aunt Maggie avowed.

A dark walnut table with turned Chippendale legs overflowed with old photograph albums and crocheted doilies. After a few minutes of chitchat Alistair glanced around. "So where's my boy?" he asked.

Aunt Maggie pointed to the stairs. "He's up in his room translating a Latin passage. He's a diligent scholar, that lad. And if he goes ahead with his schemes to stand in the pulpit someday, he'll do you proud."

"Yes, he will," Alistair agreed. "I think I'll look in on him for a minute." Alistair excused himself and bounded up the stairs, two at a time. Swinging around the newel post, he caught a glimpse, through one of the open doors, of Timothy encircled by crumpled paper.

When Timothy heard Alistair's footsteps, he vaulted to his feet and embraced his father. "Dad, it's great to see you," he exclaimed. Timothy, tall and energetic like his father, had his mother's dark hair, almond eyes, and finely chiselled nose and chin. He would soon be eighteen and excelled in the third form at high school.

Alistair released his son. "I couldn't come to town without stopping by. Besides, your mother sent along a package of oatmeal cookies."

Timothy grinned at the thought of his mother's baking. "I can't wait to get on the road tomorrow," he admitted. "Aunt Maggie fusses over me like a broody hen, but it's just not the same as home." He lowered his voice. "It's so quiet here. I'm sure looking forward to helping you build those new beehives on Saturday."

Alistair smiled and patted Timothy on his shoulder. "It'll be good to get that little job done while we've got a quiet spell. Spring'll be upon us before two shakes of a lamb's hind leg."

Timothy looked into his father's eyes. "Could we go to see Reverend Smithers after we finish the hives? I'd like you along when he helps me choose my courses for next year—the best ones for seminary." He paused, his face pensive. "Dad, I really want my life to make a difference."

Alistair searched Timothy's expression. He'd always tried hard to be a good boy. "Yes, to make a difference. That's a noble ambition, son."

Then Alistair glanced over Timothy's shoulder and out the window. "The afternoon's slipping away, and it'll be dark soon. But the snow's deep and holds the track. I'd best be going." With a final squeeze of his son's shoulder, Alistair took his leave. Then, at the foot of the stairs, he turned and considered his son's tender face. "If there's more snow down tomorrow, I'll come and fetch you with the team. Six miles is too far to walk on heavy roads."

When Alistair returned at nightfall from his errands, he carried Priscilla's supplies as far as the kitchen table.

"How are Timothy and Aunt Maggie getting along?" she inquired.

"They both send their love," Alistair said. "And Timothy's put in an order for bread pudding for supper tomorrow."

Priscilla smiled suspiciously. Bread pudding with raisins was also Alistair's favourite. "One pudding or two?" she prodded with amusement.

"Good question," Alistair said with a straight face. "You'd better make two." He stood for a minute eating a slice of warm bread and butter. "Well, I'd best put the team away," he said, leaving Priscilla to look over the supplies. "I still need to feed the sheep and give them some more straw. It's going to be bitter tonight."

Priscilla straightened her back. "Phoebe's taken her usual bowl of bread and milk to the kittens. Tell her supper's ready." She paused. "She's a little teary eyed. Says she's got a stomachache."

As Alistair led the horses into the warm stable, he smiled at the thought of bread pudding. Or was it at the thought of the woman stocking the pantry, the woman at the core of his life and concerns? After tying up the team, he hurried through the stable looking for Phoebe. Rounding a box stall, he saw tears streaming down his daughter's cheeks as she sat on a mound of straw cuddling a mother cat and three striped kittens on her lap. Heavy stockings and rubbers projected below Phoebe's navy coat while flaxen braids hung over the red scarf she had knitted before Christmas. The matching mittens lay on the cream separator beside her.

"What's wrong lass? You look as if you've lost your best friend."

Phoebe raised red eyes. "I've a desperate stomachache," she sniffled.

"You've a tummy like your mother's, my dear," Alistair comforted. "Maybe a little supper'll help it feel better."

Phoebe stared, expressionless. "No, it won't," she insisted stubbornly.

"Well, hurry along," he urged. "Supper's almost ready."

When Alistair got to the sheep shed, he crawled up the ladder into the loft. After pushing fresh hay down through the open hatch in the floor, he climbed back down to fork it into the manger. Walking toward the hay, he noticed Natasha, his Great Pyrenees, sitting on the pile. He whistled. "Come on, Natasha. Get off there." The dog turned her heavy head at the sound of her master's voice. As the big white animal trotted between the ewes with the unique rolling gait of her breed, it was hard to distinguish between her and the sheep.

Alistair had often been troubled with stray dogs and coyotes harassing the helpless flock at night. In the early hours one morning, they had stolen into the pasture and made a bloodied mess of two of Alistair's prize ewes and their lambs. Finding the carnage of the dead and disembowelled creatures in the corner of the field had sickened him. This discovery was the last straw, and he had watched the newspaper advertisements for weeks until he found a Great Pyrenees, a breed used for centuries in the rugged mountains of Spain to protect sheep from predators.

When Natasha came to his side, Alistair pulled his mitt off and reached down, patting the dog's broad head and tousling her ears. Her luxuriant coat felt thick, almost like wool. "You look just like a sheep," Alistair asserted. "And sometimes you act like one too." He took out his handkerchief to blow his nose. "Whew. You even smell like a sheep," he laughed as his hand brushed his face. "I'd wager you think you're a sheep." Natasha gazed up through brown liquid eyes and wagged her woolly tail, as if agreeing.

The huge dog had never lived outside a sheep pen or a pasture. She had been whelped in the corner of a manger and, as a cuddly puppy, she had frolicked and played with the lambs. When the sheep lay down, she lay down. When they got up to graze, she walked around and sniffed the pasture. In almost every way, her life was that of a sheep.

While Alistair looked at Natasha, a question struck him hard like the kick of a horse. *Is it possible I'm like Natasha, thinking myself to be something I'm not?* This jarring parallel illuminated his mind, allowing a flood of questions to pour in. *Am I a real Christian or am I deceived too?* Alistair's mouth drew tight. *Is a man a Christian because he's been given that assurance since childhood? Or since joining a particular persuasion? Am I a Christian just because I go to church?*

As he leaned his shoulder against the door of the sheepfold and slid the barrel bolt into place, it dawned on him that Natasha could never be a sheep. "What an obvious and simple fact," Alistair said aloud. "No matter how much she looks like a sheep, the only way Natasha can truly become one is to be born of a sheep—with a sheep's nature. There's no other way."

When Natasha heard her name she lifted her head and looked in Alistair's direction. He laughed at himself for speaking out loud in the dim light of his own barnyard.

Alistair studied her rough coat again as she sniffed around the outside paddock. He suddenly realized that he would never become a Christian simply by associating with those who professed to be Christians. He knew in his heart that he had been living the Christian life as though he were a sheepdog among sheep.

As he trudged through the gently falling snow, the swinging circle of lantern light irradiated the soft flakes as they settled around him. He pictured the supper table bright with Priscilla's geraniums and the roasting chicken resplendent with rosemary dressing. Behind him, the cry of a bleating sheep penetrated the sheepfold door. A long-remembered verse sprang to mind, as if bidden by the muted sounds of creatures kneeling down in shared warmth against the winter night: "My sheep hear My voice."[2] Alistair paused on impulse, steadied the lantern and spoke into the night air, "Loving Father, shepherd of the sheep, give birth to a new life within me. Receive me into Your fold."[3]

Two

TROUBLING QUESTIONS
Late Winter 1898

One wintry Monday morning in late February, Alistair forced the handle on the frozen pump and saw with chagrin that he had accidentally snapped the bracket to the connecting rod. Staring in frustration at the jagged casting, he slammed the loose handle against the pump and turned toward the horse stable. Through the cobwebs and dust on the barn window, he could see Priscilla emerging from the summer kitchen to sprinkle a pan of cinders along the icy path.

Spying the harnessed horse, she called out. "Where are you off to?"

"I broke this dratted casting. It's still way below zero," he explained, opening his leather palm to reveal the broken part. "I hate leaving in the middle of the forenoon without my chores done." Alistair's breath burst forth in a white cloud as he shrugged like a truant school boy. "But the stock needs water, and it's got to get fixed. I'm heading over to Stephen's shop. I reckon he'll mend it in jig time."

As it happened, Stephen McElderry had unlocked his blacksmith shop early, and the broken part gave Alistair the excuse he'd been wanting to visit Stephen anyway.

"These castings are brittle as crockery in the cold," he complained, handing Stephen the bracket.

"You're right," his soft-spoken friend replied as he examined the break thoughtfully. "But it'll be right as rain in a few minutes."

As Stephen pumped the bellows to forge the new piece, Alistair leaned against the bench. "Winter's getting away," he reflected. "I heard that Jordie flushed out a skunk and got himself sprayed when he torched his tool shed Saturday night, the old ninny. He tried to herd the dazed critter into a barrel. The Halfpenny clan never had enough sense to last out the winter."

Stephen glanced up, surprised at the tone. "Well," he rejoined with typical whimsy, "there's sense and then there's nonsense. I'd guess the world needs both."

Alistair laughed sheepishly as he moved closer to the fire. After a few minutes of staring into the flames, he ventured, "When you and Emily come over Thursday after supper, there's something—a church matter—that has me unsettled. I'd like to talk it over—get another man's opinion."

Stephen's blond hair stretched down into heavy sideburns on either side of his ruddy face. The burly young man rarely offered his opinion unless asked. He clamped the bracket in his tongs and paused, deliberating the sinews flexing in Alistair's jaw. "Something in particular, Alistair?"

"I guess I just want to know how you feel about Saint Patrick's and the drift of things there. You know, all the talk about money for a new building. It just doesn't seem right anymore."

The corners of Stephen's eyes twitched with surprise, but he gave a nod as he watched the metal turning cherry red. "I'll give it some thought." Muscles rippled in his powerful shoulders and arms as he hammered the piece into shape on his anvil. When the new bracket was finished, he plunged it into a bucket of cold water. "There. How's that?"

"That should keep the water coming," Alistair said, admiring Stephen's skill. "Well, I'd better get a move on. See you on Thursday."

Stephen stood at the shop door and watched Alistair disappearing down the road. Whatever had come over the man? Alistair had never uttered a word about his neighbours before, even when old Jordie was raving up and down the whole concession. It was other folks who finally went to the magistrate about getting him settled down. Stephen scratched his head, puzzling about Alistair's cryptic reference to Saint Patrick's as he sauntered back to his anvil. Like as not, the morning's interruption had twisted him out of humour.

As Alistair drove home, he passed the gabled cottage Stephen and Emily rented at the edge of the village. He smiled as he took in the shoveled walk and gleaming windows. Just after the McElderrys' marriage two years before, he and Priscilla, along with Bill and Alice Jones, had helped the young couple get settled.

Bill and Alice, both in their mid-thirties, lived on the next concession on a farm that Bill's father had left him in his will. If a stranger had asked at the mill or the forge or even at the store for one Llewelyn Thaddeus Jones, the assembled loafers would have tipped back their hats, felt or straw according to season, and scratched their heads in bewilderment. No citizen of Puslinch answered to such a name. As a boy of ten years, Bill Jones had deliberately sloughed off this appellation and become known to everyone simply as Bill.

Alice and her family had eked out a living on a small holding at the edge of Guelph, where her father, a rough-spoken grizzly of a man who filled a doorway, worked as a teamster for an iron foundry. When work was short, he met each train with his wagon or hauled coal. His brutal habit of beating his team extended to taking swats at any of his children who crossed him or spoke out of turn. The alienation of his family eventually drove them from home as it had his wife when Alice was ten and her two brothers were even younger. Alice had learned to keep out of her father's way by hocing the garden or cleaning the chicken house. By the age of sixteen she escaped the tyranny for good, finding employment as a maid at a fashionable residence in Guelph. Still, as she gained maturity and independence, she longed for the day when she would marry and have a home and children of her own. That day finally came into view one Saturday when Alice and a friend had found a ride to a barn dance south of Guelph. Bill, arriving fresh-faced that September evening in 1889, had caught her eye and asked her for the first square dance. Only a few weeks later the couple was married.

On the Jones family farm, Bill's mother, Tillie, retained a separate part of the roughcast house with her own bedroom and sitting room, but she shared the big farm kitchen with her daughter-in-law. The sharp side of Alice's tongue could raise blisters on anyone who crossed her, but she did love Bill's mother and her tolerant devotion to the children. It was Tillie whom Alice trusted to watch them when she and Bill got together with the Stanhopes and the McElderrys on Thursday evenings.

In spite of the range in ages, the three couples took pleasure in each other's company. Occasionally they played chequers or dominoes, but for the most part they talked and laughed around the cast-iron stove, sipping hot apple cider or eating baked sweets. The heat radiating from the roaring wood fire toasted their faces and kept the kitchen pleasantly warm.

Thursday morning dawned frosty and clear, and the trees lining the laneway cast sharp blue shadows on the fresh snow. The lane was unmarked except for fallen twigs and a maze of crisscrossed rabbit tracks. As Alistair walked to the barn, he turned over the thoughts he intended to share with his friends that evening. Once during the morning, he went to the driving shed for a brace and bit and came back with a buggy wrench. At supper time he found his feet taking him toward the sheep shed before he got himself turned around and onto the path to the house. Would anybody else feel the way he did about Saint Patrick's…or was he simply overreacting, as Priscilla claimed?

The evening was crisp, and a full moon lit the farmyard as the men helped their wives down at the house gate. Priscilla hugged Alice and Emily as they entered and helped them take off their heavy coats.

As Stephen and Bill tied their horses in the warm stable, Alistair tossed a pile of hay and half a gallon of oats into each manger. The men's boots crunched along the snow-covered path that led to the house. When they stepped inside, they, too, met an enthusiastic welcome as they laid aside their outer clothing. Bill wiped the fog off his wire-rimmed spectacles and placed them carefully on the butter churn.

Alistair threw a few chunks of hardwood into the firebox, and Priscilla passed around buttered tea biscuits and large mugs of hot milk and cocoa. The tangy smell of wood smoke gave a relaxing ambience as the men talked about the drop in hog prices, the bull Alistair had for sale, and how much hay was left in Bill's mow.

"It'll sure be good to get the cattle back out to pasture for the summer," Bill said. "They're a lot of work in the stable, feeding and cleaning them out and all. But that's a good couple of months away yet."

Stephen leaned back and hooked his thumbs behind his thick belt. "What date do you generally shoot for?"

"About the tenth of May if the pasture's dry enough. If you put the stock out too early, they punch it up with their feet and damage it."

Alistair got up and stirred the fire with the poker every few minutes, and each time he cleared his throat as if to speak.

The women clustered at the other end of the wood stove, their voices mingling with the crackle of beech and maple. "How did that recipe for buttermilk spice cake from the *Herald* turn out?" Alice asked Priscilla.

Priscilla's voice rose in mirth. "A perfect flop," she chuckled. "At the last minute I forgot the cream of tartar and the thing came out of the oven flat as a nightcap boiled, starched, and sat upon..."

Laughter ensued until Alice cut in sharply. "Sweets are going to be the bane of my kitchen. Tillie's forever slipping the lads bread and honey. With tongues *that* thick and sweet, I tell her, they'll never eat proper turnips and sprouts. She even tucks molasses cookies into their pillow slips." Her eye caught a glimpse of Emily fingering a bleached sugar sack propped against her chair leg. "Why, Emily, whatever have you got in that bag?"

Emily, as though forced to divulge a secret, reached deep inside and withdrew a tiny garment—a dainty pin-tucked gown she had sewn. Alice's round face beamed as her eyes took in the embroidered square yolk, full sleeves, scalloped hem, and lavish trimming of Valenciennes lace. In the fine white muslin, the hand stitching was nearly invisible. Priscilla met Alice's eyes. So *this* was why Emily had been hoarding her pin money.

For a moment Emily herself seemed at a loss for words. The exquisite garment lay spread over her lap, awaiting as it seemed only a starry stranger of nine months, still unshaped and unknown. Then, her breath catching in her throat, she said shyly, "It's...not as if we're beginning to hope right away." A sudden uplift of her eyes revealed alert concern and curiosity in the faces of Alice and Priscilla.

Timothy, home with a bout of the grippe, bounded down the stairs to join the men and paused at Emily's shoulder, startled by the silence among the women. He gazed blankly at the baby gown. "Looks like something the fairies brought in," he said, an unaccountable drollery in his voice.

Emily blushed and began to roll up the precious garment, but not before both Priscilla and Alice had reached out to caress its snowy loveliness. "Such fine stitching," they exclaimed in unison. "It's gorgeous."

With a glance toward the men, Emily lowered her voice. "Stephen and I have always felt bad about losing what we hoped would be our first little one," she confided. "And since then nothing seems to be happening." Her hands fluttered in a resigned gesture.

After an hour or so of rural news and pantry gossip, Alistair could hold back no longer. He raised his voice to include the women as he interposed awkwardly. "I'm sorry I didn't get a chance to stop and visit all of you this week," he said as he glanced over at Bill and Alice. "When I was at Stephen's shop, I mentioned to him that I wanted to discuss a few things about the church. I'm talking to all of you because you're my closest friends and I really want to know what you think. I just hope I won't upset any of you."

"I'm sure whatever you have to say won't leave any of us huffed," Alice assured him, smiling. "We've always been honest with each other." The stout woman's face, as open as a sunflower, beamed around the group.

Alistair paused for a moment before plunging ahead. "When Ben died, I realized that death...well, it scares me, to tell you the truth. I want to know what will happen to me after I die. It maddens me to think I may be taken away surrounded by doubts and fears." He hesitated, scratching an imaginary itch at the back of his neck. "I want to be sure. And it seems to me that church should be the place we get these answers. Why do we go, really? Isn't it to know God better? If that's so, I want to tell you, it's not working the best for me." He paused again, staring absentmindedly at the clock as if he could somehow make it run in reverse and bring Ben back. "I don't want to pretend to be a Christian or look like one without truly being one—I need to know what it really means to follow Jesus." It was the most heartfelt appeal Alistair had ever made, spilling out quickly and leaving his shoulders hunched.

Glancing up he saw Priscilla frowning as she studied her friends' faces. The others shifted in their chairs, fidgeting uncomfortably. After a couple of awkward minutes, Bill spoke up. "I have no idea what you mean, Alistair. I've been a Christian all my life." Defensiveness edged his voice.

Alistair crossed his legs. "There's not a single person at Saint Patrick's who doesn't think he's going to heaven. Until recently I thought so too. But now I'm not so sure. God's showing me that I need something more."

"Don't be so hard on yourself," Alice objected. "You're more of a Christian than most people."

"Thanks," Alistair said. "I know you mean that, but it's just not true."

Stephen's square face bore a puzzled intensity. "Just what does being a Christian mean to *you*, Alistair?"

Alistair rubbed his hand over his forehead and eyes. "In a way, I hardly know," he allowed. "I'm still groping for the light. But I'm beginning to understand that it has a lot more to do with living close to God and trusting Him than it has to do with just going to church."

"But isn't church where we learn to trust God?" Alice persisted.

"That's the point. I've been going to church all my life. Then something happens, like Ben being struck down, and I realize I hardly trust God at all." Alistair took a deep breath. "Besides, I get tired of hearing about money all the time. It hit me hard that first Sunday right after Ben died, as if the building was more important than our souls."

"Didn't you see the snow sifting in around the cracks during Ben's funeral?" Bill demanded, incredulous. "Unless people hear about the need for money, they won't give."

"Actually, you've hit the nail on the head, Bill. Frankly, I wasn't thinking about the building at all. I was thinking about Ben. And whether I really know Jesus for myself. That's what's important. I need to know Him better. As real as I know you. And to learn to trust Him for help with everyday problems and questions, not just think about Him on Sundays and at the funerals of friends."

Bill rested his elbows on his knees, cupped his hands together, and fixed his eyes on Alistair. "All right. So you don't think going to church helps," he said tensely. "What do you have in mind?"

"Well, I'm not sure. That's why I wanted to talk with you all. But one good thing's happened. About a month ago I started reading the Bible every chance I got. One thing I noticed right off is that the disciples lived with Jesus and followed Him in a very simple, practical way." As Alistair wrapped his hands around his warm mug and smiled, a new confidence, a different strength seemed to pervade his being.

Bill eyed him skeptically, ripe for debate. "Make some sense, man," he urged. "That was then and this is now. And what about the fact that Jesus isn't on earth anymore?"

When Priscilla detected resistance in Bill's voice, she cut in. "How about some more cocoa everyone?"

"No thanks, I'm just fine," Bill replied, as he sat forward on the edge of his chair. Alistair looked in Priscilla's direction and shook his head, in the silent eloquent speech of a long-married husband.

"That's partly right, Bill," Alistair said thoughtfully. "Now is now, and then was then. But Jesus is just as present in Spirit today as He was in body then. My heart needs to follow Him—even when I'm working in the barn or doing whatever. I suspect that's what'll give me happiness and peace. The thing I know for certain is this—when this body dies, my spiritual part is going to continue on someplace. I want it to be with God."

Emily's eyes softened as she looked at Alistair. "I know how Ben's death must be affecting you," she sympathized. "I was badly shaken up myself when my older sister died of pneumonia on Christmas Day, back in 1884. She was only sixteen. I knew then that I needed God, but I just didn't know how to approach Him." She stopped, hesitating for a few seconds. "For a long time part of me has been crying out as well, aching for something beyond religion, something that will bring me closer to my Maker."

Stephen gaped at Emily, admiring his tall, slender wife and yet taken aback at this uncharacteristic openness. Her sweet, thoughtful expression and pale complexion reminded him of the porcelain Eaton Beauty dolls he had seen in Crundle's store the previous Christmas season. The slight limp Emily still carried from a horse kick during childhood gave her a fragile impression of vulnerability.

Alice squinted as she listened attentively. "Sometimes I feel like the barn well in July—almost empty. When I was a girl and that happened, my pop was fit to be tied. We dasn't get in his way then or we'd get a tongue lashing or the switch. My life's better now with Bill and the young ones, but it can still be dry at times. Maybe Alistair has a point. I'd be game to talk about it again."

"All I can say is that I'll have to think about it some more," Bill muttered. "Frankly, I'm pretty skeptical. I'm not sure we can do much more than we're doing right now."

Priscilla said nothing. Although she didn't want to oppose Alistair in front of their friends, she agreed entirely with Bill.

After a little more discussion Stephen looked at the clock and stood up. "Thanks for the tea biscuits, Priscilla. Mr. Rogers' heavy team needs to be sharp shod first thing in the morning, so I think we'd better head on home."

Long after the younger couples had bidden goodnight and Alistair and Priscilla had climbed into bed, his ear picked up the distant baying of Jordie's foxhounds. Drawing steadily nearer, their rich full-throated melody rose and fell across the frozen moonlit fields as the dogs pursued their quarry through the cedar swamp. Two hours later Alistair still lay awake, replaying the evening's happenings. Priscilla was sleeping softly beside him, the goose down comforter bunched under her chin, her breath a frosty column. He could hear the house creak and a rafter, somewhere in the darkness above him, snapped with the biting cold.

He reflected on the futility and frustration his forty-six years had given him, even considering the usual joys of family life and farm labour. But now for the first time, he felt a springlike sense of hope. Maybe he could find God alone, but he preferred to seek Him with the others.

Alistair snuggled into his feather pillow. At least some of his friends seemed to understand this evening. Could he hope it would lead to genuine change? And that they'd finally made one small step toward something real? Something that would outlast life itself; something that would prepare him for the day he would follow Ben? Eventually, exhausted from the day's events, he sank into the depths of sleep.

The following morning after the breakfast dishes were dried, Priscilla shook out her pastry cloth with unusual vigour. As she sifted flour with salt, she found her hands shaking and her lips trembling. "Alistair's wayward notions could raise Bill's hackles so high that he refuses to bring Alice next Thursday," she muttered, cutting a chunk of white lard into the flour.

Priscilla's hands flew as she tore about the kitchen, her face clouded in a dark scowl. By noon, she had worked herself into a lather, watching the hands of the clock as they crept past twelve and then one.

"Forgot the way home, did you?" she fumed when Alistair finally appeared in the doorway.

"The auctioneer dragged out the sale of the bulls, and I hung on to see what they'd fetch," he defended himself.

Priscilla stared balefully at the kettle before turning an indignant face on him. "You say you love my cooking, love to hear me sing," she alleged. "You say you appreciate the sheets boiled in lavender, but you forget there's still a wife here that you need to pay some mind to. Sometimes I wonder if you really do love me. Or whether I'm just a reliable cook in your kitchen. Another one of your livestock."

The accusation in her voice irked Alistair for a moment before he sprang forward and pulled her to him. "Foolish lass," he murmured into the glistening coils of her hair. "I do love to be with you. It's just that I tried to squeeze too much into my morning."

Alistair's mind whirled as he held his sniffling wife. "I know we have some hitches between us, but what's upset the apple cart just now?" he asked sympathetically. "The discussion last night, was that it?"

Priscilla said nothing, but the slight catch in her throat acknowledged the perceptiveness of his assertion.

Alistair's face creased. "We might need to slog through some muck, but I truly believe this might be the answer, not the problem."

Seeing that Priscilla had no intention of talking further, he took his place at the table and turned back his shirt cuffs, eating his meal in silence. Later, as Alistair picked his way down the cinder-strewn path toward the barn, Priscilla stared out the window, her eyes red, her simmering emotion spent. What about the confidences Emily and Alice had shared the previous evening? Still pondering, she drummed on the windowsill with her fingertips for several minutes before turning back to her work. Could it be they might understand the loneliness she was feeling?

On the next concession, the events of Alice's week followed their natural course. But from time to time, she, too, thought back to Alistair's words and considered her respect for the man. Was it possible that his present worries were merely a prolonged grieving for the loss of a good friend and nothing more? Then she recalled the ardent concern on his face as he spoke and pondered her own weaknesses. Maybe Alistair wasn't so far off the mark after all.

Bill had made no mention of Alistair's assertions, and Alice wondered what he might be thinking as he sat silently munching an apple a few days later. His slight build, gentle manner, cool head, and stable upbringing spoke to her of all the things her father had never been. Given time, Bill would arrive at a deliberate and balanced conclusion of his own.

Meanwhile, two miles away, Stephen and Emily also earnestly considered Alistair's words. One morning after Stephen left for his anvil and forge, Emily closed her bedroom door and knelt beside their bed. "Dear God, please come to me in a more real way than ever before," she pleaded. "Help me understand what You have in mind for my life." Previously she had prayed only in times of dire distress—when all else had failed. And even then she did not always turn to God. But Alistair's recent words had found a kindred spirit in Emily.

By the following Thursday, the temperature had risen slightly and a hint of flurries drifted on the air. And, as punctual as ever, at half past seven, the Jones' and the McElderrys' sleighs turned into the lane of Wood Creek Farm. Hot bricks on the floor of the sleighs and thick buffalo robes had helped to keep them warm on the ride to the Stanhopes'. Alice brought a hamper with a hot apple pie and maple muffins wrapped in a blanket.

Once inside, Bill opened the warming closet above the cook top and set his mitts neatly on it to dry. After he opened the oven door, he put his sock feet on the door itself and leaned back in his chair. Each person settled into their regular place around the crackling stove. They had spoken about general things for only a few minutes before Bill raised the church issue.

"I've been puzzling about last week's discussion," he said. "I'm still far from being convinced, but I know Alice is interested. So we're willing to give something a try."

Alice's cheeks still flamed red from the frosty ride. "Maybe we could make every Thursday an informal Christian meeting," she suggested as everyone sipped their tea. "We could sing a few hymns around the piano."

"It might be good to read some Scripture, too, to broaden our understanding," Emily suggested. "I've never read much in the past. I was content to rely on the minister's sermons. As a result I don't have much firsthand knowledge of what the Bible actually teaches."

Alistair blinked thoughtfully in the soft lamplight, and then he added, "I've noticed that in New Testament times, little groups of believers met in each other's homes. There were no budgets, building committees, or church politics. And I can't find a shred of evidence of a salaried minister."

"But what about having someone with proper training tell us what the Bible means?" Bill challenged him. "Don't you think Reverend Smithers' sermons help us know Jesus better?"

Alistair hesitated, weighing his response carefully. "No, I guess I don't," he confessed. "I don't find much life in most of them. Nothing that touches my soul—and it gives me no pleasure to admit that."

"I think it takes something else…something no clergyman can do for us," Emily said, putting her finger on the very heart of the matter. "Since last Thursday I've found myself praying urgently, asking God to come to me in a more definite way than ever before. I can't explain just why it's happened now. I guess because of how you laid your soul bare, Alistair." She paused and caught her breath. "I've come to see that each one of us must become desperate to enter into our own private friendship with God. For myself, I'm committed to a life with Him and dozens of times this week I have earnestly prayed, 'God, be merciful. I'm such a sinner.'"[1]

Alistair's spine stiffened when Emily openly admitted to being a sinner, fearful that she might embarrass herself. He fumbled with his shirt collar, swallowing dryly, as she exposed her deepest feelings in such a vulnerable way. "It's not just you, Emily," he assured her, his voice gentle with concern, "we're *all* sinners by nature—separated from God."

Priscilla, her face a study in consternation, ran her hand over the warmth of the stove's water reservoir. She had never imagined that Emily felt desperate; she always seemed so cheerful. *And I thought I was the only one aching inside,* she mused. *But what does Emily actually mean when she speaks about being a friend of God?*

Still, Priscilla summoned the courage to state her own convictions. "Well, I don't think we should be so hasty in judging ourselves. We all make mistakes, but we just have to pull ourselves up by the bootstraps and do better. And Saint Patrick's is a good church. Reverend Smithers graduated from a fine seminary, and his sermons lay out his knowledge." Priscilla's platitudes seemed to put a damper on the others' conversation.

Stirring uneasily, Stephen locked his charcoaled fingers. When Alistair bent down to tug a burr from Teddy's shaggy coat, the sprawling collie thumped its tail against his chair leg. At that moment seminary knowledge seemed a long way from the needs of both men and dogs.

Startled by an exploding knothole in the stove, Emily jumped, and then she settled back, blushing. An awkward silence filled the kitchen as Priscilla's declarations hung in the air.

Alice scanned the tense faces around the circle. "Anybody going to turn down a slab of apple pie?" she asked, getting briskly to her feet. Stern-faced, Priscilla followed her to the table.

Reaching into her wicker basket, Alice surveyed the company with laughing eyes. "My old aunt always said apple pie without cheese is like a kiss without a squeeze."

Priscilla chuckled in spite of herself. "I've got a hoop of cheddar that wants finishing," she offered as she headed for the pantry.

As the evening drew to a close, Alistair made a suggestion. "Why don't we all read the first chapter of John's Gospel before next Thursday and come prepared to share one simple thought?"

"That's a fine idea," Alice rejoined with enthusiasm. "We can pool our thoughts and have a good discussion."

Emily set her empty cup on the end of the dough box. "Maybe we could also include any other experience or reflection we have during the week that focuses us on Jesus."

"Sounds like homework to me," Bill protested in a matter-of-fact tone as he stood up. "Anyway, I'll give it some thought and see what happens."

Alistair smiled and followed the couples to the door. "Thanks for coming this evening," he said as Bill laced up his boots. Alistair turned to help Alice on with her long coat. "The apple pie was great. People would beat a path to your door if they knew about it. No flavour like a good Spy."

"Thanks for everything, Alistair," Emily murmured as she slipped her arm into the coat he held. "It seems you've kindled a fire in my heart."

As the friends stepped from the warm kitchen into the winter night, the icy stoop crackled with frost. The farmyard lay in brilliant starlight reflected on the fresh snow that softened every ridge and curve. The winter heavens revealed the face and breath of God. Like the Milky Way sparkling overhead, His Word hovered, waiting to illuminate their hearts.

"The flurries have come and gone," Alistair remarked as he looked up. "Now remember, it's the first chapter of John's Gospel. I learned the whole thing by heart as a boy, and I recollect even then feeling its mystery and beauty. Aunt Maggie tried to explain it out to me, but I think even she got lost in the absolute vastness of it all…" He paused, lost in his memories for a minute. Then he caught himself and smiled. "Good night, all. Safe home."

And so it was, that on the following Thursday, while the cold fires of the northern lights advanced and receded toward the pole, the six friends gathered around the radiant heat of the Stanhope cookstove. After hearty greetings and a few good-natured laughs, the earnest seekers bent their heads in the lamplight over the sacred mysteries of the fourth Gospel. The room became quiet as they seemed to defer to Alistair's leading.

"Let's read a couple of verses apiece before we talk it over," he suggested. The unfamiliarity of the exercise reflected in the voices as each one carefully articulated the words on the page before them. When the entire chapter had been read, Alistair said, "The words are so simple, the meaning so deep that it can barely be fathomed."

Stephen coughed suddenly. Then, as though weighing the words, he slowly repeated the opening phrase, " 'In the beginning…' It's like a second creation story," he noted, "only here in the New Testament, the emphasis is on God the Son."

Alistair traced his right ear with his finger. "In the beginning," he repeated reflectively. "Everything has a beginning except God, and I sense our gathering tonight is the beginning of a journey that will lead us far beyond our present understanding. Have you ever noticed that in the first three verses of Genesis we see God, the Spirit, and the Light? Just like the world itself, wouldn't it be wonderful if He would reshape this formless earth out of which we are all created."

"And that the light of Christ would shine upon our hearts," Emily added softly.

In a voice diffident with self-consciousness, Stephen began to tabulate the names he had found in the first chapter. "The Word, the Light, Son of God, Lamb of God, Rabbi, Master, the Messiah, the Christ, Jesus of Nazareth, son of Joseph, King of Israel, Son of man…" He paused. "We listen to folks differently, depending on who they are. Who, I've been asking myself, is Jesus to me?"

"And Nathanael," Alice interrupted, "must have seen Him just as a carpenter, the son of Joseph. He was the doubter who asked, 'Can there any good thing come out of Nazareth?' My father used to ask that. Only he said Nassagaweya instead of Nazareth—that's where my ma came from…" A surge of discomfort rippled around the circle causing sideways glances of quiet humour.

Near the end of the meeting, Emily's voice seemed to come out of distracted concentration. "Jesus' promise in the very last verse reminds me of Jacob's dream way back in Genesis when he slept, pillowed on a stone, and saw angels ascending and descending—Jesus' very words—on a ladder to heaven." The dialogue among the friends progressed until near midnight as they pored over the realization that Jesus was indeed that stairway, their access to the kingdom of heaven.

When finally no one else had anything to add, there were a few yawns and the Jones and the McElderrys rose to leave. The snow flurries had waned, the moon was clear, and a slight frigid breeze greeted them as they hitched their cutters and turned for home.

The next morning Alistair awakened before Priscilla and crossed the cold floor to the window, where the first rays of the sun glittered across delicate, snow-covered fields. His lips moved in heartfelt conviction as he recaptured the soft spirit of the previous evening. "And *we* beheld His glory, the glory as of the only begotten of the Father, full of grace and truth."

Three

ENCOUNTER IN BERLIN
Spring 1898

Kindled by the early rays of the sun, a row of prisms blazed from the icicles that dripped and occasionally plummeted from the barn eaves. A recent thaw had exposed bare patches of earth along the gangway, and Alistair could smell the frost heaving out of the ground. Beyond the barnyard fence, on the sheltered south side of the ice house, Priscilla's snowdrops had appeared, like shivering groups of little girls who had put on their white summer dresses far too soon.

One sunny morning in early April, Alistair coaxed a finely muscled Shorthorn bull into a stout livestock crate set directly on the sleigh bunks. At a special auction for breeders in Berlin, he was assured of getting the best price for the many hours he had invested in this promising young animal. As though dazzled by the sheen of sun on snow, the bull resisted, and then, without warning, it heaved its huge bulk forward between the racks, its head lowered and forelegs splayed. Alistair smiled proudly as he reassured the bull, "You'll show 'em fella—they'll see what kind of bloodlines come from Wood Creek Farm. There won't be many set up as good as you." Climbing onto the seat behind the horses, he waved to Priscilla and started with a lurch down the lane.

White-blanketed fields lay on either side, waiting patiently for spring as though a goose down comforter had been drawn over their autumn nakedness. Alistair looked forward to the four-hour trip, and for a few miles he thought about Ben, wondering where he might be now. "Life's a voyage that's homeward bound," echoed in Alistair's ears—the sea captain's wisdom reverberating over the solid ground of Wellington County.

The team had just crossed a narrow plank bridge when a large crow swooped out of a nearby wood lot. Startlingly black against the porcelain blue sky, the solitary bird flew levelly alongside the sleigh for a few seconds. Caught in a whimsical mood, Alistair wondered how the rolling terrain of Puslinch Township would look through a crow's eye as the sleigh passed through cedar swamps, traversing the dips and hills where stands of uncut forest reached up and delicately fingered the sky.

As the miles slipped by, Alistair harked back to his previous week's reading in the book of Acts. The early church was referred to as *the way*.[1] Perhaps, he deduced, because Christians journey along a spiritual path. *We reside in one place, but don't we need the outlook of the early disciples, homeless travelers on the road with Jesus, following and trusting Him so completely that He became their way, their truth, their life?*[2] As the rolling contours of the township began to soften, Alistair's eyes meandered down snow-choked lanes and overgrown bypaths on either side. *How tragic*, he mused, *if a man wanders all of his life and never arrives at his spiritual home.*

After a couple of hours, Alistair found himself among the fertile farms of Waterloo County and could see other sleighs, also loaded with anxious and occasionally bellowing bulls, approaching the intersections of country concessions leading into Berlin.

By the time Alistair arrived at the sale barn, his stomach was growling. He unhitched the horses and tied them up in a stall. Then he led the bull to a display pen full of clean straw. The sharp frigid air surged with particles of straw dust stirred up by the feet of beasts, young and lusty, herded together in strange surroundings that struck fear to their raw instincts. A subdued bellowing rumbled from deep within their chests as they shoved and strained against the sides of confining chutes and pens.

After placing large forkfuls of hay, scoops of oats, and pails of water in front of the bull and the horses, Alistair patted his bull on the shoulder, caught up his lunch bag, and sauntered into the sale barn.

Behind a rough wooden counter, the tea lady sloshed out a steaming cup of tea as Alistair counted out two coins. "Now mind ye don't set yerself in the draught. There's a terrible lot of pewmony around, I hear. Folks that's neglected theirselves…"

A man can't move a whisker without a woman telling him how to do it, Alistair reflected in wry humour as he watched the farmers milling around, their faces tanned and weathered, the healthy complexion of men who laboured in the fresh air and sunshine.

As he finished the last of his roast beef and buttered bread, his eyes were drawn to a slim man of medium stature sitting on a bench across the room. He appeared to be about thirty years old and, like all the others, wore dark overalls, a heavy coat, and a woolen cap. What attracted Alistair's attention was the way the man paused to remove his hat and give thanks before beginning to eat. Alistair had never seen this done outside the home. The simple gesture was accomplished without an upward glance. Only then did the young fellow start his simple meal, oblivious to the hustle and bustle of men coming and going. When he had finished eating, he stroked his neatly trimmed beard to dislodge any leftover bread crumbs.

Alistair got up and went out to check on his animals. As he approached the pen, two men were leaning over the side.

"Nice straight top line and no waste in the front end," one admired, pointing at the animal's trim brisket. "And with clean shoulders like that, the heifers won't have trouble calving." He swung around toward Alistair, sensing him to be the bull's owner. "Who owns his sire?"

"Are the cows from this bloodline heavy milkers?" the other inquired.

Alistair answered their questions in detail, and before they left, the two farmers promised to bid when the bull was brought into the sale ring. A glance at his pocket watch told Alistair it was nearly one o'clock, time for the auction to begin.

A set of narrow steps led up to the higher seats around the ring and, as the bleachers filled quickly with farmers from many miles away, Alistair found a vantage point from which to observe the proceedings. The sale ring took on the air of a Roman forum as men of all ages—strapping sons, sharp-eyed fathers, deliberate uncles, and doddering grandfathers—wrapped in woolen layers from the skin out, sweated in anticipation together. Their language—half gesture and half windy rhetoric—focused on the attributes of the prospective herd sires, for this was the time of year to buy a young bull for the spring breeding season. On a platform the auctioneer bantered with the faces circling the ring, preparing to emit his staccato bombast and looking as inscrutable as the noblest Roman of them all.

Among the influx of men, Alistair again noticed the young man from the lunch area. He, too, was making his way to the upper seats, approaching closer and closer until he hesitated at the very row in which Alistair sat. Turning, he started along the row toward Alistair.

"Anyone sitting here?" he asked.

Alistair shook his head, and the man sat down beside him. His pleasant, boyish face carried a ready smile and his pale blue eyes twinkled. After sitting for a few minutes, he unfastened his coat and struggled to remove it. He turned toward Alistair, draping his coat over the back of the bench.

"G'day," the man said in a genial voice. "My name's George Farnham, from Arkell." After Alistair introduced himself, they spoke about the weather, the sale, and the price of bulls. Alistair wondered how he might find out more about this quiet farmer who had prayed unashamedly before eating his meal. Something seemed strikingly different about George Farnham. No ordinary farmer, interested only in the weather and the bulls, he exuded a kind of peace, a serenity which drew Alistair into wanting to know more about him.

The sale progressed smartly, and when Alistair's bull was led into the ring, a hushed concentration settled as the bidders studied the easy gait and powerful structure of the beast, one of the finest being offered. The bidding opened and continued briskly until the auctioneer cried out, "Sold to the man with the handsome fur hat right down here for one hundred and sixty-five dollars!" It was an excellent price, and Alistair was well pleased. Still, he felt as if he had some unfinished business. As he followed George down the steps after the sale, Alistair gathered his courage. "Sitting behind a fella with a pipe and a can of Prince Albert leaves a man's throat dry," he managed to say. "What about a cup of tea before you get on the road?"

The young man readily agreed, and a few minutes later the two men were lingering over tea in the main room, discussing calving problems and the best solutions for dipping sheep to protect against ticks. After draining his cup, George reached for his coat and fumbled in the deep pocket. He drew out a small paper bag. "Like a horehound candy for the road?" he offered with a grin.

"Thank you," Alistair said, popping a piece of the hard candy into his mouth. Just before George stood up to go, Alistair cleared his throat. "I happened to notice that you gave thanks for your food at lunch time," he ventured. "Mind telling me what church you go to?"

When George's head jerked up, his eyes startled, his lean, sunburned face wincing, Alistair wondered if he had miscalculated.

Then George's features relaxed into a smile. "Well, you know, I've gone to church on Sundays ever since I was a boy." He paused awkwardly, as if unsure of how much to say. "But to be honest, I try to be aware of God all the time. I know He watches over me, and I want to thank Him for that."

Alistair's voice betrayed his delight. "That's how I feel," he declared. "I'm trying to sense God's presence more of the time. It's a new thing for me, just started this winter when one of my closest friends passed on."

As the conversation deepened, Alistair found it hard to believe how similar their feelings were. It was apparent to him that George had an inner life with Christ. The simple act of thanksgiving was only an outward indication of something much deeper in George's heart.

Alistair broke into a smile and leaned forward. "My wife and I meet with two other couples for a Bible discussion on Thursday evenings. That exercise is helping us understand some things we never knew before." He could see the spark growing in George's eyes.

"That's very interesting," George responded. "Been meeting long?"

"No. Just a few weeks, actually."

A pensiveness crossed George's face as he toyed with his empty cup. "I've a good friend, Jack Gillan. For a long time, he and I've thrashed over the idea of inviting a few others to talk over and search the Scriptures." He stroked his beard, trying to picture the gathering. "Do you mind me asking how it went at first?"

Alistair smiled at the man's perceptiveness. "Well, a tad awkward, I have to admit. You know how it is, nobody knew just what to say. None of us were in the habit of talking about the Bible outside of church. Or even in church, for that matter. We were trained up to be listeners. Anyway, we plunged ahead and sang a few hymns to break the ice. Then we read a chapter in John's Gospel. But we're finding our feet now."

"More like a prayer meeting then, is it?"

Alistair laughed. "Not much prayer so far. I got up the nerve to share a short prayer by the third evening. And now two or three of the others have caught on too. But praying out loud with other folks listening is a bit of a stretch for most of us."

George's expression remained attentive. "I hope I didn't sound like a nosy parker," he said apologetically. "But it's just the sort of thing that really draws me."

Not wanting to lose contact, Alistair had been puzzling how he could keep in touch with this new friend. Suddenly an idea popped into his head.

"Would you consider coming along next Thursday in time for supper?" he blurted out. "I know it's a bit of a ride, but you could stay overnight and head home first thing in the morning."

George's eyes widened. "Well, if you're sure it's all right with the lady of the house, I'd be delighted," he exclaimed. Then his voice slowed. "How would you feel if Jack came along with me?"

Alistair nodded enthusiastically. "Of course. That'd be grand."

"Jack is most sincere in his search for God," George explained. "He works around the property for Reverend Chumbley in Brookville and is also the colporteur in Nassagaweya and Eramosa Townships. He distributes the Scriptures, as well as tracts and religious books. That's how we met. I was picking stones in my front field when he stopped at the fence to talk. As you know, being a church colporteur isn't too fat a living. But Jack's single, and he can scratch a living off a rock. Besides, his main idea is to help people spiritually."

Alistair's brow wrinkled as he listened. He knew of a few churches that had colporteurs. Traditionally, they were paid about a dollar per week plus some of the profits on the books they sold door-to-door. They had to find their own keep and cover their own traveling expenses. *George's friend must be mighty sincere to do that,* he thought.

George paused and stroked his sandy beard. "Even though Jack's still doing this, he told me that he's becoming disheartened. Walking up and down the roads by himself has given him plenty of time to think. He's come to feel that being a Christian is a very simple but living thing. He often meets people who are outwardly religious but few who truly want to be influenced by the Spirit of Christ. The two of us get together often."

George's voice filled with admiration as he spoke of his friend's zeal. "One evening when Jack was home visiting his folks in Eden Mills, his father and some of the neighbours were sitting around the table. They were talking on and on about the barley harvest. After a while Jack must have got tired of it, because he suddenly took hold of a Bible. 'I think we'd be better to learn something about this,' he told them, 'rather than being taken up so much with the barley.'"

Alistair listened intently, picturing the scene in the farm kitchen.

"The men were dumbfounded and the conversation stopped at once," George said. "That night Jack told his dad and the neighbours an intriguing story from his reading in English history. Seemed to help the men understand what Jack was driving at. If you ask, I'm sure he'll be happy to tell it again. It'll help you understand how much he loves Jesus."

Alistair rubbed his palms against his knees absently. "Yes, I'll be sure to do that," he replied. "I'd be very interested in hearing it."

George wrapped his scarf around his neck and buttoned his coat. "Anyway, Jack's father and his neighbours seemed to like what he had to say," George said. "News traveled fast, and for a while Jack had quite a crowd coming to his parents' place each week. But sadly, his listeners seemed to lose interest after a while and the meetings stopped."

As the two men stepped outside, Alistair extended a warm grip to George and offered him directions to Wood Creek Farm. "Goodbye," he said, "and a good road home. The snow's still heavy enough for runners."

After George had returned his handshake and met his eyes with a flash of fellow-feeling, Alistair adjusted his fur cap and watched the younger man climb into his cutter. Then he turned to his sleigh, much lighter now without his prize bull, and hitched up his team. It was certain, he felt, that God's hand had directed his day and had brought George to the very place where he had been sitting.[3]

The following Thursday afternoon was mild and foggy. Stephen McElderry looked up from the heavy anvil where he was shaping a red-hot horseshoe and gazed out the open door of the blacksmith shop. As he studied the vague horizon, it was hard to determine where the white fields met the white mist. Only yesterday Alistair had stopped by on his way home from the village and shared the news that two visitors would be joining them for their evening meeting.

The shop was busy, and Stephen concentrated on replacing a worn-out set of shoes on the Hespeler milkman's horse. Old Ned was docile and picked up his heavy feet at Stephen's prodding. The big Clydesdale's job was to pull the loaded milk wagon, stopping in front of each door. Often the children ran to feed the patient beast a lump of sugar, a carrot, or an apple as he paused instinctively along the delivery route.

Stephen steadied Old Ned's foot against his heavy leather apron as he trimmed the edges and the frog to fit the new shoe. Then he turned and pressed a row of square nails between his lips before starting to pound them into the hoof. "It's a pleasure to work on such a gentle horse," he said to the milkman when the last nail was clinched and broken off.

Just as Stephen was turning the lock on the shop door at six o'clock, he saw two strangers riding past on horseback. *Won't be the men Alistair told me about,* he concluded. *They'll be coming from the east. Like the wise men.* He chuckled at his own private joke as he hurried home. He and Emily rushed through supper in their eagerness to get to the Stanhopes' on time.

Anticipation swelled in Bill, Alice, Stephen, and Emily as they came in the door. Smiling, George scrambled to his feet and waited to be introduced as each couple entered the room. His firm handshake and his expectant blue eyes communicated the same warmth and quiet respect that Alistair had felt at the sale barn.

Jack, somewhat shorter and heavier set with broad shoulders, stood beside him. Beneath dark hair, his round wind-burned face wore a perpetual tan and his lips parted over white teeth in a friendly smile. Something about his alert brown eyes gave the impression of roguishness just below Jack's deferential manner as he stepped forward to acknowledge the hearty welcome.

As Emily slipped into her place at one end of the wood stove, she noticed the fresh polish on George's rough farm boots and that Jack's heavy plaid shirt, tucked inside a thick belt, had been carefully pressed. She listened as the others chatted affably.

After a few minutes, Alistair passed around some hymnals. "We usually begin by singing hymns," he explained.

The resonance of Jack's deep baritone harmonized wonderfully as the group sang the hymns together. Then five of the voices around the gathered circle were raised, as each felt prompted by the Holy Spirit, to offer two or three sentences of earnest prayer. Afterward, each person in turn read a short portion from the sixth chapter of John's Gospel.

Emily was the first to speak. "Several times in this chapter, Jesus associates the word 'life' with Himself. We need to be certain that our Lord is the central theme each time we meet. And indeed, each day of our existence. Otherwise we can't be blessed by the Life that He is."

Alice leaned forward. "Speaking about life, I found a broody hen patiently sitting on some eggs three weeks ago," she observed, "but they weren't fertilized by a rooster. Even if she sat there for months, they'd never hatch. It made me realize that unless God plants a divine seed in our hearts, our best efforts won't bring forth new life either." Her eyes sparkled.

Alistair then said, "That calls to mind a turkey that had nested near our woodpile years ago. I noticed she had laid eight eggs but had hatched only two turkey chicks. I saw that a weasel had made a tiny hole and sucked the insides out of the other six, leaving the shells intact in the nest. I'm sorry to say I've done that myself—presented the hollow pretense of being a Christian but without any inner life!"

"You know, I'm seeing things in a whole new light too," Stephen said. "I've been needing a couple of new handles for my mallets, so yesterday I snowshoed back to the bush to cut down a small elm. On the way through the swamp I caught a glimpse of a cottontail struggling in a snare. Somebody's going to be right annoyed, but I released the wretched creature. And when I did, I saw the rabbit had been baited with pieces of carrot and apple. That helped me to understand the craftiness and cruelty of the devil. He also has special lures to entangle each of us.[4] He knows just what'll attract us, draw us away from God, and choke off our spiritual life."

Wonderful fellowship followed, and everyone except Bill and Priscilla shared a personal experience or reflection. As the evening progressed, Alistair noted that although Bill's remarks were guarded, he did enter into the discussion, but Priscilla remained silent.

While the three women sliced and served desserts, Alistair poured the hot milk and cocoa. In the background he overheard Stephen speaking to George and Jack. "I hope you fellows can come again next week. Emily and I have a couple of shakedowns for travelers."

Alistair smiled. Kindred spirits had found each other.

After the couples had gone home, Priscilla put her hand over her mouth to stifle a yawn. "If you gentlemen will excuse me, I think I'd better go to bed."

The men said good night to Priscilla while Alistair refilled their cups and tossed another piece of wood in the stove. Then the three of them settled back in their chairs. For a few minutes they said nothing, listening as the block of cedar snapped and crackled in the firebox. The far-off howl of a brush wolf broke the spell.

"Jack, I understand you have a special story," Alistair said.

Jack looked puzzled. "I do?"

George smiled. "The message you shared with your dad and the neighbours that first night in Eden Mills. I mentioned it to Alistair when I met him at the sale barn."

"Well, it's more like a parable than anything else," Jack said, his eyebrows raised questioningly.

"That's just fine," Alistair reassured him. "Please go ahead."

"It goes like this," Jack said, clearing his throat. Carefully, he began to unfold his story as if he were handling something very precious.

"Identical twins, Adam and Joshua, lived in England during the 1620s. No one in the village of Ipswich could tell them apart. Adam was found guilty of stealing a basket of bread from a nobleman's kitchen and sentenced to die. Times were lean, and he could hardly bear the thought of leaving his wife and four small children alone. His wife's love for him was deep, and she suffered dreadfully, struggling to come to grips with the imminent catastrophe. She had no way to provide food for herself and the children. Losing her husband would inflict terrible tragedy.

"Joshua, the unmarried twin, went to visit his brother in his cell every day. Both he and his sister-in-law shed a lot of tears as the day of execution approached. One night, the innocent brother, Joshua, couldn't sleep. For hours he struggled in anguish for an answer to this seemingly insurmountable dilemma. 'What can be done?' he repeated in despair.

"Finally, just before daybreak, he fell asleep, spent from mental exhaustion. But while he slept, Joshua dreamed that he was the guilty one, convicted to die on the gallows. The dream was so powerful—so real—that he could not escape its impact even after he woke up. Yet as frightening as the dream had been, he felt a strange sense of peace.

"Later that morning when Joshua visited his brother again, he said to him, 'I had a dream last night, Adam. I dreamed that I took thy place and died on the gallows instead of thee.' The prisoner slowly raised his head and stared at his brother in confusion.

"'I will come two days before the execution and change places with thee,' the innocent brother announced.

"'Thou canst not do that,' Adam objected.

"'And why not?' Joshua replied. 'Who shall know the difference?'

"Adam looked grieved. 'But thou didst no wrong. Thou art not guilty.'

"But his brother was adamant. 'Thy wife and children need thee, Adam. I have no family. Just thyself and they.'

"The prisoner remained adamant that he couldn't let him do it, and he ended by saying that it simply wasn't fair or just.

"On his way out of the cell, Joshua stopped at the door. 'I will die so that thou canst be free and live—truly live.' Joshua left the heavy door ajar. 'I love thee, Adam. More than thou wilt ever know.'

"As he turned and walked away, the condemned man buried his face in his hands and wept. His cries of anguish drowned out the sound of his brother's footsteps as they echoed back along the stone corridor.

"When the day arrived, the wife distracted the guards while the two men exchanged clothing. After a long and emotional embrace, the guilty man walked out of the prison—totally free. But at a tremendous price.

"Filled with a mixture of pain and troubled freedom, Adam went to witness the hanging as the next of kin. He watched his innocent brother being led slowly across the cobbled prison yard and up the makeshift stairs to the scaffold. Then he saw Joshua turn, look at him,[5] and nod ever so slightly. The pain in Adam's heart became so excruciating that he had to bite his lip. He wept uncontrollably as the blindfold was placed over his brother's eyes and his hands tightly tied. Then the black-garbed hangman led him to stand on the trap door. Joshua's hour had come.[6] The prison clock struck seven times and then the trap door dropped. With one convulsive jerk Joshua was gone—into God's eternity.

"Every day of the redeemed man's life, he remembered the one who had died for him, the one who had taken his place. That thought transformed Adam's daily life. One day someone treated him miserably, and the next morning he sulked in bed, feeling sorry for himself. But as he lay there, he suddenly remembered his brother's final words: 'Adam, live every day for me.'

"The exchange was the immortal story of a wondrous love, so great, so free."

As Jack fell silent, his listeners remained in their forward crouch, transfixed under the storyteller's spell. In the flickering flame of the pungent torch, they had witnessed ill-clad men chained to the cold stone pillars of the seventeenth-century prison. They had breathed its dank and fetid air and heard the accents of Jacobean England echoing from the cobbled chambers. They had flinched at the remorseless judgment of a kingdom which, despite Henry the Second's Common Law, had invoked one code of justice for noblemen and quite another code for common labourers.

Jack tightened his fingers around his cup of cocoa, as if to warm them. "Do you know the hymn 'Was It for Me?'" he asked. Alistair looked as if he were trying to place it, so Jack hummed a couple of bars.

"Yes, I've heard it," Alistair said, his voice filled with reverence. Then he closed his eyes. In his mind he could hear Priscilla playing the piano, voices singing, and the delicate strains of a violin filling the parlour.

> Was it for me, for me alone,
> The Saviour left His glorious throne,
> The dazzling splendours of the sky:
> Was it for me He came to die?
>
> *It was for me, yes, all for me;*
> *Oh, love of God, so great, so free!*
> *Oh, wondrous love! Oh, boundless grace!*
> *He died for me, He took my place.*
>
> Was it for me He wept and prayed,
> My load of sin before Him laid
> That night within Gethsemane:
> Was it for me, that agony?
>
> Was it for me He bowed His head
> Upon the cross and freely shed
> His precious blood, that crimson tide:
> Was it for me the Saviour died?[7]

George looked up to see moistness gathering in Alistair's eyes. "God is absolutely holy and just," he said. "That's why it's impossible for Him to have direct fellowship with sinful men and women. God answered that hopeless dilemma with an unthinkable solution: He allowed Jesus to substitute His spotless, unblemished life and carry the burden of all human sin in His own body."[8]

"Sometimes I'm reduced to tears," Alistair said softly, "when I'm reminded of how willing Jesus was to accept *my* guilt and take *my* place on Calvary's cross."[9] He took out his handkerchief and blew his nose. For several minutes he sat in silent adoration. "Until two months ago, I had never realized that Jesus loved me so much. Or that it was *my* sin that killed Him."

Alistair, looking up at his two new friends, slowly shook his head as if in disbelief. "During those hours that He hung on the centre cross, Jesus received the full consequences of *my* sin and experienced rejection in *my* stead. As a result, God wiped out all the charges against me."[10]

George ran his fingers through his sandy hair. "During this past year, I've come to understand that Jesus didn't just take our sin. He also *gives* us His life. In other words, we receive the goodness or righteousness of His life.[11] It amazes me that Jesus *exchanged* His pure life for our corrupt, sinful ones at the cross of Calvary. And now, by faith, we lay hold on His perfect life, giving us the right to approach God."

Jack slipped his thumbs in behind his brown suspenders. "That's not to say," he interjected, "that we can live a sinless life as long as we're living in an earthly body with its natural tendencies. We make mistakes all the time."

"That's right," George agreed. "But if we ask for forgiveness because of our Saviour's sacrifice, we'll continue to have His righteousness. The cleansing power of Jesus' blood becomes effective each time we respond to Him by faith. So even though we can't be sinless, we can be blameless.[12] We can enter into an intimate fellowship with the Father because of Him."

The kerosene's amber glow etched lines of solemnity in the three earnest faces gathered around the oil lamp and the jug of hot cocoa.

"What you've just said is marvelous!" Alistair exclaimed. "I'd always thought of Jesus as taking our sin. But somehow, until I heard your story, Jack, I never fully realized that He begins to live His life in us *at the same time.* For me it's an awakening! It's not just a changed life, it's an *exchanged* life that Christ offers us."

"That's the good news of the gospel," George said. "Jesus' death saves us from the penalty of sin. And His life saves us from the power of sin."[13]

Jack took out his handkerchief and wiped the sweat off his forehead. Alistair sat without saying a word, engrossed with the clarity of this revelation and the power of Jack's story. George, too, seemed reluctant to break the silence. The only sound was the steady tick of the kitchen clock echoing into the shadowy corners of the room.

Eventually Alistair looked up at the hands. "Well," he said, "I guess it's time we climbed the wooden hill." He wiggled a match out of the red tin holder on the wall, struck it against the cookstove, and lit a chamber lamp. "This'll give you fellas a bit of light for the stairs."

That night Alistair lay in bed thinking about the two guests under his roof. He marveled at the providence of God and at the inexplicable way He had brought their lives together. Tonight's fellowship had reached far beyond anything he'd ever been handed in a parson's sermon. Balancing on the edge of sleep, Alistair turned over, face down on his crossed arms. "It's about traveling with Jesus and with others who are doing the same," he whispered to himself and the night. "It's about accepting an exchanged life, in faith believing."

Four

FIRST SUNDAY IN MAY
Spring 1899

George and Jack continued to make their weekly trek to Wood Creek Farm for the Thursday night meetings. Only twice in fourteen months had they been absent. In October a severely bloated cow needing urgent attention had held George back, and in February a sleet storm had iced the roads beyond any reasonable footing. The two men had found their new friends to be of like mind indeed—seekers of an authentic Christian life.

Weeks turned into months and months into seasons, and once again Puslinch Township welcomed the shy southern Ontario spring. Thin curtains of rain billowed across dimpled fields that gave the impression of rising to meet the tender ministrations of the sky as it awakened the soil for the seeds of a new season. From every marsh frogs set up their chorus in C-sharp minor, and rigid stalks of bulrushes, plundered by returning red-winged blackbirds, released their velvet filaments. It was a season of opening what had long been closed, a turning over to wind and sun of what had lain in winter's dark chambers.

Stout farm wives of sixty and mincing maids alike thumped down stovepipes heavy with soot. They aired quilts and bolsters on fence lines and invaded closets and attics reeking of mothballs. Farmers dragged seed drills out of dark implement sheds after wrestling open rusty hinges and warped doors. Straw mounds were forked away from damp foundations and cellar hatches yawned, disclosing shrivelled turnips and puckered potatoes like naughty faces suddenly exposed to the light of truth. Shivering outhouses, heaved by frost, staggered at alarming angles, as though rudely surprised by the axial tilt of spring.

Late in the afternoons schoolboys flopped belly down on the warm planks of bridges over swollen creeks. Cantilevering themselves over the edge, they plunged gangly arms up past their elbows into the transparency of the icy flow. The boldest of them rolled up their pant legs and waded knee-deep in the rushing meltwater while giggling girls, responding to the stirrings of young flesh, followed brazenly in their wake. Defying the boys' taunting, they, too, waded in, their cotton dresses hiked up to their knees as the mud, like cold velvet, oozed between their toes.

Their grandparents, who had rocked the winter away in chimney corners or dozed beside icicle-encrusted windows, now hitched themselves forward, viewing in gap-toothed amazement the miracle that spring had wrought in the April landscape. Much good advice flowed from their lips, whether it concerned the right way to open a beehive or the only way to remove rust from tin candlesticks during the annual spring cleaning.

The idle gossip of winter, spoken out of the sides of men's mouths, took on purpose and energy as the farmers compared plans and intentions for this field or that. Although Bill Jones enjoyed the rigours of farm work, he held himself apart from the small talk that passed as discourse among the men of the farming community. With the responsibility of two small children, three now since last September, he weighed each decision judiciously, his family's well-being always in mind. Years earlier, his school pals had joked that Bill's cautious, skeptical nature must have been a far cry from the fiery, impetuous little Welshmen of his ancestry.

Bill straightened up, brushed aside his thinning brown hair and adjusted his spectacles. Then he bent forward to continue his repair work on the harrows in the implement shed behind the house. Years ago, his father had sawn pine logs from the bush at the back of the farm to build this shed, but before long he would have to replace the crumbling structure with something new. Presently, Bill was preoccupied with getting ready to sow seed as soon as the fields were dry enough to get on the land.

His mind ran back over events of the past year as he unbolted a broken tooth off the set of harrows. He recalled that he had stubbornly resisted the new direction at Alistair's for most of the past summer, making little effort to enter into the Bible discussions. During those first months some disagreements and awkward moments had darkened the atmosphere of the gatherings. On one occasion Alice had objected to the order of the meeting, and in the heated discussion that followed, her sharp tongue had cut a wide swath, hurting Stephen's sensitive feelings so badly that he had risen to his feet and slunk off to the woodshed. Another time Jack had droned on with so many suppositions about the Babylonian captivity and the reign of Nebuchadnezzar the king, that some of the folks were fed up with the protracted monologue. "Jack's not feeding the flock," a disgruntled voice groused. "He's filling them with chaff."

But each time Alistair sensed a barrier to their fellowship he had pleaded, "Pray the problem into shivers, my friends. Ask Jesus to break down any walls between us."[1] So the few, including the repentant Alice, who were anxious for passage beyond the obstacle would hold an ardent prayer meeting in Stephen and Emily's back parlour, or "upper room" as Stephen sometimes called it.

Bill had perceived a mysterious yet unspoken camaraderie developing among those who had espoused this life more fully than himself. George and Jack seemed to be closer to the others than he was. And they had only been coming a few months. Did he intend to be left behind even as Alice forged ahead? Although Bill was included in every activity and discussion on Thursday evenings, still he sensed a widening fissure that couldn't be bridged by laughter or conversation.

Each Sunday as the three couples sat in their family pews at Saint Patrick's, Bill would glance up at Priscilla in the choir. He and she, he realized, were the only ones still sitting on the fence. Returning from service one morning, Bill had slumped in disheartened silence, resisting the urge to break the Sabbath and vent his spiritual turmoil by tinkering with the broken wagon wheel or mending the bridle that was too loose now for old Duke.

For much of the previous summer, Bill had dragged his feet, dithering between his loyalty to Saint Patrick's and the course the others had so wholeheartedly chosen.

But by harvest time in September, shortly after their daughter Madeleine had been born, the changes in Alice's life had become undeniable. Bill noticed that she took time to pray and to read her Bible. He saw the increased peace and joy in her eyes. But most of all, and in spite of the baby's colicky screams throughout the night, Bill heard a softer tone in her voice that had all too often been shrill with judgment. "Alice's tongue could peel the skin off a pig," a local wag had once declared.

One Friday morning after climbing the wooden rungs to the top of the hay mow, Bill had found himself stalled. He leaned against the heavy timber that braced the purlin as he pondered the glow on Stephen's face the evening before. "I feel happier, more serene, and closer to Jesus than ever before," the blacksmith had claimed, his smile emanating a peace that attracted Bill.

During the autumn, Bill had often reflected on what the others shared on Thursday evenings and he had begun to pray and to talk with God as he worked around the farm. He stumbled onto the reality of God's presence from the cow stable to the threshing floor in a way he had never known—even though he had sat among friends who had felt that awareness much earlier. Before the snow began to fly, Bill had dedicated himself to God, and as the barnyard blew full of drifts, his thinking shifted completely. Like columns of dark clouds driven before a December wind, Bill's objections dispersed to reveal the brightness of Alistair's vision. By Christmas he embraced it with his whole heart.

Then one Sunday in February, Bill had turned to Alice as he hoisted their small boys, Gilbert and Nathan, into the cutter after the morning service at Saint Patrick's. "Christians should be more like a family than what I see here," he had said, jerking his thumb toward the building. "I prefer the way we all participate at Alistair's. The back and forth helps us all to grow."

Now Bill pulled his coat tighter around him as a gust of chilly spring air swept in through the gaping holes in the roof. He reflected that Saint Patrick's was rather like this implement shed. The structure his parents had built and devoted themselves to was beginning to collapse. Perhaps it was time for something else in its place, something strong enough to withstand the winds of dissension. Before he put away his wrenches and went to supper that night, Bill had formed an irreversible decision.

On the second Thursday of April, a sudden warmth settled over the fields like a man's arm across a woman's shoulders. Blue smoke curled upwards from the brush fires and a waterfall of birdsong echoed from the greening woods. Gathering that evening at Wood Creek Farm, the friends felt a quickening spirit corresponding to nature's pulse in the air.

After they had moved into the parlour, Bill was the first to speak. "I know I dragged my feet when we first started meeting like this. At that time I thought the old church was just fine. But over the past year I've come to see the beauty in what Jesus is doing here." He paused and drew in a deep breath. "I'm tired of going to church on Sundays. I come away hungry every time. And coming here on Thursdays only makes the lack more obvious." Bill took off his glasses and wiped his eyes. "This may surprise you, but Alice and I have gone to Saint Patrick's for the last time."

The others sat silently as this fact settled in.

Bill looked around, searching for a reaction from the others. He saw George and Emily nodding and the flicker of encouragement in Alistair's lean face. Jack appeared pensive as he shuffled his wool socks back and forth against each other.

Emily discerned the fervour in Bill's face. Didn't she, too, need to become so desperate for Jesus that nothing else mattered? Otherwise, there was no way to move forward.

Then she heard Alistair's voice. "Carry on, Bill."

Bill smoothed his palms along his thighs. "Wouldn't it be better for us to meet in one of our homes on Sundays?" he appealed.

"Bill and I have been praying about this," Alice joined in. "We'd like our children to be included, too, so they can learn how adults worship God *in spirit and in truth*. Children become what they see their parents living, and most things we share here are simple enough for a child to understand." Alice's face flushed with conviction. "Bill and I feel a lack of food for our souls, an emptiness so strong that it's impossible for us to carry on as we always have."

"The Thursday meetings do fill a need," Alistair conceded. "But it's true that we would benefit more by meeting twice a week. The early church met on Sunday to break bread." The friends looked around at each other, apprehensive about abandoning a custom they had all observed since they were children.

Stephen thought for a moment and then admitted, "It would seem very strange not to be in a pew at Saint Patrick's on a Sunday morning."

"Some of our friends and family will ask a lot of questions," Emily predicted as she fit her fingertips together thoughtfully. "If we stop going, we'll have to be prepared for whatever reaction we get. It could be rough."

Alice tried to assess Emily's inference. "I don't give a fig about other people's opinions," she asserted. "This friendship with Jesus is the most important aspect of my life—no matter what the personal sacrifice."

Priscilla's stomach knotted and her pulse raced. It was one thing to continue the Thursday meetings while still retaining the comfort of her traditional Sunday service. It was quite another thing to sever those ties. She bit her lip and said nothing.

Beneath the open window, a cricket chirped from its hiding place in the damp soil as the conversation seesawed back and forth late into the evening. Clearly Bill and Alice were finished with Saint Patrick's. Emily, the most sympathetic to her feelings, also felt prompted to leave the traditional church. The others remained apprehensive but were gradually drawn by the Spirit to move forward.

"Each of us will have to choose for himself," Alistair said. "But I'm going to meet with Bill and Alice on Sundays. As you know, more than a year ago Ben's death started me on this journey, and there's no turning back now."

Priscilla's heart raced. Then a sickening thought crossed her mind: What will Timothy think? She knew her son enjoyed the Thursday evening meetings when he was able to be at home, but what if he decided to continue at Saint Patrick's? Although he had not spoken about it lately, Priscilla knew Timothy was planning to pursue a livelihood in the pulpit. Suddenly horrified at the possibility of a fracture within her family, Priscilla stiffened and pressed on her breastbone to ease the burning reflex in her stomach.

"I agree with Alistair," George offered. "There's no going back now." Looking down at his boots for a minute, he added, "God's leading us in this direction for a reason. You can count me in, too."

Priscilla sighed and looked over at George. The kindness in his narrow, boyish face looked as always, ready to spill over. As she reflected on the relentless friendship he and Alistair had forged over the past year, tiny pangs of fear and jealousy crept into her heart. It was one thing to witness other neighbourhood women, even the boldest ones, tease or hector Alistair when they encountered him at the store or the township hall in the good-natured way that a handsome and respected man finds himself addressed. But it was an entirely different matter to accept this powerful bond that George had, almost unconsciously, formed with her husband. How could such an innocuous chap, barely thirty, exert such a compelling influence on a seasoned older man?

It's George's fault, she sputtered to herself. He and Alistair were always so focused on the New Testament, and now he wielded more sway than she did. Why hadn't she put her foot down long ago? *It's high time he had a wife to keep him busy at home…* Her thoughts were interrupted by a deep melodious voice.

"It's lonely being a colporteur," Jack began soberly, "you know, going up and down the roads by yourself. All the time I was selling books, I kept my eyes open for a spiritual family. But I never found one until George brought me here. So I want to plough ahead with the rest of you." A wry grin twisted the corners of his mouth, and his dark eyes sparkled. "If you can put up with a little of my history now and then, that is."

Jack's good-natured humour was lost on Priscilla. As her face grew tight and pinched, she tried not to collapse inwardly. But she was losing the battle, and tears began to stream down her cheeks. "I'm sorry," she finally choked. "Part of me wants to go along with the rest of you, but I'm not ready for such upheaval. It's just too hard for me."[2]

A few minutes passed as Priscilla cried softly, her chin resting in dejection on her chest. As she struggled to regain her composure, Alistair stood up and walked over to sit beside her. Lifting her long dark hair, he slid his arm around her quivering shoulders and held her close. She took his other hand and squeezed it.

Emily averted her eyes as she saw her friend weeping. Instantly, an earnest plea for God's help rose from her heart.

"I'm sorry, but I just can't do it now," Priscilla sniffled. "You'll have to give me a little time." She wiped her face with her apron.

Again the room fell silent as each person absorbed Priscilla's decision—that she couldn't take the step with them. Tears welled up in Alistair's eyes. He felt sorry that she intended to go to Saint Patrick's alone. As he sat unconsciously rubbing his chapped knuckles against the palm of his other hand, he promised himself to support her in the choice she had made.

Finally, Stephen spoke. "It's difficult for me, too. Still, I know in my heart that this is the right thing for me. I'm going to make the break too."

And so, one by one, they all decided to begin meeting at Wood Creek Farm on the first Sunday in May. All of them, that is, except Priscilla.

As the sun's brilliance appeared above the dark horizon and the clear morning dawned on Sunday, May 7, 1899, each of the seven knew this day was going to be very special. Just as no man possesses the power to hold back the sun, so no one could prevent the Holy Spirit from drawing true seekers together for fellowship.

Although Saturday was the Sabbath, the Puslinch friends intended to gather on Sunday, the first day of the week, as the first-century church had done. Jesus had stepped out of the garden tomb on Sunday morning, and His disciples met to celebrate His resurrection and triumph over death. For each of them, He was alive, risen and guiding them by His Spirit.

George and Jack had arrived the night before around supper time. George had turned in at the village to spend the night with Stephen and Emily, and Jack had ridden on to stay with Bill and Alice. Like a mischievous lad, Jack hugged a parcel to his chest and when the Jones boys tore it open that evening, they shouted with glee. Inside was a worn set of treasured animals carved by Jack's old uncle. As a lion pursued a giraffe up and down Jack's legs and lap, he smiled at the roaring sounds, remembering his own boyhood antics.

On Sunday morning silence hung like a damp fog over the Stanhope breakfast table. Priscilla slowly buttered her toast and then pushed the jam pot aside, as if denying herself a pleasure sweeter than jam. Vexed to her soul, she had rebuked Timothy for ruining one of the tines of her good forks as he tried to loosen his knotted boot laces. Timothy abruptly rose to his feet and Alistair soon followed, leaving Priscilla alone at the table. While Timothy finished the chores, Alistair brushed the mare and hitched her to the buggy. His feet dragged as he led Nell to the gate, ready for Priscilla. It had been his dream that she would be beside him during the first meeting in their home. Still, he respected her gumption. Cupping her chin in his hand, he kissed her before she climbed into the buggy. "See you at dinnertime," he called out, his throat constricting as he watched her tighten her hat strings and give the mare a clip. Absorbed in a mixture of feelings, Alistair didn't hear Timothy until he felt a sudden hand on his shoulder.

"I'm sorry to see Mom going off to Saint Pat's on her own," Timothy said ruefully, "but I really want to be here for the meeting. And I know Phoebe does too. I'd hoped Mom might change her mind, but she seemed struck on going. I'm sorry I got her goat at breakfast."

Alistair swallowed hard and with a nod, turned toward the house.

The McElderry and Jones families and their overnight visitors felt a sense of exhilaration as they walked up the familiar flagstone walk to the Stanhope farmhouse that morning. Alice carried the sleeping baby while Bill guided their two lively boys. In the flower beds along the walkway, a profusion of white narcissus and yellow daffodils reached up toward the warm sunlight. The unfolding leaves on the trees were alive with insects, buzzing as they came to life after the cold winter. In the field beside the house, a bay mare had given birth to a foal overnight. The colt was running and jumping around with its own awkward beauty. All of the new life was in harmony with God's plan. And so were these friends as they came together in remembrance of the resurrection morning.

There was no need to knock when they came to the kitchen door. They were family. Besides, Alistair was there, waiting to welcome them into the house. Flowers bloomed inside as well as out, and red geraniums spilled from the three deep windowsills in the kitchen. George bent over to draw in their pungent fragrance, cradling the silky petals with his fingertips.

The occasion was solemn and reverent, yet joyful and happy all at the same time. Phoebe kneeled down and hugged Gilbert and Nathan while Alistair pretended to be formal and shook hands with each of them laughingly. Alice eased back the blanket to reveal Madeleine's chubby arms and legs as she laid the rosy-cheeked baby, oblivious to the excitement, in Phoebe's old cradle. Everyone stood talking in the kitchen for a few minutes and then one by one they made their way into the parlour.

Priscilla kept a comfortable house. The parlour floor was covered with a woven rag carpet, which had been laid over a thin layer of marsh grass to make it soft. She had tacked the carpet around the edges to hold it in place.

Alistair had arranged the chairs around the room in an informal circle. As each person quietly sat down, they noticed the small low table in the centre where a linen napkin covered a china plate. Unseen for the moment were a small loaf of bread and a cup of wine under the white cloth. As they waited for the meeting to begin, each sat facing the bread and the cup in silent contemplation. It was a solemn visual reminder that Jesus is the centre and the focus of His church, and that they had come together to remember His life, His death, and His resurrection. Only the steady ticking of the Regulator clock broke the stillness, its polished brass pendulum swinging rhythmically.

Emily passed around little packets of favourite hymns that she had painstakingly copied over the past two weeks. Even Bill and Alice's two small boys came prepared with a Bible and were given a few hymns. Nathan, the younger and more lively of the lads, kicked his feet back and forth as he stared at everyone's face.

For a few minutes the tiny assembly waited in silence.

Timothy, home from high school for the weekend, stretched his long legs out beside Phoebe. It seemed strange not to be in church on Sunday morning, and yet there was something special about being here with the others. He missed being at the Thursday gatherings when he stayed with Aunt Maggie during the school year.

Alice couldn't help but notice the reverent tranquility in the room. How different, she mused, from the old place of worship. There, she'd rarely thought of Christ as she chattered to the person beside her. More like a market than a church.

As she sat reflecting, she felt a soft draught on her shoulder. Looking up, Alice saw that the double-hung windows were lifted a few inches and the starched white curtains were stirring in the spring breeze. They reminded her of Priscilla, and she glanced at the empty chair beside Alistair. Two years ago Priscilla had refurbished the room with sage green wallpaper running up to the crisp, whitewashed ceilings. It seemed strange to be here, knowing that her closest friend was sitting in one of the cold, hard pews at Saint Patrick's. Alice was startled back to the moment when she felt a touch on her arm. Her little boy looked up. "Are we going to start soon, Mama?"

"Sssh," Alice whispered, her finger to her lips. "In a few minutes."

Alistair smiled at Nathan, husky and blond-haired like his mother. Then in a reserved voice, he asked if someone had a particular hymn to begin the first meeting of this little church.

George's voice had the inquiring tone of a child. "Could we please sing 'Lord, We Are Met Together'?"

Alistair looked across the room. "Jack, would you start the singing for us today since Priscilla's not here?"

Jack's rich baritone gave the lead as the voices of the little church swelled until the melody filled the parlour.

> Lord, we are met together,
> A weak and helpless flock,
> The powers of earth against us,
> But Thou art still our Rock;
>
> Now may we simply trust Thee,
> Depend upon Thy power;
> Extend to us Thy favour,
> Make this a hallowed hour.[3]

One by one they prayed briefly, thanking God for His continuing care and blessing upon their lives and for bringing them together. They asked

Him to be present with them, to make His will clearer to them, and to help them follow Jesus. When the last person finished praying, Alistair spoke.

"When the early church at Corinth came together, each person offered some thoughts or suggested a hymn. The apostle Paul advocated that they be ready with a word of instruction, a revelation, a tongue, or an interpretation. All of these were to be done for the strengthening of the church. They were all to prophesy in turn so that everyone could be instructed and encouraged."[4] Alistair then clarified that the words "to prophesy" meant to strengthen, encourage, and comfort.[5]

Each of the friends shared a positive thought or message in order to encourage and comfort the others. Some spoke only two or three sentences, while a few took four or five minutes to present their reflections or experiences. There was no sense of grandstanding or any attempt to give a sermon. Rather, there was a sense of humility, of brokenness, a true sincerity rarely witnessed outside of the intimacy of a family. There was no set order, and everyone tried to be sensitive in choosing when to speak. Each friend believed that the Spirit of Christ was leading their meeting.

Stephen opened his Bible and began his thoughts with a verse: "The first thing Andrew did was to find his brother Simon and tell him, 'We have *found the Messiah*'…and he brought him to Jesus."[6]

Stephen looked up from the page. "One day last fall as I was coming home from town, I noticed several people in a wheat field walking through the stubble, all in different directions. As it turned out, they were looking for a pocket watch. Someone had lost it while he was stooking sheaves. Just last week, I saw a group of children gathered in a close circle in a pasture. They had found something, a newborn lamb. They were sharing in the joy of finding such a pure and perfect life.

"In this world people are running in every direction, a sure sign they're searching for something to satisfy the emptiness they feel. On the other hand, when we, as God's children, gather in a circle, like today, we're showing that we've found something. Only that something is a Someone. We have found Jesus, the Lamb of God, the source of the abundant life."

Stephen's voice radiated a childlike delight, as though he had tasted something sweet for the first time. The reality of this revelation had touched the palate of his soul and given him profound joy.

When Stephen finished speaking, he fumbled through the little packet of handwritten hymns. "Could we please sing the hymn that speaks about having found Jesus?" he asked.

Emily's nimble fingers found it quickly. "It's the eighth one from the top," she said. The church joined in song to emphasize Stephen's message.

> All my life long I had panted
> For a drink from some cool spring,
> That I hoped would quench the burning
> Of the thirst I felt within.
>
> *Jesus, Saviour, I have found Him,*
> *Whom mine eyes with joy have seen!*
> *Jesus satisfies my longing;*
> *By His blood I am redeemed.*[7]

After everybody had shared their thoughts, Alistair paraphrased the account of the Last Supper: "During the meal Jesus took bread, gave thanks to God, and broke it. Then He gave it to His disciples saying, 'Take this and eat it. This is My body.' Jesus picked up a cup of wine and blessed it. 'Take this and drink it,' He said. 'This is My blood and with it God makes His new convenant with you. It will be poured out so many people will have their sins forgiven.' And when they had sung a hymn, they went out to the Mount of Olives."[8]

Alistair surveyed the circle of friends. "Before we break bread, could someone choose a hymn to focus our attention on the sacrifice of Christ?"

"Perhaps we can sing 'Calvary'," Bill suggested.

Their singing was soft, slow, and thoughtful.

> Lord, we gather round Thy footstool,
> Bowed in deep humility;
> As we look upon the emblems,
> We remember Calvary.
>
> *Calvary, Calvary,*
> *We remember Calvary—*
> *In the bread Thy broken body,*
> *In the wine Thy blood we see.*
>
> In that night so dark with sorrow,
> Left alone in prayer to bow,
> See Him drink our cup of anguish,
> Drops of blood upon His brow.

See Him led outside the city,
Bruised and bearing all our sin;
Cruel was the death He suffered,
Heaven's joy for us to win.

Unto Him who loved and washed us
From our sins in His own blood,
We should render thanks and plead for
Grace to love Him as we should.[9]

When the hymn finished, Alistair walked over to the little table and removed the white linen cloth. The loaf of bread and the cup were open for everyone to consider. They gave thanks to God before they shared this emblem of Christ's pierced body. Each person broke off a piece of bread to eat before passing it to the next one around the circle. As they quietly divided the tiny loaf among themselves, Alistair was reminded of Jesus' last supper with His disciples.

Similarly, the little church gave thanks for the common cup of red wine representing His blood poured out for each of them. After the empty cup was returned to its place on the table, everyone joined in a final hymn.

The first Sunday meeting was over.

It had been a spiritual awakening—personal and relevant to each one. Not only did they feel the close presence of Christ themselves, they also recognized His gentle voice speaking through each other. Alistair smiled broadly, happy with the first meeting.

~∘

When he saw the horse turning in at the laneway, Alistair hurried out to meet Priscilla, taking her arm as she stepped down from the buggy. After kissing his wife on the cheek, he led the mare to the stable. Alice and Emily hugged her at the doorway, also glad to have her back at home with them.

The three women went into the kitchen and began lifting the dinner that Priscilla had put in the oven before she left. As she carved the roast chicken, she waited for one of the women to mention something about the meeting. After a few minutes, she could no longer contain her curiosity.

"How did the meeting go this morning?" Priscilla ventured.

Alice replied with a smile. "Absolutely wonderful. It felt like a family." She paused to put her arm around her friend. "Except we missed you, Priscilla."

Emily added her impressions. "I can't help but think that the love of Christ was here and touched me, truly touched me. And the way we shared the emblems was simple and lovely."

In her mind, Priscilla compared Emily's and Alice's descriptions with her own experience at Saint Patrick's that morning. She had been part of a passive audience for Reverend Smithers' sermon. She knew the messages shared at Wood Creek Farm had been far more personal.

But as Priscilla forked the chicken onto the platter, she set her jaw. Nothing was going to deter her from her duties at Saint Patrick's. A woman needed some backbone, and she knew the choir depended on her. At any rate, taking the worship out of Reverend Smithers' hands wasn't the answer. Alistair needed more respect for the cloth—that's what he needed.

While the women were getting the meal ready, some of the men went out to look at the new foal. As they leaned over the fence, Stephen spoke first. "Is that the colt off Jim Braithewaite's big Percheron stallion?"

Alistair nodded.

"Nice looking animal," Stephen added. "Judging by the length of the cannon bone, I'd wager he's going to stand a good eighteen hands tall."

Alistair watched the foal running unsteadily. "New things wobble a bit," he said. "No doubt about it. But they certainly are filled with life."

The other men nodded in agreement.

"Judging by the smell of that roast chicken in the kitchen, I'm soon going to need a toothpick," Jack laughed, as he broke a sliver off a cedar rail and started to whittle.

"I'm beginning to understand," George said, "what Jesus meant when He said: 'You shall know the truth and the truth shall make you free.' "[10]

Jack listened attentively as he shaved the wood into a toothpick. Then he snapped his jackknife shut and slipped it back into his pocket.

"When we really know the truth as it is in Jesus, we're set free," George continued. "Free from religious tradition, formality, budgets, and church politics. Having His Spirit gives liberty."[11]

"Liberty, that's it. Liberty to share the joys of Christ. Or even the difficulties I'm facing." Alistair stretched his arms as the men started back toward the kitchen. "I feel reassured that if I talk about the feelings in my heart, I'll be embraced by all of you. I used to feel lonely for God, even before Ben died. Sometimes questions gnawed inside me, but I didn't feel comfortable sharing them with anyone else, not even Priscilla.

"I often wondered," Alistair continued, "if I don't go to church, will anybody miss me? Certainly not during the service I decided, but maybe socially. But now, if one of us is absent, we're all aware. We not only arrive physically, but also spiritually. We depend on each other, like members of a body—the body of Christ. This morning reminded me of Jesus talking to His disciples as they gathered around Him…" The brassy clang of the dinner bell cut Alistair's thought short.

Dragging their chairs back at one end of the table, Alistair and the other men fell into place before the oval of china plates. Priscilla bustled about the kitchen with oven mitts, lifting the platter of roast chicken from the warming closet and a crispy pan of scalloped potatoes from the oven. Alice set bowls of glazed onions and creamed carrots onto two folded towels before bringing a steaming dish of fiddlehead ferns. Struggling to open a jar of her green tomato pickles, Emily handed it to Stephen to unscrew. In the far corner, Phoebe finished spearing two dishes of pickled beets and hurried to the table. When everyone was finally sitting down, Alistair asked Bill to give thanks.

Then the little assembly fell into a comfortable silence as each one savoured the delicious spread before them. The light clink of knives and forks touching plates peppered quiet conversations.

"Fare like this makes a fellow regret being a bachelor," Jack joked.

"Thanks for the compliment," Priscilla responded with a smile. "You're welcome at our table anytime."

When the bowl of greens came to Alistair, he took a generous helping. "Nothing like fresh fiddleheads in butter," he remarked. "Don't last more than two or three weeks, do they?"

"There's a dandy patch in the woods behind our sugar camp," Alice said. "Be all done in another week." She gave a wry smile. "That's about all my back'll take, I reckon."

Emily found herself sitting beside George. "I feel a greater sense of unity today than ever before," she observed quietly. "How about you?"

George nodded as he buttered a thick slice of warm bread. "We've just taken a wonderful first step."

Emily reached for the pitcher of milk. "Today the word 'church' has taken on a clearer, more tangible meaning for me," she said, glancing around at the faces of her closest friends. Her eyes stopped at Stephen cutting up little Nathan's chicken for him. She nudged George with her elbow. "Now that's church," she whispered, nodding toward her husband.

"Is there an extra drumstick?" Jack asked from along the table.

Timothy grinned. "Sorry," he said. "We have a three-legged rooster around the yard, but we couldn't catch him this morning. He runs too fast."

A peal of laughter rang out from those within earshot. After polishing off two huge serving bowls of creamy tapioca pudding and a pot of tea, some of the men got up and ventured back into the parlour for a quiet doze. While the women washed and wiped the dishes, Alice retreated to the kitchen chamber and gathered nine-month-old Madeleine onto her lap for a spell of nursing.

Late in the afternoon George and Jack rode home with an overwhelming feeling of peace. Only the clip-clopping of their horses' hooves punctuated the silence of a countryside yielding to the sweet persuasion of spring. Willow trees with tousled heads of gold leaned over the creek while untilled fields swelled toward the horizon in delicate folds of green. Every farm lane they passed had been planted in a double row of rock maples, their budding tips a dusky red and the northern side of their trunks still dripping with the residual sap of March. Beyond the pine stump fences that lined the roadsides, oblivious sheep browsed while among them a scattering of billygoats raised their heads to stare insolently at George and Jack. Durham cows all facing southward grazed on fresh untouched pasture, their hides gleaming like waxed mahogany in the five o'clock sunshine. After the timbered darkness and dry fodder of their winter confinement, the farm animals, like the men on horseback, reveled in their new-found freedom under a sky as blue as wood violets on that first Sunday in May.

Five

FRUSTRATIONS AND FIRESTORMS
Spring 1899

On Monday morning Jack's first stop was at Reverend Chumbley's country home on the edge of Brookville. The congregation had purchased the prestigious manse to attract a seasoned minister. Its mansard roof and wrought iron lace seemed to mock Jack as he walked up the path, his resignation clutched in his sweating hand. His heart pounded as he recited his speech one last time before lifting the heavy brass knocker.

Reverend Chumbley swung open the door and pushed his round figure out onto the porch. "Jack, my fine fellow. I wondered if you'd be along this morning since you weren't able for church yesterday. I had to get Dugan MacGladry to fill in for you and pass the collection plate. No need for explanations," he went on with a sweep of his hand. "Most of the Breadalbane clan were ill too." He slapped Jack on the back, dismissing his attempt to speak.

Jack swallowed hard. "Actually, Reverend, I'll be missing Sunday service more often," he said. "That is, I won't be coming anymore."

The Reverend's gray eyebrows arched up into his forehead as if pulled by invisible strings. "What's that you say?"

Jack gazed out into the garden at the new buds on the rose bushes, collecting his thoughts and his courage. He turned back and looked Reverend Chumbley directly in the eye. "I feel that God is calling me to worship like the Christians did in the New Testament."

"Well, what do you think we're doing in this church? I read a passage from the Gospels every Sunday, according to the lectionary."

"The Christian life I see in the New Testament is simpler than that," Jack insisted. "It's like stepping through a gate and finding oneself walking along an entirely new path, one of quiet faith in God. I want to taste it, touch it, live it. Indeed, to radiate the very love of Jesus."

"Don't talk foolishly, boy," Reverend Chumbley scoffed. "I've sat under the finest theologians and I know what the Christian life demands—ethical living."

"Yes, and you can quote the church fathers eloquently, sir; but each one of us needs to hear Jesus' voice for ourselves and to follow Him with our heart. I'm afraid that hasn't been my experience in recent years. And I need to change that."

The Reverend leaned forward and tapped Jack on the centre of his chest with his index finger. "Listen to me. You're an employee of this church. You need to learn a little respect. Leave me to interpret the Scripture. Your job is to mow the grass and hand out the literature."

Jack blanched. "That's why I'm here." For a moment he hesitated, and then in the tone of a schoolboy reciting a text, he continued, "I can no longer be a church employee, and I've come to give you my resignation."

Reverend Chumbley stared, speechless for the first time. After recovering, he tried hard to make Jack's decision seem ridiculous. Still, Jack was certain that his new direction was guided by God, and that certainty filled him with confidence.

"Thank you for the steady work you've given me, Reverend Chumbley. I've been glad to have it, but I just can't continue." With that Jack handed him the letter and quickly walked down the sidewalk, leaving the clergyman standing dumbfounded on the porch.

As Jack hiked toward home, a feeling of disorientation swept over him. How would his acquaintances react to this news? Certainly, he wasn't the first. After all, history showed tens of thousands who lost their means of earning a crust because of what they believed, many of them taking refuge in caves and holes in the ground. Hungry, sick, ill-treated.[1] Unlike them, *he* had a warm bed and agreeable folks. Jack cast his eye over the rolling front meadow of the home farm and, in the distance, he saw the clothesline strung with wash gently billowing in the breeze. He kicked a stone into the ditch as he turned into his father's lane. "The world wasn't worthy of them," he declared aloud.

Regardless of their good intentions, the Puslinch Township couples could not have anticipated the firestorm their Sunday meetings would ignite in their small farming community. And the furor was not long in gaining momentum.

On Monday afternoon Bill hitched up the team and wagon and dropped in at the feed mill to pick up the nine hundredweight of grain he had left for milling. The feed mill manager was on Saint Patrick's church board, and he hurried along the loading dock straight to Bill's wagon.

"Good day, Bill. How's the family?"

"Just dandy, Mr. Rogers. And you?"

"Not too bad," the manager said, flexing his arms across his chest. "Were you and the McElderrys out of the township on Sunday? Or perhaps a tad under the weather?"

Bill sensed a directness in the question. "No," he replied cautiously. "Why do you ask?"

"Because your pews were empty yesterday morning."

Bill dug his fingers into a sack of pig chop and heaved it onto the wagon. "We've decided to meet at Wood Creek Farm on Sundays."

"Meeting at Wood Creek Farm? What in thunder for?"

"We're planning to follow Jesus as closely as we can. We hope to feel the Spirit of Christ more than we have at Saint Patrick's."

Mr. Rogers' eyes narrowed darkly. "And who, pray tell, is going to do your preaching?" he asked, making no attempt to disguise his sarcasm.

"Well, actually, each of us shares a simple message," Bill replied, scrubbing a groove into the dust with his boot heel. He leaned against the side of the loading dock. "Can you see how that could benefit us?"

Mr. Rogers ignored the question. "Without an ordained minister, you're going to fall into serious error, Bill Jones," he said, his voice rising. "In fact, you already have. Don't you see you'll all end up in Hell?"

Bill felt like a rabbit in a steel trap. He wanted to run but he couldn't. All he could do was stand and listen as the tirade went on.

"What about your boys? They won't learn a thing without Sunday school classes," Mr. Rogers chided. "Have you thought about that?"

Tossing another sack onto the wagon, Bill took a moment to collect his thoughts. "Yes, Mr. Rogers, I have. I'm sorry that you're so against our choice. We do teach our boys at home according to the instructions in the Bible. Parents were told to teach God's words to their children, to talk about them when they were sitting at home or walking along the road, lying down or getting up.² Every morning after breakfast, we read a Bible story and talk to them about Jesus." Bill straightened his cap. "Besides, my boys will learn more by seeing Christian love in action than by doing pantomimes for a Christmas play."

Mr. Rogers' face turned deep red, and tiny beads of sweat broke out on his brow. He directed the Christmas pageant each year. "That's nigh on to blasphemy, Bill Jones."

Bill shifted the last sack toward the center of the wagon and climbed onto the seat. "I'll be back to settle up my bill tomorrow, but don't plan on seeing us at Saint Patrick's anymore. I feel it's only decent to tell you."

As his steel-rimmed wheels started to roll, he could hear an angry voice rising over his shoulder. "We'll see about that, Bill Jones," the voice shouted above the clatter of the wheels. "No one's going to start a cult in Puslinch."

Mr. Rogers' ominous accusation pounded in Bill's ears as the team lumbered away from the mill. His mind grappled with momentary doubt. The biting remarks shocked and saddened him; after all, the two men had sat in adjoining pews at Saint Patrick's for years.

Impulsively, he turned into Stephen's blacksmith yard at the edge of the village. As he stepped through the shop door, he saw Stephen pick up a round iron scoop, dip it into a tub of water, and toss a little on the forge fire. It reacted angrily, hissing and spitting like a vindictive serpent.

At the sound of Bill stomping the mud off his boots, Stephen wheeled around. "Oh, g'day, Bill. I didn't hear you come in."

Bill bent over and beat the chop dust out of his clothes with his hands. "Just came from the mill," he explained.

Silently, Stephen nodded, studying the frown on Bill's face.

"I just stopped by to tell you that Mr. Rogers has a burr under his saddle about last Sunday," Bill went on, tossing a rasp and clincher aside to prop himself against the hoof stand. "He's as mad as a hatter, and you can bet that if Mr. Rogers feels this way, there'll be others too. As I pulled away from the mill, I noticed him heading along the road in the direction of Reverend Smithers' manse."

Stephen wiped his burly hands on his leather apron. "That's a shame. I hope they don't carry it too far. Anyway, we'll just have to wait and see and keep our irons in the fire." Stephen smiled at his own unintended wit, but Bill's face remained troubled.

"I wonder if that's Mr. Roger's idea of correcting in brotherly love," Bill said. "He'd catch more flies with honey than vinegar."

Stephen leaned back against the anvil, puzzling about the stern reaction. "I guess we were shortsighted to think folks would accept our decision without a big stir," he concluded.

"He jumped on me about Sunday school for the boys too," Bill added, his expression black. "I say it's enough if Alice and I know God's way of training children," he muttered defensively. "Showing them in everyday circumstances that we're trusting Jesus ourselves. You can't fool the young ones. They know if you're relying on God or not."

Shifting off the hard metal stand, Bill got up and rubbed his backside to restore circulation. "Well, Stephen, I'd better get this load of pig chop home. Besides, I'm going to stop in and warn Alistair as well."

～

It was shortly after supper on Tuesday that Reverend Smithers came up the Stanhope lane. Alistair's Scotch collie, Teddy, trotted out to greet the buggy, his mouth open, tongue lolling. Eager to escort the visitor to the house, he wagged his tail as he looked up, his handsome face full of friendliness. Taking no notice, the minister hurried past Teddy on his way to the front door.

The minister's long thin face expressed a more intense purpose than a social visit. Still, minutes later he was smiling cordially and full of gracious words as he sat down at the parlour table with a cup of tea. The vicar had been schooled in refined deportment since his childhood. After chatting with Priscilla for a few minutes about the weather, he uncrossed his long legs and turned to face Alistair.

"I heard an insidious rumour yesterday that you are planning to start your own church, Alistair. I knew that you wouldn't do such a foolish thing, but I did promise to come out and confirm that it's not true."

"Actually," Alistair said, "we are planning to meet here on Sundays. For fellowship. It's more a meeting of friends than anything else."

Reverend Smithers' hand shook as he balanced the teacup on the saucer. "I can hardly feature it, Alistair," he said. "Your father was one of the founding members of Saint Patrick's well over forty years ago. How could you think of breaking such a fine tradition?"

Alistair weighed his words, and replied, "I've never been heavy on traditions, and this isn't about losing faith. To tell you the truth, I seem to be needing more of Jesus than I've been getting lately."

Reverend Smithers, pretending not to hear, stared at a fly struggling to free itself from sticky flypaper hanging in the window. "It's not fitting, you realize, for Priscilla to travel to church every Sunday by herself."

"Priscilla's capable of going on her own and making her own decisions. Besides, if the weather's bad, I'll take her and fetch her after."

Briefly, a smile returned to the pastor's face. "I'm sure a new building will improve everything, Alistair. You know we're already short of men to sign on the mortgage. A woman can't do that. Without you and the others it might be years before it happens. We do want Saint Patrick's to stand proud and noble in the community, don't we?"

Unnerved by Alistair's quizzical silence, Reverend Smithers turned and peered over his glasses at Priscilla. "I'm glad you made it out to church last Sunday. You know the choir needs you to lead the singing, Priscilla. You're not going to jump ship, too, are you?"

As he spoke, it became apparent to Alistair that the Reverend was mostly concerned about making the outward shell of his organization function. It saddened him to think that this was what fellowship with Jesus primarily meant to Reverend Smithers.

"And what about Timothy?" Reverend Smithers continued, his eyes turning hard and unyielding. "He told me his application for seminary is under review by the committee. I certainly won't be able to write a very strong letter of recommendation if his father isn't supporting the church," he warned. "Without it, he'll never get into our seminary."

Priscilla twisted a damp tea towel on her lap. Even as a small girl, she had hated any kind of confrontation. She could feel her stomach cramping just as it had always done. Uncertain about her own position, she didn't want to be drawn into either side of a dog fight.

"Yes," Alistair acknowledged. "I'll share your concerns with him. It's a choice he'll have to make for himself. He's nearly a man now."

Realizing that Alistair was firmly set in his new direction, Reverend Smithers fidgeted with his starched collar before he spoke. "Priscilla, I hope you can convince your husband to give up this foolishness. There's something badly wrong with a man's head when he leaves his church. The tradition of his fathers should mean something to him." Turning again to Alistair, the Reverend warned, "I must tell you, Alistair, I shall do all I can to bring this nonsense to an end."

Then he rose abruptly from the table, offered Alistair and Priscilla a hasty handshake, seized his stiff felt hat from the hatstand, and headed for his buggy. Alistair put his arm around Priscilla as they watched him picking his way down the path.

"May God have mercy on your soul, Alistair Stanhope!" the Reverend shouted back as he started his horse with a sharp crack from the whip.

Watching the dark figure disappear down the lane, Alistair could feel his wife's shoulders shaking. He glanced down at her, surprised to see her eyes filling with tears and her hands clamped over her mouth as she tried to contain what seemed to Alistair as an uneasy giggle.

With the tension broken, she gasped for air. Her emotions still muddled, she blurted out half laughing and half crying, "Poor Reverend Smithers. He said 'May God have mercy on your soul' as though you're committing some heinous crime and are about to be hanged for it." Priscilla wiped her tears with the back of her hand, suddenly apologetic. "I'm sorry. I'm not trying to be mean. I don't agree with you about leaving the church, but it's definitely not a crime."

"It's so wonderful what God is doing in our meetings, and our poor Reverend seems as blind as a mole," Alistair said with a trace of sadness. "He's really not a bad man. In fact, he's a good person, but he just doesn't understand our spiritual need. He's satisfied with a religious shell. I suppose he figures I'm kicking over the traces, leading some kind of rebellion. I hope some day he'll understand that Christianity and conformity aren't the same thing."

~⌒∽

The following Sunday Priscilla again went to Saint Patrick's by herself. She had grown up with horses and had no trouble handling the buggy on her own. As she walked across the churchyard, she saw Mr. Rogers turning in. She nodded and he returned her greeting with a short tip of his hat.

When Priscilla walked into the church, she wondered if it was just her imagination that some of the whispers changed to silence as she made her way to her customary pew by the organ. Usually the McElderrys shared it with her and Alistair and the children, but today it was empty. No one moved to join her as she sat alone at the far end of the long bench.

Priscilla was reflecting on the events of the past week when the organist ended his prelude and Reverend Smithers stood up to give his traditional welcome and call to worship. Flattening the corners of his crisp grey moustache, he tightened his lips, creased a sheet of paper on the oak pulpit, and cleared his throat. "Dear brethren in Christ," he began. "This morning I begin our service by bringing you warning of a very serious matter. Many of you have noticed that the McElderry family, the Jones family, and Alistair Stanhope and his children were absent last week and again this morning."

Priscilla could hardly believe her ears as he gestured toward her and the empty pew. Feeling the heat of everyone's eyes on her, she slid down a little and stared blindly at the floor. Priscilla twisted her gloves as hard as she could. Not a creak or a rustle could be heard as people waited. It was as if Reverend Smithers had paused for Priscilla, to make the silence stand around her, to make her carry the weight of the others' absence.

Reverend Smithers went on. "A dangerous heresy is being fomented by these families. They've left our precious church to form a cult at Wood Creek Farm. I have spoken to my worthy fellow ministers in the other two churches in the village, and we have hit upon a solution. We need to help these misguided souls recognize that they cannot exist without their community of fellow Christians. Accordingly, I am instructing you to stop using McElderry's shop until he repents of his sin. Go out to Reuben Lafayette's or to Guelph if you want to have your horses shod, anyplace except McElderry's. The other two churchmen in the village are delivering this same message to their congregations this morning."

Dazed and numb, Priscilla heard a sudden murmur among the parishioners. She struggled to breathe, feeling as if someone were choking her. Her face burned, and she knew it must be a deep crimson by the time she heard Reverend Smithers starting to recite the opening sentences of the order of service. At first Priscilla wished she could have dropped through a hole in the floor. But then she felt a surge of anger at the attack on her gentle friends who were meeting in her own parlour. Everything within her rebelled. What was she doing sitting there? As out of place as Peter in the high priest's courtyard.³ Not more than ten minutes passed before she could bear it no longer. Reverend Smithers was preaching about the virtue of caring for each other when, in the middle of his sermon, she stood up as if jerked to her feet by a sudden vision of justice. His careful enunciation of the words, "and by chance there came down a certain priest that way: and when he saw him, he passed by on the other side,"⁴ echoed in her ears as she bolted down the aisle and out the double doors. Behind her the congregation craned their necks in stunned silence.

Priscilla hurried to the buggy and, gathering her skirts clear of the wheel, she stared resolutely ahead as the startled horse broke into a trot at the churchyard gate. It wasn't until Priscilla reached the privacy of the open fields that tears began to spill down her cheeks. Nesting in the low-lying pastures on either side, she heard the piercing, almost human cries of the killdeer as though nature herself were heeding Priscilla's pain. Her body began to shake as she cried, brokenhearted. "I should've known better," she sobbed as the buggy pressed on toward Wood Creek Farm.

She arrived part way through the meeting and stood listening outside the parlour door for a few minutes. The soft voices inside began to soothe her pain. Then slowly she walked into the room and slipped into the empty chair beside Alistair. Her pulse slackened and her breathing slowed as she listened to her friends pouring out their love for Christ and for each other. When Alistair eased his arm around her trembling body, she snuggled close and held his hand, relieved to feel its strength and warmth.

Although Priscilla was too overwrought to talk just then, her pale, tear-streaked face and the pain etched in her eyes told the story. Asking no questions, her friends embraced her, glad she had come home to them.

As soon as everyone had gone, Priscilla beckoned Alistair to the privacy of their room. Through her tears she told him what had happened. "What kind of a man would try to attack such a sensitive and hardworking couple as Emily and Stephen?" she demanded. "And in the name of God?"

Shock registered on Alistair's face as he listened to the grim news. "I hadn't expected such a severe backlash," he muttered. "Stephen and Emily are just getting started as owners of the forge, and I'm certain they don't have a lot of reserves." He turned and stared out the window. "I'll have to chew on it for a spell…"

"Reverend Smithers is beginning to show his true colours," Priscilla acknowledged. "Or maybe I'm just starting to understand, like you said, that his main concern's the outward running of Saint Patrick's. I didn't grasp it before…or maybe I didn't want to."

Alistair took her in his arms and kissed her. "It doesn't matter, my dear," he assured her. "I'm just glad we're together now."

~∘

The next morning right after breakfast, Alistair hurried over to Stephen's blacksmith shop.

"Good morning, Alistair. It's a surprise to see you so early." Stephen leaned up against the doorjamb watching for customers. "For some reason the shop's been unusually quiet for a Monday morning."

"It may be that way for a while, Stephen," Alistair said softly. "After everybody left yesterday, Priscilla told me the three ministers have ordered their congregations to stay away from your shop and go elsewhere."

Disbelief struggled with fear in Stephen's face as Alistair told him the story. As shock glazed his young friend's eyes, Alistair could feel his own muscles and joints tightening with anger. Stephen wasn't that much older than Timothy, and he felt a fatherly concern for the young man and his wife.

Looking down, Stephen slowly shook his head. "Why on earth would this happen just when I'm doing my level best to get this shop going?"

Alistair didn't have an answer for that question, but he did reach out and put his hand on Stephen's strong shoulder. "We've had good crops the last couple of years, and I've got a little extra in the bank," he said. "Priscilla and I intend to stand behind you and Emily—no matter what."

"Thanks for the offer, Alistair," Stephen said. "You're a real brother."

Like Alistair, the others offered support as well. As soon as Bill heard the news about the ban on Stephen's shop, he hurried over to promise help. And when George stayed with the McElderrys on Saturday evening, he asked Stephen if he would like to work with him on his farm. "I'd be happy to go halves with you. Besides, I'd enjoy your company."

At first, Stephen and Emily were anxious, worrying that they might have to move elsewhere or turn to farming like Bill and Alistair. Money would be very scarce before long. But as the young couple prayed about what to do, they felt a strong conviction to weather the storm and quietly put their trust in God.

Bill and Alice kept a flock of chickens in a cedar-shingled henhouse between their house and barn. The Rhode Island Reds served as meat birds for the table and the egg sales provided pin money for Alice. Every week she sold them to Mr. Crundle at the general store. Garnering a range of produce from local farmers, the storekeeper hauled it to the city each Wednesday, returning at night with a load of groceries and dry goods.

One evening, as Alice entered the henhouse to collect a basket of brown eggs, she discovered that one of the mature hens was being savagely attacked by the others. The bloodied creature was trying in vain to escape into a quiet corner so Alice put the hapless fowl outside of the henhouse to heal and recover. She knew that if hens notice something unusual about any one of them, the others will peck the unfortunate creature until it dies.

At supper, while dishing out potato cakes and sausages, Alice passed a plateful to Bill. "One of the biddies got pecked half to death this afternoon," she remarked. "Odd, isn't it, how different the nature of a chicken is from that of a lamb? I'd rather be the Master's lamb."

Bill sopped up the juice on his plate with a slice of bread. "Uproar in the henhouse and peace in the pasture," he mused aloud. "God will take care of His own."

Sectarian feelings, like the reek from manure piles, were running high. Sometimes when Bill and Alice greeted certain neighbours along the road, the drivers would avert their eyes or whip their horses into a trot. Others, however, pulled up on the grass and greeted the Jones as usual.

On her way to sell her eggs at Crundle's General Store one Tuesday morning, Alice chanced to meet old Jordie along the road. "Mighty fine day, Miss Alice," the older man declared as he tilted back his stained hat and glanced skyward. "How's them young rips of your'n?"

Alice's broad face broke into a grin. "Tearing up the turf as always."

"'Bout the meetin's at Alistair Stanhope's," Jordie began. "I don't hold with what certain folks is sayin'. After all, they're mighty fine neighbours. I'll never forget 'twasn't Alistair set the magistrate on me. And Bill's father was a right upstandin' old Welshman." Old Jordie wiped the slobber from his chin with the back of his hand. "And young McElderry's the best durn blacksmith in these parts. Honest as the day is long too." He scratched his knobby elbow and leered affably at Alice. "Keep your bloomers dry, Miss Alice," he wheezed. "By 'n' by folks'll come 'round."

Although Alice turned a shocked face on him, a smile teased her lips. "Good day, Jordie," she said as she flicked the lines and pulled away.

The steps creaked under Alice as she entered the general store to find Mr. Crundle alone at the counter.

"Good morning," she said cheerfully as she walked toward the cash register and set down her basket of fresh eggs.

A scowl spread across the storekeeper's face. "I don't want any more of your eggs," he growled as he shoved them back across the counter.

Alice's mouth gaped at the icy remark. "Why not?" she stammered, her mind racing. "Weren't the last ones fresh?" But even as the words left her mouth she suddenly realized why.

"I want to do business with honourable folks, and until you people straighten up, I'll get my eggs elsewhere," Mr. Crundle retorted, his face quivering with nervousness.

Alice felt a rush of anger. "Albert Crundle," she pronounced, her voice rising in exasperation, "don't talk to me about being *honourable folks* while Smithers and his cronies are tramping a fine couple like the McElderrys into the ground. Those three hypocrites look good on the outside—like whitewashed tombs[5]—but inside they're full of death and totally heartless. They're consumed by power and control like the great harlot.[6] Their churches are as dry as dust—full of tradition but no life. And you're backing them up, Albert. Take my advice and get out while you can."[7] The stunned storekeeper clamped his teeth as Alice lambasted the clergymen. Then, leaving him dumbstruck, she spun on her heel. "I'll sell my eggs in Guelph," she shouted over her shoulder as she slammed the door, rattling the glass in his storefront. A covey of the neighbour's chickens scattered with a squawk, their wings flapping, as she charged toward the buggy.

As she rode toward home, she cooled down quickly. She hadn't gone a mile before she felt distraught about her outburst. "Why do I always fly off like that?" Alice fretted. "I wish I were more like Bill. He'd have said nothing, just taken it." When she got in the door, she hurried to her room and fell prostrate on the bed, pleading with God for forgiveness.

Afterwards, catching sight of her reflection in the oval bedroom mirror, Alice stared with dispirited revulsion. What she had never been able to cast off, all these years later, were the haunting memories of her father brought on by the blocky shoulders, powerful arms, and fleshy face that glared back from deep within the glass and the vindictiveness she had heard spewing from her own mouth an hour earlier.

Over their noon stew, Alice broke the silence abruptly. "Bill, I did something horribly wrong this morning." Her tone conveyed deep remorse. "Mr. Crundle told me he didn't want to buy my eggs anymore. You know, because of the church ruckus. It made me think about Stephen and Emily, and I got terrible riled." Bill nodded gravely. "When he accused me of not being honourable, I tore into him and gave him both barrels. I said a lot of nasty things. I wasn't much like Christ on Calvary.[8] It's a terrible reflection on our little group and what we try to stand for." Her features crumpled.

Bill looked at the baby sleeping in a square of sunshine beside the south window. Then he leaned forward to lay a hand on Alice's arm. "You're one of God's little ones, and He's already forgiven you," he assured her. "You'll just have to leave it there and tread more softly."

"That's true," Alice sniffled. "But I've still got to make it right with Mr. Crundle. There's no excuse for a Christian to act the way I did."

After dinner Alice washed the dishes, brushed her hair, and hooked up the horse again. As she rode along, she asked God to guide her words and to soften the storekeeper's heart.

Mr. Crundle's eyes took on a hunted look when he happened to glance out the window and saw Alice cinching her horse's lead shank to the rail. "What on earth's comin' now?" he muttered.

Alice's face revealed purpose as she swung the door open and stepped over the threshold. "Mr. Crundle," she said, "I've come to say I'm sorry for what I said this morning. I hope you'll forgive me."

The storekeeper's shoulders slumped as he fiddled with his pencil. "It's no matter," he mumbled, flushing a mottled purple.

"Thank you," Alice said. "I need some red flannel and cotton batting before I go. Would you please help me measure it out?" After she paid for her things, she headed for home, at peace with herself and God.

Mr. Crundle scratched his head as she pulled away. He had understood Alice's earlier reaction, but this present one left him baffled. He screwed up his face and wound his index finger as deeply as he could into his right ear, pronouncing a single eloquent word: "Women!"

News of the little church fell from the lips of many of the neighbours in and around Puslinch Township. Even the few who never attended a church of any kind became aware of the harsh reaction of the clergymen. But not everyone's response was negative.

One evening Bill had just returned from harrowing the back field when, through the approaching darkness, the neighbour's hired man, Malachi Jackson, appeared, trudging through the freshly cultivated soil. Bill led his heavy work horses to the gate of the paddock and tied their lead shanks to a ring so he could brush them down. Malachi crossed his tanned, hairy

forearms and leaned his elbows against the rail fence, certainly a more civilized character now than his stormy arrival at Ben Aberlochy's funeral would
have attested.

"Weather's been pretty fair," he offered.

"Not bad," Bill replied, wondering why Malachi would come to visit
after a long day of hard work.

"I reckon everything works itself out."

"Guess so."

"You should take that mare over to Jim Braithewaite's stud. She'd throw
a nice foal for you."

Malachi was a leathery, fifty-eight-year-old with large ears and a missing
front tooth. He had worked for the neighbour for the past twenty-three
years after owning a farm in Haldimand County, which he had left abruptly
and for reasons that remained mysterious. When he had first arrived in
Puslinch, idle speculation among neighbourhood gossips ran the gamut from
a drunken brawl in which someone had been maimed to a dalliance with
a neighbour's wife, but whatever it was, Malachi's lips were sealed. Over
the intervening years, Bill had often witnessed the hired man's gentle way
with livestock and his quick, well-known wit and unlimited repertoire of
pithy sayings. Aside from the rare public outburst when he had slipped into
drunken despair, Malachi endured a lonely existence.

Bill was in mid-motion of pouring each horse a gallon of oats when
he heard Malachi's nasal twang. "When I went fer a dose of garglin' oil at
the store, Albert Crundle told me about them meetin's you and your missus
are takin' in over at the Stanhopes'."

Looking up into Malachi's lean face, Bill waited, wondering what was
coming next. "Yep," the hired man continued, "some of the stuffed shirts
seem hard agin it, but it's just the sort of thing I'd like to know more about."

Bill was so surprised that the oats continued to pour, unchecked. Malachi
never went to church at any time, and most folks figured that spiritual matters were the farthest thing from his mind.

Bill remembered one evening last summer when he had gone to check
on his cows in the back pasture. He had come across Malachi sound asleep
in a fence corner beside an empty bottle of rye. Bill felt sorry for him and
knew that the hired man, in his desperation and loneliness, often hid away
in some solitary place as he tried to drown his sorrows.

After he had curried out the last of the harness marks, Bill turned the
horses loose until morning. As the two men ambled up to the house, it

was settled that Malachi would catch a ride with Bill and Alice the following Thursday evening. As with the original church in Jerusalem, persecution was generating growth.[9]

Two weeks passed and Stephen's shop remained quiet. But like it or not, horses needed to be shod, and Stephen was an excellent and honest blacksmith. The next closest smith was seven miles away and not nearly as good with the horses. To his customers, religious principles were one thing, but a fine blacksmith was something else. Gradually, farmers and cart owners began to arrive until a row of patient horses could be seen standing in front of the shop by mid-mornings. Stephen and Emily had waited out the storm, and delighted at the outcome, they marveled at God's care.

One afternoon as the season lengthened into summer, old Jordie shambled onto the porch of Crundle's Store to dicker for a turnip scuffler. "That whole shunning ruckus agin young McElderry's darn near petered out," old Jordie snorted through tobacco-stained lips as the money changed hands. "I reckon even Smithers had to take in the slack of his jaw. Why, how in tarnation could he imagine Alistair Stanhope and Bill Jones turnin' Puslinch on its ear anyhow?"

"Among 'em be it," Albert Crundle grunted in curt consensus as the two men lugged the scuffler toward Jordie's stone boat.

By early June the blades of grain were well out of the ground and the air hung heavy with the sweetness of mown hay. The days were longer and farm chores crowded on each other's heels. The marshy chorus of spring peepers, shrill in May, had muted to the occasional grunt of a bullfrog.

On the weekend before his final examinations, Timothy stayed in town with his Aunt Maggie to study. Quietly, in his own bedroom on Sunday morning, he took time to pray and to meditate on some of Jesus' words.

Timothy had exams in Latin, algebra, and trigonometry early in the week, but on Wednesday afternoon he corked his inkwell with a flourish, gathered his armload of books, and bounded down the staircase of the Guelph Collegiate Institute. A pair of third form girls, reacting from examination jitters, stuck out their pointed shoes in a mock attempt to bring their hero to his knees. But just as handily, Timothy swung around with a wide grin and gave the lead girl's hair comb a playful tug, allowing her swept-up locks to tumble unceremoniously down her back. Turning, she stuck out her tongue as she and her friend flounced up the stairs.

As he strode to Aunt Maggie's for the last time, he reflected on the Latin examination. Last winter he had given the dead language priority, knowing it would be vital for the ministry. Only yesterday an embossed envelope had arrived from the college and lay like an importunate document on his washstand. Nothing now but Reverend Smithers' letter of recommendation, a character reference from his teaching master, and an application fee stood between him and ivy-clad walls. But the several times Timothy had been able to be a part of the Thursday night meetings at home had begun to shape the young scholar's thinking. Timothy was concluding that seminary attendance was not the scriptural way to prepare for the life of service he envisioned. Surely the training of Peter, James, and John was adequate for him too. Like Jesus, the carpenter, they had all experienced the dignity and responsibility of ordinary occupations before beginning to teach the gospel of life to working men and women. If the Son of God didn't ignore this practical step, certainly he couldn't either. And so Timothy had decided to settle into farm work with his father for a while.

Timothy recalled his father sitting on a three-legged stool as he milked a big roan cow in the stable. "It's not when an institution puts a piece of paper into a man's hand that he's equipped to point others to Christ," he had insisted, the pail between his knees. "It's when God puts an earnest care into his heart..."[10] Alistair's sentence had been cut short as he ducked to avoid a swat in the face from the cow's tail. "No one can give what he hasn't received, tell what he hasn't heard, or show what he hasn't seen."

This wisdom had lodged in Timothy's young mind, and as he packed his belongings that Wednesday afternoon, he resolved to spend as much time in the company of Christ as possible—watching, hearing, receiving.

When he brought his case down the stairs, Aunt Maggie was standing on the stoop, her white hair tucked in a hairnet and her scrawny arms folded in her apron bib. "Now be sure to live up to what you was taught," she admonished. "A lad can't do better than that." The two stood together in a moment of awkward tenderness, neither one meeting the other's eyes.

Then Timothy was gone, turning his face away from the coal smoke of Guelph and toward the fresher air of Puslinch Township. As the elegant spire on the Church of Our Lady, high on the hill, faded from sight, his collegiate memories slipped from his mind. In the bottom of his satchel lay a large, savoury sultana cake—Aunt Maggie's final offering to the lad whom for four years she had loved and housed as her own.

Six

REACHING OUT IN LOVE
Summer 1899

"Heavy hay in June before the waning moon," Jack grinned, quoting from *The Old Farmer's Almanac*.

"All this rain we've been having makes the alfalfa and rye grass shoot up," George remarked as his seasoned eye swept over a lush field behind a stump fence. "That clover's thick as fleas on a dog's back. Trouble is, it's a job to get it off while the sun's shining. Like as not, it could pour again tomorrow. Anyway, I'm glad it's Thursday again. Alistair and Timothy'll be pleased for us to come early and give them a spoke for the afternoon."

Jack balanced comfortably in the gentle roll of the saddle, his muscular back ramrod straight, his eyes shielded from the sun's glare by the wide brim of his straw hat. "Timothy will be one jovial fella to be rid of those Latin examinations for good. Great he finished up last week, just in the nick of time for haying."

George chuckled aloud. "He certainly can keep you in stitches when you're working along side him."

As George and Jack rode in the direction of Wood Creek Farm, they fell into the companionable silence men share when each one is thinking about a woman.

Laura Chapelton's face filled George's mind. He had met her three years earlier when she was hired to teach a second class of junior students at the one-room schoolhouse in Arkell. At the time, there were so many students that the present teacher couldn't handle the entire four forms. Laura had boarded with George's parents, who lived on a farm close to the school. Although George had his own farm, he could often be found at his mother's table during mealtime and, either by chance or design, in the chair next to the new teacher.

Laura's head barely came up to George's shoulder, making him feel a certain protectiveness for her. She had delicate features, and she often wore her thick chestnut hair in a lustrous French braid, neatly dressed. But it was her eyes that had caught and held him in a bond that George himself couldn't explain.

The two had become almost inseparable as he grew to appreciate the depth of her conversation and her thoughtful ways. She knew his little habits well and liked to tease him. "I always know when you're happy, George. You whistle to yourself without making any sound. The happiness floats out in the air but the music stays in," she laughed.

Unfortunately, as time had passed fewer children were starting school. With regret, the trustees had informed Laura that they were unable to renew her contract for the third year, but promised if the need arose again, she would be the only person considered.

Laura began to watch the postings in the *Globe* for teaching positions. With her excellent resume and letter of reference, she had been promptly hired by the school board in Mildmay, sixty miles to the northwest. The new job challenged her and the children were delightful, but after a few months Laura realized she was too far from George to be happy for long.

As George rode along, his mind raced back to the September evening nine months earlier when he and Laura had said goodbye before the long winter separated them. At the Farnham supper table during the last meal that Laura would share with them for a long time, George's parents worried aloud about the price of parsnips and cabbages at the Guelph market. While George's father grumbled about the ones that the heifers had trampled, George and Laura exchanged glances across the table in the wordless language of love. After swallowing the last of his gooseberry pie, George pushed back his chair and seemed to vanish. Laura remembered that her white high-collar blouse with the puffed sleeves, now swaying on the clothesline, had to be ironed before her travelling outfit would be ready for the next day's train journey. She had slipped out to the yard where the pink September afterglow cast its radiance eastward, framing a pair of mourning doves on the barn ridge between the tall spires of spruce. In the unseasonable warmth of the late summer evening, she noticed the Flemish

Beauty had released more of its yellow crop, leaving the windfall pears slimy with sweetness and covered by countless hornets extracting the syrup. Laura reached for her damp blouse, pinned upside down with its leg-of-mutton sleeves extended, as if appealing to an unseen figure.

Startled, Laura heard her name being called softly, insistently. Peering into the shadows, she caught a glimpse of George perched on the wood-pile, an impish grin lighting his face as he leaned toward her. She approached him and stood for a moment between his knees before impudently seizing his cap and tossing it back over her shoulder. In a moment of reverse surprise, George sprang forward, wrapped his arms around her, and planted a kiss on her lips. Laura melted into his embrace, returning his passion with soft murmurs of affection as she ran her fingers over his ears and tousled his unruly hair. "George," she teased, "why don't you pack up and come with me?" The intensity in her eyes softened as she traced a forefinger over his face. "I'm going to miss you so much." She blinked, releasing an errant tear to meander down her face. "I'm sorry…I didn't want to cry. It just makes it even harder."

"It's all right," George whispered as he stroked her hair. "You don't have to be strong." Then he raised her chin and kissed her again, his lips as gentle and warm as the darkness falling around them. Laura closed her eyes, and for a long time they held each other close, sharing the tender intimacy of these final moments together. Both felt a heartrending urgency, a consciousness of impending separation they had never felt before. The formal words George had prepared, the vision of a happy marriage—all of this escaped him. As he took Laura by the hand and walked her to the kitchen door in the darkness, his mouth felt dry, his jaw tense.

Although George had not proposed, Laura hoped that when his farm was paid off, they would marry and have children of their own. She respected George's desire to be free of debt before taking on the responsibility of a wife. And if at times she found it difficult to wait, she gave no indication, patient in the certain knowledge that they would eventually be together as man and wife.

The next morning at the train station, under the watchful eye of his parents, George and Laura had shaken hands in awkward formality while his entire body thumped painfully over the lost opportunity.

A lively exchange of letters broke the long winter silence, week by week. As the northern hemisphere turned away from the sun, and then, almost imperceptibly, toward it again, George had wondered how the next opportunity to propose would present itself. It was only yesterday that George had posted his latest letter to Laura. He thought of it now as the horses approached Alistair's lane.

Arkell, Ontario
June 10, 1899

My dearest Laura,

I can't begin to tell you how much I miss you. Life without you has been as gray and drab as a November landscape when all the leaves have gone. As the months drag by and our letters share mostly surface details of our lives, I miss the special closeness we enjoy when we're together.

Do you remember the picnic we took to Doyle's Mill and how we watched the orange glow of the sun as it disappeared behind the willows? Only the splashes of the bass catching insects broke the pond's glassy surface. And the bullfrogs sang to us from the lily pads at the water's edge. I can see you now. The sunset shining on your face made the summer evening a rare beauty.

Speaking of reflections on a pond, do you recall one of those last nights in August before you left? I sure was glad for the cool breeze as we sat close, my arm wrapped around you in the darkness. Nestled there on the stone wall of the pasture, we watched the full moon rising over Snyder's barn. That brilliant orb painted a long silvery path across the ripples of the pond almost to our feet. Only the distant sounds of a loon calling to his mate and the soft hooting of an owl pulsated through the stillness.

I think about those times often and wonder if you felt the same feelings that I did. You certainly are wonderful to hold and behold! Memories like those keep me going until I see you again. Summer—it's an agony to wait for it.

Most of all, Laura, I want to sit and talk face-to-face with you about these matters of the heart and to sing those majestic hymns of our Saviour together. I am hoping your soul will receive the same craving that mine has for the gentle Spirit of Christ. I also want you to get to know my friends better. The time you spent here last August was far too short for you to understand the love and friendship that we all share. The warmth among this little fellowship is sublime, and Jesus has breathed new life into my former tired religious self.

Well, Laura, I just felt like rambling tonight since I'm at home by myself. I miss you terribly. And I love you more deeply with each passing day. Can you really believe that we'll be seeing each other in just two weeks? Seems like forever, but I've learned that waiting is what farmers do best. I'll be at the train station when you arrive!

With my fondest love,

George

George and Jack arrived at Wood Creek Farm just as Priscilla was ready to ladle out her chicken dumplings. Phoebe was on hand, too, proudly showing off the rhubarb pie she had baked, the first one of the season.

During the fiercely hot afternoon, Jack drove one team back and forth across the field with the dump rake, tripping the lever intermittently to release the fresh cut hay into windrows to dry. Bouncing along on the rake's springy metal seat, he watched George and Timothy loading hay in the adjoining field. From time to time, he spied Alistair coming out of the barn to thrust a hand deep into the windrow, drawing out a handful of alfalfa to roll between his leathery palms. Damp hay, Jack knew, could turn mouldy, generate heat, and ignite the barn.

George drove the second team that pulled the wagon hooked to the hay loader. As the massive black horses plodded up and down the windrows, the ratchet-like teeth of the loader cranked the dry hay up and over the back rack to where Timothy, pitchfork in hand, built the load. When the wagon could hold no more, he clambered down and yanked out the draw pin, uncoupling the loader from the wagon. "Let 'em at it," he roared up.

With a cavalier wave, George guided the team to the foot of the gangway where he stopped to give them a breather. He never failed to admire the way Alistair's big Percherons leaned into their harness, straining to lug the dead weight up the steep incline and into the barn. One at a time, George unhooked each horse and led it back outside, its broad flanks squeezing between the bulky load and the side of the mow. Pausing at the watering trough, he allowed the gentle giants to press their soft noses into the cool water. George waved his straw hat over their sweaty withers as they drank, dispersing a cloud of horse flies intent on the patches of lather around their collars. The horses' shoulders flinched and their tails snapped up and down as they sought relief from the biting insects. After they had drunk their fill, George backed the team up to a second set of whippletrees, connected by a heavy rope and pulley blocks to the giant hay fork which swung the heap high over the mow. Minor dust storms smothered Alistair each time he tugged on the cord to release another dump.

When George once again eased the team across a gully at the end of the driving shed, the wagon's bunks creaked under the weight of the cumbersome load. Glancing toward the house, he noticed Priscilla hurrying past the windmill, a blue speckled jug in her hands. She beckoned to him, and when the horses turned in at the barnyard gate, she grabbed their bridles.

"Thirsty?" she called up.

He scrambled down the front rack. "Parched as a toad in a dustbin."

Priscilla dunked the small dipper into the pail. "I boiled and corked this ginger ale four days ago, so it's got plenty of fizz."

"Nothing like ginger ale to quench the thirst," George replied as he straddled the tongue of the wagon, swigging the refreshing drink.

Priscilla's womanly curiosity got the best of her as George accepted a second dipper. "Isn't it time for your friend Laura to be heading back this way?"

Startled, George looked up. "Yes, it is," he conceded. "In a fortnight." Just then, Teddy trotted around the corner of the wagon and flopped at George's feet, his tail thumping and his tongue drooling. George ran his hand over the collie's caramel head. "Teddy's so eager he upends the stooks before Timothy can pitch them up to me. Jams his long snout underneath trying to snatch a fat field mouse."

Priscilla smiled, eager to return to her subject. "It was nice you brought Laura to meet us last August," she coaxed. "Maybe this summer, you'll be bringing her regularly in the buggy—instead of bouncing along on your own on horseback." George didn't respond for a minute, tipping the bottom of the dipper toward the barn roof. In the face of silence, Priscilla persisted. "Wasn't she interested in coming to the meetings last summer?"

"Laura's a wonderful person," George acknowledged, "but any girl's apt to go along with a fella just 'cause she likes him. That's alright for some things, but in this, she needs to receive her own revelation."

"But surely you encouraged her, George, didn't you?"

"No, I didn't try to influence her one way or the other. When God speaks, she'll be here whether I come or not. That's the kind of devotion I'd like to see in a better half." He handed the cup to Priscilla. "I once knew a girl who got all heated up about fox hunting until her suitor jilted her. Then she dropped it like a hot potato. Besides, Laura was living with my folks last year, and my mother's broken leg was in plaster. She wanted to help her get to church for those few weeks. I just let it be. God works things out in His time." George wiped his face with a shirt sleeve. "Thanks for the drink, Priscilla," he said as he climbed back up the wagon racks and settled onto the sweet-smelling load, picturing the day when he and Laura, together, would be a loved and loving part of the circle at Wood Creek Farm.

The heavy crop soon filled the barn and Alistair started an outside haystack for the surplus. The men's faces were hot and flushed and their shirts wet with sweat as they made their way to the kitchen. Priscilla and Phoebe poured each man another tall glass of the fermented ginger ale. After such a blistering afternoon of field work, the Thursday evening meeting might have been called off by less zealous men, but no one here even considered such a thought. These gatherings were the highlight of their week.

The welcome coolness of the evening reminded Alistair of the previous Monday. He had dashed over to help Bill get some hay into the barn before a threatening thunderstorm. But as they struggled to finish, the storm, like a disgruntled raven, had moved off to the south. On the way home, he had yielded to an impulse and stopped at the old burial ground. Tying his horse to the sagging iron fence, he moved among the leaning gray monuments until he confronted a newer one, still bolt upright. Instead of the clasped hands and weeping willows of the others, this stone featured an anchor under which the stonecutter had chiselled, "Home is the sailor, home from the sea."

Standing at the foot of Ben's grave, Alistair bowed his head and lifted his voice. "Dear Father, as I tarry in this field of clay from whence we've all been taken, and whither we return again,[1] I'm reminded that You alone are the master potter. And that You used Ben's death to soften my heart and place Your fingers inside it.[2] Has not the potter power over the clay to turn the wheel of time and fashion his creation according to his good pleasure?[3] Father, many things I can't understand, but please do whatever is needful to shape me into a vessel that brings honour to You. And Father, continue to deal mercifully with Ben, I pray, for his soul also came from and has returned to Your eternal care. Amen." Finally, as the cool breeze picked up, Alistair moved on, almost sensing that somehow Ben knew all that Alistair couldn't say.

The combination of the cool evening and the coral sunset that lingered over the western horizon engendered a serenity as he wandered, reading the tombstones of other lives that ended long ago—some before Alistair had been born. An eight-year-old boy here, a young man there. A baby girl and her mother had died two days apart in a childbirth tragedy. Nearby, in the long grass, a crescent of smooth stones arranged themselves like milk teeth in an infant's smile. These marked the tiny graves of the diphtheria victims, all children. Alistair watched the shadows creeping across the grass, knowing that before long, each stone would be laden with heavy tears of dew. In this consecrated ground the anguished unready ones lay side by side with those who had prayed for death. Muted depressions and flat markers, worn and long-since illegible, marked the tired bones of the original settlers who, after a life full of labour and hardship, had welcomed death as a delayed friend.

After a few minutes, Alistair circled back to pause again at Ben's grave. "Goodbye, Ben. You've remained as faithful a friend in death as in life. And helped me more than you know. I'll come again."

Alistair glanced around the ancestral burying yard, reflecting on the poignant drama of lives now hidden from future generations forever. What, he wondered, could a man do to truly make a difference? And then he remembered the gospel of Jesus Christ. Yes, the gospel. It makes a difference that time can never erase. He ambled toward a boulder beneath an old apple tree standing in the fence row. But how? How could it be accomplished? As he sat down, transfixed, his eyes fell on a cluster of tiger lilies at his feet and he remembered Jesus' words: "Consider the lilies of the field and how they grow."[4]

After nearly an hour of contemplating the lilies, Alistair found himself at home with pen and paper. Setting down his thoughts, he hoped, would work some of the woolliness out of his thinking:

> *Each lily at the burial ground abounds with beauty and life. Depending upon the light and warmth of the sun, it extracts from the soil the nutrients it needs to be a lily. Little else affects its existence. In like manner, a Christian relies on God above and draws from the earth the essentials for natural life. Each lily grows exactly as God intended—a tangible expression of His creative thought. It never attempts to be a trillium, a rose, or the apple tree along the fence. What the plant is and becomes can be traced to a mystery within the original seed, a design conceived before creation. Being true to His will means accepting with grace our lot in life.*

> *Two lilies growing side by side share the same nature and are much alike—yet entirely different. Each one unfolds its leaves and extends its flowers toward heaven in a way no other lily has ever done before or will again.[5] God saw beauty in creating them similar yet distinctive. So it is with believers; the same Spirit of Christ, but each possessing a unique personality. Of course, humans have the liberty to reject His plan and fashion our own identity and destiny. Or, like the lily, we can glorify Him by lifting our heads and reflecting His beauty.*

> *A healthy plant produces fruit or seeds naturally and spontaneously. Buds burst forth in beautiful, fragrant blossoms and eventually in fruit.[6] Unfinished and imperfect at first, it matures into a work of tender sweetness. But no lily has the power to hold its breath, grit its teeth, and suddenly burst into bloom. It must wait for God.[7] Flowers or fruit prove undeniably that they are alive. No life—no fruit. Abundant life—abundant fruit.[8] The mystery is that each piece contains a seed with exactly the same desires and inner code as the seed from which it sprang weeks, months, or years before. Although the plant has no part in creating or even planting itself, it plays a vital role in faithfully reproducing seeds from which new lilies spring. The life of Christ lived out again!*

Lilies seldom grow alone. Before long a little community of plants flourish where the first seed was once planted, sustaining and protecting each other from the winds. Like members of the true church, they stand together along the quiet fence rows, tiny saints beholding the beaming face of God. Their unique nature differentiates them from all the surrounding plants of the field. In a few years grass may shroud the soil where the lily once spent its life. But no matter. It reflected God's purpose during its sojourn as He intended.

Alistair laid down his pen, placed the cork in his ink bottle, and let out a long, steady breath. Things seemed clearer as he folded up his papers and stored them away.

Until now the little gathering of believers at Wood Creek Farm had been content to be passive and somewhat introspective, but over the summer the Holy Spirit continued to influence Alistair. The seed in his heart was coming to maturity. More and more, he felt it necessary to invite his neighbours to hear about Jesus. To Alistair, the regeneration of the gospel seed should happen much like God's plan for the plant kingdom. The first seed had to be planted by an outside agent; perhaps the wind, a bird, an animal, or a Christian believer. But the agent was only the seed's transportation, never its creator. Life came from God alone.

Taking a break from the task of scuffling turnips, Alistair pulled up two chairs in the summer kitchen while Timothy, his face caked with dust, fetched two apples from the root cellar.

"The Spys have stayed hard over the winter," Timothy noted as he ran the paring knife around a giant specimen in steady concentric circles. A roguish grin dimpled his cheeks. "I wonder how hard the apple was that bounced off our friend Mr. Newton's head."

Like a man whose mind was miles away, Alistair stared at the oilcloth.

Unfazed by his father's introspective silence, Timothy persisted. "I reckon I can slip this off in one piece," he declared as the dangling peel twisted and curled.

Alistair raised his eyes, munching mechanically. "Every apple seed wants to produce a new apple tree," he mused at length. "And every apple tree wants to produce more seeds."

Timothy's almond eyes crinkled as he considered the statement.

Taking the paring knife, Alistair pried open his core and edged the glossy brown seeds into a neat row along the rim of his saucer. "You can count the seeds in an apple, but you can never count the apples in a seed. The possibilities are unlimited if we do things in God's way."

Timothy studied his father's face, trying to absorb his logic. When nothing more was forthcoming, he stood up. "Well, back to the grindstone," he said, tugging on his cap.

The possibilities also seemed unlimited to George on the last Friday of June as he stood watching the Wellington, Grey, and Bruce engine hissing into the Guelph railway station. The platform reverberated to the thunder of an exuberant crowd, some of the class of '99, newly graduated from the Ontario Veterinary College. The young men thrust triumphant fists into the air as they hoisted onto their shoulders and roared approval of the scholar who had won top honours for Wellington County. Oblivious to the boisterous graduates, George waited in a frenzy of impatience as the conductor, with maddening deliberation, elbowed down the steps a tottering parade of powdered ladies with shawls and parasols. George's smile burst across his sunburned face when at last he spied Laura negotiating the precipitous steps to the platform. He sprinted forward and folded the stylish young lady to his heart. "Laura, my girl!" he exclaimed, drawing in the fragrance of her perfume, delicate as a baby's breath.

Laura's voice, sweet and euphoric, rose above the clamour of the boarding train. "Look, George," she said with a laugh, "my landlady packed a lunch for the journey, and she put in enough for two." As she peered into the bag, her brows creased in disappointment. "But there's just *one* apple."

"Good," George said emphatically. "We'll eat that one, turn about, you and I."

Startled by the passion in his voice, Laura shyly met his eyes. The gruff old conductor, overhearing them, thumped down Laura's trunk onto the platform. "Share and share alike," he jested, his eyes twinkling.

The old road out of Guelph to Arkell was lavish with the beauty of early summer. When Laura gazed on a green field divided by a silver stream, George drew back on the lines until the right wheel creased the orchard grass along the shoulder. "Let's pull up here a bit," he suggested, "and eat that landlady's lunch." His eyes roved over the field, settling at last on a pile of granite stones, heaved aside by the pioneers when the century was young. A beech tree, its new leaves glimmering with sunlight, leaned over a large boulder as if inviting the lovers to sit in its shade.

"Just think, Laura, we have the whole summer ahead of us, and after that the rest of our lives…" George glanced sideways at Laura's slender hands folded on the lap of her periwinkle blue dress. Just at that moment she lifted her eyes to his, her smile radiant. He knew that Laura's elder sister, Abigail, had been married that winter and that the three younger sisters at home in Stratford were stretching their longsuffering papa's resources. Did George dare hope he could slip a ring on Laura's finger before the summer was out?

He helped her step nimbly down from the buggy, and the moment her trim buckled shoe touched the grassy roadside, he clasped her arms and swung her around in a circle as if she were a girl of fifteen. Then he bent, giving her the lingering kiss that had waited through the frost of winter and the flowering of spring. George's white horse, sensing something out of the ordinary, tossed his head and whinnied, but the lovers were insensible of anything except their rapture in the blissful fields of June.

The fragrant heat intensified, and one Sunday in August the sun drew shimmering columns of humidity. At ninety-six in the shade, everyone was grateful to have the day to rest. After the fellowship meeting, Priscilla and the other women prepared a tasty meal of sliced cold meats, tomatoes, cucumbers, and greens—ideal for the sultry weather.

Laura's presence during the school holidays had been like spring promise and summer fulfilment combined. It was as if she cherished an unspoken secret as she tied on her apron and trimmed a dish of radishes with girlish enthusiasm. Meanwhile, the men carried the kitchen chairs outside and sat under the big maple trees on the lawn. When the meal was ready, each person filled a plate and took it out to eat in the shade.

Among the fellowship, George's devotion to Laura had not gone unnoticed, but such was the discretion and sensitivity of the group that the young couple's love flourished and blossomed in a wholesome way, unhampered by cynical tongues or rash comments. As a testament to Laura's winsomeness, Alistair had, after only a month's acquaintance, seemed to regard her as an honorary daughter, thereby setting the tone for her summer life at Wood Creek Farm. On this Sunday afternoon she resembled a seated figure in a painting as her green summer dress fell from her waist in a series of flounces encircling her graceful form on the orchard grass. With the ending of the school year, her French braid had been released in a cascade of chestnut curls that draped her shoulders in the elegant manner of a Botticelli portrait. Her eyes, blue as the August sky, radiated joy and gaiety around the circle, especially to the children.

Priscilla took quiet note of how George and Laura always sat when lounging outdoors, as now—not side by side, lover fashion, but face-to-face, as though reading each other's expressions for the subtle meanings imprinted there. At least this had been their posture until Alice's baby girl, trying her first tentative steps across the lawn, tottered with outstretched arms into Laura's lap and sank down in a muslin heap of pink cheeks and corn-silk hair. Laura nuzzled her face against the baby's velvet cheeks, drawing in her sweet buttermilk breath.

"Sugar and spice and all things nice," Laura cooed playfully. "I could eat you up." Glancing over the child's shoulder, she caught George's eyes fastened upon her, his expression intent. For a reason she couldn't have explained, she blushed deeply as she tried to extricate her curls from the baby's determined pink fist.

As Timothy sprawled out on the grass after dinner, he noticed Malachi mopping the perspiration off his forehead. He recalled the first Thursday that the man had followed Bill and Alice meekly into the parlour. As the old bachelor had looked around, he scratched himself in abstraction and then dug his hands defensively into his armpits, fidgeting as if he felt he didn't belong amongst a group of serious Christians. But the welcoming spirit of the room soon drew the older man in, and within weeks Malachi had sensed that he had found a long sought after family to call his own. Though not his own blood, they were yet family because of the blood of another…the Christ who bound these believers in quiet unity.

Timothy rolled onto his side. "Mal, you're sweating like a hen drawing rails."

"Yeah. And if she laid an egg today, it'd be hard boiled," the hired man grunted as he stuffed his handkerchief back into his pocket.

Timothy looked away to hide an amused smile. "So you think it's hot enough for ice cream then?" he replied with a straight face.

Malachi's mouth twisted into a wry grin. "Near about."

Alistair and Timothy had cut large blocks of ice off their pond last winter, loading them onto a sleigh and hauling them into a small building tucked under the shade of an outcrop of birch trees. Buried in two feet of sawdust and chopped straw, the ice had lasted most of the summer.

Today, Timothy mixed some of that ice with rock salt and packed it around the outside of the ice cream maker. He worked hard turning the crank as the machine churned out generous servings of ice cream made from fresh cream, eggs, sugar, and vanilla beans. Phoebe carried a bowl to each person.

Alistair, too, had been turning the mental crank. As they enjoyed the dessert topped with wild raspberries, he decided to bring up his concerns about reaching out to the community. He knew that some of the parishioners at Saint Patrick's had felt that sharing the gospel was the exclusive work of a minister or an evangelist. Efforts by ordinary folks to do so had been frowned upon. Unsure of how others in the little fellowship felt, he proceeded tactfully.

"Over the last few months, I've concluded we should be inviting others to hear about Jesus. The question is, do we have the scriptural authority to do that even though we aren't ministers?" Alistair looked around as the little group mulled over his question. "How do you all feel?"

George rotated toward the sound of Alistair's voice and straightened his back. "In my reading a couple weeks back I noticed the Sunday meetings in Corinth were mainly for believers. But if you read closely you'll see that visitors were sometimes among them. It seems observers were welcome so long as they didn't disrupt the meeting."[9]

As Priscilla listened, she wondered what it would be like to have strangers sitting in on their meetings. Even though she had been slower than the others to choose this simple way of Jesus, she cherished the closeness among the little church.

"When the believers were scattered during the persecution, they went everywhere preaching the word,"[10] Bill said. "Meanwhile, the apostles stayed behind in Jerusalem. And do you remember Philip and his four daughters who lived in Caesarea? That's an example of saints expounding God's mind and will. Not one of them was ever referred to as an apostle or minister, but the eunuch, among others, received Jesus just the same.[11] So it makes sense to me that we should be able to share the same message."

"What do you mean by saints?" Laura's voice rose from the grassy swell across from George. "I'd always imagined saints were folks long gone who were granted an exalted place in heaven."

"Yes," Bill assented with a reluctant smile, "but truth is, the New Testament term for ordinary believers *is* saint. It doesn't mark off any special rank. In fact, all of us here today are saints—living ones."[12] Catching Laura's rather astonished expression, Bill gave an inclusive gesture with his arms.

George leaned forward and clasped his hands over his knee. He had been weighing Alistair's question and now he spoke. "When the apostle Paul wrote his personal letter to Timothy, as an older itinerant minister to a younger one, Timothy was traveling on a specific mission among a group of home churches. In his epistle, Paul alluded to those elders who labour in the word and doctrine,[13] meaning those saints who were mature in the faith and who spent part of their time preaching and teaching."

Jack had been quiet until now, thumbing through his Bible. "God used a saint named Ananias to instruct and baptize the apostle Paul," he said. "Surely, if Paul, who wrote more of the New Testament than any other person, became part of the church in this way, it's clearly appropriate for saints to teach and baptize. In another place, ordinary men from Cyprus and Cyrene preached the Lord Jesus to some of the Greeks. The hand of the Lord was with the men and a great number believed.[14] So I don't see why we can't do the same."

As Stephen listened to Jack speaking, another Scripture popped into his mind. "Two married saints, Priscilla and Aquila,[15] taught Apollos about the way of God when they met him in Ephesus," Stephen offered. "And even as a boy, Jesus felt He must be about His Father's business.[16] So if He's living in us, I'm sure we'll feel the same way."

While Priscilla sat envisioning people without Jesus, she remembered her last Sunday at Saint Patrick's. Until that service she had been resisting God—albeit unknowingly. She had thought she was doing right, staying the course, when, in fact, she had simply been blind. Sincere but blind. Like the apostle Paul on the road to Damascus, she had needed Jesus to break down her headstrong attachment to the old way. The episode involving Stephen and Emily had opened a chink in her heart, allowing the pure light of revelation to illuminate her darkness.

During those appalling moments when Reverend Smithers was attacking Stephen from the pulpit, she had crouched forward, tingling with shock and numbness. While the censure rained down around her ears, she had, for the first time, reached an incontrovertible conclusion. She'd never find the humble Jesus of Nazareth at Saint Patrick's.

As she had ridden home brokenhearted and disillusioned, she had finally been able to receive a clear revelation that Jesus is the only way, the only truth, and the only life. It wasn't that her mind had not already grasped that understanding, but her heart had not yet received the life of that reality. *Spiritual life,* Priscilla thought, *comes directly from God by a revelation to my own heart. And day by day it is He who continues to reveal the beauty of the Christ life.* These concerns prompted her to speak up.

"What you're all saying is fine," Priscilla cautioned. "But I'm more concerned about how we do it. The gift of eternal life can't be shared by our words alone, only by a revelation from God. Remember when Jesus said to Peter: 'Flesh and blood hath not revealed it unto thee, but my Father which is in heaven.'[17] It's the same today. We have a tendency to try to convince others, using human effort and reason. That would be a disaster. We can't produce life in anybody. Only God can do that."

"Priscilla's right," Emily agreed. "Jesus *gives* the right to become a child of God to anybody who accepts Him and puts their faith in His name. None of us are God's children because of our parents, or because of our own lofty decision, or because somebody else wanted us to be. God, Himself, is the one who made us His children.[18] We need to be careful not to persuade people as some religious folks do. We might influence a lot of people, but we'd be hindering God's real work. Churches often get drawn into this very trap because they need more and more people to contribute. Many of their converts possess only a razor-thin gloss of Christianity while underneath they may still be starving for real spiritual substance."

"Or living lives of hypocrisy," Alice pronounced. "When I went to Saint Patrick's, my weekday words were out of kilter with my fine Sunday professions. Not everybody's starving for spiritual substance. Some are happy with a sweet Christian icing on an otherwise worldly cake."

Phoebe yawned and got up from where she sat cross-legged on the grass, stretching out a hand to Bill and Alice's two little boys. "Would you like to go to the pond with me?" she asked. "We can stop and see a litter of new kittens on the way. Their eyes aren't open yet."

As Emily watched the children running lightheartedly toward the barn, she straightened her own lame knee. "We need to be sure that Jesus is alive in us," she continued. "That way we bring Him close to everyone we meet, allowing Him to work quietly and effectively through us. We need to be sensitive, speaking as He prompts, and, even then, with gentleness and love." Emily smoothed her print skirt around her ankles. "But it's better to err on the side of enthusiasm than to allow our fears to hold us back."

Alice glanced down at the red juice stains on her sturdy hands. "Yesterday I picked some wild raspberries at the edge of the woods," she said. "Later, while I was cooking them in the kitchen, I thought about that phrase: 'Christ *in you*, the hope of glory.'"[19]

"There was a batch of preserves ready to carry down to the fruit cellar just as Bill came into the kitchen. Suddenly a whimsical question popped into my mind, and I pointed to the glass jars of jelly. 'What are these?' I asked. He looked at me as if I'd lost my mind, 'Raspberries, of course!' he said. To him, the bottles were transparent. He only saw the fruit.

"When I visit my neighbours, I want them to see a lot less of Alice and more of *the fruit of Christ, in me.* The fruit of the Spirit is love, joy, peace, patience, kindness, gentleness, self-control…"[20] The face of Mr. Crundle, the storekeeper, flashed through Alice's mind when she uttered the word self-control. "Without it, our words are hollow, powerless."

Malachi, a man of few words, spoke last. "I reckon spiritual life comes by revelation, not by explanation." He propped his bony elbows on his sharp kneecaps. "I'll drop a pebble into the pool of another person's heart as often as I can. If I see any ripples, I'll try to say a little about Jesus. If folks don't cotton to it, I'll just wait until God opens their eyes."

Before the afternoon heat had burnt itself out in the sweet dampness of evening, it was settled that each would be sensitive to opportunities to reach out. As Timothy gathered the chairs and carried them into the summer kitchen, he heard a whippoorwill beginning its far-off whistling and the heavy shade trees rustling as if to welcome the summer darkness. Hoping to get advice on a change of feed for the young heifers, Timothy scanned the yard for George. In the distance he could see an eerie white mist rising, the phosphorescence that transformed the pond and beaver meadow beyond it into a mystical fairy world. George and Laura's figures, arm in arm, stood out clearly against the white mist. Timothy, with an awkward grin and a young man's nonchalance, shrugged and turned toward the stable by himself.

Seven

DROPPING PEBBLES

Autumn 1899

September paraded through Puslinch Township, heralded by a chorus of crickets in the shorn hay fields. The hedgerows and farm lanes took fire as the sugar maples, teased by Jack Frost, burst into vermilion and gold while the sunlight, warm and mellow, shone on human flesh with a touch that became cool by four o'clock in the afternoon. Alice welcomed the sharp frost at night, believing it cured her hay fever—the runny nose and stuffy headaches that had distressed her through the hot summer months when the air simmered with pollen and chaff dust.

On this bright September morning, she stood at the door of the summer kitchen. Behind her, nature's prodigality was heaped up into pyramids of apples, pears, and squash, and the baskets of Damsons she intended to stir into jam. Her two high-spirited little boys, Gilbert and Nathan, only thirteen months apart, had started school three weeks earlier, departing with bursting satchels and shining morning faces under their Tam o' Shanter caps. They had ignored little Madeleine's wails from the doorstep as they chased each other down the lane, cramming their pockets with chestnuts as they went.

With the change in seasons, Alice found herself enjoying a brisk new energy. Still, the friends' discussion remained fresh on her mind. Her insistent prayer became, "Dear God, please show me how to reach out to others." For a while no answer seemed apparent. That is, not until one afternoon when she baked two thimbleberry pies for supper. After eating the first slice that night, Bill had planted both elbows on the table and wiped his mouth. "That's the best pie I've ever tasted. You could make a king's ransom with that recipe, sweetie." He jumped up from his place at the head of the table and came around to kiss her. The next day, her eyes twinkled when she saw the door on her pie safe swinging on its hinges. Tiptoeing to the pantry, she caught Bill inside wolfing down the last slice. Laughing, they hugged and kissed before he headed back to the barn.

As Bill cut up a piece of roast beef for Nathan at supper that evening, he turned to Alice. "Any more thimbleberry pie hidden around?" he teased.

"There'll soon be more pie than you can shake a stick at," Alice declared. "I had a brainstorm this afternoon."

Grinning, he cocked his head. "Just one?"

Alice grimaced good-naturedly. "I'm going to bake pies, lots of them. And sell them at the Guelph Market along with fresh eggs. It'll give me an opportunity to meet people and maybe a chance to *drop a pebble.*"

So each Friday after school, the children helped crank the apple peeler for a dozen pies that Bill loaded into the buggy early Saturday mornings.

On the second Saturday, a short, pear-shaped lady, a tumble of gray hair escaping her bonnet, stopped at Alice's table. "Miserable weather for dryin' clothes," she complained, pitching her large black umbrella against the bedraggled rain.

Alice surveyed the lines that furrowed the woman's pale complexion like a winter field. "Yes, it is rainy," she agreed cheerily. "But the weather's in pretty good hands."

The woman stared in surprise. "Aye. Aye, Ah'm sure yer right," she faltered. "'Tis easy to overlook, isn't it?" As she selected an apple pie and counted out the coins, her face took on a forlorn expression. "Ah 'ardly ever bake since me 'usband passed away last June." She looked up, hesitant.

"Oh, I'm so sorry," Alice comforted. "I just can't imagine."

The warmth and attentiveness in Alice's face gave the widow confidence to continue. "Edmund was so sick before 'e died. And ah was too busy carin' for 'im to bake. Now there's nobody to eat it wi' me. Bread wi' sorrow, a woman allus comes to that." The woman seemed to wear her loneliness like a heavy shawl, her shoulders bent wearily under the weight.

Alice laid a reassuring hand on her customer's arm. "It must be like pulling teeth just to light the lamp and get going on these darker mornings."

The older woman, startled by Alice's perceptiveness, raised blurry eyes. "It certainly is. Ah missed 'im this mornin' when ah did t' weekly spot o' washin'. Edmund allus used to do t' manglin' for me. 'E was a far better 'elp in t' 'ouse than most men, ah'll give 'im that." She paused, raising her hand to conceal her trembling lips. "But t' worst is t' long, lonely evenin's. We used to talk about our day. Even when 'e was sick, we could still talk for 'ours about little things. We had so many…" Alice touched her hand, encouraging her to go on. "We 'ad so many good times together." The widow's voice was tired, ragged, like wind through a broken window.

A lump formed in Alice's throat as she imagined the grief of losing Bill. "My name's Alice Jones," she said gently. "I'm in the market 'til November. And thankful to have this stall, out of the wind and dust a bit."

" 'Tis so nice to meet you, Mrs. Jones," the woman replied. "Ah'm Mrs. Edmund Green."

On hearing the name, Alice's memory made a hasty connection. Edmund Green. This must be the widow of that odd little north-of-England green-grocer. He used to have a stall here years ago. She pondered Mrs. Green's mournful eyes. Was it the nostalgic memories of her times at the market with Edmund that had brought Mrs. Green along today?

"Perhaps you'd stop by next Saturday and have a cup of tea with me, Mrs. Green," Alice offered.

The widow flushed and started dabbing at her eyes with a hanky. It felt so good to talk openly about her loss that she overcame her reticence. "Aye, ah'd like that," she admitted. "Please dearie, just call me Susan."

For Alice, it was a beginning, a chance to express Christ's own love and concern for this dispirited woman in widow's weeds.

Over the next few weeks the two women became better acquainted, and one Monday, Susan Green hitched a ride with the tea peddler to spend the day with Alice's family. She met Bill's mother, Tillie, and discovered they were wound from the same ball of yarn. Susan returned to visit often and over several weeks, the two widows grew to be old cronies. They spent hours in Tillie's sitting room, sipping afternoon tea while piecing her prized Fox-and-Geese quilt. At times they were interrupted by little blonde-haired Madeleine, unsteady on her feet and dragging a corncob doll.

One day some weeks later, Susan stood looking out the farmhouse window at the golden glory of an October afternoon. "Ah likes comin' to yer 'ome, Alice," she remarked softly. "There's peace and quiet 'ere and some-thin' wonderful different about yer family. Wot is it?"

Alice had held back from telling Susan about her faith, waiting for the older lady to ask in her own time. Now, Alice felt the time was right to talk to Susan about this special presence in the Jones' home. For over an hour, they talked about Jesus and His friendship.[1]

In their separate ways, each of the saints who met at Wood Creek Farm watched for opportunities to tell others about the friend they had found in Jesus. They tried to be sensitive to what they felt was the guidance of the Holy Spirit. They *dropped pebbles*, waiting for signs of interest before they spoke of their faith. Some conversations started hesitatingly, some laughingly, and some, like the one with Susan Green, in tears.

One Thursday evening Jack brought Dugan and Hilda MacGladry, acquaintances from the picturesque village of Eden Mills, to Wood Creek Farm. Dugan's red hair and crinkly beard reflected his Scottish heritage. Lighthearted and easygoing, Hilda had the same high colour in her cheeks but was slim and lithe in contrast to her stocky husband.

Jack had first called at MacGladrys' door during his work as a colporteur. The weather had been cold, and Dugan had invited him in for a cup of tea. Once inside Jack had been intrigued by the collection of history books lined up on a shelf. Their calfskin spines had gleamed in the winter sunshine slanting into Hilda's parlour. The conversation soon shifted as both men discovered that the other was also an avid reader of history. Their friendship had deepened with every armload of books Jack carried in or out of the MacGladrys' kitchen—*The Antiquities of the Jews* by Flavius Josephus, *The Decline and Fall of the Roman Empire* by Edward Gibbon, and an anonymous account of the English Peasants' Revolt of 1381.

During the MacGladrys' first meeting, Priscilla shared her desire to make more room for Jesus. "I've been reading about the birth of Jesus in Bethlehem," she began. "His mother had to lay Him in a manger because there was no room for them in the inn.[2] No doubt the innkeepers were doing a brisk business and their rooms were full of good people. A lot of us are like that, full of the good things, the wholesome things of life. But we're too full for Jesus to have any place in our hearts."

Dugan listened attentively, his eyes as still and blue as a Scottish loch on a sunny day. He detected the intensity in Priscilla's voice.

"I've been getting acquainted with a woman in the Old Testament who lived near the village of Shunem. This prominent woman was well-off and married to an older man. But she wasn't able to have children.

"In spite of that she showed great concern for others. Of the many who passed her house, she noticed that one man, Elisha, was exceptional. 'This is a holy man of God who passes by us,' she told her husband. 'Please, let's build a small upper room so he could turn in and stay with us.' She furnished it with a bed, a table, a stool, and a candlestick, that the man could work and rest.[3] When the guest room was complete, she invited him in.

"Can you imagine how much this woman must have appreciated Elisha's godly presence in her home?" Priscilla asked. "In a similar way, I'm beginning to learn the value of making room for Jesus. Knowing that He's working and resting in my heart brings a special peace."

Dugan stroked his left ear absentmindedly, nodding slightly.

"It's amazing," Priscilla concluded, "that this Shunammite couple who, for years, had been childless were now given the miracle of a son—the result of making room for the man of God. A *new* life that was previously impossible. Jesus is passing by each of us daily. Do we make room for Him? Or are we so full that He must pass us by?" Priscilla glanced around the circle, distracted momentarily by the knowing smile that Dugan exchanged with Hilda.

Priscilla swivelled on the circular piano stool where she had been sitting and, when the friends had gathered in a half circle, began to play:

> Have you any room for Jesus?
> He who bore your load of sin.
> As He knocks and asks admission,
> Sinner, will you let Him in?
>
> Room for pleasure, room for business,
> But for Christ the crucified,
> Not a place that He can enter
> In your heart for which He died.
>
> Room for Jesus, King of glory;
> Hasten now, His word obey.
> Swing your heart's door widely open;
> Bid Him enter while you may.[4]

"That was a grand meeting," Dugan said to Jack as he helped his wife into the buggy. "They seem like a pretty close-knit bunch of folks."

Jack planted his right foot on the oval buggy step and swung up beside Hilda. "Something like the three of us," he chuckled as Dugan squeezed in on the other side of the narrow seat. "I'm glad to have them as my friends," he added solemnly. "My whole life has changed since I met them."

Dugan tightened the lines and clicked his tongue to the horse. "There's often a surface friendliness among people," he observed. "But it's clear that your friends have something much deeper."

"Maybe it's not that surprising," Hilda chimed in. "Didn't Jesus say people would recognize His disciples by the love they had for each other?"[5]

Dugan rode along in silence for a mile, occasionally running his fingers through his red beard. "If it's all right, we'd like to come again."

One chilly Monday in late October, Phoebe lingered at S.S. #3 after the other students had left for home. Dampening a cloth at the pump in the yard, she cleaned the wood-framed slate in each desk so they would be ready for the next morning's arithmetic lesson. When she had wiped off the blackboard, she offered to bring in the kindling. As the wood rolled off her arm, she shyly invited her teacher, Miss Duffield, to come for supper on Thursday and to stay afterward for the meeting. Another time, she brought her girlfriend from the next farm. Bill's mother, Tillie, also started attending with Bill and Alice and the children.

Little by little the saints were extending God's love. Still, many who were invited excused themselves from coming to hear the message of Christ. When Timothy was in Guelph running errands for Alistair, he invited a former high school chum who had opened a tinsmith shop.

"I've got so much work," his friend protested, "I'm busy making up copper gutters and rainwater leaders for a big job on Queen Street."

"That's fine," Timothy replied cheerfully. "Just wanted you to know."

"I'm going to make a lot of money before I'm thirty," his friend boasted. "That's the way to be secure and happy. You'll see."

As Timothy rode home from his friend's shop, he recalled a parable about the kingdom of heaven being like a king who prepared a wedding banquet for his son. When the king sent his servants to call those who were invited to the banquet, the guests refused to come. They paid no attention to the invitation and went their ways, one to his farm, another to his business. After that, the king said to his messengers, "The wedding feast is ready. I invited people who weren't deserving to come. So go to the street corners and invite everyone you see." So the servants gathered all the guests they could find, good and bad alike, until the banquet hall was full. Jesus had concluded that many are invited, but only a few are chosen.[6]

Timothy felt a youthful sadness for those who thought the best of life was to be found in the material world and used every ounce of their energy to mine this illusionary vein. Apparently his school chum was one of these.

Timothy remembered his father saying, "When people fail to understand that Jesus is the only source of abundant life,[7] they search for satisfaction in places and in ways it cannot be found. We're all created with an inner dryness, an emptiness, a unique inner void that can only be filled by God. Most don't realize what they're yearning for, and try to quench their thirst with the visible waters of *having and getting.* But a life dedicated to achieving happiness without God is a contradiction."

Timothy's tall dapple-gray mare trotted rhythmically through the brilliant autumn countryside, down the hill, and across the rough plank bridge. Passing over the creek, he saw four mallards floating with apparent tranquility on the pond below, but Timothy knew their webbed feet were churning beneath the smooth surface.

Easing back on the mare's bit, Timothy gazed down at the water. *Maybe people are a lot like ducks. Just when everything looks wonderful—as if they're gliding effortlessly through life—a desperate commotion may be going on beneath the serene exterior as they struggle for a toehold on peace and happiness.* Timothy shifted in the saddle, well aware that religious activity could be as frantic and disquieting as anything else.

As the saddle horse trotted homeward, sharp bursts of warm breath from its flared nostrils condensed on the frosty October air. Birds twittered and chirped in the hedgerows and a crow cawed in the distance. Riding along at peace with God, Timothy began to sing. His fine tenor voice rose and fell with an added measure of maturity:

> I tried the broken cisterns, Lord,
> But ah, the waters failed,
> E'en as I stooped to drink they fled,
> And mocked me as I wailed.
>
> *Now none but Christ can satisfy;*
> *None other name for me;*
> *There's love and life and lasting joy,*
> *Lord Jesus, found in Thee.*[8]

As the mare turned into the lane, Timothy remembered the shepherd's pie and bread pudding his mother had been preparing. His mouth watered. Closing his eyes, he imagined the headlines. "Puslinch Man Starves in His Own Lane." Timothy grinned. He could polish off the whole pie himself. Stomach rumbling, he clicked his tongue and galloped his horse to the barn.

~∽

One afternoon when Bill Jones was at the general store picking up shaving soap and a pair of bush rubbers, he met Jim Braithewaite, well-known for the imported Percheron stallion he "traveled." Jim led the powerful stallion behind his buggy to the various farms for stud service.

As Jim sat in the buggy, waiting for his youngest daughter to come outside, Bill hitched a foot up on one of the wheel spokes.

"A father's always waiting for one of his girls," Jim said, grinning, the late sun picking out gray hairs below the brim of his rumpled felt hat. "But I can't complain. They've never given the missus or me an ounce of trouble."

"You can be proud of them," Bill replied. "You've put a lot of hard work into raising your family." He smiled as he looked up into the fatherly eyes. "Someday when you're an old man they'll take as good a care of you."

Jim beamed as his daughter hopped into the buggy and opened her satchel. "Father, isn't this simply beautiful?" she exclaimed, drawing out a length of soft navy velveteen.

Jim ran the back of his hand over the fabric. "My girls never pick out the thriftiest material in the store," he chuckled. His daughter kissed his cheek as he turned to Bill. "Your mare showing any signs yet?"

"Looks as if she's safely in foal now," Bill said. "I want to straighten up with you on the stud fee. When can you call in?"

"How about right after supper?" Jim proposed. "My two boys can look after the chores tonight."

"Yes, sir," Bill answered. "I'll have the money ready."

Bill had always found Jim Braithewaite, a wealthy farmer, to be forthright and pleasant in his business dealings. He also knew that Jim didn't belong to any church. As the bank notes changed hands that evening, Bill looked into the older man's face. "It hasn't anything to do with livestock," he began, "but I was wondering whether you might like to come along and enjoy an evening at the Stanhopes'. You've no doubt heard about the meetings…"

"I've no time for that kind of thing right now," Jim said flatly. "I go to my other farm near Corwhin every evening. The land's producing some heavy crops, and I'm busy adding a piece to the small barn that's there. I need to build a bigger granary before the threshing gang comes."

Bill knew that it was only an excuse, but he let the subject drop.

A few weeks later when Malachi hustled across the fields with the jarring news that Jim Braithewaite had died suddenly, Bill recoiled in shock. Apparently, Jim had been trying to jack up one of the floor timbers in the old barn. Gossip had it that he had ruptured some of his insides while straining to lift a heavy beam all by himself. He had collapsed and stopped breathing shortly after coming home from Corwhin that evening.[9]

When Bill and Alice went to pay their last respects at the Braithewaite home, they found the family huddled around the casket, lost for words. The sons of fourteen and seventeen, both of them the image of their father, were sombre and withdrawn in their stiff collars and black suits. Bill and Alice shook hands and offered their condolences.

"I know you have two nearly grown boys, Mrs. Braithewaite," Bill said quietly, "but if there's anything either Alice or I can do with winter coming on and all, please let us know."

Standing between her two oldest girls, Jim's widow nodded, her tearful eyes filled with appreciation. "Thanks, Bill. I may just need to do that. It's not as if the lads have had a lifetime of experience...though both of them were close to their pa."

The neighbours fumbled with their hands, hardly knowing what to say in the face of this calamity. The men spoke in low voices as they stood in the spacious front hall, their arms crossed, their faces grave.

After a few minutes, Alice hurried to the buggy and brought in two apple pies and a pot of stew to leave on the kitchen table. Then she located Bill and the couple started for home, sorrowing for this family's loss, praying for their comfort, thanking God for His presence.

"It must be absolutely terrible to have to face that..." Alice's words trailed off as the raw wind tore the hesitant leaves from their branches. She huddled closer against Bill, gripping his arm as they rode along.

～

One bleak day Alistair stood at the grist mill waiting to have some grain ground into pig feed. As he leaned his tall thin frame against a grain bin,

Alistair noticed Andrew Gillespie, the miller's helper, approaching slowly, a question forming on his lips.

"God loves everybody, doesn't He?" the young fellow blurted out.

Alistair was surprised at the bluntness. "Yes, His love *is* constant and unconditional," he replied. "God makes the sun rise on both good and bad, and He sends rain for the ones who do right and for those who don't."[10]

The young man, covered from head to toe with white flour dust, cocked his head. "Well then," he said, "if God loves everybody as much as you say, He wouldn't allow them to go to hell, would He?"

Alistair hesitated. He didn't want to be drawn into a pointless argument. *Unless someone really wants to hear the truth,* he thought, *it's better to be quiet.*

Alistair scrutinized Andrew's face. He had always liked the boy. In fact, Andrew's parents had rented the place across the road from S.S. #3 when he and Priscilla were newly married. The country doctor could not be reached quickly, and Andrew's father had run to ask for Priscilla's help on the cold January night of Andrew's birth. After they hurried over on snowshoes, Alistair had paced back and forth in the kitchen while Priscilla, upstairs in the north bedroom, waited to deliver this squalling first child into the wintry world.

Now, as he studied Andrew's face, he sensed a seriousness behind the boy's apparently controversial questions. "Well, Andrew, can I tell you about something that happened to me?"

At first the boy didn't answer. But then he crossed his arms, leaned back against a grain bin, and gave a relenting nod.

Alistair took this as a sign to go ahead. "I was only ten when a tragedy befell us, but I remember like it was yesterday. My pa was driving the team up and down the windrows, loading the seasoned hay. I'd been pestering him all day to give me a turn, and finally he gave in. I had only been holding the lines for a few minutes when I drove the Percherons over a hidden wasps' nest by mistake. An infuriated cloud of wasps erupted and began to sting the horses' bellies. The team went wild and started to run. No matter how hard I pulled and sawed on the lines, they galloped faster and faster dragging the hay loader behind the bouncing wagon."

Alistair's voice betrayed a hint of melancholy as he continued. "My three-year-old brother, Cory, was pitched off the wagon. Pa grabbed for his little arm, but it was too late. He tumbled over the edge and was crushed by the steel wheel of the careening loader. My father flung himself off and ran to where his body lay in the stubble.

"When the team finally tangled themselves up in the far fence corner, I ran behind Pa toward the house, crying hysterically. I heard him groan as he carried Cory's limp form into the kitchen and laid him tenderly on the couch. Pa met me inside the door. 'It's not your fault, Alistair,' he said through his tears. 'It could have happened to me just as easy.'"

The young miller's dust-laden form, like a mute statue, stared straight ahead as Alistair closed his eyes, reliving the pain.

"The next morning Pa asked me to help him haul down some rough oak that was stored overhead on the collar ties of the driving shed. He'd a good set of hands on him, and without a word he gathered up his tools and laid them out on the bench. I wasn't sure what it was he intended until he flipped open his wooden rule and measured off a short board—about the height of Cory. Pa's face was stiff as shoe leather as he sawed and planed. After a bit he paused and handed me a chunk of gritty paper. He nodded toward the boards. Even at the best of times, Pa was never a big talker, but he didn't utter a word as he twisted the brass screws into the corners of that dismal box. I scrubbed the sandpaper back and forth until the oak came up smooth as marble and my fingers raw, but I didn't care. I was crying anyway. Pa didn't shed a tear until he made the lid and set it on top. But then he couldn't hold back any longer. It was awful..."

Blinking, Alistair gazed into the distance. "After a while I calmed down a bit, but the memory of it still gives me a sick feeling in the pit of my stomach. It was a terrible time for the whole family, and I felt so guilty, even though I hadn't done anything wrong. It took years of reassurance before I finally accepted my father's words."

Alistair's blue eyes softened, his face crinkled, and a certain tenderness crept into his voice. "I can still picture the two black horses in front of the hearse and my father carrying my little brother's casket to the open grave. His grief was almost more than he could bear. There, at the side of the grave, Pa laid him down. He paused for a minute, loath to leave Cory for the last time. Then he turned and walked slowly back to stand with us, tears streaming down his face.

"Did he love him? Absolutely! Why did my father leave him there in the cemetery if he loved him so much? Because he couldn't communicate with him. Cory wasn't alive. So too, unless a person's alive and responsive to our heavenly Father, He, too, must eventually leave us. We're either warm, alive, and responsive to God, or cold, dead, and unresponsive. Just as with human life, there's no middle state. Each one of us must ask: Am I spiritually alive? Most folks ignore the question. Some deceive themselves by believing they have spiritual life when they don't. But when our journey's over, we'll all want to be part of God's eternal family."

Andrew Gillespie stood silent, his confusion dispersed like the clouds of flour that had settled around him. It all seemed so clear. *If I died tonight,* he agonized, *would I be part of God's eternal family?*

A couple of weeks later, while Alistair was having more grain ground, Andrew came out and dusted off his hand to shake Alistair's. Again he asked several questions, but this time he was more eager to hear the older man's answers. Each time Alistair went to the mill, he and the young miller got into a lively exchange. Eventually, the softness in Andrew's attitude prompted Alistair to invite him to meet the saints at Wood Creek Farm.

"I don't have much in the way of fancy duds," Andrew replied, his tone apologetic.

Alistair smiled. "Just dust off your overalls and come right along."

Two of George's heifers had freshened that June, and now, on the final Thursday of October, their frisky calves found themselves loaded onto a wagon, tethered in place, and carted off to the adjoining township of Nassagaweya. At the farm gate George stood and watched them out of sight as their intermittent bawling grew fainter in the distance. In his pocket lay rolled the sixty dollars from the sale, and on Friday morning at ten he stood at the wicket of the Canadian Bank of Commerce. His farm mortgage shrank before his eyes as Mr. Butterwick, the assistant manager counted out the small pile of cash, his long thin fingers snapping each bill.

Morgan Butterwick was tall and storklike with a port wine stain on his right temple which he fingered unconsciously. He wore his striped trousers high on his narrow waist and altogether gave the impression of fastidiousness both in his person and in his work.

"I like your accent, sir," George remarked. "English, is it?"

"Yes, indeed," Morgan laughed as he handed George a receipt. "It sailed with me all the way from Liverpool two years ago."

"Liverpool," George echoed. "That's a dock city, isn't it?"

"A huge port. The White Star liners sail down the Mersey and into the Irish Sea."

"Do you have family there?" George inquired with genuine interest.

"They're all in Liverpool, and I miss them greatly," Mr. Butterwick said wistfully. "I suppose you're able to spend a lot of time with your family." He glanced up at George. It was more a question than a statement.

"Well, you know, we *are* a close family. I enjoy a good meal with my folks a couple times a week, and my younger brother's still there on the home place. No doubt you've seen the Guelph lamplighter on his rounds. My sister's married to him. And my older brother works just up the street."

When a pensive expression clouded the young banker's face, George felt a strong unexplainable urge to drop a pebble. "But I've got spiritual brothers and sisters who are dear to me too."

Morgan looked up with swift interest. "Would you have time to step into my office?" he offered.

George smiled. "I'm in no big hurry this forenoon," he replied as the banker led him into his sparsely furnished office and closed the door.

When they were seated, Morgan continued. "The walls have ears in a place like this. Now, just what did you mean when you said spiritual brothers and sisters?"[11]

As George spoke about the little church at Wood Creek Farm and the transformation in his life, the banker's eyebrows drew together in concentration. George's frank and friendly conversation disarmed him.

"Spiritual matters have been close to my heart for a long time," Morgan admitted. "Ever since my aunt took me along with her to a little country chapel in Wales. She had a house near the seaside, and I helped her in the summers until I was eighteen." Tipping forward in his oak chair, he took a deep breath. "I've been searching for spiritual substance for years. I guess that's why it's so interesting to meet you."

"So which church do you go to now?" George asked politely.

Morgan Butterwick winced. "I don't belong to any church."

George's forehead wrinkled in surprise. "Oh, I see," he said.

Morgan hastened to explain. "I've attended many groups, but after a few weeks I come away empty. At the end of the day, each one seems to have a different emphasis, a different way of adding things up." He tapped his pencil on the spine of the open ledger book, missing the unconscious irony of his remark. "To some high churches, it's the ritual of participating in the sacraments, while to other groups, it's the practice of wailing at the mourner's bench. To some, the ultimate is the conversion experience, for others it's *living right.*" Morgan glanced down at his desk and sighed. "And to yet others, it's more praying or reading of the Bible that's needed. Each one presents an element of truth, but something seems to be lacking." He stared into George's face. "It's most confusing. Maybe I'm the hitch."

George eyed his new friend with compassion, remembering his own search for truth. "No, it's not you, Morgan. Several of us have felt the same desperation." George placed both hands on the edge of the wide oak desk. "Why not come along on Thursday evening?" he suggested as he stood up to leave. "You can see for yourself what it's like at Wood Creek Farm."

Sharp at six o'clock on Thursday evening, Morgan turned the shiny handles on the door of the bank's vault and smiled with satisfaction as the heavy cylinders thunked into place. Then he brushed a speck of lint from his top hat, smoothed his broad lapels, and hurried down Wyndham Street toward the livery stable. A groom would have his high-spirited driver brushed and harnessed. He didn't want to keep George's hosts waiting on this first appointment.

The early darkness of autumn shadowed the lane at Wood Creek Farm as Morgan's rig pulled up beside the farmhouse. Alistair's eager face showed surprise and pleasure as he hurried out to shake Morgan's hand.

Sitting through his first meeting, Morgan observed the devoted and reverent way these friends spoke of God. Afterward he witnessed the unpretentious way in which they spoke to each other, in the comfortable manner of a family. Each person knew they belonged and conveyed this in smiles, in laughter, in tears, in a gentle touch, or in a knowing nod.

They talked about their faith as easily as they discussed their cattle. As Morgan walked to the kitchen, he overheard Timothy talking to Bill about a pregnant mare. In a snatch of another conversation, George was saying to Emily, "Being willing to have our bodies as tents for God to live in gives us the three keys to the kingdom of heaven."[12] One at a time, he extended three fingers. "Christ revealed to me, born in me, and living through me."[13]

In the kitchen, Stephen was helping Priscilla cut egg salad sandwiches into triangles while they spoke about believing in a person—Jesus—not in a doctrine. And through the woodshed door, Morgan noticed Alistair listening in confidence to an older lady whose silver-rimmed spectacles glinted with tears. In gentle tones he comforted her as she cried.

Morgan steepled his fingertips, pressing them against his upper lip. *Different blokes, these,* he concluded. *They certainly seem committed to each other.*

As he sat beside Alice, eating a sandwich with his tea, he ventured to ask, "What, precisely, would you say is the difference between this little church of yours and the multitude of others?"

"I can't speak for others," Alice answered. "But we feel a bond among us that springs from a love for Christ. Our union with Him is intended to be lasting—like an ideal marriage. If you try to live with one foot in and one foot out of a marriage, it's more likely to fail."

Morgan's eyebrows shot up. "Well, I've never been in that jolly predicament myself," he blurted out, "but I'll take your word for it."

As Morgan nursed his tea, he excused himself to wander into the parlour, trying to sense the atmosphere, the tone of the gathering. After a few minutes, he circled back to a chair beside George. "Your friends possess a distinct gentleness," he observed. "Do you figure a body has to be contemplative to be a Christian?"

George turned slightly, his elbow on the arm of the horsehair settee. "Oh, no," he insisted, "but we do believe there's a blessing to the extent we practise a *listening* attitude."

Morgan's brows flexed. "Do you suppose, that's what it means to hear the voice of Jesus?"

George swished his tea leaves reflectively in the bottom of his cup. "I can hardly put it into words, Morgan. Somehow maintaining an expectant desire for God's presence fosters spiritual growth. Earnest desire is one form of unceasing prayer."

As Morgan relaxed, draping one gangly leg across the opposite pinstriped knee, he absorbed the happy chatter of the room and took note of the animated faces. He realized that this was, perhaps, the first time he had witnessed such unity among brethren.[14] Slowly, like gathering beads of dew, his impressions distilled into a single conclusion: *Their persistent sense of God's love and nearness inspires this joyful peace among them.*[15] However, the profundity of the unseen changes in these friends—being entirely the work of the Spirit—remained a mystery to the young banker.

Over the weeks that followed, Morgan often received bids for supper from George, Alistair and Priscilla, or some of the other friends. He discovered that throughout each day, they sought out quiet moments of solitude with their Lord. Morgan saw clearly that His living presence had become central to their lives, and that they lived and practised the things of which they spoke. In them he witnessed a childlike dependence on God and a gentle love and caring that flowed out to others in a humble way.

One afternoon he left the bank early to visit George. When he arrived at the farm, he found Timothy and George in the stable root cellar chopping turnips for the cattle. Their upturned faces greeted Morgan in cheerful surprise. After a few minutes the banker tugged his white sleeves up behind his springy metal armbands and began passing turnips to the men.

"Fine vegetable, the turnip," Timothy joked as he cranked the wheel of the cast iron pulper. "But not much glory in it."

"Not like a tomato," Morgan said, laughing as he handed over another one.

"Good for cattle though."

"I wouldn't know about cattle, but turnips give me indigestion. I prefer tomatoes myself."

George's blue eyes twinkled as he listened to the banter.

As the pile of cattle feed grew at their feet, the conversation among the men deepened. When Morgan asked about the unassuming attitude of the friends at Wood Creek Farm, he felt the passion in George's answer.

"I can't put into words how utterly humbled I was, brought to my knees, when, for the first time, I comprehended God's overwhelming majesty and realized that whole nations were just a drop in the bucket before Him.[16] My pride was crushed. It was no longer a question of how much Scripture I knew or even how good I thought I was; it all hinged upon Jesus. I begged Him to come and live in me, knowing that it's not what I do for Him, but what He does for me that matters."

"But doesn't religion help us?" Morgan persevered.

"Religion," George said ruefully, "was my attempt to reach God by my own efforts. But it only drew attention to me and didn't bring me one iota closer to God. It's not a matter of me living for God because, sooner or later, I will fail—every time. The good news of the gospel is that Christ lives *in us,* He lives *for us,* He lives *through us. He* has become wisdom and righteousness *for us*—not any holiness that we achieve ourselves."[17]

Noting the confusion in Morgan's earnest face, Timothy paused, balancing a turnip on the edge of the pulper. "Do you reckon anyone can produce more of God?" He watched surprise spread across his friend's sharp features. No doubt, to Morgan, the insinuation bordered on absurdity.

"Absolutely not."

"The Scripture says God Himself *is* love," Timothy persisted. "But we've been taught that we can create love in our hearts by adhering to certain religious teachings."

"I don't get your drift."

"Because God *is* love, it's only to the extent that *He* lives in us that self-less love can truly be expressed."

Morgan's tone conveyed his mystification. "I need to consider that one for a bit." Turning, he glanced out the stable door. "The days are drawing in," he noted as he adjusted his top hat and smoothed his silk scarf under his long black greatcoat. "I'd better be on my way before it gets dark."

A half hour later, his horse and buggy had just passed the Ontario Veterinary College and was making its way down the hill into the city when suddenly he recalled a passage he had read earlier. "I can see it," he exclaimed aloud. "It's *Christ's* presence *in me* that is my hope of glory."[18]

It was a gray, windy day in late November. Clouds scudded across the leaden sky, and the impudent beauty of the summer marigolds, succumbing to the hard night frost, had withered and faded. On a fence post beside the lane, a raucous crow warned all within earshot of lean days to come. The last brittle leaves on the towering maples were being wrenched from the branches to blanket the ground against the coming freeze. An unaccountable reflectiveness had engulfed Priscilla, so much so that between the batches of bread dough she shone the already sparkling lamp chimneys. Strings of drying apples, cut and quartered, hung over the heat of the cookstove while russet jars of apple butter gleamed from the sideboard, still warm from her morning's work.

As Priscilla paused in the parlour to glance out the window, her eye caught sight of two leaves dancing toward the ground. In her mind they took on personality as she followed their lively yet inevitable swan dance toward the ground. *All leaves,* she thought, *like all lives—from a natural point of view—eventually come to the same level. The ones from the highest branch with the ones from the lowest.* Absentmindedly Priscilla scraped a shred of dough stuck to her fingernail, rolled it into a tiny ball, and dropped it into her apron pocket. *In death, they all return to dust.*[19]

On her way back to the bread she was mixing, Priscilla stopped at the piano. With her thoughts on the falling leaves, the end of the season, and the brevity of life, she thumbed through her worn hymn book. Sometimes she missed singing in the choir, but never for one minute did she consider going back. Pressing the pages flat, she began to play and sing, her voice filling the parlour as it had once done at Saint Patrick's.

> Life at best is very brief,
> Like the falling of a leaf,
> Like the binding of a sheaf:
> Be in time.
>
> Fairest flowers soon decay,
> Youth and beauty pass away,
> Oh, you have not long to stay,
> Be in time.[20]

With the chorus still echoing in her mind, Priscilla went back to forming the spongy white dough into loaves and placing them in buttered pans. As she watched the bread rise, a smile broke across her pretty features. *But even in the brevity of life, what blessing, what joy, what serenity and gladness God often bestows.*

As she kneaded another batch, she glanced out the window periodically, watching for Phoebe to come home, bursting with chatter and anecdotes about her schoolmates. The fourteen-year-old filled the kitchen with gaiety and made Priscilla laugh while they prepared supper together. On one of these forays to the front window, she noticed a tall, lanky figure at the end of the laneway. The person hesitated and appeared to be studying the wooden gate posts. Then, turning, he began to walk slowly up the lane between the two rows of almost bare, windblown trees.

Priscilla squinted through the rippled glass, straining to pick out the details, wondering who on earth it could be as the silhouette drew closer. A man. Tall and angular with a dark beard. He reminded her of Abraham Lincoln. Stiff gusts tore at the man's long coat as he leaned into the wind, approaching step by step. When he turned up the path, she could see his lean face, corrugated by years of wind and sun. His drab overcoat, too short in the sleeves, had been mended with multi-coloured yarn.

Priscilla opened the door before he had a chance to knock, and he quickly doffed his cap. He twisted it in his hands, and his nervous gray eyes studied her as he spoke. "I was wonderin' if ye could give me some work in exchange for somethin' t' eat," the stranger asked quietly.

Although something in the man's eyes told her he was harmless, she hesitated, retying her apron strings. But a quick decision had to be made.

"Please step in out of the wind," Priscilla offered hospitably. "I'm Mrs. Stanhope. My husband will be in from the barn in a few minutes." The man stamped the dirt off his boots and followed Priscilla through the woodshed and into the kitchen.

"What name do you go by?" she asked cheerfully.

"Angus," the man mumbled. "Angus Kincaid."

The man was what her parents had called a tramp. Such homeless people drifted from place to place without family or permanent roots. When traveling longer distances, they "rode the rods"—climbing aboard a train as it gathered speed at the edge of town. *What*, Priscilla wondered, *caused Mr. Kincaid to turn in at the gate of Wood Creek Farm?*

"We'll be having supper shortly, and you're welcome to join us," she said, pointing to a chair at the end of the cookstove. Then, suddenly a thought sprang to mind. She had heard that tramps could tell by looking at marks on the gate post whether they would be received. Previous wanderers left a secret code that only they could decipher.

As Priscilla peeled a few extra potatoes for the pot, she kept an eye on the man who sat patiently, hunched forward, waiting. His eyes darted around the kitchen, out the windows, and across the barren ploughed fields with a faraway look. She noticed his rough, calloused hands and wondered what thoughts this forlorn traveler might entertain in the inner sanctum of his mind. And whether he had a family or a friend who loved him.

The acrid smell of sweat saturated wool assaulted her nostrils as she passed Angus on her way to the pantry for flour. Her delicate nose flexed. *The man's odor is ranker than a barrel of Limburger cheese on a muggy day,* Priscilla stewed as she breaded the pork chops and added a chunk of lard to the frying pan. But now that he is in the house, what can I do?

When she caught sight of Timothy heading toward the woodshed, a notion struck her. With an expression that boded ill toward all unwashed men, she dipped a pail of hot water from the copper boiler on the stove and lugged it to the woodshed. She intercepted Timothy at the back door. "There's a tramp in the kitchen, here for supper." Priscilla pinched her slender nose. "But he's so strong I can't stomach having him at the table. You'll have to give him the ultimatum…"

Timothy recoiled in horror. "Me?"

"Yes, you. Your father's not here," Priscilla whispered hoarsely. She stabbed a finger in the direction of the wooden washtub normally reserved for Saturday evening sponge baths. "Drag it over behind that screen."

In resignation Timothy trudged into the kitchen. "Sir," Priscilla over-heard him saying, "my mother's drawing you a bath. Before supper."

Angus shot bolt upright in his chair, hearing with alarm the scraping of heavy objects across the woodshed floor. He raised a hand to object, but seeing Timothy's arched eyebrows and resolute expression, his face collapsed. He drew in a savoury breath of the frying pork chops and followed Timothy meekly to the woodshed.

George and Morgan Butterwick had been helping Alistair replace some loose barn boards before winter, and by supper time they, along with Alistair, thumped into the woodshed. They were met by the unusual scent of lye soap and the even more unusual sight of steam rising from the washing tub, now screened in a corner.

"Surely Priscilla hasn't taken a notion…" Alistair muttered as he strode toward the corner and turned aside the makeshift screen. The dilated eyes of a startled man looked up at Alistair. Only his head, shoulders and knees bobbed above the steam. Alistair turned hastily away, having taken in the situation at a glance. "C'mon into supper, fellas," he said.

At supper, Angus, seated beside Timothy, felt fortunate to be invited into such a home. Being a leaf on one of the lowest branches in society, he was used to having a dry crust of bread shoved into his hand. Sometimes he was hurried off with nothing more than the sound of a slamming door. Occasionally some rude farmer would swear at him and, more than once, someone had set a vicious dog on him, biting at his legs as he ran.

"Help yourself to more potatoes and gravy," Alistair urged from the head of the table. "And slide another pork chop onto your plate." Hot tea and mincemeat pie rounded out the best meal Angus had eaten in weeks.

Normally shy and introverted, he sat listening as the men talked. He felt warm and full, and after Priscilla's insistence on soap and water, unusu-ally clean. Above his dark beard, his weathered face shone like a burnished chestnut in the lamplight. He was basking at the end of the cookstove when Timothy startled him.

"Mr. Kincaid, what's your life been like?" Perhaps it was the rare kind-ness of the home that gave Angus the confidence to answer. Everybody sat nursing a cup of steaming tea as he began to unfold the riveting tale.

"Me mama an' papa died o' this here influenza when I was jist a wee laddie," he began. "I became a ward o' th' county, so th' Glasgow council shipped me oot t' Ontario as a *home boy* when I was eight."

Alistair remembered hearing about farmers who would feed and care for one of these lads in exchange for the work he would do. Some boys found loving hospitable homes and were adopted by their new parents. But Alistair also knew that in some places mean, skinflint men took orphans in and worked them, one way or another.

Angus hesitated, uncertain whether to say anything more. "At th' first place I was stayin', the man hit me with th' horse whip if I did nae work fast enough. His wife gave me th' leftover food off their own bairns' plates. Once there was even maggots in th' fried eggs."

The second and third homes were better, the tramp told them, but without love. Angus had learned to protect himself by withdrawing. When he was old enough, he had run away and kept running. It took a long time for Angus to stop looking over his shoulder to see who was chasing him. His world was full of strangers whose eyes he wouldn't, or couldn't, meet.

Some tramps were lazy and wouldn't work if they could beg. But Angus's work ethic drove him to support himself. "I grab any task I can get me hands on, fer a wee spell. After me purse is full, I shift along."

Angus ran a coarse hand over his scraggly dark beard. "I travel light as I can. I round up a coat and hat in th' fall an' give it away in th' spring." Dressed in a clean pair of Alistair's trousers and shirt, Angus glanced at his own clothes drying over the stove guard, freshly washed in lye soap by Priscilla. "I keep one change of clothes. An' a woolen blanket fer sleepin'."

Timothy squinted at the grimy sack lying on the floor beside Angus. "So where do you sleep, Mr. Kincaid?"

"Jist where I'm workin'." Angus tapped his bag. "I wrap this here blanket around me like a cocoon. If I'm oot o' work, I keep an eye peeled fer the underside of a railway bridge. Or rig up a lean-to o' spruce boughs to break th' wind."

Angus was seated with a group of men who thrived on, and admired, hard work. It puzzled them why Angus remained itinerant. Listening to his story, Morgan suddenly realized that the man's willingness to make do with very little gave him a freedom to move about unencumbered. He had traveled from Peggy's Cove to Vancouver Island and had even picked oranges in the groves as far south as Homestead, Florida.

"With all those travels behind you," Alistair said, "you better turn in here for the night." A mischievous glint flickered in his eyes. "I'm sure the flannels were turned over last spring."

Angus readily accepted the invitation. As usual, the conversation got around to spiritual things while the men talked, feet propped on the stove door. To everyone's surprise, Angus withdrew a small New Testament from his sparse bag, its cover as frayed and worn as an orphan's shirt.

He chuckled at the astonishment evident around him, as if a fellow in his position didn't need the Lord. "I could nae exist without me wee book," he confided. "Livin' the way I do makes a chap depend on God. Often I feel it's jist Him an' me. I've got this hymn that I sing as I walk along."

Timothy smiled. "Could you sing it for us, Mr. Kincaid?"

Angus's face tensed, and then he acquiesced. "No odds to me, my son." He reached for Timothy's old flat-top guitar leaning in the corner. "I skidded logs all one winter at a bush camp twenty mile out o' Huntsville. I had nae a thing to do but sit around all evenin'. If I washed the supper dishes, this here cook, he'd give me a lesson," he said as he began to strum and sing softly. By the emotion in his tenor voice and the ease with which he scaled the notes, it was obvious that this tune was one of his favourites.

I must have You, Jesus, with me,
For I dare not walk alone;
I must feel You close beside me
And Your arm around me thrown.

Then my soul shall fear no ill,
Lead me gently where You will;
I will go without a murmur
And Your footsteps follow still.

I must have You, Jesus, with me,
For my faith at best is weak;
You can whisper words of comfort
That no other voice can speak.[21]

The guitar notes slowed to a sweet, meditative ending as Angus's voice faded into the darkened corners of the room. He had held the kitchen spellbound, but now the clock was striking ten as the night air shuddered in the stovepipe. Alistair uncrossed his long legs as though to rise and follow the invisible footsteps of which their guest had sung. "Beautiful words," he acknowledged. "We're one with you in spirit, Angus."

"And you lay a deft touch on the strings," Timothy added. "I could learn from you in lots of ways."

Untying her apron, Priscilla briskly stood up. Filling and corking a stone pig, she handed it to Angus. "When you're ready," she offered, her voice compassionate, "Timothy'll show you to your room."

Angus smiled bashfully. "And from there to the Land of Nod."

The traveler had rarely slept in a shakedown as comfortable as the rope-hung spool bed at Wood Creek Farm. The next day he insisted on helping Alistair and Timothy dig potatoes and parsnips for the root cellar. The all-day job was heavy and dirty, but Angus felt satisfied as he spent the second night at the Stanhopes'. After a hearty breakfast the following morning, he thanked Alistair and Priscilla for their kindness and set out once again.

A few hours into his journey, he found a roadside apple tree, its branches denuded of leaves but showing a myriad of sharp red globes hanging against the cerulean blue of the November sky. Throwing a stick up into its branches, the tree yielded a cascade of Red Sweetings. Filling his pockets, he recalled a barren tree into which he had thrown a stick only a few weeks ago. No fruit came back, only the hard stick. Now, as he thought about the warmth and generosity of Alistair and Priscilla, one of Jesus' teachings sprang to mind: A good tree cannot produce bad fruit. People do good deeds because of the good in their hearts.[22]

Unbuttoning his shambles of a coat, Angus gazed thoughtfully toward the upper branches. *A lot o' folks bounce back a hard response t' a difficult request or an awkward sitchyation,* he ruminated, *but real Christians shower th' sweet fruit o' their substance on those in downright need.*

As autumn turned to winter and the dark days of December showed candles in the city windows by four o'clock in the afternoon, Morgan pondered Angus's way of life. On his daily constitutional to the Canadian Bank of Commerce on Wyndham Street, Morgan recalled the peculiar, even comical, figure that Angus had presented at Wood Creek Farm. Nevertheless, a confident faith had seemed to surround the man, different as he was from any other saint in Morgan's memory.

Returning home each evening, Morgan gazed appreciatively around at the ancestral suite of furniture on which he had paid ocean passage from Liverpool. The carved wood of the heavy table and chairs and the heirloom pewter that was known to have survived from the days of Cromwell had the power to soothe and reassure him in his self-imposed exile from the familiar world of his youth.

The smart limestone row house which he now called home symbolized to Morgan the success of his recent immigration to the New World. He had dreamed of the day he would post a steamship ticket to a pretty young lady back in the Cotswolds—a girl he had courted since boarding school. Each time he arrived home, he imagined himself carrying her across the threshold of his address on Suffolk Street.

During the second year of Morgan's life in Canada, however, fate or the capricious will of a woman had intervened and the series of letters that he had been exchanging with her had slowed and then stopped altogether. Absorbing the pain of this loss, Morgan craved more than ever a sense of belonging. The circle of faith that had welcomed both him and Angus Kincaid alike to the table at Wood Creek Farm now sustained him.

Morgan was accustomed to fine manners, to the ownership of a stylish horse and rig, and a number of small luxuries, such as his subscription to the *Times* of London that linked him with the genteel English manner of life he had left so far behind. News from Britain—weeks old by the time it reached Wellington County—had offered him a stability. But now, even the *Illustrated London News* seemed tawdry and inconsequential, unlike the events that were writing themselves on Morgan's heart.

One evening Morgan sat at his ivory inlaid desk companioned only by the reflection of his visage in the oval mirror across the room. Angus, he concluded, might be a shrewder man than himself. Hearing the low rumble and squeal of the train's brakes as it slowed for the Guelph station, Morgan shook off the mood of sober contemplation and stood up. He buttered a plate of rusks and brewed himself a scalding pot of Ceylon tea.

The following afternoon George appeared at the bank without warning and extracted a fold of banknotes from a pocket in the bib of his overalls. "I was in town picking up a sieve for the fanning mill, and I thought I'd stop by and straighten up on the December first payment."

Morgan motioned to a chair and drew a blank receipt out of his desk drawer. But before lifting a pen, he tilted back in his rounded armchair, folding his hands across a silver tie pin. "George, I've been thinking about Angus Kincaid," the banker began. "A man's freedom often hinges on his willingness to let go of the material world. It's not that I envy Angus or would trade places with him, you understand, but I do have a question."

He peered sharply at George. "Do you fancy the way he lives is compatible with the commitment needed in a group of believers?"

George's face registered the new thought. "Perhaps not for you or me," he replied. "But can anyone say how another believer should live? I think there's a lot we can learn from Angus."

Morgan tightened his lips. "I feel I should be spending more time sharing the gospel, but to be honest I'm a bit strapped—what with living in that stone house and buying that fancy driver and rig." He ran his hands over his pinstripe suit. "And goodness knows, I do like decent attire."

"I don't think there's anything wrong with a saint appreciating and even enjoying natural things," George offered. "Just that he needs to see all things in relation to God's greater purpose on the earth."

Morgan nodded. "If my attachment to material things hinders me from following Jesus," he stated emphatically, "I intend to release my hold."

"Maybe so," George cautioned. "But it'll be impossible without God's power. Once when I tried to give myself more wholly to God, I realized I was just getting self-righteous and stuffy, looking down on other folks who weren't doing the same. I took on a kind of syrupy humility that wasn't real at all, and it took a long time to shake it off."

"Yes, I can see the pitfalls," Morgan assented. He drummed the end of his pencil on a pad of paper. "I figure that by working ten hours less each week, I'll still be able to cover my expenses—provided I let my charlady go and pare my expenditures down to essentials. I don't intend to fritter away the time I could spend reaching out to others."

"That's a noble intention, Morgan," George encouraged him. "I'm sure God will guide you."

Dimmed by a veil of driving sleet, the lamps of the city flickered around George as he headed into the dwindling December light. A cold finger ran down his spine when he tried to picture Angus bedding down somewhere under a frozen railway bridge on this bitter night. As the buggy's steel rims clattered over the icy ruts, it suddenly occurred to him that Jesus and His disciples slept under the stars, and he wondered if the sophisticated people of Jerusalem might have perceived them as a band of tramps. Drawing the warm buffalo robe across his legs, George settled back for the dreary ride home. *Perhaps,* he mused, *some of us should become homeless wanderers for Christ.*

Eight

THE EPIPHANY
Winter 1900

The fierce storm had blown itself out and the furious dance of powdery snow had slackened into swirling dervishes under the cold noon sun. Happening to glance down the lane, Alice could discern the dark shape of a sleigh cutting through the blowing snow. She watched it stop and drop off a passenger, a woman in black cloak and shawl, who waded to the door with the purposeful air of one returning after a long absence.

"Susan!" exclaimed Alice. "And in weather not fit for a dog. Nobody here's stirred from home for a week, the school's been closed, and here you are blown in by the wind."

"'Twasn't t' wind, 'twas Edmund's nephew. 'E came poundin' on me door and got 'imself storm-stayed five days ago. T' young blade's only been married t' month, you know, and 'e was champin' at t' bit to git home to Hespeler." Susan winked at Alice. "Who'd want to be stuck with an awd biddie of an aunt when yer bird o' four weeks is clean crazy to have ye 'ome in t' nest?" She cackled so loudly that Alice's sleeping child stirred on the kitchen lounge.

"Well, well," Alice chuckled. "Here, let me brush your coat and hang it by the fire."

Susan Green's face glowed fiery red from the cutting wind that had driven the sleigh from Guelph to the seventh concession. "'Twas like Edmund allus said, 'Only a bloomin' Scot or a mad dog would 'ead out on a dirty day like this.''E'd turn clean over in 'is grave, so 'e would, if 'e knew ah was out traipsin' about in this to-do tryin' to catch me death."

Awakened from her nap, little Madeleine sat up, warm and tousled. For a moment the sleepy-eyed beauty, startled out of her dreams, looked as if she might cry. Then focusing on Susan, she brightened and a smile lit her flushed cheeks.

"And you, little one," Susan teased, divested of her snowy garments, "a springtime face in t' winter if I ever saw one—a marigold in t' button'ole o' blustery awd January." She eased herself down and cuddled the child in the hollow of her lap while Alice set the kettle on the stove.

Hearing Susan's infectious laugh, Tillie poked her head through the doorway and joined the women for a cup of tea around the kitchen stove. Afterward, when Susan opened her bag and drew out a partially tatted anti-macassar, Tillie retrieved the red socks she was knitting for Bill's birthday. As the afternoon wore on, Alice bustled about baking a chocolate cake for supper.

Susan was sprinkling nutmeg and parsley flakes over the mashed turnips when Bill and the boys arrived from the barn at six o'clock. "Ah declare, ye 'ave an 'ole kitchen full o' cluckin' biddics," she chortled as she threw her arms around Bill and the boys.

"Always room for one more at a hen party," Bill joked as the boys tore across the kitchen to stick their fingers into the bowl of chocolate icing.

After the meal Susan dried the dishes. She watched Gilbert and Nathan wrestling on the kitchen lounge as she polished the plates with her towel, her smile reflecting back from the white china.

"Seems so long ago since I met you and t' others," she remarked. "Ah know it's only been a few months, but ah feel likes ah've allus knowed you." She hesitated pensively. "D' you remember that rainy day ye told me t' weather was in pretty good 'ands?"

Alice smiled. "Yes, Susan, I do."

"Well, it wasn't just t' weather. Me life was pretty rainy and dreary at that stage too. But since then ah've come to see that ah was in good 'ands. In t' best 'ands, in fact. Just when me future's lookin' right dismal, God's 'and was leading me to you, and now ah've everythin'; I 'ave Christ and 'is love…" Susan wheeled around at the sound of a hard thud behind her. Nathan let out a howl as he crashed onto the floor. "And a family o' friends wi' plenty o' ruckus," Susan laughed as she helped the lad to his feet.

"I can't believe that saying one small thing about the weather gave me such a loyal friend," Alice replied. "God's blessed me with your friendship too." Dropping her towel on the trestle table, she gave Susan a hug.

～

Dugan and Hilda, the young couple from Eden Mills, also marveled at the good friends they had come to know. Shortly after becoming part of the circle of believers at Wood Creek Farm, they had consciously made room for Jesus as an honoured guest in their home. The secular history books, written by hard-eyed scholars, found their way to the back of the shelves, while an old Fletcher's Bible, complete with illustrations, was often left open at a current reading. During the autumn it had become clear that Hilda and Dugan were about to entertain yet another guest—a human one this time—but also sent from heaven.

By late January Hilda's gait was showing an unmistakable forward lurch. Although she had often spent her afternoons with the other young wives in the village, she now retreated to the patch of winter sunshine that warmed the cozy wing chair, absorbed utterly in the booties, tiny sweaters, and slips that sprang from her lap as if by magic. Hilda laughingly remarked that the baby drawers and nightshirts bore an absurd resemblance in miniature to Dugan's own. Dugan himself spent his evenings sawing lengths of pine and turning spindles for a tiny crib. Gone were the evenings that he had formerly idled away in reading about the Wars of the Roses or playing chequers with his neighbour.

"Samuel, if it's a boy," Dugan insisted.

"And Ruby or Agnes, if it's a girl," Hilda countered.

"And if she's twins," Dugan teased, "we'll hand one to old Maisie down the lane. She's had nothing to do for a hundred years but suck her pipe. Maisie'll make a model child of her…"

Hilda sprang to stand in front of Dugan, playfully threading her fingers into his thick beard. "She'll suck her pipe for a hundred more years before any daughter of mine lands on *her* lap, the old harridan." She sank down at his knees, drawing his hands to her cheeks. "Dugan stop teasing, do. It makes the baby kick."

"A little spice of Highland temper," Dugan approved, gathering his wife in his arms.

It was only a few days later that Dugan arrived home from work to find the fire out, no supper started, and his wife tensing with sporadic pain. "Hilda!" he cried, stricken at her look. "How long has it been this way with you?"

Hilda began to laugh but sharply caught her breath. "Oh, Dugan, ever since you left at noon. Old Isaac's wife, the curious soul, came yoo-hooing at the door with a basket of canning jars, as if it were the season. I tried to help her take them down cellar and put them on the shelves but I…I didn't feel right. I'm chilly…" Hilda's voice broke. She shivered and leaned back against Dugan, who wrapped his arms about her shoulders.

"Oh, dear God," he muttered, feeling suddenly weak in the knees. "Hilda, let me tuck you up on the couch—here under this blanket. Please, don't move. I'll be back as soon as…"

Dugan sprinted for the door, his coat and hat still flung on the newel post. Tripping on the stone doorsill, he sprawled headlong into the fresh snow on the porch.

"Take a few deep breaths," Hilda coached from the kitchen lounge.

"Sure, sure," he sputtered, leaping to his feet. He grabbed his coat and shot out the door like a startled partridge to fetch the midwife who lived at the edge of Eden Mills. The good woman was immersed in a leisure cup of tea after her supper and seemed as immovable as Gibraltar.

"Sure and there's no hurry about it, first child and all, I do be thinking," she drawled. "Not so fast, lad. Rome wasn't built in a day."

But Dugan's despairing appeal found them hurrying along the snowy lanes by lantern light. They returned to find Hilda shivering and drenched in sweat as another labour pain racked her body. Wisps of fair hair stuck to her pasty forehead. In the eight hours of darkness that followed, she struggled to the point of exhaustion, giving Dugan cause to consider that the Roman Empire could have risen, declined, and fallen in less time than it was taking Hilda to give birth. As the gong in the downstairs clock called off the hours, Hilda's labour grew more excruciating and at times he heard her moaning. Almost unrecognizable as his wife's voice, it sounded like the keening of an animal kept too long in captivity.

When he could not bear to watch the woman he loved in such distress for one more minute, he got up and clutched the window frame as if to will the dark sky into dawn. Involuntarily, from deep within his chest, he felt his prolonged anxiety rising to a pitch of near panic that frightened him. Clammy with perspiration, his shirt clung to his skin as he stared muttering into the blackened night.

An irrepressible Irishwoman, the midwife turned on him in exasperation. "Go on and boil another kettle of water. Your usefulness around here ended nine months ago, lad. Get on with you…"

Another half hour dragged past. Dugan was growing desperate when, like a sudden expression of his own pain, he heard a sharp cry from the bedroom and a moment later the midwife calling his name.

"For the love of Mike, hold your hands out like a man," she ordered, feigning rebuke as she placed into his rough palms the most beautiful baby boy Dugan had ever seen. The baby's eyes, like those of a blind cherub, were tightly shut against the kerosene glow. His damp scalp glistened with his father's red hair, and his tiny hands folded as if entreating forgiveness for the anguish his birth had cost. Dugan's eyes burned with sudden tears.

The midwife looked the child over approvingly, and in her droll manner she cautioned Dugan, "Now raise him aright, in the fear o' the Lord and the fellowship o' the saints!" She pursed her lips as she poured a basin of water. "What name do you be intending to lay on the lad?"

"Samuel. Dugan picked it," Hilda offered, pale and tremulous.

"Yes," he acknowledged. "Samuel in the Old Testament was a good man. And he started out as a good boy."

Standing beside the bed, the midwife gripped her stout sides and roared. "They all start out as good boys. It's what goes awry as they age. That's the rub. Now hand me the child so's I can mop him down."

In the weeks and months that followed, Dugan and Hilda rode a wave of elation, cheering at the baby's latest antics. Anybody who would listen heard about Samuel's ability to roll over, to hold a spoon and bang it on the side of his cradle. Surely a musician had been born. The transformation worked so powerfully, so completely, that their friends could hardly believe they were the same couple. Sometimes the new mother and father could barely grasp the change themselves. Samuel was the deepest joy they had ever shared.

One day as Dugan graded a pile of green lumber at the saw mill, his rendition of a verse from Isaiah, the Old Testament gospel preacher, crossed his mind: Unto us a Child is born, unto us a Son is given; and the government will be upon His shoulder. His name will be called Wonderful, Counselor, Mighty God, Everlasting Father, Prince of Peace.[1]

Dugan laid down some cross spacers so the air would dry the next row of planks. As in the dawning of a new day, he began to see that the Christ life had changed his daily activities just as profoundly as little Samuel had.

In the middle of supper that evening, Hilda heard a cry that sent her scurrying to the baby's basket. As Dugan sat at the table eating by himself, he again pondered the conception of Christ within a human heart. He slowly stirred the edges of his barley soup, concluding at length that Hilda's pain in bringing Samuel into the world was like a spiritual birth. Both involved some inner conflict, even tears.[2] He remembered his own struggle. And how different it had been from any other religious experience he'd ever had.

Hilda cradled the little fellow in her arms, his chubby red face peeking out through the flannel blanket. "Poor wee lad," she sympathized. "Only three months old and already having bad dreams."

"I'll never forget the thrill of hearing his first cry," Dugan said as he rocked his son, still whimpering softly. "I couldn't wait to hold him in my arms." Samuel snuggled up against his father's chest. "I got to thinking this afternoon that's what touches God too. When He hears us pleading for His presence, He reaches down with compassion and draws us to Himself."[3]

Hilda scoured the pot bottoms as she considered Dugan's analogy.

"In the womb each part of Samuel's body developed so he'd be prepared for this life," Dugan went on. "Those nine months had little meaning to him until he was born. And it's the same today. We grow spiritually so we'll be able to rejoice in the kingdom of heaven."

Hilda glanced over at the baby squirming on her husband's lap.

"So what I'm saying is that immortality will confirm the meaning of the life we're living today."

Dugan looked down as Samuel's chubby fist groped its way to his shirt collar, fiddling with the button. Wincing, he extracted a chest hair from Samuel's tiny grip. "He never worries where a thing's coming from, does he?" he observed. "Neither the porridge or the mortgage."

As if on cue, Samuel began to fuss, his face reddening with displeasure. When the fidgeting shrilled into a wail, Dugan thrust the baby toward her. "Here," he urged, "You've got a charm I don't have."

Draping the towel over her arm, Hilda suppressed a giggle. "You're just hungry, aren't you, sweetie pie?" she cooed as she drew the baby to her breast. "You need to eat to grow into a big man like your daddy."

As he watched her cuddle their son, Dugan smiled at his slender wife. It was marvellous how easily she'd slipped into motherhood. Then as Samuel settled into the contented sounds of nursing, Dugan's mind returned to his thoughts. Spiritual nourishment, he mused, enables us to grow up into Christ in every way.[4]

Later that evening, Dugan adjusted the wick in the kerosene lamp and carefully wiped off the oilskin tablecloth. Then he brought his Bible and a tattered history book from the parlour shelf. Thumbing through the pages, Dugan found the excerpt of a letter written in fifteenth-century England. Once again, the words of Thomas Kittlewell of Worcester, a poor Lollard preacher, swayed his heart as he pored over their timeless wisdom:

> The beauty of Christ exceedeth my comprehension. Like a child, He is the living issue of a union—one of singular love and chaste desire.[5] He entered the centre of my being, conferring life upon me.[6] Even as the virgin Mary conceived the incarnate Jesus by the power of the Holy Spirit, so the conception of the Christ life cometh of immortal seed untouched by human intervention.[7]

> It hath been made known to me that the traditional Christ I had formerly sought and beseeched each Lord's Day was not Christ in any form, but a strong delusion.[8] Like treasure buried in a field, His kingdom remained hidden while I did struggle vigorously for earthly attainments, heedless of the underlying truths of life.

> Only when I came to the end of myself could the Christ child become my counsellor for every doubt or trouble. Passing beyond this gate of humility truly placed the government upon His shoulder. No other power remotely compares, no created or imagined thing—even unto the final enemy—can wrench me from His hand. I walk and talk with Him; and He with me. The contentment He grants remaineth incomprehensible to the mind of man…[9]

The kitchen clock struck one in the morning as Dugan finished reading about the trial of Thomas Kittlewell before the Archbishop of Canterbury. When the former tailor refused to stop preaching and distributing the Scriptures in English, he had been declared a heretic and an enemy of the Church. Dugan felt inspired by the deep peace that Thomas had radiated as his jailers bound him with chains to the stake in the Smithfield village square. Even after a barrel had been thrust over Thomas and wood piled around it, his voice could still be heard praising God as the fire was lit.

Dugan bowed his head and thanked God for his own fortunate circumstances. He closed the heavy volume and carried it back to its place on the shelf. Leaving his Bible at the head of the table, he checked the wood fire, blew out the lamp, and tiptoed gingerly up the wooden stairs, trying to avoid the squeaky treads. Feeling blessed and at peace, he burrowed under the covers and cuddled up against Hilda's warm slim body without waking little Samuel. When she turned over sleepily, he rubbed her back and whispered, "I love you, Hillie."

In the little fellowship, the new life affected every person differently. The rays of God's love shone through Christ like a magnifying glass in summer until each heart burst into a flame of service. In their own way, each of them grew more devoted to their Lord and His work.

At the Canadian Bank of Commerce, Morgan Butterwick's heart burned within him and he, too, felt sharply accountable for his time. His voice rose as he addressed the bank manager. "It's fewer hours that I'm asking for, sir. There's a new priority in my life now."

The manager hooked a thumb into his waistcoat pocket and stared into his assistant's face. "That's a most unusual request, I must say. Most of the tellers are asking for extra hours, not less. Money's in short supply for most folks these days, you know." As he absorbed Morgan's earnest intentions, the banker's full face strained with incredulity. "And that's your only reason?"

"I'm, as you'd say, wanting to put first things first."

"You're a fine employee, Mr. Butterwick, and you have an excellent knowledge of British banking. I don't want to lose you." He hesitated, taking in the row of teller's cages. "Just don't step over the line and do anything that might discredit our institution."

Morgan's thin face broke into a smile. "Yes, I'll be careful, sir. And thank you for your consideration."

The manager shook his head in skepticism as he turned away. "It's your look out, my good man. I wish you well."

With more free time, Morgan intended to use every opportunity to speak to people, privately and publicly. He noticed that folks tended to linger and congregate on market days near the livery stables. Picking his way past the long line of horses and rigs, he found himself standing beside the gray stone walls of a ironmonger's shop one day in late February. Underneath his pin-stripe trousers, his knee caps tensed, his toes arched in his shoes, and his legs prepared for flight. Morgan fidgeted, his eyes sweeping the street. Open air preaching was most unnerving. Maybe he'd shift along and come back in warmer weather.

Then taking a firm grip on his emotions, he cleared his throat as a well-dressed passerby approached. "Good afternoon, sir." The man paused, smiled warmly, and then caught sight of the Bible clenched in Morgan's right hand. Abruptly the man's face turned to stone, and he brushed Morgan aside with an icy stare. The long line of storefronts on Wyndham Street swayed before Morgan's eyes. A woman, taking her daughter by the hand, skirted Morgan as stiffly as if she had encountered a leper.

Morgan retreated to the security of the stone wall, taking several deep breaths as he struggled to collect his thoughts. As his pulse slowed, it was as if the stones behind him were crying out, encouraging him to simply read some Scriptures aloud.[10] His long fingers trembled as he fumbled for a verse. He had not yet found his page when a chubby-faced boy on the way home from Central School stopped.

"Are you going to read something, sir?" the lad asked, his eyes round.

Morgan smiled down at this diminutive source of encouragement "Yes, sonny, I am. Would you prefer Noah and the ark or Daniel in the lion's den?"

"Daniel," the boy replied in a word and plopped down on his satchel.

Forthwith, Morgan's clipped Liverpudlian accent rose on the chilly air of late afternoon, his voice thin and strained. A small band of listeners soon gathered, some intent on his words and others waiting to engage Morgan in heckling. They heard how Daniel, uprooted and far from his birthplace, threw open the windows of his heart and communicated with God con-tinually—even at risk of being ripped apart by wild beasts.[11]

Morgan's impassioned tone and transparent sincerity caught even the veriest cynic by surprise. With the ebb and flow of his pulse, the port wine birthmark that stained his temple turned from blood-red to purple.

"Got the mark of Cain, that one," he heard a voice from the crowd. Morgan flinched, reminded of this painful derision years ago by school-mates.

"From Liverpool, y' say?"

"Pay no mind to the addle-brain," his companion urged.

"Hey, mate," another voice taunted in mock cockney accent. "Do ye fancy you're at Speakers' Corner upon Hyde Park?"

To Morgan's left, a matron, wicker basket on her arm, nudged her friend. "Isn't that the banker my husband had dealings with at the Bank of Commerce last week? Fine fellow, but the Good Book tells me you can't serve God and mammon." She rolled her eyes as the pair turned away.

Morgan, feeling as if he himself were ringed by bloodthirsty lions, looked around and forced a tight smile. He determined to get used to the hostility, to be a fool for Christ's sake.[12]

One by one, the knot of listeners dissolved. Only the small boy and a blind man on his way home from selling brooms on Wyndham Street remained. The man reached out tentatively to touch Morgan's sleeve. "I can tell by your tongue you're a long piece from home, friend. Thanks for the message." As he turned to go, his armful of brooms brushed Morgan.

"Thanks to you as well," Morgan replied. "Hope to see you again."

When he had finished speaking, the boy, chubby-faced as Daniel and his fellow captives, jumped to his feet. "Are you coming here again, sir?"[13]

"Yes," Morgan said. "Next Wednesday about the same time."

"Wowsers," the lad said, kicking a pebble into the gutter. "I'll be here."

Before he left, the sun had broken through and suffused the limestone wall behind Morgan in shades of warm ochre.

As the weeks unfolded Morgan became less anxious about street preaching. Nevertheless, he preferred more personal visits and sought out quiet opportunities for his spiritual discussions. He hesitated to knock on private doors and confront people, knowing it wouldn't be right to try forcing his beliefs on others. Even if it satisfied his own desire to spread the word, it would be of no benefit to God. At the same time, Jesus had instructed His followers to go into all the world and preach the gospel to everyone.[14] So Morgan waited for the proper times to plant a seed.

One day an older farmer came into the bank to arrange a loan for the purchase of a McCormick harvester and binder. He talked as Morgan filled out the loan agreement and promissory note.

"The machinery'll save me a lot of time," he said. "And goodness knows, I need it. Between the farm and my bee yard in the Paisley Block, I can hardly get through all the work."

Morgan raised his head. "What's involved in keeping bees?"

"When the wax combs are full," the apiarist explained, "I extract the honey. My old woman used to sell it at the Guelph Market, but she's laid up. The stall takes far more time than I can spare right now."

Morgan stroked his forehead. "I've been looking for some extra work that'll get me out on the street meeting folks," he ventured.

The farmer's eyes widened at the thought of a banker selling honey. *"You,* are you sure?" he stammered. "Well…if you're bent on it."

Before they parted, Morgan had agreed to buy all the honey the bee-keeper could produce. He intended to sell it door-to-door and at the farmers' market. It was the perfect way to earn a modest living and at the same time meet people without alienating them.

Later that week Priscilla, determined to finish Phoebe's new dress for her violin recital at the school concert, hurried off to Crundle's general store. She found Albert Crundle and three of his grizzled cohorts propped on nail kegs around the potbellied stove.

"Winter's back is pretty well broken when you can hear the train whistle kind of low and melancholy-like," she heard Mr. Crundle observe.

"The ice is gettin' rotten," another declared. "I oughta know, I misjudged the creek behind the barn and fell clean though up to my…" He glanced discreetly in the direction of Priscilla and patted his backside.

"A thaw makes a man mighty restless," said the third. "I plan on a-gettin' my sowin' done by mid-May. Don't know as I'll live to reap it."

"Jordie, you fool. Your old man hung on long past the allotted span—eighty-three, wasn't it? And more ornery than a billy goat with mange. Take heart, you've already lived into the new century."

"Yaas, nineteen hundert sounds kind of funny. Not rightly legal."

While the men raked each other with sarcasm, Priscilla ignored their sparring to examine some hooks and eyes for Phoebe's spring dress. She was comparing them when she heard Jordie's voice, low and portentous.

"Somebody that ain't going to live past spring is Joe Purves. If he don't get help, and soon, he'll be a goner afore her."

"Why, whatever are you meaning?" a man's voice asked.

"It's Bella. They tell me she ain't pullin' around. Didn't y' hear? Seems she took an apoplectic attack three weeks past."

Priscilla faltered, her heart suddenly heavy at the news.

"That's a durn shame," the second voice acknowledged. "And Joe's a right decent chap, too."

Old Jordie's tone lightened. "But bashful as a schoolgirl. And since he was knee-high. Why when we was young, a gang of us lads hiked it down to the swimmin' hole one hot evenin'," he croaked when Priscilla had moved behind a forest of fabric bolts. "But Joe beat it soon's we peeled off the first stitch. Can't figure what scairt him about being barefoot all over."

Setting her bag down on a table incubator, Priscilla held up a length of white pearl fringe. She cut off two yards and moved along the aisle.

"Time and again, when anything to do with them matters came up at the harness shop, Joe allus changed the topic right quick," another voice rasped. "Married all these years and likely never laid eyes on the soles of Bella's feet. She could a had twelve toes for all he knew."

Great gusts of ribald laughter emanated from around the cherry-red stove. "If his bed took fire," the second man snickered, "you can be mighty sure he'd hitch up his suspenders afore he'd grab a pail o' water."

"Yaas, and it was told around he sired 'em nine young uns without so much as doffing his cap."

Priscilla's lips twitched in spite of herself. "Such foolishness," she muttered. From behind the screen of dry goods, she heard old Jordie's wheezy belly laugh degenerate into a fit of coughing. *Serves the old geezer right,* she thought as she added a box of cream of tarter to her bag and approached the counter. Albert Crundle rose to total up her purchases.

"I couldn't help but overhear you men speaking about Joe Purves," Priscilla said apologetically. "Isn't his family able to help out?"

"Nope," Mr. Crundle said. "She raised nine of 'em and nary a one handy by. Every last one of 'em up and moved away to get hitched or work. Now isn't that a fine how-do-you-do?"

"What about his neighbours?" Priscilla persisted.

"Guess they're plumb busy with their own affairs like the rest of us. Talking about it lots, but nobody's showed their face as far's I've heard."

"It's a corker if nobody's helping them," Priscilla lamented as she turned toward the door.

That evening Priscilla was praying to experience a deeper love when an image of Joe's worn face snapped into her mind. The image lingered as she bustled about her kitchen the next day. *I'll fetch over a pot of stew,* she resolved. *First thing in the morning.*

~⊙~

Joe and Bella Purves had been fixtures in Puslinch for as long as Priscilla could remember. In his younger years, Joe had worked long hours in the shop of a saddler and harness-maker near Goldie's Mill. Priscilla could still remember the pungent smells of horse sweat, fresh leather, and linseed oil as she stood beside her father watching Joe stitch together a broken hame strap. Much like Priscilla's own parents, he and Bella had also struggled to raise their large family. Priscilla had grown up with some of their children, but she hadn't seen them for a long time. *Do they actually know,* she wondered, *how grave their mother's plight has become?*

Dwarfed by an ancient maple, the Purves's clapboard cottage knelt beside the main road to town, and Priscilla set out for it immediately after breakfast. When Joe's haggard face appeared at the door, she assessed his weary eyes, rumpled shirt, and faded overalls. He braced himself, one elbow on the jamb as he changed position, taking the pressure off his arthritic knee. She smiled warmly at his dazed expression. *Coming here today,* she discerned, *was the right thing.*

"Joe," she began kindly, "I've come to sit with Bella so you can rest a spell."

Joe halted in the doorway, staring. Tears stung his eyes. He seemed unable to move. Priscilla shifted her blue granite pot to one arm and put her other hand on his elbow, gently guiding him back inside.

"I'll watch over Bella while you're lying down," she promised. "I'll call you if she takes a notion for you."

Joe fell into an exhausted sleep that lasted most of the day while Priscilla sat at Bella's bedside, knitting a pair of wool socks for Timothy. As she looked at Bella lying fast asleep, Priscilla noticed how feeble her aged body had become. Her once work-hardened hands lay helpless on her chest and masses of varicose veins knotted above her ankles. Priscilla's thoughts returned to her childhood days. How strong and rugged the old woman had once been. According to the season, Bella had worked for the local farmers pulling flax, tying sheaves, or picking potatoes and turnips in the fields from morning to night. She had often had one baby on her hip and a toddler at her feet as she did the backbreaking work. When she thought of Bella as a mother, Priscilla felt a sadness deep inside, recognizing in the enfeebled body before her images of her own mother.

This recollection opened a floodgate. Never before had Priscilla considered how busy her mother's life must have been. She felt ashamed and relieved at the same time. For the first time she could appreciate her mother's love and sacrifice. Tears began to roll down Priscilla's cheeks as memories came surging back. Whatever the daily scoldings had been among the eleven brothers and sisters, it was not memories of loneliness or rebuke that Priscilla remembered, but those of her mother's gentle kiss each night, long after Priscilla had snuggled under her quilt. She recalled her mother's white-gowned form passing from bed to bed on a summer's night as a thunderstorm shook the house, ensuring that her brood was safe and sleeping. With greater clarity, she remembered many thoughtful things her mother had taken time to do for her—despite the staggering amount of work that had to be done each day.

Suddenly an overwhelming love for Bella caught Priscilla off guard. It was as if every wall of anger and resentment that she had ever constructed was now dissolving like a sand castle at high tide. As God's love rose within her heart, it began to release her from the bitterness and pain hidden there. Her own mother was no longer with her, but Bella's need called out to her now. And Priscilla intended to give her love to Bella as long as the old woman was alive.

Bella rested comfortably most of the time. But when she stirred, Priscilla chatted to her, brought weak tea, or helped her to manage a few spoonfuls of chicken broth.

Waking late in the afternoon, Joe entered the kitchen with a yawn and bashful gratitude. "Thank you, Priscilla. Reckon I slept like a January coon in a hollow log."

As Priscilla pressed a cup of tea into his hands, she could see that he looked a little better. Both of them sat down at the dinner table, and Joe began to tell her about the previous three weeks.

"Bella and I were having breakfast when suddenly I noticed she couldn't get her porridge into her mouth," he explained. "Her spoon was bumping into her chin and cheeks, spilling cream and oatmeal down the front of her dress. Her eyes were different; they didn't focus proper-like. She seemed to be staring at something behind my chair. Her face, which was usually smiling, had gone blank. I shook her shoulder and said, 'Bella, what's wrong?' but she didn't seem to hear. Then the spoon fell out of her hand and onto the floor. Somehow, I got her to our bed and sent for the doctor. When he came, he told me he couldn't do anything and that she could take another spell at any moment. Prepare yourself for the worst, he said. She might not last very long." Joe cried softly, and Priscilla realized how much in love this couple was even after forty-three years.

Before she left, Priscilla warmed some of the hash she had brought and promised to pay another visit in a few days. Thanking her again and again, the older man radiated such gratitude that Priscilla regretted not having come sooner. But even as she surveyed the wrinkles at the corners of his cavernous eyes, she reassured herself that the Holy Spirit hadn't touched her heart until yesterday. And that God's timing was always best.

Trudging home in the light drizzle, Priscilla thanked God for answering her prayer. She shook her head to disperse the droplets of water obscuring her vision. *The gist of it,* she realized, *is that the only way to please God lies in the way of love. But it must be practical to be real—good words alone don't amount to a hill of beans. It's our love for others that confirms we belong to the truth.*[15]

Priscilla rubbed her wet palms briskly when she remembered how cold Bella's hands had been. Turning in the home lane, she suddenly felt inspired to send Phoebe along on Saturday with a roast chicken and the warm afghan Aunt Maggie had knitted.

When Priscilla walked in the kitchen door, Alistair stood washing the supper dishes while Phoebe dried, both of them encircled in the warm lamplight. With water dripping from her dark hair and still wearing her wet coat, she walked straight to Alistair and threw her arms around him. As she buried her face into his shoulder, he could feel the dampness finding its way through his shirt. Surprised, he asked, "What's wrong, my dear?"

"I love you so much," was all she could say, thinking of Bella slipping away from Joe. After Alistair held her for a few minutes, he heard what had happened at the Purves's. Alistair had learned by now that the best way to love his wife was to listen when she needed listening to, and to hold her when she needed holding. He didn't need to have answers for all her woes.

Over the months, Priscilla had begun to know a contentment and quietness in her soul as never before. God actually loved *her,* irrespective of her flaws, she marveled as she stirred the pancake batter one morning. Her mind raced, struggling to take it in. She was acceptable just because she'd embraced His Son in faith—nothing more. This discovery that her own merit, or lack of it, had no special significance gave her great liberty of heart. It wasn't even her will to love God, but His will to love her that made all the difference. This assurance gave her such peace that she no longer looked to Alistair to fill the void that she had once known. It was God's love abundantly overflowing to her that she, in turn, shared with Joe and Bella.

Priscilla would often sit at the piano and sing a hymn in which each verse carried special meaning for her now:

> Not what these hands have done can save my guilty soul;
> Not what this toiling flesh has borne can make my spirit whole.
> Not what I feel or do can give me peace with God;
> Not all my prayers and sighs and tears can bear this awful load.
>
> Your work alone, O Christ, can ease this weight of sin;
> Your blood alone, O Lamb of God, can give me peace within.
> Your love to me, O God, not mine, O Lord, to Thee,
> Can rid me of this dark unrest and set my spirit free.
>
> I praise the Christ of God; I rest on love divine;
> And with unfaltering lip and heart I call this Saviour mine.
> My Lord has saved my life and pardon freely gives;
> I love because He first loved me, I live because He lives.[16]

Getting up from the piano stool one evening when she and Alistair were alone, she walked to where he was sitting beside the window, tilting the *Guelph Daily Herald* toward the last weak sunlight. She reached down and took his wind burned face between her hands. "Alistair," she said tenderly, "God's finally broken through. He's helped me understand that I was blessed with a good mother and a wonderful husband. I know you've got your own struggles, but I feel closer to you on account of it. Thank you for being you." When she bent over to kiss him, he swept her onto his lap.

~⌀

As winter turned to spring, the believers at Wood Creek Farm were being built up in love. They were touching truth, the reality of God. Transparency of heart before God and openness with each other could be a fearful thing, but they all seemed to want more of it in order to experience their Lord's presence more fully. And as time passed He added new souls to the little group[17]—a safe bed in which a new plant could sprout.

But even in the midst of this happy situation, Alistair offered some words of caution: "We must be careful to focus on the bridegroom, never on the bride.[18] If Christ, our bridegroom, ever becomes secondary to our own little assembly which is part of His bride, we're in desperate straits. All through history, the church has suffered from this insidious problem of drawing people to herself. Little by little as she took on a life of her own, the life and Spirit of Christ was sifted out until only a shell remained. That's what happened at Saint Patrick's—the candlestick was removed and for a while we didn't even know it was gone."[19]

This lack of the Spirit betrayed itself in many ways. Occasionally a visitor came who would do a lot of loud talking about Christ, but with little evidence of His humble Spirit. These strangers seemed to think their abundance of words and knowledge of the Scriptures would impress the saints at Wood Creek Farm.

This dissension troubled Priscilla for weeks, and finally one Sunday when the friends were together for dinner, she raised the subject. "Sometimes we have visitors who profess to be Christians, but when they come they monopolize the entire conversation or want a heated debate. If this type of self-centred person chooses to become a permanent part of our church, it could spoil the unity and close fellowship we enjoy."

Alice's forehead furrowed as she looked over at Priscilla. "Don't you think a church needs to be open to anyone?" she objected. "We don't want to become an exclusive sect."

"Absolutely," Priscilla conceded. "It needs to be open for anybody to hear the gospel. But we're also a family. The question is how to balance the two. Most people won't be able to understand that concern because they can't grasp the intimacy of our fellowship. But if you suggested they adopt every pompous individual that comes along into their own family, to listen to that stranger talking across the table at every meal, to discuss their most private concerns in front of this visitor, they'd object strongly."

Emily nodded in instant agreement. "Priscilla's right. I just can't imagine pouring out the sorrows and burdens in my heart in that sort of situation. As it is now, I sometimes shed tears in front of you. And that's all right because I trust you. You're my brothers and sisters. But some of these folks talk about God in a most casual and offhanded way. I just don't think some of them would understand the yearning of my heart. And that would make me uncomfortable. On the other hand, we definitely want to embrace those who are needy, who are honestly searching for Jesus."

"Folks who seek God's presence aren't able to be contentious or casual about these matters of the heart," Alistair added. "On the contrary, we feel a powerful conviction to love Him with *all* of our heart, our soul, our strength, and our mind.[20] That means total surrender, taking up our cross and submitting ourselves to His Spirit."

Timothy leaned forward from his place at the corner of the harvest table. "Religion can spawn a heap of talking, but Christianity is about walking. Walking with Jesus. Maybe I could be a little quieter myself," he added with a self-deprecating grin.

"I can see Priscilla's point about people who want to give a lecture," Bill said. "One Thursday, I said something I thought was clever. But even while I was speaking, my words felt heavy and sluggish as though the Holy Spirit had left me on my own. After I turned it over for a few days, I realized that a well-rehearsed sermon gives a lot less nourishment than a simple, timely thought."

Bill fell silent as he remembered the shock of realizing that his mind was as keen to manufacture its own viewpoint as any human hand had ever been to fabricate a gold idol.[21]

Emily folded her slender hands on her lap. "I agree with Bill," she said with a smile. "I like it best when someone shares an experience that's taught them a spiritual lesson and helped them know God better."

Jack crossed his short legs. "Dugan and I'd never want to say anything negative about studying history," he said, winking at his old friend. "But having known Abraham Lincoln as an intimate friend would be vastly different than being able to rhyme off a set of historical facts about his life. And knowing Jesus is infinitely more valuable than simply knowing *about* Him. Intellectual discussions feed the mind but rarely the heart."

Malachi's voice took them by surprise. "Some folks seem to have busy minds and blind hearts," he interjected. "It's humble minds and open hearts as God wants—like little children.[22] That's the only kind of soil the gospel seed can take a good root in."

Bill took off his thick glasses and polished them on the edge of the table cloth. "Human beings like big splashes, and it might make us feel good to have larger numbers. But unless a listener hears the voice of Jesus, the invisible church will never grow."

Phoebe's youthful higher-pitched voice startled them all. "Invisible church," she blurted out. "What's that mean?"

Bill squinted in Phoebe's direction as he bent the wire frames slightly, trying to make them comfortable behind his ears. "The true church is made up of everyone who's become alive to God—from every nation and age since the beginning of time," he explained. "Their invisible connection with God is what makes them part of His great universal church. Simply attaching one's self to a group, even ours, will never do that."

The growing concern that people with busy minds and blind hearts would inhibit the warm family spirit and sense of oneness within the little church caused the saints a lot of soul-searching.

"What would you think of inviting visitors on Thursday evenings to hear the gospel message?" Alistair finally asked. "If it seems these folks are in harmony with the Spirit and teachings of Christ, then we could invite them along on Sunday to break bread in the fellowship meeting."

Catching the nods all around, George seemed to speak for the entire group. "Sounds like a fine idea to me," he declared.

In addition to the meetings at the Stanhopes', Jack often stopped by George's farm for fellowship. When the two friends met, they usually pored over some Scripture together. One April evening they sat at the kitchen table as usual, their open Bibles lying flat before them. George's voice resonated with carefulness as he rephrased a passage into his own words: "Jesus went around teaching from village to village. Then He called together the twelve disciples and sent them out two by two with power over evil spirits. He told them, 'You may take along a walking stick, but don't carry food in a bag or money in your belts. It's all right to wear sandals, but don't take along an extra change of clothes. When you are welcomed into a house, stay there until you leave that town.' Then the apostles left and started telling people to repent and turn to God."[23]

Suddenly, George stopped short and raised his head. "Doesn't that sound familiar, Jack?"

Jack bent lower over his Bible, squinting in the dim lamplight. "I'm not sure what you're getting at."

"We read some verses last week," George reminded him as he found a place in Luke's Gospel. After quickly scanning the passage, he looked into Jack's puzzled face. "It says that after this the Lord appointed another seventy and also sent them two by two into every city and place where He Himself was about to go."[24]

George ran his fingers up into his sandy hair and scratched his scalp pensively. "When did God change this?" he questioned. "Or does He intend that the same two by two itinerant ministry should continue today?"

Jack paused, gently pinching his upper lip. "I don't suppose it should be any different today, really," he finally replied.

"It seems that even after the resurrection, the New Testament ministers refused to become established in one place," George added. "They took their model from Jesus."

Jack chewed tentatively on his toothpick for a few minutes. "You're exactly right. Jesus' followers practised what He had initiated, a constant traveling mission among the towns and villages of the Roman Empire. And they must have been brave to live as perpetual strangers in an empire ruled at times by barbarous brutes—the likes of Nero or Diocletian."

George nodded. "The book of Acts and the inferences in the Epistles confirm that Paul and his companions never settled in one place either."

The two men talked until the kitchen clock struck twelve times.

"Let's bring it up with the others and see what they think," Jack said as he got up and reached for his boots. "See you next week, George."

The following Thursday, George stopped in mid-motion as he shoveled out his pig pens. Had he heard an unmistakable trumpetlike call approaching from the south? Dashing to the stable door he caught sight of a pair of snowy trumpeter swans as they swept low over his barnyard, the whistle of their great wings slicing through the velvet fog. He stared after them until their resonating sound had faded away. All that remained was the crystalized tinkle of brittle ice as, under the insistent influence of the warm mist, it collapsed, leaving ragged edges along the receding creek.

That evening at Wood Creek Farm, the company of friends gathered around the kitchen table, their Bibles spread before them. As the study drew to a close, George looked around the circle, a new light in his eyes.

"Jack and I've been puzzling about the New Testament ministry," he declared. "You know, how it actually worked."

The others listened with keen interest as he and Jack outlined the passages they had found.

Bill let out a low whistle. "Whew. Now isn't that an eye-opener."

Alistair nodded slowly, his forearms crossed on the table. "You're right," he acknowledged. "Anybody here ever seen hide or hair of a voluntarily poor, itinerant ministry in these parts?" He glanced around, noting the small group of shaking heads.

"Nor in Haldimand," Malachi added from one end of the table.

This new revelation about the first-century ministry was a milestone and a moment of truth for the little group of believers at Wood Creek Farm. Promising to read, pray, and think about the matter until the following Sunday, the friends separated into the warm moonlit evening. Frogs croaked in the roadside ponds as their horses' hoofs beat a dull staccato on the homeward road, soft now and yielding to spring's gentle influence.

On Sunday morning the spirit in the meeting was unusually tender and soft. Each person shared some simple thought encouraging the others to remain strong and faithful in union with Jesus. No one ever thought of preaching a sermon, but in genuine humility they offered a brief word of comfort and support.

After the meeting everybody stayed for dinner. While the women prepared the table with roast beef, mashed potatoes, turnips, sliced beets, sweet pickles, and shoofly pie, the men strolled out to look at the new beehives Alistair had put in the orchard behind the house.

"I'm hoping the bees'll help pollinate the blossoms," Alistair explained as the men gathered in a semicircle around his workmanship. "And give a few extra bushels of apples and pears."

Morgan bent forward to peer under the hives. "Good thing you've set them up from the ground a bit. Skunks got into the bee yard out on the Paisley Block. Made quite a mess of the hives, the farmer said."

"I didn't know skunks liked honey," Timothy rejoined.

"It's not the honey they're after," Morgan insisted. "It's the bees. At least according to my beekeeper friend."

Alistair ran his thumbs behind his suspenders. "They dig a lot of grubs and critters out of the ground," he noted. "And beetles out of rotten logs."

"And fresh eggs out of henhouses," Bill snorted. "Some of the beggars got into Alice's laying hens a while back."

"I reckon you'll have to flag down old Jordie," Timothy chuckled. "He's an old hand in dealing with skunks."

The men grinned as they headed toward the kitchen.

In the middle of dinner, while everyone was laughing and talking like one big happy family, Timothy quietly jabbed Phoebe in the ribs.

"Do you remember last week when Bill set his cup of tea on the floor?" he whispered, his eyes sparkling. "He joked that the tea was so weak he was afraid it would fall off the table."

Phoebe nodded and smiled, wondering what was coming next.

"Let's cut a thick crust of bread and put it in the bottom of his cup," Timothy suggested. "Then we'll get a spoon and stick it in the crust before we fill the cup with tea."

Timothy set the teacup on the table in front of Bill. The spoon was standing straight up and not touching the sides of the cup at all. "I hope the tea's strong enough today, Bill!"

The farmer's jaw dropped as he stared at the spoon, mesmerized. Everybody roared at the colour rising in Bill's face. "Just wait until I get one on you, Mr. Timothy," he sputtered sheepishly.

Slapping his knee, Malachi's crimson face convulsed in silent paroxysms of laughter. "The look on Bill would've made a horse laugh," he wheezed when he could finally catch his breath.

George smiled as he watched the antics. *And some people,* he mused, *assume that Christians lead dour, despondent lives.*

When the last of the dinner dishes had been cleared away, the little church returned to the parlour and the atmosphere became more serious. The subject that each had been grappling with since Thursday now confronted them: What was ministry like during the first century and was there ever any suggestion that it be otherwise today?

George glanced around the circle. "When Jack and I were reading together, we noticed that Jesus sent out a traveling ministry that moved from place to place teaching His simple truths. Even after the church matured, its ministers deliberately chose to remain poor, unpaid, and itinerant. Seemingly, they went wherever the Holy Spirit led them to satisfy a particular spiritual need."

"What do you mean unpaid?" Bill asked. "Don't you reckon they received a stipend or at least something for their keep?"

"There's no evidence of it," George asserted. "It doesn't look as if they ever took a collection for their own use. Or preached with any expectation of reward.[25] I doubt they even considered their endeavour as a job or a position."

"I think it was an individual calling from God to which they responded in faith," Jack added.

Alistair scanned the eager faces around the room. "I'm sure that's right," he said. "I've been reading about it since Thursday, and I can see that Jesus not only established these conditions for His first disciples, but also for the men who followed. Paul, Barnabas, Silas, Timothy, Titus. They all respected and adhered to the same pattern."

"My history books indicate that little change took place until the church in Rome deteriorated in the second century," Jack said. "Clearly, our present-day, professional clergy has drifted a long way from the original plan of Jesus. And by that I'm not speaking of any particular man. Most ministers are very fine people. It's just that they've grown up like all of us—in a system that doesn't line up with Scripture. All too often, the living Christ gets squeezed out by the outward form of tradition."

George, balancing his open Bible on his knee, leaned forward. "I've been reading in the Old Testament too, and I can see that a temple-like structure and a resident priest supported by a tithing system has much more in common with the old synagogue system under the Mosaic Law than with the Christian life of grace."

Bill squinted as George's statement took hold. "Yes, you're right," he acknowledged. "Receiving a salary and being provided with a residence and a church building definitely reminds me of the Jewish system—which Jesus specifically rejected. There's a big difference between that and the simple methods He chose."

"Why *did* Jesus establish such methods?" Alice wondered aloud.

Alistair's elbows rested on the arms of his chair, his fingers interlocked across his slim waist. "If a man doesn't have the necessary faith to believe that God will provide his everyday needs," he theorized, "he would never leave his home to preach the gospel without the assurance of financial backing. And without possessing the reality of this faith and trust in God, he's unable to share these vital elements of the Christian life with others. In other words, he can't give what he doesn't have."

George stroked his beard thoughtfully. "And if a man's love isn't powerful enough to compel him to share the gospel of love without personal reward or recognition, then he cannot be the selfless, humble preacher of Christian love that Jesus requires."

Like people walking out of a thick blanket of fog into the bright light of the sun, the saints began to understand that such a life sets apart those who have a genuine love and faith from those who don't. As the little group mused on these matters, they were struck by the awesome wisdom of Jesus.

For days George pondered their discussion and began to think about the impact the first itinerant preachers had had on the world. Would such a ministry still work if there were men who were actually willing to forsake all and follow Christ? *They'd need a strong faith*, he reasoned, *depending entirely on God to supply their daily needs.*

The ensuing fortnight throbbed with the overtures of spring, but George seemed oblivious to it all. Often on his way to the barn he found himself halting at the windmill and gazing off into the distance, deep in thought. *There's only one way to go about preaching, and that's the way that Jesus went. With no promise of provision, except from God. If we refuse His practical methods, we face the risk of rejecting Jesus Himself.*

As the April calendar counted off its final days with stronger sun and a fine green mist on the deciduous woods, the question became pointed, more personal. It lay like a live coal on George's heart. Night after night as he stirred in bed, he asked himself, *Would I be willing to forsake all?*

Nine

THE BAPTISM
Spring 1900

Sunday morning's fiery dawn succumbed to a gray mantle of overcast sky. A light drizzle had already set in before Bill Jones hurried to the house for breakfast after finishing his early chores. Later, as his family made their way to the neighbour's farm to pick up Malachi, Alice tried to shelter her quarrelsome brood under dripping mackintoshes. The horse's shoes threw splatters of mud against the buggy's dashboard and rain soaked Bill's coat as he strained forward scanning the milk house and smoke house beside it where Malachi usually waited. But there was no sign of the older man's gaunt frame and lean face.

At Bill's knock, the neighbour's wife answered the side door, and before Bill could speak, she said, "Malachi got up and struck out first thing this morning," she said. "Hain't seen him since. Land's sakes, it's his stinkin' habit again, don't you know."

Bill searched the woman's face. "Did he say anything, Maude?"

She pressed her lips tightly together and shook her head. "No," she said slowly, "but last night he seemed terrible down in the dumps." Maude ran her hand over the bristles on her chin. "I'd have gone to check on him," she apologized, "but my old man's in bed with a bad dose of the shakes. All out in a rash too. He's sick as a dog." She turned at the sizzle of a kettle boiling over, tiny beads of water dancing across the stove top. "But it's the rattle in his chest that worries me most. I'm fixin' him a hot mustard plaster."

Bill nodded and cautioned her, "Don't overheat your good man." A reluctant smile like the stingy sunshine of a December day passed over Maude's pinched features as she watched Bill hurry back to the buggy.

"Alice, something's wrong with Mal," Bill said somberly. "Maybe it's his old troubles. You take the young ones and go on to Alistair's. I'm going to hunt him up."

Alice's full face looked petulant. "Hasn't the man an ounce of resistance?" She reached over and took the leather lines. "We'll come straight home after the meeting. See you at noon." When she clicked her tongue, the horse lurched forward with a jerk. "Gilbert, hang on to your sister. I won't tell you again..."

"Oh, honey," Bill added as he took a few quick strides, raising his hand to the side of the buggy, "please have the little church pray for Mal and me." As she looked down and nodded, he caught the remorse in her eyes.

"Sorry, Bill. It's my sharp tongue again. Maybe it's me the devil's got hold of." She switched the reins, flustered. "Right now, Mal probably needs you far more than I do."

Bill headed down the back lane, stepping around puddles of iodine-coloured runoff from the manure pile. He looked inside the driving shed, his eyes sweeping it from corner to corner as he called Malachi's name. But there was no response—only the sound of startled sparrows fluttering in the rafters of the empty building.

When Malachi, sitting quietly in the loft, heard Bill calling in the stable below, he shrank into his smock. He had presumed that when he wasn't waiting, Bill and Alice would have gone on without him. Bill called again, but Malachi still didn't answer. Instead he slunk down behind a pile of hay and slid the bottle along the side of a vertical timber. Then he heard the squeak of the small door opening into the loft of the barn. He held his breath, listening as the footsteps approached, and then stopped in the centre of the barn floor.

"Hello, Mal. Are you up here?" Bill's voice echoed among the beams.

Malachi twisted in his hiding spot as Bill called out anxiously once again. The old bachelor clenched his fingernails into his palms and took a deep breath. "Over here, Bill."

He heard the sound of Bill's feet scrambling up the side of the mow, saw the concern on his face as he spotted him, felt the warmth in the hand Bill extended. Malachi's eyes fell as the younger man flopped down in the hay beside him. He lowered his head and stared at his feet.

"I'm rotten sorry, Bill." His voice was strained and tight. "I didn't want you to find me in this shambles."

Bill looked into the drawn face and bloodshot eyes. "It's alright, Mal."

"You and Alice and everybody at Alistair's have been so good to me. And now I've let you all down—blamed terrible."

"Mal, we don't just love you when things are good." Bill reached over and gripped Malachi's shoulder. "We love you. No matter what."

"Nobody ever did before," Malachi mumbled. "Even when I was a kid, my Pop would grab me by the scruff of the neck and shake me. The way a dog shakes a kitten. He'd a skinning knife he'd shove in my face when I didn't move right quick and swore he'd skin me alive. The same knife he used for to skin muskrats or castrate pigs." Malachi devoured a sudden sob. "What use could I be to Pop with that knife in my face?"

The muscles in Bill's jaw tensed and he clenched his hands. "I'm sorry you were tormented like that. But it's different now."

As though trying to cushion a betrayed confidence, Malachi resumed in a nostalgic tone. "But Pop weren't always mean. Like as not he'd be weepy and morose. Maw was thin in her mind, and I reckon Pop had his hands full. I mind the time she took a shovel out beyond the lilacs and allowed she'd try to bury her sins. She'd no sooner brought the shovel down but the blade sliced into her bare foot. Pop heard her shriekin' and tore out of the barn. When he yanked out the shovel, the tip of her little toe rolled into the dirt. At the sight Maw screeched and fainted in a dead heap. Pop tried to bring her around and ran to pump a pail of water. He sloshed it on her face with his hands, gentle like, 'til finally she stirred and began to mumble." The anecdote died in Malachi's throat with a pathetic strangled sound. "Livin' proof," he asserted mournfully, "that a father's nightmares are visited upon his son. I ached for a happy home. And why did a young fella like me end up with a wife as couldn't honour her vows?"

Suddenly, he threw his head forward, grinding his brow into his knees. His gnarled knuckles entwined themselves, tense and white, at the back of his stubbly neck. "It's always in April I miss her most," he wailed. "It was the 17th, right before we lost the farm. She walked out and I've not seen hide nor hair of her. I asked all over, but she'd vanished into thin air."

Bill felt a cold fist tighten over his heart, leaving him speechless. "I had no idea," he finally gasped. "I'm so sorry, so sorry." He threw his arm around the older man's shoulders.

"I've never told anyone in these parts. I was so ashamed when I cleared out of Haldimand County that I vowed I'd never ever utter another peep about it…" Malachi unclasped his fingers and straightened slightly. "And until today, I never did."

Bill tried to picture the girl in his mind. "What was her name, Mal?"

One corner of Malachi's mouth twisted. "Stella. She was the bonniest thing going. But she didn't intend to put up with a man as couldn't provide for her proper-like." The half smile faltered. "Or give her young uns."

Like cold steel thrust into Bill's heart, Malachi's vulnerability silenced him. The wind intensified and, in the distance, slammed a creaky door open and then, after a bit, closed again. For a long time, the two sat quietly, listening as the rain increased, pounding diamond spikes on the roof.

Malachi pulled a handkerchief out of his dusty overalls and snorted into it. "I tried so hard, but I've hit the dust again," he choked. "I don't reckon I can go on as a Christian. You'd be best to forget about me."

"Never, Mal!" Bill's reply was quick and firm. "You're as much a part of this family as any of us. We've all got hitches of some form or other. That's why God's placed us in a church—to help each other along."

"But I keep falling. I don't want to, but I can't seem to stop. It's like a black cloud settles inside me and I feel so miserable and lonely."

"Mal, what child do you know who began to walk without stumbling?" Bill reasoned gently. "It took years for us to grow and develop into men. And it's going to take time to mature into the fullness of Christ."[1]

Without getting up, Malachi reached down and yanked a tall dark-brown bottle from its hiding place. When he wrenched out the cork, rank fumes mingled seductively with the soft scent of hay. For a moment Malachi scowled at the gold label and then, with a sudden grimace, he thrust the glass neck through a knothole in the barn boards. The amber contents trickled down the side of the building and dripped into the mud. "I've got to learn to trust Jesus when things seem so black. Not lean on this old stuff." Malachi peered out through the knothole as if viewing his past, pinned in the frame of this tiny aperture. The drizzle, slanting across the stark gray of a weathered shed, swelled the dismal puddles in the barnyard.

Malachi's tone lightened as though consciously repressing past tragedy in favour of recent comedy. "I'd a rope around a steer's neck the other day when the dog spooked him," he grinned ruefully. "Couldn't get unhooked fast enough and the ding-busted critter dragged me through the slop and manure until I was plastered from head to toe."

Bill smiled. "You must've been a sight for sore eyes," he chuckled as he hauled out his pocket watch. "It's almost noon, Mal," he said as he stood up. "Come on over for dinner. Alice has a pork brisket in the oven."

Malachi's revelation to Bill was not without consequence. After vocalizing Stella's name and retelling their nuptial story, pitiful and brief, his long repressed agony, like an infected thorn in the hand, had at last burst and opened itself to healing and comfort.

On the Wednesday after Bill's visit, Malachi awakened in the middle of the night, his heart pounding—the dream had been so vivid, so devastating. The tortured bed sheets, wound around his ankles, held him like leg irons. In his dream he had been racing from room to room, up and down the stairs, searching frantically for Stella. Where was she? Her dresses had vanished, the blankets out of the travel chest lay heaped in the corner, and before he checked he knew that the extra bank notes squirreled away to stall foreclosure were missing.

Outside a desolate rain beat against the window as Malachi twisted on his bed. *Why, why am I such a failure?* He buried his face into the pillow and wept. *Why can't a man marry again if his wife's run off and left him?* In the thick darkness, Malachi listened to the incessant drip from the ceiling, drenching his floor in a pool of black sorrow. His spirits sank. Where had he left that bottle?

It was then he remembered the distress in Bill's face as he scrambled over the edge of the mow. "The same nightmare, the same old corn mash, the same rotten guilt," Malachi muttered. "I've got to learn to let go of that rope." Rolling onto his stomach, Malachi kicked the sheets free from his legs and began to pray. "God, you know all about my nightmares. I'm turning them over to you because they drag me through the muck. Please release me and take them away." Then, he drew in several deep breaths, consciously turning his mind to the happiness he felt each Sunday when the little church gathered.

But Malachi not only turned to God in times of trouble; he made a point of conversing with Him as he worked on the land or cared for the stock. In the evenings after his day's work, he sprawled his long form out on his bed and read the Scriptures, trying to understand and follow their teaching more carefully. It gave him great satisfaction to carry his Bible to the fence corner, the hay mow, the very places he had once taken his bottle.

~∘

One sultry evening in June, Malachi tossed and squirmed on his bed tick, unable to sleep. After a little while he got up, struck a match, and lit the candle. Immediately, a velvet cloud of moths clustered around the flame while a bat retreated to a corner of Malachi's chamber, eerily ruffling its taffeta wings. He reached for his Bible and sat down on the edge of the bed. Its delicate pages fell open at a passage in the book of Acts about an Ethiopian minister of finance. Malachi's rough forefinger followed line by line as he mouthed the words in the flickering light:

> Then Philip opened his mouth, and...preached unto him Jesus. And as they went on their way, they came unto a certain water: and the eunuch said, See, here is water; what doth hinder me to be baptized? And Philip said, If thou believest with all thine heart, thou mayest. And he answered and said, I believe that Jesus Christ is the Son of God. And he commanded the chariot to stand still: and they went down both to the water, both Philip and the eunuch; and he baptized him. And when they were come up out of the water, the Spirit of the Lord caught away Philip, that the eunuch saw him no more: and he went on his way rejoicing.[2]

Malachi laid the large Bible back on the table and blew out the tiny flame. *Why*, he puzzled, *did Pop not have me baptized as a child? Likely 'cause he never darkened a church door himself.*

As Malachi went about his daily chores, he became increasingly troubled by thoughts about baptism. After the Sunday fellowship meeting, he took advantage of a lull in the conversation to broach his concern. "I reckon you've all been baptized." The parlour fell silent and the intent faces around the circle turned at his voice. "You wouldn't have any way of knowing, but that never happened to me," he divulged. "The more I read in the Scriptures, the more I figure it should've. What do you all make of it?"

The women and younger men turned toward Alistair, but it was Bill who spoke up from the opposite corner. "You've asked a good question, Mal," he began "But I don't know enough to give you solid counsel."

Alistair glanced around the group; his gaze hesitated at George. But seeing the younger man shaking his head, he flattened the clip on one of his suspenders. "Nor me. Let's all take the week to read up and pray about it—make it a subject of study like we generally do when something out of the ordinary comes up."

On the following Sunday, the buggy wheels raised powdery dust along the country roads as the various friends made for the Stanhope farm. After the dinner dishes were dried the church returned to the parlour.

"Mal's baptism question from last week has given me some serious thinking," Alistair admitted. "It's like trying to get hold of the end in a pile of string. I'm hoping the rest of you have some light to shed. I did read that before Jesus began His public ministry, He asked John the Baptist to baptize Him. When he objected, Jesus explained it was necessary to do all that God had planned.[3] So I reckon every saint needs to be baptized."

"But only if they believe with their whole heart," Bill cautioned. "Not just as a matter of ritual. The only people John baptized in the Jordan[4] were those who'd repented and confessed their sins.[5] That's why he refused to baptize some of the religious leaders. He told them to first show by their lives that they'd indeed given up their sins."[6] Before closing his Bible, Bill earmarked his three verses.

Emily flipped her pages to the Gospel of John. "It says here that Jesus baptized in the Judean countryside,"[7] she attested. "But farther along it appears as if He also gave that authority to His disciples.[8] And before He ascended into heaven, He definitely told the eleven to go and make disciples of all nations, baptizing them in the name of the Father and the Son and the Holy Ghost."[9]

Malachi sat listening, his hairy forearms crossed, as he tried to absorb all of the implications. "I don't much care for the notion, but do you reckon it has to be done by an ordained minister?" he asked tentatively.

George raised his head, keeping his finger on Emily's reference. "Only people who were filled with the Spirit themselves baptized others as far as I can see. The apostles did, of course. But also men like Ananias and Philip, for example.[10] Although they weren't apostles, they were saints, born of the Spirit. That's why God entrusted them to baptize Paul and the eunuch." He looked around the gathering. "It seems to me that *any* child of God can baptize another believer."

Looks of astonishment glanced back and forth around the assembly.

Caught off guard, Dugan hitched himself forward. "You don't mean—anyone of *us?*"

"Yes," George replied. "Anybody under this roof."

"Well, suppose it was fitting for one of you men to baptize Malachi," Alice asked, "how would you go about it?"

Jack hefted a thick Bible dictionary onto his lap and began to read aloud. "Baptism—derived from the Greek word *baptizo*, meaning to dip, immerse, or plunge." He closed the heavy volume, balancing it on his knee. "The only method of baptism in the New Testament appears to be by immersion," he said. "Jesus *came up out of* the water after His baptism,[11] as did the Ethiopian eunuch. And certainly before He could come *up and out*, He must have gone *down and in*. Baptism locations were specifically chosen because of their plentiful supply of water."[12]

"Are you saying there's something wrong with being sprinkled?" Alice demanded, thinking of her own baptism.

"Well, it's just like Jack says, sprinkling has no foundation in the Scripture," her husband replied.

Malachi grinned. "If I get baptized, I want to go right under," he chuckled. "Down with the old man, up with the new."

Seeing the tension building in Alice's face, Priscilla stood up and went to fetch the teapot.

"Baptism symbolizes our death, burial, and resurrection with Christ," George explained. "When one dies, he's buried and placed under the ground. Baptism by immersion shows that we've died, been buried, and then risen with Christ. Sprinkling doesn't give that impression at all."

Bill got up and walked over to the cistern pump for a glass of water. He set it on the table in front of Alice. "I don't mean to make a joke, but do you think there's enough water here to be buried in?" The others smiled broadly at Bill's illustration.

"All right, then," Alice shot back. "Suppose I agree with what you say. Where's that leave the rest of us? I hadn't yet cut a tooth or spoken my first word when somebody sprinkled me in the sign of the cross. And I simply don't know anything about the minister who sprinkled me."

"Alice has a good point," Emily said. "It was the same for me. I neither chose nor rejected Jesus. I had absolutely no faith in Christ nor had I experienced His indwelling Spirit. To be honest, it's only been during these past two years that I've known the first thing about the Spirit of Christ." She drew one corner of her lower lip between her teeth in thoughtful introspection. "Aren't we all in the same boat as Mal?"

"You're right, Emily," George replied. "If unconditional commitment is the sole basis for baptism, then I need to be baptized as much as Mal.

Water baptism is the outward expression of the inward purification that comes with the Spirit of Christ. We need to express that before each other."

Priscilla's face registered dismay at George's last comment. "Don't you think our former baptism carries any weight?"

"I doubt it," George said quietly. "Anyway, I would definitely like to be baptized again. At the same time as Mal."

Alistair looked over at Bill's glass of water. "I think we all agree that sharing in Jesus' death is the only way to be resurrected to a new life with Him. And that immersion is the scriptural way." Glancing around, he saw that most of the little church were nodding. "So anybody who wants to be rebaptized next Sunday morning better bring along a change of clothes."

Later that week, Malachi skirted the field of sprouting barley and cut through a patch of red alders on the line fence of the Jones farm. Rounding the corner of the driving shed, he spied Bill on his knees beside the binder.

"Got a hitch?" he asked.

Bill settled back on his haunches and looked up. "Needs a set of new canvases and the knotter's been jamming lately."

Malachi gave a preoccupied snort. "Bill, I know I need to be baptized. But maybe I'm not worthy yet. I mean, it's not that long since I was near about pickled with Walker's Kilmarnock."

Bill straightened up and looked at Malachi. "You believe in Jesus with all your heart, don't you?"

"And all my strength too."

"And in the power of His precious blood?"

Malachi didn't respond in words. He closed his eyes, his face twisting like a child's as he nodded.

Bill's eyes softened as he laid down his wrench. "We've all seen the changes in your life, Mal. Even if you do have problems now and then— like the rest of us. If we wait until we have everything perfect in our life, we'll never be baptized."

Everybody arrived early on Sunday morning, well in advance of the fellowship meeting. Overnight, the sky had cleared to a cloudless turquoise and the warmth of the summer day extracted a pungent fragrance from the cedars lining the small oval pond at Wood Creek Farm. Timothy noted the sunlight glinting off the branches and recalled from his course in botany that the cedar was the *arbor vitae*, the tree of life. Nature reflected newness of life as the songs and meditative piping of birds filled the air.

Timothy uneasily remembered the tension that had made itself felt under the Stanhope roof the previous evening. His mother's lips had been set in a straight line as she went about her Saturday baking, as if she had encountered unexpected resistance to her well-laid plans for the morrow.

"What's the matter, my girl?" Timothy had overheard his father ask. "Finding weevils in the flour barrel?" His mother had turned a distressed face on Alistair and whispered a few words.

Feeling slightly guilty at his inadvertent presence in the pantry, where he was spreading bread with honey, Timothy saw, in the reflection of the pantry cupboard glass, his father wrap a reassuring arm around his mother.

"Give her time," Alistair had said in a low tone. "She's only fifteen. Besides, it's far better for her to hold back than to jump into something she's not ready for. In fact, I admire her decision to wait until she's certain."

His mother had stiffened her back and wrenched away, turning toward the stairs. "I worry that she's not ready to be baptized along with the rest of us," she muttered as Alistair trailed her to the foot of the stairs.

"Everything in God's time, my dear," he declared, prophetically.

Close to his sister in spite of their natural friction, Timothy had suddenly felt hollow, his assumptions about Phoebe shaken. Although he marveled at the independence of her choice, a characteristic he had not recognized before, he was unnerved at this minor rift in the family.

Timothy's reverie was interrupted at the sound of a splash, and he caught sight of Teddy paddling up to his chin in the water. He bounded forward and called the collie to his side, stifling a chuckle at Phoebe's exasperation when the dog shook his heavy golden coat and flopped down at her feet. Only the grunt of a bullfrog at the far side of the pond balanced the sweetness of bird song as the little church prepared for baptism. Timothy felt a wet swish and looked down to see Teddy's tail slapping between his own bare foot and his sister's shoe. Smiling, he reached over and placed a hand on Phoebe's shoulder as the little company of believers assembled at the water's edge. Each person was dressed in everyday clothing and stood barefoot in the tall grass, silently waiting for the purpose of their gathering.

When they were all present, Alistair asked George to pray for God's blessing. Then they sang a hymn together:

> Dying with Jesus, by death reckoned mine;
> Living with Jesus, a new life divine;
> Looking to Jesus till glory doth shine;
> Moment by moment, O Lord I am thine.
>
> Moment by moment I'm kept in His love,
> Moment by moment I've life from above,
> Looking to Jesus 'til glory doth shine;
> Moment by moment, O Lord, I am thine.[13]

As the singing died away, Alistair and Bill slowly waded out into the water. In spite of the unseasonably warm weather, the water felt chilly as it inched up their legs. When they got to waist depth, Alistair found a firm footing on the sandy bottom and Bill stood sideways in front of him. Without any further ado, Alistair placed his left hand on Bill's forearm and his right hand on his upper back, and then he spoke loudly and clearly, "Bill Jones, I baptize you in the name of the Father, and of the Son, and of the Holy Ghost." He laid Bill backwards into the water until he was totally immersed. After the water closed over Bill's body, Alistair raised him to a standing position again. Bill's thin brown hair was plastered to his head and the water dripped from his shirt. The two men exchanged positions and Bill baptized Alistair in the same way.

One by one the believers were baptized by Alistair, neatly and without splashing. Taking the hand of each sister at the water's edge, Bill steadied the women as they waded out to Alistair. Each one had pulled her long hair back into a bun and covered it with a kerchief to keep it from clinging to her cheeks like seaweed. They also wore rain cloaks to keep their full dresses from billowing up and floating on the surface. This made them perspire as they stood in the sun, but nothing could take away from the tenderness of the scene. A few tears were shed as each saint was buried with Christ through baptism into His death.[14]

After the women had all been baptized, Malachi rolled up his pant legs halfway to his knees and stepped quickly into the water. He considered it a privilege to be baptized in such a simple setting. In some ways the little church gathered on the shore reminded him of the crowds that had flocked to the Jordan River. As Malachi waded through the water toward Alistair, the Ethiopian eunuch came back to his mind. Nearly nineteen hundred years had passed since the African brother had taken this same simple step, confirming that the gospel of Christ had come alive in his life too. Malachi moved to a place directly in front of Alistair.

"That's good, Mal. Maybe a little more this way," Alistair murmured as he gently maneuvred Malachi into position. The warmth in Alistair's steady blue eyes gave Malachi confidence.

When he felt Alistair's strong hands gripping his arm and supporting his back, he relaxed and crossed his hands at his waist. A surprising peace took hold of him as he closed his eyes and waited. Then he heard Alistair's unwavering voice in his left ear. "Malachi Jackson, I baptize you in the name of the Father, and of the Son, and of the Holy Ghost." After he came up out of the water, Malachi wiped his face with both hands and smiled to himself. Turning, he saw Priscilla on the grassy bank with a coarse towel.

As Malachi watched the other men being baptized, he flexed his shoulders at the sensation of wet clothes clinging to his skin. Gradually, the heat of the morning sunshine penetrated his shirt and began to dry his hairy neck. He felt satisfied and blessed as if standing on holy ground. Malachi's mind wandered back to that first evening when he and Bill had talked over the rail fence. His life had changed so much since then. *I haven't got soused up since Bill found me in the mow,* he reflected. *Funny how that old habit's just dying away.*

When the last person had been baptized, Alistair returned to the shore. Together, the little church sang another hymn before going into the house to dry off and change their clothes for the fellowship meeting. They hadn't thought that it was possible to feel any closer to each other than they already did, but by fulfilling one of the last specific commands of Jesus, they felt His presence in a unique and special way. "I am with you always," He had promised, "even unto the end of the world."

Ten

TEAR-SHAPED BEADS OF DEW
Summer 1900

The hot summer days ripened the wheat into a rich gold, and the heads of the mature grain bent over with fullness. In every garden the sunflowers pushed upwards like drowsy peasants rising from a nap. Overnight the morning glory vines, with an impish sense of fun, scrambled up the handles of shovels and hoes, opening eyes of heavenly blue to meet the first light of dawn. Tear-shaped beads of dew, like drops of mercury, trembled in the heart of the squash blossoms until late in the dazzling summer mornings. Laura and Phoebe picked baskets of elderberries, black currants, gooseberries, and wild plums, which Priscilla boiled into jams and jellies and garnered into the fruit cellar. Ears of sweet corn, juicy tomatoes, and sliced cucumbers were served on the long harvest table at every meal.

Summer holidays allowed Laura to arrive back in Puslinch in early July, and although she was sorry to have missed the June baptism, she thoroughly enjoyed the meetings at Wood Creek Farm. Her gaiety and joy seemed to incarnate the summer's burnished beauty, fitting like a daughter of the house as she did into the Stanhope family and the little church.

"Those pesky goats are in the garden again," Laura laughed as she raced out the woodshed door. When the recalcitrant goats heard the slam of the screen door and saw her advancing, broom over her head, they bolted back through the narrow gate.

During her stays Laura helped Phoebe with her violin practice, and at times they whispered late into the night, as Phoebe shyly presented a litany of questions intriguing to a young woman.

Knowing that Phoebe had always coveted a sister to share her secrets, Laura invited her home to Stratford where three younger sisters impatiently awaited Laura's two week visit. Her lately married sister, Abigail, had set up housekeeping on a street facing the Avon River. Having unpacked the contents of her hope chest, the recent bride had taken on the dignity of a matron and now considered herself an authority on all things matrimonial.

One sweltering evening a few days after the train bound for Stratford had whirled the girls away, George pushed a bit into his horse's mouth with the air of a man on an irreversible mission. The scents and sounds of high summer hung all around him as he took an unaccustomed shortcut through the old Beaver property, newly acquired by George's neighbour, Jacob Pillman. Glistening snail trails crisscrossed the path as his horse felt out the unfamiliar footing through the scrubby underbrush. Moist spider webs draped themselves over George's face and ears in the dim recesses where blackberry bushes tried to reach the scant sun, and the sinister fruit of deadly nightshade and doll's eyes gleamed in the half twilight.

Coming upon a fence stile, George slowed when his eye caught a white apron flung over the post, and now he could see it was freshly stained with red. Startled, he pulled up the horse and leaned down. At that moment, in the delicate country silence, he heard or thought he heard the shriek of what must have been an animal—a cottontail perhaps, at the first terrifying touch of an owl's talons. But the cry burst into laughter, and a girl's voice, gasping and breathless, broke the eerie spell. A second voice made itself heard, deeper, entreating. When the horse, already spooked, witnessed the thorny brambles thrashing ahead, it whinnied and snorted, its nostrils flared and eyes wild. Instantly the laughter was startled into silence.

A sense of propriety urged George to wheel his mount and take a side path to the left. But even as the horses's flanks swayed in a wide turn and George strained sideways to avoid the overhanging branches, he couldn't help but see on the mossy floor of the thicket, the tumbled golden hair of a plump girl in a blue frock. In the next moment, he recognized her. It was Gertie Whitacombe, flushed and beautiful, pinioned in the strong arms of a lad—the lanky Randall Pillman. A half-filled tin pail of raspberries had spilled its sweetness and lay crushed and unheeded. In spite of himself, a scalding flush rose upwards from George's heart to his neck and cheeks. He tightened his grip on the reins and dug his heels into the horse's ribs.

As the underbrush thinned out, George pulled a wry smile. *Must be all of fifteen and going to town already,* he marveled. *Hope they don't get the cart before the horse.* As the Beaver property fell away behind him, George's face gradually reverted to its earlier preoccupation.

Alistair was just stepping out of the woodshed door at Wood Creek Farm when George rode into the yard, catching him unaware.

"Good day, Alistair. How are you faring?"

"Real good, thanks. How is it with you, George?"

"Fair to middling," George answered, but the tone in his voice told Alistair that something was preying on George's mind. The two men chatted about the weather and the crops, but Alistair's concern remained.

"I've a three-year-old Durham heifer that's having trouble calving," he said, nodding at the pail of warm water in his right hand. "It's her first calf, and she's been trying for over two hours now." He looked sharply at George. "I'd best check her again. You might as well join me."

After reaching the privacy of the stable, George announced abruptly, "Alistair, I've decided to sell my farm and stock!"

Alistair's eyes widened with alarm, but he held his peace as he made his way along the passage toward the heifer's pen. He knew that George loved farming and was working hard to pay down his mortgage. It was difficult to imagine a more diligent farmer.

The two men paused at the side of the pen. "Ever since our talk a couple of months ago," George confided, "I've had a feeling that won't go away. I think God's calling me into homeless ministry we talked about."

Alistair stalled in bewilderment. "What do you *mean*, George?"

"Jesus told one man to sell everything he had and to give the money to the poor. Then, the man was to take up his cross and follow Jesus."[1]

"Do you think that's for today—to accept Jesus' teaching so literally?" George nodded. "I'm sure it is."

Alistair ran a hand over his face thoughtfully. "So where would you expect to take shelter?"

"Well, I don't rightly know," George admitted. "But I have faith in Jesus' promise that anyone who leaves his home or farm, brothers or sisters, mother or father, wife or children, for the sake of the gospel will receive a hundred times as many...and in the ages to come, eternal life."[2]

"But Jesus had no permanent place to lay his head,"[3] Alistair persisted. "He was a traveler, a *sojourner*. Is that really what you have in mind?"

George's face was set like flint. "Yes, it is. I'm convinced that Jesus is entreating me to follow Him."[4]

Alistair grimaced, drawing back as if he had discovered a thistle in his pocket. *Maybe this is going just a little too far,* he worried as he entered the heifer's stall. *Perhaps God doesn't intend such a literal step now that we're not living in apostolic times.* An image of Priscilla baking an elderberry pie, another of Phoebe practising her violin, and one of the Sunday meetings in his parlour flashed before him. He glanced into a pen at the trio of sleek Yorkshire gilts that Timothy intended to exhibit at the Aberfoyle Fall Fair. Alistair surveyed his own stable of choice cattle accumulated over years of judicious breeding. Not only did he have a snug home and a livelihood, but around him was a circle of saints by whom he felt utterly loved and accepted. Alistair knew it would be difficult—if he were truly honest, impossible—to give up all of this and live such a Spartan, courageous life.

"George," Alistair said, "I'm going to have to think on this awhile. You may be right, but it seems to be a mighty big step of faith."

Alistair set the pail of warm water down in the straw and turned his attention to the heifer, her neck veins bulging and legs outstretched, sprawling on her side before him. "This has been going on long enough," he decided aloud. "I'd best have a feel inside." He squatted at the heifer's back end and patted her haunch. "It's alright, Marigold lass. You're coming along."

Alistair rolled his shirt sleeves up to his armpits before tugging a threadbare towel out of one pocket and handing it to George. He fished a chunk of gritty soap from his hip pocket and knelt before the bucket, scrubbing and lathering his lean arms. Then, lying stomach down on the floor, he braced himself on one elbow and gently inserted his right hand into the cow. The entry of his arm provoked an answering strain from the animal and her muscles tightened involuntarily around his wrist. Her hooves scrabbled on the concrete floor and for a minute Alistair thought she might try to get onto her knees. But as he reassured her in a low tone, Marigold seemed to calm down, and he was able to reach deeper into her.

At length Alistair's fingers located the calf's head, its nose kinked behind the pelvic bone. "I need to lift the jaw and straighten one front leg," he muttered, resting his cheek against Marigold's damp flank and grinding his chest into the soiled straw bedding. He struggled time and again trying to force his fingers around the slippery muzzle. "Seems locked tight," he grunted as the perspiration began to trickle into his eyes. "I'm nearly beat."

"Suppose you could slip a noose of twine around its lower jaw?"

"I'll have to try something." Alistair winced. "It'd be a shame to lose the calf. Or worse, the cow."

George sprang forward. "Maybe it'd help if she changed position." With the intuition of an experienced herdsman, he jammed his kneecap against Marigold's sleek hide to one side of her backbone.

It happened then. Without warning the heifer straightened her back and offered a sudden cooperative heave giving Alistair just enough room to seize the jaw. With one strenuous jerk from his cupped hand, he lifted the calf's nose and legs into the birth canal. Alistair gave a weak smile of triumph and began to wiggle free. His rubber boots scrubbed on the floor as he withdrew his arm gingerly and rolled onto his knees. "I reckon she can do better on her own now. We'll give her a bit more time."

He tried to read George's face as he re-soaped and rinsed in the tepid water. "You realize that every day for the rest of your life will be radically altered by this one decision," he said finally, his words heavy with concern.

George handed the frayed towel to Alistair. "I've hardly thought of any-thing else." His voice sounded weary. "It's dogged me all through haying. I love my farmwork, Alistair. You know how it is, to talk to your cattle as you feed them. But every time I go to the barn and look at them, I think about being unencumbered like Jesus' apostles. It seems as if God wants more from me. And somehow, I guess I want more too." George shifted his forearms along the top of the pen. "More by having less."

Alistair detected dark circles below George's eyes and, in that instant, discerned that he had outstripped the rest of them in maturing spiritu-ally…that George's outward actions were catching up with an inward journey he'd already taken in his heart. Alistair felt the small hairs on the back of his neck prickle as he realized how foolish George's actions would appear to his acquaintances. And to his father, the height of folly.

George broke into Alistair's thoughts. "But how can people ask the Lord to save them if they've never had faith? Someone needs to show them that if they put their trust in Him, they'll never be disappointed."[5]

Alistair tossed aside an empty tea can he used to scoop oats out of a sack. "I reckon you're right," he acknowledged as he settled into the depres-sion in the top of the nearly full bag of grain. "And folks will benefit most when they can see that the faith they're hearing about is backed up by the preacher's life." He motioned for George to join him.

George dragged another sack a little closer. "Faith comes when a person listens to the message of Christ and allows God to speak to their soul. He seems to have chosen me to share this good news with others."[6]

The men fell silent as they leaned against the whitewashed stone of the stable wall. George's chest heaved with relief at having shared such a serious decision with a close friend like Alistair. A coal oil lantern, hanging from the heavy timber above, cast a dim golden glow over the two men and the red heifer. Alistair heard her laboured breathing, but there was little he could do to assist as she trembled in the pen beside them. The heifer's struggle mirrored, in a small measure, the labour and pain that would be involved as the Holy Spirit gave birth to a truly scriptural ministry.

Alistair looked over, and even in the dim light, he could see the anguish in the younger man's eyes. Alistair put his hand on George's shoulder. "I know this is difficult, George, and that you're concerned about hurting others with this news." He stopped. Words seemed so empty. Suddenly, he was reminded of George's love for Laura. There'd even been hints of marriage. Now, all of that seemed to hang in the balance. "You're very brave, George. I admire your courage and your willingness to follow the Spirit. I wish I had as strong a conviction as you have." As Alistair studied the stress lines forming on George's forehead, he ground the heel of his boot into the straw. "I wish I could help with your struggle, but there's precious little I can do." Then he added quietly, "But you can count on me to pray for you, George. I'm behind you one hundred percent."

George lifted his eyes to look steadfastly into Alistair's sober face. He knew the hardest work lay just ahead. "Thanks, Alistair," he said, barely audible. "I know I can always count on you."

Yet another hour ticked past as they talked of the spiritual union that every person desperately needs with Christ, and of individuals being transformed and rescued from a meaningless and selfish existence.

George's face lit up momentarily. "Can you visualize people in other towns getting to know Jesus just as we have?"

Alistair smiled as he tried to picture another little Sunday meeting.

"On the other hand," George continued, "how will I feel when Jesus comes back if I've hidden this treasure in a napkin, so to speak?"[7]

At length, he stood up and leaned over the side of the pen again, his eyes riveted on the straining heifer. As if on impulse, George turned back to the sack and thrust his hand deep into the loose oats. Raising a fistful he allowed the golden stream to run out between his fingers until only a single kernel rested in his narrow palm. "This one will never be more than a single seed unless it dies," he said, rolling it gently with his fingertip. "But if it dies, it'll produce lots of grain." George paused. "If a man hangs onto his life for all he's worth, he'll lose it. But if he gives it up in this world, he's promised eternal life. We can't serve Jesus without following Him."[8]

Silently, George twisted a piece of straw around his third finger and tied it in a knot. "Giving up my dream of owning a farm and getting married seems like dying to me," he confessed. "But you know, somehow I feel as if God wants to use my life as a seed so others can grow and be included in God's harvest. If I knowingly reject His call and turn aside to pursue my own dreams, do you reckon I run the risk of degenerating into a spiritual castaway?[9] Might my name be blotted out of the Book of Life?"[10]

A few minutes passed without either man saying a word. Alistair swallowed and then, in a voice trembling with feeling, said, "No, George I don't reckon that would happen. But I agree that it would be selfish to refuse to sow one's life as seed."

Instinctively, both men knelt in the passageway between the pens. Face down on the bags of grain, they prayed with silent fervour, pleading for God to use their lives. When George stood up again, tears streamed down his face. He wiped his eyes with the back of his hand and slumped back onto the sack. Staring up at the dusty lantern through blurred eyes, a slight movement on the beam caught his attention. He blinked, then gave a droll grin at the sharp face and beady eyes inspecting him from the shadow above the lantern's hood. When Alistair rose, fumbled in his pocket for his handkerchief, and blew his nose, the mouse rustled into the darkness.

An insistent grunt summoned Alistair to the pen, and shoving the gate ajar, he stepped over Marigold's outstretched legs. When he crouched down again to examine the expectant mother in the faint light, he saw a pair of soft cloven hoofs already presenting themselves. "Push hard, girl," he urged as he patted her heaving side. "It's nearly over. A couple of good shoves and you'll be done." Alistair reached down, wrapped the slippery forelegs with a burlap sack and tugged until a nose appeared. But then the cow relaxed and the tiny head withdrew from the dim outside world. Marigold's brown eyes stared at the wall for several moments before her bulging abdomen contracted in one prolonged push and forced the gasping calf onto the hard floor. After clearing its nostrils, Alistair rubbed the calf briskly with the dry sack, and within minutes, the wide-eyed newborn lifted its head and struggled to stand up. Marigold, already back on her feet, craned her neck, let out a soft bellow, and began to lick the shaky calf with long coarse strokes. Alistair wrapped one arm around the bull calf's supple body and guided its mouth to the taut udder. Before the men left the barn, the new mother was feeding her offspring its first swallows of warm milk.

After Alistair secured the barn door, the men walked in the shadowy darkness to the narrow gate leading to the house. George's white horse stood tethered nearby, and they could hear it ripping off and chewing blades of grass. At the sound of George's voice, it paused to give a muffled nicker through the gloom. Alistair looked up to see a beeswax candle sitting on the upstairs windowsill where Priscilla was preparing for bed. *Even a candle,* he thought, *must accept the flame and allow itself to be consumed in order to give light to the house.* "It's late, George," he spoke up. "Why not sleep here tonight and leave for home in the morning?"

"Thanks, Alistair, but I'd better be on my way." Then almost as an after-thought, he added, "I know you'll keep this to yourself for the time being. I want to talk to Laura first…" His voice trailed off into the night.

Alistair nodded and put his arm across George's shoulder in the dark-ness. "It's just between you and me," he assured him in a voice thick with emotion. "Goodnight, George. Safe home."

Bright stars twinkled overhead and a light mist lay in the hollows. As George rode along in the cool night air, the sound of croaking frogs and the damp smell of the cedar swamps overtook his senses. Coal oil lamps flickered in the windows of the farm homes he passed at first, but after an hour or more, all was dark as the countryside slept. His mind throbbed with questions that only God could answer. He felt uneasy, a little scared even as his heart alternately pounded and slowed—like a runner's at the start of a race. But in spite of his natural uncertainty, he felt the peace that comes from total acceptance of whatever God plans—so much to let go of, but so much more to reach toward.

Exhausted, George went straight to bed, but he tossed and turned. When he finally did doze off, he slept fitfully. He had been asleep only a few hours when he woke up sweating, his face warm from the bright sun shining in his open window. He could hear the cows bawling in the barnyard as they waited to be fed and milked. Pulling on his overalls and smock, he hur-ried out to the stable. As he went about his chores, he suddenly realized how tedious they seemed—feeding and milking, morning and evening, feeding and milking, morning and evening. Harvesting grain that he would never use himself seemed less meaningful now than it had a few weeks ear-lier. Still, he needed to keep at the work until he could tidy up his affairs and distribute the belongings God had given him.

But what about Laura? The thought of a life without her tore George apart. No matter how hard he resisted, images of her forced their way back into his thoughts and dreams: her voice bantering with Timothy or Malachi, her dainty cotton waists swinging on the clothesline with sleeves billowed in the wind, the lavish summer flowers she picked and propped up in the big cream jug. For days the inner conflict raged and he prayed desperately to know what path he should take.

One hot afternoon during harvest, as George stooked oats alone at the edge of his backfield, his emotions finally overwhelmed him. Knowing he couldn't fight any more, he staggered toward the fence now and leaned over the top rail, burying his face in his hands. He cried, heartbroken, aching inside as he thought of Laura—her eyes, her hands, her hair.

If he asked her, he felt certain that she would marry him and go along with him. But as far as he knew, she had never been called by God into this kind of homeless ministry. And even if she did choose to go with him now, would that be for the best? It would be perfectly natural for her to want to have children before long. But how would that be possible if he never intended to have a home? Any woman, even Laura, might become resentful of his constant devotion to others—particularly if it stood in the way of having her own family and home. His promise to dedicate his entire life to traveling and preaching would almost certainly be threatened then.

It wouldn't be fair, George reasoned, to Laura or to any children they might have. It's one thing for a fellow to follow God's call into a life of voluntary poverty, but it's another issue altogether to invite someone else to share such a life just because she loves him.

In mid-August, Laura returned with Phoebe on the afternoon train from Stratford to stay with Alistair and Priscilla for the last two weeks of the summer. The day after Laura's arrival, George hastened across the township to Wood Creek Farm. Unlike his usual visits on horseback, this time he had borrowed his father's buggy and packed a wicker lunch hamper along with a red chequered tablecloth and woolen blanket.

After tethering his horse to Alistair's gate, George hurried into the kitchen. "G'day, Priscilla," he greeted her distractedly. "It's a lovely day."

"George, what a surprise!" Priscilla said turning, her jam ladle in the air. Then she gave George a knowing wink. "I guess you're looking for someone special. She's in the garden, getting rid of some pesky bugs."

George leaned against the icebox in a deceptively casual stance. "What's Alistair busy at today?"

"He and Timothy went to help Bill cradle grain in a couple of fields that are too hilly for the binder. I don't expect them back until sundown."

Priscilla knew something was on George's mind when he walked right by a fresh batch of raisin cookies cooling on the kitchen table. It wasn't like George not to notice warm cookies.

He found Phoebe and Laura shaking potato bugs off the plants and into a shallow pan with a little kerosene in the bottom. His shadow fell across the row before the girls were aware of him. Startled, Laura glanced up, high colour rushing to her cheeks as a momentary shyness wrung her.

Phoebe leaned back on her bare heels and squinted against the sun. "What are you doing here, George?" she blurted out, her voice shrill with girlish innocence.

George blushed a scalding red. "I've come to take Laura on a picnic," he mumbled, his voice strained, his expression faraway.

Phoebe's eyes roved from one face to another. When no invitation to join them was forthcoming, she turned in mock resignation to the potato bugs. Catching George's eye, Laura ran upstairs to comb her hair and change into her green organdy dress. After splashing cold water on her flushed face, she glanced in the dresser mirror and recognized the soft sheen of giddy excitement. What could be important enough for George to arrange a surprise picnic in midmorning when most farmers were hard at work? *But,* she decided with a smile, *it's foolish to guess that this might be George's way of proposing. That'll come in its proper time.* Meanwhile, she was elated as she climbed up into the buggy and slipped onto the seat beside him for the six-mile ride to their favourite picnic spot at Doyle's Mill. Her cheeks were pink with pleasure as she glanced up at the cottony clouds drifting across a blue sky into the face of the morning sun.

Laura unloaded the picnic basket and stood waiting while George unhitched the horse and tethered it to a black cherry tree. A path led around the crest of a knoll where wild flowers bloomed among the orchard grass and the meadow blazed with red and yellow paintbrush and purple vetch. After spreading out the blanket in the shade of a weeping willow, they sat beside the pond and watched the stream cascading over the water wheel at the end of the millrace. The field stones in the mill wall glowed with mineral lustre, and here and there a speck of granite gleamed in the sun.

Leaning against George, Laura suddenly raised her hand, pointing across the water. "Look, George, there's a blue heron...fishing." Not waiting for a response she chattered on about the superb surroundings. "George," she said, her curiosity finally getting the best of her, "this is lovely. I'm both surprised and flattered that you took the day off to be with me when it's such fine weather for harvesting."

Praying silently for wisdom and courage, George could feel the blood draining from his face and a tiny muscle trembling in his cheek.

"What's *wrong*, George?" Laura asked anxiously. She probed his features in alarm. "Are you sick?"

"No, Laura. I'm not sick. But I have something I must tell you." George's voice was flat and grim.

"Does it have to do with us?" Laura asked, her heart racing.

"Yes, it does." George looked down at the grass and took a deep breath before plunging ahead. "Laura, the truth of the matter is I've decided to become an itinerant preacher. For quite a while now I've had an aching feeling that just won't go away. I'm sure it's God calling me."

Laura waited, her face perplexed.

"I'll have to sell my farm and all my things," he continued, his voice sad, apologetic. "I always thought I would pay down the mortgage so I'd have a home for the two of us. But for now, I feel that I need to stay single, like the apostle Paul, so I can go where God leads me."

The words struck Laura like a blow. Her breath caught in her throat as she realized George's future plans did not include marriage. Not to her, not to anyone. George was not asking her to marry him. He was telling her things between them, understandings, glances, hopes, were over.

Although she tried valiantly to control her emotions, she couldn't stop her lower lip from quivering as she sat in numb silence.

"Laura, say something, please." George's voice sounded heart-struck as it reached out to her.

"George, I'll go wherever you want me to," she pleaded, hopeful eyes rising to catch his response. "We could still be married." Tears began to course down her cheeks.

"I know, my sweetheart. But I just *can't* do that now. Forgive me."

Laura's pretty face, like an upturned flower, visibly wilted in the anguish of rejection. She sobbed, heartbroken, as the reality set in that George intended to remain single.

George, feeling horrible misgivings, cried too. Tears covered his face as he gently wrapped his arms around her shaking body, rocking her to and fro in a gesture as old as instinct itself. Her slim shoulders were hunched as he put his cheek against her face and held her tight. He could feel her long eyelashes wet against his skin. Even though he was now sitting still, his chest heaved and patches of sweat broke through his shirt.

"I love you more than you'll ever know, Laura," he whispered hoarsely. "I always will." He hesitated, biting hard on his upper lip. "But I can't escape God's call to take the gospel to perishing men and women."

"But where does that leave me, George?" She wrenched away from him and turned toward the meadow, its beauty suddenly faded.

Laura's arms tightened around her legs as she pressed her forehead against her bent knees, tears soaking through her long dress. Waves of anger taunted her mind and she wanted to lash out at George. What about all the promises you made me? Don't they count for anything? I've waited three years and now in three minutes you tell me it's over. But she bit her lip and held her peace.

After a while, Laura's eyes searched George's face and her voice rose uncertainly above the sound of the foaming mill race. "When Abigail was married, I helped her get settled and put out all her pretty things—her hem-stitched linen and doilies and Grandma Chapelton's tea service. When she'd been a wife a fortnight, it was as if she'd always been married…And I was letting myself hope…" Laura swallowed the words she couldn't say.

At length she tried again. "George, I can't bear a future apart from you. Would I ever see you if your home's gone and you're away traveling?"

"Sweetheart, you can *never* be out of my heart and thoughts. I want you to feel my loving concern for you—always." The tenderness in George's voice defied the emotional constraint of his upbringing.

Laura's response to this declaration was a fresh burst of tears. When she turned to George again, she could tell by his sunken eyes that he was hurting as much as she was. Languishing in long spells of silence, they talked only now and then, and by three o'clock their words had been carried away on the summer air. When Laura rose to her knees in what seemed to George a supplicating gesture, he looked up to read her expression.

Clasping her hands, she leaned forward. "It's getting along in the afternoon," she said softly, her voice not far from tears. "I've never walked the far bank of the millrace, and I fancy seeing it from the other side."

George reached for his cap and bounded to his feet. "Sounds a good plan," he said, eager to dispel the cloud of melancholy. But Laura stood rigid, impassive as he held out his hand. In her graceful dress that blended with the hues of summer, she seemed, momentarily at least, far removed from him. Nothing about her had changed, yet he sensed a mysterious guardedness. Had he lost the loving trust she'd always shown him?

"It's just by myself I want to walk," she protested, turning a troubled face on George. "I need some time to wander alone, to think over what you've told me…I'll be back after a bit."

Intuition warned George to relent and retreat. His searching eyes watched Laura's figure grow smaller until she rounded a curve and disappeared through the untamed swale grass along the river.

For a time George entertained himself, eating some buttered bread, checking the horse, and tossing twigs into the water. Finally, glancing at his pocket watch, he saw with alarm that an hour had passed. As the moments dragged on, George, caught in a swirl of conflicting emotions, wrapped his arms around his bent knees and breathed a prayer for Laura's understanding and well-being. The second hour without any sign of her more than tried his patience as he huddled enmeshed in a paralysis of will and emotion.

When day waned into late afternoon and cooler air currents rose from the water wheel, George began to shiver. Each beat of his heart seemed to last an unbearable moment. Had Laura been so distraught that she slipped or lost her footing on the uneven bank? George stood up and paced in front of the massive trunk, his wistful eyes alert for her return. Misgiving assailed him as he recalled how her girlish laughter and chatter had so suddenly been silenced by his words. Torn between his desire to honour her wish and his need to know she was safe, George clenched his fists. Across the pond, he could see the master of the mill locking the oak doors while his bluff and hearty laughter echoed across the yard. A covey of white geese scattered before the departing mill hands. It was supper time…

Laura, in the meantime, had wandered from Doyle's Mill among the patriarchal willows whose fronds swept the mounded bank. Between their trunks she scarcely saw the yellow fields that rolled in waves to meet the blue of the summer sky or the sun-dappled clouds that rose in stately palaces on the southern horizon. In her mind she understood, she saw it all—George's passion to serve God and his love for her. Strangely, the two forces were at odds. As Laura pursued her pathless rambling, the turbulent currents and shoals gave way at length to smooth untroubled water, and by the time the arching crests of the willows on the far bank had cut into the sun's slanting rays, her first flash of bitterness had faded.

When at last George spied Laura emerging from the goldenrod, her hat swinging on her arm, he ran to meet her. With wordless empathy he gathered her to him, his beard brushing her satin cheek. Only after a few minutes did Laura pull back slightly and whisper, "The sun's getting low, George. Let's gather the picnic things. It'll be dark by the time we get home, and they'll be expecting us."

The shadows began to stretch across the dark water as they packed their things. The wicker basket on her arm, Laura glanced wistfully at the flattened grass while George shook out the crumbs and folded the blanket. Although they gripped each other's hands as the white horse trotted home, for the first time, a shadow of uncertainty fell across Laura's heart.

After turning into the gate at Wood Creek Farm, George pulled up short under the rustling maples. He leaned over and squeezed Laura tightly before helping her alight from the buggy. "Laura, my girl, I love you. You'll always be my dearest friend—the *only* lady of my life." His eyes met hers as she hesitated by the front wheel.

Laura forced a wan smile. "Goodnight," she managed in a choked voice, turning away from the conciliatory kiss that hovered on his lips.

George drew back. "I'll see you Thursday, for sure…"

Knowing her eyes would be red and puffy, Laura slipped in through the parlour door and headed for the staircase. She felt tired and hurried straight to her bedroom to nurse a headache. Closing the door behind her, she flung herself across the bed and buried her face in the pillow. The house at Wood Creek Farm had witnessed the full range of human utterance from the cries of birth to the groans of death. But until tonight its walls had never heard the suffocating, nearly soundless sobs of a woman as she tried to relinquish her first love. Priscilla, alarmed and distressed, paced the upstairs hall with a candle but instinct warned her not to intrude upon the little room nor to question Laura's unspoken suffering.

George rode on through the suddenly darkened landscape where the fields and lanes lay in the melancholy light of evening. As his afternoon with Laura kept flashing across his inner vision, he agonized that he had made a colossal blunder. Like bread beyond reach of a starving man, his hapless remembrance of Gertie and Randall rose up before him, mocking his self-denial. Surely God's call was not intended to deny him the treasure of a wife, the hopes for a family, and the sweet joys granted to other men. Yet he had read somewhere that shared grief was as intense an experience as shared ecstasy, and he knew by instinct that any true bond was incomplete without both of these. Now, for the first time, he and Laura were bound together in pain. Over the dark hours of a sleepless night, George came to acknowledge that he could love Laura just as deeply as before, even if their love remained sacred and untouched by the imprint of earthly desires. With this conviction and with the twittering of the first birds of dawn, George slid face down onto the hard rocks of sleep.

~⌐

At the close of the Thursday meeting, George raised a hand. "Could I just say a word?" Everyone relaxed back in their chairs, waiting for him to continue. Only Alistair and Laura had any idea of what was coming.

George leaned forward, fingers splayed on his knees. "Back in the spring we sat around this circle and talked about the New Testament ministry— as best we could tell. Well, you know, it's been hounding me ever since— that I should actually be doing something about it. I tried my level best to shrug the notion off, but it keeps haunting me." When George looked up he saw a ring of faces, each a study of frozen concentration. "Finally, I realized that God was speaking to me, troubling me…" George's voice cracked as he struggled to share his deepest feelings with the people he loved so much. With a final sigh, he choked, "Well, the long and short of it is, I plan to sell my farm and become an itinerant minister. The part that hurts most is that it'll take me away from the people dearest to my heart—all of you." George half turned and placed his hand on Laura's shoulder. "And Laura."

Beside him, Laura could feel his tension. Her own heart pounded as she tried to concentrate on George's words, afraid she might burst out crying once again. On Laura's left, Priscilla impulsively grasped her hand.

Across the room, Stephen silently grappled with George's words while beside him Emily's eyes widened in alarm. Her arms blossomed with goose bumps as her thin hand instinctively found its way into the comfort of Stephen's muscular grip. Her delicate complexion creased and tears began to streak down her pale cheeks as she glanced at Laura's downcast head. Beside her Emily felt Stephen shudder, and his breath sounded raw.

The room sat silent for a moment. "Does that mean you wouldn't be here for our meetings?" Bill finally asked in a husky voice.

George scanned the glazed reactions. "I just don't know where this will all lead to," he admitted, "but probably not."

As the weight of this monumental decision fell, its bittersweet implication infused the parlour. George's overflowing love and compassion for seeking souls carried a cost the others could barely comprehend. Spontaneously they all stood and gathered in a close circle around George as he embraced Laura. Priscilla began to sing and others soon joined in:

> There is no gain but by a loss:
> Thus Jesus taught, who bore the cross;
> A corn of wheat, to multiply,
> Must fall into the ground and die;
> Oh, should a soul alone remain,
> When it a hundredfold may gain?
>
> Wherever you ripe fields behold,
> Waving to God their sheaves of gold,
> Be sure some corn of wheat has died,
> Some faithful life been crucified;
> Someone has suffered, wept and prayed,
> And fought hell's legions undismayed.[11]

George's next step was to inform his parents, hardworking farm people who had been born, raised, and married not more than eight miles from their home. The following evening his father pulled up at the head of the long table, his mother on one side and George opposite. George glanced at the three empty chairs where his siblings had once taken their places.

Arthur, George's older brother, worked at the Raymond Sewing Machine Company and had married Olga, a German girl from Berlin, twelve miles to the west. She always fussed over George, preparing one of his favourites, a kettle of sauerkraut and pork hocks, when he stopped by their quaint frame cottage. Their two boys clamoured until Uncle George hauled them back and forth along the wooden sidewalk in their red wagon.

His sister, Lizzie, had married the Guelph lamplighter who, from his one-horse wagon laden with barrels of coal oil, filled the lamps along the city streets. He lit the lamps before dusk and let them burn until midnight.

And Cyril. George was glad his bachelor brother was away tonight at a meeting of the Aberfoyle Fair board. For now, he could only bear the weight of telling his parents, and he wanted to be alone with them.

During supper George played over the scene at Wood Creek Farm the previous evening, sensing tonight's task would not go as smoothly. After the meal he helped his mother clear the dishes, stacking them at one end of the table. After dipping a pan of steaming water from the reservoir of the Findlay Oval, he slid it onto the table beside the supper dishes. His mother washed and he dried while his father rocked in his chair beside the firebox, engrossed in the *Daily Herald*. Their old tabby, Miss Orangey Morangey, lay stretched out full-length on the linoleum floor behind the stove.

The candle above the wash counter flickered slightly as George braced himself. He hated to upset his folks. Children of any age, he knew, had the power to bring the greatest joy and the deepest sorrow to their parents. Still, God was leading and he had to follow, even if they couldn't understand.

Focusing on the white china plate in his hands, he drew in a deep breath. "There's something I need to tell you both," he began. "I've decided to sell my farm and go out to preach the gospel."

Neither of his parents spoke. George heard his dad snort and looked up to see the anger on his face. His mother let out a slow measured breath.

"You, a *preacher?* Have you taken leave of your senses?" George's father scoffed. "You've never been to college."

George encountered his father's eyes, weighing the benefit of an explanation. "Dad, the New Testament preachers never went to college. Jesus called them to spend time with Him, to learn His ways. Afterwards He sent them out to preach—"[12]

"I'm not for meddling with snakes of any stripe. They're all out of the same nest."

George winced like a soft-eyed hound that had been kicked in the ribs, its wind gone. Years ago, his father had been in a fight with a minister who had refused to bury George's grandfather in the church cemetery because the old man had spoken openly against the practice of tithing. George's father had been so furious that he had vowed never to darken the door of a church again. And the Farnham disposition was known to have a streak as unyielding as granite. Despite her husband's embittered resolve, George's mother attended the church in Arkell regularly.

All the ministers whom George's parents knew had studied at a theological seminary where it was possible to become an academic and to learn about Jesus without ever actually experiencing Him. Indeed, the clergyman who had offended George's father at the cemetery gates had been a brilliant graduate of this system—able to debate the most subtle questions of doctrine or the finest points of ethics, yet he seemingly lacked any compelling desire to adopt and practice such principles.

George, on the other hand, concluded that Jesus drew men to Himself rather like apprentices, teaching them in real-life experiences. Over time an indentured apprentice would develop an affinity for his master's trade. As the disciples listened and watched, they, too, grew to love Jesus and His work before setting out to share the good news of His kingdom. Like all apprentices, their failures taught them to depend more on their Master.[13]

More than once that year, George had tried to tell his father about his newfound understanding. "I'm not interested in religion," had been his father's brusque retort. And that was that. He brushed George's comments off like a horse switching its tail at a bothersome fly. But now it was going to affect his life, and that made all the difference.

George struggled to share his vision of a New Testament preacher. "The disciples learned by seeing the love and compassion that Jesus modeled in ordinary circumstances," he began, "the same practical way an apprentice works alongside a master carpenter. Over the past two years, I feel like Jesus has been building a house of faith before my eyes. Now I need to tell others what it is that I've witnessed."

As George's story unfolded, his father's jaw hardened and his eyes raked the room. "That's the most scatterbrained idea I've ever heard," he shouted. "You've worked your fingers to the bone to pay down the mortgage on that farm, and now you're going to throw it all away. It's the most idiotic malarkey I've ever heard."

"I know this doesn't add up in your books," George interjected.

Scarlet-faced, his father spewed his words with venom. "That stupid Jack Gillan. I've no idea why he comes loafing around your place anyway. Hasn't he got better things to do than wander around the township blathering on about religion and putting crazy ideas into your head? He'd be doing some good if he bought a farm and made something of himself."

Mr. Farnham smouldered. "And Stanhope. He's a man of fifty, you say. By that age a man of any account would set his sights on passing something worthwhile along to the next generation, not baiting people with pie in the sky." He cast a withering glance at George's bowed head. "I've heard about Malachi Jackson for years too, the old sot. They say he hasn't got the brains of a louse. I wouldn't want to be caught dead in the same yard as the man. Who knows what folks might take from it?" His tirade ranted on, reducing the McElderry clan to charred cinders.

"You don't know one of them firsthand," George countered weakly.

"No! And I don't know why you'd fall in with a dizzy bunch like that either. We reared you better 'n that. You owe it to your mother and me to straighten up and get back in the harness."

When George failed to reply, his father jumped to his feet. "There's no point in wasting my breath," he said sarcastically. "I can see you won't hear common sense. Maybe starvation'll teach you a thing or two. Have you thought about that?" Yanking on his boots, he stormed out of the house.

Alone now with his mother, George opened up, telling her more about his hopes and outlining the itinerancy of the New Testament ministers.

"I want you to be happy, George," she said, straining to understand and accept. "But where will you stay at night?" Her voice was laced with concern. "And what if you get sick and don't know anybody?"

"Mum, I could get sick and die right here at home. Besides, I trust in God. He'll care for me."

"That's fine in principle, but I've seen too many disasters. God takes care of folks who mind themselves. This whole thing worries me sick."

George raised sad eyes. "I love you, Mum," he assured her. "You've bent over backward to take good care of me since I was a little boy. It makes me feel bad to think of you worrying about me now." He stood up and walked to his mother, putting his hand on her shoulder. "What can I say to relieve your concerns, Mum?"

"Nothing, George. It's just part of being a mother." She sat on the chair by the china cabinet, her hand cradling her forehead in mute appeal.

Across the room, Miss Orangey Morangey opened her eyes and stood up, extending her hind legs and back into a protracted stretch. Then, after licking her front legs and raking a block of firewood with her claws, she strolled under the kitchen table and sprang onto Mrs. Farnham's lap. The sudden action seemed to arrest the older woman's downward spiral, and she looked up at George. "What about Laura?" she questioned, her tone softening. Secretly, she had looked forward to having Laura as her daughter-in-law. After boarding with them for three years, she was like a second daughter. "It's not natural for a man to remain single, George."

"It's not that I don't want to marry Laura," George said quietly. "I do, far more than you can imagine. But I feel that God is wanting me to stay single for the sake of the kingdom of heaven."[14]

His mother's troubled look darkened. "The whole idea seems strange."

"The gift of singleness isn't for everybody, Mum. Only for those who are able to accept it."

After talking with his mother for over an hour in the kitchen, George decided it best to leave before his father returned from the barn. As he turned to go, his mother reached out and laid a careworn hand on his arm. "Please, George, don't do it. Just for me."

The raw desperation in her voice broke his heart. He bowed his head and sighed. "I'm sorry, Mother. I have no choice."

Walking sadly down the long lane, George moved with the gait of an older man, his head bent forward. He barely noticed the first leaves of autumn that had detached themselves from the overhead branches and were swaying to the ground around him. As he trudged along, he remembered Jesus saying that He hadn't come to bring peace to the earth, but a sword. He would set a man against his father, a daughter against her mother, and a man's enemies might well be those of his own household. "Anyone," George sighed, "who loves his father or mother more than Jesus and does not take his cross and follow Him is not worthy of Him."[15]

Eleven

GIVING EVERYTHING TO THE POOR
Fall 1900

One November evening as George's neighbour, Jake Pillman, lumbered up the narrow lane, he detected the scent of burning pine mingled with the eerie fog that shrouded George's farm. A short, squat fellow whose suspenders often strained with loud guffaws, Jake resembled his biblical namesake in one respect only: He was the proud father of a flourishing tribe of twelve children. Six strapping sons bristling with ambition had each been set up with land to call their own, and if their acres were not in fact patrilineal, they were the next thing to it. After Jake had acquired the adjoining Pocklington farm to the east, and shystered a deal to get the Beaver place to the north, his neighbours had begun to refer to him as "Tent Peg Pillman"—owing to his shrewd negotiations in extending his holdings. Tonight, catching sight of a puff of smoke from George's kitchen chimney and the ruddy glow of a lamp in the window, Jake smiled to himself. His hefty legs stumped up the porch steps, and he pounded on the side door.

Jumping up from his half-eaten supper, George hurried to answer the unrelenting knock. Startled to find his neighbour waiting in the darkness, he offered a greeting. "How're you faring, Jake? I'm surprised to see you before milking. Come in and have a chair."

Jake spat his plug of chewing tobacco into a honeysuckle bush beside the porch. "Naw, I can't stay," he declared, as he sprawled against the door frame. A grin spread across his heavy jowls. "Recollect, George, I've my nine oldest married off, and all thrivin'. What you prob'ly don't know is my two youngest fellows both got their eyes on two lovely lasses, Gertie and Floss," he announced proudly. "The pair of 'em's been courtin' for months. They'll be hitched before winter's over 'n one of them'll need another place to live. 'Course, the youngest gets the home place. Soon's I heard the rumour you're sellin', I skinned right over to see if it's true."

"True enough," George said, an odd edge on his voice.

Jake puffed out his chest. "Neither of 'em girls is a day over sixteen. That's how to do it, I always say. Get 'em young and train 'em up. A well-trained woman and a hundert good acres. So I'd be mighty glad to get yours, George, for one of my lads. My Randall can carry on a fine family tradition on yer acres, seein' as how you can't. The old woman 'n me, we agree it'll not be hard to see our last two young fellows set up with a wife apiece, and a pair of 'em as ain't too hard on the eyes neither…"

Jake's eyes gleamed. "So, George, what'll you take fer the place?"

George slid his right hand inside the front of his smock and leaned forward. "The Neil Black place on the next line sold last summer for fifty-four hundred," he began. "This set of buildings is in far better repair, but I'd like to wind things up quickly. How about four thousand, Jake?"

"Twenty-seven hundert," his neighbour broke in. "Remember, the swamp's not drained."

George looked beyond Jake to his freshly painted barn doors. "I'm sorry," he said, his tone resolute, "but I guess I'll need to ask around a bit. Maybe somebody else'll take a notion of it."

The neighbour shifted from one foot to the other and stroked his short chin. He had hoped to bend George's eagerness to sell to his advantage, but clearly he'd miscalculated. "Well…it is a good piece o' land" he muttered, grasping for a way to save face. His eyes darted around George's well-kept kitchen. "And you've got it all set up so's a woman could move right in. I can picture my Randall and his missus bein' real happy in yer house." He ran his grubby fingers over his gray stubble as if assessing a crop about to be taken off. "If you'll throw in yer team of horses, we'll call it a deal."

George swallowed hard, remembering how he and Laura had spent a Saturday gaily mixing flour paste and hanging the wallpaper in this kitchen. Their laughter and tomfoolery came back to him now as he recalled how the first roll, bulging with paste, had unfurled and flopped back over Laura's chestnut tresses. When Jake ran an appraising hand down the door moulding, George snapped back to the present. Then, setting his jaw, he extended his right hand to Jake, sealing the transaction in silence. The farm would change hands on December first.

George invited his family and a few close friends to choose any items of special interest before the auction. When his dad refused to come, he helped his mother carry home the family effects she wanted. And in that week's mail, Emily received a short pathetic note, the contents of which had puzzled her. But her womanly intuition directed her to wrap up a con-voluted parcel and put it in the mail to Laura. It contained the log-cabin quilt and goose-feather pillow off George's bed. Emily instinctively knew that Laura would not want someone else sleeping on George's pillow.

The local auctioneer arrived early one Saturday morning in the middle of November to sell the rest of the animals, tools, and household effects. George stood watching as strangers bid on his broad axe, his adze, his prize Hereford bull, his spool bed, and a variety of other possessions. *It's like a dream,* George thought, *or like watching my life through the eyes of someone else.* He remembered searching for, bargaining over, and buying each of these items. At the time they had seemed so important. Now they were only encumbrances—and of no further interest to him.

On December first, George rode into Guelph to meet Mr. McMillan, the senior partner in the McMillan and Dunbar Law Office, to pick up the certified cheque from the closing of his farm. From there he went to deposit the funds at the Canadian Bank of Commerce, a solid stone struc-ture with arched windows overlooking St. George's Square.

Heading for the teller's wicket, George could see Morgan out of the corner of his eye as the assistant manager sat at his desk, head down over a stack of lined ledger sheets. At that moment, Morgan, glancing around for a file, noticed George and beckoned him over with a friendly nod.

"This is a momentous day," he observed as he drew George a chair.

George nodded, his Adam's apple bobbing up and down. "It sure feels strange to have all my earthly possessions in a single travel bag," he admitted. "I dropped it off at Alistair's last evening. In fact, it's his dapple gray I'm riding today." He paused, suddenly thoughtful. "But in a way, it's a mar-vellous release." George eased back into the oak chair. "All the responsi-bilities attached to settled life are gone. No animals. No chores."

"I can't help but envy you, George. I've been trying to cut back but still I'm chained to this ball." Morgan tapped the desk with his knuckles. "You, on the other hand, have freed yourself totally for God's work."

George smiled, feeling the warm wash of peace that comes from letting go. His eyes met Morgan's. "It was God who freed me," he said. "In fact, He pried me loose. And your turn'll come too if that's what He has in mind." He drew the certified cheque out of his pocket and flattened it on the desk. "Hard to imagine that a little piece of paper can represent years of milking cows, getting up in the middle of the night with sows that are farrowing, forking sheaves until your shirt's sopping wet..."

Morgan ran the cheque between his long fingers. "I enter hundreds of these every week, but I hardly ever think of the toil they stand for." Turning it over, he scrawled "for deposit only" and pushed it back for George's endorsement. "So what type of investment would you like to place this in?"

"I don't want an investment. I just want the money in a bank account."

Morgan looked surprised. "But an investment pays better interest."

"That may be, but an investment strikes me as being like a farm. Something that's not part of the New Testament ministry."

Morgan's fingers drifted to the port wine birthmark as he mulled over George's words. "At the bank here, we consider a savings account to be as much an asset as anything else, " he offered tentatively.

George eyes widened. "I hadn't thought of that," he conceded. "I'll need to chew that over for a day or two."

Riding along the road to Alistair's, George puzzled about his motives for keeping a bank account. *Surely Jesus and His disciples owned no such thing*, he mused. *All they possessed in the bag Judas carried were a few coins to buy the day's bread.*

Drained from the day's events, George wanted to spend the evening quietly with God. After checking with Priscilla about breakfast time, he climbed the steep stairs to the attic room where he had stayed many times before. On those occasions he had always known that soon he would be in his own familiar bed again—but not tonight. He looked around. Nothing had changed. And yet it felt different now that he had no place to call his own.

The tiny room had a white sloped ceiling with a rough plaster finish and a four-pane window facing east. The walls were painted soft green, and the pine plank floor had been worn smooth over the last forty years. It was a modest room with a wooden table, a straight chair, and two single beds covered with patchwork quilts. Tucked discreetly under the edge of one bed sat a white porcelain chamber pot.

As George adjusted the wick and lit the coal oil lamp, he thought of Laura. Her face, her eyes, her elegant French braid came vividly before him in the hazy kerosene glow, like the ever-present genie of the lamp in his boyhood tales. He felt a wistful melancholy knowing that this had been her room last summer. Since the recent events that had spelled an end to their future together, Laura wrote to George often—letters that concealed the heartbreak between the lines. Still, she seemed to be accepting of the sudden turn of events and encouraged him to trust God's leading. George prayed for her daily, and he felt certain that she was doing the same for him.

Kneeling on the hooked rug at the side of the bed, George stretched his forearms across the mattress, his face pressed against the log cabin pattern. Below him, he heard muted household sounds—the cellar hatch banging shut for the night and the rattling of stove grates. For a couple of minutes George drew slow deep breaths, mindful of God as he forced the distractions aside. "Dear Father, I'm thankful that You hear each earnest prayer. Help me to forsake all, and direct my next steps, wherever they may lead. Grant me the grace to conduct myself in a godly way in other folk's homes. May I feel the closeness of Your presence as I follow the long succession of men who, through the ages, were described simply as Your *servants*.[1] These favours I ask in the name of Jesus. Amen."

A strange feeling crept over him as he dropped off to sleep in the little attic room. He owned nothing and yet had everything he needed. Each member of the little church had made it clear that their homes were to be his home from this day forward. In many ways he felt closer to these believers than to his own sister and brothers. He recalled the apostle Peter speaking for every itinerant preacher when he asked: We have left everything and followed You. What will we get out of it? George was beginning to understand Jesus' answer: Everyone who has left home or lands, brothers or sisters, mother or father, wife or children, for My sake and the gospel's will receive a hundred times as many in this present age. And in the age to come, eternal life.[2]

Long before daylight, George awoke with a start. His heart was pounding, and for a moment he didn't know where he was. Before the sun appeared on the eastern horizon, he knelt to pray again and found comfort. The first light of dawn seemed to renew God's promises. As he looked out the window, a line of Scripture presented itself to his consciousness: Sell whatever thou hast, and give to the poor, and thou shalt have treasure in heaven: and come, take up the cross, and follow me.[3]

Give to the poor. *Give to the poor.* The words drummed in his mind. He'd been so intent on selling and following that he'd overlooked the giving part.

George sat on the bed again and listened to the routines of a home that was not his own. He heard Alistair get up and go down the creaky stairs. The lids on the stove rattled as he lit the kindling. The door slammed when Alistair went outside to fetch a pail of water. Then, after setting the kettle on the stove top, he went to feed the livestock.

Upstairs, Priscilla snuggled in bed until she heard the kettle begin to whistle. Then she stretched, yawned, and got up to start breakfast.

Alistair had not yet returned from the barn when George came downstairs, smelling fresh coffee and frying bacon. When Priscilla caught a glimpse of Alistair coming from the barn, a pail of warm milk in his hand, she ladled out hot oatmeal and set it on the table with cream, brown sugar, blackstrap molasses, and maple syrup. The porridge was followed by soft-boiled eggs, bacon, and toast with strawberry jam.

In the weeks prior to selling his farm, George had wondered what activity would fill his days without his own chores. But now, on his first free day, he turned to Alistair. "I hope to go to town today, but I was wondering if you could find a job for an able-bodied fellow this forenoon."

Alistair rocked his mug on the table. "George, I don't want you to feel like you need to earn your keep when you're bunking in here. You're in God's service now, and it's our pleasure to support that work."

George smiled. "Thanks. But I'm still feeling my way about how to use my time," he admitted. "It isn't easy to know what God has in mind."

Alistair nodded. "Some of the bottom boards on the cow stalls are rotting out, and I'm going to replace them. Timothy's planning to clean out pens and sprinkle them with lime. We've got a dose of the scours in that new litter of pigs, and we need to nip it in the bud. Anyway, we'd be happy for your help."

"Sounds good," George said. "I'd like to help Priscilla clean up, and then I'll be right along."

After breakfast, Alistair and Timothy pulled on their smocks and left for the barn while George dried the dishes. He suspected this small token of his appreciation would not only become his lifelong habit as a guest in someone else's home, but might give him a splendid opportunity to listen and learn from others' experiences. Most people, he knew, found it strange for a man to help in the kitchen, but it felt right, so he did it anyway.

After the last dish was put away, George went out to help Alistair. Afterward he saddled the mare and set out for Guelph. He'd had little contact with destitute people in the past, but he wanted desperately to obey his calling and give what he had to the poor.

After George left Alistair's dapple gray at the livery stable, he walked toward Carden Street. He knew a few people lived in squalor farther along the Grand Trunk Railway tracks. Stepping over the steel rails, he strode along the cinder-strewn railway bed, surveying the area beyond. After a few minutes he came to a dozen or so tiny shacks huddled on a sandy knoll where the land was driest. A knot of ragtag boys, digging pointed sticks into the freezing mud, turned to stare at him. When a mangy dog bristled and bounded stiff-legged toward George, barking ferociously, a door cracked open and a man with a surly expression glowered in his direction.

George took a deep breath, moistened his lips, and headed toward the closest shanty. The outside walls were sheathed with slabs of scrap wood and bark from the sawmill. George cleared his throat and knocked on the door. No one answered, and after a couple of minutes he knocked again. An unshaven man in shabby clothing and bare feet opened the door, and George saw a shield of distrust pass over the man's face.

"What do y' want?" the man snapped, staring at George's neatly trimmed beard and clean clothes.

"My name's George. I have a little extra money, and I was wondering if you could use some help."

"Help?" The man's lips, stained with chewing tobacco, curled in an ugly snarl as he spat the words into George's face. "What would you know about help? Your sort are all the same. You won't give us jobs, but you come here wanting to do some high and mighty thing so you can tell all your friends. Get out of here before I set the dog on you." A stream of curses flowed out of him as he slammed the door in George's face.

George's legs quivered at the unpleasant exchange. As he stood, dumbfounded that someone would refuse his offer, his first thought was to hightail it from this shantytown as quickly as possible. But then he heard Jesus' words echoing through his mind. "Give to the poor."

Looking around, George spotted a dilapidated shack standing by itself at the far edge of the group. As he approached warily, he saw that the faded door, bare and chipped in spots, badly needed repair and paint. One of the windows was broken, and he could hear a child crying pathetically inside. When he knocked, the door swung open and George looked into a world he had never witnessed before. A thin woman, wearing what looked like shrewdly patched rags, held a little boy in her arms. She tightened a thread-bare blanket around him against the cold December wind.

"Would you be looking for someone?" she asked apprehensively.

At first George couldn't find words. "My name's George," he replied lamely. "I thought perhaps someone here could use some help. I've some money that I don't need. I want to use part of it to help somebody else." Then he stalled again, searching for words. The little fellow in the woman's arms squirmed around and looked up, intent on the stranger's voice.

The woman, naturally suspicious, scanned his face. Why on earth would a strange man knock at *her* door and offer her money? What would folks think if she invited him inside? Still, as she looked into the man's inno-cent blue eyes and noted his obvious awkwardness and quiet manner, she felt reassured. He looked harmless enough, and if what he said was true, she was in no position to turn down an offer of help. She glanced toward her neighbour's window, a tide of red rising in her cheeks.

"Please, step in out of the wind," she offered. "I would be Mrs. Muldoon." She paused and looked away from his eyes. "Would you be having a cup of tea with me while we talk?" She gestured with embarrassment toward a single chair at a rickety table.

Accepting her suggestion, George couldn't help but notice the empty shelves against the wall. Even with the door closed he could feel the cold draft. The woman had a pitiful pile of firewood that might last four or five days at the most, and winter was already whistling along the Speed River. Reaching for an old pot, she brewed the tea from a bunch of dried gold-enrod hanging from the ceiling. George thanked her for the cup just as it was placed in front of him. No sugar or milk was set out, but George sipped the hot drink and showed his appreciation for her hospitality all the same. As he glanced around, he could see she was a tidy housekeeper.

"Have you been here long, Mrs. Muldoon?"

"Oh, no. Just since my husband was killed."

George flinched. "I'm sorry," he said softly. "I meant have you been in Canada long?"

The young widow reached forward to shield her child from the wood stove. "We sailed out o' Dun Laoghaire in the fall of '97, so we did. I had high hopes for a quiet life but no sooner would we be settling on a plot than my husband was impatient for more. One day he got wind of fifty acres of bush near Guelph. That's what fetched us away out here."

Her little fellow plopped down on the dirt floor at George's feet and seized one of his boot laces. "Now come away, me brisk young man, and leave the gentleman alone, do," his mother remonstrated.

"There, there," George said, hoisting the lad onto his lap. "He's just curious. What's your name, young fellow?"

Lena Muldoon beamed. "Patrick. After his grandfather."

"It must've been hard to leave your family behind in Ireland," George noted sympathetically.

Lena Muldoon clasped her hands at her waist. "Seamus had been taking the notion to immigrate to the colonies for months," she revealed. "Nothing for him in Tipperary, he thought.' Tis the dashing young fellow he was— but no staying-power atall. Seamus was in his element here. From sunup 'til dark he'd be cutting and burning slash like a madman."

George's eyes followed her lips intently. "I see," he said, "but you say he's gone now."

"Just in April," she assented sadly. "Seamus was ridding the paddock of a pine stump. When the dynamite didn't be firing, he must've been dashing back and it blasted up into his face. Two neighbour men dragged him off the field into our shanty, bleeding like a stricken deer, the pitiful mortal. The Good Man above would be having no mercy, and Seamus took his last gasp through a hole in his throat, for there was nary a feature left on his face. No cheek to be kissing, no eyes to be closing." Lena's face was a mask of tragedy, caught in recollection of that terrible hour.

George straightened up, his chest tight, his hands and feet achingly cold. In the darkness of Lena's catastrophe, his sacrifices seemed of lesser moment. He stirred, trying to shake off the chill her story had laid upon him. "I can't imagine the horror," he murmured at last. "I suppose you wanted to get away from the farm after that..."

"No, I'd have been content there," Lena resumed. "But I could not be scratching up the mortgage payment, and I was by way o' being forced to give it up. The grass grows over Seamus—green as Tipperary—and now there's but little Patrick and meself. At least me boy'll be showing his pappy's black hair and blue eyes—and the same grand cockalorum, I'm thinking." Lena's eyes fastened imploringly on George's face. "And now 'tis work of any kind I'm wanting, but 'tis so hard to be finding." Her voice drifted off in discouragement. "I've spent days tramping from place to place with nary a bit o' luck. I'd be taking work at any wage, but nobody is wanting to hire a woman. Especially one with a child hanging to her hand." Silence hung between them for a few moments.

"Yes," George sympathized, "with the closing of so many factories, I know it's very difficult to get a job." He drained the cup of tea and moved to perch on a block of wood. With a change of tone, he asked, "What would you do if you had a little extra put aside?"

Lena's eyes met his as she thought for a few moments. "I'd be buying a sewing machine," she said, her voice filled with purpose. "And some dry goods, so I could be making clothes to sell. Then I could support little Patrick and keep the wolf from the door."

"Would you ever think of going home to Tipperary?"

"No," she replied. "Never. My folks were groveling for a few 'taties the last days of their lives. Besides a woman daresn't try to change a man's mind after he's gone. Better Seamus lie buried in the soil o' the New World than the peat bogs o' the Old." With the tenacity inbred from her ancestors, Lena had seized upon the vision of a happier future in the land that Seamus had chosen for his son.

They talked for over an hour about her dilemma and her sisters back in Tipperary. Finally George stood and buttoned his coat. "I'll come back again tomorrow morning," he promised. "For sure."

Shortly after breakfast the next day, George returned, and he and Lena began the search for a warm place for her and Patrick to live. They soon discovered a cosy room with a cooking range above one of the shops along Wyndham Street. He prepaid the rent until spring and gave Lena a size-able sum to buy food. George purchased a sewing machine from the company where his brother, Arthur, worked. They went shopping for the supplies of thread, muslin, and wincey that she needed to realize her dream. When the last of her scant possessions had been carried up the long flight of stairs, Lena invited George to stay for supper.

"I just can't believe it," she said, beaming. "I've hardly been having a joint o' beef or dessert since Seamus was alive. No need for me to be sitting about with a long face now. 'Tis wonderful!" Her happy voice rose and fell with the soft rural lilt of southern Ireland. "Thank you so much, George. But how can I *ever* be repaying you?"

Her smiling face and laughing eyes were thanks enough. Patrick seemed excited, too, as he toddled around the warm room, his stomach full for the first time in weeks. As the little fellow stopped to steady himself, he placed his tiny hands on George's knee and looked up into his face. The child's beseeching gaze reminded George of the prospects he had given up.

Finishing his tea, he glanced toward the window. "It's getting dark and I must go," he observed. "But I'll see you again." He said goodbye without leaving more than his first name and the memory of his soft blue eyes and gentle generosity. Although Lena asked many people if they knew George, he had disappeared into a world seemingly as remote as that of Seamus.

~

Over the next few weeks George deliberately invested his money with his eternal destiny in mind. Seeking out the poorest of the poor, he gave them what they needed to move forward with hope. He looked for struggling people who, with modest assistance, would persevere in improving their situation. After earnest prayer, each bequest was given as anonymously as the situation would permit, allowing George to be guided by Jesus' teaching that if a man tries to show off when he does good deeds, he'll have no heavenly reward. Instead, he wasn't to let his left hand know what his right hand was doing. "Give in secret" the man was counseled, "and your Father who sees all things will reward you openly."[4] Like Jesus and His disciples, George felt it necessary to learn the lessons that come by living sparingly. Voluntary poverty had emptied his mind of the concerns of daily life.

George had stopped riding horseback for the most part. Alistair's fine dapple gray would soon be left behind, and even now it was often a burden, needing to be stabled at a livery while he visited various people. When Alistair discovered that George was walking back and forth to Guelph each day, he snuffled around in the dingy corners of the driving shed. "Let's reinvent the wheel," he quipped as he dragged a dusty old bicycle out into the daylight and brushed off the cobwebs.

After pumping up the tires, George pedaled over to Stephen's blacksmith shop. Waiting for Stephen to finish a span of heavy grays, he plucked a newspaper from the pile of kindling. Under the headline, "Sizeable Sum Donated to Erect Public Monument," he read an article glamourizing the wealthy donor. A photograph of the proud industrialist, surrounded by the mayor and the town council, leaped off the front page.

"That's quite a generous donation," Stephen broke in from behind the horse. "But I remember someone saying it's better not to give than to do so like a hen that lays an egg and then cackles to the whole henhouse."

George nodded, laying the paper aside. "A man needs conviction to carry a full cup without splashing it around," he replied.

Two hours later, George stood back and admired the sturdy rack that Stephen had fashioned over the rear wheel to support the travel bag. Afterward, George walked or, if the weather was mild, cycled wherever he went, returning at night to Alistair's attic.

Occasionally, the niggling voice of conventional wisdom disturbed George as he gave away his hard-earned money. *What if your father is right?* But still he persisted in pedaling back and forth to town. On the way back to Wood Creek Farm, he would fly down the steep hill in the sixth concession, the fingers of the wind tearing at his cap and tousling his beard. *Life's like chasing the wind,* he thought, *a fleeting shadow across the road.*[5] *And being overly focused on possessions, rather than on the Spirit is misguided.* Sometimes he would run a hand over his empty pocket and smile. *The truly spiritual man,* he concluded, *considers himself a stranger and a pilgrim*[6] *and lets go of things superfluous to his journey of faith.*[7]

George was particularly impressed with the gentleness and compassion of one poor man he found hunkered in front of the Golden Lion dry goods store on Wyndham Street. The man had lost his sight when a vat of lye had splashed into his face at a soap factory. Since then, he had been forced to earn a crust for his family by selling brooms on the sidewalk. On that hard stone, the blind man's character had blossomed.

George often stopped to chat with his new friend, crouching alongside him until his legs cramped. *Why,* he wondered, looking into the bleak eyes, *has God allowed this gentle soul to lose his sight?* But even as George struggled to understand, his own eyes were opened. For the first time, he saw how clearly God's work was being demonstrated through his friend's blindness.[8] Just as George's prosperity had come from God, so, perhaps, had this man's adversity.[9] Through it he had received profound lessons.[10] George discerned it was spiritual maturity that enabled his friend to be content with his frugal existence and thankful for the *inner* light of Christ.

On the last Thursday evening of the old year, the wind moaned prophetically in the Stanhope chimney as the gathering of friends put on their wraps. Alistair cautioned his visitors, "The wind's got around northeast, and there'll be a blow before midnight. Safe home, everyone." Then, putting a detaining hand on Jack's shoulder, he advised, "Better bunk in here. In an hour's time the roads'll be fit for neither man nor beast."

George turned to Jack. "Remember, there's an extra bed in the attic room I'm using," he said. "It'll be like old times to have a good talk."

When the door had squeaked shut, the two men undressed quickly and scrambled under the chilly bed clothes. "It'll take a few minutes to get the flannels up to temperature tonight," Jack chuckled as he rubbed his socked feet together.

George propped himself up on his elbow and peered through the darkness at Jack. "That wind drives the cold right through the walls. Alistair says they're filled with sawdust, but at times you'd hardly know it."

"I hope they mixed some lime into the sawdust to keep the vermin at bay. The carpenter at home didn't do that, and some nights there's so much scratching and scurrying, it sounds as if all the mice in Nassagaweya have gathered for a box social."

George listened to the wind rattling the lightening rods and whistling around the window sash. "Jack," he observed at length, "you've never been caught up with wealth, working like you did as a colporteur for years. Did you ever notice that Jesus spoke more about a man's relation to money than any other single thing?"

"Can't say as I did, but maybe it's not that strange. After all, He drove the moneychangers out of the temple." Jack paused. "They say true wealth isn't what you accumulate, but what you give away."

George's face reddened, suddenly warm in the cold darkness. Although unwilling to admit his own largesse, even to himself, he was, nevertheless, eager to hear Jack's perspective. "Paul says it's the *desire* to be rich that's a temptation and a snare, that the *love* of money is the root of all kinds of evil."[11] George heard Jack stirring before he replied.

"Yes," Jack agreed, "it's the insidious desire, not the money itself, that's inherently destructive. On the other hand, some people in history despised wealth and used their poverty to draw attention to themselves. I don't think that motive's any more virtuous than outright greed."

George tucked the quilt around his neck. "I suppose any child of God can enjoy the wholesome things of life, but in moderation. And with an awareness of the kingdom of heaven.[12] As he matures, he'll handle his time and resources differently."

"In my opinion, hoarding is idolatry," Jack declared. "Why only a few days ago, I was reading one of Dugan's books about a martyr called Thomas

Kittlewell. He was a tailor in Worcester who became a poor Lollard preacher in the fifteenth century. Although the man didn't own a thing, he wrote that possessions are neither good nor bad, that they were created by God for our use and in themselves are neutral. What's bad is the false impression that happiness can be realized through them. If a man's reason for having things is to draw attention to himself, then the motive is wrong.

"Thomas spent a lot of time under lock and key, so he knew something about cells. He figured everybody starts out in a cell, so to speak. Well-off folks just have one with gold bars instead of iron bars. Thomas said some of them are so dazzled by the glitter that they often forget they're captives as well—to their own false sense of importance."

"You've certainly given me some things to chew on," George said as he relaxed back on his bed tick. "I want to value everything by the price God places on it."

On Saturday George went to visit a frail couple in their seventies who could no longer work or provide for themselves adequately. Their sons had heard of the Klondike gold rush and one by one they had moved to the Yukon. Their only daughter, who had stayed at home to care for her parents, had contracted influenza and died.

As George listened to their tragic story, he suddenly realized how indebted he was to his own aging parents. During his childhood, they had worked long and hard, scrimping and saving to give their children the best they could. When the time came that they could no longer work, George would be unable to assist them in any material way.

After supper that evening, fortified by a feed of ham and baked beans, George turned to Timothy. "How about a night off, lad? If it's all right with your father, I'll go along to the barn and help with the milking."

Alistair nodded. "Sounds fine to me," he said as he and George pulled on their barn smocks.

Later as the two men sat back to back, each of their hands directing a stream of warm frothy milk into their pails, George cocked his head toward Alistair. "What do you make of those religious folks who gave gifts to the temple in order to gain public recognition?"

Alistair hesitated, trying to pinpoint the Scripture. "You mean the ones who refused to care for their aged parents?"

"Yes, that's the ones."

"What do you mean, what do I make of them?"

"Well, do you think a man has an obligation to care for his folks?"

Alistair paused, ruminating. "Didn't Jesus tell the Jewish leaders that God had commanded children to honour their father and mother?"

George leaned forward, resting his head against the cow's side. "I take it that the Pharisees taught that a man could weasel out of his responsibility by simply telling his parents that whatever help they were expecting had already been offered to God."[13]

"Sounds like a handy loophole," Alistair observed. "The money could then flow directly to the temple coffers. And God's commandment be conveniently bypassed."

When a striped tabby rubbed against George's pant leg and placed its front paws expectantly on the rim of the pail, he diverted a teatful of creamy milk into its mouth. He smiled as the cat's pink tongue absorbed the stray droplets from its whiskers.

"Thanks for hearing me out, Alistair." He kicked aside his milking stool. "I've been pondering about a man's obligation to his folks."

George arrived at his parents' farm in the middle of the next morning. He had been back several times since he had told them about his plans, and each time his father had been inhospitable, sometimes delivering biting remarks, which George tried to ignore. At times he felt the urge to respond. *But what,* he asked himself, *would be gained by getting into a nasty and useless confrontation?* Hopefully it would be different this time.

As his mother cleared away the dinner dishes, he edged forward on his chair. "You know," he began, "I won't be able to offer much help when you get up in years if I don't have a regular line of work."

His dad glared at him, saying nothing.

"Yes, George," his mother said, "we can understand that."

"Well, you know, I have some money now that I would like to give you. It's money I'd have used to help you later on…"

"I don't want your money," his father interrupted icily. "I just want a normal son, not some religious oddball. Already you've lost the best farm in the district, and now you're wasting your life.[14] The whole settlement's buzzing about your strange behaviour. I should have known something would give way when you joined that idiotic church. What's more, you're walking out on a girl who's going to make a perfect wife for some other man. What'll you think then?"

Absently George fingered a penny out of his homespun pocket, his face twisting as he recalled Laura's tearful features. The image of Victoria Regina gazed impassively towards the rim of the coin.

"And do you ever give a thought to Laura's folks? I 'spect they're big-feelin' people, her father the Stratford doctor and all. You can't do better than that. Word'll soon get back here that they can't hold their heads up in their own town, what with only the one girl married and their Laura looking jilted. George, when a man goes back on his word to a woman…" His father's voice halted with unyielding implication. Then, in his usual way, Mr. Farnham got up and slammed the door, stomping off to the barn.

George stared down at the floor, rocking the heel of his boot on the chair rung. "I'm sorry, Mum," he apologized. "I know it's hard on you, too…And Dad might rant on for quite a spell."

"Don't worry about me, George," his mother's voice reassured him. "I'll get through it."

George's mother was going into Guelph to spend a couple of days with her eldest son, Arthur, and his family, and she agreed to meet George there. Arthur would open a bank account and the money would be available for both of George's parents when it was needed.

"Thank you, George. You've always been very considerate," she said as she tearfully hugged him goodbye. "It's a wonderful thing you're doing for us. Pay no mind to your father. He'll come around. He was so proud of you and the way you were running your farm, that's all. Now he thinks the neighbours are all laughing at us. And somehow he had a special place in his heart for Laura, just as I have. But we both love you very much. Just give him a little time, George. It's a long road that has no turning."

Twelve

THE INAUDIBLE VOICE
Spring 1901

On January 22, 1901, the peaceful farming settlement of Puslinch Township reverberated with shock to a dispatch that had been flashed by telegraph across five time zones, an ocean, and half a continent. The roads of Wellington County were livelier than usual as cutters and sleighs stopped to pass the news, pausing momentarily to compare reactions and reminiscences. A few of the oldest inhabitants could recall the summer of 1837 when the Sailor King had died, leaving the throne to his niece, Alexandrina Victoria Guelph. And now the girl of eighteen who had come, by the grace of God, to the British throne as Queen Victoria, was dead. The public buildings in Guelph were draped in black bunting, for had not the Queen bestowed her family name on the young city?

Late into the night, lamps and candles gleamed through farmhouse windows as dazed families reread and folded the pages of the *Guelph Daily Herald.* Alistair read the headline aloud as Priscilla peeled onions for the next day's stew. "The Glorious Victorian Era Has at Last Ended—Queen Said Affectionate Farewells to Her Children at Noon, Whispering a Few Words of Consolation to Each." The impact of the death, like the dark drapery seen everywhere, lay like a sorrowful pall over the snowy fields.

In time the lengthening days of February and March brought a brighter crystalline glow to the wind-whipped snowdrifts along the Downey Road. By April winter had blustered its way through the township, and in the woods a few early bloodroot were springing up in the wavering shade of the deciduous trees. Although George had not yet set out to preach the gospel, his days had been filled with milking cows, cutting ice, sawing wood, and fixing harness, all of which he enjoyed. He and Alistair had jacked up a sagging beam in the stable and hewn sturdy posts to support it. When supper was over, he always helped Priscilla with the dishes.

Bill and Alice's three children adored this extra uncle whose deft fingers could fashion porcupines out of teasels or owl faces out of a walnut shell. Invariably George read them a bedtime story before heading back to the attic room at Alistair's. Although he sometimes stayed overnight with Bill and Alice or Stephen and Emily, he felt the strongest pull to Wood Creek Farm, where his influence had touched Timothy's heart.

Having now graduated with his senior matriculation, Timothy put in long days around the farm. At twenty years, he had stretched up to a height outstripping his father's, and although his good looks and easy charm wreaked havoc among the aspiring young ladies of Puslinch Township, he seemed blissfully unaware of their coy looks and flirtatious advances.

As he ran errands in the district, Timothy grew increasingly aware of the deep respect accorded his father by the surrounding farmers. Indeed, when Timothy had taken a broken spoke for repair at the wheelwright's, he had overheard old Sandy MacPherson expounding as he leaned against a stack of carriage wheels. "A good and decent man, Alistair Stanhope. And plenty of backbone too. Why, when Jordie's barn burnt to the ground last spring, he was the first on hand. Him and Bill Jones hauled timbers near steady 'til we got her raised again." Sandy's Scottish burr had made the waiting farmers laugh in unison, but heads nodded as he spoke with quiet approbation of the men who gathered each week at Wood Creek Farm.

In spite of his natural aptitude for tomfoolery, Timothy's presence in the meetings bespoke his serious commitment to the simple way of faith. And although he was still a youth at heart, he held a profound admiration for the nobility of George's sacrifice and a fascination with the New Testament ministry. Long after the rest of the family had turned in for the night, he and George would angle their Bibles toward the circle of weak lamplight as they delved into various Scriptures and compared their interpretations. Both men were intent on memorizing verses so that they could enjoy them as they worked or traveled. Sometimes, like a sheep chewing its cud, George would turn over a single verse in his mind for days until he had extracted its very essence for his spiritual nourishment.

One afternoon the pair were replacing a broken board in the bottom of the wheelbarrow when Timothy stopped sawing. "What do you fancy Jesus meant when He told the man to let the dead bury their dead?"[1]

George squirted some oil onto the rusty bolt he was struggling to loosen. "Don't you reckon He was tickling the man's imagination, encouraging him to question why a dead man would be depicted as doing anything? Or he might wonder, was Jesus alluding to something else, perhaps to a man living, but as if he *were* dead?"

Timothy mused as he finished cutting the board. "Far too many people pass this way untouched by any compelling vision, especially a spiritual one. Like the man living among the tombs, we could be alive but living in the cemetery of this world."[2]

"So what would it take to leave that land, that way of life?"

"A complete change of outlook, I reckon."

George tried to jam the board into the open space. "This piece is as tight as a barrel stave." He reached for the block plane. "Jesus never forced anyone to accept His teachings. He hardly ever said, 'Do this!' or 'Don't do that!' Most of His sayings and parables were intended to unlatch a gate in the minds of His listeners, affording them glimpses of the kingdom of heaven. For those who saw, the pristine image of what lay beyond the impenetrable wall of the natural world would alter their perspective and beautify their lives forever."

Timothy braced one foot against the steel wheel of the upended barrow. "His healing of the blind man would demonstrate to folks that they needed spiritual sight. Jesus spoke about men who have eyes but don't see—suffering a kind of blindness that plagues men from birth."

"I was in the dark much of my life too," George admitted. "But now I'm getting a glimmer of the path leading out of the land of the dead. Like the man who left the underground tombs after Jesus healed him."

Timothy's face lit up. "That's what happened to you," he exclaimed.

George looked up from his shavings, puzzled. "What do you mean?"

"Right after Jesus spoke about letting the dead bury the dead, He added, 'But go thou and preach the kingdom of God.' Your enlightenment, your new way of seeing is what enabled you to reevaluate, to sell your farm, to leave your own father, and to go preaching. Just like Jesus instructed."

The pile of curly birch shavings grew at George's feet as he struggled to fit the board into place. "I guess I never connected the two parts of the verse before. But it isn't just me. All of us are seeing things differently."

For several weeks George puzzled over the mission ahead, conscious that the New Testament ministers almost always worked and traveled in twos. Although George searched diligently, he found little evidence of a minister on his own, unless for a temporary period or for a specific reason. Jesus had sent the twelve disciples out in pairs in Matthew 10, and again in Luke 10, when He appointed and sent another seventy. George turned to the Acts of the Apostles and reaffirmed that the Holy Spirit chose Barnabas and Paul, for *the work*.[3] Even when a sharp difference of opinion caused them to part company, Barnabas took Mark, and Paul traveled with Silas.

Throughout the cold and stormy March of 1901, George wrestled with this troubling question and prayed for understanding. Surprisingly, he never discussed his concern with the others. God, he felt confident, would solve every dilemma in due course. Although eager to begin the work, George knew that God often taught His true messengers over a considerable length of time and in relative solitude: Joseph in an Egyptian prison, Moses in a remote part of the desert, John the Baptist in the wilderness, Jesus at the carpenter shop, and Paul in Arabia. And so George waited patiently on a Puslinch Township farm for God to indicate the proper time and direction. All the while God was preparing His labourer for the harvest field.[4]

After resigning from Reverend Chumbley's employment nearly two years before, Jack Gillan had been without a job. Although he had loved his work as colporteur, his new convictions would not permit him to move among people under the auspices of his former denomination. When he returned home to his parents' farm near Eden Mills, his mother was thrilled to have her son back in his old bedroom rather than boarding near the Reverend's manse. Jack's dad, well over sixty, was pleased to have the extra help and paid him the usual two dollars per week that any hired man would receive. For his parents, it was a comfortable arrangement, not one they were eager to see ended.

But for Jack, the high points of his week were the Thursday and Sunday fellowship meetings, even though it was lonely now, riding back and forth without George. If the day was blustery, he would start out early and afterwards spend the night with Stephen and Emily. The waxing moon of April often witnessed him on his horse, a lonely silhouette moving across the Eramosa bridge at a fair clip. For Jack, it was a time of reflection, of looking backward at the boy he had been, a devoted reader of the Henty books, devouring adventures from faraway and long ago. In school, both history and literature had pulled him to the past. Now, at a time of inexplicable change, Jack sensed that the text of his future lay in the pages of the most sublime Book of all time. An unseen finger seemed poised to turn a page and reveal a new script for his life.

In early May, a week of ideal seeding weather promised new hope to the tilled fields. From every hedgerow and orchard, the sweet voices of spring called insistently to each other. On the second anniversary of the Sunday meetings, the spirit of the gathering was pensive and gentle as each person offered a reflection from the two years of their shared lives.

Emily stirred beside Stephen. "God's literally transformed my life," she said, her voice as soft as rainwater. "The thoughts that come to me are so different now that I'm attuned to Him. Yesterday, a tiny hummingbird found its way to our wild plum tree. As it hovered at each blossom, it extracted the nectar and left the rest behind. It's only the sweetness of each conversation, of each event, that I intend to absorb. What feeds our minds will come out in our lives and, sooner or later, we'll all arrive at the secret thoughts of our hearts."

Malachi swallowed the last of his peppermint. "Funny, I been thinkin' about flowers too," he said. "Last night I was readin' about Samson findin' honey in the lion's carcass. I reckon that took two things—the death of the lion and the life of the bees. My old drinkin' habit's near about dead, and the Spirit's comin' alive in me. God can produce a tad of sweetness, y' know, even in a twisted old stick like me."

Bill nodded thoughtfully, mindful of the faith and grit Malachi had shown. Each time he stumbled, he had picked himself up and started along the path again. He was determined, Bill knew, to depend on God when dark thoughts settled like a flock of starlings on the branches of a cherry tree. In fact, one March afternoon as they had cut up a hollow elm that crashed across the line fence, the older man confided he had found peace at last. As the two men had sat side by side on the fallen trunk, the raw east wind in their faces, Malachi thanked Bill for the many times he had hurried over encouraging him to keep on in the journey of faith. The sudden rustle of pages in Susan Green's Bible startled Bill's mind back to the meeting.

Straight from the Yorkshire dales, Susan's earthy dialect warmed the hearts of her adoptive family. "'Tis nigh onto a year and a 'alf since ah met Alice at t' market," she began. "T' bottom 'ad dropped clean out of me world when Edmund died, so it did. There was days it near drove me daft. Ah almost wished it'd been me, not 'im. Ah 'aven't made much of a fist o' servin' God," she admitted, "but ah'm so glad to be part o' this warm-'earted family." With a spontaneous flourish, she extended her arm as if to encompass the whole circle.

Sitting beside Malachi, Priscilla caught the glint of a tiny tear in his eye when Susan spoke of losing her mate. When Priscilla reached out and laid her hand across his, Malachi smiled and leaned toward her. "Susan's learned," he whispered, "that every sunset bears promise of a fairer day."

Priscilla cupped her hand. "A child of God should have finer and more delicate feelings than other folks," she murmured. "The more we appreciate God's compassion and care, the more tender we can be to others."

Malachi sucked softly through the gap in his front teeth and nodded.

As usual, each person spoke as the Spirit prompted, and on this particular Sunday, Jack was the last. With the air of a man struggling to reveal his soul, he tried to speak, but his voice broke. Tears welled up, his brow furrowed, and his face began to flush. "I've known for months," he blurted out, "that God's been calling me into the ministry…" His emotions overcame him, and he stopped in mid-sentence. A moment passed before Jack could clear the feelings that clogged his throat. Finally he confessed, "Although I don't have many things, I've been fighting against His call. It's so hard to give up my dream of owning a nice place someday and instead just to go wherever God will lead. But I know it's best, and I'm ready for that now."

Victorious in his struggle, he searched out George's face. The very sight of him gave Jack comfort. Then, speaking directly toward George but addressing all of his friends, he continued. "George," he choked, "you've been a brother to me ever since that first day we met in your front field. If I can be of use, I'd dearly like to go along with you in the work."

George blinked, his eyes red and hazy as he got up to meet Jack in the centre of the parlour, throwing his arms around him. "That would be wonderful, Jack," he managed to say. "I've been praying for understanding about a companion, but I had no notion that God had His hand on you."

In unison the friends rose and gathered around George and Jack, shedding the same tears of joy and appreciation as they had when George had taken this same step a few months earlier. Gradually the cluster of friends drifted apart, each one taking an opportunity to hug Jack and express the rejoicing they felt in their hearts.

Eventually Alistair raised his voice. "Could you all take a chair for just a minute?" he asked. When the friends were again seated, he resumed, his voice soft and fatherly. "We're witnessing today what the little church at Antioch experienced over eighteen centuries ago. This is not merely a noble human decision; this is God at work in our very midst."

Morgan entwined his long legs around the chair rung, his face solemn.

People barely breathed as Alistair continued. "On that occasion, the Holy Spirit said, 'Set apart Barnabas and Paul for the work to which I have called them.' God did the calling, but the Antioch saints had a role as well. They fasted and prayed and then they laid their hands on the two men and sent them on their way. Barnabas and Paul, being directed by the Spirit, went down to the seaport and sailed from there. I don't know just what God has in mind, but perhaps all of us, not just George and Jack, could be sober and prayerful about the next steps."

Afterward, George slipped upstairs to his room and knelt to thank God. When dinner was over, he invited Jack to join him for a walk along the back lane. On either side, thorny shrubs abounded with chirping birds among the damp mosses, while the hepatica unfolded their pink and purple blooms. From the beaver meadow came the sweet adagio of spring peepers, interposed by the hoarse squawk of a blue heron in ponderous flight. George placed his right hand on his friend's broad shoulder. "Jack, I'm so happy to have you as a companion. I felt hesitant to go alone, and yet I knew that God had called me. His call to you is an answer to my prayers."

"I'm very glad to be setting out with you, George. I hope I can be useful to God as I meet new people." For a few minutes Jack walked, head down as if examining the wild flowers. Then he stopped abruptly, turning to his friend. "There's one thing I need to tell you, something you don't know about me." When he read the startled expression on George's face, his eyes softened. "It's nothing awful, just something private that no one knows about except my folks." He closed his eyes for a couple of seconds before forging ahead. "I was adopted as a baby. My mother was only fifteen. I guess she fell into a bad way and was sent here to Guelph until after I was born. I expect she went home to her own family afterwards as if nothing had happened. My mother said that she and Pop didn't know the girl's name or where she came from." He winced at the inevitable conclusion. "That makes me a bastard," he added, spitting the word out as if it were a mouthful of dirt.

George noticed his friend's face redden, scalded by the shedding of his protective mask. "Jack, that's not your fault at all," he hastily reassured him. "You had nothing to do with it. You weren't even born."

"I know. I've told myself that hundreds of times, but I just can't make peace with it all. At times I wonder if I ran across some of my own kin whether it would ease the shame. I find myself searching every face I meet to see if it bears any resemblance to my own." He paused. "It's not that Ma and Pop aren't wonderful, because they are. It's just that I'm intrigued, maybe even lonely for a brother or a sister, born of my own stock."

As the men turned around to retrace their steps, George looked into Jack's eyes, brown pools of integrity. "Thank you for trusting me with your secret, Jack," he said softly. "Your openness binds me even closer to you."

As the two men crossed a plank bridge and stopped to gaze into the translucent water, Jack's words plucked a chord in George's heart. Staring down at his own reflection, he realized that he, too, searched the face of every person he met, looking for the gentle character of Christ. *Every child of God possesses the longing,* he conjectured, *to meet brothers and sisters born of the same Spirit.* On his left, George caught a twitching among the bulrushes as a frightened muskrat plunged into the water, its ripples distorting George's thoughtful image. *Why is this craving for fellowship such a mystery to unbelievers?*

The stars shone brightly as the friends parted at the end of the flagstone walkway. Bill's and Stephen's rigs pulled out, and Jack followed them on his saddle horse, trotting down the lane into the cool darkness of the spring night. The profusion of emerging buds on the trees sharpened against the backdrop of the full moon as he stopped at the crossroads to bid the others goodnight. Jack squeezed his heels against the sides of his tall roan gelding and felt its steady rhythm beneath him. This early in the spring, the gravel road lay pocked with potholes and the boggy corduroy sections were ribbed from the logs pushing up through the muddy surface. The potholes and logs were dangerous for a horse in the dark, and Jack reined in his mount over the swampy stretches. Riding along, Jack pondered the task of disbursing his possessions. Even though they were few, it would be hard to give up the cherished history books he had acquired so painstakingly over the years. As he turned in the moonlit lane at home, he wondered how soon he could get packed and be ready to join George. Meanwhile, oblivious to his plans, his parents shifted in their sleep.

One evening in early June, Jack climbed the stairs at home with greater purpose than ever before. From the attic he retrieved an old Gladstone bag left by a tea pedlar long ago at the Gillan farm. He dropped on one knee in front of his bookcase and began to extract book after book. By the time he had jammed them into the bag, he had handled the entire history of the human race from Adam to the Zulu War of 1879. Dugan MacGladry would while away many a winter evening with them. And in an apple crate, Jack lined up his collection of Henty books earmarked for Bill and Alice's boys, now eager lads learning to read stories more challenging than the animal fables in their primer.

Finally, Jack pulled open a small dresser drawer and withdrew a photograph that had been tendered him on his sixteenth birthday. His parents had seemed oddly preoccupied as, together, they had held out the portrait of a girl whose dark eyes now gazed back at him with the intensity of secrets withheld for many years. He turned it over and read the initials M.S.W. written in a schoolgirl's hand. Jack felt his chest tighten as he tucked the picture, along with another of his mother and father, between the pages of his Bible and slipped it into his traveling case. Only a single change of clothes and a straight razor along with a towel, tooth powder, and a few cakes of his mother's soap made up his goods for the journey.

On the day of departure, Jack hugged his mother and father at the back door of the summer kitchen. Behind them on the cookstove, the sweetness of strawberry jam mingled with the sharp scent of wood smoke on the morning air. Everything called to hearth and home, but Jack's mind focused on his journey. "I love you both," he reassured his folks. "Please don't worry. George and I will be together. I couldn't have a better friend. We'll look out for each other."

"When will we see you again, Jack?"

"I really don't know. It could be quite a while."

Jack saw his mother struggling to keep a stiff upper lip and trying to sound enthusiastic as he promised to write regularly and visit when he could. At last he looked into his father's misty eyes. "Goodbye, Pop."

Jack tied his travel bag onto the bicycle rack and tossed his jacket across the top. Doing his best to appear nonchalant, Jack leaned over and patted the dog's head. "Keep those groundhogs on the run, old Collie."

Then he pedaled down the laneway to join George at Wood Creek Farm. Stopping at the end of the lane, he looked back and saw his dad still standing with his arm around his mother in the doorway. They both waved vigorously as he turned and disappeared down the road. Tears blurred Jack's eyes and his heart ached.

"These two people took me in when I was a stranger and couldn't care for myself," he agonized.[5] "Now I'm walking out on them just when they're getting older and need me most." His short muscular legs churned the pedals as he sought to work out the tension and assuage his regret.

That evening George and Jack shared the little attic room on the third floor of Alistair and Priscilla's home. A melodious refrain of crickets flooded through the open window, and in the distance a cow bawled for her missing calf. The next day the two men helped Alistair fulfill his statutory obligation of dressing and graveling the road in front of Wood Creek Farm. Each spring he spent three days hauling material from the wayside pit with his heavy team and gravel box. Tipping back their straw hats in the pouring sunshine, George and Jack talked over their plans as they shoveled stones and sand. Where should they go and how should they start? George had been waiting for months, and now the time seemed right. After much prayer, they decided to start in the village of Elora in two weeks.

On the Sunday before George and Jack left, the friends spent the day together. Before parting, they gathered around the brothers and laid their hands on them to show they were all united in Christ and supportive of their mission. Even though the men would soon be many miles from the Puslinch church, each person knew that distance would not sever this bond.

Early the next morning George and Jack, clad in their rough farm clothing, said goodbye to Alistair, Priscilla, Timothy, and Phoebe. High hopes and a rare euphoria buoyed them as they cycled down the lane and into an unknown future. They estimated that the ride to Elora would take at least three hours, and they hoped to arrive in plenty of time to find lodging. Two miles past the village of Ponsonby, they coasted down the long hill and stopped at a grassy meadow beside Swan Creek. Priscilla had packed a generous lunch, and each man was thankful as he bit into thick sandwiches and rested comfortably within earshot of the gurgling stream.

This was George's first picnic, if it could be called that, since the day he had taken Laura to Doyle's Mill nearly a year before. She was still teaching at Mildmay, and the envelope he had received from her yesterday had been bittersweet with memories of their times together. When George read her words, it seemed as if he could hear her voice whispering into his ear. As he had carefully folded and saved the letter, he had thanked God for her continuing friendship. George knew he had made the right choice for his life, but he also knew that he still loved Laura and indeed, since he had committed to the Lord's call, that his feelings for her had intensified. In the torment of their denial, his body often betrayed him. Had he been a woman, he could have wept openly and found relief. As a man, he had been taught to crush and hide his pain—alone. Yet sometimes, in the dead of night, he jerked awake from a dream in which he heard her voice calling him.

Jack broke the silence. "I'm really looking forward to being in Elora, but I'm going to miss seeing our friends at the meetings."

George agreed, his face flushing. "It's hard to be separated, especially from Laura." He brushed the crumbs out of his beard as he remembered searching for and finding the first kiss she had given him and the surprise each had felt in the other at the insistence of their passion, of youth calling to youth. Inadvertently, too, and as though from a long distance he recalled Lena Muldoon's shack, smothered with soot from the passing engines, and her muted anguish as she intoned, "No cheek to be kissing, no eyes to be closing." He pondered her face, later creased with joy and gratitude, and the touch of her child's hands, as if on George's heart.

Lena…and Laura, George mused silently. *Two women I must leave behind—but both strong enough to stand alone.* His thoughts took a gentler tone. *Laura…Elora,* he played with the resonant names. *At least I can take her name with me to Elora—and my love for her…*

Jack's voice cut into George's meditation. "Did you see my pocket knife around here?" He began shaking the ants out of the lunch.

George shook his head, moving slowly, as if his mind was far away. Then he tightened his jaw and changed the subject. "It's a little unnerving to go to a strange settlement, not knowing where we'll spend the night."

A grin tugged at the corners of Jack's mouth. "I guess we can sleep in a farmer's haystack if worst comes to worst." He let out a good-natured snort as he climbed back onto his bicycle.

In 1901 Elora was a bustling village of nearly 1200 people. Nevertheless, everyone noticed a stranger on the street, his features in sharp contrast with the meticulous delineation of family lines that had been etched into their cognition from school days to funeral wakes.

George and Jack leaned their bicycles up against the hitching rail in front of Foster's General Store and strolled inside. Two ladies were fingering the chintz in one corner while the thickset storekeeper, in a slightly soiled white butcher's apron, leaned on the counter. He was attentively writing out a grocery order when the brass bell rang throughout the quiet stone store. Straightening up, he smiled at the two men. His full face sported a double chin, gold-rimmed spectacles perched upon his ample nose, and the reek of carbolic soap pervaded his person.

"Good day, fellows. Lovely afternoon out there."

"Yes, indeed," Jack agreed. "Summer heat coming on and all."

"What can I do for you today?"

George spoke up. "We're looking to find a place to room and board."

The grocer raised his eyebrows, glancing outside at the dusty bicycles.

"Mrs. Applebee sometimes takes in boarders," he suggested helpfully. "You could try there." The grocer was curious and full of questions about these two strangers, but he held back. Mrs. Applebee would fill him in the next time she came to the store. She could be counted on for that, he knew.

After getting directions, they thanked Mr. Foster and wheeled their bikes along the sidewalk. It was only two blocks from Geddes Street to Victoria Street where Mrs. Applebee lived. The elegant two-storey brick home had an inviting wooden veranda and an arched Gothic window. A narrow lane led to a driving shed along one side, and a neat picket fence surrounded an array of blue lupins and white peonies. In the corner of Mrs. Applebee's yard a huge lilac bush flaunted its purple glory.

After leaning their bicycles at the front gate, George and Jack threaded their way around the flower beds to the door. George's knock was greeted by a cheery voice, "Come in." They stepped inside and were immediately received by the plump Mrs. Applebee. True to her name, she had round rosy cheeks set in a congenial face, and her white hair was pulled up into a neat bun on the top of her head.

"Good afternoon. My name's George Farnham and this is my friend Jack Gillan. Are you Mrs. Applebee?"

Mrs. Applebee smiled warmly. "Yes, I am. How can I help you?" When she extended a hospitable hand, she took note of their firm shakes.

"We're looking for a place to board for a few weeks," George began. "And Mr. Foster at the general store suggested that we check with you."

"Well, boys, I might be able to help." Mrs. Applebee hesitated. "Tell me, what brings you to Elora?"

As they explained their intentions, they could see surprise spreading across her grandmotherly face.

"Where were you preaching before you came here?"

"Nowhere," George said, "we were farming."

"We're just starting out," Jack added.

Mrs. Applebee's scrutiny dropped from their sunburned faces to their calloused palms. She had not lived her seventy-six years without becoming an astute judge of character. "If you lads can stand my cooking, you're welcome here," she concluded, eyes twinkling. "And Jenny L.'s singing."

"Does Jenny board with you as well?" George asked politely.

Mrs. Applebee's cheeks puffed out in merriment. "Well, you might put it that way," she chortled. "I'll introduce you." Beckoning the men to follow, Mrs. Applebee turned to lead the way inside.

Jack met George's eyes. *It certainly would be pleasant,* he thought, *to have someone else on hand who liked to sing too.* He glanced around as they followed Mrs. Applebee into the parlour. No sign of the lady yet.

Stepping into the bay window, Mrs. Applebee drew back the lace curtain, revealing a gilded cage. "Jenny," she said to the yellow canary, "I'd like you to meet George and Jack. They're going to be with us for a spell."

The two men burst out laughing as the canary's pale eye blinked impassively and her wiry feet edged along the centre perch. "You certainly pulled the wool over our eyes on that one," Jack chuckled.

"She's named after my favourite opera singer, Jenny Lind," Mrs. Applebee explained. "I've loved opera since I was a girl, and she was just five years older than me."

Only the price needed to be settled, and George explained their need to be frugal. "But we're willing to help in whatever way we can," he added. "We aren't asking for any handouts. We are able-bodied men, after all."

After reflecting for a few seconds, Mrs. Applebee replied, "I'm a widow, so there's nobody to do the heavy work around the house. My husband passed away six years ago. Even if one can afford to hire a man, they all seem to be busy as red ants on a hot stove at this time of year. Would you two be willing to cut and split my winter firewood?"

"We'd be glad to," George exclaimed, anxious to handle an axe again.

After agreeing to a slightly lower rate in exchange for the work, Mrs. Applebee showed them to an upstairs bedroom that overlooked the side yard. Somewhere a clock chimed five times and Jack met George's eyes in a conspiratorial grin. Everything, it seemed, had unfolded almost too easily.

They could hear Mrs. Applebee preparing supper while they unpacked their things into a tall oak armoire. Jack took off his boots and stretched out on the bed while George went down to put their bicycles in the driving shed. They had decided it would be easier to meet folks if they walked wherever they needed to go.

On his way down the carpeted stairs, George noticed a few family tintypes along the wall. A parlour table stood on the landing, and above it hung a pigmented enlargement of a small boy dressed in a sailor suit. The late afternoon sunshine kissed the child's rosy cheeks as his vivid eyes looked back at George. *Mrs. Applebee didn't mention any family,* George mused. *Must be a nephew or some other lad in her circle.*

In the driving shed, George took note of the brass trim and stylish harness hanging on the wall, now laden with dust. He studied an elegant two-wheeled jaunting cart, its plush horsehair seat protected with an old blanket and its shafts tipped up for storage. He stroked his beard thoughtfully. *Mr. Applebee must've been quite a man.* Turning away, George closed the door, careful to secure the bolt. As he ambled toward the house, he leaned forward and drew a fragrant cluster of lilacs to his nose.

Mrs. Applebee called them to supper in a tone that implied she had been calling hungry lads to supper all her life. As the three of them sat down, a moment of silence ensued. The travelers bowed their heads, and after an awkward pause, Mrs. Applebee cleared her throat. "George, would you be good enough to ask the blessing?"

George nodded. "Dear Father," he began. "We thank You for leading us safely to this home and for the hospitality so generously given. We're reminded of the two travelers on the road to Emmaus and how Jesus drew near and blessed their food as they sat at meat together.[6] May those favours be ours as well as we gather around the bounty of this meal. We are mindful, Father, that every person in Elora is also on the road to Emmaus. And that

Your Son desires to draw near and to walk with each of us. Open our spiritual eyes to truly see Him. This we ask in Jesus' name. Amen."

Mrs. Applebee appeared momentarily preoccupied as she raised her head, but she quickly reached for the platter of glazed pork chops and handed them to Jack. "It's nice to hear a man give thanks at the table," she observed. "I don't always say grace when I'm alone. But I know I should."

As she spoke, George recalled the sale barn in Berlin and how the simple act of silently bowing his head had caught Alistair's eye. So much had happened as a result of that one expression of thanksgiving.

Mrs. Applebee looked up at George, quietly enjoying his supper. "I've never heard anyone mention the road to Emmaus in just that way."

George paused and laid his knife on the edge of his plate. "Of late, I've become particularly aware that Emmaus happens over and over. It's a road that runs through every man's heart. We forget the risen Christ is journeying with us, whether we recognize Him or not. Sometimes we get a glimpse of Him—as real and present today as at that quiet meal long ago. And in a split second, our course of life is forever altered."

As thoughtful reflection descended upon the table, Mrs. Applebee's eyes appeared searching and faraway. Stirring herself, she passed the bowl of mashed potatoes around for the second time. "Now, tell me a little about your families," she urged. With a self-deprecating grin, Jack began with his boyhood in Eden Mills, and as the three of them ate, they became acquainted.

The next morning after a hearty breakfast of waffles and maple syrup and lots of hot tea, the brothers set out to explore Elora and find a place to have some meetings. As they walked along Geddes Street, the two men discussed the apostle Paul's use of synagogues.

"Synagogues are as scarce as hens' teeth in this part of Ontario," Jack laughed, "so we'll have to think of something else."

"Do you remember that Paul preached in the school of Tyrannus?"[7]

Jack slid his toothpick to the corner of his mouth. "Yes, I do."

"He probably used the school after Tyrannus had finished his teaching."

Jack smiled. "Maybe we could do the same if the Tyrannus of Elora is sympathetic to our cause."

The men stopped first at the post office to leave their names in case any mail arrived and then asked the postmaster for directions to the school.

It was morning recess at the schoolhouse on Mill Street when George and Jack arrived at the gate. A group of boys played baseball in one corner of the yard while the girls pushed each other on a swing hung from the limb of a large oak. As the men approached the door, the teacher stepped out of the vestibule with a bell in her hand. She seemed surprised to be greeted by two young men walking up the path. "You gentlemen are a little old for school, aren't you?" Her dark brown eyes glimmered with merriment.

"Don't worry, we finished the *First Reader,*" Jack said, smiling. "Besides, it might be tough to teach us anything." All three of them laughed. "Actually, we came to see if it would be possible to hold public meetings in the school during the evenings."

Distracted momentarily by a fist fight between two young scrappers, the teacher raised her hand. "Please excuse me for just a minute," she interjected. "I have to get these rascals inside or they'll never settle down." She rang the bell and the students formed two lines. As the children filed in to their desks, Miss Keats returned to George and Jack. "It's fine with me," she said, "but you'll need permission from our three school trustees." A few minutes later, with the address of each trustee in hand, the brothers set out on foot.

They called first on Mr. Summers, owner of the dry goods store. He and his son, Eddie, were sorting through swatches of fabric when George and Jack arrived. They explained that they were planning to preach the simple gospel message and were not attached to any denomination. Mr. Summers weighed the request. It wasn't every day that something as innocent and intriguing as two traveling preachers came to Elora.

Stalling for a minute, he removed his spectacles and cleaned them, even though they already sparkled. Then he smiled, displaying a gold front tooth. "I can't see how it can do any harm," he said, putting his glasses back on. "I'd be happy to let you use the school as long as the other trustees are agreeable too."

Eddie, about the same age as George and Jack, looked on approvingly. "I hope things go well for you in Elora." His voice followed them as they started for the door. "If there's anything I can do, just let me know."

The rest of the day was spent finding the other two trustees, Mr. MacQuarrie and Mr. Coffer, and by supper time all three men had given their permission. Gratified with the trustees' response, George and Jack entered the kitchen just as Mrs. Applebee was laying pieces of chicken into an iron skillet where a chunk of lard sputtered and danced. Before long, the two hungry men were digging eagerly into hash browns, green beans, and crusty chicken dressed with pear chutney. For dessert each man heaped his bowl with the fresh strawberries that Mrs. Applebee had picked from her garden and then smothered in rich cream from her neighbour's Jersey cow. After supper they showed their gratitude by helping with the dishes and then, thanking her for the delicious meal, they headed upstairs.

At this moment, a crone-like person with bristling silver hair stuck her head in Mrs. Applebee's screen door. "Them's your boarders?" she rasped.

Mrs. Applebee nodded, putting a finger to her lips. "Nice young men," she whispered. "Well-bred. They say they're traveling preachers."

Mrs. Quinn pulled her bonnet strings tighter, nodded portentously, and hobbled back across the road. "Well-bred young men," she muttered under her breath. "At least they won't *murther* her in her bed."

Meanwhile, up in their room, the brothers discussed the best way to invite people in the community to the meetings. George suggested they make notices and post them around the village.

Waking before daylight, George lay in bed and listened to the steady patter of raindrops on the roof. It was the kind that would be good for Mrs. Applebee's garden. After breakfast, he and Jack sat down with a small pile of paper, two quill pens, and a bottle of ink borrowed from Mrs. Applebee.

"What shall we use as a heading?" George asked.

Jack unscrewed the lid of the ink bottle. "How about 'Public Meeting'?"

"Might be a little too vague," George reflected. "What do you think of 'Evangelical Meeting'?"

"That sounds kind of religious," Jack responded. Finally they settled on 'Gospel Meeting,' because, after all, it was the *gospel* or *good news* that they wanted to share. Writing carefully, and without spelling mistakes, was slow going for men far more accustomed to wielding a hay fork than a pen. But after much labour, they had a neat stack of notices to distribute.

That night, before going to bed, George wrote a letter to the church at Alistair's, telling them about the progress so far. George considered the Puslinch church to be a vital part of this work, knowing that without their prayers it would be difficult for him and Jack to continue.

He penned a few thoughts that had strengthened him spiritually during the past couple of days. Recalling the apostle Paul's letters to the churches, he added: "The grace of our Lord Jesus Christ be with you all."[8] When he had finished, he folded the letter and blew out the lamp. Then he knelt beside his bed and prayed earnestly, asking that each one who would attend the Elora meetings would indeed receive this essential, unmerited favour of the Lord.

The rain passed overnight, and by morning the sun shone warmly upon the damp soil, revealing jeweled cobwebs and glistening drops of moisture on green leaves. At the picket gate, the white peonies lolled on the grass, a shower of fallen diamonds sparkling from every heavy-headed globe.

After breakfast Jenny L.'s high melodious voice could be heard from the parlour as Mrs. Applebee untied her apron and packed a market basket. "I'm going down the village to see my sister, Verity. She's been laid up all spring with bronchitis. Short of breath but long on gossip, I always say. Can you men heat your stew at noon?"

"Of course!" George assured her as he dried the porridge pot. "Don't worry about a thing."

"Just slam the screen door behind you to keep the flies out," Mrs. Applebee cautioned.

～◌

The heat and humidity of the day increased as George and Jack posted their notices in various public places. They received Mr. Foster's immediate approval to tack one on the tongue-and-groove wall just inside the entrance of his store. Full of questions, Mr. Foster leaned back against the counter and crossed his arms. "Now, who would it be that you fellows represent?"

"We represent Christ, and Him only," George replied.

"I mean," the storekeeper asked, rather awkwardly, "which church ordained you or sent you?"

"Jack and I each made a individual decision to do this work. Entirely on our own. Only then did we share it with a few others. We feel this way of life is a specific *calling* by the Holy Spirit. Without the assurance that God called us, we wouldn't be able to do this."

"In a way, we hardly have a choice," Jack added. "We don't feel we can refuse the call to tell other people about God's love for them and about their need of a Saviour."

"Well, if you don't represent a group, then who supports you?" the store-keeper persisted. "You know, your expenses."

"Nobody is supporting us in that way," Jack admitted. "We're trusting the Father who called us to also care for us." His voice radiated the trans-parent faith of a child, while his brown eyes shone with intensity.

Mr. Foster gawked in stunned silence; his mouth opened and closed without a word. Suddenly he caught himself and forced a smile. "Well, all the best then," he managed as he reached to open the door for the men.

"Past belief," he murmured as he watched them walk away. "And yet it does make sense. Good sense. God's work done in God's way should result in God's care."

When he closed the store for an hour at noon, Hugh Foster, a man who often read the Bible as he ate his dinner, turned to the verse: "Paul, a servant of Jesus Christ, *called* to be an apostle, separated unto the gospel of God."[9] He smiled as the authenticity of George's explanation registered.

~⌒

At the Elora Post Office, George slid his letter through the wicket grate to Mr. Chambers. "Would it be all right to put up a notice for some gospel meetings here?" he asked, handing the young postmaster a copy.

"I suppose that would be just fine," Herb Chambers said stiffly, after an odd hesitation. "It *is* a public notice board." Reading the paper care-fully, he asked if their mail might come addressed to an organizational name.

Jack explained, "We're simply Christians following the path set down by Jesus."

"You must be Protestants though," Herb ventured.

"No, we're not. We're neither Protestant nor Catholic." The postmaster's eyes narrowed with suspicion. "And when you think about it," Jack continued,

"Protestants began as a splinter group off the Catholic church. Although they were somewhat modified by Martin Luther, they spring from the self-same root."

"I've never heard of that before," Herb replied. "But if you're neither, then what are you?"

"We're part of a brotherhood of Christian believers. And free to serve God without any traditions."

"Well, are you a denomination of some sort?"

"I'm sorry, this must be confusing," Jack apologized. "We aren't part of any denomination. The New Testament believers never took a label. And we don't want one either." His face flushed with conviction.

Herb looked bewildered. "Do you think it's wrong to have a name?"

"Whether or not it's wrong is up to our Lord," Jack explained. "We certainly harbour no ill feelings toward anyone who loves our Saviour.[10] But for us, we believe God has called us to simply bear the name of Christ. No other name can save."[11]

Herb Chambers pressed his thumb and forefinger against his eyes as if to shut out Jack and his disturbing words. "So...you think a divided Christianity grieves the heart of God?" he ventured at last.

Jack's composure softened as he absorbed the young man's turmoil. "Not long ago I felt just like you," he sympathized. "If you had a dying family member, how important do you reckon his last request would be?" Jack studied Herb's face. "Very important, wouldn't you agree?"

Herb nodded, his eyes glazed.

"Well," Jack continued, "Jesus' last prayer was a plea that His followers might all be one.[12] Having a label promotes a sense of 'I'm different than you' or even 'I'm better than you.' That kind of thinking leads to divisions.[13] If people would abandon their labels and dogmas—and come together in the Spirit of Christ—we'd have unity."

Herb swayed slightly in front of the grid of pigeon holes. "I'll speak to my wife," he said. "Maybe we'll see you on Sunday evening."

Back on the sidewalk, George spoke first. "The Scripture says the whole family of God—in heaven and on the earth—is named after Christ, and only Christ.[14] His name is above every name.[15] I can't fathom why any Christian would want to be known by something different." As they passed a small clapboard barber shop, George reached down to tickle an orange kitten sleeping on a warm bench in the morning sunshine. "How can people be so divided on earth, even to the point of fighting each other, and still expect to be united in heaven? But each group is sure that *they* are part of the body of Christ."

Jack's sides shook as a soft chuckle erupted. "I've never seen one part of a body walking up the left side of a street while another part walked down the right side."

George smiled at Jack's wry wit. Then he changed the subject. "I think we should give an invitation to each of the trustees, as a courtesy." When they stopped at Summers' Dry Goods to deliver the notice of the meeting, there was no sign of Eddie.

"I don't see your son today, Mr. Summers...." George hesitated.

"Eddie is the traveler for the wholesale part of our business," Mr. Summers explained. "He calls on proprietors of dry goods stores from Stratford to Toronto, and he'll be gone until tomorrow."

"Maybe you can let him know about the meetings as well," Jack suggested, remembering Eddie's cheerful remarks on their last visit.

"I'll definitely mention it to him," Mr. Summers promised. "He does a little preaching himself at times, so he'll be eager to go."

The morning passed quickly as the men walked from place to place, putting up notices and speaking to people here and there. As they knocked at the doors of various homes east of Geddes Street, George noticed that many of the homes were built of limestone from the nearby quarry. Jack covered one side of each street while George worked on the opposite side. Most visits were brief as they met busy housewives hanging out their wash, baking bread, or weeding gardens. Although most people were courteous, some were clearly disinterested, and a few were downright rude.

"We have our own church," one lady retorted, cutting George off in mid-sentence. "Beats me why the likes of you would come to Elora anyway when there are lots of fine churches here already." Her bright terrier eyes snapped as she shook her spindly finger in his face. "Do you hear?"

George blinked as he took a step backward. "I'm sorry, ma'am," he apologized. "I just wanted to make sure you had an invitation." His face burned red as the door slammed in his face. It reminded him of his first attempt to give away his money. *Jesus never promised that being a Christian would be easy,* he thought as he hurried down the path. *But He did teach us to love those who dislike us.* An instant prayer formed as he forged on to the next door.[16]

Occasionally George and Jack were invited in for a cup of tea and neighbourly conversation. One such visit occurred just before noon. Jack knocked on the door of a little frame cottage, the closest house to the Elora public school. A young woman with wavy blonde hair answered the door and listened attentively to Jack's invitation.

Her eyebrows drew together in discernment. "Are you having these meetings by yourself?"

"Oh, no!" Jack rejoined hastily. "My companion is on the opposite side of the street, giving out invitations there too."

"Where do you men live?"

"Well, right now we're staying with Mrs. Applebee on Victoria Street, but we don't have any permanent address."

The woman broke into a knowing smile. "I'm Jessie Liddle and my husband's name is Lyman." She shook Jack's hand vigorously. "We've been studying the New Testament and praying for a simpler form of church life. One day we discussed the traveling pairs of preachers that Jesus sent out, but we doubted if we'd ever meet men like that in our day. My husband'll be home soon. Would you join us for dinner?"

A dusty pair of work boots had been neatly set together on the front stoop when George and Jack returned. Lyman Liddle, a small man with deep-set eyes, greeted them at the front door and shook their hands heartily. As he led them through the parlour, the brothers noticed the threadbare carpet and the plain but tidy furnishings. The aroma of muffins met them as they entered Jessie's freshly scrubbed kitchen.

"Do you think we should shake again?" she laughed, extending her right oven mitt toward Jack as Lyman pointed them to the table.

An immediate feeling of trust resonated among the four of them. Before long Lyman plunged into some questions, eager to hear what the two men had to say. Although Jessie said little, she listened intently as the brothers told about their background and mission. The cream of leek soup and corn-meal muffins were delicious to George and Jack, but they were almost overlooked by the Liddles. Hungry for the fellowship they had been reading about in the Scripture, Lyman and Jessie could only pick at their meal as Jack recounted his dissatisfaction as a colporteur. And how he had searched for a spiritual family until he met George over a roadside fence.

Before Lyman returned to the Mundell Furniture factory at one o'clock, he promised to be at the Sunday night meeting. George was deeply pleased; he felt that same warm feeling with Lyman and Jessie that he had when he met Alistair. The noon hour had opened up in a most hospitable way.

Keeping their eye on the town clock, George and Jack arranged their afternoon to arrive at the school just before class was dismissed. When they came to the door, Katie Keats worked her way down the aisle.

"Miss Keats," Jack said, "do you think it'd be appropriate to announce the gospel meeting times to the children, so they can tell their parents?"

"Certainly," she exclaimed and led them to the front of the class. Their invitation to hear the simple message of Christ was carried to many homes that evening. Before they left the school, George asked Miss Keats if she played the piano.

Her eyes sparkled mischievously. "Do you have a sudden thirst for a piano concerto by Tchaikovsky or Beethoven?"

Jack laughed. "George might prefer 'The Flight of the Bumble Bee.'"

"I'm afraid I don't know any of those," George admitted with a smile. "Actually, I was going to ask if you'd play the hymns during our meeting."

"I guess I could do that." Miss Keats smiled. "But pianists in Elora don't come cheap," she added with a straight face.

~⌒

In a small Ontario village ripe for tantalizing news, the two stranger preachers had quickly become the talk of the town, just as Paul and Barnabas must have been centuries before. Women prattled about them at quilting bees; families mentioned them at the supper table; neighbours spoke of them over backyard fences; men debated their activities at the barbershop; and Mr. Foster announced the meetings to everyone who came into his general store. Although a gamut of heated opinions rose from around his counter, many planned to be at the school on Sunday evening.

Outside in the shade of Hugh Foster's porch, a red-faced matron settled down at one end of the bench, untied her bonnet strings and fanned herself expansively. "The way Hugh Foster goes on about these preachers, you'd think they were the new Moody and Sankey."

Holding forth from the other end of the bench was a tall fair-haired spinster, her voice rising in shrill indignation. "Why in the name of time do we need more religion in this village? Five churches going strong already. Full to bustin' and spewin' out."

"Maybe so, but if they stay on a spell, I'd like to hear them out." The fretful voice belonged to a portly woman with black-stockinged ankles the colour and shape of stove pipes. "Unless my gout lets up, I don't get further than the store these days," she added as she heaved herself down onto the centre of the bench. Her round elbow jostled her neighbour, tipping her sideways on a broken slat.

Dropping her fan, the flustered matron hastily drew her parcel onto her lap. "Mind them eggs, Thyra. You near about set down on 'em. Then we'd hear some squawking." Her lips pursed as she turned back the brown paper and extracted a length of fabric. "Look at the shameful quality of this dotted Henrietta, will you? Seventy-five cents a yard and the warp all tangled. No selvedge edge to speak of. I've never seen the like of it in all my years of dressmaking. I don't know why Hugh Foster doesn't keep better stock. The man's tighter than skin on a louse."

Ignoring the matron's complaint, the comely spinster edged forward on the arm of the bench. "Hugh claims these men are bachelors, but that's a likely story. A pair of disgruntled young wives are at home, I expect."

The matron's eyes twinkled. "It'd behoove you to find out," she said. "You're still in the running and rattling around in that big house alone."

Out of the corner of her eye, the spinster caught sight of a handsome young man angling up to the porch, his hat drawn down to his eyebrows. She detected his deliberate attempt to avoid eye contact. "Why, if it isn't the town's most eligible bachelor," she sang out perversely as she stuck out a foot to bar the door. "Let's hear what Lord Summers has got to say about these traveling preachers."

The young man tipped his fedora gallantly. "I certainly plan on a front row seat on Sunday." A grin flickered across his refined features. "I'd say if the mighty Billy Sunday himself arrived in Elora, you good ladies would tar and feather him and run him out of town." Eddie Summers disappeared through the screen door to a shrill and scornful chorus of outrage.

Oblivious to public speculations and the stir they were causing, George and Jack retired to their bedroom at Mrs. Applebee's. Kneeling at their bedsides, they prayed earnestly to be in harmony with the Holy Spirit so there would be a truly spiritual benefit to the hearts of both the speakers and the listeners. They didn't want to draw attention to themselves, other than what was needed to present the gospel invitation.

Before turning in that night, George stood thoughtfully at the bedroom window and looked out at the dimming village lights. Afar in the west, a single large planet sparkled with the intensity of early summer. "If just one person hears the inaudible voice of Jesus," he said, "and truly follows Him, it will be all worthwhile."

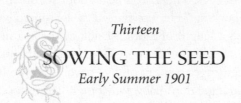

Thirteen

SOWING THE SEED
Early Summer 1901

"I'll see to it that the roast's cut and the gravy stirred up by five o'clock," Mrs. Applebee called upstairs.

George stuck his head out of the bedroom door. "Thanks, Mrs. Applebee. We'd like to go in good time tonight—our first meeting and all."

The landlady smiled, one foot on the bottom step. "The meat peddler said it was a sirloin piece, and cautioned me not to overcook it or it would get stringy. Besides, I want to get a good seat myself," she added with a toss of her head. "The entire village will want to hear what my boarders have to say…"

George and Jack set out right after supper. A few of the older children playing in the yards recognized the men and extended shy greetings while the smaller ones stared inquisitively as the brothers passed by. Inside, most adults had taken advantage of the warm Sunday afternoon to rest.

Katie Keats, who had promised to unlock the school, was already moving desks when George and Jack stepped into the cloakroom. As George surveyed the classroom, he noticed some blue spots on the white ceiling above the stove. Astutely he guessed their source: last winter someone must have set a frozen ink bottle to thaw on the hottest part of the stove and then forgotten to remove it in time. George smiled to himself as he pictured how the cork would have shot into the air, pursued by a blue liquid tail.

On either side of the room four tall windows extended the full height of the ceiling. The maple plank floor, waxed and shiny, was worn in the centre aisle by years of scuffling feet. Above the wainscotting and chair rail, bright canary walls displayed samples of the pupils' penmanship, maps of the British Empire, and the results of a spelling bee. Behind the teacher's desk, a blackboard ran across the front of the classroom, and on an upright Bell piano in the front left corner sat a nature study of various birds' eggs.

The brothers laid their Bibles on Miss Keats's desk and quickly arranged the desks and chairs to accommodate as many as possible. A number of coal oil lanterns were set out, but they would hardly be needed as the meeting would surely be over before dark.

Just as they finished setting up the room, a few children came in, having run ahead of their parents, who were enjoying their leisurely stroll in the coolness of the evening. In sharp contrast to the boisterousness of a school day, the youngsters behaved with subdued respect as they hesitated in the porch, where the dry smell of chalk and books assailed everyone's nose. Around the school, twittering swallows dived for insects as people arrived in groups of twos and threes. Some visited outside while others went in early, eager to find a strategic place to see and hear the preachers.

Mr. Foster, from the general store, arrived with his wife, Gertrude, an outgoing lady with a contagious smile and a figure that strained the seams of her tight drugget dress. She greeted everyone enthusiastically as she moved along. Their son and his wife and two grandchildren had joined them for the outing.

Mrs. Applebee entered the schoolhouse with her neighbour, Mrs. Quinn. The fragile sticklike widow followed Mrs. Applebee stiffly to a seat in the third row. In every way, the pair played out the contrast between a rosy-cheeked apple and the thin twig from which it hangs.

As George scanned the rapidly filling room, he noticed Mr. Summers, the owner of the dry goods store, with his son, Eddie. It was only at the last minute that Eddie Summers had arrived home from a cricket match. He had met his father coming down the oak staircase of their stately home, its entrance recessed between a copper-roofed bay and an imposing corner turret. The senior Summers was elegantly attired in his Sunday best. As the village clothier, he felt obliged to be one of the best-dressed men in Elora.

George watched Eddie chatting with Mrs. Applebee and Hugh Foster. He noted the young draper's genial diplomacy among the crowd. With his centre-parted, carefully oiled hair, groomed moustache, and fastidious turn-out, Eddie gave the impression of a prince moving among lesser nobility.

Although the meeting was scheduled to begin at seven o'clock, the room was almost full by a quarter to the hour. Unknown to the brothers, many people saw the duo as a kind of entertainment in a village where time itself seemed to stand still, watching its reflection in the shopwindows.

George and Jack were greeting people when, in the midst of the activity, Jack suddenly realized they were going to be short of seats. George sensed the concern on Jack's face and beckoned him outside.

"I remember seeing some planks in a stack beside the fence," George said, "and some blocks of hardwood in the woodpile. We'd better bring a few inside." Without another word, they each grabbed a big block of maple and carried it inside, setting it along the side wall. Returning, they carried a thick pine plank and placed each end on a block. Several men saw what was needed and followed them out for more. A few boys moved to sit on the makeshift benches, grinning as they elbowed each other. By seven o'clock every seat was filled and a line of men leaned against the rear wall.

George stood motionless at the back of the room. In one way he felt anxious and jittery, and yet, on a deeper level, he was filled with an inner peace, knowing this was not his work but the work of God. Standing in front of a crowd was the very last place he would choose to be—but he wasn't doing the choosing. A quiet man by nature, he much preferred to work alone under the open sky. Only his strong faith in the One who had called him into this work gave the gentle farm boy strength to continue. Now the hour had come, and with a deep breath, George followed Jack up the centre aisle. Taking his seat, he glanced at the crowd with an expression of warmth and goodwill. As he surveyed the rows of unfamiliar faces, he had the calm realization that even though he'd never met any of these folks before, somehow he felt a love for them. He knew that behind the masks that shield the human heart, all people were the same. All needed love and hope. His insight was suspended as Jack moved to stand in front of the teacher's desk.

Jack nervously cleared his throat. "George and I want to thank you all for coming out this evening," he began. "We hope you'll be comfortable in spite of the tight quarters. To start our meeting, we have asked Miss Keats to play 'Tell Me the Story of Jesus.'"

With that, Katie Keats moved from her seat on the front row to the piano stool. She paused for a moment as if to centre herself, and then she adjusted the hymn book and began to play. Everyone joined in heartily:

Tell me the story of Jesus;
Write on my heart every word.
Tell me the story most precious,
Sweetest that ever was heard.

Tell how the angels, in chorus,
Sang as they welcomed His birth,
"Glory to God in the highest!
Peace and good tidings to earth."

Love in that story so tender,
Clearer than ever I see;
Stay, let me say, "I will follow
Him who has suffered for me."[1]

Jack's deep baritone voice led the singing, and George marveled at his calmness and apparent comfort in front of the crowd.

As the last notes died out, Jack clasped his hands at his waist. "Would you please join me in bowing our heads as we ask for God's favour this evening?" As people closed their eyes, the room went quiet.

Lowering his head, George hunched forward, elbows on his knees, fingers resting lightly against his temples. In the fleeting moment before Jack began, the prescribed reading from the prayer book flashed through his mind. What a difference between truly praying and simply offering a string of words, elegant as they may be. Then Jack's words—spoken slowly, deliberately, and in the simplest of language—washed over him, silencing his distracting thoughts.

"Our gracious Father," Jack prayed, his voice trembling with intensity and fervour, "may each of us assembled in this room feel Your presence as never before. George and I stand before You in all weakness and inability, pleading that the Holy Spirit may add life to our words. We thank You for each soul who has turned aside from the natural affairs of the evening to give ear to Your glorious gospel. According to Your eternal purpose, may Jesus speak to each of our hearts. These favours we ask through the precious blood of our Lord and Saviour. Amen."

Although Jack's prayer was over almost before it began, a hearty "Amen" resounded from the audience. George had barely opened his eyes when with a start he heard Jack say, "My companion, George, will share a few thoughts with you now."

As he exchanged places with Jack, George looked into the eager faces and whispered a prayer. "Dear Father, please reveal Your Son through me." Neither of the brothers had thought of using a prepared script as they had seen other preachers do. Mindful of Jesus' teaching that in the hour of need a believer would be given appropriate words, they thought of themselves solely as living instruments to transmit a message inspired by the Spirit.

George opened his New Testament and swallowed. "Tonight I'd like to read a passage from the Gospel of John, chapter one. It tells us about the day after John the Baptist had baptized Jesus. Friends, can you imagine John standing with two of his disciples, perhaps under the shade of an olive tree? About four o'clock in the afternoon, Jesus walked past them, and John said, 'Behold, the Lamb of God!' The whole purpose of these gospel meetings is to help each of us *see* Jesus, the Lamb of God, in a deeper and more profound way than ever before."

Glancing down at the printed page, George went on, paraphrasing the text in his own words: "When the two disciples heard John speak, they began to follow Jesus. Then He turned and saw them. '*What seek ye?*' He asked. 'Teacher,' they replied, '*Where dwellest Thou?*' Then Jesus said to them, '*Come and see.*' So they went and saw where He was staying and spent that day with Him."[2] George closed his Bible and looked up, scanning the attentive faces before him. "What seek *ye?*" George paused for a few seconds. "In other words, what are *you* looking for…here, tonight?"

The crowd stirred as each person pondered, "Why *am* I here tonight?"

"Although you're hearing my voice," George persisted, "it's Jesus who asks that question, not me. Some of us may never have confronted the all-important issue: What desire is foremost in *my* life? Is it to be prosperous and secure? Or just to eke out a living, week by week? Is it to be well thought of in the district? Perhaps as a good farmer, a talented tradesman, or an upstanding shop owner? Could it be we desire a certain status or influence in the settlement or in our church? All of these may be fine in their place, but should they be our *chief* ambition? Or are we, like Andrew and John, truly seeking the sacred, the divine, the spiritual? If you can honestly respond as they did, 'Teacher, where do You live?' then you, too, can benefit from Jesus' answer. In other words, those two fishermen aspired to grasp the very essence of His life. And indirectly, of their own.

"Our homes are the centre of our living. We may leave them for work, for laying in supplies, for visiting, for various reasons. And yet we always come back to them. But do we really want to know firsthand the place where Jesus lives? And what wisdom we can gain there?

"Andrew and John weren't interested in a quick how-do-you-do along the side of some road. They wanted a much deeper, more purposeful discussion. Earlier in my own life, my desire for Christ's presence was limited to a casual how-do-you-do on a Sunday morning. But each of us has the ability to follow Him with our hearts to His place of tranquillity. He'll invite us in, help us to lay aside our burdens, and truly rest."

Lyman and Jessie Liddle sat on the front row with their three children. As Jack listened to George, he noticed their oldest son, Jimmy, draw his hand out of his pocket, raise it to his mouth, and pretend to cough. Beside him, his father sat with his arms crossed, looking straight ahead at George. With a sleight of hand befitting any magician, the lad deftly slipped a Scotch mint into his mouth. A smug smile flickered across Jimmy's mischievous face as he lifted his head again to look at the preachers. Jack smiled warmly when the boy's startled gaze met his own.

"Have you ever wished you could sit around a camp fire with Jesus and His disciples,[3] and converse with Him and truly get to know Him?" George asked. "Well, let me assure you that it's entirely possible. If we acknowledge His nearness and listen for Him in our hearts, we will sense a still, small voice.[4] And as our awareness of God deepens, what has previously been a mere existence can break out into a richer, more consequential life. Just as an eggshell must open for the chick to live, so our heart must open for our soul to abound.

"This spiritual relationship with Christ is essential," George continued. "It's a living bond that forms now and never ends. Jesus didn't preach a fancy sermon to explain this to Andrew and John. He used three simple words: 'Come and see.' Jesus extends the same invitation to each of us."

George felt the attention of the room focused on his words, but now that he was in the midst of it, his apprehension lifted. His time alone with God had prepared him for this moment. As he heard the words pouring out of him like a fountain, he realized the value of the hours that he had spent reading, praying, and meeting with the friends in Puslinch. He found himself repeating some of the thoughts and even the phrases he had garnered among the little church.

"Can you visualize an exhausted traveler, parched and dusty, on a desert trail and burdened under an oppressive pack? And beside that road waits a man with a cup of cold water and an eagerness to lift and carry the biting load. In a way, that picture describes each person on the road of life. All of mankind is thirsty and fatigued, labouring under a heavy weight as they strive to live life to the full. Some become so familiar with the strain they barely lift their eyes to fairer prospects. Yet every hour of every day Jesus invites the weary and heavy-laden traveler to come to Him and receive rest.[5] For life without God can never be satisfying."

For several more minutes George spoke the simple message from his heart, and then he concluded by going back to the Scripture and repeating the strikingly simple dialogue: "Master, what is your life all about?" "Come and see."

Closing his Bible, George asked Miss Keats to play "Jesus, I My Cross Have Taken." The piano filled the room and the voices rang out the final chorus with enthusiasm. When the hymn finished, he sat down.

Jack seemed to bound to his feet. "A woman from Nova Scotia once told me about walking into a strong headwind along a low wharf. It was just before nightfall. As she looked out to sea, she noticed a storm brewing. Ahead of her, two small girls walked and chattered, oblivious to their surroundings. One had a little dog who followed her closely. Although he was almost blind, he, too, seemed to enjoy the wind and the seaside. Then, without warning, the dog ventured too close, misjudged his step, and tumbled off the edge of the wharf into the choppy water. The girls didn't notice at first, and the dog tried to find them in the gathering darkness. He paddled furiously, thinking he knew the right direction, but his strokes only carried him the wrong way, out to the open sea and certain death. His struggling was of absolutely no benefit to him. In fact, it took him farther away. Suddenly, his little mistress saw he was missing and called out for him. The dog heard her voice and paused to listen. Again she called, loudly and clearly. Now, knowing the direction in the mounting waves, he turned and swam straight toward her. When he approached the wharf, she scooped him into her arms and hugged him. The exhausted little dog was safe as his young mistress carried him home.

"This is the story of each of us until we hear the call of Jesus, giving direction and meaning to our lives," Jack explained. "Until we answer Him, all of our efforts, even religious ones, no matter how well intentioned or vigorous, will only take us farther from Him."

Jack rephrased Jesus' parable to the religious Pharisees: "The man who enters by the door is the shepherd of the sheep. They recognize their shepherd's voice. He calls each of them *by name* and *leads them out*. But you do not believe because you are not My sheep. My sheep hear my voice and I know them. They follow Me and I give them eternal life."[6]

Mrs. Applebee thumbed through her big Bible until she found the verses Jack had just quoted. Then she nudged Mrs. Quinn with her elbow and pointed out the text. Mrs. Quinn's spectacles glinted in the soft evening light as she craned her neck to read.

"During Jesus' time," Jack continued, "there were communal sheepfolds in every village. A doorkeeper guarded the entrance during the night. Early in the morning, each shepherd came to the door and called his own sheep *by name* and led them out to find pasture. His own sheep had come to know the distinctive sound, the unique tone of his voice. They had learned that their shepherd came daily to lead and nurture them. And they responded joyfully to his familiar call. Sheep belonging to someone else would not respond to that voice and were left behind. This story tells of the intimate bond between the Shepherd and each of His flock.

"Everyone here this evening is also a sheep, a spiritual sheep, who needs God's care—whether we know it or not. Like the natural sheep in the parable, Jesus wants to lead us out from the crowded walls and soiled conditions of our human nature and into the expansiveness of His life.

"The Christian life is the response to a call from One who has no audible voice. He speaks to us from the depths of our own soul. Jesus said that God's kingdom is not something you can see. There's no use saying, 'Look! Here it is,' or 'Look! There it is,' for the kingdom of God is within you.'"[7]

Jack hooked a thumb behind his left suspender as he studied the faces confronting him. "God speaks to us out of every circumstance of life," he said quietly. "If we rely on our intellect and our five senses alone, we'll miss the whole meaning of life. But if we learn to listen for the inner voice, we'll find peace and joy, here and forever. Although many other elusive voices call out to each of us daily, none of these lead to a lasting happiness.

"Later in this parable Jesus said: 'I am the door of the sheep...If anyone enters by Me, he will be saved, and he will go in and out and find pasture.' This part of the parable describes isolated folds, high on the hills, that often consisted of only a circular stone wall without any door. During warm weather, the flocks stayed in these hillside folds at night while the shepherd stretched out across the opening. Nothing and no one could enter the fold except past him. In effect he was the door. Sheep could not live without a shepherd[8] in the Judean mountains, and those who wandered alone eventually starved or were killed by predators.

"Jesus taught us that He is the only door, the only way, and the only entrance into a new life in the Spirit. This Shepherd of our soul gently calls us to come in and go out with Him as He influences both the inside and the outside of our lives. He not only protects, comforts, and heals our inner hurts, but He leads us into wider fields of spiritual growth when He knows the time is right. Remember, real life can never be experienced without the great Shepherd[9] becoming the most important influence in our lives."

Jack nodded his head in Katie's direction and asked her to play "Why I Love Jesus" to the popular tune of "When You and I Were Young, Maggie." In George's mind the image of the shepherd calling for his sheep blurred with the one of the little girl standing in the storm, calling for her dog. It seemed to him as if everyone in the school sang with feeling.

> You ask why I love and adore Jesus,
> Perhaps you have never been told,
> Of the thorn path He trod all alone for me,
> To carry me back to the fold.
>
> And all through the night with the storm raging,
> He called and He searched after me,
> And that's why I love and adore Jesus
> And Jesus has proved He loves me.[10]

When the last notes had died away, George glanced up at the school-house clock. Just seven minutes short of an hour.

Again Jack moved to the front of the desk and stood, looking into the shining faces of the crowd. "Once again we'd like to thank you for enduring the tight quarters," he said earnestly, lacing his fingers. "Especially you men standing along the back wall. God willing, we intend to have a meeting each night of the coming week. We hope to see you all again."

As he and George worked their way to the rear door, people got to their feet and slowly spilled outside into the cool night air. Many bid farewell to the men and said how much they appreciated their messages.

When the Liddles were well away from the crowd, Lyman spoke quietly. "I've never been to a church meeting like that before. It certainly didn't follow any of the traditional rules."

Jessie nodded. "Strange to see a minister without a starched clerical collar or black frock coat."

"Indeed," Lyman agreed as he unlocked the door to the house, allowing the children to race inside. "I know you can't judge a book by its cover, but it seems that those fellows are living exactly what they're talking about. And it wasn't just what they said, but the humble way they said it. No pretense at all."

After Jessie had tucked the children into bed and kissed them good-night, the couple sat down for a hot drink and a dish of raspberries. "I'm certainly looking forward to getting to know George and Jack better," Jesse reflected as she sipped her tea. "What they spoke about tonight was so simple yet so clear. I can't wait to hear what they have to say tomorrow."

"What Jack said about sheep tonight," Lyman noted, "reminds me about the story of an old shepherd. He gathered in the stragglers by leading his most dependable sheep among them. The wayward sheep would be drawn into the safety of the fold by following the ones who were listening to the shepherd. George and Jack really do seem to be following Jesus."

"It's wonderful the way God has answered our prayers." Jessie swirled her tea leaves. "I wonder if others feel the same as we do."

～℗

As Hugh Foster undressed for bed in his apartment above the general store, he puzzled over the evening's events. "I just can't believe those two fellows forgot to pass around a collection plate at the end of the service," he said to Gertrude as he buttoned his nightshirt. "I've never seen an evangelist forget *that* part before."

"Maybe they get a salary from a church somewhere," his wife speculated.

"But they don't. That's just it. When I asked them how they supported themselves, they told me very clearly that God is going to supply their needs." Hugh scratched his head. "I just assumed that they'd take an offering. I had a ten-cent piece ready in my pocket."

Gertrude's voluminous nightgown resembled a full-rigged schooner as she sailed past the open window. "It's kind of a vital detail to overlook, don't you think?" she chuckled.

"Oh, well," Hugh sighed. "They seem like nice lads, but I guess they're just beginners. By tomorrow night, they'll have realized their mistake. I'll take along a twenty-five cent shinplaster so they aren't short."

~◯

Across the village, Eddie Summers lounged on the front porch with a glass of chilled lemonade, watching the lights blink out one by one as his neighbours retired. The new electric streetlights in the village, all four of them, would be turned off at midnight. While he reflected on the evening's happenings, the second hymn drummed over and over in his mind:

> Jesus, I my cross have taken,
> All to leave and follow Thee,
> Destitute, despised, forsaken,
> Thou, from hence, my all shalt be.
>
> Perish every fond ambition,
> All I've sought and hoped and known;
> Yet how rich is my condition!
> God and heaven are still mine own.
>
> I will follow Thee, my Saviour:
> Thou hast shed Thy blood for me;
> And though all the world forsake Thee,
> By Thy grace I will follow Thee.[11]

Until tonight the words of this familiar hymn had always seemed passive to Eddie. But now he could picture a sublime purpose as he saw two men actively demonstrating the reality of taking a cross, of leaving all, of setting aside every fond ambition and following their Saviour. Although Eddie had been in church services of many stripes and done a good bit of preaching himself, nothing held a candle to what he had witnessed tonight. He recalled the time when the disciples saw that Jesus lived by a power beyond their comprehension. In amazement they had asked themselves, "What kind of man is this?"[12]

He was still puzzling about what kind of men these were, and whether his own preaching would engender such a question, when his father, Oliver, thrust his head out of the door. "I'm heading off to bed, Eddie. Just wanted to say goodnight."

"Yes, goodnight, Dad." Eddie set his lemonade on a small rattan table beside the chair. "By the way, what did you make of the men tonight?"

"Well," Oliver said, tightening his imported night robe around him, "they're certainly marching to a different drummer than most."

"I'll say," Eddie acknowledged. "I've been to a lot of revivals, but I've never seen an evangelist in rugged farm duds and work boots."

"Right. Quite a contrast to the usual spit and polish."

Eddie grinned up at his father. "But who are we to talk. Fine clothes are our bread and butter."

Oliver's face took on a sober cast. "Still, I'd have to say I was touched by their sincerity. They're the plainest preachers I've heard, but they might also be the most genuine." He stared off at the distant lights. "Anyway, it's getting late. Enjoy the night air, son."

Among those gathering that night had been Harold MacQuarrie, whose shingle, dangling under a stone archway, advertised "Joiner and Undertaker." Folks said he could have made a fortune when diphtheria swept through the village and carried away so many of their children. But it was known that he did not charge any of the fathers for the coffins that he made during the epidemic. His own fair-haired twins had both been taken away during the same night, their faces of laughter turning to granite. They had been laid out in the chilly air of the MacQuarrie's stone cottage while the heat of July blistered the very grass outside. From that day forward, Harold MacQuarrie had never smiled.

On the second morning after the girls' death, the minister had come to the crepe-wreathed door and laid a hand on Harold's shoulder. "It's time," he kindly remonstrated, "time to give the children a Christian burial. Harold, you can't hold them to yourself any longer. You need to lay them to rest."

All Elora knew of the secret that allowed Harold to pursue the terrible necessities of his trade. "Like his father before him," people reminded each other in dark undertones. But tonight at the schoolhouse he had been sober.

As he made his way back to the darkened stone cottage, he reflected uneasily on the irony that his skill as a joiner only led toward the final separation of loved ones. He reflected, too, on the young men with the fervent voices who had asserted that, "God speaks to us out of every circumstance of life." The words drew a painful response in Harold's heart.

Stepping into the silent cottage, he listened, as was his habit. When only the impassive tick of the kitchen clock echoed back, he struck a match and lit the oil lamp beside the door. In the flickering light, he made his way to a cabinet under the cellar stairs and took a draught from a dark bottle, hoping to silence the voices within. Long after midnight Harold stumbled up the stairs and heaved himself across the double bed.

Meanwhile, upstairs in their room, Jack blew out the candle. "I'll write to Alistair in the morning," he said. "I'm sure the others will want to know how the meeting went."

"That's a fine idea," George agreed as he lifted the window sash at the head of his bed. "I just hope that this beginning is the work of the Holy Spirit. Otherwise all of our efforts will be worthless." Then George knelt in the darkness.

The delicate incense of Mrs. Applebee's locust tree wafted through the open window as George arose, stretched, and then settled onto his bed. *The Spirit is more penetrating than the fragrance of the locust trees scattered through the yards and gardens of Elora,* he thought. *Everyone breathes the same sweet air, yet only a few will respond in awe to the breath of God.*

Fourteen

BEHOLDING THE GLORY
Mid-Summer 1901

The freshness of early summer wilted under the sullen heat of July when a month of drought visited Wellington County. Day after day cumulus clouds piled themselves high in the southwest but laboured futilely to bring forth rain. A desiccating wind seared men working under the pitiless sun, their faces turned heavenward, imploring the rain to come. Nightfall brought fitful sleep punctuated by gasps of exhaustion as heads tossed to and fro, away from the heat generated by feather pillows and straw ticks. Husbands and wives turned from each other and sighed in their sleep, as though nature herself decreed isolation.

In Elora nearly every cistern had run dry and word spread of shallow wells dropping drastically. Kitchen gardens withered and toads languished under yellow rhubarb leaves. Ribbons of dust curled off stagecoach and wagon wheels, choking pedestrians and casting a haze of brown powder over Geddes Street. Hugh Foster plugged every crack and hung an oiled sheet over the screen door while the men on his front porch muttered about the risk of fire. Dragonflies skimmed the mud flats of the Grand River and sucked briefly at the trickle in the riverbed. The cracked mud bottom resembled ghastly faces, tortured by unending thirst, and village lads in dusty knickerbockers tossed aside their fishing lines in disgust.

In the languorous afternoons at Wood Creek Farm, the granite field-stones of the cellar walls sweated great beads of condensation while across the yard gusts of hot wind slammed the barn doors. Alistair and Timothy's labours hung heavily upon them as their trousers and boots became caked with dust and sweat. In the evenings sheets of strange hypnotic lightning irradiated the sky over the cedar bush while thunder shook the chimneys and echoed around the outbuildings.

By mid-July, the goldfinches that had hatched in the nest above the well had flown and the barn cats, lean from suckling, had raised their spring litters and now, with smouldering eyes, pondered a summer batch. Phoebe's school friends, merry girls who fancied themselves young ladies, visited the farm in droves for the express purpose of choosing a kitten, not to speak of exchanging confidences and sharing patterns for lace berthas. Occasionally, a boy's name fell under debate, and Andrew Gillespie would have reddened to overhear his strength whispered about and giggled over.

Over the past year, Bella Purves' iron constitution had wrestled her back to a measure of strength and, to Joe's delight, she had rallied considerably. Although still bedridden, she had been easier for him to care for, smiling and speaking in slurred fragments. But a fortnight ago, the doctor's dire prediction had fulfilled itself and a second attack had shaken her body.

Priscilla again began to relieve Joe Purves by taking care of Bella two or three times each week. After her supper dishes were finished, she would set the table for breakfast and then start out on foot to visit the old couple. She could make the walk in three quarters of an hour and usually arrived late in the evening when Joe was the most weary and grateful for some sleep. Priscilla would sit through the long dark night with Bella, doing needlework, mending clothes, or reading beside the kerosene lamp.

One sultry morning well before daybreak, Joe's mantel clock struck four times from somewhere in the shadows, stirring Priscilla from her fitful dozing. As her mind cleared, she pictured Alistair and her children sleeping peacefully at home and thanked God for blessing her life in so many ways. As the first light began to creep through the hedgerows, her memory drifted back over the weeks since George and Jack had left. Every week the church had received a letter from one or the other of them. Just last Sunday Alistair had produced the latest envelope from his shirt pocket after the concluding hymn had been sung. Fishing his jackknife out of his trousers, he had slit it open and unfolded the letter.

"This arrived from George in Friday's mail," he had explained as he glanced down at the signature. "I'll read it aloud." Leaning forward, he began, articulating each word as distinctly as a school boy at the head of his class.

Elora, Ontario
July 12, 1901

Dear friends,

We hope this finds each of you as happy and healthy as Jack and me. It was good to hear the drought hasn't burned the crops off so far. Mrs. Quinn's aunt is one of the oldest inhabitants here in Elora. Claims she was born in 1812 as General Brock's redcoats and the Americans exchanged cannon fire across the Niagara River. The old lady can't call to memory the likes of this dearth of rain with such scalding temperatures. Jack teases that the ravens will soon be bringing me bread and meat beside the Grand River. But I told him we're past that stage; we're already being sustained by a generous widow.[1] And Mrs. Applebee's certainly been fussing over us.

What a rare privilege we are enjoying as we try to share the good news. We've started to hand out invitations at the neighbouring farms, and although there's more legwork getting around, Jack and I feel pleased to be moving among farmers again. On occasion we get into a friendly visit, and yesterday the man at one place was short of help, so we rolled up our sleeves and pitched in. Our shoulders ached after lugging water to his stock for most of the afternoon. Over supper we got to share our story with the whole family. Among other things, I told them about the day we met in the sale barn in Berlin, Alistair. And about the circle of friends at Wood Creek Farm that has grown from the original three couples. Thank you all for being principal characters in the story of my life.

The schoolhouse continues to be packed most evenings but especially on Sundays when we start at seven so folks can bring their children. During the week we hold the meetings at eight P.M. to give farmers enough time to finish their barn chores first. People will likely come in good numbers until the message touches a nerve. But, for now, it's still early days.

The village barber has started to attend—Tony Ortello, an Italian man. He always sits near the back and slips out quickly afterwards, never saying more than, "Nice a meeting, Georga." But the glow on his round face says more than a thousand words. Jack's planning to give Tony some business soon, so maybe he'll get better acquainted with Mr. Ortello then. In the meantime, Jack's begun to call me "Georga" when he's in that humorous mood of his—which, as you know, is often.

We ate a crackerjack of a supper at the Summers' last night. Their cook, fresh from the Old Sod, had two forks and a linen napkin on the left of the plate and a knife and two spoons on the right. Although I've heard of fancy spreads before, I had no idea how to begin or which fork to use first. It left me in the lurch, so I watched Eddie lay his napkin across his lap and then I followed suit. We began with something called toad-in-the-hole and finished up with coffee and a wedge of Sally Lunn cake. Anyway, it certainly was an experience. Seems there isn't any Mrs. Summers on hand.

Herb and Harriet Chambers have invited us for tea next Thursday after he closes the post office. Herb's rather nervous and intense, but I admire his sincerity, and Harriet's warm hospitality speaks for them both. They come early to the meetings and always sit in the second row, right behind the Liddles. Funny how people adopt a pattern so quickly.

Well, it's almost six o'clock and Mrs. Applebee will soon be calling us for supper. The smells of roast chicken and hot bread pudding are finding their way up through the floor grate in the hall and making my mouth water. As Timothy will understand, it wouldn't show good manners to keep her waiting after she's gone to all the trouble of making bread pudding.

Jack says he's busy pressing the sheets on his bed, but it looks a lot like sleeping to me. He sends along his warmest greetings as well.

Your brother in the gospel of Christ,

George

Priscilla eased forward in the rocking chair and stared into the pearl-gray dawn. She remembered that as Alistair had lowered the letter, Emily's face was brimming. "It's simply marvelous the way folks are responding."

"Sounds like Elora boasts a downright decent lot," Alice had observed.

Hiding his mouth behind his cupped hand, Morgan leaned toward Timothy. "Anybody who serves toad-in-the-hole or bangers and beans has got to be of pretty fine stock," he joked.

Timothy grinned. "I saw a toad under the edge of the water trough this morning," he whispered back. "I'll see if he'll oblige your palate."

"Who'd have guessed that folks would crowd in like that to hear two farm boys?" It was Tillie's high-pitched voice from beside Bill.

"Maybe that's part of it, Mother," Bill had offered. "George and Jack definitely aren't your run-of-the-mill preachers."

"Whatever the reason, I'm thrilled to hear of their success," Priscilla declared. Balancing on the piano stool, she straightened her back. "I'm convinced the mission of the itinerant preachers is mainly to extend the gospel to communities beyond the reach of saints in a home church—just like the New Testament."

Alice's forehead furrowed in thought. "Right," she quickly agreed. "Once a church is established, any saints worth their salt will be eager to take over the responsibility of pointing others to Christ."

Priscilla nodded as she shifted to a more comfortable seat beside Alistair. "That's what I'm picturing."

"Our own church proves that," Emily noted. "Why, there were only eight of us, including Timothy and Phoebe, that first Sunday in May. Not including the children, that is. Now, we're a family of twice that number."

Alistair's eyes ran around the circle taking in the array of recent friends. Next to Alice, sat Susan Green; at the opposite end of the parlour, Hilda leaned against Dugan as she bounced little Samuel on her lap; in the same overalls he wore to the feed mill, Andrew Gillespie, silent as usual, lounged back on his chair between Malachi and Morgan; sitting in front of the windows, Tillie ran her hand over the blonde braids of her little granddaughter. "One minor correction," Alistair chuckled. "Priscilla was at Saint Patrick's that first Sunday." He wrapped his right arm around her shoulders. "But she's very much here today," he said, giving her an affectionate squeeze. "Body and soul."

Priscilla remembered smiling back at Alistair. "Time flies by," she had said, "and we should use every opportunity to give an account of our faith."

"Like Morgan," Alice blurted out. "He's as busy as a honey bee."

The tall thin banker had blushed, his hand instinctively reaching for his temple. "It's just that I'm footloose and fancy free," he had stammered. "I've more time to be out and about than the rest of you…"

The lively response to George and Jack's weekly letters had absorbed Priscilla as she darned a pair of Joe's socks under the dim light. But now a long ruffling snore from the other bedroom brought her thoughts back to Joe's dedication. He tried to remain cheerful in spite of Bella's steady deterioration. Each day he cut a fresh bouquet of pink-and-white larkspur from his garden and placed the vase beside her bed. But as his wife's breathing became erratic and her death seemed imminent, he turned to Priscilla, knowing that she tried to live close to God.

One night she was sitting at the kitchen table, reading her Bible by the soft light of the candle. Joe was rocking slowly, his chin on his chest, when he suddenly raised his head. "Priscilla," he asked, "I'm worried about Bella. How can I know where she's going—by and by…?"

Priscilla looked into Joe's eyes, artesian wells of concern for his beloved Bella. "I take comfort from knowing that God held each of us in His arms before we were born," she replied. "And that He's eager to receive us back at the appointed time. The Creator of the earth does right for every person in every situation."[2]

In the shadows the soft rhythm of Joe's rocker ground back and forth on the battleship linoleum. "I know I'm a sinner," he admitted, "even though I've tried to live a pretty honourable life. How can a man who's made many mistakes ever come to peace with his Maker?"

Looking up, Priscilla wondered what to say. Then she began to tell Joe the story of a man who had repaired roofs for a living. She had heard it from a rag-and-bone man whose Yorkshire accent still rang in her ears.

"One day the roofer was hired to repair the slate on the steeple of a village church. He disliked wearing a rope because it hampered his work. His safety record made him cocksure even at lofty heights. So he worked on the belfry, paying no attention to the ground far below. A few white Dorsets grazed in the churchyard to keep the grass clipped around the graves. In this tranquil setting, tragedy struck when the man caught his toe on a copper flashing. He lost his balance and plunged headlong.

"The vicar heard his horrified scream and ran to the rear of the church, expecting to find a shattered body on the hard ground. He approached with trepidation. Miraculously, the roofer was still alive. The reason was immediately apparent. Beneath him lay the body of a lamb that had been feeding under the edge of the church's roof. The lamb had died under the human load, but the man's life had been saved."

Priscilla explained that this innocent lamb was like Christ, the Lamb of God, who died willingly under the load of human sin. "Man may struggle diligently, twisting and trying to land *upright*, but without the Lamb he will surely die.[3] Man's hunger for wisdom started in the Garden of Eden when our first parents reached out for the Tree of the Knowledge of Good and Evil.[4] Perhaps they felt that armed with this knowledge, they could make better choices than God about how to live to the fullest. Since then, mankind has attempted to live without God, the source of all life. Ultimately, sorrow and death come to all of us when we try to do that."

Joe's eyes rested on Priscilla's face as her words spoke to his soul. "Yes," he murmured. "The Lamb of God. He's the only answer."

On the last evening of the month, the July air was languid, the milk for supper had soured, and the humidity threatened a thunderstorm. As Priscilla hurried across the fields toward the Purves', she eyed a thunderhead on the southeast horizon. Out of the cloud shot flashes of lightning that gave the sky an eerie radiance. Cutting through a hedgerow, Priscilla broke into a sprint, brambles and thistles tearing at her skirt.

When she arrived, Bella lay unconscious, her thin eyelids twitching. Her breathing, heavy and laboured, puffed her left cheek as the air blew out the corner of her mouth. Priscilla went to stir up some supper for Joe, and when she returned, she found him holding Bella's hand as he wiped spittle from her chin. Although the dark circles under his eyes disclosed both physical and mental exhaustion, he had never once complained. Joe ate in silence and then, with a slight smile, he left the room to rest.

Not long after Priscilla had started the night's vigil, she felt the air chill as the first splats of rain began to pelt the darkened glass. Smiling at the rising crescendo, she lit a lamp and hastened to the kitchen to close the windows. She paused at the open door and drew in deep breaths, absorbing the welcome smell of rain. Overhead a torrent gurgled along the wooden trough and funnelled into the rain barrel at the corner of Joe's woodshed. Through the palpable curtain of darkness, she detected a cascade flowing over the barrel staves. An ancient maple rustled appreciatively in the patter that bathed its dusty leaves. It seemed as if the tears of heaven were washing away the travail of Bella's decline. When a single hailstone bounced against the threshold, Priscilla stooped and held it tight until the celestial crystal vanished between her fingers.

She had just returned to her chair when Bella made an unusual noise. Priscilla sensed that something critical was imminent and ran to call Joe. He hurried to the bedside and had just taken hold of Bella's hand when she sat bolt upright, staring straight ahead, unseeing, her jaw and tongue moving as if she were trying to speak. Then, with a single guttural groan, she collapsed back onto her pillow, gone into God's eternity.

Tenderly, Priscilla closed Bella's eyelids. Then she put her arm around Joe's hunched shoulders and the two of them wept together, wrapped in the sudden silence. Priscilla knew that nothing she might say could ease his pain. After a few minutes she drew the sheet over Bella's face with an air of finality and led Joe to the kitchen for a strong pot of tea.

The thunderstorm slashed the window panes and the parlour stove reeked of damp soot as the two sat up with the body in the quiet house.

As they drew together in the glow of the kerosene lamp, Priscilla frowned and stirred her tea. "Joe, for the next two or three days while Bella lies in the parlour, either Alistair or I will be here with you," she reassured him. "After that, won't you please come and stay with us for a few weeks?"

Joe sat huddled in a shroud of shock and numbness. The phantom he had feared had come at last, unlike any of his imaginings. Like a kindly, reluctant guest, with sad eyes but purposeful demeanour, Death had crossed the threshold and taken Bella away. In the instant of her passing, all sense of "home" had departed with her.

"I can't think of being alone here—not right now," Joe confessed. "Your family has been so good to me…" His voice rose in a thin wail.

As the Regulator edged toward eight o'clock, Priscilla covered her head with a shawl and dashed through the sheeting rain to the neighbour's back stoop. Word needed to be sent for the doctor to come and sign the death certificate. And after that, for the undertaker.

Three days later the old burying ground at the crossroads received its latest guest. Only four of the Purves' children had been able to make the journey home and stand by Joe as their mother was returned to the earth under the fragrant pines. During her funeral, the clack of the hay rake in a distant field, the loud buzz of the cicadas, and the sharp cry of the meadow-lark all sang of high summer. Afterward, Bella's family and old friends ambled slowly back to the long line of horses that stood shaking their manes and snapping their tails until the mourners climbed into the buggies. When the last rig had pulled away, Alistair, Bill, Morgan, and Timothy removed their ties and collars, laid their suit jackets over a convenient headstone and retrieved four round-mouth shovels from the fence row.

Over the weeks, Joe regained some of his former vigour and well-being. He appreciated being with the Stanhopes and life at Wood Creek Farm gave him a fresh perspective. Their friends were kind, and the softness of the meetings touched his grieving heart. In the quietness and sorrow after Bella's death, he had begun to pray that God would speak to him. He discovered that after the day's work was done, the Stanhopes often gathered around the piano. One Sunday evening, when Laura was there with her violin, Joe requested a song that reminded him of Priscilla:

> Live for others every day:
> Be a blessing while you may,
> Ever loving, kind and true,
> Jesus-like in all you do.

Live for others, spend, be spent:
'Tis the life the Master meant—
Giving with a lavish hand,
Meeting ever love's demand.[5]

Joe noticed that Morgan Butterwick seemed to sing the hymn with particular fervour. During the last few weeks of Bella's life, the gangly young man had made a habit of stopping for a few minutes when he passed by on his way to Wood Creek Farm. Even though Bella had hardly known Morgan was there, Joe always appreciated his cheerful visits and amber bottles of honey.

When Priscilla and Laura had finished playing the hymn, they hurried to put on the kettle and fix a lunch. Joe moved to the chair beside Morgan. "The Stanhopes certainly are gracious, aren't they?" he murmured.

Morgan looked into Joe's tired eyes. "The spirit of this home is very soothing." He hesitated, as if remembering an event of long ago. "I noticed that the first time I came here—the warmth, the lack of pretense, the commitment of these friends to each other. You don't need to advertise that you're a Christian if you have the goods."

Joe's face wrinkled in confusion. "I don't get your drift…"

Just then Timothy sauntered back into the parlour balancing a slice of toast on a mug. "Hot chocolate and raisin toast are coming," he announced.

"Care to join us?" Morgan asked. "I was just about to tell Joe a story."

Timothy grinned as he flopped down. "Nothing beats a good yarn from an Englishman."

Morgan loosened his shirt collar. "On Friday I was working in my office with the door open when I overheard a customer talking to one of our tellers in a loud voice. Each sentence was sprinkled with some token religious phrase as if the man was desperate to convince everyone within earshot that he was a Christian." Morgan ran his fingers into his hair and smoothed it back. "Did you ever wonder if Christ speaks through a person who draws so much attention to himself?"

Timothy took a long swig of hot chocolate. "At least the chap had the courage of his convictions," he averred. "Still, we'd better not covet the power to cast out demons if we can't get control of our own tongues." He glanced sideways and saw Joe rubbing his arthritic knee. "Seriously, we're not to believe everyone who claims to be a Christian," he went on, "but to test their spirit to find out if they really do come from God."[6]

"This chap at the front of the line seemed to present another Jesus," Morgan said. "A very different spirit⁷ than I feel among our friends here."

Joe smiled, suddenly grasping the essence of Morgan's story.

"Sadly, I felt repelled by, rather than drawn to, the Jesus this man knows," Morgan added. "His whole manner was one of agitation rather than of peace. It made me want to withdraw."

"It's vital to have the Spirit's influence," Timothy mused as his mother handed Joe and Morgan each a cup of tea and a chunk of sharp cheddar on hot buttered toast. "Otherwise we could do more harm than good, turning people away from Jesus instead of toward Him."

After Morgan turned the lock on his desk drawer each day, he loaded his two-wheeled handcart with golden bottles of clover and buckwheat honey. As the cart jolted along from door to door, the jars tinkled and rattled, heralding his arrival like a wise man bearing gifts of gold. His disarming nature drew such business that a second farmer agreed to supplement his supply. Morgan's main purpose, however, was to meet people in honest, open settings where he might detect a spiritual need, a loneliness for God. Never hurrying, he always took time to listen as his customers shared the daily dramas of their lives. He refrained from speaking hastily or rashly in case he might disturb the work of God in someone else's heart. Although he was happy to tell of his own relationship with Christ, he was also reticent, hesitant to plunge into idle chatter about something so precious, so beyond a purely rational explanation.

Morgan knew that the seed pods of some delicate woodland flowers burst open with the lightest touch. Praying for this same sensitivity to release the gospel seed at just the right time, he spoke to people of God's infinite love, offering assurance that even in the struggles and trials of life the Lord cared about them. He often sang as he pulled his cart, laden with sweetness, from house to house.

Alistair, too, was experiencing deeper dimensions in his spiritual life. One hot afternoon he was cobbling together a piece of fence the cattle had knocked down at the back of the farm. A long section of thirty rods needed to be rebuilt. Each morning he copied out a few verses on a slip of paper, and as he worked he tried to memorize one or two of them. He was amazed at how that simple exercise helped in opening up the Scripture. After taking apart some broken rails, he pulled the slip of paper out to check the words again: We all, with unveiled face, *beholding the glory of the Lord,* are being transformed into the same image—by the Spirit of the Lord.[8]

Suddenly it dawned on Alistair that if he could focus on the glory of the Lord Jesus, he would gradually be transformed by the Spirit of Christ into His likeness. But what is the best way to behold that glory? Alistair stared, unseeing, at a solitary cloud far to the east. *Through the Gospels,* he mused. *In them we see His true glory.*[9] *The Son—perfectly divine and fully God*[10]*—reflects the radiant glory of the Father and shows His kindness and character in human form.*[11]

Alistair's features clouded as he repeated the phrase *with unveiled face* several times. Could that simply mean looking to the Lord with total receptiveness? He smiled at the inspiration. Being like soft clay in a potter's hands would allow the Spirit of Christ to shape him.[12] Because he was God's workmanship, any transformation in the inner workshop of his soul would be accomplished by the Spirit. Not by himself.

For days Alistair pondered a practical way of seeing Jesus. He imagined actually meeting Him face-to-face. That was impossible, he knew, but still, the thought of it brought him a lot of pleasure.

Then one day, as he stood upon the same ground pounding a crowbar into a post hole for the broken fence, a startling idea halted him like the resistant rock below. Why not use his imagination to picture Jesus? Initially, at least. Then, when he'd immersed himself in the setting, he could leave his mind behind and wait for the Spirit to draw close. Alistair smiled. His time with Jesus could be unlimited.

He felt an unexpected longing to see Jesus and he gazed around. No one was nearby; the fields lay quiet and empty. He chose a patch of grass under a big beech and sat down. Leaning back against its sturdy trunk, he stretched out comfortably on the ground. At first he found it difficult to lay aside the concerns of the day and all the tasks he had planned. His mind flitted from place to place, like an unruly child who refuses to quiet down. He felt as if he were wasting time. But then he remembered his friend, Ben Aberlochy, and he was certain that if Ben could speak now, he would tell him to spend more time with God, even in the middle of a busy day.

Alistair crossed his ankles, aware that Jesus often slipped away to be alone in the solitude of a garden or on a mountainside.

Alistair regarded the landscape before him, trying to shut out every noise, both within and beyond himself. He closed his eyes and breathed deeply, expanding his chest to the maximum. He relaxed his mind, careful not to pressure himself to blot out all of the distractions. Struggle, in itself, could create anxiety and come between him and God. Instead, he simply allowed wandering thoughts to pass on without engaging them. Gradually, his mind stilled and a soft muted serenity overtook him.

The warbling melody of a Baltimore oriole broke into Alistair's silence. He looked up into the thick branches of the beech. Then he took out the verses he had written down that morning:

> And when he was gone forth into the way, there came one running, and kneeled to him, and asked him, Good Master, what shall I do that I may inherit eternal life?...Then Jesus beholding him loved him, and said unto him, One thing thou lackest: go thy way, sell what-soever thou hast, and give to the poor, and thou shalt have treasure in heaven: and come, take up the cross, and follow me. And he was sad at that saying, and went away grieved: for he had great posses-sions.[13]

Alistair read the passage carefully. He concentrated on each word and phrase, allowing it to settle. Turning each one over, he tried to taste and sense its meaning and depth, like the psalmist who wrote: "How sweet are thy words unto my taste! Yea, sweeter than honey to my mouth!"[14] Alistair pondered the simple phrases that Jesus spoke. He slowly read the verses twice more, picturing each detail of the setting from the viewpoint of an actual observer.

Closing his eyes again, he let the fields, the tree, and the oriole fade away. Slowly, the path in the story came into view—the hard-packed surface, the weeds, and dusty stones on either side. A thin layer of soil covered outcroppings of stony shale in places. On the other side, thorns and thistles flourished. The heat of the blazing sun accentuated the arid climate. Alistair could see parched, barren hills. A shepherd sat on a distant rock tending his flock. Here and there, scattered plots of wheat stood ready for harvest, but few people were gathering it in. He could hear a sparrow chirping in a nearby fig tree.

Alistair saw the tanned hands and lean faces of the disciples and the texture of their rough clothing as they made their way toward the next village. He had never understood, until now, how poor these itinerant Galilean peasants were. Only a couple of them wore sandals; the others were barefoot. Although the man in the centre of the little company was no different in appearance from the rest, the others seemed to listen attentively when he spoke. Alistair's eyes widened. That must be Jesus.

Then something extraordinary happened. His vantage point had shifted from below the beech tree, and now he was suddenly walking along among them. As they all walked together, Jesus spoke quietly to the men on either side, something about permitting little children to come to Him. Who were these men? Perhaps, Peter on the left and James and John on the right?

What were the other disciples talking about? Was it about the parents in the last village who had insisted that Jesus touch and bless their little ones? Or about Jesus' indignation at their own hard-hearted reaction? What did He mean by saying that they must become like little children themselves in order to enter the kingdom of God? One of the men, carrying a bag, smiled affably at his fellows. Alistair's hand went instinctively to his throat and his face took on a pained look. *That's likely Judas. His fate could befall any of us under certain circumstances.*

Alistair heard a disturbance and looked around to see someone running. Jesus, he could tell, had heard the man too. Alistair watched Him stop and turn around, waiting for the young man to join them. When he came puffing up to the group, Alistair noticed his soft and sumptuous robe.

As the disciples gathered around, Alistair stood among them. He watched the rich young man kneel before Jesus. "Good Teacher, what shall I do that I may inherit eternal life?" he said, his voice fraught with concern. In the sincerity of that question, Alistair could hear his own voice.

Shifting his gaze to Jesus, Alistair saw the tender wrinkles in His tanned face and at the corners of His eyes. Those eyes. Never before had Alistair seen such eyes. Warm, gentle, caring. He felt comforted by the reassuring smile, the unmistakable love.

The man explained that he had obeyed all the commandments since youth.

"One thing you lack," Jesus said. "Go, sell everything and give to the poor, and you will have treasure in heaven. Then come and follow Me."

Alistair watched as shock fossilized the rich young ruler's face. He said nothing, stared at the ground, and then walked away dejected because he had great wealth. Alistair was staggered when he realized that the man had turned down Jesus' invitation.

Standing in the shimmering heat, Alistair shook his head, disbelieving. How could anyone turn down the chance to follow Jesus? Or refuse to take a place among His disciples as they walk or recline or eat with Him? He knew Jesus' gentle instructions and wise answers would resonate with a depth of compassion and discernment never before witnessed. Alistair wished he could sprint after the young ruler, place a fatherly hand on the shoulder of his tunic and urge him to reconsider. He would insist the man was missing the opportunity to experience divine love in a human body, God in the flesh. Unlike the departing figure, Alistair had read the Gospels—as yet unwritten—and wanted to call out, "You're going to bungle the chance to hear the most profound words ever uttered. Words that in the future thousands will forfeit their lives to honour. Why not listen as He teaches the unlearned or comforts the downtrodden? Grasp the wisdom when He confronts religious critics?

"Blind men will receive sight, the crippled will walk, those who have leprosy will be cured, and the deaf will hear. Before your eyes, He'll return the dead to life again. Each time Jesus meets someone—perhaps for the first time—you can step into their sandals. His answer, His touch, His love will be for you and me as well. Friend, you'll be blessed if you don't turn away." But the words died on Alistair's lips, unspoken. What could he add, when Jesus Himself had already spoken?

After the rich young ruler had disappeared into a maze of sagging clay houses, Alistair edged closer to Jesus. By faith he had come into God's presence. His rational mind was quiet, absent from this part of the experience with his Lord. Waiting his turn, immeasurable appreciation filled his heart as he regarded this humble man of Galilee.

Being lean and vigorous lent height to Jesus' stature. His hands, calloused from carpenter work, were strong yet supple and moved with easy grace when He gestured. Above His beard His face was narrow but showed a gentle ruggedness while His dove-gray eyes conveyed a striking sensitivity. His acorn hair, not recently trimmed, fell in thick wavy coils around His ears and neck. When He turned to see Alistair, delight shone through the burnished tan and His eyes crinkled in instant recognition.

He knows everything about me and still He wants to be my dearest friend, Alistair marveled. *I've often worshiped Him in spirit.*[15] *Now I can tell Him face-to-face how much I love Him.*

Falling to his knees, Alistair again looked up into the gentleness of those eyes. Eyes that looked deep into his own soul, not critically but with a rare compassion. They filled him with the confidence to pour out his anxiety and concerns for the future.

The answer was simple and reassuring: "Rest and don't worry.[16] I am going to prepare a place for you. Remember, I will always be with you, even until the end of the world."[17] Silently, Alistair felt an overwhelming calmness transfer to himself, filling him with the power and sweetness of Christ. Clearly every question and burden could be left safely behind.

When Alistair tried to speak of his failures, Jesus responded with compassion and assurance. "Neither do I condemn you; go and sin no more."[18]

After lingering a few moments, Alistair perceived a light passing over his face. He opened his eyes to see a chord of sunlight, breaking through the leaves of the beech tree. He lay on the grass as he had done as a boy, wondering how long he had been in that other, luminous world. Again he could hear the oriole singing its golden song. Then, as Alistair went back to repairing the fence, Jesus seemed more real, more touchable than ever before.

At the supper table that evening, Alistair recounted his experience and his reaction to the rich man's decision. "What an awesome invitation! Can you imagine? The possibility to travel with Jesus, to observe Him daily, even hourly." From his vantage point at the head of the table, Alistair watched Timothy's smile lines soften into reflection. Beside him, Joe stopped mashing his potatoes and laid his knife and fork down and turned to listen. Across the table, Phoebe continued to ladle gravy over her potatoes and green peas before handing the bowl to her mother.

Alistair rested his elbows on the table. "The man passed up the chance to stand among the crowds and hear Jesus' parables, chock-full of wisdom and warning. He could have squeezed into the circle of disciples and absorbed Jesus' private teaching. Most of all, he had the privilege of becoming a friend of the Saviour. But something came between him and this life *in the Way*."[19]

"Maybe the man loved his things too much," Phoebe exclaimed, thinking of the hair ribbons she had given to a girl at school who had none. "He didn't want to give away his fancy clothes."

Priscilla smiled at Phoebe's perception. "Do you think if he had truly believed in Jesus, he'd have been so reluctant?"

Phoebe mulled over the question so long that finally Timothy answered for her. "Of course not. His love of things was just a sign of something worse—he lacked faith. He thought his belongings would make him happier than following Jesus."

Alistair soaked up the last of his gravy with a slice of bread and nodded. "Without faith, our possessions, whether scant or plentiful, will always be our first choice. They'll seem more important than life with Jesus. Without faith it's impossible to please God because anyone who comes to Him must believe that He's real. And that He rewards those who search diligently for Him."[20]

Alistair salted the last radish on his plate and crunched into it thoughtfully. "Each of us makes a choice too," he continued. "Will we turn away sorrowfully from Jesus because of a lack of faith, clutching our possessions? Anything that's more important than following Him will prevent us from traveling in the narrow way."[21]

"Pass the sugar, please," Joe said as he reached for the spooner.

Phoebe maneuvred the bowl across the tablecloth before turning to her mother. "You all keep talking about possessions," she said, flipping her thick flaxen braids over her shoulders. "Just what do you mean by that?"

Priscilla swallowed her tea. "Possessions are things we own, honey," she explained. "You know, things like…like all the things put away in the rag room. Things that call out to us. And, in the end, they possess us."

Phoebe looked mystified, and then with a short laugh she responded, "Oh, you mean those bags of buttons and beads hanging on the wall. And the piles of hand-me-downs and scraps of cloth." She pushed back her chair. "Anyway, thanks for supper, Mom. I've got to practise my violin." She dashed up the stairs, leaving the adults to talk.

Alistair stacked his cup and saucer on his plate. "There's more to it than meets the eye," he added. "Possessions can include our own strongly held opinions, our pride in our appearance or abilities, or our status in the district—in fact, lots of things very acceptable in the broad way."

"When we first left Saint Patrick's, I was afraid of losing my position in the choir," Priscilla remembered. "And of being ridiculed by our friends and relatives. But I had to leave that burden behind to follow Jesus."

"There's no indication that the things the young ruler possessed were bad," Alistair concluded as he stood, "only that they had the power to hold him back. He loved them more than Jesus. It's not what most people label bad things that separate us from eternal life. It's the *good* things we love more than Him."

Following Alistair's lead, Joe struggled to his feet. "My knee's seizing up," he muttered, using his arms to push himself up from the table. "The old arthritis acting up. Reckon we're in for a bout of dirty weather."

Alistair glanced out the east window as he placed a steadying hand under Joe's elbow. "I'd better head out to check the doors and the stock before dark. Would it do your game leg good to take a little stroll?"

Joe smiled. "That's just what the doctor ordered before bed."

Daybreak the following morning found Priscilla on her knees in the rag room, gathering swatches of fabric and stuffing them into flour sacks. "Silk, satin, velvet—all these scraps I hoped to make a crazy quilt from—just another possession to rob my time," she scolded herself aloud. "Bella carried nothing out of this world in her thin old hands. The fabric of my life needs to be woven of loving deeds and time devoted to God." Priscilla reached for a ball of twine and tied the necks of the three bags with a flourish. "I'll get Timothy to take them along to Aunt Maggie's neighbour the next time he's in Guelph," she said aloud. "And good riddance."

The following moment a spectator in the Stanhope farmyard would have witnessed the sash of the north window being hoisted, three lumpy flour sacks ejected, and a woman's triumphant face thrust over the sill.

Fifteen

LOCKED OUT
Late Summer 1901

As though compensating for the torrid month of July, nature came bearing showers and fruition in August. The gooseberries, though smaller, were sweeter on account of the heat, and the first tomatoes in the village gardens found themselves jealously guarded by scarecrows, whose bleached burlap arms warded off conniving birds. The drought-defiant corn swelled into full ear, and the wheat, though shorter, darkened to burnt sienna as the gospel harvest continued in Elora. Although the numbers attending the schoolhouse had dwindled, George and Jack continued to present straightforward lessons from the Scriptures each evening.

Returning home from the meeting, Eddie Summers cracked his knuckles as he walked along the dim streets. Head cast downward, his face burned with the powerful conviction he was receiving from the messages. *Jesus' teaching,* he remembered, *provoked this same reaction in His hearers. And wasn't the audience of the early apostles also pricked in their hearts? Yes, so much so that they were moved to action and had said to Peter and the other apostles, "Brothers, what shall we do?"*[1]

In the falling darkness, Eddie turned up his own street. His handsome features twisted as questions gnawed at his soul. For the first time, he had heard a message that actually *pricked* his heart. Every point seemed sharp and searching. Why should that be if he was a Christian already?

When Oliver Summers arrived home a few minutes later, Eddie raised his concerns. "Dad, do you sense that George and Jack are speaking about a more fundamental change in people's lives than we normally hear presented in church?"

Oliver looked squarely into his son's eager face. "In the beginning these meetings seemed a pleasant place to spend an evening, to have one's ears tickled. But as time goes on, it's becoming clear that these men have a very different understanding of Christianity than our local churches."

Eddie nodded as he poured two glasses of black currant cordial. "By something George said tonight, I take it that he doesn't think a church building is scriptural." He set a glass in front of his father. "It won't be long before that kind of talk lands him in hot water and starts to rankle some of the traditional-minded folks in the village," he added with a grin. "Anyway, I'm going to look up the references for myself."

Mr. Coffer, the school trustee, first twigged to the difference in the tenor of the message as he listened to Jack Gillan describe Jesus of Nazareth as being *a man of very ordinary circumstances* whom the common people heard gladly.[2] He was offended when Jack stated that most churchgoing people see the Saviour as *a gentleman Jesus* and that the real Jesus was not, and never would be, the favourite of the religious establishment—who only use Him for their own purposes.

Mr. Coffer enjoyed his prominence in Elora. His muscular build and trim Van Dyke beard gave an imposing look while his steel-gray eyes revealed a canny intelligence. Fiercely proud of his competence and integrity as a member of the Church of Scotland's finance committee and as the village treasurer, he had whittled the municipality debentures to half.

At the finance meeting the following evening, Mr. Coffer listened as several members of the church session spoke disapprovingly of the evening activities at the Elora school.

"These upstart preachers need to be shut down before they draw away some of our parishioners," one of the members fumed. "Why, they're not even educated or trained."[3]

The presiding clerk pursed his lips. "Not as many of our congregants go now as in the beginning," he said bitterly, "but some, like Miss Keats and Hugh and Gertrude Foster, never miss a meeting. The kind of cow-stable religion these tramp preachers advocate is a threat to every upstanding church in this village."

A round fatherly looking man to the right of the clerk doodled on the corner of the budget before him, his pulse throbbing in his temples. "My feeling is that they're stirring people up for good. Maybe folks'll attend church more regularly if they're on fire for the Lord."

The elder across the table glared back. "That's just the way I had it figured at first," he retorted. "But now I can see that they're turning the village upside down, undermining the very foundation of the Church of Scotland.[4] I say they're twisting people's thinking, and it's high time we take this situation into hand."

"I can see I'm the odd man out here," his fellow member replied gingerly, "but I'd rather that than to be found fighting against God.[5] There's a good number in the village who seem to like their preaching. I'd say let's not act too hastily."

With the enigmatic expression of a bureaucrat, Mr. Coffer glanced around at the other members of the session, taking in their obvious indignation. He knew all too well that the church budget could not afford any decimation. Something, it was clear, would have to be done. He fingered the point of his carefully barbered beard and cleared his throat. "I could have a brotherly talk with the other two trustees on the school board. Perhaps," he said, lifting an eyebrow, "I'll discover a little dissension in the ranks." The clerk tightened his lips to suppress a smile.

The next morning Mr. Coffer opened the town office at nine o'clock sharp and quickly assigned a mill rate calculation to his assistant. Excusing himself, he then marched along Geddes Street to Summers' Dry Goods.

"Morning, Oliver," he said to Mr. Summers with uncharacteristic joviality. "Before long I'll be needing a new suit. Since I have a few minutes this morning, I thought I'd call in." He feigned interest as the clothier eagerly presented him with a broad array of fabrics and styles.

Mr. Summers draped a smart herringbone tweed over his forearm. "This one's straight from one of the best looms in the Highlands," he avowed. "And fine enough to make any man look gallant."

"Even our chief tax collector," Eddie quipped as he stepped out of the window he was draping.

Mr. Coffer gave a weak laugh. "Guess any tax collector's not too popular," he admitted as he touched two or three of the bolts abstractedly. Mr. Summers put on his spectacles, preparing to take some measurements.

"Say, Oliver, what do you make of those meetings over at the school?" Mr. Coffer remarked in the most offhanded manner.

Mr. Summers' reply was instant. "Why, I think they're the dandiest preachers I've ever listened to."

Mr. Coffer deftly switched topics, but not before Eddie, who was assembling some bolts of cloth, noticed his jaw clench disapprovingly. When Mr.

Coffer looked at only one more swatch before hastily excusing himself, Eddie met his father's eyes.

As Mr. Coffer's back disappeared down the street, Eddie touched a finger to the point of the scissors. "Your fellow trustee looked a mite testy. A little strain in the fabric of our village," he suggested cryptically.

The third trustee, Mr. MacQuarrie, lived behind the stone arch that his father, a proud Scottish stonemason, had built forty years earlier. Mr. Coffer's stylish buggy pulled up to the limestone cottage shortly after noon. Here the visit was more productive. Mr. MacQuarrie was not opposed to these servants of God, but at the same time Mr. Coffer and the establishment represented the clientele he served—at least at their latter end. Conveniently, Mr. Coffer withdrew a prepared notice from his leather case. Harold MacQuarrie held it in his long deliberate fingers and scanned it. Instantly, the school meeting flashed before him and, just as swiftly, unresolved anger with the God who had given and had so suddenly taken away. In memory, he viewed again the short—pitiably short—coffins of his children. There had been no need to measure them; he had known to the inch how the twin girls had grown, like a pair of tender plants. The muscles in his inscrutable face tightened as he took the pen from Mr. Coffer, bent down, and signed. For a second he looked with misgiving at his slanting scrawl. Then, he returned the paper to Mr. Coffer's outstretched hand.

When the brothers arrived early that evening to set up the chairs in the schoolhouse, they found the door padlocked and a notice posted. It read: "Mr. George Farnham and Mr. Jack Gillan are to discontinue the use of the Elora Public School forthwith." As they stared at the sign and at each other in shock and disbelief, people began to arrive. They, too, read the notice and reacted swiftly. An angry current ran through the crowd.

"Who do Coffer and MacQuarrie think they are?" the tanner growled.

"That's right, we pay taxes. This school is ours, and we have every right to use it," another man snapped, giving the door a resounding kick.

Loud voices erupted among a knot of younger men, their faces flushed and tempers flaring. "I say we round up Coffer and MacQuarrie and haul them over here to justify their actions," the cooper's apprentice threatened.

Jack stood quietly discussing what to do with a few of the men at the corner of the school, but George was nowhere to be seen. Several of the women stood off to one side, gathered in a sullen circle. When George returned a few minutes later, he and Jack climbed the steps to the little porch outside the school door. As George raised one hand to appeal for quietness, Eddie noticed fresh grass stains on the knees of his trousers. George, he suddenly realized, had gone behind the school to pray.

"Friends, again we thank you for your support. First of all, I'd like you to do one special thing for Jack and me."

Everyone stood in silent anticipation.

"Please don't think poorly of Mr. Coffer or Mr. MacQuarrie." George paused, staring into the throng of angry faces. "Although they seem intent on hindering the open preaching of the gospel, we should forgive them.[6] Perhaps God's hand is in this, for we all need to realize that if we are true Christians, we'll face opposition. We should be more concerned if there is no resistance."[7]

The tension in the irate crowd began to dissolve as people focused on George's face and mollifying words.

"When you get home, I'd like each of you to memorize the following words of Jesus." George opened his Bible and began to read: "Think not that I am come to send peace on earth: I came not to send peace, but a sword…he that taketh not his cross, and followeth after me, is not worthy of me."[8] When George looked up from the page and toward the crowd, he saw a golden reflection on the Grand River beyond them. "We don't have a piano," he said, "but let's sing a hymn anyway."

The sound of their voices, united in song, could be heard all through the neighbourhood.

> The waves rolled high, fierce raged the angry deep;
> Danger seemed nigh—the Saviour lay fast asleep.
> His Father's hand controlled the winds and sea,
> And daily led the Man of Galilee.
>
> Be of good cheer when storms around you rise,
> Should threatening clouds appear in darkening skies.
> Our Father's hand shall guide through storm and sea;
> His guarding grace shall lead to victory.[9]

As the melody drifted into the evening shadows, George bowed his head and began to pray. "Our Father, we thank You for Jesus, for His life and death and for our privilege of following Him—even in what our human minds perceive to be adverse circumstances. Help us to understand that You have a purpose in all of this. We ask for the power and the willing-ness to accept it and indeed to rejoice if we are rejected like our Master.

We pray, dear Father, that You will forgive those who are turning against the simplicity of Christ. We ask these favours in Jesus' name. Amen."

Then George looked up and spoke again. "As soon as God opens another door, Jack and I will resume the gospel meetings. In the meantime, we'll all need to be patient. Goodnight, everyone."

The yard was silent as everybody looked toward the two brothers, who were cast in the fading light. No further words, however, came from them. An unfamiliar democrat, pulled by a team of handsome horses, rolled past the dispirited stragglers separating onto the roadside. "Give way, you country hicks," the driver shouted as if he were a nobleman scattering the ragtag and bobtail of London's narrow streets.

Pumping his fist, the tanner let out a derisive whoop.

After returning to Mrs. Applebee's, Jack opened his Bible and read about the apostle Paul being put out of the synagogue in a similar experience more than 1800 years earlier.[10]

"Traveling preachers presenting the gospel of Christ have never been the toast of the town," he said pensively as he closed his Bible. "But the question remains, where else can we hold meetings?"

George scratched thoughtfully behind his ear. "It's a kick in the pants alright—just when we've got nicely started. But let's not forget God's in control. I'm sure something'll work out."

"I noticed an empty shed down near the mill. It's just got a dirt floor but it might be fine. We could haul over some planks for folks to sit on."

George frowned. "Sounds pretty rustic."

Undeterred, Jack responded with a jocular grin. "Can you picture Mr. Coffer and his cronies hunkered down in an implement shed listening to a couple of hayseeds in work boots?"

George got up and pressed the door closed before lowering his voice. "But what about Eddie and his father? Or Mrs. Applebee, for that matter?"

Jack's face creased into a grimace. "We certainly don't want to scare them off," he replied solemnly. "It'll definitely sort out serious listeners from the gadabouts. Still, it's a shame the trustees got their backs up."

George undressed and hung up his clothes. "I don't like to raise anyone's ire," he said. "But challenging people is a vital part of the gospel. Many listeners hated Jesus and His unorthodox and outspoken teaching. And He warned His followers to expect the same. This resistance is a sure sign that our message is striking home and convicting people's hearts."

"You're exactly right, George. Most people prefer a flowery Sunday sermon that makes them feel virtuous."

George perched on the edge of his bed. "If we contend earnestly for the faith—as it was committed to the first-century saints[11]—and try to separate it from the traditions of men,[12] we can't help but ruffle the feathers of some religious folks. The way we live is so contrary to the methods of the established churches, and Mr. Coffer and Mr. MacQuarrie intend to keep things the way they are now."

"And they have four hundred years of tradition behind them," Jack added as he tossed his socks across his boots.

As George lay in the dark, he thought of God's children throughout the ages. They neither sought the approval of others nor attempted to provoke their disapproval, because the opinions of others had ceased to be significant in their lives. They had paid the price of freedom by honouring the pattern that Jesus had entrusted to His disciples.

~⌐

As Eddie dressed for work the following morning, he mused about the turn of events. Mr. Coffer and the church board were staunchly traditional, and the closure of the school had not surprised him. But what about the brothers' unusual reaction? He lifted an eyebrow as he leaned into the mirror to adjust the knot on his tie. It certainly wasn't the work of the mind; it must've come from a deeper source.

Throughout the forenoon, Eddie kept a sharp eye out for the brothers to pass Summers' Dry Goods on their way to the post office. The noon hour had passed, and he was beginning to presume that he had missed them, when he caught a glimpse of George walking briskly along the street.

"George," Eddie said, rushing out of the store. "Good afternoon."

George stopped, smiling and squinting into the sun.

"Well, what did you make of last night's shenanigans?" Eddie demanded, curiosity brimming. "The way you handled the trustees' notice was astonishing. Turning the other cheek, I'd say."[13]

George looked down at the sidewalk, unwilling to accept any merit, as if their reaction was commonplace. But Eddie persisted.

Finally, George offered a simple illustration. "Suppose there are two men," he began. "One a lawless killer, the other an honest constable attempting to uphold the laws of the frontier. The constable has to transport the murderer across a barren, uninhabited wilderness to a jail, a journey of several days' walk. Every night the evildoer sleeps soundly beside the glowing campfire and wakes up refreshed. His guard sleeps fitfully, always afraid his companion might attack him. As the days drag on, the exhausted constable, who has done no wrong, becomes more and more drawn until he's barely able to keep on going from lack of sleep. Meanwhile, the murderer enjoys the scenic journey. Because the good man can't release the evil man, he becomes the prisoner." George moved his foot to one side, allowing an ant to continue its journey across the sidewalk.

"The constable had no choice; it was his job to stay handcuffed to the criminal. But we have the option to do otherwise. We can't afford to chain ourselves to evil by letting it occupy our thoughts and control our actions. Only when we forgive immediately and set each other free can we enjoy the journey of each day."[14]

Eddie's eyes brightened before he changed the subject. "Any ideas about another place for your meetings yet?"

George drew in a deep breath. "Jack and I are going to size up that old implement shed down on Mill Street later this afternoon."

"*That'll* separate the sheep from the goats," Eddie exclaimed.

"Would your father be likely to come along there?" George asked, a tentative air in his voice.

"Oh, absolutely. My father and I are keen to hear you men out."

The lines at the corners of George's eyes relaxed. "That'll be good if the place pans out then," he said as he left for his mail.

A few minutes later, Eddie glanced out through the storefront and saw George whistling as he walked back along the opposite side of Geddes Street, envelopes clutched in his hand. As he noticed the lightness of George's step, the practicality of the message rang crystal clear.

Eddie narrowed one eye in the manner of a man deep in thought. He realized for the first time that he had never truly understood the power and importance of forgiveness. Eddie took a deep breath and turned from the window. *When we forgive, we become free and light. Guided more by the Spirit and less by emotion.*

Meanwhile, in the sanctity of her kitchen, Mrs. Applebee awaited her boarders' return. As she crimped the pastry on a meat pie for supper, an importunate rapping on the screen door heralded Mrs. Quinn's arrival.

"Plantar warts, they tell me. Would ya have any remedy atall?" Her shrill voice cracked into every corner of the kitchen. "I've rubbed tater juice on 'em. And poulticed 'em with slippy elm, but I'm fearful o' gettin' the gang greens. It runs in the O' Makins. 'Twasn't any time atall after my great uncle got the gang greens 'til he breathed his last. His big toe rotted clean off."

"Well, I can't judge your warts without a look," Mrs. Applebee reasoned. "Have you soaked them in a solution of weak lye?"

"Musta sowed the garden wrong time o' the moon," Mrs. Quinn went on, ignoring the question. "Wait'll you see the likes of these." With dire significance, she backed into the pantry and sat down on the step stool. "Them young men's nowhere around, is they?" she hesitated. "Cryin' shame what our village done to 'em. But I smell a nice meat pie all ready for 'em."

First her stocking, then her drawers inadvertently puddled around her ankles as she struggled to hoist her right heel across her knee and into her bony grasp. Purple veins in her hands stood out with the effort as painful and unsightly plantar warts appeared on the sole of her foot.

Mrs. Applebee drew back in horror, her tongue not bothering to find its way around the felicities of language. "Mercy sakes, woman! That's the filthiest foot in Wellington County."

Moira Quinn rose to the bait. Her thinly lidded black eyes sparkled with merriment. Her cheeks, which had collapsed with age, hung well forward of her nose like a pair of shrivelled peaches. "Wellington, Wentworth, Waterloo," she intoned, as if the names formed a witch's incantation. "You ain't seen the half of it. Let me hist t'other stocking off." She twisted grotesquely until her black lisle stocking and garter lay in a heap like a spider's web ingloriously tangled. In triumph she pronounced, "Here's a foot even *filthier.*"

A sudden scrubbing of boots on the back stoop alerted the women to the young men's arrival. "Here, quick, get yourself looking decent," Mrs. Applebee ordered, pulling the pantry door behind her. Inside, Mrs. Quinn cackled as she fumbled in the sliver of light to pull her garments together.

After her neighbour had limped out the front door, bearing her verbal triumph like the spoils of war, Mrs. Applebee tightened her apron strings and opened the oven. Her bosom was still heaving with suppressed laughter as she slid the meat pie onto a hot pad and took a seat at the table.

"Well," George said after they had given thanks for supper, "we got turned down on the implement shed this afternoon."

Mrs. Applebee stiffened. "I can't imagine that Abe Prichard turning you down on his rubbishy old shed," she chafed. "What harm could you possibly do to it?"

"He said he was afraid somebody might turn an ankle and then come back on him," George explained.

Mrs. Applebee's rosy cheeks ripened into a brilliant red. "That's only a bald-headed excuse," she bristled. "His wife's a first cousin of Mr. Coffer. There's the hitch…" A sharp rap on the screen door cut her censure short.

When Evelyn Applebee returned to the kitchen, she had Lyman Liddle in tow. "Have a seat at the table, Lyman," she offered, shooing her cat off a chair. "I'll pour you a cup of tea."

Lyman turned to the men. "It seems odd not to be heading over to your meeting this evening," he confided.

"Yes, for us too," Jack commiserated.

Lyman's tea sat untouched. "Jessie and I got to talking last night and again this morning," he announced. "We've been counting up the folks who've been coming along of late, and there's scarcely two dozen at most."

George and Jack listened attentively while Lyman went on as if staking out the boundaries of a building. "Jessie sat some chairs around today and she figures everybody can squeeze into our cottage, what with it being so open and all."

George caught the sincerity in Lyman's deep-set eyes. Across the table, he saw Jack's head nodding slightly.

"If you wish, you can have your meetings there," Lyman offered. "Jessie and I would be honoured."

Gratitude softened George's face. "What do you think, Jack?"

"A wonderful offer, Lyman," Jack declared. "Thank you so much."

Jubilantly, Mrs. Applebee plunked down a slice of hot apple pie in front of Lyman, pleased with his suggestion.

"It's astonishing how quickly God's provided for our mutual needs," George observed. "We'll shake a leg and spread the word in the forenoon."

"Why didn't I think of that?" Mrs. Applebee chided herself after Lyman had left. "You could've had the meetings right here."

George laid a hand on her soft gingham shoulder. "Maybe God had something else in mind. Let's just trust His judgement."

Jack's face lit up. "When the authorities opposed and maligned Paul, he moved to the house of Titius Justus, who lived next to the synagogue."

Mrs. Applebee laughed. "And the Liddles live next to the school."

The following evening Lyman and Jessie's parlour was packed, some eager to hear the Word of God and some curious to discover why these men had been barred from the school. Children sat side by side on the stairs that overlooked the stuffy room, poking and making faces at each other, and occasionally stifling a giggle. Lyman had borrowed chairs and George and Jack set up the modest room so they could face the door, their backs against the kitchen wall and the open staircase on their right. On the warm air of the summer night, the muted squeals of girls playing hide-and-go-seek in a neighbour's yard echoed through the open windows. A rooster crowed in the distance as Lyman watched the hour hand on the clock creeping toward eight. Just as the gong finished striking, a man with a bulbous nose and sparse eyebrows slipped through the door. Dragging off his hat, he revealed a high-domed forehead as he slid into the back row beside Tony Ortello.

Everyone fell silent when George stood to address the room. "Jesus said that no one pours new wine into old wineskins. The new wine would swell and burst the old wineskins. Then the wine would be spilled and lost, and the skins ruined. New wine can only be put into new wineskins.[15]

"In the past few weeks, we have been attempting to pour new wine, but some people don't want it. They're like old inflexible wineskins in their response to the gospel invitation. A genuine awakening to God requires a new expression, a new way of seeing. In other words, the practical life of Christ won't fit into our selfish, egotistical natures or into the old religious system we have been brought up with. Why? Because the new wine is alive and developing. It causes a pressure that bursts the old wineskins. That's what happened at the school last night! To have expected otherwise would be to contradict the teaching of our Saviour. The pure, unadorned gospel offends because it levels all social distinctions. It takes away the power, the prestige, the pride that attracts some people to organized religion."

A slight movement drew George's attention to the tall man in the back row. He noticed the contrast between the man's clenched jaw and haughty stare that bored into him with that of Tony Ortello. The barber's charcoal eyes blinked slowly and his soft double chin folded into his swarthy neck as he relaxed, arms crossed, absorbing the gist of the message.

"When Jesus preached in Judea," George continued, "the Pharisees and the chief priests felt threatened. They resented His straightforward gospel of love. Has human nature changed?" George extended his hands, palms up. "No! Has the true gospel changed?" He looked around at his listeners. Many were shaking their heads. "No! And so the reaction we are experiencing now has developed because the gospel is simple and true. It's not watered down to fit the old, but human, system. New wine needs new wine-skins." George smiled as he saw people nodding.

"Jesus also said that no one uses a new piece of cloth to patch old clothes. The patch would shrink and make the hole even bigger. And the new piece wouldn't match the old.[16] What was our Saviour teaching in this illustration? Just that it's impossible to change our old self-nature or the old system by attaching a shred of something new. This totally new garment is symbolic of the divine nature of Christ."

George smiled at one of the small girls sitting on the floor and beckoned her to stand beside him. Then, after draping a long coat over her thin shoulders, he touched the sleeve.

"Just as a garment covers our bodies, so the purity of Christ's righteousness covers our sin. We can't improve our human nature, or fill in what we lack, by adding some of the teaching of Jesus to our own efforts. That won't please God. Rather, we must abandon any reliance on our own attempts to produce a Christian life and recognize that all of our own righteous acts are like filthy and ragged clothing before God.[17] But there's good news: The gift of salvation, the new garment that Jesus provided on Calvary's cross, is entirely free to those who are willing to receive it. Unfortunately, many refuse."[18]

The bawling of cows from the pasture fence beside the Liddle's house interrupted George's message. Catching sight of several contagious smiles when the racket persisted, George grinned back. "I'm not sure whether they're agreeing or protesting," he said, raising his voice above the uproar.

"This parable of the new garment illustrates how Christ covers our sin and makes us acceptable before God," he continued. "The parable of the new wine depicts how Christ lives within and enables us to reveal His life and nature before men. The first deals with our past, the second with our future."

George thanked the little girl for helping and as she sat down, he cast the coat over the back of a nearby chair.

"God planned this new way before He created the universe. The new life was brought to earth by Christ and lived by the church during the first century. From the beginning of time, it's been quietly lived by individuals enjoying an inner communion with God. And it's still offered today.

"What is this new wine that goes inside the wineskin? It's the Spirit of Christ." George stroked his sideburns, thoughtful for a moment. "Think about a man who drinks a lot of wine," he suggested. "His complexion becomes colourful, and for a short time he's confident, happy—even blissful. Of course too much wine debilitates a man, and when its influence wears off, often plunges him into despair. With the Spirit, it's different. The effect is always uplifting and refreshing. But remember, you can talk about a forty gallon cask of wine until the cows come home, but it will have no effect whatsoever—unless you drink it. In the past, I was drawn into a lot of religious talk myself. But talking never brought satisfaction.

"Not until we drink in the Spirit of Christ will the character of God be reflected in our words and actions. We'll have an inner glow that can't be hidden. But that can only happen if we've been emptied of the old life. We must be willing to turn away from the traditions of men, and even from one's own self-nature. Both will try to kill the Christ life. The Bible says that any person who is entirely satisfied with the old wine will not desire the new wine. For to him the old seems better.[19] Until we feel disquieted and incomplete in ourselves, we'll never desire the new life and new way."

George paused and looked earnestly into the faces before him. "This brings me to a question that I'd like each of you to take home and think about." Waiting, no one stirred. "Are you content with the old wine and the old system? Or, spiritually speaking, are you looking for a new wine, a new life, and a new way? Do you want to be the closest you can be to Christ?"

The warm room and the intensity of his message had left George drenched with perspiration. But as he mopped his forehead and looked into the soft eyes of his listeners, he was sure that some of them understood.

After George took his seat again, Jack led the group in a hymn.

> There is a way, a narrow way,
> That leads to life above—
> A way of peace and holiness,
> Of purity and love.
>
> My yearning soul desires to find
> This hidden path of bliss;
> Lord, hear my prayer and lead me in
> The way of holiness.[20]

The humidity of the late August evening enveloped the yard as the group dispersed, and the eerie whistling of the whippoorwill could be heard above the occasional whinnying of the horses tied to the school fence.

As the men walked home to Mrs. Applebee's that night, Jack spoke up. "Did you notice the man who came in late and sat near the door?"

"He didn't look very happy, did he?"

"No, he didn't. And he left pretty quickly too. Lyman told me that he and Mr. Coffer and their wives play whist on Saturday evenings."

George smiled ruefully. "I saw him grit his teeth and shake his head when I started to talk about how rigid and unbending old wineskins were," he said. "And about a new way being needed for a new awakening."

"While you were speaking it occurred to me that the gospel of Christ is good news for bad people,[21] but bad news for good people."[22]

"Tell me what you mean by that."

"Well," Jack elaborated, "folks who understand that we're all born with a sinful nature will treasure the pure garment of righteousness that Jesus offers. But people who consider themselves fine folks will be annoyed by the suggestion that their righteous acts are just filthy rags as far as God is concerned."

"You're right, Jack," George said as the two men turned in at Mrs. Applebee's gate. "Prisoners of traditional thinking won't be able to grasp the key to that simple truth. It's beyond their reach. Besides, if they're satisfied in captivity, why would they search for freedom?"

Jack grinned and offered a lighter note. "I noticed the cows did their share of bellyaching too."

"Yes, but they simmered down in a hurry when the farmer let out their calves. It might not be so easy with Mr. Coffer's friend."

~

News of the opposition to the gospel stirred the hearts of the Puslinch church. Alistair was near the edge of the beaver meadow in the back forty cutting more fence posts when Priscilla brought him the letter. When he first saw her, long skirt gathered in one hand as she hurried through the field dotted with Queen Anne's lace and goldenrod, he ran to meet her.

As he stood under a little stand of white birch, slowly reading and rereading the brothers' news, his face clouded with both sadness and joy. He thanked God for the brothers' unshaken resolve to carry on in spite of adversity. Beneath the last sentence of the letter, George had printed the essence of one of Jesus' sayings: Blessed are you when people insult you, persecute you, and falsely say all kinds of evil against you because of Me.

Rejoice and be glad because great is your reward in heaven, for they per-
secuted the ancient prophets in the same way.[23]

Alistair studied the strength in George's upright script. "Thanks for
bringing the letter away back here," he said as he carefully folded the letter.

Priscilla caught the thickness in his voice. "The reaction to Jesus'
preaching was just the same," she noted as she tucked the letter back into
its envelope. "Some people heard Him gladly. Others became bitter."

"I know," Alistair replied softly. "But it stings just the same to think of
George and Jack being insulted." He picked up the bucksaw, balancing its
sharp teeth on the soft bark. "It's like these posts," he observed. "The same
moisture that rots a cedar fencepost makes a cedar tree grow and thrive.
The fibre's the same, but only one is alive."

Stephen and Emily reacted to the news with a compelling urge to visit
the brothers, and on Monday they wrote to tell them they were coming.
Stephen closed the blacksmith shop by mid-afternoon the following Saturday
and harnessed their high-spirited driver. Emily carried out a battered leather
suitcase borrowed from her neighbour and climbed up beside Stephen. As
they drove through the countryside, the warbling of countless flocks of blackbirds reminded them that the autumn migration was already on the wing.

The horse, partly of Thoroughbred bloodlines, was a pacer and covered the ground quickly. But even so, with a couple of stops for the horse,
it was supper time before the couple reached Elora. They had barely pulled
up in front of the house when George and Jack sprinted out to the buggy
and threw their arms around them. George led Stephen and Emily inside
to meet their landlady while Jack stabled the black gelding in the shed.
Mrs. Applebee beamed as she showed the young couple to their bedroom.
She had spread her double wedding-ring quilt over the freshly made up
four-poster bed and set a bowl of golden pears on the dresser. After she
turned in, the four friends talked late into the night.

The following morning was Sunday and the brothers had been sorely
missing the weekly fellowship of the Puslinch saints. When George heard
Mrs. Applebee starting to prepare breakfast, he hurried down to ask if they
could use her parlour for a fellowship meeting. She quickly gave her permission and seemed pleased when George invited her to join them.

Like all the meetings at Wood Creek Farm, the spirit of the tiny gathering was soft and gentle. George had procured a loaf of unleavened bread
and a cup of wine to enable them to remember Jesus in the way He had taught
His disciples. Mrs. Applebee seemed genuinely moved by the intimacy of

this simple memorial of Christ. Her sterling perception showed at the close of the meeting when she turned a shining face on the group.

"In this parlour," she declared, "Wilson used to dispute with lawyers and barristers from all over Wellington County. They'd smoke their pipes and argue the law's finer points till the wee hours. They'd bicker back and forth, debating everything from the new Criminal Code to the Admiralty Act, but now there's a different spirit here. This morning the Scripture, 'peace be within thy walls' was fulfilled in this very room.[24] What a lovely spirit of life and joy you've brought to my summer." Jenny L., silent in the presence of unfamiliar guests, opened her beak at the sound of Mrs. Applebee's cheerful voice and began her sweet trilling scales. "And Jenny agrees," she added as she bustled off to the kitchen.

After dinner Stephen and Emily stretched out for a nap, staying on for the gospel meeting that evening. It was thrilling for them to meet Lyman and Jessie Liddle, Hugh and Gertrude Foster, Oliver Summers and his son, Eddie, and others they knew through George and Jack's letters.

Early Monday morning before the mists had evaporated, Stephen and Emily packed their bags, their hearts filled with wonderful news for the Puslinch church. As their rig pulled away, Emily sat half turned, waving her white hat in the air until they rounded a corner and slipped from view.

"I feel a little homesick," Jack admitted as he and George turned back toward the house. "There's often a letter from my folks on a Monday. I'll stop by the post office after the train passes through." When George failed to reply, Jack looked sharply at him. "I'm sorry your mother never learned how to write, George. And that your father won't."

George kicked a stone aside. "It's all right. I never expected otherwise."

As Herb Chambers slid an envelope under the wicket, he was rewarded by a broad smile on Jack's round face. Recognizing his mother's hand, Jack thanked the postmaster and turned toward the street. He tore open the seal and began to read as he sauntered toward Mrs. Applebee's.

Eden Mills, Ontario
August 28, 1901

Dear Son,

Summer's getting away seems a long spell since June. I see the raccoons is at the corn. Come fall when my preserves is done I mean to start on some rag rugs out of Grandpa's wool trousers. Your Pop will tear the strips for me he gets them so nice and even. Jack, dearest son, something is laying heavy on our hearts these days and nights. It might be we should have told you long afore this.

When Iris the midwife brought you to us along with the picture of your little mother she made us promise to give it to you on your 16th birthday. She gave us to understand your mother had growed up on a farm outside of Belwood afore she got taken advantage of by some neighbour man. Then she was sent to her cousin's in Guelph until you was borned. We was to tell you she was from Belwood when we gave you the picture but to be honest Jack I was afeared you might get taken up with finding her. I didn't want to take a chance on losing you. Your father backed me up. But now as yer in that district and a grown man it's only right you should know.

Jack's hands trembled as he turned the single page over. His heart pounded and his tongue felt suddenly dry. He lost all sense of Geddes Street, its stores and passers-by as he continued.

Your dear mother who was hardly more than a child—well she may be living around Fergus or Belwood yet. Maybe working out someplace as a washerwoman or a dressmaker for a genteel family. It may be that your paths will cross if she's still in that district. We leave this in your hands. We are sorry to put this surprise onto you but as the Good Book says there is nothing hidden that shall not be uncovered. I am broke up about this. Forgive us for holding back.

Your loving folks,

Mother and Pop

Jack leaned against a paling fence where hollyhocks poked sunburned faces through the missing slats, as if reading over his shoulder. He took a heaving breath, turned the page over, and read it all again. His eyes stung with the possibilities, with the uncertainties, and with the sudden need to be alone, away from anyone's eyes, even George's. He folded the letter along its original crease and tucked it back into the envelope from which had sprung such jarring news.

Hobbling around the end of the fence, Mrs. Quinn accosted him like a meddlesome gnome in her brocaded wrap and tasslled earrings. "Mercy on us, young man, I say you don't look so well." She reached out a clawlike hand. "You're white as a scairt rabbit. Best go home and have Mrs. Applebee brew you a tonic. My, she enjoys her boarders—so she was telling me today. Men—they don't require the starching and ironing women folk do." Her face thrust itself upward, inviting dialogue, but Jack ducked aside as if eluding an unwelcome swarm of gnats.

Sixteen

RENDER UNTO CAESAR

Early Autumn 1901

George and Jack had already split and piled several face cords of maple and beech in Mrs. Applebee's shed. But the shorter days and cooler evenings heralded autumn's approach, and they wanted to lay in a plentiful supply— at least six bush cords—for the winter. Early one morning they strapped a lunch bucket onto their bicycles and rode out to Mrs. Applebee's sister's farm to cut more wood.

Admiring the foliage, George smiled and drew in a deep breath of the clear air as he took a moment to stretch in the sun. He offered Jack a piece of horehound candy from the brown bag in his pocket before picking up the crosscut saw. He enjoyed working with Jack on the other end of the long blade. Some men leaned on the saw, rather than letting the sharp teeth bite into the hardwood at its own rate. Not Jack.

"Do you remember that sawing bee, back about six years?" George asked. "At the old Barclay place. We were partners."

Jack grinned back across the log. "Sure do. Out of twenty-four teams, we finished second."

While the two men took a breather from the saw later in the morning, George listened to the chatter of the red squirrels scolding as they chased each other along the rail fence. Stooping, he turned up a leaf on a milkweed plant beside a rusty sap pail and located the cocoon of a Monarch butterfly. When he and Jack had started cutting logs three weeks ago, he had noticed a caterpillar which seemed intent on eating as much milkweed as possible.

One evening, standing in front of Mrs. Applebee's tall bookcase, George had taken a volume from the shelf entitled *Flora and Fauna of Southern Ontario*. He had been startled to learn that the Monarch's consumption went on night and day until the larva's weight had increased many times. Then a dramatic change occurred, and the caterpillar entered its chrysalis in less than a minute. Inside the cocoon all the internal parts of the larva dissolved into a greenish liquid, except for its steadily beating heart. Everything else—its body, legs, stomach, nervous system, and eyes—had essentially perished and disappeared.

Now George gazed in awe as he watched the final stage in this metamorphosis of a once blind chrysalis into a beautiful new creature. The elegant orange and black wings flexed as they dried in the September sunshine and then, before his very eyes, the butterfly lifted on the breeze, released from the earth at last. Far away on a remote mountain in Mexico, this Monarch would join millions of its kind in a paradise it had never seen.

"Beautiful, isn't it," he heard Jack say at his elbow.

George turned to his friend. "You know, I was like that caterpillar," he said. "I started out as a consumer, and my whole life revolved around my farm. The having and the getting stage, I call it. But what a marvelous transformation when God touched my soul—I became alive to His love."

"Someday we'll leave these old earth-bound bodies behind just like that critter did," Jack said, nodding in the direction of the tiny Monarch, floating high overhead. "We'll fly away to the mountaintop of New Jerusalem to be with the Lord forever."

George flexed his shoulders in the warm sun, visualizing the joyous crowd from every nation gathered around the throne of God. "What a thrill to invite others to be part of that company," he declared. "Anyone who belongs to Christ is a new creation. Old things have passed away."[1]

Reaching down again, George cradled the empty green cocoon in his narrow palm. "This cocoon's just like the empty garden tomb," he noted.

Jack crouched down to take a closer look. "And like all the graves that will be left behind on the resurrection morning." Standing up, he put his hands on his hips and arched his back. "I'll just head back to the wood pile and stretch out for five minutes until you come along."

George nodded as he uncorked a wine bottle he used for carrying water. The butterfly's ascent on the morning breeze made him think of all those who would rise because of their faith in Christ. As he tipped back his head to take a cool drink, he gazed into the distant clouds, thinking about Christ's return. *Those who have already died will rise first,* he mused. *After that, believers who are still alive will be taken up into the clouds to meet the Lord in the air. From that time on, we'll be with Him forever.*[2]

George knelt at a tree stump on the leafy forest floor and once again consecrated his life and efforts to God. "Dear Father, please reveal Your Son through *my* life."

Later as the pair chopped limbs off a twisted log, George returned to the subject. "Jack, I feel sorry for Mr. Coffer and the others who oppose the preaching of the gospel. I hope they don't get stuck in the caterpillar stage and miss the joy of the transformation."

"Yep," Jack agreed. "They'd miss out on life altogether. A real shame."

The next day at breakfast, Jack announced that he needed a haircut. "When I'm finished, I'll meet you back here," he told George as he left the house. After walking briskly for a few minutes, he turned down Church Lane, a narrow side street, and disappeared behind the red-and-white striped pole in front of Tony's Barbershop.

The shop was quiet at this early hour, and Tony sat reading yesterday's *Elora News Express.* The bracing fragrance of aftershave, mingled with that of talcum powder and lemon pomade, had permeated the room and its fixtures. The barber's chair sat in the centre of the room with four straight chairs along the wall for waiting patrons. Opposite, a small shoeshine stand vied for attention with a hat shelf and a row of coat hooks.

Tony, a short dark-haired man, looked up from his paper and greeted Jack with a thick Italian accent and a jovial grin. "Shave and haircut?"

"Just a haircut for today," Jack said as he climbed into the chair.

"You sava the shave for you wedding day?"

Jack laughed. "We'll have to see about that."

Clipping around Jack's ears with the scissors, Tony kept up a steady patter. He told Jack that upon immigrating he had first settled in Toronto, but that his rural roots had brought him westward to Elora. Initially he had been cold-shouldered in the Scottish and English neighbourhood, but over the years he had made friends and established a dedicated clientele.

At first, Tony's ramblings seemed only those of a congenial barber, but soon Jack realized why their paths had crossed. "I grow uppa in the Alps westa of Torino. Provincia of Piemonte," Tony explained. "An olda people liva there during the Middle Age. They travel and preacha lika you do."

Jack sat spellbound. All he could think of was his own strong conviction that in different times and places isolated pockets of believers had practised their faith in the simple manner of the New Testament.

Tony's voice broke into Jack's thoughts. "When I was twenty, I studia to be a priesta," he continued. "One time in the seminary library I stumble acrossa something about these early people. Their lives and teaching were differenta from what I wasa use to. I wasa so intrigue that I spenda days searching the Vatican archiva for mora information.

"One day I getta so fed up with organize religion and so convince that it's not like the Bible that I quita school. My papa, he wasa mad. He want a son in the priestahood. Things at home getta so hot that I packa up and leava Piemonte for good. I tella my papa that I hava nothing to do with the church again." After settling in Canada, Tony said, he had written a journal to keep his findings fresh. "I quite interest in your gospel meetings," he confided. "They're the only religious thing I attenda since I leava the churcha."

As Jack slipped out of the chair and stood in the circle of hair clippings at his feet, Tony made a promise. "When I coma to Lyman Liddle's, I bringa my papers," he said. "Then you can reada for yourself."

"Sounds interesting. I can hardly wait," Jack exclaimed, drawing his coins from his pocket. "That's the usual fifteen cents, Tony?"

The barber jammed both hands into his pockets. "Not a thing."

Jack's eyebrows shot up. "Oh, no," he insisted. "I need to pay you."

"You no taka a collection. This isa my way to helpa you work."

Catching the resolve in Tony's charcoal eyes, Jack hesitated. He didn't want to offend the older man or slight his generosity. "Thank you very much," he murmured as he slipped his cap onto his head and reached out to shake the barber's hand. "We'll see you soon."

∽

Each Saturday evening after supper, George paid Mrs. Applebee the room and board. But one afternoon as he carefully counted out the money on his bed, he realized that he and Jack had only enough for the coming week. *We'll soon be down to the wire,* he fretted to himself.

Then he remembered what Jesus had told His disciples: "Don't worry or ask yourselves, 'Will we have anything to eat or drink?' or 'What will we have to wear?' Only people who don't know God worry about such things. Your Father in heaven knows what you need. Put His work first and all things will be yours. Don't worry about tomorrow. It will take care of itself."[3] George took a deep breath, confident as he set about his day's work. He wouldn't mention it to Jack for now.

At supper that evening, Mrs. Applebee handed George and Jack two huge bowls of hot apple pudding with honey drizzled over the crust. "Used to be Wilson's favourite," she said with a smile. "Here, cut yourself a nice chunk of cheese to go with it." Her eyes had an added depth that bespoke her large and generous soul.

The following night, after the Sunday meeting, a lady with a sombre and uncertain countenance invited George and Jack for a visit. "A cup of tea," she said, "and a few suggestions for your ministry."

"Thank you," George replied. "We'll see you about nine o'clock, if that's all right."

At the agreed hour, the two men called at Mrs. Ravenshaw's home on Mill Street. As they talked over morning tea, their hostess's intent became clearer. Her forehead furrowed as she began. "My husband and I really need a bigger house," she said. "Something on a nicer street and close to the shops." She took a deep breath and smiled. "I hope you'll pray with me. That's the benefit of being a Christian, isn't it? When we want something, we can expect it. After all, we're children of the King."

George thought of the prayers of Jesus and of the apostle Paul. He couldn't remember either of them ever praying for a new house or anything remotely close. Jesus had prayed that His disciples would have the constant presence of the Holy Spirit, be kept from the evil around them, and enjoy unity among themselves.[4] Paul, too, had prayed for spiritual, not material concerns: that the saints' love would flourish. And with it their insight to discern what is best so they could be pure and faultless until Christ returns.[5]

Mrs. Ravenshaw smiled. "We should also ask God for a horse and rig so you men can get around easier. And maybe your own cottage to live in."

"I don't mean to be contrary," George clarified. "But we're not expecting any of those things. What's more, I question whether any Christian should be asking God for a fancier house."[6]

Mrs. Ravenshaw's surprise was evident. "Well," she retorted. "I can't imagine why not."

George and Jack exchanged wary glances.

"We've often been taught that we need only to believe in Jesus to have salvation," Jack said. "But even though some people in Jerusalem believed in Him, Jesus didn't commit Himself to them."[7]

Mrs. Ravenshaw's face took on a guarded expression. "Strange, I don't recall hearing that before," she protested.

Sensing her skepticism, Jack opened his Bible to John's gospel. "Jesus knew that many were drawn solely by the things He could give them to improve their natural lives," he explained. "They wanted to be filled with the loaves and the fish, so to speak.[8] Although they definitely believed that Jesus could supply those things, they had no desire to receive the source of power behind the miracles and no real thirst in their soul for His life and teachings. Believing in Christ with only our intellect, or coming to Him primarily for material blessings, will never produce eternal life."

"So what did they do?" Mrs. Ravenshaw asked, one eyebrow raised. "Those people in Jerusalem."

"I expect they just drifted away," Jack said. "Many of Jesus' disciples stopped following when they realized that it wasn't material prosperity He promised, but eternal life."[9]

"But why would they turn their backs on Him?" she persisted. "He was their Messiah, after all."

"They left because He said that they must eat His flesh and drink His blood.[10] Or in other words, participate in the life of self-sacrifice which He taught and practiced. After losing some of His followers, Jesus said to the twelve, 'Do you also want to go away?' But Peter answered, 'Lord, to whom shall we go? You have the words of eternal life.'"

Mrs. Ravenshaw sat silently for a moment, and then she straightened herself in her chair. "I understand what you're saying, but I have a lot of faith in my pastor. He says Christians should expect better health and more prosperity than the ordinary man. Besides, I felt a real power when he spoke in some kind of an ecstatic utterance at our church yesterday morning." Her face flushed in the telling. "I've never heard anything quite like it before."

"Well, you know," George began. "I've no question that you felt a power. But what was its source? God cares for His creation, and we wouldn't want to question His power. But often the power that people feel has nothing to do with God."

Mrs. Ravenshaw leaned back in her chair and folded her arms. The brothers could only hope that she wasn't folding her mind against what they were trying to show her.

"When I was a boy," George went on, "a friend asked me to go fishing one morning. I was to be at his farm before daybreak. I set off in the darkness and took a shortcut through the woods. As I walked among the misty trees, I caught sight of a stranger in a thicket a hundred feet ahead. He waited eerily just behind the trunk of a gnarled old elm. I froze in absolute horror, unable to move. A shadow hid his face, but I could see his head turning to peer in different directions. He appeared to be over six feet tall, so I knew he could catch me if I ran. But I wasn't sure he'd seen me, so I stood petrified in my tracks. My heart pounded and cold sweat trickled down my neck. My breath came in shallow gasps that he must surely have heard. But still the stranger waited for my next move and pretended to look the other way." George saw Mrs. Ravenshaw's eyes widening with alarm.

"The terror held me to the ground as the sky grew lighter. Then, all of a sudden, as the sun began to crack through the trees, the stranger's head flew off his shoulders. It soared up into the sky with a slight hooting sound and left only a dead stump standing where the horned owl had perched.

"You see, the morning light dispelled my fear. There's no question that a gripping power affected my body—but it was all manufactured in my mind. The illusion itself was lifeless; it possessed no power at all."

As the message of the story penetrated, Mrs. Ravenshaw's colour rose. "So you're saying it was all in my head?" Her voice carried a hard edge.

"Well, you know, sometimes our minds do give a power to something that seems so real. But it's only a delusion. According to the apostle Peter, we do well to heed the gospel as a light that shines in a dark place until the day dawns and the morning star rises in our hearts.[11] Only Christ, the light of the world can illuminate the darkness of the mind and dispel its forceful power."[12]

"Well, I know *my* mind wasn't deceiving me," she sputtered defensively. "There's a power in those services no matter what you say!"

Meeting George's eyes, Jack changed the subject by commenting on a photograph of Mrs. Ravenshaw's family. Although the three of them chatted for a few more minutes, the atmosphere had cooled considerably.

Jack spoke first as they wended their way along Geddes Street. Ahead, two boys, like nimble puppets, performed hand springs over the hitching rail in front of Foster's General Store. "I doubt if Mrs. Ravenshaw's ever going to be receptive to what we said in there," Jack declared. "In a way, I'm surprised she's kept coming to our meetings."

"Maybe so," George conceded, "but I think she's a very spiritual lady who just got a dose of bad teaching. I sense that something struck a chord with her today." He paused to admire the acrobats. "Were you ever that agile?"

"My hamstrings weren't designed for somersaults," Jack laughed.

Skirting the antics, the men moved on. "If Mrs. Ravenshaw's honest with herself, she'll pray for understanding," George asserted. "I hope she'll realize the Holy Spirit's more interested in doing an eternal work in our hearts than a temporary one in our pocketbooks."

After lunch George and Jack began scraping Mrs. Applebee's shutters and window frames. The tedious work gave George plenty of time to think, grappling with the contrast between his perspective and that of Mrs. Ravenshaw. Suddenly his own image confronted him from the elaborate curved pane of the glass. Was she in it merely for what she could get out of it? He now did a careful check to be sure that this did not describe him as well. Eventually, he spoke up. "I sometimes question my own motives for being a Christian. Maybe I've no right to doubt Mrs. Ravenshaw's."

Jack looked sharply at George from his ladder. "Don't you think there's a big difference?" he asked. "God promised to supply our *essentials* if our first concern is His kingdom.[13] That's quite different from her view that Christians are better off than other folks." He stretched up to reach the top of the sash. "Don't forget, you got rid of everything to follow Jesus."

After mulling it over, George knew that he had no thought of getting anything material out of his relationship with God. If he had, he would never have sold his farm, his animals, his furniture. And aside from tangible things, he certainly would never have broken off his understanding with Laura. Her smile and laughter came flooding back as he scraped the peeling paint. For a minute she was there, bantering with him on the ladder, and then she was gone again. He felt a dull pain in his chest when he thought of what might have flowered from their love. He wiped his eyes with the back of one hand.

"Remember Job?" Jack's voice jolted him back to the present. "Being true to God cost him all his wealth. And more than that, he had terrible anguish over the death of his children. His entire body was covered with boils, so disfigured that even his friends didn't recognize him."[14]

George smiled weakly at Jack's attempt to encourage him. "And in spite of all that," he returned, "Job never lost faith in God's goodness."

"Exactly right," Jack declared. "And what about Paul? He prayed that the thorn in his flesh would be removed. But the Lord replied, 'My presence is all you need, My power is strongest when you are weak.'[15] So you see, being a Christian is no sure-fire recipe for health or abundance or for an easier life. Sometimes the opposite is true."[16]

George relaxed his grip on the rung and flexed his fingers. "Even if God allows me to wilt under the hot sun of affliction, He still cares for me," he found himself muttering to the shutter. "Adverse circumstances may very well be blessings in disguise, part of God's *special recipe* for me."[17]

"What's that you said, George?"

"Oh, I was just talking to myself," George answered as he sanded off the last bits of old paint and pried loose a chunk of hard putty.

Jack grinned. "Are you answering your own questions, George?"

"Not yet." George smiled as he brushed off the windowsill with an old cloth. "The Scripture says that all things work together for good to those who love God.[18] *All things* may very well include hunger or suffering. That's the opposite of pleasure, but not necessarily the opposite of peace."

Jack climbed down his ladder and stood looking up at George. "Even Jesus learned obedience by suffering,"[19] he said. "And He made it clear His followers would face the same.[20] In fact, many of the first apostles suffered a martyr's death. But they didn't lose their peace or hope and run away."

George nodded. *Would the prosperity preachers be willing to accept pain or poverty,* he wondered, *if it brought them closer to Jesus? Or were they simply trying to entice folks by appealing to the normal desire for more things and a pleasant, trouble-free life?*

"Do you remember Malachi pointing out that the same boiling water that softens a potato makes an egg hard? Circumstances don't matter, he said, just our reaction to them."

George rolled a lump of putty, allowing it to absorb the warmth of his hands. *A fellow needs to be soft,* he reasoned, *not hard and bitter when he feels the heat and sorrows of life.* He thumbed the fresh bead along the pane of bubbled glass. *But it takes the faith of Job and the stamina of Paul.*

Jack stepped back to survey the work. "I'm going to walk around the house and check our progress." He returned in a few minutes. "We're nearly done scraping," he announced enthusiastically. "So maybe I'll stop and get more paint on my way back from the post office."

Like a jaunty boy heading off to dig worms for bait, Jack had been calling for the mail with a lighter heart since the surprising letter of his birth mother's whereabouts had arrived from Eden Mills. He had responded to the revealing note with tender reassurance for his parents, despite their ill-advised reticence. Since then he often tucked the photograph of his young mother into his shirt pocket, allowing it to breathe with fresh life, her eyes and lips taking on a previously unknown expressiveness.

The crisp sunny afternoon held a touch of fall in the air as George crouched precariously on the veranda roof. Glancing up at the cloudless sky, he began to prime the window frames. *Ideal weather for drying paint,* he thought. Startled by the squeak of the gate, he twisted and looked down to see a well-turned-out man in a business suit and felt hat.

"Excuse me," the man called up. "Is Mrs. Applebee at home?"

"Yes, sir," George replied. "She's in…" Then he heard the landlady's burst of welcome.

Mr. Applebee had been the senior partner in the law firm of Applebee & Peterson prior to his death in the summer of 1896. Mr. Peterson, the only lawyer in Elora now, delivered a monthly payment to Mrs. Applebee according to an agreement he had struck with his former partner.

"Well, John, it's nice to see you," George heard Mrs. Applebee exclaim. "You're always so prompt. Come on in for a cup of tea."

While Mr. Peterson, leather satchel in hand, settled in a kitchen arm-chair, she went to call George down from the roof.

Mr. Peterson regarded George with approval as the wiry young man bit into a hot buttermilk scone slathered with peach jam. "Every able-bodied man in this town is so busy at this time of year that it's like pulling teeth to get good help," the solicitor remarked.

"You're right about that," Mrs. Applebee agreed. "I'm fortunate to have George and Jack. Thanks to them, I'm all ready for cold weather. Just a little painting to finish today and everything will be done." George pondered his teacup as Mrs. Applebee and her visitor talked about the shorter days and how business was at the law office.

After finishing his tea, Mr. Peterson folded his napkin and rose to leave. As he lifted his wide-brimmed hat off the hall tree at the door, he asked, almost as an afterthought, "George, do you think you fellows would have time to do a little yard work for me too?"

George hesitated, wondering what response God would want him to give. "Thank you for the kind offer," he replied. "I'd like to speak to Jack. Could we come by your office tomorrow with an answer?"

"Perfect," Mr. Peterson agreed with a nod. Then, shaking hands with George and Mrs. Applebee, he left.

Back outside, George climbed the wooden ladder again. As he brushed a fresh coat of white paint on the Gothic window, he wondered how the apostles and other itinerants had been supplied with their natural needs. The apostle Paul, he recalled, had made tents with Aquila and Priscilla in Corinth. Every Sabbath he went to the synagogue, trying to persuade and win over both Jews and Gentiles.[21] Clearly, Paul offered a solid example of preaching in conjunction with physical work to support himself.

After supper, the two men took a stroll along the edge of the rugged limestone gorge that circumscribed the west side of the village. The sun's rays played on clumps of grass and scrub that clung to the rock face like cautious climbers, leaving the churning river buried in deep shade.

"How far down do you reckon the water is?" Jack asked as he rested his husky forearms across the rail of the David Street bridge.

"Pretty near a hundred feet, give or take."

As the two men watched the shadow line inching its way up the east wall, George outlined Mr. Peterson's request. "As far as I can tell, it's well within the scope of Paul's letter to the Christians at Thessalonica. Wasn't that the commercial centre of Macedonia?"

"Yes, I think that's right," Jack replied as the men turned to meander along the precipice.

"Anyway, Paul wrote to the church saying that he and his companion hadn't been idle when they were there. And that they hadn't eaten anyone's food without paying for it. On the contrary, they had worked night and day so they wouldn't be a burden. He said they had the right to assistance, but they worked to make themselves a model for the church to follow."[22]

Jack nodded thoughtfully as he scooped up a stone at Lover's Leap and hurled it far out over the gorge, watching it curve and plummet into the swift current. "It wasn't just in Thessalonica," he remarked. "Paul displayed a shining example of the true ministry in other communities as well. Ten years later he stated emphatically to the elders in Ephesus that he hadn't coveted anyone's silver or gold or clothing. And that his own hands had supplied both his needs and those of his companions. He said that by working hard he had shown the Ephesians the need of helping the weak."[23]

The two young men stopped upstream of the mill to watch the sun being eclipsed by the magical mist that veiled the Tooth of Time. The tiny islet of rock and cedar clung precariously to the brink of the falls.

"I'd say it's appropriate for preachers to earn their basic needs by working with their hands," George concluded above the roar of the current.

"Yes," Jack agreed, "but it's also scriptural to receive some support from believers given as a token of love. Both Jesus and Paul enjoyed the support of others with whom they were in fellowship."

A couple of days later, George opened a soiled envelope from Malachi Jackson and found a one dollar bank note for each of them tucked into a letter. Malachi's scrawly handwriting was almost illegible, but the warmth of his love was crystal clear and spoke volumes to the brothers. George thanked God for such a loyal friend. Malachi worked hard, he knew, and this was his wage for an entire week. He couldn't help but think of the poor widow of the New Testament who had given away her last two coins.[24]

Later, when George wrote to Malachi, he borrowed some of Paul's words to the church at Philippi: When I began to preach the gospel and left from Puslinch to go to Elora, you sent aid more than once for my necessities.[25] The way of love is repeating itself again.

~⊙~

"There's something miraculous about depending on God to supply our needs," George said as he and Jack cut across a field of thistles on their way to Mr. Peterson's office the next morning. "Our allegiance is to Him, and no one else. We can preach what He lays on our hearts without worrying what the audience wants to hear."

"That's where the clergy are bound hand and foot," Jack said. "They can't do that. They're accountable to the congregation who hired them."

"You can't find a single servant of God in the Bible who was controlled by his audience," George said solemnly.

A grin spread across Jack's face. "What kind of message do you think you'd have to preach to soften up Mr. Coffer's friend? You know, the tall man with the high forehead who came to Lyman's a while back."

"I don't think he'll be happy until he sees our backs as we walk out of Elora," George said with a chuckle.

The solid oak door of the law office was inset with a thick pane elegantly bevelled around the edges. The name Applebee & Peterson—Barristers and Solicitors had been painted on the glass in gold Roman-style letters. Grasping the heavy brass door handle, George led the way inside. A law clerk sat in the reception area clacking on a black Underwood typewriter. He turned to look up at the two men.

"We've come to see Mr. Peterson, if he's free," George said politely.

With a courteous nod, the man directed them to the lawyer's office. Stacks of legal files and official documents lay piled upon his desk.

The busy attorney peered over his gold-framed spectacles and beckoned them into his mahogany office. "Good day, George. Nice to see you again." As Mr. Peterson rose, George introduced him to Jack, and after shaking hands, the men sat down in comfortable leather chairs.

"This used to be Mr. Applebee's office," the lawyer offered with an expansive sweep of his hand.

"It's certainly a nice place to work," George replied.

Mr. Peterson smiled proudly.

"Jack and I've talked about your offer and we'd be happy to accept, if it's still available," George went on.

"That sounds fine. When can you start?"

"Well, we came prepared to start right away, if you wish."

"Wonderful," the lawyer rejoined.

George looked at Mr. Peterson. "Our first concern has to be our ministry, and we'll need to visit people now and then. You should also know that we plan to leave the village in a few weeks. Is it agreeable to you if we quit by late afternoon to prepare for our evening meetings?"

"Absolutely," Mr. Peterson replied, smiling. "You look like two strong men. Perhaps you can gather some of the vegetables out of the garden and store them in the root cellar. You'll find the tools in the back shed. And some bushel baskets too."

Mr. Peterson possessed one of the old village gardens that had been enriched with decades of kitchen compost. It showed the rank growth and sweet decay of vegetables born out of bloated rinds, peelings, and seeds that lay among the picturesque and colourful wrack of seasons past. Between the

rows an empty rabbit's nest sent up soft fluff while bits of broken Derbyshire
pottery gleamed among the glossy cucumbers and overripe tomatoes that
had collapsed and hung suspended from dejected vines. The knobby Hubbard
squash, swelled into monstrous shapes, sunned their fat bellies while their
lesser cousins, the acorns and butternuts, entwined themselves around them
like emissaries paying homage to noble sultans.

Jack heaped the ripe squash into baskets while George took a fork and
dug the carrots out of the damp earth.

"These carrots are like oversized toothpicks," he announced. "I guess
Mr. Peterson was too busy to thin them out."

Jack walked over to take a closer look. "It always seems funny to pull
out perfectly good carrots after they start to sprout. But this is a great lesson.
Unless you do, none of them will reach their full potential."

"It's like life, Jack," George said as he knocked the dirt off another bunch
of scrubby carrots and tossed them into the wooden wheelbarrow. "There's
lots of good deeds one can do. But if we do each of them halfheartedly,
none of them will amount to much. It's better to give up some aspects of
life so others can develop fully."

Jack piled two squash on the heaping basket. "You mean our choices?"

"Right," George said. "Every day believers choose from a range of activities that are perfectly wholesome. But if they occupy too much room in
our hearts, they crowd out Christ and reduce our reward."[26]

"So we've got to keep thinning the carrots." Jack hoisted a heavy bushel
of squash and headed for the root cellar.

Once again the brothers had no idea of the stir their work for Mr.
Peterson would ignite among the townsfolk who pictured them as clergymen and, therefore, above labourers' work. The brothers had been helping
Mr. Peterson for only two days when Eddie Summers urged them to come
to the store for morning tea. He quickly came to the point.

"It's not just me either. There are others too. We didn't know you needed
money." He laid ten dollars on the table for each of them. "Otherwise we'd
have given you some."

"We really *don't* need any money," George asserted, taking care that the
tone of his words conveyed respect and not insult.

"But why are you working," Eddie countered, "if you don't need it?"

George flexed his back. "God provided for our needs by introducing
us to Mr. Peterson. We don't just want to talk about Christianity, we want
to live it. God promised to care for us and that's what He's doing."

"But it doesn't look good to the community," Eddie insisted. "You know, two preachers having to work like common labourers."

"Eddie," Jack said gently, "Let me assure you, we're not the least bit concerned about appearances. We want to be like Jesus in every way. Even though He was the Son of God, He lived a very humble life. Besides, we're not above honest work. You know, ordinary toil bears its own nobility."

Eddie Summers was mystified as he put the twenty dollars back into his morocco pocketbook. He understood, and yet he didn't. It was all so different from any other evangelist or minister he had ever encountered.

Walking back to Mr. Peterson's yard, George turned to Jack. "We can't take money from anybody who hasn't fully accepted the simple teaching of Jesus we're trying to present and live out—even if we wanted to. The apostle John's fellow preachers didn't accept help from anyone who wasn't a follower either."[27]

"Exactly right," Jack replied. "On the other hand, John encouraged those who had become followers to show hospitality to the itinerants and to receive them into their homes. After their visit, the Christians sent them on their mission in a way God's servants deserve."[28]

The two men walked a full block before George spoke again. "Do you remember what Paul said about his reward for preaching the gospel?"

Jack shook his head slowly. "No, I don't."

"He said, 'What then is my reward? Just this, that in preaching the gospel of Christ, I may offer it *free of charge*, that I may not abuse my authority in the gospel.'"[29]

Nodding, Jack swung open the picket gate into Mr. Peterson's yard.

A few days later, when Hugh Foster saw the brothers at his grocery store, he, too, urged them to take a few dollars to help with their expenses.

"Thank you for your generous offer, Hugh," George said, "but we feel that we just can't accept money for sharing the wonderful story of Jesus."

The storekeeper assumed their principles prevented them from taking a private gift from an individual. "Well then, you should take up a collection like other preachers," he suggested.

Jack raised a rough boot to balance it on a nail keg. "We're not hesitating because it's *your* money, Hugh," he said softly. "It's just that we feel the New Testament doesn't permit us to take money as payment for preaching. Perhaps we're mistaken, but that's how we feel."

As Jack spoke, George prayed silently that the shopkeeper would not have his feelings hurt. Hugh, he knew, wanted to give them money because he admired them and thought they were doing good. But he and Jack felt there were important things Hugh needed to learn about being a Christian, about letting Christ lead him daily. George stared at the sawdust under the butcher block. How *could* they accept Hugh's support? He hardly knew what they stood for. Hugh and Eddie would first need to become brothers in the simple way of Jesus.

George shifted uneasily against the front edge of the counter. "At some point we'll be cycling on to another village," he explained. "If you are united with us in Spirit and feel led to mail us a few dollars, that might be different. It would no longer be payment for work, but a gift of love."

Hugh tugged at his double chin, struggling to comprehend.

George and Jack also wanted Hugh to understand that giving money wouldn't buy anyone access to heaven and that they had chosen this life out of a love for Christ, not for any personal gain. They could not exchange the message of love for money. They both remembered when they, too, had thought that doing good deeds or giving money would merit eternal reward.

"But the Scripture speaks about a collection and about giving a tenth of your income to the church," Hugh protested.

"A collection is mentioned only once," Jack said, smiling. "And it was not for Paul or any other minister's use, or for an organization. It was a special gathering of goods by saints in home churches for the special needs of destitute Christians in Jerusalem. This one-time gift expressed the Gentile Christians' love for their Jewish brethren."

Hugh was stumped. "But giving tithes is scriptural, isn't it?"

"Contrary to what we've been taught," George said, "there's absolutely no evidence of tithing in the New Testament. Most of the churches we grew up in fail miserably when it comes to *rightly dividing* the word of truth."[30]

Hugh looked perplexed. "I just don't get your drift," he confessed.

"Here's a way to see it more clearly," said George. "Do you have a will written up, for when you die?"

"Yes. Yes, of course."

"And when does your will or testament come into effect, Hugh?"

"Well, I guess it would be at the time I die."

"That's right," George continued. "The moment of your death will draw a sharp dividing line between the old way of doing things and the new way which will be governed by the will."

Hugh nodded, still wondering what George was driving at.

"At the time of Jesus' death, the New Testament, or new will, came into being.[31] The old will and the old way were finished forever. According to God's divine plan, Jesus' death divided the old way from the new way. Quite accurately, the churches preach the New Testament gospel of full and free salvation by grace, but then they mix it up with the methods of the Old Testament. In other words, they don't understand or divide the Scriptures rightly. They worship in temples made of stone and mortar, like the Old Testament. It's directed by a resident priest, like the Old Testament. And the whole thing is supported by the Old Testament practice of collections or tithing. The old way was largely outward and physical, but the new way is inward and spiritual. Jesus taught us that it's crucial to worship the Father *in spirit and in truth*.[32] For human beings this is so simple, yet so difficult. And we stumble over it."

Jack spoke up. "George and I've read a lot in the New Testament, but we've never found anything about Christians tithing. In fact, I learned from an old history book that there is no evidence of Christians participating in such a religious system until three hundred years after Jesus' resurrection. This corrupt and erroneous practice was instituted by a superstitious emperor in Rome during the fourth century."

For several days Hugh struggled with this new vision. He kept his Bible on a little table beside his rocking chair, and he spent each spare moment carefully searching for something to prove that George and Jack were mistaken. One evening, he finally had to accept the truth of what the brothers had said, that the existing religious system he was most familiar with functioned, to some extent, on commercial principles.

Leaning forward onto the front of the rockers, Hugh pressed the heels of his thick palms against his eyes. *If the money stops coming in, there'd be no church*, he concluded. *That's very different from the first-century church. Its lifeblood was the love of Christ in its members. Money had nothing to do with it.* He closed his Bible and sat staring out the kitchen window, dumbfounded by this startling revelation. The sun had set hours before, and everything was cast in a darkness that exposed no shape. Yet, when he concentrated his eyes and looked closely, he could make out a somewhat lighter shade that must have been the tree line joining with the sky. "Just ponder that, would you," he murmured to himself. "Two men working outside of any system for love, and love alone."

Seventeen

ANCIENT AFFIRMATION
Early Autumn 1901

Eyes narrowed in concentration, Jack lowered a row of wicks on the candle rod into the pot of melted tallow while George soaked the cotton wicks in limewater and saltpetre. It was more than a week after Jack had been at Tony's barbershop when an autumn storm hindered their yard and garden work for Mr. Peterson. After watching gusts of wind and rain toss the fallen leaves in fury, George and Jake decided to stay inside and help Mrs. Applebee make her winter supply of candles.

As they worked, Mrs. Applebee was riding a full tide of reminiscence. Striking a match to test one of the new wicks, she turned to the men, her eyes alight with devilment. "I remember a teacher challenging us to memorize some lines from *The Merchant of Venice*. There was a prize offered and I won it. I chose the passage, 'How far that little candle throws his beams! So shines a good deed in a naughty world.' That's over sixty-five years ago now."

"What a memory," George exclaimed.

"It certainly is," Jack acknowledged. "And speaking of Italy, I'm surprised we haven't seen Tony. He seemed so definite when he told me that he'd see us at Lyman and Jessie's one of these evenings."

George shrugged, without reply.

All of this, however, turned out to be a concern in haste; for that very evening Tony slipped through the door of the Liddle's modest cottage, a brown envelope in hand. After shaking hands with Lyman and his son Jimmy, Tony took his usual seat near the back. From off to his right, Eddie

Summers, sitting beside his father, glanced over his shoulder and winked, his slick oiled hair glistening in the lamplight. As Tony's eyes adjusted to the low-ceilinged room, the cheerful ruby glow from the two vase lamps brought into focus the familiar faces, some animated, others reposeful.

From the yard he heard a loud guffaw and in a couple of minutes the Fosters and Mrs. Applebee bustled into the room. As Gertrude made her way up the narrow aisle, she nudged empty chairs aside before squeezing into an armchair next to Harriet and Herb Chambers. Hugh, following behind, realigned the chairs in her wake and then, casting a smile in George and Jack's direction, settled back and crossed his arms.

"Mrs. Quinn is not coming along tonight?" Katie Keats whispered as Mrs. Applebee opened her Bible.

Evelyn pursed her lips and shook her head. "Says she's heard enough gospel for now. Can't understand it myself, but it's up to her."

The young tanner leaned toward Mrs. Applebee. "Maybe someday she'll have heard enough *gossip* too," he jested under his breath. "One of these days she's agoin' to get hung up in the brambles by her earrings."

On the other side of him, his wife, a bashful new mother, wrestled with a squirming baby on her lap, a fat-cheeked son who had inherited his father's lungs. Relentless screams vibrated through the room until his mother hustled him into the adjoining bedroom. When the wailing suddenly stopped and the sounds of nursing drifted out through the door, Jessie smiled, knowing that only a mother could offer the antidote.

Glancing at the clock, George stood up and led the group in a hymn. Afterward he shared his message, trying to help each person understand the need of taking another step in their journey of faith. "We'll all experience either one birth and two deaths, or two births and one death."

George noted the confused intensity in Harriet Chamber's face as she strained to comprehend the meaning. "We were all born once in a natural birth," he explained. "But we can be born a second time as well—born of the Spirit as a result of the divine seed being planted in our hearts. It's this second birth that establishes our connection to God.

"We'll also experience death," he cautioned, leaning forward slightly. "Death doesn't mean annihilation; it means separation. The first death will mark our separation from family and friends, from this physical world."

George paused, both to add emphasis and to create a moment for reflection. "If we reject the second birth, the Spirit of Christ, we have no life with our Creator. The result is that after we die and leave this earth, we'll face a second death as well—eternal separation from God. Now you can understand why we say that each of us will experience *one birth and two deaths*, or *two births and one death*." Even in the dim light, George could see Tony's dark eyebrows arching in concentration. "How does one experience this second birth, you ask? Simply by not hardening the soil of our hearts, by not rejecting Christ—God's divine seed."

As George spoke, he noticed the tanner's wife tiptoeing back to her seat beside her husband, her little lad sound asleep in her arms. "As a bachelor, I've never seen a newborn take its first breath," he admitted. When he caught sight of Eddie stifling a grin and noted the twinkle in Katie's dark eyes, he hesitated, wondering what had struck their funny bones. "But life is much more than just breathing air. It's a miracle. And the second birth is an even greater mystery. It awakens a consciousness that's less occupied with ourselves and more and more centred in God." With a smile, George sat down and Jack got up to speak.

Mindful of men who had started work before daylight, Jack checked his pocket watch, careful the meeting wouldn't extend longer than an hour. After wrapping up his words and singing the last hymn, he glanced up to see Tony making his way toward the front of the room, envelope in hand.

"Sorry it taka so long, but I forgota that my notes are in Italian," he apologized as he handed Jack the package. "I writa a letter and posta to a friend. He's a smarta man and changa into English."

Jack raised a quizzical eyebrow as he accepted the papers.

"Don'ta worry, it'sa ver good English," Tony chuckled. "See you tomorrow nighta." Then he was gone with his lantern into the darkness.

The envelope felt thick in Jack's hand, and he could hardly wait to read what it contained. After accompanying Mrs. Applebee home and wishing her goodnight, George and Jack hurried to their room and eagerly tore open the package. George bunched up his pillow and leaned across his bed, his eyes closed as Jack sat at the desk and began reading aloud.

Elora, Ontario
September 24, 1901

Dear Jack and George,

I'm very glad you came to my shop last week, Jack. For years I've hoped to meet men living and preaching in the manner of the New Testament. At times I wondered if I ever would.

During my studies at the seminary, I became increasingly disenchanted with the backbiting among the priests, and I began to examine the New Testament more closely to see how the early church functioned. I wondered if any of the original practices—established during the first century—might have continued after the advent of organized religion. Books written by historians years ago confirmed my suspicions. I discovered that a primitive church had flourished in the Alpine valleys of Italy and France during the Middle Ages and before the Protestant Reformation. I was amazed at how closely their manner of worship resembled the first-century church.

For twenty years, Pierre de Brueys braved severe dangers as he traveled throughout France, drawing multitudes away from their superstitions and back to New Testament teachings. Using the Bible, he showed that baptism should not occur until people are old enough to understand its meaning and that it was useless to build churches because God accepts sincere worship anywhere, even when only two or three are gathered. Pierre de Brueys taught that the bread and wine are not changed into the body and blood of Christ but are simply symbols commemorating His death, and that the prayers and good works of the living cannot benefit the dead. Church authorities squelched his voice by publicly burning him in 1126.

A few decades later, Peter Waldo, a successful merchant and banker living in Lyon, France, was awakened to his need of salvation by the sudden death of a guest at a feast he had given. After hiring clerks to translate parts of the Bible into the common dialect, Waldo became aware of a teaching of Jesus that would transform his life: "If thou wilt be perfect, go and sell that thou hast, and give to the poor, and thou shalt have treasure in heaven: and come and follow me."[1]

In 1173, he transferred his home to his wife, sold his assets, and distributed the money among the poor. Initially, he devoted himself to studying the Bible, but in 1180 he began to travel and preach, taking these words as a guide: "The Lord appointed other seventy also, and sent them two and two before his face into every city and place, whither he himself would come... Behold, I send you forth as lambs among wolves."[2]

Companions joined Waldo, and traveling and preaching in this unpretentious manner, they were labeled "The Poor Men of Lyon." They tried to bring people a sense of the simplicity of the church as it was during the first century. Peter Waldo and his companions directed many to the New Testament, where they learned to draw fresh and inexhaustible water from the well of salvation. These poor itinerant preachers disputed openly and called the people to solemn meetings in homes, in the marketplaces, or in the open fields. All classes received their message: nobility and common folks, rich and poor, men and women. Primitive home churches were scattered throughout Europe. In some regions they enjoyed a large measure of freedom, and in others they were subjected to cruel persecution.

During the early 1200s, these believers were tortured horribly—burned alive at the stake or forced into bags and drowned in rivers. Simon de Montfort, a churchman of boundless ambition and ruthless cruelty, was a leader in persecuting and ravaging them. On one occasion 140 believers were captured. The women were found in one house, men in another, engaging in prayer as they awaited their doom. De Montfort had a great pile of wood prepared and demanded they convert to the Catholic faith or mount the pile. They answered, "We are not under any papal or priestly authority, only that of Christ and His Word." The fire was ignited and the confessors, their eyes filled with pain and glory, died in the flames.

In 1229, the council of Toulouse instituted the Inquisition and decreed that common people could neither read the Bible nor translate any part of it into their own language. The scattered believers, on the other hand, asserted that the Bible must be much more than a sacred book in Latin, reserved for the sole and exclusive use of the priests. Rather, it should be understood and meditated upon daily by all people.

During times when the terror of the Inquisition made public preaching impossible, the believers kept the faith alive within the walls of their homes, indeed within the recesses of their own hearts. When the streets were closed to them, they would gather around their ovens, at their washing places by the streams, in their livestock stables and shops—any place where they could strengthen each other in their faith. They constantly reached beyond their familiar circle, strongly desiring to communicate, to evangelize, and to teach. One inquisitor remarked, "Not one of them, young or old, man or woman, day or night, ever stops learning and teaching others."

When Jack heard George turning over, bunching his pillow into a different shape, he looked up at his friend.

"They surely faced opposition for their faith," George said pensively. His pale blue eyes carried a distant look. "They had the courage of their convictions. And they were ready to die for them—just like the first apostles."

"We have our convictions too, George."

George twisted sideways. "But would you be willing *to die* for them?"

Jack crossed and uncrossed his legs. He stroked his upper lip and frowned. "Those were different times—times of great power and control by the Roman church. We don't burn people at the stake anymore. We deal with conflicts in a more humane and civilized manner now."

"But the tremendous sacrifice…"

"You gave up your farm, everything you worked for all those years. You even ran headlong into your father's opposition. You've sacrificed a lot, George, and given up your life too. Given it to others to help spread the same word as these messengers."

"It's a spark in an ash bucket compared with the fiery martyrdom of these believers. How can I hope to share heaven with men and women like them?"[3] George stared at a dark stain on the ceiling. "Besides, it wasn't just me," he resumed. "You gave up your old life too. It has nothing to do with *how much* either of us gave up, Jack. It's that we tried to let go of *everything* that held us back from doing God's work."

"I think you've just answered your own question," Jack said with a smile as he turned back to the letter. He searched for his place on the page:

> Outsiders often called these little churches by the name of some prominent man among them. Their opponents denied their right to simply call themselves "Christians" and labeled them Petrobrussians or Waldensians— names they never acknowledged. In fact, they rejected utterly the idea of any name. Bernard of Clairvaux, the most powerful religious man in Europe at that time, complained bitterly of their objection to taking the name of anyone as their founder: "Inquire of them the author of their sect and they will assign none." Although these people were called by many names, they were essentially one in Spirit and kept in touch with each other.
>
> For centuries little gatherings of believers existed in the Alpine valleys of Piedmont. Such groups did not spring from any reformation within the Roman or Greek system, and bore no trace of their influence. On the contrary, they were the continuation of something handed down from quite another source—the teaching of the New Testament and the practice of the early church. Their existence proves that there have always been men and women of faith and spiritual power who maintained a manner of fellowship close to that of the apostolic days and far removed from the rituals of the dominant churches.
>
> In 1630 a sympathetic prior in the St. Roch monastery wrote about these people: "They are so ancient as to afford no absolute certainty with regard

to the precise time of their origin. Even in the ninth and tenth centuries they were not a new sect. They can assert without fear of contradiction that their faith has continued from one generation to the next, through time immemorial, even from the very age of the apostles. They state: 'This religion which we live is not merely our religion of the present day, or something discovered for the first time only a few years ago, as our enemies falsely pretend. It is the faith of our fathers and of our grandfathers, yea of predecessors still more remote. It is the religion of the saints and of the martyrs, of the confessors and of the apostles.'

"It would not be difficult to prove that this poor band of the faithful was in the valleys of Piedmont more than four centuries before Luther and Calvin. They may very well be descendants of those refugees from Rome, who after Paul preached the gospel there, abandoned their beautiful country and fled to these wild mountains like the woman mentioned in the Apocalypse. To this day, they have handed down the gospel, from father to son, in the same pure and simple way as it was preached by the apostle Paul."

While most of these saints remained in their homes, other Spirit-taught laymen became itinerant ministers, sharing the message of Jesus and establishing home churches. These men left behind their property, goods, home, and family for their life was one of self-denial, hardship, and danger. Traveling in utmost simplicity, with neither money nor a second suit, their needs were supplied by the believers among whom they moved. They normally traveled in pairs, often an older man aided by his younger companion. No formal education was required, only the genuine willingness to follow the simple teaching of Christ. In times of persecution, the itinerants often visited the little churches secretly and at night. Their visits were highly esteemed, and they were treated with great respect and affection.

The saints recognized that not all were called to travel and the majority served Christ while remaining with their families and continuing in their usual occupations, acknowledging that they, and everything they owned belonged to Him. This distinction was based on the fact that in the Gospels some were called to sell all that they had and to follow Jesus while others of His disciples served Him in the surroundings in which He found them.

Apart from the Scriptures, the believers had no special creed or any rules. No man, no matter how eminent, was allowed to set aside the authority of the Bible. Yet, throughout the centuries, and in all parts of Europe, these believers professed the same truths and shared the same practices. Regarding both doctrine and church order, they considered the Scriptures to be binding for all time and not to be rendered obsolete by any change of circumstances. They valued Christ's own words in the Gospels as the highest revelation. Any time they were unable to reconcile any of the words of Jesus with other portions of Scripture, while they accepted all, they acted on what seemed to be the plain meaning of the Gospels.

"The Spirit of Christ is effective to the measure in which any man obeys the words of Christ and is His true follower," they said. "Only Christ can give the ability to understand His words. If anyone loves Him, he will keep His words." A few great truths were looked upon as essential to fellowship, but otherwise, in matters open to doubt or to difference in opinion, large liberty was allowed. They maintained that the testimony of the indwelling Spirit is of greatest importance, since the highest truths come from the heart to the mind.

They viewed the Sermon on the Mount as essential—the rule of life for God's children. These obscure brethren opposed the shedding of blood, even for capital punishment. In matters of faith, they would not use force or retaliate against those who harmed them. They refused to take oaths and did not use the name of God casually. They did not agree with the claim of the great organized church that it could open or close the way of salvation. Nor did they believe that salvation came through any sacraments or by anything but faith in Christ. They held the doctrine of the sovereignty of God in election, together with that of man's free will.

These followers of Christ had no love for theological controversy; rather, they esteemed practical piety and serving God in quietness. Although they practiced simplicity in matters of church order, the elders of these little churches accepted their responsibilities with the utmost seriousness. Regular individual reading of the Scriptures, along with daily family worship and occasional larger gatherings or conventions, were a highly prized means of maintaining spiritual life. These saints took no part in government or in courts of law, but when they were brought before judges themselves, they were ready to die for their faith.

In May 1872, a good friend and I visited Torre Pellice, a small village on the eastern slopes of the Italian Alps. Both of us were seminary students at the time. The sharp contrast between what I felt in these mountains and what I learned each day in becoming a parish priest finally gave me the conviction to abandon my studies. Leaving the village and climbing high into the Alps on increasingly narrow trails, we passed spectacular scenery and rugged, rocky terrain. We were on our way up to Pra del Torno, hidden deep in the Angrogna Valley. Surrounded closely on all sides by high mountains, it was the refuge of the believers when they were in danger of attack. A steep, unscalable mountain named Rocciaglia runs across the valley, except where some convolution of nature has ripped the mountains, forming a long dark chasm through which the Angrogna torrent falls. Many of the believers lived in this valley, and it was the place to which a number of the itinerant ministers resorted during the winter months.

Eventually our horse and cart could go no farther, so we set out on foot to finish the steep ascent. At the top of our climb we found a modest stone cottage which had once served as a retreat for the travel-weary preachers during the fourteenth to sixteenth centuries. It was from here and from many similar places that they fanned out across the landscape of Europe, carrying the good news of Christ to Germany, Hungary, Sicily, Spain, and beyond.

This rugged cottage was built in a lightly wooded area, high on a steep slope. A clear mountain stream supplied water for both drinking and washing. The one-room building, approximately fourteen by eighteen feet, had a primitive fireplace and a massive flat stone for a table. A strange awestruck feeling swept over me as I ran my hands across its smooth surface, and I imagined myself sitting around it with the brothers of six hundred years earlier. I could almost hear them telling of their narrow escapes as they tried to share the wonderful gospel story. I envisioned the love in their faces as they spoke of Jesus.

Three small additions to the cottage offered sleeping quarters. Inside, we saw a thick layer of dry leaves on the floor, typical of a medieval bed. I couldn't resist stretching out on it. I closed my eyes and drew in a deep breath, savouring the pungent smell of the damp earth floor and thick stone walls surrounding me. When I opened my eyes, I saw that the roof had been constructed of thin, flat stones laid up like shingles upon a frame of hand-hewn poles.

The itinerant ministers arrived here for rest and fellowship when the harsh Alpine winters choked the valleys with deep snow and prevented them from traveling. Lacking printed Bibles, they used the time to study and to copy manuscripts. They memorized much of the New Testament and the Psalms, carrying the Scriptures in their hearts and minds during an age when it would have been dangerous to be found in possession of the actual writings.

It was here, within these stalwart walls, that they met with new companions before setting out for another year. The young, novice preachers would spend their first winter around this table learning from their seasoned companions and growing in spiritual maturity as they consecrated themselves to God's ministry. A little sign on the outside of the stone cottage read: "They went out into the world in twos for their bitter and often dangerous task. Their mission lasted a lifetime, until their force was spent or until they fell to martyrdom."

During dangerous times, they often traveled as traders, selling their wares and speaking to their customers of the Bible at opportune moments. Just as the Jewish leaders had spoken of Christ as never having learned letters,[4] the enemies of the itinerants maintained they were simple unlettered peasants and, therefore, unworthy of credence.

The primitive church did not hesitate to include women among their preachers, a practice which profoundly shocked the whole clerical and lay establishment of the time. Although the women were fewer, I was reminded of an account from secular Roman history: About 112 A.D. the Roman governor, Pliny the Younger, interrogated two young women who were preaching the gospel in Bithynia. They were willing to die for their faith in the arena.

As we hiked back down the steep trail, my friend asked a very pointed question. One that eventually changed my life.

"When we looked inside that austere cottage and I saw you lying in the leaves," he said, "I was reminded that Jesus was born in a stable. And His followers were dirt poor. Just like these itinerants of the Middle Ages."

I nodded, wondering what he was getting at.

"Well, it made me think about the Holy Father," he continued. "He's living and working in the Vatican—a palace with 1100 rooms. If God's own Son was born in a manger, would He arrange to have His Son's servants living in a palace—like the kings and rulers that Jesus warned against?"[5] He paused for a minute. "Unless God has drastically changed His way of doing things in the last 1800 years, those things just don't go together, Tony."

I must have stumbled along in a daze for several minutes before I could say a word. "That's a very good question," I finally agreed. "There's no comparison at all. I'm quite sure that God hasn't changed, but I don't have any answer."

For several weeks I tried to explain away the troubling disparity. But the facts were inescapable. That day in the mountains had been a turning point in my life. In spite of the many admirable attributes of the pope, I could never again see him as a simple follower of Christ—like Peter and the early apostles. It's doubtful if Jesus and His disciples had more than a few small coins among all of them. In contrast, the manner in which the leaders of our churches have chosen to live speaks volumes about what is most important to them.[6] For me, the spirit of humility, the hallmark of Christ, is absent. As I mentioned before, I eventually left the Roman Catholic Church.

For many years I considered joining a different denomination. Then one day I read Jesus' words: "There will be one flock and one shepherd. My sheep hear My voice, and I know them, and they follow Me." Jesus didn't say to follow the pope to his fold. Nor the Archbishop of Canterbury to his fold. Nor any other man to any other fold. "No," Jesus said, "they follow Me."[7]

I perceived this thought as a God-given revelation, and from that time forward I tried to focus directly on Jesus. I began to watch for someone who might be described only as a follower of His. Or for a little group free from the ritual and organization that have drawn so many away from the New Testament pattern. The simplicity of such a church would make it adaptable to various conditions, a trait of particular value in times of persecution. I knew the church I was looking for would likely be little known, even in the religious world. Their anonymity would give their work a quiet effectiveness. For a long time I never saw or heard of such a person or group. Yet, I felt sure that people like that must exist somewhere and contain within themselves the power to carry the "word of life" to others.[8]

Then a few weeks ago one of my customers told me about two strangers going from house to house inviting people to a gospel meeting at the Elora school. As the words fell from his lips, I felt a strange blend of hope and excitement. Was this the very thing I was looking for? Nevertheless I held my anticipation in check, afraid of disappointment. I slipped into one of the back seats of your gospel meeting wondering, like all the rest, what to expect. When I heard you quote that exact same verse—"My sheep hear My voice and they follow Me"—in your very first meeting, I took it to be a sign.

For a while I pondered whether you might indeed be a branch of the movement that my friend and I had observed in the mountains. Particularly because I recalled seeing a sign inside the cottage stating that there were many similar places in Europe. I wondered if that ancient group, relatively unknown, might have spread to Canada.

After you talked to me in my barbershop, I realized that you were not connected by a direct historical means to the little churches of the Middle Ages, but that you were being guided by the same Holy Spirit. I hope to get to know each of you better and look forward to a more spiritual visit whenever you get a chance.

Yours very sincerely,

Tony Ortello

Neither man said a word for several minutes after Jack finished reading. Finally George shook his head as if in a daze.

"It's beyond me to grasp the magnitude of this whole thing," he said. "I had no idea we were doing something so many others have done before." George fell silent again. "It's so amazing—miraculous, really. I mean that this same vision of Christ and His church was also revealed to us."

"I guess the same seed'll produce the same fruit in every generation," Jack asserted. "It gives me courage to carry on, no matter what."

George propped himself up on his left elbow. "God has continued to add to His church in every age," he mused, "according to *His* vision for her. He wants her to express the life of His Son in a dark world."

They read the letter once again before blowing out the lamp. As tired as they both were, they found themselves on their knees thanking God for His church and for calling them to be part of it.

Afterward George lay awake thinking about all the men who had set out as homeless preachers in the same way that he and Jack were doing now. In the darkness he could hear his companion's heels bumping the footboard as he turned over in bed for nearly an hour. When a barn owl settled onto Mrs. Applebee's clothesline post and began its ghostly hooting, George relaxed into the soft rhythms of sleep.

Eighteen

JUST AS I AM
Mid-Autumn 1901

The warm friendly atmosphere in Lyman and Jessie's home reminded George and Jack of the gatherings at Wood Creek Farm. They knew it would be easy for them to stay here among these folks whom they had grown to love. But in the minds of the two men, Tony's letter had underlined the itinerant nature of their work.

"I feel certain," George said one morning as they scrubbed out Mrs. Applebee's cistern, "that after we leave, some of these people will want to meet on Sundays for fellowship."

"Folks'll need to make a firm decision to either accept or reject this new way," Jack responded. "No one can serve two masters."[1] He paused. "So, when we leave here, where do you think we should strike out for?"

George sloshed a pail of clean water on the cement floor. "I hardly know," he replied. "Someplace close enough that we can get back here for at least a few Sundays."

"We can easily walk ten miles in half a day, even in winter."

"Heading west, that would take us as far as West Montrose or even St. Jacobs. Fergus and Belwood are just up the line to the east, a bit closer."

A deep reminiscent longing, like that of a man going home, flickered in Jack's eyes. "Belwood sounds good to me."

"I reckon we should be prayerful about it and see what settles."

The following Sunday night in Lyman's parlour, Jack opened the meeting with a hymn that spoke about responding to the Saviour's call:

My soul desires to walk with God,
Along the path His chosen trod;
I hear Him calling "Come away,"
And joyfully I now obey.

I hear Him call, I hear Him call
From all that would my soul enthral;
I haste away to walk with God,
Along the path His chosen trod.[2]

When the hymn was finished, Jack stepped forward, looking into the faces of many whom he and George had come to love. It was time, he knew, to give them the privilege of expressing openly how they felt in their hearts about following Christ.

Jack began to speak about how Jesus and His disciples had celebrated their last supper together in Jerusalem—the feast of the Passover.[3] After reading a short portion from the Old Testament, he closed his Bible and looked up again. "The twelfth chapter of Exodus is about the very first Passover," he said. "Exodus means 'the way out,' similar to the English word 'exit.' A group of Jewish slaves were about to break free from captivity and begin a journey to a promised land.

"God offers an eternal place of promise to us as well—the kingdom of heaven. The Israelites took a physical journey; we must take a spiritual one. Their quest for a new land was tortuous, filled with obstacles and difficulties. Are we willing to face the same? To abandon the familiar and visible, in exchange for a journey by faith into the unknown and spiritual.

"If we look at this historic trek as a spiritual illustration, we might say that Egypt represents our human nature with its attachment to this world. From that state we need *a way out*, an exodus, because human nature ends at the grave—unable to enter the kingdom of heaven."

A slight movement of Lyman and Jessie's front door caught Jack's attention. At first he wondered if the wind had blown it ajar, but as he continued to speak he could see that Jimmy Liddle, slouched next to his father, was edging it open with his boot. Every few minutes, after peering sharply at Lyman, and then at Tony Ortello to confirm their absolute concentration on Jack's words, the boy would inch the door a little further.

"Tonight," Jack went on, "I want to focus on how the Israelites relied on the blood of a sacrificed lamb in order to escape Egypt's bondage. The lamb was to be perfect, without blemish. Isolated from the flock, it was brought into the house and cared for by the family for four days."

Jack looked over at the young woman with wavy blonde hair sitting near the staircase. "Jessie, you're a mother. Can you imagine how attached your children would have become to this lively little lamb after four days?" Jack surveyed the solemn faces in the room. "And you grown-ups would have admired its perfection and innocence, knowing all along that you would have to slaughter it at twilight."

At the sound of his mother's name, Jimmy Liddle's head swiveled, like the released mainspring of a clock, back to gape at Jack. Temporarily distracted from coaxing the neighbour's cat inside, the sheepish lad stiffened reflexively when Jack smiled back at him. And although Jack's voice never hesitated, the pair locked eyes for a fleeting second before the gray tomcat was scooted back outside by Jimmy's toe.

"The lamb's death represents the loneliness and rejection that Jesus experienced, the sacrifice of a perfect and innocent man who died for each of us. Our sin was placed on Him and He died alone, outside Jerusalem's city wall on the cross of Calvary.[4]

"The Hebrews were instructed to eat the lamb in their homes." Jack turned to a page and began reading aloud, "If any household is too small for a whole lamb, they must share one with their nearest neighbour, taking into account the number of people."[5] Jack looked up from the passage. "Can you picture these tiny one-room homes scattered throughout the country? Neighbouring families hurriedly gathering for the Passover celebration. This was extremely serious! To be found outside the house, or in the house but without the blood of the lamb, meant certain death. The number in each home depended upon the size of the lamb, but I suspect it would likely have been about a dozen or so."

Jack scanned the intent expressions of his listeners. He could see the perspiration glistening on Hugh Foster's bald spot when the storekeeper shifted to stretch his arm along the back of Gertrude's chair. "Centuries later Jesus and His twelve disciples also celebrated the Passover in the simple setting of a home," Jack asserted. "There Jesus told them that He was to become the Passover Lamb of the New Testament. During the meal He blessed the bread and gave it to His disciples to eat, just as the children of Israel had consumed the lamb. Then Jesus picked up a cup of wine and gave thanks to God. He gave it to His disciples and said, 'This is My blood, and with it God makes His new covenant with you.'[6]

"Back in the book of Exodus, the children of Israel were given specific instructions: No meat was to be eaten raw or cooked in water, but roasted over the fire.[7] That suggests that the way of Christ is not to be boiled or diluted, but prepared by a flame of love. Many of us have experienced watered-down Christianity. They were to eat the entire lamb, including its head, legs, and inner parts. Nothing was to be left until the morning. Each of us may prefer certain parts of Jesus' life and teaching. Perhaps we value the mind and fancy the wisdom of the head but reject the lowly feet—His simple walk and humble way of life. Others may turn away from the inner parts such as the heart—His Spirit of kindness, goodness, gentleness. Are patience, faithfulness, and self-control unappealing or even repulsive? But, my friends, we either accept it all or remain in slavery.

"In the Exodus story, certain death came to every household that failed to sacrifice a lamb and put its blood on the sides and top of the door frame." Jack tapped the centre of his chest with his forefinger. "We can only be saved by having Christ's blood on the doorways of our hearts.

"Can you fathom the pain, the anguish at midnight?" Jack's brow tensed into sympathetic creases. "In every Egyptian family the oldest child suddenly died. No home was spared by the death angel, and there was loud wailing throughout Egypt."

As though gripped on both her shoulders, Mrs. Applebee looked up beseechingly toward Jack. Her stricken face could not hide the long concealed pain that now broke forth, manifesting itself in anguished memory. All the village of Elora had supported her and Wilson in the loss of their first and only child, just as, years later, Evelyn had helped sustain the young MacQuarries when their children had perished. But now Jack's voice was pulling her back into the darkness of the Egyptian night.

"Pharaoh and his officials got up during the night and summoned Moses and Aaron. 'Rise up immediately and leave my people,' he urged. 'Go and worship the Lord as you requested. And pray for me also.'[8]

"The Hebrews ate in haste, sandals on their feet and a staff in their hand. Like those folks, we must be ready to take the next step. The Christian journey is a movement forward—not a static condition. That's the essence of our message this evening.

"Although Moses had been adopted as a baby by Pharaoh's daughter, he refused to be called Pharaoh's grandson. He left Egypt, knowing that its elusive treasures could never compare with the promises of God."[9]

Jack laid his Bible on the table beside him. "We can't please God without traveling by faith either. Imagine a person on a bicycle trip for three months. Someone offers him a beautifully carved desk at an absurdly low price. Just a minute, he says to himself and goes out to study his bicycle. Is there any place it will fit? The oak desk is so handsome and such a bargain that he hates to leave it behind. But it just doesn't fit. He must choose—either abandon his journey or abandon the desk. Like the Hebrews, he must be resolute to travel onward."

As Jack paused, the lamplight seemed to irradiate his features. "With that in mind, I want to encourage you to start on your own spiritual journey. Some of you may have felt the Holy Spirit leading you out of Egypt and have already begun to follow. Perhaps others are still holding back. Until you give Jesus the lordship of your life and begin to journey in His lowly way, you will never be released from the bondage of your own nature and from the temptations of the world around you."

Jack sat down with the fixed look of a visionary, one not looking back at the darkness of Egypt, but forward, beyond the desert, to the shimmering brightness of a land flowing with milk and honey.[10]

George stood up, hymn book in hand. "In a few minutes, we're going to conclude our meeting by singing 'Just As I Am.' It emphasizes the precious, saving blood of Christ. Jack has been telling us about the need of leaving our self-nature and the world behind and about a journey that begins with the blood of the Lamb. In our first meeting, we spoke about the Lamb of God. We said that every hour of every day Jesus is calling: 'Come to Me, all you who are weary and heavily burdened and I will give you rest.' And in our first hymn this evening, we sang: 'I hear Him calling, "Come away" and joyfully I now obey.' Tonight each of us will have an opportunity to sing this hymn—'Just As I Am'—as our personal response to Christ's invitation."

George paused, remembering his own beginning with Jesus. "For any of you who might feel that you must somehow improve your life before you can follow Jesus, I want to share the story of the author of this hymn.

"Charlotte Elliott was in her early twenties when she recognized her own sinfulness. How, she often asked herself, can a person such as myself ever see God's face? She visited several churches and talked to many pastors, asking each one what she must do to be saved. Some told her to wait until she had improved her life while others suggested she spend more time praying or reading the Bible. Yet others recommended that she undertake some charitable activities. This went on for many years, and during that time our sister actually felt that she was drifting farther from God."

As Jack listened, he noticed a gradual transformation in Katie's expression. She had, at first, been relaxed, listening casually as the story began, but now her round face took on a severity as if she were Charlotte Elliott herself. Katie leaned forward, propping her elbow on the back of Harriet's chair, the knuckles of her clenched hand pressed hard against her ruddy cheek. When she shifted position, a white dimple remained.

Seemingly oblivious to Katie's reaction, George continued, "Finally, Charlotte met a wise preacher, stricken in years, and explained her predicament. 'What must I do to be saved?' she asked him.

"This gentle old brother stepped close to her and put his hand on her shoulder. 'Sister,' he said, 'go and meet your God just as you are!'

"Charlotte resisted. 'But don't I need to perfect my life before God will receive me?'

"'Not at all,' the old preacher assured her. 'If you have truly repented, you can come just as you are. You are saved by grace through faith in God. Salvation comes as His gift to you, not because of anything that you've done to earn it.[11] The necessary changes will take place when Christ comes to live in you.'

"'But it seems too easy,' Charlotte protested. 'There must be more needed than that.'

"Patiently, the elderly worker explained: 'When we hear and believe the gospel of our Lord Jesus, we understand that He died for us. We claim this free gift of salvation by trusting in Him and in what *He* has done.'"

A slow smile blossomed across Katie's features, softening her secret distress. She folded her hands and leaned back into her chair, savouring George's words. How strange it felt to be—for the first time—utterly acceptable before God. She closed her eyes for a moment. No one knew the release she felt in her soul. Even Mrs. Applebee, squeezed tightly beside her, could have no sense of the revelation that had come to her.

Hooking his left thumb into his pocket, George bent forward. "As the message of grace unfolded, Charlotte's eyes widened as if she were seeing something for the first time. 'I'm beginning to understand why the word "gospel" means the "good news,"' she blurted out. 'He does what I've never been able to do. I used to try so hard, but I always fell flat on my face.'

"The old preacher smiled. 'It's not what you do for God that counts,' he affirmed, 'it's what *God* has done *for you* that makes all the difference. When you place your faith in Jesus' provision of love, a new life begins.'

"Charlotte looked a bit perplexed. 'You mentioned changes coming,' she said. 'What did you mean by that?'

"'Well,' the old man continued, 'this new life will change your whole manner of living. Christian works are the *product* of salvation. Just like the *fruit* on a grape vine, they are the *evidence* that new life is flowing through the branches. Works are the *result*, the *confirmation*[12] that the Spirit is alive and producing the character of Christ in you.'

"'Oh. I see it now,' Charlotte exclaimed. *'Works are the cart, not the horse.'* Her face brightened with relief. 'Thank you so much,' she added. 'Your explanation of God's unconditional love are the most comforting words I've ever heard.'"

George smoothed open his hymn book. "It was during Charlotte's new life that she wrote these reassuring words: 'Just as I am...I come, I come.' I hope each of us can sing this from the depths of our hearts." When George nodded in her direction, Katie slipped onto the stool and, after planting her feet squarely on the pedals, began to pump the parlour organ. The old instrument wheezed to life as she fingered the opening chords.

> Just as I am, without one plea,
> But that Thy blood was shed for me,
> And that Thou bidst me come to Thee,
> O Lamb of God, I come, I come.
>
> Just as I am, Thou wilt receive,
> Wilt welcome, pardon, cleanse, relieve;
> Because Thy promise I believe,
> O Lamb of God, I come, I come.
>
> Just as I am, Thy love unknown,
> Has broken every barrier down;
> Now to be Thine, yea, Thine alone,
> O Lamb of God, I come, I come.[13]

When the last notes died away, George addressed the group again. "Friends, this is our last gospel meeting for the time being." There was a general gasp of surprise. Faces betrayed shock and disappointment. "Jack and I plan to leave for Belwood next week. Thank you for coming so faithfully to our meetings. And for the open door you've given us in so many ways."

An overwhelming sadness filled the room as George offered a few final words. "Before the apostle Paul and his companion left a community, they would encourage believers to gather for regular fellowship. Some of you may have made an inner commitment to journey with our Lord and feel that you'd like to worship in the same way as the New Testament churches. If that's how you feel, please speak to us in the next few days. We'll be staying with Mrs. Applebee for the rest of this week. Once again, thank you very, very much." George paused to draw his handkerchief out of his pocket, crumpling it in his palm before raising it to his eyes. "Jack and I've grown to love you all, and it will be hard to say goodbye."

As people stood to leave, some were still bewildered. Because of their traditional background, they hadn't understood that the New Testament ministry was itinerant.

"Why would they up and leave just now?" Gertrude remonstrated to Harriet in a voice choked with indignation. "There aren't a lot of us, but it could be the start of a congregation for one of them at least."

"I hate to see them go," Harriet admitted. "They're such fine fellows."

Gertrude shrugged. "Oh, well, I guess the grass is greener in Belwood. Anyway, I'm sure Hugh'll want to invite them over to find out what George meant by a New Testament church."

One by one they came to George and Jack and a few expressed their appreciation with hugs, with best wishes for the future, and even with tears. Before the last couple left, George and Jack had made several promises to visit people during the remainder of the week.

As each person gathered their Bibles and donned their coats for home, the Liddles pressed the brothers to stay for a few minutes. While Jessie set the table with tea and fruitcake, Lyman opened his heart. "From the first day you knocked on our door, Jessie and I knew that your ministry was scriptural. Since then we've seen the love you have for people. Now that you're moving on to Belwood, we wonder what to do next. As you know, we left our last church before you came, and now we sit down with our children each Sunday morning to talk about Jesus."

"That's very commendable," George said, encouragingly. "It's best when believers gather for fellowship every week. Maybe some of the others will be interested in doing that too."

"But if you're not here, who'll deliver the messages?" Lyman replied.

George told them about the Puslinch church and how each person at Wood Creek Farm participated. He suggested that the Elora friends could worship in a similar way. "Jack and I could come back to be with you on Sundays for the first few weeks."

Lyman gave a start of surprise. "You mean Jessie and I and the others would preach in the meetings?"

"Well, not exactly preach." George hesitated. "It would be more like sharing what God has laid on your hearts."

Although Lyman and Jessie seemed a little uncertain, they trusted George and Jack's counsel. For a few minutes not much was said as the couple sipped their tea and reflected. In the parlour, Jimmy sat Turk-fashion on the hearth rug quietly absorbed in *King Solomon's Mines.*

Lyman spoke first. "The meetings have worked out well in our house for the past few weeks," he said. "But if we were meeting permanently, wouldn't we need a small building?"

"Archaeology finds no evidence that the early Christians ever built special meeting places," Jack answered. "They usually met in homes. Or in times of persecution, secretly, in caves or catacombs. The emperor Constantine, who claimed to be a Christian, constructed most of the first church buildings after 312 A.D. These false churches reflected the practices of the Roman pagan temples and bore no resemblance to first-century Christianity. Churches, oriented around a building, were constructed far and wide throughout the Middle Ages. First by the Roman Catholic Church, and then after some changes, by Martin Luther and his successors. It's still the church pattern we see today. But these enormous palaces would have been completely foreign to the early saints."

Lyman cupped his chin in his palm. "So without the burdens of holding property," he said, "the New Testament church was free and alive. And able to focus on Christ."

"Exactly right," said Jack. "With the waves of persecution that came, buildings would have been confiscated and Christians made more vulnerable. In fact, their own hearts were to be used as God's temple."[14]

Caught by surprise, Jessie gave a short laugh. "But there's nothing wrong with having a building, is there?"

George swallowed the last bite of his fruitcake. "The Jews used a building-centred organization with synagogues, a temple, and resident priests," he said looking over at Jessie. "But Jesus specifically rejected that system in its entirety. Since His followers also avoided that kind of arrangement and worshiped in a much simpler way, I'd be very reluctant to drift back to the methods of the Pharisees."

Jessie drew in her breath sharply as George brushed the crumbs into his saucer before offering a speculation. "Maybe God allowed the absolute destruction of the temple so people would shift their focus from its majesty to that of His Son[15]—and begin to worship Him in spirit and in truth.[16] Picture a buggy wheel with a centre hub," he suggested. "The spokes are drawn tightly to the hub by the steel rim. Like these spokes, the closer the brethren were to Jesus, the closer they were to each other. They were drawn to Him, not to a building or an organization, and they were held together by love, not by rigidly enforced rules or a membership roll."

Jessie and Lyman listened, captivated by George's explanation of a simple Christ-centred church. "In that case, we'd be happy to have the meetings continue right here in our home," Jessie proposed.

As the brothers prepared to leave, she offered a final declaration that warmed their hearts. "I want you to know," she said, looking into their eyes, "that for the first time I've begun to feel Jesus as a living presence. Until you came He was only a historical figure to me." She reached out and grasped one hand of each man. "Thank you for coming," she whispered.

George and Jack walked slowly home, accompanied by swirling leaves and a windy-looking harvest moon.

Jack tucked his Bible up under one arm and stuffed both hands into his pockets. "It's starting to get nippy," he observed.

George nodded and then changed the subject. "I'm glad we decided to tell Mrs. Applebee before the meeting about our plans to leave next week."

"It was the only considerate thing to do," Jack declared. "She's been most obliging, and I wouldn't want to have sprung it on her."

George's fingers danced along the top of Mrs. Applebee's picket fence as far as the little gate. "Even so, her round face bobbed up and her fore-head crinkled when I elaborated tonight. And she left pretty quick after the last hymn. I hope she's not flustered."

It was well past Mrs. Applebee's bedtime, and the two men opened the door quietly, intending to tiptoe upstairs. But to their surprise she was still up, reading her old family Bible by candlelight. A plate of fresh tea bis-cuits sat in front of her on the kitchen table and the kettle was singing on the cookstove. "I'll make a cup of lemon balm tea," she called out cheerily. The brothers thanked her and sat down on the kitchen couch, sensing that she had something on her mind.

"I always knew you were going to leave," she began, "but I didn't know when. I've grown to love you two boys as if you were my own sons, and I'm sorry to see you go. You've been so good to me." She let out a long sigh and dabbed at a tea leaf. "But I understand your concern to bring the gospel to others. From that weekend when Stephen and Emily came to visit, I knew I'd waited all my life for the warmth of this simple fellowship. I could never have put into words what I was looking for before you came. But when I saw your practical faith, I knew I needed Jesus myself."

Mrs. Applebee patted the Bible beside her. "I know you're tired, so take your drink and a biscuit upstairs. I just wanted to tell you that I'm hearing Jesus' call—in a way that never happened before. I've given my life to Him now. And I want to follow Him, no matter what."

The two men didn't go anywhere. They stayed fixed to their seats, listening to the sincere words of this kind soul who was now touching them as much as they must have touched her. As she poured out her heart, the brothers sat spellbound.

"You're a real inspiration, Mrs. Applebee," George offered quietly.

The brothers climbed the stairs in amazed silence. As they undressed for bed, Jack spoke first. "It's a marvel to see how alive the gospel has become in Mrs. Applebee's heart."

"It surely is." George hung up his clothes in the wardrobe. "But there's one thing we have to make very clear."

"What's that?"

"These folks need to understand that they're not joining anything. Not a sect. Not another denomination. What we're encouraging people to do is to simply become continuing disciples of Jesus. And then, as a result of that, they will enjoy fellowship with others who are doing the same. Like Tony pointed out near the end of his letter, believers are not to be following any man other than Jesus to any other fold. That includes any fold George and Jack could produce."

Jack nodded pensively. "What brought that to mind?"

"When we were talking to Lyman and Jessie tonight, the thought came to me that we must be careful to avoid giving people the idea that we're creating another system, even a better one. We need to point people to Jesus, and to Him alone. I'm sure Mrs. Applebee has grasped it, but I don't know about the others."

Jack unbuttoned his heavy plaid shirt. "You're right," he agreed, "people could presume that attendance at meetings is the vital part when in fact, the ongoing presence of God is far more important."

"Even if it means being a solitary disciple," George added as he blew out the light and knelt to pray. "Goodnight, Jack."

Above Wellington County that evening, the constellations of autumn glittered in the violet sky. Job's Coffin and the Northern Cross flamed to the west while the winged horse, Pegasus, galloped overhead. When dawn broke, the first light of the clear October morning shone brighter than usual. Walking with buoyant steps through the autumn leaves on the sidewalk, George and Jack began calling on the people who had requested a visit the night before. George whistled happily to himself as they made their way to visit Eddie Summers and his dad, Oliver.

Eddie was creating a display in the store window. When he saw the brothers, he quickly laid down the bolt of Gaelic tartan and led them to the office. "Father and I want to continue in fellowship with the others," he declared as he dragged three extra chairs into a half-circle around the desk.

Oliver beamed in affirmation as Eddie described their newfound joy.

After a few minutes George fingered his sandy beard reflectively. "What would you think of meeting in one of your homes?"

"Yes, that's what happened in the Scriptures," Eddie acknowledged. "Mary was one of the first in Jerusalem to open her home. After the apostle Peter had been miraculously released from prison, he made his way through the dark streets to find his friends gathered there in prayer."[17]

George settled back in his chair. "Paul kept in touch with many little assemblies of believers as he traveled from place to place.[18] When he wrote to the saints in Rome, he asked them to greet Priscilla and Aquila and the church that met *in their house.*"[19]

Eddie rolled up the cloth measuring tape draped around his neck and removed a Bible from his desk drawer. He opened it to a place that had been marked with a gold ribbon. "At the end of Paul's letter to the Colossians, he asks that greetings be extended to the brethren in Laodicea, and to Nymphas and the church which meets *in his house.*"[20]

"Exactly right," Jack said. "And later, when Paul and Timothy wrote to Philemon, they referred again to the church *in your house.* "[21] Eddie's eyes shone with excitement.

Mr. Summers took his glasses off and started to clean them. "If that's so, why did the apostles go to the Jewish synagogue in each community?"

George leaned forward earnestly. "It wasn't to worship or break bread, Oliver. They went there hoping to preach to God-fearing listeners. During New Testament times, there were two kinds of meetings. Initially, the preachers conducted public gospel meetings, like those we were having in the school before we were locked out. That message was presented to a mixed audience. Afterwards, those who believed and accepted the life of Christ gathered in one of their homes to worship and break bread."

Oliver Summers nodded as he readjusted his spectacles on his nose.

"The messengers never burdened themselves with a building," Jack explained. "They'd have been appalled at the notion of spending time and energy to erect and maintain a structure. Instead, the apostles dedicated their entire effort to sharing the invitation of Jesus with the most people in the most efficient manner. Many listened to them, and a few rejoiced to be added to the body of Christ, the way, the truth, and the life.[22] These very words suggest a mobile, living body, not a rigid, inflexible edifice."

Oliver Summers sat in thoughtful silence, like a father among sons. When George and Jack got up, both he and Eddie walked to the front door, giving each man a firm handshake before they stepped onto the sidewalk.

George and Jack had expected to hear from Herb Chambers, the postmaster, and his wife, Harriet. They seemed to be with the brothers in spirit in every meeting. But no invitation came, and George noticed that Herb avoided him whenever he went into the post office. Herb would nod and then disappear into the back, leaving his assistant to hand over the mail. George prayed about it, but no answer came. Then a few days before the brothers were to leave, George happened to see Harriet coming out of Hugh Foster's store with a wicker basket on her arm. He walked across Geddes Street to chat with her. "Good day, Harriet," he said. "How is it with you?"

The young woman looked strained. "Not very well, George."

"Oh, I'm sorry. I didn't know you had problems."

"It's the meetings, George." Harriet breathed a sigh, seemingly relieved to finally unburden herself. "Herb just doesn't feel ready to give up his job. We want to follow Jesus, but it's too big a step for us right now."

Lifting his wool cap, George ran his fingers through his sandy hair. "What do you mean about Herb giving up his job?" he asked. "Doesn't he like his work at the post office?"

"Yes, he does. That's the problem," Harriet said, wiping away a tear with the back of her hand. "But if we follow Jesus like you and Jack, he'll have to quit his job."

"Oh, Harriet, I think you've misunderstood us. There's no reason that Herb couldn't continue at the post office."

"He could?" Harriet said incredulously. "But one evening you mentioned that people who were raising families should have homes and jobs. As you know, George, we don't have any children. Doesn't that mean we'd need to sell everything and do what you and Jack are doing?"

The sincerity in her face gave George a pang. *Imagine,* he thought, *if following Jesus means becoming itinerant, Harriet would actually be willing to leave Elora.* He stroked his narrow jaw. "Oh, no. That's not something for all Christians," he clarified, smiling into Harriet's face. "Most people are called to follow Jesus as the carpenter, at which time He had a home and earned a living. Only later, are some called to follow Jesus as an itinerant preacher, without a permanent home."

"But didn't Jesus tell the crowds that unless they renounced everything they couldn't be disciples of His?"[23]

"That's right, Harriet. After we renounce everything, we realize we're no longer the owners of our possessions and our time. We become stewards for God and begin to use these assets as He directs. Most continue to live in their homes and carry on with their work, but they live moderately, considering God's wishes in the way they spend their time and talents."

George could see relief spreading over Harriet's face.

"I was farming when God first began to reveal Jesus to me. Little by little I realized everything I possessed belonged to God. When I had decisions to make about buying or selling something, or about how to use my time, I talked to Him. Sometimes I got clear answers, and sometimes I didn't. I lived that way for a few years. Later, when God called me into the ministry, it was easier to sell those things and give the money away because I already recognized they were no longer mine—they belonged to God.

In following His simple command to let go of them, my time has become even more available for Him to use."

Harriet tossed her shawl back on her shoulders and gripped George's hand tightly with both of hers. "Please come for supper tonight. I'll go and tell Herb right away."

As George walked back to Mrs. Applebee's, he thanked God that he had met Harriet in front of the general store. Their conversation turned his thoughts to Morgan Butterwick, the honey man in Guelph. Although Morgan had not been called to be an itinerant preacher, he had clearly renounced everything. As a steward of the gospel,[24] he arranged his time and resources so that he could reach out to strangers in his own community. George remembered Morgan once saying, "I could hardly be in fellowship with men who have chosen voluntary poverty for the sake of the gospel and continue to live extravagantly. My conscience wouldn't allow it."

That evening as promised, George and Jack stepped over Herb and Harriet's threshold. A lavish table was spread for supper, and against the vase of red maple leaves in the centre, a telegram stood propped up. On gripping the brothers' hands, Herb showed unusual liveliness. "Grand news!" he exclaimed. "Had a telegram delivered at four o'clock. The stationmaster's boy ran up with it. My young brother's returning from the war in South Africa. Seems he got himself wounded at the battle of Blood River. Remember, 'twas written up in the Guelph paper some weeks back. His arm's in a sling, but he's safe and well. Nineteen years old."

"I never felt right about our boys leaving for that squabble," Harriet conceded. "None of them ever did a lick of harm in their lives. But anyway, let us hope the Boer generals will soon be suing for peace."

As the four friends sat around the table late into the evening, they shared a spirit of deep thankfulness.

The next morning George and Jack called on Tony Ortello at his barbershop and afterward they had dinner at Hugh and Gertrude Foster's. When some offered to have the Sunday meetings in their home, the brothers prayed about which place would be the right choice. As the days passed, they felt it best to keep the meeting at Lyman and Jessie's. They seemed settled in their conviction and had adequate space for everyone.

Meanwhile, Katie Keats struggled with the brothers' invitation. There were times when she could hardly keep her mind on teaching her classes. She desperately wanted to be part of the little church that was being formed, but she knew she would face harsh opposition from her mother. As each day dragged by, she felt torn between her desire to be part of the church and her need for her mother's acceptance.

On Friday morning Mr. Richardson, a father of one of the boys in the school, approached Katie before class. "I plan to come back around noon," he said. "I want to take my son to the Fergus Fall Fair. Any of the other children are welcome to go along for the outing too."

Miss Keats announced the invitation to the class and told them that she would call them in from the school yard when Mr. Richardson arrived at noon hour. "But please come quickly when I call," she cautioned. "We don't want to keep him waiting."

The children were playing outside at lunch when a frisky dog bounded into the school yard. They tried to catch the black and white collie as he raced around the yard, a shoe in his mouth. In the middle of this exciting and noisy pursuit, Katie called to the children several times. Each one heard the call, but their new playmate's appeal was strong and only five responded. The rest continued the chase. Afterward, several disappointed pupils complained bitterly when they realized they had missed the special trip. One girl sniffled at her desk for much of the afternoon.

Katie was still musing as she wiped off the blackboard at four o'clock. *Every person*, she concluded, *hears the gospel call at different times. But most don't respond to the offer to join the Father and His Son on a spiritual journey. The chase and excitement of life captivates and holds them back.*

The dreadful conviction held by one church that some people were born to be saved and others born to be lost had never sat well in Katie's mind. *No! That would be unjust and completely outside of God's nature of love*, Katie reasoned. *Everyone hears the call, but some reject it; others simply neglect it.*[25] What is preplanned or predestined is that there will be a *group* going with the Father. We can reject our place in that group, the church, the bride of Christ. Remembering the brothers' invitation, she determined not to miss her place in the newly planted church.

⌒⌒

On Saturday, as the brothers were preparing for the first Sunday meeting of the Elora church, a knock came at the door. Mrs. Applebee answered to find Miss Keats standing on the porch.

When George and Jack came downstairs, Katie Keats was sitting on the lounge, stroking the tabby cat between its ears. The cookstove crackled with the hard maple the brothers had chopped. Then, suspecting that Katie might prefer to talk privately, Mrs. Applebee excused herself.

Katie looked uncomfortable. There was a flush to her skin, and she kept fiddling with the buttons on her coat as she spoke absentmindedly of the weather and other goings-on in Elora. George and Jack were beginning to wonder what the purpose of her visit was, when she suddenly seemed to pull herself together.

Katie lowered her voice. "I came to talk to you about the meetings."

"We're glad you came," George reassured her.

"Well, I've been kind of upset since you told us you're going to leave." Her voice shook a little as she spoke. "I wanted to ask you for tea like the others, but my mother's been dead set against me going to your meetings. She wouldn't have been happy if I'd invited you home. She's proud that I play the organ at church, and she'll be hopping mad if I quit."

She swallowed a hard lump. "The other thing is that I go to the same church as Mr. Coffer and Mr. MacQuarrie, the school trustees."

Both George and Jack could see Katie's predicament as she took out a white hanky and wiped off her round cheeks.

"But, George, you've given me assurance that God still loves me. What you said about Charlotte Elliot left me breathless. I've never heard it put that way before." A scarlet flush rose from Katie's cheeks as she buried her face in her hanky. "I've tried so hard to toe the line and failed," she choked. "I've done some things that shouldn't be part of any woman's life."

"There's nobody without a dark side," George consoled her. "If your pupils had to get a hundred percent in each and every grade, how many would graduate into the first form of grammar school?"

Behind her hanky Katie shook her head. "Not one."

"The Scripture says the person who manages to keep every law of God but makes one little slip is just as guilty as the man who breaks them all.[26] That means one slip in an entire lifetime." George's forehead wrinkled, his eyes soft. "We love to compare ourselves with others. Usually there's some poor soul we reckon to be worse than us, but that has nothing to do with it."

Sensitively, George leaned forward and lowered his voice. "Whatever situation you might have stumbled into, Katie, doesn't make you one iota more of a sinner than the best living woman in Elora. We're *all* equally reliant upon the precious blood of Christ."

After a minute or two, Katie lowered her hands and stared at the pattern in the linoleum. "Thanks for picking me up again," she murmured before changing the subject. "I've been going to the Church of Scotland all my life. I usually enjoyed being there, but I never felt what I feel in your meetings. Maybe it's the Holy Spirit."

She looked at her restless hands and then up to the brothers' faces. "To be honest, I'm not willing to turn back. For the first time I'm beginning to hear a call. My perspective's changing. God's giving me the strength to walk with Him, even if it does rile things at home or at school."

"That's wonderful," George said. "I know He'll be with you and will help you in your difficulties. We'll be praying for you too, Katie." He reached out and squeezed her arm reassuringly. "We're going to have a fellowship meeting in the morning at Lyman Liddle's. It will be at half past ten if you'd like to join us." Each felt the special closeness among them as Katie promised to see the brothers in the morning.

As she floated home, Katie felt like a butterfly released from a net. She hardly noticed the yards where people were raking leaves and harvesting the last of their pumpkins and squash. Filled with a sense of peace, Katie sang to herself as she hurried along.

> Though powers of earth and hell oppose,
> I rest in this—my Father knows;
> His word is sure, it cannot fail:
> Rejoice, my soul, thou shalt prevail!
>
> I hear Him call, I hear Him call
> From all that would my soul enthrall;
> I haste away to walk with God,
> Along the path His chosen trod.

After successive rounds of hot oatmeal, bacon and eggs, toast and preserves, and more coffee, Jack threw up his hands in mock despair. "Please, Mrs. Applebee, I beg you. Please, no more food or I'll have to roll to the meeting!" George burst out laughing. Mrs. Applebee's chin dropped as she surveyed the abundance she had made to keep, as she put it, *body and soul together* for her two hardworking boys.

The three of them set out for the short walk to Lyman and Jessie's. It was the last Sunday in October. Most of the leaves had been raked into neat piles as neighbours disposed of the autumn foliage. Although the acrid smell of burning leaves had been drifting on the breeze all week, the air was still and fresh.

Jack drew in a deep breath and declared, "This is my favourite time of year—Indian summer."

"Mine, too," replied Mrs. Applebee. "The smells remind me of my father's farm when I was a girl. My mother made the most delicious pumpkin pies in all of Nichol Township. Very heavy on cinnamon and nutmeg, and the lightest touch of lard you ever saw."

Trailing a few steps behind, George noticed a MacIntosh tree in one yard. Among the leaves lay a scattering of windfall apples. Unconsciously, he slowed his pace, stopping to pick up an apple that had rolled into the ditch. With the hand of a gardener, he turned it over, examining it closely. *Interesting,* he thought, *how the ripe apples from the youngest branch are indistinguishable from those of the most mature.* George dawdled, unaware of time, before tossing the apple next to the trunk of the tree. *The sap flowing from the root,[1]* he concluded, *has produced the same glorious fruit at the tips of all the branches. Because the age of the limb has little bearing, all of the fruit displays the same beauty and contains the same sweetness.*

It's like that with these friends in Elora, he mused as the apple image settled in his mind. *Marvelous how they possess the same sweet spirit as those in Puslinch. The pure love of Christ, the fruit of His Spirit is the same no matter whose life it flows through.[2]* George glanced up to see that Jack and Mrs. Applebee had gained a good half block on him.

The three arrived to find Lyman and Jessie waiting to greet them at the door. After hugging them and helping Mrs. Applebee off with her coat, George scanned the room, noticing the sheen on the hardwood floor and the smell of furniture wax. "Everything looks lovely, Jessie," he remarked. "You've certainly gone to a lot of effort." Jessie smiled at the compliment and ushered Mrs. Applebee to a soft armchair beside the staircase.

George noted that Lyman and Jessie had set up chairs just as they had for the gospel meetings—all facing the same way. Knowing they were trying to be helpful, he took extra care not to sound critical. "How would you feel if we set the chairs in a circle, something a little less formal?"

Lyman looked surprised. "Sure, if you think that would be better."

George smiled. "Initially, the New Testament ministers preached to an audience of unbelievers," he explained. "But I suspect that after some had received the gospel, they'd sit in such a way that each person could share from the heart—like members of a family gathered around the table."

"That's most interesting," Lyman said, raising a hand to his chin. "We presumed you'd be in front speaking."

Cheerfully, Jessie joined the men and began to rearrange the chairs. "I like the idea of a circle of fellowship where everyone can participate," she noted as the room took shape.

Jack lugged a few chairs to one side of the parlour. "I don't think Jesus ever intended that His followers would sit and listen to one or two men preach every Sunday," he said as he slid them into position. "Rather, they were to minister to each other, sharing thoughts they'd received from the Spirit."

George placed a small table in the center of the room, and on it he set a cup of wine and a loaf of unleavened bread. As Alistair had done years ago, he covered these emblems of Christ's sacrifice with a linen napkin.

As they waited for the others to arrive, Jack's mind flashed back to his history books. *Over the centuries the two distinctly different types of meetings have been muddled together,* he thought sadly. *Why do churches persist in using speaker-to-congregation preaching when believers gather to worship on Sunday mornings—a practice that chokes off any real fellowship, putting one man in authority and creating an instant hierarchy?*

Jack noticed Lyman greeting people at the front door and was struck by the familiarity of the scene. Standing there, welcoming people into his home, Lyman reminded him of the way Alistair embraced his visitors as they came in. Jack was proud of this—proud, not for himself, but for this fellowship of true brothers and sisters. After laying their coats on the spare bed, Lyman guided his guests to the parlour. His youngest sat wide-eyed beside Jessie, watching each newcomer find a chair around the circle.

When everyone was settled, George spoke softly. "It's wonderful to be together. God has been a Father of children and a God of families from the beginning of human history. I hope we can always meet like this—in the spirit of a family. Now, let's begin our meeting with a hymn."

Let us draw near to God[3]
We know that He is here;
Oh, may His presence fill our souls
With reverent, godly fear.

Let us draw near to God
He will forgive our sin:
Christ's precious blood has opened heaven,
And we may enter in.[4]

George's voice was warm and resonant. "In a gathering like this one, audible prayer softens our hearts as we listen to each other speaking to our Father. I would encourage as many of you as possible to share in a simple heartfelt prayer. A single sentence from the heart is far more powerful than an eloquent string of words that may go no higher than the ceiling. Sometimes folks are nervous about speaking in front of others, and if you're afraid you won't know the right words to say, remember what Jesus said about the man who trusted in his natural ability."

Lacing his fingers over the spine of his Bible, George rocked forward. "In the parable, a Pharisee and a tax collector went up to the temple to pray. The Pharisee stood and prayed with himself. 'God, I thank You that

I'm not like other men—robbers, evildoers, adulterers—especially that tax collector. I fast twice a week and give a tenth of all I earn.' But the tax collector stood off at a distance. He would not even look up to heaven, but beat on his chest and prayed, 'God, be merciful to me, a sinner!' When the two men went home, it was the tax collector, not the Pharisee, who was pleasing to God."[5]

George's expression grew solemn. "Jesus described the first man as praying with himself. This proud, religious man, full of his own importance, prayed to impress himself and others. On the other hand, the humble tax collector uttered seven short words that actually reached the Father's ear. Perhaps we, too, can offer a simple one or two sentence prayer today. There's a hymn that might encourage us. Jack, would you lead us in singing 'Teach Me to Pray'?"

> Teach me to pray, Lord, teach me to pray,
> This is my heart cry day unto day;
> I long to know Your will and Your way;
> Teach me to pray, Lord, teach me to pray.
>
> Living in You, Lord, and You in me,
> Constant abiding: this is my plea;
> Grant me the power, boundless and free,
> Power with men, Lord, power from Thee.[6]

The little company bowed their heads and, one by one, as the Holy Spirit guided, they gave thanks to God for His great love. While Mrs. Applebee prayed for her sister and nephew, tears rolled down her cheeks. The other prayers were in harmony with this elderly woman's pleadings—all of them so natural, so real, that they sounded like petitions of a family.

Katie took out her hanky and blew her nose as she listened to Tony asking God's forgiveness in simple, unrehearsed words—his accent thick with emotion. "Thank You, Father," she whispered, mindful of her own life.

The innocent requests and expressions of thanksgiving were refreshingly different from the ritualistic readings from the prayer book that many of them had endured in their former churches. Oliver, Herb, and Katie found it impossible to pray audibly during that first meeting. Perhaps they were uncomfortable praying aloud with others present, or perhaps they were too filled with the wonder of it all to speak.

After the little church finished praying, George spoke up. "I want to thank each of you for your earnest petitions this morning. They truly touched my heart." As he paused for a moment, glancing around the circle, he saw Katie dabbing her eyes. "And for those of you who prayed silently or crystallized your prayer in a tear, remember that God heard you just as clearly. The tiniest tear holds enough water to float a desire to God." George turned to his left. "Now, Jack's going to share a few thoughts."

Jack edged forward in his chair, his open Bible draped over one knee. "When we come together to worship on Sunday mornings, our purpose should be to build each other up in our faith and walk with Christ. You might suggest a hymn or offer a word of instruction. Perhaps you could tell about something that God has revealed to you. We should speak one at a time so that everyone will be able to learn and be encouraged."[7]

As George listened to Jack, he recalled how nervous he had been in their first meeting at the school. It had become a little easier with time, but still he found it difficult. For a brief minute, his mind wandered from Jack's voice. How *would* a person know if he was sharing only empty words? He shifted on the straight back chair. When it became easy to speak, when the words flowed unimpeded—but without the gentle leading of the Spirit. A sudden movement of Jack's wrist drew his thoughts back to the parlour.

Jack opened his Bible at the epistle to the Hebrews and paraphrased three sentences: "The blood of Jesus gives us courage to enter the most holy place by *a new and living way.*[8] This way that leads to life takes us through the curtain that is Christ Himself. So *let us draw near to God* with pure hearts and a confidence that comes from having faith, encouraging each other toward love and good deeds."

Jack looked up at his friends again. They completed the circle at both sides of George and himself. "In the past we attended church services to receive a sermon from the minister. But here we minister to each other in order to stir up our love for Christ. Love is a choice we make every day. It is to a little church what breath is to our bodies. Authentic love allows us to safely bare our souls. When we reveal our frailties and shortcomings, our fears and weaknesses, we know we'll be heard with understanding. We're assured our secrets will be held close and that we'll receive a prayerful and loving response. Sometimes the most welcome responses come without words: just a knowing smile, a meeting of the eyes, a gentle touch. Or in the days that follow, a letter in the post, a brief visit, a helping hand, a standing by. In the depth of this shared love, we find comfort and solace for the rough parts of the homeward road.

"The body of Christ is like our own in many ways. Each member both serves and is served by other members. Last summer my toe got a sliver embedded in it. My finger and thumb gently withdrew the splinter and comforted the injured toe." With an appreciative grin, Jack glanced toward the kitchen. "When my eyes fall upon a plate of roast turkey with all the trimmings, my hands and my mouth get busy and work together to nourish my whole body. If our digestive tract is invaded by something harmful, producing pain and fever, the whole body shivers and shakes and rests until danger passes.[9]

"Any tiny church who struggles to afford each other this generous measure of tenderness and compassion will discern the gentle nature of the Lord Jesus in their presence. But the intensity that arises in living so close to brothers and sisters demands that we learn to *deny ourselves*.[10] In this *new and living way* we set our relationships and everyday affairs in the framework of Christian love by submitting to and caring for each other. And by accepting each other's care."

Jack paused to gaze upon his friends, his brown eyes mirroring the tenderness of which he spoke. "Everyone in the village of Elora will know that you are His disciples," he said, "*if* you truly love one another."[11] A certain cautionary tone crept into Jack's voice. "Until we learn, even earnestly desire, to carry each other's burdens, we're not fulfilling the law of Christ.[12] That was the nature and closeness of the first-century church. And that's how it is with us. We're one body in Christ, and each member belongs to all the others."[13]

Jack held up the tip of his little finger. "In 1858 a German scientist discovered that each living body develops from a single cell that grows and multiplies until it reaches maturity. The mystery of our natural bodies is that each system possesses this same life—the original spark—the indwelling Holy Spirit. Once again we come to two churches—the false church and the true church. One is only an organization, the other is a *body* sharing the common life of Christ."

Some nodded as they listened while others, eyes thoughtful, sat entranced by the depth and wisdom of Jack's words.

Although George had spent time on Saturday preparing for the meeting, he now felt that perhaps the Lord was bringing a different thought. *God alone,* he acknowledged, *knows the spiritual needs of each person here this morning. My part is to be sensitive.*

When his turn came, George spoke about the apple tree he had seen on the way over. "God never hangs sweet red apples on the end of a branch," he explained. "Rather, they're formed day by day as the life of the root flows through the branch. We may pray for spiritual fruit, but it never appears as an instant gift either. We only fool ourselves if we expect that to happen. It always comes by having more of Christ's life flowing through us, and by drawing on Jesus as our root, our source of spiritual strength."

George encouraged everyone to open his heart by taking time to reflect on the Scripture and to pray each day. "A soft receptiveness to God supplies nourishment for our soul and gives us something to share with others on Sunday." Then he looked around. "Lyman, could you please read how Jesus celebrated His last supper with the twelve?"

At this, Lyman opened his Bible. With his calloused palm, he pressed down upon the binding, cleared his throat, and began to read about Jesus blessing the bread and the cup before He gave it to His disciples.[14]

Hugh Foster read from Paul's letter to the house church in Corinth. "The Lord Jesus the same night in which he was betrayed took bread: And when he had given thanks, He brake it, and said, 'Take, eat: this is my body which is broken for you: do this in remembrance of me.'"[15] Hugh met George's eyes tentatively. "I believe verse seventeen in the previous chapter means that by sharing the same loaf we become *one bread* and *one body.*"[16]

"That is an excellent point," George agreed as he thanked Hugh and leaned forward so he could see everyone's face. "When we partake of the Spirit of Christ, that one bread, we become unified with each other in His eternal body. Each kernel of wheat has been broken and ground to become part of the bread. Each individual grape has been crushed to become part of the cup. By laying aside our individual natures and by accepting the loving nature of Christ, we all become one.

"The most important reason for gathering is to hear and to remember Jesus. Through this memorial, His blood communes with us, speaking to the depth of our souls. Breaking bread in such a simple manner reminds us of Him and takes away all the elaborate trappings of ritual. It compels each of us to stand humbly before God and to contemplate the awesome act He performed at Calvary. Many, over the centuries, have been taught that celebrating these elements, as a purely physical act, will bring eternal blessing. Unfortunately that's just not true. Partaking of the bread and the cup is meaningless unless accompanied by a deep conviction to receive the Spirit of Christ, no matter the cost to our human nature."

Before the little group broke bread, George recited some of Jesus' words: "Unless you *eat the flesh* of the Son of Man and *drink His blood,* you have *no life* in you."[17] George closed his Bible and propped it against the chair leg. "Strictly speaking, this verse, taken in its historical setting, did not pertain to partaking of these emblems in a meeting," he said. "However, it does illustrate a vital matter.

"When our faith in Christ is real and present, it compels us to adopt His self-sacrificing way of life. By eating the bread and drinking from the cup, we are making a silent declaration before each other. We are saying: 'By the grace of God, I want to imbibe the very essence of Jesus' life. I'm willing to take up my cross and follow Him.' This is not a gospel of self-improvement; it's a gospel of self-denial. By faith we reckon ourselves dead to our own self-nature, thereby allowing Christ to reign in us.

"Perhaps we can sing 'Calvary' to focus our attention on His sacrifice?" George had chosen the same hymn as the friends had sung at the first meeting of the Puslinch church:

> Lord, we gather round Thy footstool,
> Bowed in deep humility;
> As we look upon the emblems,
> We remember Calvary.

> Unto him who loved and washed us
> From our sins in His own blood,
> We would render thanks and plead for
> Grace to love Him as we should.[18]

After the last notes faded away, the room fell silent as George asked Lyman to remove the white linen cloth. The loaf of bread and the cup were open for everyone to consider. George gave thanks before they shared this symbol of Christ's broken body. When he saw Lyman carrying the tiny loaf in his direction, he motioned toward Mrs. Applebee. Tears ran down Evelyn's soft cheeks as she broke off the first piece and handed it carefully to Katie. Evelyn's lifespan of seventy-seven years had encompassed much of the nineteenth century, yet nothing in her long years could have prepared her for the joy that bubbled over as she met the radiance of Katie's face. From hand to hand, the friends passed the bread around the circle, dividing it among themselves as each person broke off a piece.

When the broken loaf paused at a gap in the circle, Eddie got up and carried the bread to his father, offering him a piece before he took one for himself. As George watched the respectful and tender way Eddie treated his father, he remembered the love Joseph had shown Jacob in the land of Goshen. Leaping from his chariot, Joseph had thrown his arms around his father and wept, extending to him the bountiful provision of the land.[19]

When the bread had been consumed, George spoke again. "Lyman, would you please give thanks for the common cup?" Moments later, after the empty cup was returned to its place, the assembly sang another hymn to end the first meeting of the Elora church.

The little church remained silent as Lyman arose and carried the napkin, the crumb-covered plate, and the cup into the kitchen, returning to take a seat as people began to visit quietly with the person on either side.

During the last half-hour of the meeting, a tantalizing smell had been wafting from the kitchen cookstove. Now Jessie stood up and announced, "You're all invited to stay for dinner."

Not one person was in a hurry to leave. When the women went into the kitchen and tied on aprons, George got up to help too. "Jessie," he said, "if you tell me where the knives and forks are, I'll set the table."

Jessie pointed to a shallow drawer in the kitchen sideboard. "I counted heads and if I'm right there are thirteen grownups. And three not-so-little scallywags," she added, smiling at Jimmy.

Before long, the little church was seated on either side of the harvest table enjoying a roasted wild turkey that Lyman had shot in the woods at the edge of Elora. Hot vegetables, gravy, cranberries from the bog, fresh bread, and pumpkin pie were food for both body and soul. From the dining room wall, the majestic stag in Landseer's *Monarch of the Glen* gazed down with deep, almost human intensity.

During a lull in the dinner conversation, George announced, "Tomorrow morning Jack and I are going to cycle to Belwood to see if the Lord provides an opening there. If all is well, we intend to return next Saturday afternoon to be with you on Sunday again." Turning he asked, "Herb, would you be able to bring our mail here next Sunday?"

Herb nodded. "Oh, yes," he replied. "I'd be glad to do that, George."

Like every other person at the table, the postmaster had wondered how this meeting would go. Would he feel comfortable? Or stiff? But as the last of the dishes were dried and everyone was leaving for home, he savoured the warm family-like feeling and the wonder and simplicity of it all. Looking at the faces of the others, Herb could tell they, too, felt blessed.

In his next letter to Alistair and Priscilla, George wrote of the plans to move on to Belwood and asked for their prayers. The friends at Wood Creek Farm were overjoyed to hear about the outcome of the mission in Elora and to learn that George and Jack would soon be carrying the gospel to another community.

As George wrote he pondered the closeness of the friends in Puslinch and now in Elora. He felt sad and a bit lonesome for his own family. Both he and Jack had kept in touch with their parents to let them know how much they loved them. Although Jack's mother corresponded regularly, the others never answered. At times the absence of news made George feel disheartened. Nevertheless, a letter addressed in his upright script found its way along the lane of his parents' farm every two weeks.

Twenty

CONSCIENTIOUS PLOUGHMEN
Late Fall 1901

The bicycle ride through Nichol Township led George and Jack into the teeth of a raw east wind. Stopping briefly near the bridge that crossed the river to the village of Aboyne, they looked down on the old oatmeal mill now used to manufacture linseed cake and oil. As they rested, wooden barrels were being loaded onto a solid green wagon hitched to a massive team of dapple gray Percherons. The millpond spilled through the race, driving the colossal wooden wheel. From the end of the Aboyne bridge, the winding road looped up and up to meet the sky, providing a picturesque view of the river valley below.

"I could easily spend the whole day here," George said. "But we'd better keep shanks' ponies on the move."

As they passed through Fergus, the men met farmers hauling fattened livestock and wagon loads of waxed turnips to the train bound for Cataract. Cycling along St. Andrews Street, George and Jack were amazed at the natural beauty of the Grand River, crashing through the channel it had worn into the limestone.

The air was fresh and cold, but the hard frost had not yet set in, and farmers were finishing the last of their fall ploughing. They walked up and down the long rows behind their teams, turning over fresh furrows of rich dark soil. George recalled his own walking plough and his pains to make straight furrows by fixing his vision on a point at the far end of the field. As he watched one conscientious ploughman out of the corner of his eye,

George thought of Jesus' teaching that no one who puts his hand to the plough and keeps looking back is fit for service in God's kingdom.[1]

As he rode George prayed silently that both he and Jack in the full-time ministry, and the saints in the Elora and Puslinch churches, would be forward-looking and resolute in *the new and living way.* Softening the heart's soil and turning down the weeds of life were never-ending tasks.

The two men breathed heavily as they pedaled up the hills, now gaining in steepness. Beneath rows of naked sugar maples, scattered piles of stones lined the curving roadside. The pioneers had sweated and toiled as they picked these rocks to make their fields as productive as possible.

Although neither of the men had ever been in Belwood before, a cautious confidence swept over George as they coasted into the village, their feet lifted well away from the flailing pedals. They now had a little experience and some idea of how to make a beginning in an unfamiliar place.

George pulled over and dismounted on the grass. "It's almost dinner-time. Maybe we should find the general store," he suggested. "We can buy something for a sandwich and ask about a boarding place." Jack nodded and they cycled down Broadway Street to Rankin's General Store.

After purchasing a half pound of hard cheese, a loaf of bread, and two apples, Jack passed George the change and asked the proprietor if anybody in town might be willing to rent them a room.

Alexander Rankin thumped his pipe on the stove. "You could try Mrs. Shepton. She's got space aplenty. Family all gone, you know."

After receiving directions, the pair took their lunch and walked their bicycles down past the Belwood railway station to a grassy place at the river's edge. They sat with their backs against the cool wind, gave thanks, and ate their sandwiches.

After they finished eating, they made their way to Mrs. Shepton's house. When Jack knocked on the door, an older lady with high cheek bones and loose curls of gray hair opened it halfway.

"My name's Jack Gillan," he offered courteously. "My companion and I are itinerant ministers."

"I have my own church, thank you," the lady cut in rather stiffly and stepped back from the door.

"No, no," Jack blurted out, "we need a place to board for a few weeks, and we wondered if you might be interested."

The lady looked Jack up and down, examining his face and rough clothing. "No," she said tartly. "I'm sorry. I don't have any extra room."

"Perhaps you might know somebody else who might?" Jack persisted.

"'Tisn't likely," Mrs. Shepton rebutted, closing the door in his face.

Stung by the unexpected rejection, Jack turned and headed back down the steps. The two men stood on the sidewalk in front of the big house. As they pondered their alternatives, George's eye caught a slight movement behind one of Mrs. Shepton's curtains. "Don't look now, but I think we're being given the eye," he murmured to Jack. "We're making Mrs. Shepton uncomfortable. Maybe we'd better shift along."

Jack grunted and glanced up and down the street. "The only thing we can do is to start knocking at doors." Throwing his leg over the crossbars, he forced a smile as he pushed off.

During the next four hours, they tried every home in the village. Most people were pleasant, a few rude. But the answer was the same: They had no lodging for two strangers. As the sun pulled gray clouds over its face, the evening grew sharp and the daylight disappeared down the river valley.

"I think we'd better look around outside of the village," George said. "Maybe we can find a farmer's barn or an implement shed to sleep in."

Jack hunkered into his coat. "Not the best night to sleep in the open."

As the brothers pedaled out of the village, they kept a keen eye for a place to bed down. After a mile or so, George spotted a haystack in a three-sided field, sheltered by thick cedar woods. "What do you make of that?" he asked, pointing into the gathering darkness.

Jack gave a mock shiver. "It'll be my first time to sleep rough."

"I'd prefer to talk to the owner first," George declared, "but there's no sign of buildings." He paused. "We'll have to leave it just as we found it."

The two men lifted their bicycles over the rail fence and pushed them through the long grass toward the stack. Propping his bike against the hay, George walked around to the lee side and hollowed out a hole away from the wind. Jack, too, began to fashion a shallow cave under the edge.

"It's got all the comforts of home," Jack laughed when they had finished scooping out two recesses about six feet long. "I'm going to put a bit of loose stuff on the bottom. The rest can be the bolster and blanket."

"Be sure to pull it right up to your chin," George chuckled as he rubbed his hands briskly. "I'm glad we still have some cheese and part of this loaf." Sitting side by side in the darkness, the two young men looked toward the murky outline of the cedar bush as they ate their bread.

"If we'd known we were going to be outside tonight, we could have bought a few more apples." Jack snuggled his back into the soft curvature of the hay. Abruptly, he sprang to his feet. "I just remembered something."

George watched Jack's stocky form disappear into the blackness.

In a few minutes Jack came back with a pocket of apples. "I found dessert," he said, passing a couple to George, "but watch for the holes."

George grimaced. "I can't see my hand let alone any marks," he said amiably. "Besides, it's not the holes that worry me. It's the critter inside."

"It's a far cry from our first night at Mrs. Applebee's," Jack observed. "You know, the fried chicken with all the trimmings."

George didn't speak for several seconds. "Yes, it is," he said finally. "But it's no less a part of this kind of ministry. Jesus and His disciples must have spent a lot of nights under the stars."[2] He chewed another bite of apple. "Can you imagine how they felt when Lazarus and Mary and Martha welcomed them into their home in Bethany?"[3]

"And Lyman and Jessie, and Mrs. Applebee in Elora," Jack added thoughtfully. "Paul mentioned being hungry and sleepless too. It was a lot rougher in those days than it is now."[4]

Tired from the day's journey, the brothers decided they needed to get some sleep. They expected frost before morning and took the few extra clothes they had out of their travel bags. George struggled to pull his second shirt and pants over those he already had on.

"Goodnight, Jack," he said. "I just want you to know how much I appreciate you as a companion. Especially at a time like this."

"Thanks, George. I feel the same way." Jack's voice sounded muffled as if he had wrapped his extra shirt around his head. "It's wonderful how God planned that His ministers would travel in pairs."

Then George pulled his coat over him and lay face down to pray. "Dear Father, thank You for Your abiding care. And for the wonderful privilege of following Jesus in circumstances like these. It helps me to appreciate and understand the depth of His love. Please overshadow us tonight and be with us in the morning. Help us to be sensitive enough to know where you wish to lead us." Before George finished, he asked God to draw close to each of his friends in the Elora and Puslinch churches and help them in their spiritual journey as well.

George slept soundly for a couple of hours, but as the cold penetrated, he drifted in and out of sleep. Suddenly, the long lonely howl of a brush wolf rose from the nearby swamp. Although he knew the wolf would not harm them, the eerie sound made the hairs on his neck stand up. He burrowed deeper into his prickly nest and for a long time he lay awake listening to the noises of the night. Just before dawn, he finally fell asleep.

After the men had carefully tramped the loose hay back into the stack, they walked down into the cedar woods and found a stream. Kneeling down, George splashed cold water on his face and drank. Then, after combing his hair, he and Jack pushed their bicycles back to the rail fence.

At the first two farms where they asked for lodging, the same rebuff met them as they had received in the village. "I didn't think it would be this hard to find a place," Jack said as they pedaled along the gravel road.

"God must have a particular place He wants us to be for the next few weeks." George's voice was steady with conviction. "We really need to be responsive so He can lead us there."

At a narrow crossroads Jack braked and dismounted. "Which way do you think we should go here?"

"Maybe we should climb up there and see what we can see," George replied, pointing to the crest of a steep hill ahead. Frosted plumes of goldenrod bent down along the roadsides, seemed to frame the hill's crest, now slickly wet from the melting frost. When the brothers reached the top of the grade, they could see three farmsteads in the distance.

"I've a feeling we should try that place," George said, pointing to a large red brick house, its slate roof glinting in the sun.

Jack's eyes fastened on the set of buildings at the end of George's finger. "Looks like a half mile on, I reckon."

In a few minutes the men pulled up in front of two matching gate posts and a framed white sign with the name Hunters' Hollow inscribed in stylish Gothic letters. The farm, like a picture in a child's storybook, appeared to be folded between two hills. On the left of the long lane, between the house and the road, an orchard of apple, plum, and pear trees had been planted in precise rows. As the two men drew closer, they could see that the house was trimmed with gingerbread, scrolls, steep gables, and buff, quoined corners. Farther back and secluded among tall spruce trees, no doubt planted to break the strong west wind, a nice-looking paddock, a gray weathered barn, and a few outbuildings clustered around the farmyard.

At the south side of the woodshed, next to the lane, patches of raspberries, gooseberries, and thimbleberries had been set out. George puzzled as he and Jack cycled up the lane. It was obvious the property had been planned and cared for by a meticulous owner. But what could account for the somewhat tangled and overgrown appearance of it now?

He waited at the gate while Jack stepped onto the spacious porch and knocked. The outline of an approaching woman, swathed from collar to ankles in a muslin apron, could be seen darkly through the screen.

Jack stepped back as the door swung out. "Hello. Lovely day, although it's a bit breezy."

"Yes, it's not bad now," the lady said cordially, "but it looks like a storm may be blowing in from the east. What can I help you with?"

"I'm Jack Gillan. My friend, George Farnham, and I are hoping to hold some gospel meetings in Belwood, and we need a place to board."

"Amelia Hunter." She smiled warmly and held out her hand. Jack shook it and was surprised that the slight woman had such a firm grip. Her ash gray hair and sharpened features were the only things that gave away her age. After asking a few questions, she invited the men into the parlour, gesturing toward two Queen Anne chairs. But George and Jack stood tentatively, caps in hands.

"Do sit down," she insisted, taking a chair herself and folding her hands on her lap. "Now, tell me a little more about yourselves." When the men had finished their story, she smiled. "I'd like to ask my husband before I say yes or no." She excused herself and hurried upstairs.

George noticed dust on the dark furniture and a few cobwebs in the corners of the high medallioned ceilings. *Must be a lot of work to look after such a big house,* he thought as they sat waiting.

It seemed a long time before Mrs. Hunter returned, and George feared they would be turned away yet again. When she reappeared at the parlour door, her narrow shoulders seemed stiff and tense. Elbows tight to her body, she clasped her hands decisively. George detected a tiny twitch at the corner of her right eye. They'd likely had a disagreement about taking on two boarders. He shifted uneasily on the Queen Anne chair.

Mrs. Hunter frowned. "My husband says he's willing to give it a try for a week." She paused, biting her lip. "If he changes his mind, there won't be any trouble, will there?"

Jack smiled warmly. "None at all, Mrs. Hunter. We appreciate you taking a chance on us."

"There'll be three square meals," Amelia volunteered. "Nothing fancy but plenty of it. I'm more attuned to cooking for farmers than clergymen."

Jack ran a hand under his suspenders and laughed, "I've been eating like a farmer for thirty years and seemed to flourish so far."

Amelia relaxed slightly. "My husband reckons twelve dollars a month would be reasonable for each of you. Would that be fair?"

"Just fine," Jack agreed. "And we'll try not to be any bother."

Nodding, Amelia beckoned. "If you'd like to follow me then, I'll show you to the rooms." She led George and Jack up the wide staircase and along a spacious hall to separate bedrooms in the rear wing of the second floor. Although it was yet autumn, the upper hall exuded the chill of long-uninhabited chambers and a dispirited sense of loss and emptiness.

"I'm sorry this room is not quite ready," she apologized, gesturing toward the second room, "but I've been distracted and wasn't expecting company." Amelia Hunter bustled around and found sheets and pillow slips. "Make yourselves at home. If there's anything you need just let me know." She finished making the bed, buttoning the pillow slips and turning down the quilt. "Supper will be ready at six."

The raw wind outside made Amelia shiver as she returned to the kitchen, so she tossed another block of wood into the stove and adjusted the damper. Outside, the tip of a spruce branch scratched back and forth against the window pane. She took out some beef and carrots and wondered if the men would like turnips and barley in their stew. When everything was cut into pieces, she placed the iron pot on the burner over the firebox. As she started on pastry for an apple pie, she thought about her prayers and about her husband's needs. Small and dainty, Amelia moved nimbly about her kitchen. First sprinkling a dusting of flour on the tabletop and reaching for her rolling pin and then crimping the pastry, her deliberate gestures resembled those of a bird building its nest. Even her voice, when she spoke, sounded like the muted yet musical chatter of a chickadee in November.

George and Jack, with clean shirts and combed hair, dutifully presented themselves in the kitchen at 5:50. They were surprised to see the table set for only three.

"Won't Mr. Hunter be joining us for supper?" Jack asked politely.

Mrs. Hunter's face looked troubled. "Robert was gored by the bull more than a month ago, so he can't get out of bed," she lamented. "The bull's normally quiet, but for some reason when my husband went into the pen to give him fresh straw that day, he turned on him. He slammed Robert with his horns and pinned him against the stone wall."

Jack exhaled sharply. "Oh, I'm so sorry." He knew firsthand about that kind of tragedy. Years ago, his uncle had been killed by a bull while crossing a pasture field. "I certainly hope your husband's on the mend."

"Well, his pelvis was broken." She paused, putting her hand over her face. For a minute George thought she was going to cry. "Seems as if his innards are damaged too," she added, a slight tremor in her voice. "We just don't know how it'll turn out, him being sixty and all…"

"Who's doing the farm work now?" George ventured. Amelia explained that she had been doing it as best she could on her own.

While Amelia took Robert's meal to him on a tray, the brothers exchanged glances, reflecting on the misfortune that had befallen these kind people. Now they understood why the property was looking neglected.

When Amelia returned, George spoke for both of them. "Mrs. Hunter, now that we're here, we hope you'll let us help you out a bit until your husband gets back on his feet."

Amelia Hunter dropped her eyes for a moment and when she looked up, a smile had rearranged the careworn lines of her face. "That would be lovely," she murmured.

The wind whistling in the eaves and the fire crackling in the stove were the only sounds as the two men ate, mindful of Amelia's delicious stew and the workings of the Holy Spirit. After eating a few spoonfuls, she added, "I'd like you to meet Robert after supper. Never mind that the man's flat on his back. After nothing but a woman's company for nearly a fortnight, he'll be glad to chew the fat with another man or two…"

After supper as the men followed Amelia upstairs, the potent reek of Doctor Sloan's Liniment assailed their nostrils. When they entered the room,

Robert was propped up in bed on pillows. "Come in," he said, drawing a homespun blanket up to his waist as they approached. Amelia's husband, a big powerful man with craggy features, looked awkward lying helplessly in his nightshirt. No doubt he would have preferred to meet two strangers in his barn where a man appeared less vulnerable.

Amelia walked to Robert's side and put her hand on her husband's hunched shoulder. His unshaven face was pale, gaunt, the skin on his hands slack and sallow. It was obvious the man had endured a great deal of pain.

George stepped close to the bed and reached out to shake hands. "Evening, sir. My name's George Farnham. I'm pleased to meet you."

When George stepped aside, Jack introduced himself. "We very much appreciate you letting us board in your home," he added.

Robert eyed the two strangers carefully. "It's fine," he allowed. "Years ago, Amelia boarded out when she was a teacher. She thinks it'd be good to put the shoe on the other foot. So we'll give it a whirl and see how it works out." His wife had drawn three chairs up to the bed and he asked the men to take a seat.

"We're sorry to hear about your accident," Jack commiserated.

"It's come at a bad time," Robert responded. "Anyway, I'm thankful to be alive." When he looked at Amelia and gave a small tight smile, she squeezed his shoulder. He went on to explain what had happened, reliving the seconds of terror as the bull had thrown him around like a rag doll.

Then a peace washed over his eyes "Amelia mentioned that you two are preachers." When he asked a few polite questions about their plans, he liked their simple, direct answers.

As the conversation went along, he learned that both George and Jack had been farming. This gave Robert a sense of confidence as he looked into their tanned faces. He could understand farmers. He listened eagerly as the two young men talked about the farms they had grown up on, about their families, and about the reason they had both left to preach the gospel.

Later that night, Amelia changed the dressing on Robert's wound and then got into bed and blew out the lamp. She was on the edge of sleep when she heard a hoarse whisper. Amelia turned over and leaned close enough to hear her husband's breathing. "Those fellows," he whispered again, "they're two decent men."

The next day George and Jack paid a visit to the Belwood schoolhouse on Broadway Street. As in Elora, they looked up the trustees and made the necessary arrangements. Following their pattern, they planned gospel

346   CONSCIENTIOUS PLOUGHMEN

meetings for each Tuesday, Wednesday, Thursday, and Friday evenings, and set to work on some notices. While they were putting up a notice at the post office the following day, they left their names for incoming mail. They were surprised to find a letter already awaiting them from Mrs. Applebee.

Elora, Ontario
November 2, 1901

Dear George and Jack,

It's only been a couple of days since you left for Belwood, but already I'm missing you boys. It was wonderful to have you around the house these past few weeks. I didn't know how lonely I really was until you came. It's so good to know that you'll be back on Sundays for a while. Now I realize how hard it must have been for your friends in Puslinch when you left there to come to us.

Katie stopped by yesterday. When she went home after the Sunday meeting, her mother was livid and told her she had twenty-four hours to pack up and get out. She came and talked to me before school on Monday, and I'm delighted that she's going to board here. I wanted to let you know so you won't be surprised when you arrive. Katie is using the third bedroom, so your beds are still waiting. As long as I'm alive there will always be a spot here for each of you.

It's a tremendous thing that you've undertaken, but there'll be many who will turn their backs on your message. If only they could see the difference it has made in my life and the lives of so many others. And they say miracles don't happen anymore! The thing that had the biggest effect on so many of our little group in Elora was the way you handled being kicked out of the school. The extra mile you went in showing forgiveness was alien to many of us who let anger rule our voices and actions. Over my life, I've seen a lot of that in my husband's law practice. People want to get even. The gentle way of reason and forgiveness is so much better.

Well, it's almost four o'clock and time to get the potatoes peeled for supper. Katie'll be along soon. With every good wish, I remain,

Your faithful friend in Christ,

Evelyn

Amelia Hunter had been feeding the animals since Robert's accident, but cleaning the stable was beyond her. Two weeks ago she had hired a neighbour to clean the stalls, but they were beginning to pile up again.

George felt a certain nostalgia working in the stable and thought of his own barn and livestock. The fact was that he liked looking after pigs and cattle, even shoveling out the manure. As he worked, he took a good look at each of the animals. The horses were high-spirited, and George could tell that they hadn't been out of the stable for exercise in a good while. After supper that evening, the brothers visited with Robert, and he encouraged them to harness up his driving horse to use on their trips to the village.

"Using Robert's horse might give the wrong impression in the settlement," George said after returning to their bedrooms. "Two preachers who claim to be homeless, trotting about town in a stylish rig and driver."

"It doesn't seem to go together," Jack agreed. "We'd better leave the horse at home unless Amelia needs to go to town."

"Or unless we need to haul some heavy supplies for the farm."

George and Jack fed and bedded down the livestock morning and night during the week. When Robert had suggested that they do this in exchange for part of their room and board, they accepted happily. However, the twice daily chores only maintained the animals, so they worked a little every day, bringing the barn back to what it had been before Robert's accident.

On Saturday, as planned, the men prepared to leave for Elora after the morning chores. They apologized for not being able to do all the work and promised to be back late on Sunday.

"That's fine. I'm just thankful to have the extra help during the week," Amelia exclaimed. "Enjoy your holiday."

As they walked to their bicycles, the men exchanged glances.

"Holiday," Jack chuckled under his breath.

That evening Amelia went to the barn for the first time in four days. When she stepped into the stable, she could hardly believe her eyes. The stalls were cleaned out and the animals bedded with fresh straw. The horses had been brushed and curried, and a sheen rippled on their coats. Even the cobwebs had received a swipe. Amelia moved through the stable in a daze. All the pig pens had been shoveled out. There were even fresh tracks leading away from the manure pile at the back of the barn. Amelia followed the tracks to the field where the brothers had hauled and spread it. Amelia quickly fed the animals and then ran to tell Robert the startling news.

When Robert heard Amelia's footsteps pounding up the stairs, he heaved himself up in the bed, suddenly oblivious to the jolting pain. Eyes wide, his mouth gaped as she recounted all the work done in the stable. After rehearsing the details for the second time, Amelia plumped Robert's pillows and he eased himself back. "I can hardly take it in," he panted as the two of them marveled at the kindness and efficiency of the men. But then a sickening thought suddenly crossed Robert's mind. "You can bet your bottom dollar they're expecting to get paid."

Shock and disappointment registered in Amelia's eyes. "But they seem like such accommodating young fellows."

"But they're likely as short of money as the rest of us. One thing's for certain. Nobody does extra work for nothing." The more the couple talked, the more convinced they became that this was the case.

"They should've had enough sense to ask first," Robert muttered. "We could have explained how poor the crop turned out this past summer, between the wheat smut and that dashed drought at haying time..."

Amelia looked down at the floor. "I didn't want to worry you," she said. "But the bank's already pressing me for last month's mortgage payment. And there isn't enough in our account." She hesitated. "That's why I was so insistent we take George and Jack on as boarders."

Robert let out a deep sigh, staring angrily at his bandage. "I just wish I could get back on my feet," he grumbled. "I thought that having these two men might be a help. But it looks as if they're adding toads to our soup."

～

George and Jack arrived at Mrs. Applebee's in time for a late supper. After Katie and the brothers finished the dishes, they lounged around the kitchen, laughing and talking with Evelyn as if she were their favourite aunt, and they her preferred niece and nephews. They all played Parcheesi until eleven o'clock, when Katie folded up the board and Mrs. Applebee, with deliberate unction, lit three of the new candles. "Off to bed now, the lot of you," she concluded with a flourish.

The next morning the Elora saints arrived at the Liddles ten or fifteen minutes before the meeting. After a hearty welcome, they sat waiting in reverent anticipation of God's presence. The meeting unfolded just as the brothers had hoped, and each person prayed briefly and fervently. George and Jack thrilled to the simple petitions that the Spirit presented through each one.[5]

Lyman Liddle told of a recent experience. He had purchased a coloured jigsaw puzzle of the world for his oldest son. "Katie has the pupils in the *Third Reader* memorizing the countries of the British Empire," he said. "I wanted Jimmy to understand the geography of the globe. When I gave him the puzzle, he took the pieces to his bedroom. In a few minutes he came back with the whole thing together. I was amazed that a nine-year-old could do that, so I asked him, 'How did you get it together so quickly?'

"He told me that he had looked on the back of the box that the puzzle came in and saw a line sketch of a father holding his little boy's hand. The back of the puzzle had the same outline. So he turned the puzzle upside down and arranged the pieces according to that sketch. 'When I turned it over, the world was also together and perfect,' Jimmy told me.

"I've discovered too," Lyman said, "that if I reach out and take the Father's hand, the rest of my world fits together perfectly as well."

Eddie spoke about waiting expectantly for Christ's return, and then he shared an illustration. "When I was twelve, I overheard our washerwoman telling the neighbour lady this story at the clothesline." Eddie glowed, as if envisioning a magnificent painting. "Two young people lived near the seashore on a remote island. They loved each other, and each Saturday evening they went to a secluded part of the beach to make a campfire and talk together. As time passed their love grew stronger, and the girl wrote a poem expressing how she felt. Eventually she composed music and sang the beautiful song to her friend. Months passed and they talked about marriage, but jobs and money were scarce, and the young man wanted some security before starting a family. Hearing that prospects were better on the mainland, the couple agreed that he should go there to prepare a place for himself and his bride. He promised to return for her as soon as possible.

"Their little village had no harbour, so the massive ship dropped anchor well offshore. The young man took his beloved into his arms at the water's edge and embraced her until the last possible moment. But when the heavy foghorn blasted through the drizzle for the third time, he knew he had to tear himself away. As he released her reluctantly, he made a parting request: 'Promise that you'll go to our special place on the beach every Saturday evening. Build a fire and sing your song for me. When I come back, I'll meet you there.' She promised and then he was gone, a crewman paddling him out in a rowboat to the huge ship. Tears streamed down the young woman's cheeks as her friend climbed the rope ladder that was lowered. After he reached the deck, she waved until the tiny speck faded into the mist. Weeping, she turned and headed for home, hoping the memory of his tender love would sustain her until he came again.

"Each Saturday night she remembered her promise and went to that quiet place, built the fire, and sang her song of love for him. But as the months passed, she often wondered if he'd ever come back. Gossipmongers in the village started rumours that he had another girl and would never return. Eventually, she wavered and questions appeared in her mind. 'Shall I go again this week?' she asked herself. 'Will it even matter?'

"And one cold, damp winter evening she decided not to go anymore. 'I know he won't come back tonight.' But at the last minute, she made up her mind to go, just one more time. A wet, bone-chilling wind was sweeping in from the darkness of the sea. The moonless night was black, and it took considerable effort to light the fire. She huddled in her coat and after a while she sang her song. From off the shore she heard a little splash, which she presumed was a fisherman coming home late. Then, as she hunched her back against the ocean wind, the returning bridegroom-to-be emerged from the darkness. When his gentle hand cupped her shoulder, she turned in surprise. They embraced—never to be separated again."

In the silence that followed, George gazed intently at the storyteller. The young man had seemed so sure of himself, so sophisticated. Had Eddie ever known the presence in his life of a love so powerful, so overwhelming, that, like Laura, even in her absence, she kept her hand over his heart? Then George heard Eddie's voice resuming.

"We're the espoused of Christ, and I know He is coming back for each of us," Eddie affirmed. "I want to be here each week to kindle the fire of my love for Him."[6] He thumbed through his hymn book. "Could we please sing the song 'I Am Waiting for the Dawning'?"

> I am waiting for the dawning
> Of that bright and blessed day,
> When this dreary night of sorrow
> Shall have vanished far away,
>
> I am waiting for the coming
> Of the Lord who died for me;
> O, His words have thrilled my spirit:
> "I will come again for thee."[7]

Each person shared a thought reflecting love for Christ, and as they finished singing the final hymn, Eddie glanced down at his gold pocket watch. *How,* he marveled, *could an hour and a half have flown by so quickly?* The thought that George and Jack would be leaving shortly gave Eddie a twinge of disappointment until he remembered that he would soon be making a sales trip to Orangeville. He would stop in to see the brothers when he passed through Belwood.

By mid-afternoon, George and Jack were back on the road. It was well after nightfall when they rode up the Hunters' lane. As they approached the house in the darkness, they saw a coal oil lantern burning in the kitchen, as well as a candle flickering in the upper bedroom. When Amelia heard the door opening, she bustled downstairs.

"I'm glad you're back safe and sound," she welcomed them. "It's a long journey." As they hung up their coats, she asked, "Could you join Robert and me for a visit? I'll bring some chairs and a pot of tea."

As the brothers carried their overnight bags to their bedrooms, Jack whispered under his breath, "Robert's usually sleeping by this time of night. And Amelia looks a little tense. I wonder if there's a problem?"

George looked bleak. "I guess we'll soon find out."

Robert turned when the men tapped on his door, the colour in his face more robust than usual. "Amelia's cooking—never had any hitch with it until that darn bull crushed me," he announced. "But today I was able to eat a good piece of mutton again." He asked how the trip had gone and about the folks in Elora. After Amelia brought in the teapot and a plateful of oatmeal cookies, Robert hitched himself forward and cleared his throat.

"We can't thank you enough for all the extra work you've done in the barn," he began. "Amelia tells me the barn's cleaned out and the animals freshly bedded." He hesitated, unsure how to continue. "The problem is that we have no money, and it might be months before we can pay you."

An involuntary quiver spread across Amelia's chin. Already she had come to appreciate these two young men. She didn't want to hurt their feelings, but she couldn't ignore the bills or have the men thinking that there was money to make when there was none.

George smiled and leaned toward them. "Thank you for the thought," he said, "but we couldn't take money for that. If we wanted to be paid, we would have talked to you beforehand. We appreciate the comforts of your home, and we can see you need some help. When I see somebody in need, that person becomes my neighbour. Something inside of me wants to help. Besides, this is our way of saying thank you for receiving us into your home. You didn't know us. You could have turned us away."

Amelia could not hold back. Tears of gratitude gathered in her eyes, spilling down her cheeks as she smiled and cried simultaneously. Robert sat speechless, his gaze riveted on George's guileless face. When at last he found his voice, the tone was husky. "I feel we've gained a pair of nephews— full grown. We just can't believe it. How can we ever thank you?"

George placed a reassuring hand on the older man's shoulder. "You already have, Robert—when you and Amelia took us under your roof. None of us is an island unto himself."

As Amelia lay in bed that night, wondering about these two travelers, something she had heard from the Bible flashed through her mind: Be sure to welcome strangers into your home. By doing this, some people have welcomed angels without even knowing it.[8] *Funny,* she thought, *how Scripture could do that, could hide away in your mind and come back just at the right time.* Although Amelia didn't honestly think these men were angels, she couldn't escape the fact that they were very different from anybody she had ever met. And they, too, had come just when she needed them. *Would I have accepted George and Jack into our home,* she wondered, *if I had not been at my wits' end?*

Amelia woke early the next morning with George's words repeating in her mind: "When I see somebody in need, that person becomes my neighbour." As dawn broke she wrapped herself in a quilt and tiptoed down to the parlour. Lighting a candle, she took out the old family Bible, sat on the hassock and began thumbing through its delicate onionskin pages. It was the word "neighbour" that she was searching for. After a few minutes, she found the occasion in Luke's Gospel where an expert in the law had stood up and asked Jesus what he must do to inherit eternal life. She could see that the man, when asked what was written in the law, had a well-rehearsed rejoinder:

"Love the Lord your God with all your heart, all your soul, all your strength, and all your mind," the lawyer had answered. "And love your neighbour as yourself." But he wanted to justify himself. "Who is my neighbour?" he had persisted.

Amelia mused over the parable that Jesus related about a man going down from Jerusalem to Jericho who fell into the hands of thieves. They stripped him of his clothing, wounded him, and ran off, leaving him half dead. A priest happened to be going down the same road. But when he saw the man, he walked past on the other side. A man from Samaria also came traveling along that road. When he saw the man, he felt sorry for him and went over to him. He treated his wounds with olive oil and wine and bandaged them. Then he put the man on his own donkey and brought him to an inn, where he took care of him. The next day he gave the innkeeper two silver coins and said, "Please take care of the man. If you spend more than this on him, I will repay you when I return."

Amelia envisioned Jesus looking at the legal expert. "So which of these do you think was a real neighbour to the man who was beaten up by robbers?"

"The one who showed mercy to him," the lawyer replied.

Then Jesus had told him, "Go and do likewise." [9]

As the sun broke free from the horizon, Amelia watched the parlour growing brighter. The portraits of Robert's ancestors gleamed in their oval frames where the sun's rays struck them, but Amelia's mind was focused on the strangers who were helping in her time of need. *Have I ever met anybody,* she tried to recall, *who came as close as these men do in loving their neighbour as themselves?* [10] Because of Robert's illness, Amelia had not attended any of the brothers' meetings. But now, even though she saw their sermon in action daily, she wanted to hear what they preached.

That evening the potbellied stove at the Belwood schoolhouse crackled with broken ends of barrel staves, the hot wax spitting against the mica window. Like a schoolmarm once again, Amelia stepped briskly over the threshold of the girls' entrance and took a desk near the front. Behind her a former pupil, now a Justice of the Peace, leaned forward and tapped her on the shoulder. "Don't be taken in too quick by this pair of shysters, Mrs. Hunter. I've heard they don't come on anybody's recommendation—except maybe from Balaam's ass." [11] Beside him a thin austere man with a head of silver hair and side whiskers folded his arms across his chest as if rejecting the preachers' words as yet unspoken. Amelia recognized him as one of the stewards from the Methodist church.

As Amelia settled back into the curve of the seat, she turned over the man's caustic scepticism and the wary reaction around the village to the meetings. A tinware peddler, rattling his way from door to door, had first spread the titillating tale of stalwart churches in Elora being broken up by "the irresponsible proselytizing of the two strangers." Had Amelia not been privy to the unembellished details, she might have been swayed herself. But the brothers' daily lives spoke powerfully and, from their own lips, she learned of the handful of humble seekers who gathered weekly in the home of Lyman and Jessie Liddle.

The schoolhouse door creaked open and a hoarse whisper could be heard throughout the classroom. "Brush them wet leaves off the back of my coat, would ya?" a woman's voice rasped. Gathering her shawl over her shoulders, Amelia shifted discreetly to see Sissy Boggins unbuttoning her bulky fur coat while her boarder, the young apprentice from the tinsmith's shop, reached obediently for the corn broom. Behind them stood Alexander Rankin and his wife, smiling as they waited for the cloakroom to clear.

Gazing out in the lamplight as the schoolhouse filled, Jack scrutinized the faces confronting him, wondering if any among them might be of his own kin. When a dark-haired woman, who appeared to be in her mid-forties, entered the door, he instinctively matched her features with that of the photograph, but as she drew closer in the faint light he discounted his first impressions. Then glancing at the clock, Jack stood up, thanked the crowd for coming, and gave out the first hymn.

Amelia listened astutely as the meeting got underway. After the opening hymn and prayer, it was George who spoke first, his face clouding with intensity as he scanned his audience. "Imagine yourself living two thousand years ago within the stone walls of an ancient city," he proposed. "Your people have been at war for many months with another city state, and you're afraid. Afraid to venture outside the heavy wooden gates where, without warning, you might find yourself besieged and under attack, afraid to till your gardens and crops, afraid to harvest your vineyards and olive trees. Daily life has become miserable with hunger, confinement, uncertainty.

Gripping his Bible, George leaned forward. "But now," he continued, "the fighting men of your city have slipped out under the cover of last night's darkness to engage the enemy in battle a few miles hence. The safety and future of your entire clan and your neighbours hang in the balance. From the first light of dawn, you position yourself on the massive outer wall, shielding your eyes against the sun as you scrutinize the horizon. Suddenly, about mid-afternoon, you catch sight of a movement, a dark speck, a lonely figure. The solitary runner grows larger and larger as he sprints toward the city, and you abandon your post to dash down and greet him. Other haggard, anxious faces cluster at the gate seeking news of the battle's outcome. The messenger arrives, chest heaving, face blazing with fatigue, tunic saturated with sweat. 'Victory,' he gasps, 'has been won.'"

"At his words the knot of eager listeners breaks into jubilant exultation." George paused, permitting the listeners in the Belwood schoolhouse to react to the runner's report. "*Evangelion* was the Greek word for that kind of message," he explained. "Translated as 'gospel' in the Bible. And indeed, what Jack and I hope to share in these meetings is wonderful news as well: The victory has been won by Christ on Calvary's cross, releasing each of us from spiritual hunger, bondage, and fearful uncertainty."

George glanced down the aisle at Amelia, her demeanour one of rapt attention. "Why is this finished work on Calvary such marvelous news?" he challenged. "Because, before Christ came, diligent, God-fearing men and women had tried for thousands of years to live without sin. But without exception, they had failed. Jesus' message wouldn't have been good news if we'd been told that by living perfect lives we merit God's eternal favour. That's impossible for anyone, and it would've set us up only to have our hopes dashed! But the good news is that victory has *already* been won on Calvary's cross—a demonstration of God's undeniable love toward mankind. Our part is simply to accept in faith that incredible fact. And to live each day in that reality.

"But what if you stood at that ancient city gate and rejected the message?" Foreheads wrinkled as some in the schoolhouse stared at George. What further point was he making? "Because you couldn't believe, your daily life would remain unchanged. You would continue to live in hunger, bondage, and uncertainty, still bound by the old order." George glanced over rows of earnest faces. "May each of us here tonight, step beyond the limiting walls of our humanness with its suffocating traditions and accept the gift of the cross, in faith believing."

After the crowd had dispersed, Amelia squeezed onto the frosty leather seat between George and Jack. The flickering lights of the village fell away as the horse broke into a trot, dusting through the fallen leaves on the track towards Hunters' Hollow.

As the darkness closed around the buggy's single lantern, Amelia turned to George. "What a message of hope you brought us tonight," she exclaimed.

"I've never heard the likes of it before, and I can't wait to share it with Robert."

Softening the tension on the lines, George gave the horse its head. "Until four years ago, it was all a mystery to me too."

◦

Every Saturday afternoon the brothers cycled to Elora to spend Sunday with the saints. The church often ate dinner together, and George noticed that each woman set a covered dish in the kitchen before the meeting.

One Sunday during the meal, Jessie raised the subject of baptism. George explained why he and Jack and the friends in Puslinch had been rebaptized as adults and suggested the Elora friends consider the same.

"When should that be done?" Lyman asked.

George washed down his apple cobbler with a swallow of tea. "We feel a person should be baptized immediately after he decides to follow Christ.[12] If the weather permits, that is. But because it's so cold at this time of year, that's out of the question just now. Jack and I could be on hand early next summer if any of you wish to take that step."

After the meal was finished, Eddie motioned George outside to the woodshed. "I've been earning a pretty fair income," he confided. "And I'd like to contribute most of it to assist you and Jack."

"Thank you, Eddie. That's most generous." George's eyes met his. "But Jack and I've got all the money we can use for the present. However, I'm sure your concern's been prompted by God. Maybe He has something in mind other than your money. We should all be praying for more workers. In God's harvest field, there's not only a tremendous need for saints to help in the gathering of souls in their own districts, but also for some to travel farther afield."[13]

Eddie nodded thoughtfully as he and George made their way back to the house. "Certainly food for thought. I'll puzzle who might fit the bill."

After kicking off his boots on Lyman's stoop, George turned to face his friend. "Thanks again for your generous offer, Eddie. I'm certain you'll know what to do when the time is right."

◦

Eddie Summers always made it a point to stop at Hunters' Hollow when he called on Stevens' Dry Goods in Belwood or passed by on his way north. Sometimes he arranged with Amelia to come for supper and to stay overnight after the gospel meeting. Being on company business, he always paid Amelia the going rate for bed and breakfast. She objected because the brothers were so good to her and Robert, but Eddie did the right thing anyway.

Long before meeting George and Jack, Eddie had done a bit of informal preaching throughout Ontario as he traveled for his father. He had a habit of speaking to his customers about eternal things, and in his own way, he seemed fairly successful. People were charmed by his debonair looks and dynamic personality and could be persuaded to accept his point of view. But Eddie was often disappointed later when he would discover that after the first flush of enthusiasm, people often lost their zeal and drifted back to their old life. Much of what he had planted had withered and died.[14]

More than a year before the brothers had come to Elora, Eddie had reluctantly begun to acknowledge that his methods relied upon human persuasion. And that he, like many evangelists, was primarily a master of the quick catch. Eddie's listeners had heard nothing more than his natural voice. They had neither heard Jesus, nor felt His Spirit. Eddie recognized immediately that George and Jack were men of no ordinary stamp.

Since the two brothers had come along and Eddie had begun to hear Jesus speaking to his own heart, his old self-assured feeling was gone. Now when he shared a message in the Belwood gospel meeting, it was with a deepened sense of humility. He had become less confident in his own ability and more dependent on the Holy Spirit.

One night in a gospel meeting in Belwood, Jack again used the phrase *a gentleman Jesus* as part of his message. As Eddie sat listening, he remembered how much this phrase had offended Mr. Coffer and the other church elders in Elora. Only a few weeks ago, Eddie had taken out his diary and written about his own first reaction to this unusual expression:

> *At the time it sounded strange, irreverent, and repulsive to my Pharisee ears. Others felt the same way too. So much so that some took offence and rejected the meetings from that day on. Yet none of us could contradict the truth in that simple phrase, which, in the end, had a very healthy and corrective effect on me. My perception changed completely from the fictitious gentleman Jesus to the New Testament Jesus, whom the common people heard gladly. From the manger to the grave, He*

was one of the poorest and lowliest. God hides His truth from the wise and prudent and reveals it to those who, with childlike simplicity, are willing to identify with the lowly man of Galilee.[15] Looking back, I stand amazed at how little humility could be found in either my preaching or my home and social life. I tried to appear holy when, in fact, that was just a glossy veneer.

I now consider the use of this seemingly insignificant yet rather peculiar expression—a gentleman Jesus—to be of great import. Most people are unwilling to accept the distinction between their Jesus and the Jesus of the New Testament. The addressing of that issue, in itself, contains a test of spiritual character, because to admit its truth means to level all economic and social distinctions. Instead most folks conjure up a Jesus and a heaven of their own imagination and not those of the Bible. He is made to suit their own aspirations, and they see in Him only what they want to see. In effect they follow a powerless Jesus who has been made to reflect themselves. However, anyone who wants to be a disciple of Jesus of Nazareth, a poor, unsalaried, itinerant preacher, must be content to do things as He did them and not as the world does them.[16]

As Eddie heard Jack mention the phrase again here in Belwood, something stirred in him. Was he, too, being called to do things as Jesus did them, as a homeless preacher? At the Hunters' that evening, Eddie talked about the tremendous need for other communities to hear the gospel.

Listening to his friend, George recalled Jesus' concern when He saw the crowds, confused and helpless, like sheep without a shepherd. "The harvest is plentiful," Jesus had told His disciples, "but the workers are few. Ask the Lord of the harvest to send out workers into His harvest field."

The next day after a morning's work in the stable, Jack stamped the manure and straw off his soles on the way to the house for dinner. As he yanked his heavy boots off with the bootjack, he burst out chuckling.

"That Eddie," he said, "he could charm the skin off a snake. Did you notice his patent leather shoes with the buckles? They say clothes make the man, but there's a lot more to Eddie than his fine suit and onyx ring."

George grinned in agreement. "Yes, a *lot* more."

"Dinner's a little behind," Amelia apologized as the brothers padded into the kitchen in their thick wool socks.

George surveyed the table. "What can I do to help out?"

"You could mash the potatoes, if you like."

"Something for a second pair of hands?" Jack offered expectantly.

Amelia glanced around the kitchen. "I can't think of another thing until the roast comes out of the oven. Why don't you prop up your feet in the parlour, and I'll call you when it's ready to cut?"

Settling back into one of the Queen Anne chairs, Jack reached for an album of photographs sitting on a round walnut table. He found it intriguing to scan the pictorial record of Robert and Amelia's lives together. A picture of a bearded man holding a small baby was captioned "Robert and Grandpa Hunter." On another page, a gang of barn builders crouched on their hands and knees nailing cedar shingles on a steep barn roof. Underneath was the phrase "In Time for Winter, November 1883." A family of seven children stood in a stiff semicircle around their mother and father seated in chairs, hands clasped on knees. "The Hunter Family," it said. Jack flipped through the album, stopping here and there. On the left side of one page, a pair of lads with wide smiles and missing front teeth displayed a string of trout while a droopy-eared hound sprawled in the forefront. The picture, slid behind an oval cutout, was titled "Robert and Frederick with Laddie." On the other side two girls of about fourteen, arms around each other, smiled at the photographer from the back of a huge Clydesdale led by a young woman. Jack's eyes moved easily from face to face. Suddenly they stopped, staring at the second girl on the horse. Her radiant smile and dark eyes seemed familiar. Jack bent forward and squinted, tipping the album to catch the light. A sudden anticipatory shiver ran up his spine, and he felt the hair on his neck prickling as he stared at the handwritten caption "Amelia with Warmington Girls, Nettie and Miranda on Duchess—1869." Again, Jack studied the second face, absorbing its vibrancy emanating from the photograph. As he slumped back, a rush of heat engulfed his face and neck.

"The roast's ready," Amelia's cheerful voice sang out from the kitchen for the second time. Forcing himself to his feet, Jack fastened the clasp and returned the album to its place. Taking a moment to collect himself, he stumbled in a daze toward the kitchen.

"Jack! You look as if you've been dragged through a knothole," Amelia exclaimed when she saw him. "Are you under the weather?"

Jack's voice was uncharacteristically passive. "I'm a bit dizzy. Maybe I'm coming down with the blind staggers," he mumbled. "If it's all right, I'll go upstairs and stretch out. Please, just go ahead and eat without me."

With a quizzical expression George picked up the carving knife. "There's been something on Jack's mind," he confided to Amelia. "I've sensed it for a while—something that catches up with him once in so long."

"It's more likely those sausages at breakfast are coming back on him," Amelia rejoined briskly. "I'll offer him a dose of sarsaparilla if he's not right before bedtime."

Back in his room, Jack crouched down and drew the worn photograph of his mother out of his travel bag. In the searching November sunlight that played over the room, he pondered it again. Turning it over, he saw the mysterious initials M.S.W. leap off the lower right corner. "Miranda," he whispered softly. "Miranda Warmington."

Twenty-One

THE HOME VISIT
Winter 1902

As the brothers pitched straw down from the mow into the Hunters' stable, hidden from the low January sun, George suddenly stopped to lean on his fork. "Do you realize it's only been six months since we left Puslinch?" he asked. "With everything that's happened and all the new friends we've made, it certainly seems a lot longer."

Jack's cheeks broadened into a sheepish smile. "I could get a bit homesick if I dwelled on it," he confessed. "What would you think of going home for a visit next week?"

George grinned. "That's exactly what I was thinking. Before long we'll want to move on again. Maybe to Orangeville. It might be a good idea to visit now before we get much farther away."

Although the train whistled into Belwood each morning, the brothers felt it would be better to save the eighteen-cent fares and make the journey on foot. After the Friday evening meeting, they announced that there would be no gospel meetings the following week, but that they would resume the week after. Amelia packed them a lunch, and the two men set out Saturday morning through the eerie darkness of a winter dawn. With the heavy snow on the road, George and Jack thought the trip would take about ten hours.

After stopping at noon for a spicy bowl of beef tongue soup at the Ennotville inn, the men started out again, their energy restored. They had only tramped a mile or so when a faded black cutter, loaded with pelts, overtook them. The pendulous-jowled driver, his ears jammed under a muskrat cap, pulled up alongside. "You chaps care for a lift into town? There's no point in hoofin' it when I've got a smidgen of space."

"Best offer we've had all day," Jack beamed as he scrambled in. "Our boots seem to have gathered some lead since we struck out this morning."

"The furrier on Quebec Street pays a premium for skins as prime as these," the trapper divulged as he jostled a stack of raccoon and fox furs to one side. "Y' know, no buckshot holes or rips from hounds' teeth."

George winced at the words. "I'll squeeze in behind the seat," he offered, nestling himself against the heap of raw pelts. Facing backwards, he watched laneways and fence posts melt into the distance as the runners sliced through the snow. Pulling his mitts off, George ran a tentative finger over the stiff oily leather, his nose wrinkling at the pungent musk permeating his coat and beard. After a while, he hitched himself forward on one elbow and listened to Jack and the trapper swapping yarns. When the horse finally drew up in front of the Guelph Free Library on Norfolk Street, the two men thanked their host and parted with a hearty handshake.

It was dark again by the time they plodded up the laneway toward the beckoning lights that shone from the windows of Wood Creek Farm. Inside at the stove, Priscilla heard, or thought she heard, the stomping of boots and the shaking of coats in the woodshed.

When she opened the kitchen door, the brothers' weary faces were cast in the soft kerosene glow. "George! Jack! Of all people. What are *you* doing home?" Priscilla exclaimed. "Is something wrong?"

"Not a thing," Jack chuckled. "We just popped by for a spot o' tea," he added, mimicking Morgan's clipped Liverpudlian accent.

Priscilla's face brightened. "Well, don't just stand there, come on inside," she said, wrapping her arms around George first and then Jack.

Over her shoulder Alistair and Timothy could be seen jumping up from the table, their eyes shining with surprise. Alistair threw an arm across each man's shoulders while Timothy clapped them on the back. As they pulled up chairs, Priscilla fetched extra plates from the sideboard.

"You're in the nick of time. Supper's just been lifted," Alistair said, ladling each of them a generous dollop of mashed potatoes and beef stew.

After the conversation had slackened and the men's appetites had been satiated, Priscilla got up and poured a fresh pot of tea. "Any news of Laura lately?" she asked as she strained the tea leaves.

Gripping his saucer, George held Priscilla's gaze. "She's really taken a shine to the children in Mildmay." He stirred thick cream into his tea, a smile playing on his lips. "And needless to say, they just love her." George took a tentative sip. "But she's missing you all here…"

"Do you suppose we'll see her around the end of June?"

George pursed his lips. "It's possible she'll stop here on her way to Stratford. She's the maid of honour for one of her younger sisters in July."

Phoebe, sitting opposite, brightened. "Maybe she'll invite me again," she said hopefully. "I've been to a couple of weddings. But neither of them elegant affairs, like a doctor's daughter will have. She'll likely have a lacy gown with a train. And a reception in their garden with a band playing."

Jack winked across the table. "So Phoebe, any up-and-coming lads along the concession?"

"Along the concession nothing," Timothy cut in. "She's drawn a bead on our Mr. Gillespie. Problem is, he doesn't know he's in her sights yet."

Phoebe's face turned scarlet as she glared at Timothy. "You've got less facts than a goose has sense when it comes to that," she sputtered.

Timothy folded his arms and grinned. "Aunt Maggie says you catch a man by his ankles and hang on with your teeth."

Alistair cleared his throat, signaling an end to the sparring. "I'm eager to hear about Belwood," he interjected. "How's Robert Hunter getting on?"

George and Jack both answered at once and then instantly stopped and deferred with a laugh to the other. The conversation took on more serious tones as the men visited with nods and gestures interrupted by an occasional comment from Phoebe as she grated carrots and potatoes for a suet pudding. On a layer of newspaper at the other end of the table, Priscilla cleaned a fat goose for the Sunday dinner. Before long the soothing heat of the stove worked its magic, and George and Jack began to yawn and rub their eyes, fiery with fatigue.

When Priscilla saw their eyelids drooping, she handed each of them a stone pig filled with scalding water to warm the flannels. "Up you go now," she ordered in a tone of finality.

As George climbed the familiar stairs to the green attic bedroom, he felt dizzy with all the good memories, and he looked forward to the smell of Priscilla's fresh bread in the morning. This was so much like coming home, but still, he wanted to visit his parents and his sister and brothers. Except for a single letter from Lizzie, he hadn't seen or heard from any of them since last summer. And crush the thought as he would, George both feared and longed to walk the laneway of his own farm and witness the changes— no doubt good ones—that Randall Pillman had made.

Nearly thirty chairs had to be set up the next morning for the Sunday meeting. Although the Puslinch church had written to George and Jack every time someone was added to their number, the brothers were still surprised to see the size of the gathering firsthand. The folks were delighted to find George and Jack standing in the kitchen when they arrived. They flung their arms around the brothers and hugged them tightly.

Alice was the first of the Jones family to catch a glimpse of George when she bustled in through the kitchen door. Still bundled in her heavy coat, she dropped her daughter's hand and dashed over, drawing him into an energetic hug. "George, I can't believe it," she spouted. "Home from the far corners of the earth."

As George looked into her robust face, ablaze with cold and exhilaration, he felt her arms tighten against his ribs. "It's wonderful to be back," he responded as she released him like a mother bear its cub.

In between these outbursts of affection, Alistair took care to introduce the brothers to each of the newer members. "I'd like you to meet Edgar and Jean," he said when George and Jack had caught their breath. "They've been coming along since September."

Edgar Ritchie, a tall man with ginger whiskers, stepped forward and gripped George's hand. "I'm pleased to meet you face-to-face," he said respectfully. "Jean and I've heard a heap of good things about you men."

All the friends stayed for dinner together. Each family supplied what they could, bringing a hot dish, some vegetables, or something sweet. Alistair carved the goose with a flourish, carefully placing the giblets—the gizzard, heart, and liver—at one end of the large oval platter. Jean Ritchie had brought along a dish of honeyed parsnips and a gleaming loaf of bread while Edgar sheepishly produced some of his fudge, lumpy with walnuts.

As George watched everyone waiting patiently, he was reminded of a specific problem in the early church. Before all of the saints could make their way to the meeting in Corinth, many of the people had started to eat.[1] A few even became drunk. Meanwhile, the poorer brothers and sisters who couldn't get there early enough remained hungry—all because a few lacked genuine love. Paul had told the gluttons to eat at home if all they wanted to do was to race ahead for the satisfaction of their own stomachs. To Paul, the lack of consideration was intolerable: "Don't you have homes where you can eat and drink?" he had asked. "Do you despise the church of God? Do you want to embarrass the ones who don't have anything?"

Under normal circumstances, the common meal was a lovely New Testament custom where heart-to-heart fellowship could take place over the table. For the desperately poor among the Mediterranean saints, it was, perhaps, the only substantial meal of their week. As George reflected on that scene, he appreciated even more the maturity of the saints at Wood Creek Farm. He knew firsthand of their practical love for others. And he felt grateful that he and Jack could be home with them for a few days.

After eating, some retired to the parlour and sang hymns while others sat around Priscilla's kitchen table and talked. Everybody was eager to get news of the church in Elora and the mission in Belwood. Like a family, they wanted to hear about their brothers and sisters who couldn't be with them. Jack filled them in with ease, never short of interesting anecdotes.

"You'd like that Jimmy Liddle," Jack was telling Timothy and Malachi. "He's a rascal, just like you were at that age, Timothy."

"Maybe that makes four of us," Timothy shot back with a grin.

Jack nodded affably. "After meeting one Sunday, Jimmy sat beside me at dinner. He leaned toward me. 'Uncle Jack,' he said very seriously, 'do cows go to heaven?'" Jack looked into Malachi and Timothy's quizzical faces. "'No, Jimmy,' I said, 'heaven's just for people, as far's we know.' I had just taken a swallow of water when he looked up with a perfectly straight face. 'Oh,' he said, 'I heard heaven was a place of *udder* delight, and I thought there'd be some cows there.' Well, when he said that I started to choke. I couldn't hold back and the water sprayed all over Mrs. Applebee."

Timothy rocked back on his chair legs and held his sides while Malachi slapped his knees, his face crimson with laughter.

"When you see Jimmy, ask him why it's so noisy in a barn," Timothy suggested.

Jack quirked his eyebrows. "And the answer...?"

"Because the cows all have horns."

When Jack finished chuckling, he wiped his eyes. "So cows from Quebec would have French horns, would they?" He reached down to loosen his laces. "I've one for you. How tall was the shortest man in the Bible?"

Flummoxed, Malachi and Timothy shook their heads.

Jack tugged up his pant leg to expose the top of one boot. "Bildad. It says he was a shoe height."[2]

"I'll have to remember that one," Malachi laughed as little Madeleine tore through the kitchen, her unbraided hair a golden torrent behind her.

The children romped with each other like puppies from different litters while their parents visited. All week they looked forward to joining their playmates on Sundays. The girls, with their long dresses and pinafores, liked to help the women at dinnertime by filling the water glasses or by putting the silverware beside each plate. They often brought along their dolls and played house in one of the bedrooms during the afternoon.

Sometimes the older children would go out after dinner to play hide-and-go-seek in the barn. Or, in the thick of winter, they might shovel the snow off Alistair's pond and play hockey, using crooked branches for sticks and a piece of frozen horse manure for a puck. When the snow was crusty, they would drag the two old bobsleds out of the driving shed and scramble to the top of a steep hill to see who could coast the farthest.

Emily soothed her crippled leg beside the warm stove while she chatted with Ashleigh Duffield, Phoebe's former teacher. "Stephen and I were wondering if *the friends* could all come to our house for a hymn sing on Saturday," she announced.

As Jack listened to various conversations throughout the afternoon, these two words—the friends—caught his ear several times. "Emily," he asked, "what do you mean by *the* friends? The word 'the' makes it sound like a distinctive group. Like high society," he added with a wink.

Emily laughed. "You've got a sharp ear, Jack. We talked about that term a few weeks ago. Do you remember Jesus telling His disciples that He no longer called them servants, but friends?"[3]

Jack nodded. "I suppose I do."

Emily's sweet, thoughtful expression and pale complexion radiated enthusiasm. "The friends of Christ are a special little company indeed. And I'm thrilled to be part of this humblest, highest society that I know of."[4]

"Because Christians are *the friends* of Christ," Ashleigh interposed, "they're also friends of each other. And they love each other's company," she added as she motioned in the direction of the kitchen table where George was chatting with Edgar Ritchie and his wife, Jean.

"Edgar," George was asking, "how did you hear about this little church at Wood Creek Farm?"

Edgar met George's eyes. "I was part of the same beef ring as Bill Jones," he began. "Every Friday night, a different person brought an animal to be slaughtered at our farm. Sometimes Bill helped with the butchering." Edgar went on to explain that on Saturday mornings the fresh meat was delivered to each of the eighteen men who were part of the ring. "The ladies sewed bags made from old sugar sacks, and we put a roast, a steak, and a boiling piece in each one. That way we had fresh meat every week."

Priscilla laid aside her tea towel and pulled a chair up beside George. "Can I join you folks?" she asked.

"Anytime," Edgar said with a smile. Then, turning back to George, he continued his story. "I saw how conscientious and honest Bill was in the way he divvied up the meat. One time in particular, I noticed that he put a slightly smaller piece in his own bag. I didn't say anything, but after that I watched whenever Bill was butchering. Although the pieces were cut as closely as possible to the same weight, if there was any slight discrepancy, Bill always dropped the smaller portion into his own bag when he thought no one was looking. I wondered what kind of person would do that." Edgar frowned slightly and looked directly at George. "Some men might take the smaller piece, but they'd always drop a remark to make sure you knew it.

"A few weeks later when the two of us were working alone, Bill made a comment and right then, I knew that he was living for something beyond this world." Edgar took his wife's hand and smiled. "Shortly afterward, he invited Jean and me to come along one Thursday evening."

Edgar leaned forward and his voice dropped a little. "But it hasn't been an easy row to hoe. After we yielded our hearts to Jesus, we were faced with a lot of opposition from Jean's family."

Jean spoke up. "When Edgar and I left the old church, my sisters were downright bitter. They wouldn't speak to us anymore." She forced a smile. "In fact, they still refuse to have anything to do with us." She looked as if she might cry and stopped for a moment to collect herself. "Just knowing that they're celebrating a birthday, Thanksgiving, or a family reunion and that Edgar and I are being deliberately excluded is really painful."

Edgar squeezed his wife's hand tighter. "It's all been tremendously hard for Jean to bear."

Jean wiped her eyes. "It wasn't as if we said much about our new faith," she lamented. "But my sisters are stiff and traditional, and the changes in our lives obviously annoy them. Maybe because we spend less time with the old group we mingled with for years."

"Perhaps they realize we left the old church because we found it to be dust and ashes in our mouths," Edgar asserted. "And Jean's sisters just can't loosen their grip."

"I guess we've all experienced rejection of some sort for choosing to follow Jesus," George sympathized. "There's a price for everything."

Edgar nodded. "Yes, I know. Some people have come here for a few Thursday evenings and seemed to enjoy it," he said. "But when the pressure and ridicule start to mount from their family and friends, they stop coming." He paused, twisting a strand in his thick whiskers. "One man in our beef ring came for quite a while. He talked a lot about the meetings, but then he suddenly quit coming. I heard later that two of his cousins had teased him about being the deacon at Wood Creek Farm. I feel sorry that some aren't strong enough, that they turn away when they begin to see the cost of discipleship." Edgar's eyes were shining, and it seemed clear to both George and Priscilla that he was settled and happy in his own convictions.

Priscilla beamed at the couple. "It's a blessing to have you among us," she said, putting one arm around Jean.

Jean smiled in response. "Our troubles just make us appreciate the friends even more." Then she noticed Edgar hauling out his pocket watch. "Anyway, it looks as if my man's ready to head for home," she added.

"But not before you take your hot bricks," Priscilla insisted, deftly extracting them from the warming oven and wrapping them in paper.

Late in the January afternoon as Edgar and Jean drove home, their sleigh bells rang out across the snowy fields, suffused now by the pink glow of sunset. With wind-ruddy cheeks, Edgar turned to his wife. "I always wondered what George and Jack would be like," he said. "They're very different men than I had expected."

Drawing her attention back from the sheen of the encrusted countryside, Jean shifted on the cold seat. "Somehow I'd placed them on a pedestal, making them kind of unapproachable," she reflected. "But now that I've met them, I feel only the warmth and closeness of a pair of brothers."

"I presumed they might think themselves better than the rest of us who haven't left our homes," Edgar confided. "But their manner and humility make it clear there's no second-class citizens in this family of God."

Jean tightened her scarf around her face and neck. "I remember Alistair telling us that this fellowship is different—that it's a brotherhood of equals,"[5] she added. "He said there's no clergy, no laity, no hierarchy, no regulations, no human control."

Edgar nodded. "But until today I could hardly believe it was true." He tightened the lines as the horse and cutter approached their own laneway. "Alistair also said the freedom from rules is not to make our journey easier, it's to make us rely more on the *direct* influence of the Holy Spirit. To make us struggle to feel God's presence. He said rules and regulations only divide people. Those who conform become self-righteous, and those who don't become rebellious."

Jean smiled and patted her husband's knee as they drew up at the house. "I'll get the fire stirred up while you unharness the horse."

"It was nice to meet Edgar and Jean today," Jack said as he traveled home with his old friends Dugan and Hilda MacGladry and their little two-year-old, Samuel. "Do we pass their place on the way?"

"No," Dugan replied. "They live out in the other direction, south of Bill and Alice."

Jack nodded, changing the subject. "I'm looking forward to being with the three of you tonight. It's a long time since I've been in Eden Mills. I want to go on to my parents' in the morning, but if it's all right I might come back for an hour or two and thumb through your history books."

"Some things never change," Dugan laughed. "Come over anytime."

Jack spent his evening with Hilda and Dugan, catching up on news of old friends and neighbours. As they talked, little Samuel played among his blocks on the floor, occasionally bringing something to show his father.

"Look, Pappy," Samuel said, patting his chubby hand on Dugan's knee. He pointed to the cat stretched in front of the cookstove. "Kitty's sleeping." Samuel's cloud of reddish curls bounced as he walked closer. When he felt the heat radiating from the stove, he turned to his mother. "Stove hot." He held out his dimpled hands and sucked in his breath.

"There are no flies on him," Jack quipped. "He's a real talker, isn't he?" He opened a book and touched a picture. "What's this, Samuel?"

The little boy craned his neck to see in the dim light. "Spiderweb."

"It's impressive to see how quickly children absorb information," Jack remarked. "Even when they're knee high to a grasshopper."

Hilda settled back in her chair. "Every day his mind grows by leaps and bounds. I love to watch him meandering around the yard behind Dugan, taking in everything. He's like a little sponge." Her face glowed with a mother's pride. "I just don't know where he gets it."

Jack laughed. "Why, from watching and listening to the pair of you. And if you were speaking Chinese, he'd learn that as easily as English."

"I've heard Chinese is pretty complicated," Dugan cut in. "It would be a lot harder for him to learn that."

Leaning back in his chair, Jack crossed his legs. "I doubt he'd have to exert any more effort than he's doing now. That's how the gospel works."

Hilda raised her eyebrows. "It is?"

"Sure," Jack said. "If we watch, listen, and spend time with our Father and walk with Him, we'll mature and learn everything we need. Studious efforts may very well harm rather than help the process.[6] Unless we become like a little child, we'll never get into the kingdom of heaven.[7] I've particularly noticed that trait in our new friends in Elora. Little by little the wisdom and character of Christ is being formed in them.

"The path of God's children is like the first gleam of dawn," Jack concluded. "It shines brighter and brighter until the full light of day."[8] Subconsciously he placed his boots flat on the linoleum. "The Father's revelation of a living Christ to the individual heart is the solid rock on which His church is built.[9] The more we practise, the more we're given."

Dugan stood up to make a cup of tea. "Jack, you can get bread out of a stone," he exclaimed.

"I think we're all like that to some extent," Jack demurred. "A Christian sees God in all of creation. It declares His character and power. That's why there's no excuse for not acknowledging Him."[10]

After spending Sunday night with Stephen and Emily, George awoke to find ice in the bottom of his cup on the dresser. He shivered as he swung out of bed, fingers of frigid air clutching at him. His bare feet danced on the cold floor while he yanked on his socks. His breath condensed as he scratched a hole in the ice particles to peer out through the window. A crystalline layer of frost shrouded the outside world like plumes of white eiderdown. After breakfast the three friends lingered beside the fire and enjoyed a steaming pot of black tea as they discussed George's work and the beauty of the homeless ministry.

Stephen looked up at the kitchen clock and rose reluctantly. "I'm afraid I have to repair a set of sleigh runners in a few minutes." He beckoned to George. "You've a lot of visiting to do, George. Why don't you take our Prince for the week? He'll help you get around."

"Are you sure you won't be needing the horse yourself?"

"Yes, I'm sure. We can borrow Bill's or Alistair's if need be."

After bundling up, the two men stepped outside. The mercury in the thermometer had plunged to twenty-four degrees below zero, and the snow crunched crisply under foot as they walked to the blacksmith shop to saddle up.

George planned to visit his parents and siblings as well as several of the saints before the Thursday evening meeting. As he rode with a heavy woolen scarf wrapped around his face, he was amazed at the excitement he felt building when he thought of being in the familiar surroundings of home again. But a sense of apprehensiveness tempered his exhilaration when he remembered his dad's rancour during his last visit. George rehearsed the things that he could share comfortably with his family.

With his head bent forward to protect his eyes and forehead from the biting air, George reflected on Edgar and Jean's story. Being disowned was not uncommon, for others of the friends, including George himself, had encountered varying degrees of rejection for choosing the simple way of Jesus. But having once tasted the sweetness of an intimate friendship with Jesus, there was no turning back, and the love and support of the saints was edifying. The special empathy that George felt for Jean and Edgar was almost palpable as he rode toward his own uncertain reception.

"This new life in Christ is not for people lacking the conviction of His Spirit," George declared under his breath. He remembered Jesus asking the disciples, "Do you also want to go away?" In a voice made strong and confident by his solitude on the horse, George repeated Peter's response aloud: "Lord, to whom shall we go? *You* have the words of eternal life."[11]

Sharp crests of unmarked snow angled across his parents' laneway. Footprints where George's brother, Cyril, and his father had waded back and forth between the house and the barn were the only signs of life. An almost vertical column of smoke rose from the chimney, brick red against the cobalt blue of the winter sky. After finding a stall in the well-known stable, George followed the path to the house. He could see his mother at the window, beaming as he approached. Throwing the door open as he bounded up the steps, she rushed outside in her slippers to hug him.

"George, you're home in one piece!" she cried. "I'm so glad to see you safe and sound." Finally she released him, wiping her eyes with the corners of her apron.

Getting up from the rocking chair, his father halted a moment and then pronounced in a tone less ironic than his words implied, "Well, well. So the prodigal's finally home. Winter storms and lean granaries, I imagine."

Cyril came down from upstairs when he heard George's voice in the kitchen. When Miss Orangey Morangey trotted from her bed behind the cookstove to spring purring into his lap, George smiled and braced his knees together to form a nest for her to curl up in. Drawing in a deep breath, he savoured the familiar aroma as he looked up at his mother, absorbing the care in her eyes. "Molasses and beans. I haven't had even a whiff of that since I left home. I loved that smell when I opened the door after school on a frosty evening," he acknowledged. Eyeing his father, he took another breath and asked about the farm, the cattle, and his family's health. Even his father's near silence couldn't dampen George's spirits as he told them later of all that he had seen and all that God had done in the last few months.

His father stared at the floor while George spoke about his time away, but he didn't leave the room or grumble. There also seemed to be less hostility in his eyes. George could see that and felt encouraged, even though he knew his dad was still disgusted that he had sold his farm.

Cyril, who had not been home during George's last visit, interrupted with some questions of his own—searching ones that showed Cyril's curiosity about his brother's life and faith.

After dinner the four sat around the wood stove in the searing heat, their conversation drifting to the neighbours and the happenings in the district. Apparently Jake Pillman had his eye on the sandy knoll that overlooked the Arkell plain. As the afternoon wore on toward supper, Cyril whittled a duck decoy from a cedar log while George helped his mother tear a basketful of strips for a rag rug. That evening his father retired early, but George's mother and Cyril stayed up and talked with George into the wee hours.

The next morning after swallowing the last of his oatmeal, George's father raised his bowl and drank the extra cream. His tea rattled noisily down his throat before he shoved his chair back from the head of the table. "It's the first open day for a spell, and we've got a pile of manure to spread." He shot a barbed look at Cyril, still lounging, his hands in his pockets.

"Thanks for having me overnight, Dad," George said. "There's no place quite like home. I'm off to Arthur and Olga's, then to see Lizzie." His father nodded and reached for his smock without comment.

After the door had slammed shut, George turned to his mother and Cyril. "Thanks for the good visit last night," he said. "I need to get on the road, but I want you to know that I'd be over the moon if you cared to join me at the Stanhopes' on Thursday evening."

Through the frosted window, Cyril studied his father's dark receding form. "Well, I'll see," he said. "But no promises."

After saying goodbye, George deliberately rode past his old farm on the way to Guelph. He pulled Stephen's horse up at the end of the laneway and gazed with painful ambivalence at the house to which he had hoped to take Laura as his bride. Snow sparkled on the steep roof and the windows reflected diamonds in the morning sunshine. He heard the sharp echo of a door slamming and watched a distant figure heading for the barn that was no longer his. But when Prince shook his black mane and snorted jets of steam into the cold air, George turned resolutely away.

George then went to visit his older brother, Arthur, and his sister-in-law, Olga. It was hard to believe how much his only nephew and niece had stretched up. While he was there, his sister, Lizzie, came over too. It felt good to be together again and the four spent Tuesday afternoon and evening laughing and catching up. The following day George moved from place to place, visiting each of the saints before he returned to Wood Creek Farm on Thursday morning.

Alistair and Timothy were hauling blocks of ice from the pond to the ice house when George arrived. Alistair, looking a little flushed, seemed uncharacteristically solemn as the men worked together in the forenoon.

After they finished eating dinner, Timothy turned to George. "We're running low on shavings and sawdust," he said. "I'm taking the team to the lumberyard for more. Going to come along?"

Something in Timothy's voice made George look sharply in the young man's direction. This was more than a casual request. "Sure," he replied. "I'd be happy to ride along."

They left Alistair shoveling sawdust around the blocks of ice as they set out on the sleigh. On either side of the road, the split rail fences had caused the snow to drift heavily in certain places. As teams and cutters had crossed the dense ridges, they had gouged pitch holes that grew wider and deeper with every passage. If the holes were severe enough, they could damage a cutter, particularly if the horse was excitable and the cutter ran up on his heels. In a couple of spots, Timothy steered the team off the road as they traveled through a field to avoid a series of heavy drifts.

They had just come back onto the road from one of these detours when Timothy broke his silence and revealed his motive for wanting to spend time with George. "George, I wanted to tell you that I feel God calling me into the ministry." He paused, but George stared ahead awestruck. "Just like you and Jack," Timothy continued. "Nobody else knows yet but my folks. I'm planning to tell the church on Sunday."

"That's splendid news, Timothy," George exclaimed as the team breasted a soft swell of snow angling down from the corner of a rail fence.

George's mind flashed back to that summer evening nearly two years before when he had shared the same message with Alistair. He recalled the conviction of a force pulling him, something he couldn't quite understand or describe, but something he knew he had to trust. When George remembered his own reactions, he thought of Alistair. That's why he had seemed so reflective when they had left him tramping sawdust. Timothy was young and his life offered many prospects. No doubt when Alistair slowed down, he intended to hand his well-established farm to his only son. Like Alistair, George instinctively drew back in the face of such a sacrificial commitment, but also like Alistair, he felt convinced that this was the Holy Spirit leading.

As the farms began to be interspersed with stone houses and the spires of the city rose to greet them, Timothy spoke again. "When I was in school, I always planned to be what Aunt Maggie calls 'a man of the cloth.' But after we received the gospel in its simplicity, I began to feel that studying divinity would be a way of training my mind to discuss theological matters, not a way of learning to let God lead. God's way is to have people experience Jesus for themselves and to put His love in their hearts. Only then will they have something genuine to give."

George smiled. "Mal used to say that the heart of us is the part of us that makes us acceptable to God."[12]

Timothy turned to George. "What do you suppose a man who lives by revelation from God feels he can gain by taking training from other men at a religious institution?" When the heavy black Percherons broke into a trot on the hill leading down to the bridge, Timothy drew on the leather lines. As the team settled back against the breeching, he continued. "God often prepared His true servants by being alone with them, like Moses on the far side of the desert and Paul in Arabia for three years. So I promised myself to walk with Jesus for three years before going further. Even now I don't feel capable, but I hear Him calling and I must begin somewhere. What do you think I should do next?"

George sat without answering for so long that Timothy looked over to see if he had heard him. "Well, Timothy," he said eventually, "we'll both need to pray about what you should do." There was another long pause. "How do your folks feel about this?"

"They think it's wonderful." Timothy hesitated. "But even so, it's very hard for them to see me go. There's the farm and Grandpa's wish that it pass down the generations and all..."

"I can understand that." George stared off into the distance. "I'd like to talk to Jack about it," he said reflectively. Then he smiled. "But it would seem just fine to me if you wish to join us in Belwood." He leaned over and put his arm on the younger man's shoulder. Words could not add to the spiritual bond that embraced them equally as they rode in silent peace.

Little more was said as they loaded the sawdust and shavings into the sleigh. But on the way home, Timothy, filled with a young man's eagerness, began to speak again. "The apostle Paul studied at the feet of Gamaliel, a doctor of the law and the most renowned professor of his time.[13] But that didn't prepare him for the ministry. Because the gospel he preached wasn't based on human reasoning, he needed a direct revelation from Christ. Nothing from other men. In fact, when Paul first heard God's call, he didn't talk it over with anyone—including the other apostles. Instead, he went immediately to Arabia. Then after three years, he finally went to visit Peter and James in Jerusalem for a few days."[14]

George's blue eyes twinkled. "Imagine if the church world adopted such a revolutionary policy today."

"It'd fall apart," Timothy said with the quick untempered confidence of youth. "Religious colleges would go bankrupt without tuition fees."

"Isn't each college run by a particular church?" George asked.

"Yes," Timothy said. "That's why I'm suspicious that they're designed to produce denominationalists, each according to its own kind."[15]

"You're likely right," George conceded. "But it never hurts to be open-minded enough to consider someone else's heritage and point of view."

Timothy's voice softened. "Sorry I got on my high horse there for a minute. Although I eventually decided not to go to college, something rankled when Reverend Smithers threatened to cut off that possibility if I left Saint Patrick's. That goes to show I haven't truly forgiven the man. I'd best say goodbye to him before I leave Puslinch."

George grabbed for the sleigh box as the runners lurched on the uneven snow. "I've found that for me religion seems to work against the simple life of faith…but I can only speak for myself. I wouldn't criticize anybody in his walk with God. Each man must stand or fall to his own master."[16]

For nearly an hour as the team navigated pitch holes and detours along the Downey Road, the two men continued deep in conversation, mulling over Timothy's convictions. Several times the road deteriorated, forcing Timothy to halt the big team and then, after a few minutes, start out again. Nervous of losing their footing on the slippery shoulder of the hard-packed track, one horse or the other would crowd to the centre, jostling its mate into the same precarious situation. Their constant pushing against each other made the trek laborious.

"Old Jordie's boys need to get out and cut this stretch of snow down with the disk a bit," Timothy muttered. "Otherwise some horse's going to fall and twist a leg."

George nodded. "Once they start crowding, it's a pretty tough go. Three years ago I had a bay mare that got down in the harness. It was an awful mess to get her untangled and back on her feet again." He peered over the edge of the sleigh. "Looks like the track's built up a good two feet."

Occasionally another driver would appear in the distance, a black form tracing a tedious line through the arctic landscape. As they met, Timothy and George hailed each neighbour and eased down into the soft snow, making room for the approaching team to pass safely.

At length the load of sawdust turned in at the lane of Wood Creek Farm. "I'd be ready to join you and Jack in a month's time," Timothy said earnestly, "but first I'll need to say goodbye to Aunt Maggie. She deserves to know…I remember her saying, 'Be sure to live up to what you were taught.' Maybe *she* has to learn that a fellow needs to live *beyond* what he's been taught." When the team pulled up in front of the ice house, George discerned the lines of strain on Alistair's face as he hurried out, scoop shovel in hand, to unload the mound of shavings.

~∽~

That night before they went to sleep, Alistair and Priscilla thrashed over Timothy's decision for the third night in a row. "Do you remember the July night when Timothy was born?" Priscilla asked. "Your pa was still alive then, striding up and down the kitchen while he waited, and finally he bounded up the stairs before the wee mite was barely dried and dressed. He took Timothy up in his big hands. 'Another man for the farm,' he said."

Alistair nodded wearily. "Our whole future's been changed in a single stroke," he lamented. "I'd always pictured Timothy taking over this place when you and I got up in years. And bringing a wife here when the time was right. Some wholesome, sensible girl who would take a hold and work right along beside him."

"And raise us a family of grandchildren…" Priscilla rejoined with a sigh that caught in her throat. "I pictured that too. It's part of being a mother, I suppose." She hesitated, absently tracing the outline of the quilt design with her index finger. "But I'm not surprised at the way things are working out. Even as a boy, Timothy was softhearted and concerned about others. Do you remember when he was just six? Some roughneck at school was going to beat up little Ronny Middleton. He was frightened and crying. Our Timothy stepped in and said, 'If you feel like you need to punch somebody, then hit me.'"

The darkness seemed to hang so heavy that Alistair felt robbed of air. "Yes, I remember," he managed to say. "But now his concern for others is going to take him away from home and from us."

"Only tender, softhearted people will ever be in heaven," Priscilla whispered as she reached out to soothe him, sensing his need.

Alistair felt the warmth of her palms on his shoulder blades. The pounding of his heart subsided and the fountain within him turned to tears. He turned face downward into the pillow, as men do, while the emotion drained from his eyes.

After a few minutes Priscilla slipped her hand under his cheek and eased his head toward her. His face appeared over the quilt, eyes hollow, like a woodcut illustration in a book. When he spoke, his voice was hoarse. "I'm mindful of the Father's grief. What He must have felt as He watched His Son accept the cross, measuring the separation it would bring."

There was a quiet but unwavering resignation in Priscilla's voice. "Yes, I know. Nevertheless, it's not what we will, but what He wills."[17] Priscilla rolled onto her back and began to sing gently.

> Dear Jesus, as Thou wilt:
> Oh may Thy will be mine!
> Each shifting changing future scene
> To Thee I would resign.

> Through sorrow or through joy,
> Conduct me as Thine own
> And help me still to say to Thee:
> "My Lord, Thy will be done."[18]

The cloud passed as Priscilla's voice filled the room and silver moonlight began to stream through the window panes. Alistair lay in silence, absorbing the words. When he finally turned back into the soft light, he caught a glimpse of the tiny mole on Priscilla's cheek, of the glistening in her almond eyes.

"I'm fortunate to have you as my wife," he whispered as his fingers played over her face, "especially at a hard time like this." He paused. "But still I wonder if a father can ever truly come to grips with his only son being far away from the home place..."

Priscilla stared out into the night sky. "This gives us another opportunity to enter the narrow gate," she said at last.

Alistair's hand hesitated. "I don't understand."

"Well," she said, raising up on her right elbow, "it's natural to travel through life using our own ideas and hard work to get along the best way we can. Many hurry along the broad road of reason. But rarely do we turn aside to seek out that obscure gate beyond which stretches the sublime path of complete faith. I want to be among that tiny band of pilgrims who trust God with each detail, each step along life's journey. The narrow way isn't about folks meeting here on Sundays. Or about young men like Timothy going into the work. It's about placing every aspect of our existence into God's hand."

Alistair sighed, wrapping his arms around Priscilla. "You're absolutely right, my dear. Please pray that once again I can step through the gate seldom found."

Twenty-Two

SETTLEMENT OF BELWOOD
Late Winter 1902

Each evening of the winter mission in Belwood, Amelia Hunter would step nimbly into the waiting cutter for George and Jack to take her along to the meeting. As the runners broke free and the horse pulled away, the three would return Robert's wistful wave from the upstairs window. They had all been elated when Doc Pipgrass had finally told Robert, after being bedfast for months, that he could take a few steps each day. Amelia had immediately baked a maple cake to celebrate the event. Before marrying into the Hunter clan, Amelia had taught at the local school and still kept in touch with many friends and former students. She told them about the kindness and generosity of the men and all the extra work they had taken on. This strange news of two preachers looking after Robert Hunter's farm spread like a rumour on a hired man's tongue, and curiosity brought some to the gospel meetings who otherwise might well have avoided them. But one of the people who did not attend was the minister of the Belwood Methodist Church, Reverend Walter Merrick.

One brisk morning in January brought stinging flakes of snow on the east wind. A lanky hound snuffled through a heap of stained ice emptied outside the butcher shop on Lower Broadway as Reverend Merrick approached. Rumpling the loose skin on the dog's shoulders, he cracked the door just enough to slip through without allowing the eager animal to follow its nostrils inside.

"Morning, Walter. It's a cold one. How can I help you?"

Stamping off his boots, Walter Merrick looked up to see Nelson Borthwick, the recording steward at the Methodist church, boning knife in hand. A hind quarter of beef lay before him on the cutting table, while along the wall three carcasses dangled from ceiling hooks. The smooth hardwood floor was strewn with sawdust to absorb any drops of blood. Reverend Merrick's trim moustache flexed slightly as he drew in the odour of raw meat, noting how different it was from the summer stench that pervaded the makeshift slaughterhouse Nelson kept at the rear.

Straightening his frame to its full height of six-foot-four, the minister approached the counter with the poise of a diplomat. "Ida Rose sent me to fetch a sirloin tip roast," he replied affably. "About four pounds, she said."

Nelson Borthwick reached for his cleaver and turned over the flank. "This beast's nice and tender, grain fed. Marbled enough for you?"

Reverend Merrick leaned forward. "That's just fine. Takes plenty of fat to bring out the flavour."

"Say," the butcher began as he pushed aside his bone saw, "I was planning on talking to you Sunday. You mind that ox roast they held in Orton when they opened the new church last year?"

Reverend Merrick nodded. He and his wife, Ida Rose, had picked up Nelson and his wife with their driver and together, the four had passed a delightful afternoon following the dedication of the Orton church.

The butcher placed the roast on the scales and adjusted the weights. "They fetched quite a crowd, and at ten cents a head, quite profitable too. We could use a boost like that here in Belwood."

"You can count on Methodists to show up in droves for good food," Reverend Merrick joked. "I should know, I've been a Methodist from my cradle. And my pappy and grandpappy before me. Why, I even met Ida Rose that way. When I was a young gaffer, the Methodist college held a Victoria Day picnic. There was a thunderclap, and when the rain poured down, everyone dove for cover. I found myself under the same table as Ida Rose." He smiled at the memory. "Why don't you bring up your notion at the next stewards' meeting?"

"Right," Nelson assented. "I'll do that." Lowering his voice, he continued. "Have you heard about the two farming preachers in the district? Those characters staying out at Robert and Amelia Hunter's?"

Reverend Merrick studied the tight lines forming on Nelson's face. "Heard a little but I didn't feel inclined to go to any of their meetings."

"Well," Nelson divulged, "word's going around that they're cattle thieves. Some are saying they're fixing to bilk the Hunters, to get Robert to sign over the deed of the place." He paused, trying to read the minister's reaction. "Robert Hunter's a parishioner here. But he doesn't take telling too good, so I'll leave it to somebody else to bell the cat."

Reverend Merrick glanced at the brown paper package on the counter. "By the way, do you have an extra bone for my friend outside the door?" he asked, as he reached into his pocket.

After placing sixteen cents in the butcher's blood-spattered hand, Reverend Merrick headed for home. He'd have to pay a social call to Robert and Amelia someday soon. Maybe he'd get a chance to meet the two men and size them up for himself.

Reverend Merrick turned onto St. Andrews Street, still puzzling who the strangers might be and what persuasion they might hold. Approaching the Belwood Town Hall, he glanced south across the river to see a hazy wisp of smoke angling from the direction of the lime kiln. What would people say about *him* if they were privy to the yearnings of his own heart?

As a young man he'd had what he thought were religious experiences and felt convinced he was doing God's will. But after several years, at what should have been his best time in life, he found himself empty. Ignoring the feeling, he simply worked harder, hoping it would go away. At first, he had buried himself in more activity at increasingly larger congregations in Toronto. Then, in quiet desperation, he had resigned and accepted a charge in Belwood, praying the slower pace would bring the peace for which he longed.

Reverend Merrick smiled when he saw Sissy Boggins' broad back swaying from side to side as she shoveled snow from her woodshed door. "Here, here," he said coming up behind her. "That's no job for a lady."

Sissy's petulant face swung around to confront the voice. "Shore 'nuff it ain't," she puffed. "But my boarder run off early. Said he had to put on the fire at the tinsmith's and didn't have no time."

"Maybe your man plans to come back after he gets the fire going."

"Like a pig's eye he does," Sissy blustered.

The Reverend took in Sissy Boggins' indignant eyes and bowl-shaped hat with its curled brim and an ostrich feather only slightly redder than her face. Draped in an ankle-length muskrat coat, her rotund form bore strong resemblance, he thought, to the garment's original owner. Smiling, Walter Merrick balanced his roast on a fence post and took the scoop shovel.

"Thanks," Sissy panted. "I needed more wood than I figured on."

"Leave it to me," Reverend Merrick replied. "I'll bring a good jag to the door in a few minutes."

Sissy had returned to her usual good humour by the time he had the drift cleared. "As ya can see, I got a nice batch of pies," she sang out as he rolled the last armload of wood into the apple crate beside her stove. "Take one along for you and Ida Rose. Mincemeat or butter tart, yer choice."

"Butter tart pie?"

Sissy grinned at his surprise. "Shore 'nuff is. And chock-full of raisins and walnuts, don't ya know." She cocked her head, impishly. "A slice at every meal's a surefire remedy to get rid of wrinkles." Sissy's chubby jowls stretched into a broad smooth grin as if to back up her extravagant claim.

The minister took off his felt hat, revealing a head of thick wavy hair, shot with iron-gray at the temples. "What's the occasion?" he exclaimed as she pressed the hot pie into his hands.

"Just my 'preciation for the pair of ya," she bubbled. "I can't imagine leaving a prosperous big church in Toronto to come out here to the sticks."

Reverend Merrick shifted the pie to the other hand. "Thank you, Sissy. The fact is, time is slower in Belwood. It's wonderful to stroll through the village and know most every face, Methodist or otherwise." After a few minutes of small talk, he brushed off his coat, retrieved the roast from the fence post and sauntered home, still thinking of his assertion to Sissy Boggins. The Belwood parishioners had welcomed the Merricks with open arms and a comfortable parsonage. Why then did he continue to struggle with feelings of loneliness? Even in the midst of his own congregation?

As Reverend Merrick drove his horse and cutter up the Hunter lane a few days later, he wondered who these two strangers might be. Before tying up his horse in the stable, he knocked on Amelia's door to make sure it was a convenient time to pay a call. Normally, someone else would take the minister's horse for him, but with Robert sick the clergyman headed for the barn himself, glancing about inquisitively for any sign of the men.

He was just leaving the horse stable when he heard a deep baritone voice singing in the hay mow above. "It won't do any harm to say hello," he said to himself and climbed the steep stairs. Lifting the hatch door, he came face to face with Jack. Startled, he blurted out, "I'm Reverend Merrick, the minister, and I heard you singing."

Jack grinned as he held out a hand. "I'm Jack, and I'm pleased to meet you. I hope I wasn't too far off key." Gesturing toward the door, he said, "Let's go down to the stable again. It's warmer there."

Jack followed the minister down, wondering if he had come to tell them to leave Belwood. He pulled a couple of half-full sacks of grain together and they sat down. "Sorry I can't offer you a better seat," he laughed. George was pouring buckets of swill into the pigs' trough at the other end of the barn, and Jack had to shout above their hungry squeals. "Hello, George! We've got company!"

They were soon joined by George, who also greeted the pastor warmly. Smiling, Reverend Merrick stood up and pumped George's hand, surprised to receive such a hospitable and sincere welcome. The men were covered with straw and dirt and, far from having an aversion to hot sweaty work, they actually seemed to be enjoying it.

The minister asked politely about their meetings and where they had been before Belwood. The men answered his questions in a straightforward manner and appeared genuinely interested in hearing about his family.

"Did you grow up in West Garafraxa?" Jack asked.

"Oh, no," the minister replied. "Mrs. Merrick and I moved out from Toronto two years ago. Our three boys are married and still living near College and Spadina."

"Have they studied theology too?"

"My word, no. The eldest is a master at Upper Canada College. The other two lads are in the printing business."

Jack dug his heel into the side of the sack and cradled his chin on his knee. "So what do you folks do aside from your church work?"

Reverend Merrick shrugged. "I like music," he said. "Any kind but especially choral music. And reading. Literature, theology, that sort of thing. Mrs. Merrick prefers to get out into the vegetable garden as soon as the weather's decent."

Out of the corner of his eye, Jack noticed George fishing in his pocket. "That's nigh onto coincidence," he exclaimed. "I read history every chance I get and George can't keep his green thumb in his pockets. Or his candy."

George smiled and held a brown paper bag open so Walter could peek inside. "It's horehound for my sweet tooth. Could you stand a piece?" When the minister nodded, George shook three or four chunks out into the man's soft outstretched palm before twisting the neck on the bag and tossing it toward Jack.

The three men didn't discuss spiritual things, but the ease of their conversation caused the time to fly by as if they were old friends. Taking out his pocket watch, Reverend Merrick was amazed to see that more than an hour had passed.

"Please excuse me," he said, scrambling to his feet. "I've got to get a move on. I told Mrs. Hunter I'd be right back to visit with her and Robert."

"Well, it certainly was nice to meet you, Reverend Merrick," George said affably. "Thanks for taking time to say hello."

"The pleasure was all mine. I've enjoyed our chat." He paused, one hand on the calf pen. "Mrs. Merrick and I are off to visit our sons for a few days, but maybe we'll cross paths after that."

A week later, Walter and Ida Rose Merrick's planned visits with their sons had ended and the couple boarded the train bound for Belwood at Union Station. Walter leaned back, staring at the blur beyond the train window as the city's outline fell away behind the caboose. He and Ida Rose had enjoyed their time in Toronto—a day and a night with each son. Last evening had been spent with Reverend Slade, a pastor friend from seminary days, and his wife, Julia. The Slades had graciously invited two other friends, also clergymen, and their wives for dinner. The four couples greeted each other in the effusive manner of folks whose lives had been intertwined for more than thirty years. For several summers when their children were young, the families had vacationed together at a lodge on Lake Muskoka.

After dainty crackers and pâté around the fire, Mrs. Slade ushered her guests to a table spread with her finest bone china and silverware. When Reverend Slade had given thanks, the four couples settled into a flavourful dinner of poached pickerel and roast vegetables. Although it was certainly the most elegant meal Walter had eaten in a long time, he swallowed his food almost mechanically, his mind racing ahead to the questions reserved for his friends. The pleasantries had worn on after dessert until the four ministers retired to the library, church matters on their minds, while the ladies moved into the parlour, allowing Mrs. Slade's maid to clear the table.

As Reverend Slade pushed back the pocket door, the library exuded the air of theological tomes long unopened and a silence that seemed to follow the echoes of ecclesiastical debate over the decades. When the men's conversation had fallen quiet after an hour or more, Walter cleared his throat. "I've been feeling a growing despair, a sense of emptiness," he confessed. After a brief hesitation, he continued, "I'm not really the man of faith people think I am. There was a time when I even had myself fooled. But when the lamp is blown out and I lie on my bed in the dark, I realize I've been deluding myself. Frankly it troubles me. Over and over Jesus told individuals that their *faith* had made them whole.[1] Those folks knew less about Him than I do, but they became entire and complete—relieved of their affliction—because they believed in His power. Why can't I be whole...?" The pleading words hung on Walter's lips like the beads of sweat that dampened his brow. He glanced at the three intent faces cast in the flickering glow of the fire and oil lamp. "I was wondering if any of you have grappled with these doubts too."

Reverend Slade, the most senior of the men, had responded first. "Maybe you're not busy enough out there in Belwood, Walter. Have you considered applying for an extra charge to keep your mind challenged?"

Walter gripped the smooth sculpted ends of the chair's arms. "I tried working harder when I was still here in the city, but that only made it worse. So we moved to Belwood, hoping the quietness of a country village might be the answer." His gaze concentrated on a solitary ember, dying outside the ring of flames. "The tranquility in Belwood is lovely but this isn't about my emotions. There's something deeper missing—something in my heart. A lack of connection to God."

Thoughtful and sympathetic questions followed, but none of the three seemed to have experienced the same concerns, or even have the capability to understand Walter's quandary. In the end, his friends' well-intentioned responses had fallen short, bordering on theological abstraction and long-windedness that did nothing to relieve his empty feeling. An unseen tear had formed in Walter's eye as the spent ember had crumpled into ash.

Twisting on the train's leather seat, Walter could see that the rocking motion of the coach and the warmth from its coal stove at the rear of the car had carried Ida Rose into the illusive land of dreams. A copy of George MacDonald's latest novel, *Salted with Fire,* lay open on her lap.

Walter regarded his wife with admiration. Her strong oval face bobbed up and down on her high bosom as the train rocked and chattered over a switch that curved off to the Erin freight siding. Twin waves of salt-and-pepper hair swept gracefully under her bonnet and over her ears to converge in a stylish coil low on the nape of her neck. Although Ida Rose's padded shoulders gave a decidedly military dash to her navy ulster, the delicate lines of her wan cheeks bespoke a Victorian femininity. Walter turned back to the window, anxious to rouse her but, at the same time, hesitant. What would he say?

Plumes of powdery snow obscured the soft countryside each time the plough on the front of the engine crashed through a drift that had buried the track bed between embankments. At times, white canyon walls confronted Walter before the train burst clear over a railway trestle or frozen stream. Behind the plough the muted whistle signaled each road crossing, and the soothing click of the rails eroded the miles. But Walter wasn't thinking of the majesty or sounds of an Ontario winter.

The train squealed to a standstill at the Orton station and people bustled along the aisle of the coach, children and luggage in hand. When Ida Rose's eyelids flickered open at the commotion, Walter leaned toward her. "I've been thinking about those two preachers I met in Robert Hunter's barn," he admitted. "I can hardly get them out of my mind. They're itinerant—rather like Wesley's circuit riders."

Ida Rose peered sleepily at her husband. "You've mentioned them at least once a day since last week." Folding a lace hanky to mark her place, she closed the book on her lap. "Why don't we go and hear them out?"

Walter's brow knit in frustration but he said nothing.

"Well," Ida Rose persisted, "what do you think?"

"How would it look in the settlement if I were to go and sit under the preaching of such men?" he protested sharply.

"To stay away because of what people might think is outright pride, Walter. Your sermon last Sunday urged folks to guard against that. Besides, you won't find out what they preach unless you go and listen."

The conductor worked his way through the car punching the tickets of passengers who had boarded at Orton. "Belwood, next stop," he announced.

Walter shrugged; his wife's wisdom was irrefutable. Far ahead he heard the protracted quaver of the whistle as the train slowed for the long curve into the Belwood station. Rising to his feet, he swayed as he retrieved their luggage from the overhead racks. "What about this evening?" he blurted out. "Do you have any engagements arranged?"

Smiling, Ida Rose hurried along the aisle. "I don't. We'll go together."

The stone schoolhouse on Broadway Street had two entrances—one for boys and one for girls. The boys' door was closest, and Walter stepped inside, hurrying Ida Rose along the center aisle. Out of the corner of his eye, he anxiously surveyed the room to see if any of his congregation were there, all the time trying to appear relaxed.

Walter was unimpressed as the gospel meeting got underway. The singing was off key, the piano needed tuning, and Jack's preaching struck Walter's theological mind as being so elementary that one could have almost thought a child had prepared the message. And yet, as Walter continued to listen, he sensed the sincerity, gentle confidence, and quiet authority in Jack's voice. "But where does it come from?" he puzzled. "Certainly not from years of experience."

George spoke last, and it was during his message that the reality of the farmer's words began to take hold of Walter. Gradually, he lost all awareness of the room and the people around him. He heard George saying, "You can go to church each Sunday, listen attentively to the sermon, and eat the bread and drink from the cup, but unless you have the Spirit of Christ, you cannot enter the kingdom of heaven." Walter closed his eyes as George's voice continued to penetrate. "You can sing in the choir, help around the church, and give generously when the collection plate passes, but unless the Spirit of Christ lives in your heart, you will be barred from heaven. In fact, you can even graduate as a minister, take degrees, be ordained, and receive a call from the congregation, but unless the Spirit of Christ controls your life, you will have no admission to eternity with God."

When Walter looked up, he noted the searching intensity in George's eyes. These men, he suddenly realized, had a burning love for souls—those who had not yet opened their hearts to Christ. A staggering thought struck him for the first time. Could it be that his gnawing unsettledness had come because he had never truly possessed the Spirit of Christ himself?

On his way out the door, Walter made a point of shaking hands with George and Jack. "I appreciated your sermon this evening." He tried to sound casual and offhand, but in his heart, the plain forthright message had touched a raw nerve. As he bid them goodnight, he somehow felt strangely drawn to these modest preachers.

"Well, what did you think of that?" he asked Ida Rose as they picked their way through the snowy ruts.

"I'm glad we went," she said. "Their messages were so understandable and direct. It wasn't just preaching; it was more like kindling a fire. I felt a real earnestness when they spoke." Ida Rose tightened her scarf around her neck. "I've listened to a lot of airy theoretical Christian talk in my life," she added. "But I believe those two men meant every word they spoke."

Walter agreed reluctantly. "When the second man spoke, I felt something that I don't think I've ever felt before."

Walter felt Ida Rose's eyes upon him, searching for further clarification. But he simply stared into the darkness ahead, his face masking a single burning question. If *that* was the gospel, what were his own sermons?

Although Ida Rose's heart wrenched with empathy, no further words passed between husband and wife the rest of the way home.

No longer concerned about how it would appear, or what it would lead to, the couple continued to attend the meetings regularly, unless they conflicted with Walter's own church services. What other people thought didn't matter anymore. He and Ida Rose were beginning to hear Jesus' call in a way they never had before. A call that was setting them free from the bondage of other people's opinions.[2]

~⊘

Two weeks later the Merricks invited the brothers for dinner at noon. At the first knock, Walter hurried to the front door. Doffing their wool caps, George and Jack stepped into the hall and unlaced their boots, positioning them neatly at one end of the homespun matting.

Appearing at Walter's elbow, Ida Rose added her own warm welcome. "Come on into the dining room," she said leading the way. "Everything's laid out." The fire in the dining room grate played over the embossed gilt wallpaper, and a bevy of Christmas cactus vaunted their exquisite pink blooms from a wicker stand in front of the lace-curtained window.

Somehow Walter sensed that George and Jack would not be critical or judgmental in any way, and in no time at all they were discussing spiritual matters. Perhaps it was the obvious kindness and sincerity of these two men from Puslinch, who were helping at the Hunters' farm, that prompted Walter to express his simmering questions and doubts.

He heard his own voice saying, "I'm not a very good husband in many ways." He stared down at his roast beef and Yorkshire pudding. "Don't get me wrong here. Ida Rose is a wonderful wife. The problem's with me." Walter was surprised at himself, but now he plunged ahead almost cathartically, desperate for an answer to his dilemma. "I find myself living a life during the week that's vastly different from the messages I preach on Sundays. How can a church teddy bear become a porcupine at home? I'm prickly and difficult to live with much of the time. It's ruining our marriage. And I worry that my angry outbursts make me just as guilty as any murderer or immoral person."[3] Walter picked up his napkin and then laid it back across his lap with a sigh. "But I seem powerless to change."

Ida Rose reached across the corner of the table, closing the space between Walter and herself. Gently, she laid her hand on his forearm, knowing her husband's deep frustration stemmed from his inability to supply the answers to his own problems. The fact that he had spent years studying and then performing as a pastor at several churches only accentuated his disappointment.

"At times I question whether I've ever truly experienced the Spirit of Christ myself," Walter admitted, in a confession that cost him his dignity.

He could see that these two humble men lived what they spoke about. They didn't have much to say and replied to his questions in few words and to the point. But their simple, practical responses satisfied him. When Walter asked about his difficulty in living the Christian life, George's reply was straightforward: "A Christian lives not by trying harder, but by trusting more. That's the way we say yes to Jesus and no to self."

Walter had never spoken to George about how hard he tried to be a Christian, and he wondered how George could know so much about him. Then it dawned on him. *George doesn't know*, he thought, *but the Holy Spirit does, and He's speaking through George's lips.*

As Walter and Ida Rose watched them go down the path, they felt an inexplicable bond with these two men who seemed to trust God for everything. "It wasn't so much what they said as the way they said it," Ida Rose observed as the brothers disappeared down the street. "It's the Spirit in them that allows them to live the answer, not just talk about it. Only when the Spirit is leading us, too, will we be able to live as we should."

Later as Walter walked back to his office at the church, he turned over Ida Rose's comment. *My training has given me all the right words*, he thought,

but I've been denied the power to live them. Those two men have something I
don't have—something beyond mere learning or doctrine.

~◡

One cracking cold evening in February, just before supper, a driver and
sleigh from Johnston's Livery Stable pulled up in the Hunters' yard with
a passenger. "Could you fetch me again at nine in the morning?" Eddie
asked as he jumped out. "I'll straighten up with you then if that's all right."
The man tipped his cap and the cutter pulled away.

Amelia was always pleased to see the young merchant and quickly added
a few more parsnips to the stew. Sitting around the big oak table laden
with food, Eddie asked why the brothers had stayed in Belwood for the
past two Sundays.

"If we go to Elora too often, the friends could start depending upon
us," George confided. "The church must learn to function without us and
to rely on God instead. Each person needs to bear the burden of the Lord
by feeding His lambs and sheep.[4] And by reaching out to others."[5]

Jack fished a toothpick out of his shirt pocket. "We'll be moving again
before long and won't be able to go at all because of the distance. Besides,
if some of the Belwood folks choose to follow in the way of Jesus, we'll
need to be with them for a few weeks."

"I see your point," Eddie acknowledged as he drew out his gold watch.

At the gospel meeting that night, white frost crystals climbed up the
school windows in spite of the roaring fire. When a neighbouring family
by the name of Stonehouse arrived, the children sat around the stove on
their coats rubbing each other's stockinged feet to keep them warm. Sissy
Boggins positioned herself on the front row next to the centre aisle, the
dull sheen of her muskrat coat catching the lamplight. The bedraggled
feather on her bowl-shaped hat tipped back as she gazed up at George,
absorbing the message. Behind her, Walter Merrick smiled and stretched
his long legs underneath her chair, his arm draped around Ida Rose's shoulders.

"The kernel of the Christian message is to love and be loved," George
asserted in closing. "The whole creation groans for love, for compassion,
for understanding.[6] We can't exist without it; we crave it like the very air
we breathe. The hardened criminal aches for it as much as the tenderest
infant—even if he doesn't know it. Over years a prolonged lack of love can

marshal a precious child to a prison cell." George smiled at a girl with long braids, her arm cradling her younger brother beside the stove. "Our Lord transferred His love to the disciples by breathing on them. Then He sent them to carry that love and peace to others.[7] Truly receiving God's love will compel us to love others.[8] But remember, love is only love if it can be rejected. May each of us embrace the Father who loved the world to such an extent that He gave us His only Son."[9]

When Eddie stepped out onto the snowy steps, he adjusted his silk scarf and drew in a sharp breath of the frosty air. At the click of the door behind him, the young draper moved to one side. Over his shoulder, he saw Sissy Boggins tightening her ancient fur coat around her ample waist.

Sissy's eyes darted appraisingly over the dapper stranger before her. "The old devil took a fearful larrupin' in there tonight, don't ya know," she said to no one in particular as she waddled off into the darkness.

On the way home, the runners crisped on the hard-packed snow and the string of brass sleigh bells echoed across the barren fields. When Amelia and the three men shook off their coats, they found that Robert had the kettle boiling and a plate of Christmas cake sliced on the table. He listened eagerly as Amelia recounted her impression of the meeting while George sat quietly, sipping his tea.

Climbing the stairs afterwards, George caught Eddie's uncertainty. "Bunk in with me, Eddie," he suggested. "There's a spare bed in my room."

Sitting on a cedar chest in George's bedroom, Jack took off his wool socks and laid them across the tops of his boots. George turned back his covers and started to undress while Eddie dug abstractedly in his pockets. As he talked it became obvious that Eddie had no intention of calling it a night. George studied the lines on his friend's face. Could it be that the Holy Spirit was troubling him about the ministry?

"I want to help you in any way I can," Eddie persisted. "So you can keep on reaching out to others." Then he offered the brothers most of his salary as a commercial traveler—a hundred dollars per month or so.

Jack's eyes widened, startled at such an impressive sum.

"Thanks, Eddie," George said, "we appreciate your generosity, but there's just the two of us and we're able to work during the day. Maybe some of it could be used to help a few of the poorer folks in Elora."

Jack slipped his suspenders off his shoulders and started to unbutton them from the waistband of his trousers. "Of course, there's a crying need for workers. When a person considers the vastness of the harvest field, he can't help but realize that."

"I know," Eddie sighed. "I've been thinking about it. But I can't just abandon responsibilities like mine to go and preach." Eddie squirmed uneasily in his chair as he tried to escape the issue in one way or another. "Can't I give you the money so you can use it for evangelizing?"

George raised his eyebrows. "Perhaps it isn't your money the Lord wants. Remember the rich young ruler. Jesus asked two things of him. Only one was the abandonment of his wealth."

Eddie stood up and began to pace distractedly. But the Spirit persevered, impressing upon him the urgency of the call. George and Jack were careful not to coerce Eddie themselves, having both accepted the Spirit's call without anyone's influence. He would have to make this choice on his own.

"My dad really needs me," Eddie said, his face tense and twisted. He sat back down and drummed his fingers on the desk. After a few minutes, he added, "But I suppose he could hire somebody else to do my job. Or just scale back a bit." He looked over at George wearily. "The extra business won't matter much in a hundred years, will it?"

George shook his head slowly. "Not a whit, Eddie."

"I've got to get some air," Eddie gasped. "I'll be back in a little while."

George listened to the stairs squeaking, and then he heard the front door latch click shut. "This is as tough on Eddie as it was on me," he said.

"And me," Jack responded. "I can't tell you how many times I woke up in the middle of the night. After a spell I'd get frustrated and light a lamp and read a book 'til morning." Jack unbuttoned his plaid shirt. "It's quite a thing for a man to walk away from a fine home and a business like Summers' Dry Goods. Eddie's the only son and heir."

Nodding, George kneeled down at his bedside and drew his arms around his head. "Dear Father, You created the healthy desires of the human heart, but You are also the Lord of the harvest. It appears to me as if You are calling Eddie into the harvest field, but I could easily be wrong. Please help Eddie to accept Your will, whatever that may be. And help me to trust that the decision he makes is best. As Eddie wanders alone in this dark hour of decision, please grant him the clarity to understand and the willingness to obey. All I ask is in the name of Your Beloved Son. Amen."

For nearly an hour, Eddie stumbled through the transparent darkness of the moonlit night, wandering aimlessly along the back lane. Only the sounds of his boots punching holes in the crusty snow and the rail fences cracking with frost on either side fractured the silence. Hewn long before he was born, the ancient rails seemed to guide him toward an unknown destiny. A waxing moon, white and cratered against the winter sky, cast sharp shadows beyond the thorn trees and across the undulating swells of bluish snow. He turned up his collar to break the biting wind that stung his ears and nose as he racked himself with reasons why he shouldn't go into the work. When a long-legged jackrabbit burst from beneath a pile of brush, dodging this way and that, Eddie barely noticed.

George's pocket watch ticked past three o'clock as he and Jack lay awake, awaiting the return of their friend. From the dresser the oil lamp glimmered, its warm circle enveloping the patient men. From his bed, George stared up at the wavering rings of light on the ceiling. After an hour or more he jerked awake from fitful dozing as soft footsteps padded up the stairs and the bedroom door creaked open.

"It's over." The voice was weary yet triumphant like that of a man who had just won a marathon. "I've surrendered." When the brothers realized that Eddie had capitulated, they embraced him with tears of joy.

Feeling as if he had just crossed the finish line, Eddie undressed and flopped across the extra bed in George's room. His usually impeccable suit dangled like a scarecrow from a single coat hook.

"I feel like a load's been taken off my shoulders," he conceded. "That's been gnawing at me for months, and I'm relieved to have it settled at last." Resolving to give up his home and position, Eddie, too, would become a traveler for Jesus.

"I really appreciate you hearing me out last night," Eddie said the next morning. "I'll be along with my travel bag in late March as we discussed."

George held up his hand, shielding his face from the sun as Eddie's hired sleigh drove out the lane. "We know how he's going to feel when it comes time to say goodbye, don't we, Jack?"

Nodding, Jack kicked at a snowbank. "I still recall how it felt to cycle down the lane and look back at my folks waving in the distance."

~◦

"Fine day for February," George noted over porridge one morning. "Anything in particular you'd like us to do, Robert? We'll be away in a few weeks."

Robert's craggy brows raised from his bowl. "There *is* a little job, if you'd be up to it."

"Anything you say," George replied.

"Well, I've been thinking about the bull. When the weather's fit we'll want him out to pasture with the cows. And I'm afeared now he might hurt somebody. You know, like a lad cutting across the farm."

Jack's eyes narrowed as he nodded thoughtfully, again reminded of his own uncle who had been killed in a field by a bull.

"So just what did you have in mind?" George asked, mystified.

"I reckon we could put a ring in his nose and attach a short chunk of chain. Then if he puts his head down to take a run, he'll step on the chain. That'd haul him up short."

"I've seen that done," Jack spoke up. "So long as the bull's careful, he can graze without a problem, but if he gets fired up and takes after somebody, it'll control him." He looked over at George, sitting quietly. "What do y' say, George? Can we handle that?"

"Yes, I'm sure we can," George replied, trying to conceal the measure of tension he suddenly felt inside. "Winter's a good time of year for it. No flies to bother him afterwards."

After drying the breakfast dishes, George and Jack pulled on their smocks and headed for the stable. "I didn't expect to get into ringing a bull today," George confided once they had reached the privacy of the barn. "Anyway, we'd better get on with it." He led the way past the cow stalls and along the passage to the bull's pen in the corner of the stable.

As Jack looked over the half door, the bull seemed larger than life. "He's a big brute," he noted. "There's a mountain of muscle in that thick neck of his." Standing sideways to the door, the bull's eye looked small and mean in the massive head. The cold black pupil set in a large white eyeball glared back imperiously.

"Grab that heavy rope from the horse stable, would you?" George instructed. "I'll get a pitchfork."

Sensing the buzz of activity, the bull raked the point of one horn against the stone wall, leaving score marks in the whitewash as George wound the rope several times around a nearby pillar. After fashioning a lasso of sorts, he poured a half gallon of chop into the bull's manger. For several minutes the bull stood shaking his woolly head menacingly, but eventually he took a few unhurried steps and thrust his muzzle through the side of the pen and into the manger. With a single deft movement, George dropped a loop over the bull's horns and snubbed the rope tight.

Even with the leverage on their side, the two men sawed back and forth on the rope while the bull thrashed and slammed his lethal weapons against the side of the opening, bellowing in unmitigated rage.

"Good," George grunted when the taut rope was finally anchored. "Let's get another one around his nose quick. He's got to be perfectly still." Perspiration poured off the men's faces as they struggled to limit the bull's lunging. The dry lumber creaked ominously as the powerful shoulders strained against the pen.

The stress lines on Jack's brow deepened. "I hope nothing gives way."

"Good thing Robert's a pretty solid builder," George panted as the bull's hot rank breath deflected off his wrists. Although the massive head was held motionless now, the deep rumble from within the bulky chest attested to the venom surging through the creature's brain.

"Nice looking beast, but he's sure got one ugly streak." George tied a couple of extra knots. "Robert's lucky to have escaped with his life."

Jack stroked his round face. "This bull's the same roan colour as the one that killed my Uncle Ethan. He was my favourite uncle. Carved me a set of wooden animals for my fifth birthday." Jack tipped back his cap and pressed his palm against his forehead. "Ten years later I helped my dad carry him off the pasture."

"What a task for a fifteen-year-old," George empathized. "I'm sorry."

"Time has deadened some of the pain, but it still hurts. I loved Uncle Ethan, and I hated to lose him. And my mother. I lost her before I ever knew her, but I miss her just the same." Jack straightened his back. "Well, let's get on with the nasty deed." He reached into his pocket and drew out the split ring, hinged on one side. "I've got the screwdriver too."

George ran his hand along the bull's jutting shoulder and sensed the raw energy. Running his hand forward, he scratched the animal's shaggy forehead. "This is going to sting, fella. But we'll do our best to make it quick." With that George picked up the pitchfork and ran his thumb over the tines. "I sharpened this one and passed it over a flame," he said as he placed the prong against the bull's leathery septum.

The bull stiffened but did not move or make a noise as George gave a sudden jab, creating a small round incision between the two nostrils. When Jack handed him the ring, he pressed one end through the opening. Taking the screwdriver, George threaded the tiny screw to hold the two parts of the split ring in a perfect circle.

"Hardly more than a trickle of blood," Jack observed. "Farmer turned preacher now turned veterinarian."

George tackled a stubborn knot. "Anyway, let's untie this big fella and see what happens."

Jack loosened one of the short ropes from the bull's nose. "Or maybe you'll go into the business of piercing sailors' ears," he proposed. "They used to suspicion that it gave them sharper eyesight. And the Romans associated ear piercing with wealth or luxury."

As the ropes fell away, the bull stood like a rock, seemingly stunned. Then, with an enraged bellow, he spun around in the box stall, his momentary lethargy vanished. Snorting, he pawed the straw bedding with his front hoofs before exploding into the wall of the pen. Flakes of whitewash bounced off the outside of the boards as a ton of crazed bull thudded against the other side.

Jack jumped back from the door. "A teaspoon of that energy would beat a gallon of Dr. Miles' heart tonic all hollow!" he exclaimed as he hustled down the passage.

Smiling, George turned to follow him, the coil of rope draped over his shoulder. "Let's give him a few minutes to cool off," he suggested. "Maybe if we beat a retreat, he'll get interested in the grain again. Let's head up to the granary and put the oats in that last bin through the fanning mill."

After a few minutes, Jack slipped out to the mow and stole a glance down through a hatch over the bull's pen. "Your patient's recovering nicely, doctor," he quipped when he returned to the granary.

George shoveled the oats into the hopper while Jack turned the crank. After a moment George spoke up. "What would you think of moving along by the end of the month?"

Jack straightened up and rubbed his right shoulder. "Yes, it's getting to have that feel, and there haven't been any new faces for three weeks or so. Amelia and the Merricks have been coming pretty steady."

"I doubt Walter and Ida Rose would walk away from the Methodist Church," George cautioned. "When we visited his church last Sunday, I could see how attentively the congregation listened. He's a good man." George scooped another shovelful of oats. "And Sissy comes most nights."

"Speaking of Sissy," Jack chuckled. "I must've turned as red as a beet when she tore over and threw her arms around me after Walter's service. She's definitely not backward about coming forward."

George twisted a length of twine around the neck of the sack, "Let's pray further about it and see if we still feel it's best after a few days."

⁓

On the last Sunday evening of February, George invited the residents of Belwood to speak to him and Jack if they had felt the Spirit of Christ touching their hearts. As he unfolded their plans to move on to Orangeville before spring, Walter Merrick leaned forward on his seat, his moustache tensing. He suddenly realized that a turning of the ways lay just ahead.

Later at home, after hanging his top coat on the hall stand, Walter flopped down on the sitting room lounge and ran his long fingers into his wavy hair. "Our feet are being held to the fire now," he declared as Ida Rose joined him. "We're forced to make a move." He glanced over at a stack of dilapidated hymnals, their spines loose and covers soiled. "No church can tolerate a minister who's busy every Sunday morning. A Methodist pastor can't be part of a little home church."

To Walter's left, the vase lamp, a vibrant carnation hand-painted on its upper globe, illuminated a coloured portrait of Winterhalter's *Queen Victoria and Prince Albert*. As though questioning any breach in tradition, the royal faces looked down from the frame with forbidding intensity.

Ida Rose sighed. "Oil and water don't mix, do they?" Balancing on the edge of the lounge, she reached for her husband's hand. "Maybe you'll have to consider what's best for your heart, Walter. You can't spend the rest of your days always being at sixes and sevens. You've come through a long spell of dissatisfaction. Since the men joined us for dinner earlier this month, you've started to smile, and a couple of times I've actually heard you singing again. You bound up the steps like you used to do at seminary."

"I know, I know," Walter agreed reluctantly, "but even students need to eat. Why, we don't even have a roof to call our own."

"I'd certainly miss the parsonage," Ida Rose acknowledged. "It's got one of the nicest gardens I've ever had. And the sunrise over the river is simply sublime. But I suppose the first hurdle would be for you to find satisfactory work."

"I could teach school, but then we'd have to move to a different school district and we like Belwood."

Getting to her feet, Ida Rose released the gold curtain loop and drew the burgundy damask across the dark glass. "What other work would there be around the village? You like fixing things. Would you ever consider working with your hands?"

Walter's body stiffened. "I just don't know. In the spring they'll need labourers out at Fuller's brickyard, but I doubt my back would stand that heavy slugging…"

In spite of the blazing fire, Ida Rose felt a sudden chill. "No," she replied. "I don't mean manual labour. I meant repairing clocks or making cabinets or the like."

"How could I?" Walter lamented. "I've never learned a trade…"

Ida Rose caressed her husband's forlorn face. Poor Walter. How could this happen to such a caring man? One with a fine mind, eager to learn and always ready to help somebody else. What a waste for a man his age to eke out a living digging clay or straining under the weight of a brick hod. As she wrapped her arms around Walter's shoulders, her heart melted into a pool of pity.

"Maybe we'd better back off," she choked. "I can't bear to think of you breaking your back."

"Besides," Walter continued, "what would our boys say?"

"That should be the least of your concerns," she reassured him. "You've raised them to see the worth in all manner of work. For years, they've spoken to me about your distress, and they'll want you to be happy. In fact, they'd likely press you to help with their printing business."

One by one the lights in their neighbours' windows had been extinguished. By eleven o'clock the village lay in darkness, but it was well after midnight before Ida Rose stood up. "Let's get some rest," she counseled. "We'll think straighter in the morning."

Walter's troubled face tipped up. In other circumstances he might have admired his wife's gracious bearing and resolute shoulders. But all this was lost on him for the present. "I'll be up in a few minutes," he murmured.

Hours later Ida Rose awoke with a start, squinting toward the south window, barely discernible as a translucent rectangle. Where was Walter? When she ran her fingers across the flannel sheets to his side of the bed, her hand and mind recoiled as one. The bed lay cold and empty. Straining to glimpse the bedpost between her and the window, she saw the limp outline of his rumpled nightshirt. Walter hadn't come upstairs. Ida Rose bolted from the bed. Her outstretched hands parted the darkness as she groped toward the top of the stairs. As her palm flew down the smooth bannister, she caught the flicker of lamplight from the sitting room door.

Walter lay slumped face down on the flowered lounge, his right arm dangling limply over the side, his leg twisted against the hooked rug. Fearing the worst, Ida Rose cried out as she raced to him, clutching at his arm. She shook his shoulders. "Walter! Walter! What's happened?" she sobbed frantically. When Walter groaned and opened his red eyes, she could see he had been crying.

"I guess I fell asleep while I was praying," he muttered as he turned heavily on one knee and sat on the floor, his back supported by the lounge.

Kneeling before him, Ida Rose wept softly as he took her into his arms. "Walter, finding you in a heap on the floor gave me the fright of my life."

"I'm sorry, my love," he apologized. "I didn't intend that."

The first gray streaks of winter dawn had begun to creep around the curtain before Ida Rose's breathing slowed.

Walter regarded the dark circles under her eyes. "Did you get some sleep?" he whispered.

"Not much," she admitted. "But I'm feeling some better."

"Me too," he replied, savouring her embrace. "Let's get some breakfast. And then I need to visit Mrs. Semple. She's staying with her daughter out at the Living Springs settlement. Don't worry if I'm a little late coming back. I may swing past the brickyard to see Silas Fuller."

Ida Rose winced at the Fuller name. "Please, not that." Then in an attempt to lighten the mood, she ran her fingers over Walter's stubbled cheek. "I know Mrs. Semple has poor eyesight, but you'd better shave while I scramble the eggs."

That evening after putting away the supper dishes, Ida Rose joined her husband in the sitting room. Curling up in the Morris chair beside the round upright stove, she turned to him. "How did you find Mrs. Semple?"

"Oh, just the usual," Walter said. "When I knocked on the door all bedlam broke loose inside. Her daughter's dogs were jumping on the window glass and yelping to get at me but she sequestered them in the woodshed before she opened the door."

"And the old lady?" Ida Rose reminded him.

"Oh, yes," Walter continued, "we had a lovely talk. Mrs. Semple was in good spirits and as cheerful as a magpie. Eighty-nine this spring. Wanted to know about all her old friends. I admire her. She wears a wool shawl around her head these days and keeps the bed clothes hauled up to her chin. The only thing showing is her face. She's getting more shriveled all the time. Rather like a giant golden raisin with two sparkling eyes, framed in the frill of her nightcap. I reckon she doesn't weigh much more than the big cat curled up on the foot of her bed." Turning his head, Walter stroked his ear lobe thoughtfully. "As I left she said, 'Thank you for coming, Reverend. A body never knows when they're having their last visitation.'"

After adding a scoop of anthracite to the fire, Ida Rose moved through the darkness to sit beside Walter on the lounge. She made no attempt to light the lamp, choosing instead to watch the delicate intertwining of blue and orange flames as they danced against the mica window in the stove.

Walter clasped his hands behind his neck. "Sometimes I visit an ailing person, hoping to leave an encouraging thought. But instead, they present a gift to me. Mrs. Semple's words were like that today. They nattered at me all the way home and convinced me that George's invitation might be *my* moment of visitation.[10] Throughout the centuries, it was people's faith that made them whole. And now Jesus has invited me into a truly spiritual path. What if my faith's so weak I turn away, only to be hemmed in on every side like never before? That could destroy me." He strained through the darkness beyond the window's outline, catching the muffled whinny of his horse as it nickered to another passing along the block. Across the street a door slammed and the neighbour's dog barked into the night air. "Can you quote that passage you had the children memorize in Sunday school last summer? What Ruth said to Naomi on that hot dusty road in Moab?"[11]

Ida Rose's voice, with the confidence of a settled truth, penetrated the darkness. "Entreat me not to leave thee, or to return from following after thee: for whither thou goest, I will go; and where thou lodgest, I will lodge: thy people shall be my people, and thy God my God. Where thou diest, will I die, and there will I be buried: the LORD do so to me, and more also, if aught but death part thee and me."[12]

"That's it," Walter exclaimed as he slipped his arm around his wife's shoulders and drew her close. "Then it says when Naomi saw Ruth was determined to join her, she stopped speaking and the two of them went on until they came to Bethlehem." In the faint glow from the stove, Walter said softly. "There's no turning back now. The Lord Jesus has given me a glimpse of something too precious to miss. I *must* go foward; no matter what."

Ida Rose snuggled against Walter's protective warmth. "But are you certain now is the right time?"

"As certain as I've ever been about anything," he vowed. "More than that—I'm elated, for once, to be so sure. No matter the cost, I need to follow Jesus. It's time to leave the land of Moab where I've known so much discontent."

Even in the dim light, Ida Rose could discern the vision in her husband's impassioned eyes. "While you were out to Living Springs today, I came to that conclusion myself," she assured him. "I just wanted to be sure I wasn't influencing you." She kissed him lightly. "We'll make out all right. Besides, I remember Mrs. Rankin saying Alexander needs an extra pair of hands at the store. I'll ask him about the job when I go for sugar and tea in the morning."

"Very good," Walter said. "And tomorrow afternoon we'll take the cutter to Hunters' Hollow and chat with George and Jack. I've got a few questions that need to be answered."

Two days later Walter called a meeting of the church stewards. Squalls of wind drove in around the flaps of his overcoat as he unlocked the vestry door and entered the room, where the cold air struck a chill to his heart. His hand trembled only slightly as he knelt at the stove and touched a match to the remnants of a fire from the preceding Sunday. Along the wall his clerical robes hung in black-and-white distinction, the only clear-cut shapes in the shadowy room. Above them on the shelf reposed the top hat he wore for funerals, an unwelcome reminder of his own mortality.

"The weather's turned its back on us," Nelson Borthwick huffed as he shook the sleet off his ulster, tossing it over an armchair in the vestry. "It's unmercifully raw out there." As the recording steward rubbed his hands and took his place at the end of the oak table, he glanced up at the clock. "The others should be along in a few minutes." He looked sharply at Walter, but if he was curious about the purpose of the meeting he held his tongue.

Tracing the table's ornate moulding with his finger, Walter scanned the door at the sound of stamping boots. In the next moment, Mr. Hampton was offering a warm dumpling smile and reaching across the table to shake hands. Jed Boyle, a silver-haired steward, plucked a few pellets of sleet from an equally silver beard as he nodded and scraped his chair into place. More than once some tardy parishioner had felt Mr. Boyle's unbridled censure as he tried to slip unnoticed into the last pew. Walter looked into the thin austere face. What remarks might Jed Boyle unleash tonight?

Walter lifted his lapel and withdrew a folded sheet of paper from his inside pocket. "Thanks for pulling away from the hearth on such a dirty night," he apologized. "I won't keep you long, but something urgent has arisen. And it's pressing me." He felt the weight of curious eyes upon him as he fumbled with the paper. "Perhaps it's easiest if I just read it to you."

In spite of the frost on the black windows, Walter felt his skin grow clammy. "Dear Stewards," he began. "I would like to be relieved of my duties as minister of the Belwood Methodist Church effective immediately. This decision comes after great soul-searching and grave deliberation on the part of Mrs. Merrick and myself. It's only fair to explain that we intend to become part of a home church to be founded in the district. I apologize for the suddenness of this decision and will accommodate the new minister in any way I can. I have valued your support, and indeed that of the entire congregation, since I arrived in Belwood. We will make every effort to find suitable accommodation immediately and will turn the residence over to the parsonage committee in a timely fashion. Both Mrs. Merrick and I hope to retain the many friendships we enjoy among our Methodist families. I forthwith tender my resignation. Yours very truly, Walter Merrick."

Hesitating to look up, Walter refolded the paper with painstaking care.

"Is it those blasted tramp preachers who've taken you in?" he heard Jed Boyle croak in disbelief.

Taken aback at the flabbergasted faces around the table, Walter attempted to clarify. "I hope you gentlemen can understand that Ida Rose and I are hearing a voice we've never heard before. We simply can't ignore this call to our souls." But even as he tried to explain, he saw in the blank expressions their inability to comprehend an inaudible call.

Nelson Borthwick's mouth quirked in annoyance at the passion in Walter's voice. "This here voice you're on about," he said incredulously. "Are you giving us to understand that you didn't hear it until these harebrained preachers drifted into the settlement?"

Walter nodded. "Yes, Nelson, that's right."

The butcher's jaw jutted with defiance. "But they've no credentials what-soever."

"In one way that's true. But they've got something I don't have. For a while I couldn't fathom just what it was, but now I know: God's planted a living seed in their hearts."

The point on Jed Boyle's beard quivered. "Living seeds," he snapped. "They're a pair of *hay*seeds, nothing more. I only had to listen for five minutes to catch that. That's when I up and walked out. How a scholarly minister of your calibre could get taken in by the likes of them beats all."

"I've been practising well-bred Christianity all of my life," Walter responded, his tone melancholy. "And I'm sorry to say that after fifty years I find myself wanting."

Archie Hampton, the round, spaniel-eyed steward, had sat in attentive silence. "You're leaving us in a bit of a lurch, Walter," he said softly. "It'd be desperate hard to find a pulpit replacement before Sunday. Would you be willing to conduct the service this week?"

"Yes, of course," Walter assured him, "I want to make the change as easy as possible for everyone. However, there are two conditions."

Mr. Hampton fixed his moist brown eyes on Walter. "Yes, go on."

"First, that someone else looks after the collection. And second, that my church salary be terminated today."

Jed Boyle tightened his lips in suppressed outrage, but Mr. Hampton simply smiled. "That's just fine, Walter. We can look after the collection."

Nelson Borthwick rapped his fingernails impatiently on the table. "For a man of your experience, you're making a terrible gaffe. You're bringing a cankerous blight upon our settlement. I hope you'll reconsider."

With that Nelson Borthwick and Jed Boyle offered a hasty handshake, gathered their coats, and hurried into the night.

"I'll wait while you shake down the grates so we can walk together," Archie Hampton suggested.

After Walter turned up his collar and secured the lock, he fell in step with Mr. Hampton, noting that a slight rise in the mercury had turned the sleet to freezing rain. "Thanks for respecting my position tonight," he said as the pair passed an open lot, the raw wind tearing the words from his lips.

"Frankly, I have no idea what you see in these preachers," Archie Hampton admitted. "But I've always admired the meticulous way you approach any subject. So maybe there's something to them. Where there's smoke there's usually fire. In the meantime they've certainly turned our church upside down."[13]

When they came to the corner of Broadway and St. Andrews the two men paused, tipping their hats against the rain. Placing one hand on Archie Hampton's damp shoulder, Walter sighed. "I'm glad to have this piece of church business behind me. Thanks again for your understanding."

That Sunday, Walter spoke to his parishioners for the last time as their minister. After the closing hymn, he stepped forward and clasped his hands: "I have a special matter I need to talk to you about this morning."

The box pews creaked with concentration as every row sat upright. Although the grapevine running through the village had already conveyed a semblance of the impending truth, a deathly stillness like that before a looming thunderstorm filled the airless sanctuary. Not a page turned.

Walter took a deep breath. "Mrs. Merrick and I've spent more time praying in recent weeks than ever before. But we've done more than that. We've been listening too. Over the past few weeks, we've received a revelation from God that has profoundly changed our lives."

The people were astonished by their minister's voice. When Reverend Merrick had first come to Belwood, they had thrilled to its full melodious quality, smooth and sweet as Devon cream. It was not just the natural richness of his tone that entranced his listeners, but also his considerable skill as an orator. Years of pulpit experience had afforded Walter Merrick full command of pitch, pause, and poise, adjusting the length and inflection of his sentences to suffice their task. At will his voice could melt into irresistible gentleness drawing fainthearted souls to the altar while evoking tears of emotion among the Methodist faithful. At other times his sonorous appeals rang like a call to arms, inducing short-lived fervour in even the most lethargic of his flock.

There was, however, another side to Reverend Merrick, little known in the country settlement. In his early days with all his powers and faculties unrestrained, he had been known as "the formidable thresher" among adversaries of Methodism. His voice, like a sharp-toothed instrument, had threshed mountains of rival doctrines, beating them small and reducing them to chaff. He had tackled contenders as few others could.

But today as his parishioners listened in puzzlement, their minister's voice sounded subdued. All sense of drama had dissipated. It was an unfamiliar voice, one that sounded less like that of a preacher and more like a friend sharing a crisis of conscience.

Walter glanced toward his wife, catching the steady look in her eye as he continued. "Both Mrs. Merrick and I hear God calling us to do something different from what we've been doing. We feel that we are being called to really follow Him, to trust Him, and to do this without relying on the Methodist Church. I'm sorry to be leaving you, but the call's too great. We want to remain in the village if I can find another means of livelihood. Although I can no longer be your minister, my leaving has nothing to do with being offended or dissatisfied with the stipend. The church stewards have been most gracious in every way. It's just that God is leading us in a new direction and we need to follow Him."

The congregation sat dead still. No one moved a muscle as Walter uttered his solemn words of farewell.

"Mrs. Merrick and I hope each of you will continue to visit us at home," he concluded. "Your friendships mean a lot, and we want to do everything we can to maintain them." Then he closed the service with a simple prayer.

Standing in the chancel in front of the congregation, Walter was suddenly overcome by a strange loneliness he had never felt before. As he looked into their bewildered faces, he felt compelled to sing one last solo. Rustling in the pulpit, he handed a sheet of music to the organist and waited for her to get settled. The crowd hushed as they watched their minister struggling to begin. Drawing up his impressive frame under his black clerical frock, he straightened his shoulders and drew in his breath. His deep, rich voice started low and quiet, swelling into a crescendo that filled the entire building. Bathed in the glow of oil lamps set in the chandelier, Reverend Merrick's crimson face radiated peace and happiness. He stared upward as if penetrating the varnished ceiling and listening to a distant voice.

> I hear my dying Saviour say:
> "Follow Me! Come follow Me!
> For thee I gave My life away—
> Follow Me! Come follow Me!
>
> In all thy changeful life I'll be
> Thy God and Guide o'er land and sea,
> Thy bliss through all eternity
> Follow Me! come, follow Me!"[14]

With the last words, Walter bowed his head. In the past after singing a solo, he had often raised his eyes to bask in the warm approval of radiant faces. But today he took a moment to silently thank God for the call he and Ida Rose had heard in their hearts. When he did look up, Walter's sober features disclosed no trace of his old pride.

Among the flock Sissy Boggin's ostrich feather pitched forward like a shot bird. When her reeling face could finally be picked out between the hats in front of her, she was gaping pop-eyed, her thoughts in scattered confusion. Had she heard Reverend Merrick right? Is *this* what the school-house preachers were driving at?

All around Sissy the paralysed congregation began to stir. Several ladies could be seen dabbing lace at the corners of their eyes. Even a few of the men were getting out handkerchiefs and blowing their noses as Walter stepped down from the sanctuary for the last time. Ida Rose got up from her seat in the front pew and reached out to her husband. Together they walked arm in arm down the centre aisle and out the heavy double doors onto the step, where they stood shaking hands and thanking each of the families for their understanding.

At least one person in the church sensed, to some degree, the sacrifice that Walter and Ida Rose were making. In the days following the stewards' meeting, Archie Hampton, always the astute businessman, had done a lot of thinking. Now as he swiveled his stocky neck, elbow on the back of the pew, to watch Walter Merrick walk away from a security built over many years, Archie Hampton made himself a promise to visit the Merricks soon.

Although Robert Hunter had been unable to attend the meetings, one of the brothers had spent a few minutes each day talking with him about Jesus of Nazareth. Over the weeks Amelia also tried to share what she felt in the gospel meetings with her husband. Little by little the Hunters began to realize that the Holy Spirit was giving birth in their hearts to a simple faith. Both Amelia and Robert felt drawn to become part of the new church.

There were others, as well, including Sissy Boggins and Wilbur and Florence Stonehouse with their six lively children. Having heard from these few, the brothers suggested gathering at the Hunters' so that Robert could participate too. Robert and Amelia were delighted, and the first meeting was planned for the following Sunday morning.

Walter Merrick spent several days trudging from place to place, searching for employment of any kind. For a while every door seemed to close in his face, but he never, for a moment, considered turning back. Eventually, when he found work sorting and piling cedar shingles at Skene's Shingle and Sawmill, he recognized it as a blessing. His thoughts were his own, and he enjoyed being alone with God as he bound the bundles together.

One day as he was hauling a load of lumber to the sash-and-door factory, Walter remembered an old friend from his seminary days with whom he corresponded now and then. His friend's last letter had been filled with doubts, and Walter knew that the minister was struggling with the same questions and emptiness as he had done before meeting George and Jack. So that evening Walter sat down and wrote a long letter to the unhappy man, outlining the dramatic changes that had taken place in his own life and the peace that had followed. His final paragraphs said it all:

> Because of their simple trust in God, these two men are able to lead praiseful Spirit-filled lives. This life is accepted and taught by Methodism—in theory at least. As you know, there is plenty of talk about it and praying for it. Some claim to be living the Spirit-filled life and doubtless many sincere souls often stretch to obtain it. Yet somehow the majority miss it. I did myself. I had rarely met anyone whose Christian life seemed to be the real thing until I met these men. People may appear holy but often it's just a mannerism. I tried to display that demeanour myself until I realized it was a snare and my own nature deviously presenting itself as something it wasn't. All the time, I laboured under a misconception of the character of Jesus.
>
> Even though I preached the gospel with some clarity, His method was largely ignored. I had never received the living Christ—only an intellectual understanding. When George and Jack first came, they were completely abandoned to their Master. They hesitated at nothing while we, minister and people alike, failed to see that holiness consists of following Jesus in a practical way. The Holy Spirit lives in those who obey Him, and in those only. These men translated into action things about which we had been thinking and talking, reading and writing, praying and preaching, but weren't willing to do. Lack of absolute trust and simple obedience, it seems to me, is the one thing that always quenches the Spirit.[15]
>
> For years I claimed to be trusting God, and at times I thought I was, but there was never any change in my life because there was no obedience to the teachings of Jesus. Faith alone is not enough, for hour-by-hour these truths

demand obedience. Faith and works can only be separated in men's minds; for works flow spontaneously from ardent faith. In our daily walk, we need to both trust and obey. George and Jack's practical lives illustrated both.

We had prayed loud and long for the power experienced by the church on the day of Pentecost and often sang, "My all is on the altar, I'm waiting for the fire." But if the fire had even singed our garments, never mind being consumed by it, we would probably have run away as soon as we smelled it, afraid we might lose somebody's esteem or our social status. Then here come two men, complete strangers, without any credentials worth naming except being on fire with love for God and souls. Unfettered by traditions or opinions of men, they have an untiring energy and a consuming zeal and dare to obey God, even if it might entail personal suffering. Although some in the village spread malicious rumours, they continued quietly and patiently in the face of opposition.[16] In a short time, the men became the wonder and admiration of a few and the object of envy and opposition of many others. Even those who only came to a meeting or two had to admit that they had never before seen anyone who lived as close to the way that Jesus must have lived.[17]

The simple Sunday morning meetings bring me a joy that I never found in the traditional church. I am hoping that you will find these revelations as inspiring and refreshing as I have and that what we have found can be of some benefit to you. I know it would be a bit of a journey, but both Ida Rose and I would love to have you and Madge spend a few days with us anytime.

Ida Rose sends her best regards to both of you.

Your longtime friend,

Walter

Like the early Christians who had avoided any use of titles, Walter had ceased to be a *Reverend* in any way. He liked being just Walter, one of the brothers, doing his best. He knew Jesus, speaking of the religious leaders of his day, had prohibited titles that elevate one person over another.[18]

The Sunday afternoon sun slanted across the kitchen table as Walter spread out his Bible and Cruden's concordance. The early church, he could see, used terms—elders, deacons, evangelists and prophets— that referred to the function of certain individuals. But these had never been conferred as titles or offices of preeminence. Although all Christians were called *saints*, Walter felt sure they would have been appalled to be called Saint Luke, Elder Aquila, Deacon Stephen, or Prophet Silas. If believers received acknowledgment, it was for their efforts as a servant: "I commend unto you Phoebe our sister, who is a servant of the church."[19]

This matter of titles stimulated Walter's interest, and using his concordance, he counted the number of times certain words were used in the New Testament. To his amazement he discovered that the word "pastor," meaning "shepherd," was used only once. Clergyman…zero. Reverend… zero. The word "servant," however, appeared thirty-six times, while "brother" was used a total of one hundred and eighty-four times. *If we call each other anything,* he decided, *perhaps "brother" should be used more.*

In early March George and Jack received a letter from Timothy, advising them that he would be arriving on the stage line on the fourteenth. George spoke to Amelia on the morning of Timothy's arrival. "Do you think we could have bread pudding for dessert tonight, Amelia?"

She regarded George quizzically. "Why, of course," she said, "that's easy. But this is the first time you've ever asked for anything special. Is it a favourite of yours?"

George just smiled as he and Jack hurried out the door. "We'll bring home some extra raisins," he called back over his shoulder.

While the brothers stood waiting at the depot on Broadway Street, George's forehead began to wrinkle. He remembered his own first day in the work. And the strange feeling that had crept over him in the little green bedroom at Alistair and Priscilla's. "This will be a totally new experience for Timothy," he said. "He's never been this far from home before."

Jack grunted his agreement as he leaned against the hitching rail.

After a half hour, George caught a glimpse of the coach rounding the corner. When the horses pulled up and the high wheels ground to a stop, Timothy swung down, a broad smile spreading across his face at the sight of the brothers. George and Jack stepped forward to hug and welcome their new companion. Then George shouldered Timothy's travel bag, and they headed off, three abreast, in the direction of the Hunters' farm.

Framed in the doorway and lit by the lamp behind her, Amelia stood ready to welcome yet the fourth young man to cross her threshold. Surprise brightened her face as she saw Timothy's boyishness and eager manner. How young he seemed—hardly more than a fresh-faced lad. "Welcome to Hunters' Hollow," she exclaimed, gripping his hand in a vigorous shake.

Over supper Timothy disclosed some startling news. "Three weeks ago the friends started a second church at Morgan's. You know, with the growing numbers and all. If too many gather in one home, we might lose our closeness. Having come from big churches, some worried about the impersonal atmosphere that can develop. In the end, we decided the ideal number was about the size of a large family—like Jesus and His disciples."

"Sounds like a good decision to me," George said. "Besides, it's vital that each person bring something to share spiritually. If the assembly becomes too large, some might feel their words of encouragement were less important, less needed." He slid the bread pudding along the table, smiling as he watched Timothy's eyes widen with delight.

"And just who all's going to Morgan's?" Jack inquired.

"Bill and Alice, Joe Purves, and Susan Green. Along with Mrs. Alec Delaney and her boy, and two younger couples who live right there in Guelph," Timothy replied. "It cuts out the long journey, and it's better for the little ones. The length of the meeting was getting wearisome for them." Timothy poured cream over his bowl of bread pudding. "At first we found it painful to be apart, like apple seeds cut from the core. But we knew it was best. There has to be separation and space to grow properly—sort of like leaving home. The marvelous thing is that even in the very first meeting at Morgan's there was that same strong spirit of oneness."

"They'll miss not seeing each other though," George observed.

Timothy's face glowed. "We talked about that," he went on. "So it's been planned that the two churches will meet together on the first Sunday of each month. The 'union meeting' we call it."

Jack shook a couple of toothpicks out of a holder. "So how's Joe getting along on his own these days? He must miss Bella."

"Oh, pretty fair, I suppose." Timothy shoveled down the last bites of pudding. Then his eyes brightened. "Alice insists that Joe's taken a notion of Susan…" He clanked his spoon into the empty bowl. "And you know that when Alice holds forth, you might as well save your breath. Beats me how she'd know the first thing about the workings of Joe's head."

Jack looked solemnly in Amelia's direction. "Long-married women hone the fine art of discerning obscure matters that simple bachelors like us can't begin to grasp," he intoned prophetically.

George burst out laughing as Amelia shook her index finger in mock indignation. "Pipe down, Jack Gillan," she admonished in a tone long reserved for errant schoolboys. "You wouldn't dare offer that sort of drivel *before* dessert."

With supper over, everyone sat for a while in comfortable silence until Amelia, ever the schoolteacher, asked Timothy about his years at Guelph Collegiate. A bemused smile played across her face as Timothy told her about the odes of Horace he'd had to translate from Latin and the tough trigonometry examination.

Absorbing the wave of youthful enthusiasm around her table, Amelia stroked her cheek. First George and Jack, then Eddie, and now Timothy. Her reflectiveness blossomed as she rejoiced within herself. At last she and Robert had a family coming and going. Four smart chaps, but more than that, young men eager to make sacrifices because of their love for Christ.

Robert's strength, showing signs of improvement, allowed him to be outside for an hour or two each day. One afternoon the big man hobbled to the sugar camp near the back of his farm and eased himself gingerly onto a flat stump. As he sat and watched the three brothers making maple syrup, Jack staggered toward the low sleigh, a brimming pail in each hand.

"Take a break, lad," Robert called out in a husky voice.

Stepping closer, Jack set the buckets down, balancing them with his ankles on the spongy humus. "Sap's really running today, Robert," he noted with a grin. "But I reckon it'll be a day or two yet before you're up to running. Too bad that bull set you back so bad."

Robert nodded, his coarse features set in thoughtful cast. "Maybe so. But there's another way to look at it. If that bull hadn't gored me," he conjectured, "Amelia and I might well have turned you men away from our door." He looked up into Jack's broad wind-burned face, and then beyond into the profound blue of the March sky. "And missed this way of love."

Jack tugged at his tweed cap, gripped the metal handles of the sap buckets and straightened up. "It's certainly a mystery how God works, rearranging our lives." He paused, setting the pails back down, his eyes suddenly distant. "Robert, I've been wondering," he said tentatively, "does the Warmington clan live nearby?"

"Warmington. Warmington." Robert's face clouded. "Can't say as I know anybody around these parts by that name…"

"I noticed it in the album," Jack broke in. "It's not a common name."

Robert's eyes glimmered, suddenly making the connection. "That's the family Amelia taught the first year she landed into Belwood. They rented a farm close to the school. If I recall right, they had a drove of kids—but a smart bunch. The two girls in the picture took a shine to Amelia when she prepared the oldest one for the entrance exams. Had her over for supper some."

Jack tried to sound nonchalant. "Either of them keep in touch?"

"Nothing more than an odd letter. The family up and left West Gary, y' know. Headed back to someplace near Elora where they come from. Eventually Nettie married a farmer around Tiverton." When Robert shifted to avoid the glare of the sun, a sharp pain shot across his face. "This rotten thing catches me every time I move the wrong way," he muttered, bracing himself forward with his left arm.

Jack waited until Robert was comfortable again. "And the other girl?"

"Oh, yeah. Miranda. The black sheep of the family. Got taken up with book learning and packed off to Toronto. Amelia had a letter around Christmas if I remember right. Says Miranda's one of these that thinks women should be able to vote right along like a man." Robert eased himself back on the stump. "At the time some folks gave out that she was part of the reason they all hightailed it out of here. Got herself into desperate straits, I heard."

Jack's heart pounded as he reached down and picked up the buckets for the second time, his face a strange mixture of hope and disappointment. "Better get along with these, Robert," he said. "Thanks for the breather."

Sunny days and frosty nights made the sap run abundantly, and the brothers tapped about two hundred and fifty trees with spiles made from small branches hollowed in the centre. Every day they collected and emptied the buckets into a wooden barrel on the sleigh, boiling the contents in a cast-iron kettle until much of the water had evaporated. The sap was then poured into a second and a third kettle. Amelia did the final boiling on the kitchen cookstove after straining out the twigs and impurities with cheese cloth. Forty gallons of sap were needed to make a single gallon of the rich amber syrup. When the season finished, there was more maple syrup than Robert and Amelia had ever produced before. The extra money would be used to hire a man until Robert had fully recovered.

As expected, Eddie arrived near the end of March. His face betrayed the inevitable pain of the parting from father and home, knowing his future would lie among strangers. Like Abraham offering Isaac on Mount Moriah, Oliver Summers had leaned forward, placed both hands on the shoulders of his only son and embraced him. Then holding back his tears, he released Eddie and sent him willingly on his way.[20]

That evening, after the four brothers had supper with Robert and Amelia, they gathered in the parlour to discuss their travel arrangements. They had all been praying for the Holy Spirit's guidance and felt it would be best if George and Timothy traveled together while Jack and Eddie set out in a different direction. Each pair of brothers would map out their own plans.

George and Timothy decided to go north to Orangeville, where they would be close enough to return for the Sunday morning meeting in Belwood. Eddie and Jack felt they should travel south to Milton. A strong south wind, blowing for two days, had dried the spring mud and made cycling possible again.

After nine months as constant companions, it was hard for George and Jack to think of parting company. And yet each man gained comfort from the knowledge that wherever they went, no matter how far apart, each of them would carry the same closeness in his heart. Nothing could separate them from the love of Christ that lived within them equally.[21] George, too, intuited the unknown preoccupation in Jack's mind, something deeper than his friend had yet shared.

As they stood together at the side of the lane the next morning, George spoke first. "I'm going to miss you, Jack. It's been wonderful to be together. I hope things go well for you and Eddie." He put his arms around his old friend. They gave each other a heartfelt hug. "We'll be praying for you," George went on. "Please do the same for Timothy and me."

"That we will," Jack promised. "We'll write regularly too." He glanced up and saw Robert waving from the upstairs window. Smiling, Jack signaled in return. Then he picked up his travel bag and straddled his bicycle. "Good days to all of you," he said as he pushed off.

George and Timothy stood with Amelia at the little gate and watched Eddie and Jack cycle down the lane. When they looked back a couple of times, everybody waved until they had disappeared from sight. George tried to swallow the lump in his throat. He was going to miss Jack a lot, not having him to discuss things or to laugh with. He noticed Amelia holding back tears too, and when he stepped closer and put his hand on her shoulder, she cried softly.

"It's hard to say goodbye," she sniffed and then turned to George. "But someday we won't ever have to say goodbye again, will we?"

"No, Amelia, we won't," he replied, his tone gentle.

George and Timothy packed up the next day and took their leave of the Hunters as well, promising to return for the Sunday morning meeting. Amelia resisted the flood of tears that threatened her as the red brick house yawned with emptiness. Instead she briskly mopped the floors, set her winter shawls to soak, yanked up the summer kitchen window and trimmed away the Virginia creeper vines to let the sun shine in. Then she plopped down beside Robert's bed, playfully taking off his socks to rub his feet. Something new's afoot," she chirped. "Our four young men have made tracks out of here with the greatest invitation anyone can hear. I hope someone will receive them…"

When April's sun charmed the rolling landscape into a warmer hue and dried the ruts along the township roads, farmers visited their granaries and tentatively hoisted dusty bags of seed grain.

One Monday morning after spending Sunday with the Belwood church, George and Timothy wended their way back to Orangeville along the chequerboarded concessions and side roads of East Garafraxa. They had just puffed up the side of a steep gully when a farmer crested the hill, a set of red harrows, freshly painted, overhanging his weathered wagon.

After stepping aside into the grassy ditch and waving, George turned to watch the team negotiate the precipitous slope. "You know," he said when the load had safely reached the bottom, "Robert's still not able for a full day of work in the fields."

"And seeding time's just around the corner," Timothy added instantly.

George walked the length of a farm before he spoke again. "We'd better tell the folks who are coming to the Orangeville meetings that we'll be away for a couple of weeks and go back to Robert and Amelia's," he said at last. "We'll need to put the crop in for them this year."

The farm boy grinned. "They're lucky we know wheat from toadflax."

A serious look swept over George's features. "Jesus must have loved the process of sowing. One of his richest parables begins: 'Behold, a sower went forth to sow. And when he sowed…'"[22] George's voice trailed off as he considered the different types of soil Jesus had spoken about.

Timothy glanced over at his older companion, trying to interpret his silence. George seemed to be staring off into the distant fields as he stumbled over a rutted wash in the road.

When George turned back and spoke again, his voice was pensive. "Isn't it a wonderful privilege to be called to sow that same heavenly seed of God's kingdom?"

When Robert and Amelia first received the welcome news, they were touched by the amazing offer. Again, it reminded them that this way of Christ was a way of divine love, expressed in practical ways. Still, their reaction was mild compared to the neighbouring farmers, who were flabbergasted. For people who lived untouched by the Lord's gracious Spirit, the brothers' generosity remained beyond their comprehension. And yet that simple act did much to engender a respect for the little church that gathered in the Hunters' home.

Both George and Timothy were farmers at heart, and working on the fertile land brought back good memories. For them the warbling song of the returning birds and the first buds of springtime were renewed evidence of God's care for His creation.

Carrying the grain in a canvas bag, George walked up and down the rich brown fields, scattering the seed as he went. He vigorously turned a little handle on the side of the bag, causing the spreading mechanism underneath to broadcast the oats evenly on both sides. As George stepped through the soft soil, he began to sing.

> Sowing the seed by the wayside high,
> Sowing the seed on the rocks to die;
> Sowing the seed where the thorns will spoil,
> Sowing the seed in the fertile soil.
>
> Sowing the seed with an aching heart,
> Sowing the seed while the teardrops start.
> Sowing in hope till the reapers come:
> Gladly to gather the harvest home.[23]

As the oats were breaking the crust and beginning to sprout delicate patterns of green, one of the seeds planted by the brothers' gracious gesture motivated Archie Hampton, the church steward, to pay a call. When Walter and Ida Rose had walked out of the Methodist church for the last time, Archie Hampton had promised himself to visit them soon. But he was a busy man, pencil behind one ear and irons in several village fires, and the months had got away from him. Only when he heard the story of the brothers coming back to help the Hunters was he reminded of his first impulse to find out more about the love these people had for each other. One evening after dark, the church steward finally rapped on Walter Merrick's door and was welcomed in for the first of several lively discussions. And later that summer Archie Hampton professed a new awakening and a desire to follow Christ in a simpler manner.

The small church at Belwood had grown by one more.

Twenty-Three

LAURA'S DILEMMA
Spring 1902

Spring was approaching the village of Mildmay like a barefoot girl with the sun at her back, tiptoeing around the last traces of snow and bearing mayflowers and violets in her arms. Throughout Bruce County the tinkle of fairy bells could be heard as crystallized ice on the creeks shattered under the flirtatious eye of the sun. Spring peepers tuned up in the rivulets of meltwater that had drained the snowfall off the brown landscape. The undulations made by the fall ploughing gave the fields an open and vulnerable look. The heavy snow had regenerated their moisture, making them ready to receive the seeds of a new season.

One April afternoon as Laura carried her books home from school, the honking of Canada geese high overhead on their way north turned her face upward. What *was* the mysterious yearning that called them home to nest? To a world far removed from their winter habitat. They reminded her of the unspoken feeling stirring within her own heart. For weeks she had been sorely missing George and the friends in Puslinch and, to her, Mildmay seemed on the far side of the continent. After the wedge-shaped formation had disappeared beyond a church weathervane, stark against the blue sky, she began to walk again, still deep in reflection. Geese always traveled in a flock. Perhaps, like them, she couldn't thrive on her own either—at least not happily. Wasn't she, after all, the child of another world too?

Laura was still preoccupied as she turned in at an elegant two-storey home of yellow clay brick. In the vegetable garden she could see Mrs.

Brunstedder kneeling on an empty sack as she scattered seeds along a tiny trench. As Laura walked over to greet her landlady, she recalled the quiet winter evening when the older woman had taken her into her confidence.

"Herman and me, ve alvays vanted a family," Mrs. Brunstedder had said wistfully, "but God never sent us vun." Her spectacles misted with memory. "Zat's vy ve are here in Mildmay. Visout a son to take over ze place, Herman had to sell out ven he got to be seventy. Ze verk vas shust too much for him." She had raised expectant eyes. "You're like a daughter to me, Laura," she had said softly. "I shust hope you stay for a long time."

At the sight of Laura, Mrs. Brunstedder's full lips widened into a cheerful smile across her moon-shaped face. "Velcome, velcome," she exclaimed, planting her fists in the soft soil and pushing herself up on two stout arms. "Zere's a slice of apfel pie in ze kitchen."

Walking along the path to the vine-covered summer kitchen behind Mrs. Brunstedder, Laura's thoughts returned to George and her spiritual family at Wood Creek Farm. Although she boasted many new friends in Mildmay, she couldn't exchange heart fellowship with a single one of them. They spoiled her shamefully, but they couldn't seem to understand her soul. *Friendship,* she reasoned, *is vastly different from fellowship.*

Tying an apron around her square body, Mrs. Brunstedder reached for the pie lifter. Pulling down the oven door, she inserted the wooden stick into the heat and deftly hooked the two wires over each side of the metal pie plate. "Shust give it a few minutes to cool and ve have a piece," she beamed, setting it onto a hot pad. "Herman should be along soon. He vent down street to have his vatch fixed at Oakin's Jewelry."

Laura leaned forward and patted the older woman's round shoulder. "With your cooking, Mrs. Brunstedder, I'm as spoiled as an old maid's cat." Winking, she ran her hands over her hips. "And that's what I'll be, an old maid, if I don't soon practice restraint."

Mrs. Brunstedder pulled a look of mock distress.

"But there's no point starting in the middle of the week," Laura laughed as she tossed her book satchel onto a chair. The late afternoon sun slanting across the sheet music on the piano reminded her that she had promised to give a neighbour girl her first lesson at seven that evening.

Each day after school, Laura looked forward to a quiet time of prayer before Mrs. Brunstedder called for supper. After tucking into her landlady's apple pie, she extracted Palgrave's *Golden Treasury* from her book bag and paused thoughtfully at the foot of the stairs, her hand on the curved oak volute. Again she felt the pang of loneliness that had been her recent companion. She must find a way to have more fellowship—even if it meant switching professions or taking a lower salary.

Laura closed her bedroom door, slipped off her shoes, and loosened her French braid, allowing her dark chestnut hair to cascade over her shoulders. She folded up the Eaton's pattern and a length of dimity muslin for a summer dress that she had left stretched across her bed. Then she lifted her violin out of its case and began to play. The sweetness of her voice permeated the room as it followed the violin's soaring melody. As she sang, she found comfort in the words and her loneliness began to dissolve.

> When storms of life are round me beating,
> When rough the path that I have trod,
> Within my closed door retreating,
> I love to be alone with God.
>
> Alone with God, the world forbidden;
> Alone with God, oh, blest retreat!
> Alone with God and in Him hidden,
> To hold with Him communion sweet.[1]

Warmth filled her heart as she realized that she was not alone. She was with God. Then, setting her violin aside, Laura knelt by her bed. As always, she finished by asking for God's continued favour toward George and the others. After her time in communion she washed her face before supper.

Although the lingering pain of separation had subsided, Laura often wondered how George was faring in his new life and when she would see him again. His letters were positive, but she knew that he always tried to put the best face on everything. She wanted to see his expression and eyes while he talked about his feelings. Being on her own, she suspected that Jesus had sent His workers in pairs for companionship and mutual support, and she was glad that Timothy and George were now together. As the sweet buds of April unfolded into the blossoming thickets of May, Laura found new strength and came to a firm decision.

The following Sunday morning after the Brunstedders had left for church, she spread three sheets of ivory linen stationery out on the kitchen table. After much deliberation and several false starts, she had two neat envelopes ready to post. Her third and last letter was addressed to George. Sometimes writing was almost like talking to him.

Mildmay, Ontario
Sunday, May 11, 1902

My dearest George,

April the first often spurs an epidemic of either spring fever or tom-foolery. What you wrote about Timothy throwing his gangly legs across the backs of those two Shetland ponies threw me into fits of laughter. I can just picture the spectacle—him straddling the pair as they tore around that paddock, bucking and kicking their heels toward the clouds. And then the ultimate when they veered around opposite sides of that puddle. How deep was it where Mr. Timothy landed on his back? And pray tell, where were you during the shenanigans? In the fence corner splitting your sides, I expect.

No doubt your reaction's what prompted Timothy to pinch your watch off the dresser that night and set it ahead by a full hour. I can see you in the morning stretching and climbing leisurely out of bed. Then, finding you'd over slept, shaking Timothy awake and tearing downstairs like a madman—full of apologies for being late. Only to find the kitchen empty. Did you think your breakfast had come and gone? You like a good laugh as much as the next fellow, even if you're seldom the instigator. If I thought about it enough, George, I could easily envy Timothy spending so much time with you…

I'm pleased you've found lodging in Orangeville even if the new land-lady isn't a Mrs. Applebee or Amelia Hunter. I wonder what it's like having gospel meetings in a drafty old carriage works. It thrills me to hear about the folks you and Timothy are meeting. The cattle dealer's wife sounds like a jewel. Although I'd dearly love to see more of you, I truly can discern the beauty in your ministry.

Now to some serious news. I want you to be among the first to know that I'm planning to leave Mildmay as soon as school closes. My letter of resignation lies before me, together with one to Alistair and Priscilla telling them I'm coming home. And to let me know if they hear of any employ-ment in Puslinch. I'll accept any kind of work, provided it's within walking distance of regular fellowship.

My time in Mildmay has enriched me in many ways, and I've made some dear friends. Herman Brunstedder's a prince of a man and, after school, Mrs. Brunstedder always manages to be sliding hot apple strudel or a German shensel cake out of the oven just as I arrive. Then she'll slather two wedges with whipped cream and push them across the table to Herman and me. But if she doesn't stop soon, I'll have to let out my dresses.

But now, George, I need to leave this village to fully savour what God has handed to me. Although I've loyal friends here, I long for the intensity of the fellowship at Wood Creek Farm—where the Christ in me reaches out and unites me with the Christ in another. I've learned this year, in a way I never understood before, that it's only by His Life that people can be in perfect unity.[2]

Each Tuesday evening I give one of the neighbour girls a piano lesson. Her first was based on middle C—the white key at the centre of the keyboard. As I explained that any two notes in harmony with middle C are in harmony with each other, I suddenly realized that middle C is none other than Christ in the centre of our lives. We must first be in spiritual harmony with Him to be in harmony with each other. As each of us lives by revelation from the Father, we become one. It isn't enough to have a common interest in Bible discussion or in helping others or in singing gospel music or in any other religious activity. We need inner communion with the Master Tuner, who adjusts each string to its proper pitch.

On a lighter tone, George, do you remember our last meal with Dad and Mother Farnham that September night before I ever came to Mildmay? Your father was plenty riled over the young heifers. Just that morning they'd broken down a length of fence and marauded through his vegetable patch, treating themselves to the curly Savoy cabbages he'd been raising for market. In a way, George, we were like those eager young Guernseys, you and I. We had our own notions of what life's greatest gifts might be, and although we never broke down any fences to reach them, we still allowed ourselves to dream. And now life has given us far greater gifts than we could ever have imagined.

I expect to be back from the wedding in Stratford by the middle of July, and I'm hoping that you and Timothy will find occasion to pass by Wood Creek Farm before the summer's over. I hope you'll find time to tell someone who's waiting to hear that you still miss your girl…

Laura got no further before crossing her arms on the table and putting her head down on the letter before her, her eyes moist and blinking.

~

Throughout the month Laura prepared her four senior students for their entrance class examinations, three of whom aspired to go on to the

Walkerton Collegiate. Their thoughtful abstraction contrasted with the ram-
bunctiousness of the younger fry who continually made mischief or gazed
out the classroom windows where colts rollicked in the spring sunshine.

Laura's nerves had been frazzled that week by several untoward events.
Not the least of these had been the gruff inspector's visit, during which
he had expressed gratification with her pupils' progress but disgust at the
rainwater barrel where the younger ones were hoping to hatch frogs out
of tadpoles. Ten-year-old Zillah had sat at her desk all one morning, head
down on her arms in soundless sobbing. In response to her teacher's gentle
probing she would only offer the laconic word "toothache." Indeed, her
jaw was swollen, and Laura had bent over the girl in concern, suddenly
noticing through her thin sleeve the marks of inexplicable bruising.
Unnerved, Laura determined to pay a prompt visit to the ill-assorted family
known as the "Hipple tribe." And finally, the bigger boys had lugged a dead
cat to school, an unfortunate puss whose inglorious carcase was tossed onto
the outhouse roof by the hooligans taunting the tearful girls with cries of
"Here, puss. Poor pussy." Opening the *Third Reader* with a reminiscent sigh,
Laura struggled to focus her charges' attention on the story of the greedy
dog in the manger.

The second Friday in May was Arbour Day and the students looked
forward to the day out of the classroom to tidy the school yard. Laura had
promised to take them fishing at Otter Creek if they finished early. Many
brought rakes and piled the old leaves and rubbish beside the road. Then
Laura struck a match, and the children watched as the flames crept through
the heap until a hot blaze was shooting up. The boys pushed and shoved
as they yanked out the weeds hidden among the hollyhocks and honeysuckle while the girls planted a double ring of blue and yellow pansies around
the base of the flagpole. Nostalgia swept over Laura as she thought of the
happy times she and George had spent in his garden. His appreciation for
flowers and nature made him different from most other men she knew.

Mr. Hindley, one of the school trustees, arrived at four o'clock, just as
the children were leaving for home. Dave Hindley's thick eyebrows carried a sprinkling of sawdust as he leaned against the doorjamb, waiting for
the last dawdler to shoulder her books and head down the path. When,
suddenly, he remembered his manners and yanked off his cap, the square
carpenter's pencil peeping from beneath its band tumbled out.

"Afternoon, Miss Chapelton," he said amicably. "I'm working next door,
cutting a dormer into the Oatkin's attic. I reckoned I'd take a break." When

he brushed some cobwebs from his flannel shirt, bits of cedar shingle fell on the floor. "Now there I go messing up your cloakroom," he laughed.

"Don't give it a second thought," Laura insisted. "I've got to sweep up anyway." Her eyes twinkled. "It's the time of year when schoolboys squish through every mud puddle in the village."

Nodding, Dave Hindley straightened his shoulders. "Sarah and I were wondering if you could come for a visit tomorrow evening. We plan to invite the other two trustees along as well, if that's all right."

"That will be lovely, Mr. Hindley," Laura answered cheerfully. "Thank you for the invitation." But as she watched him walk away, she felt a queasiness in the pit of her stomach. Were the trustees disgruntled at her decision to leave?

The following evening Laura arrived at the Hindleys' promptly at seven. She greeted the two other trustees and shared some friendly chatter with their wives as Mrs. Hindley served tea and cranberry muffins. Eventually their discussion turned to the school and Laura's influence on the children. The taller of the other two men said how tidy the yard looked after it had been raked and the flowers planted.

Mr. Oatkin, the bespectacled village jeweller, gave the impression of being studious. He mentioned how charming the school was with all the children's work displayed upon the walls. After a little pause, he looked directly at Laura. "You're one of the most gifted teachers we've ever had, Miss Chapelton," he said solemnly. "You've introduced the children to art for the first time in their lives. And the music they're learning is delightful. The parents are so happy that you're teaching some of the older students to play the piano and others the violin." Faint but deepening shades of pink like the first sunburn of spring appeared in Laura's cheeks.

"Even more important," Mr. Hindley added, "the parents say you've been good for the children. Good inside, you know. They seem happier, more lively, and they're doing good work." Then his face took on a more pointed concentration. "We were very sorry to receive your resignation. Is there anything we can do to sway your decision?"

"Is it the salary?" the tall man blurted out before Laura could reply. "Or problems with any of the parents?"

As she shook her head, Laura's eyes bore a wounded look. "The work is very gratifying and I love the children," she tried to explain. "It's just that I'm part of a little church in Puslinch Township." A heavy feeling filled her chest and a lump swelled in her throat. "I miss them terribly, and I want to be closer to them."

The tall trustee, a well-intentioned man, promptly spoke up. "It's good to have a young teacher serious about her faith," he asserted. "My wife and I'd be pleased to fetch you along to St. Andrews every Sunday."

Laura raised her eyes to the trustee's face. "I appreciate your invitation," she said softly. "I'm sure St. Andrews is a fine place of worship, but it's a little home church that I've been a part of." Delicately, she told them about her desire to gather in the manner and spirit of the early church. Mr. Hindley listened intently as Laura spoke about her convictions.

When the other trustee tried offering her a large raise to $460 for the next school term, Laura caught her breath. It was $150 more than most teachers received and well above her present salary. For a fleeting moment she pictured the silk flowered dresses, the kid gloves, and the Leghorn hats trimmed in chiffon that she had admired in the shop window. But the milliner's hats had always seemed just a little more than her slim purse could pay. Laura's imagination contrasted the colourful spring bonnets with the plain sailor she wore to school. In her ingenuous manner she could not know that the girlish uplift of her eyes and luminous smile under the straw brim conveyed far more charm than any lavish headgear could ever express. But even as she reflected, something from the Bible came to her: What will you profit if you gain the whole world, yet forfeit your own soul?[3] The trustees were making an exceptional offer, but she knew she had to refuse.

After Laura thanked them and she and everyone else had left, Dave Hindley turned to his wife. "Miss Chapelton's a most unusual person. How many young women do you know who would turn down a salary like that just so they could be close to their church friends?"

Sarah Hindley shook her head. "I can't think of a single one."

"Her faith's got a powerful hold on her," Dave Hindley observed, picking up his newspaper. "It certainly seems essential to her happiness."

⁓

Coming home from school a few days later, Laura spotted a blue envelope on the kitchen table. Her heart skipped a beat as she recognized Emily McElderry's distinctive handwriting. Savouring the thought of fresh news, Laura slipped off to her favourite place near the village's artesian well. The fresh clear water, from deep in the bedrock, overflowed night and day into

Otter Creek. Laura knelt down, cupped her hands, and scooped up a drink of the cold water. The day was unseasonably warm and humid, and she splashed her face before she sat down to digest the welcome words.

Hespeler, Ontario
May 23, 1902

My dear Laura,

We are counting the days until we hear your laugh and see your smile again. There are so many things that I want to tell you face-to-face. I hope you are healthy and happy as you near the end of the school year. We recently received the letter that you mailed to the Puslinch church c/o Alistair and Priscilla. In part, that is my reason for writing. I hardly know how to begin, so I will plunge right in.

Stephen and I have felt prompted to begin in God's great harvest field the same as George and Jack. And then Timothy and Eddie, a couple months ago. But perhaps I should back up a bit. One weekend last August, Stephen and I went to visit the brothers in Elora. I can't describe the overwhelming feelings we both felt there. Ever since, the work of the gospel has gripped our thoughts. We talked at length of the work that George and Jack are doing, but we never breathed a word to each other of being in the work ourselves. That is, not until one morning in December when I was praying, unaware that Stephen had come back into the house. I was so moved by the tremendous sacrifice of our Lord, knowing He would have given His life even if it was only for me, that tears flowed down my cheeks. Suddenly I wondered about others who have never known this Friend who understands my every need.

Just then Stephen came into our room. Seeing my tears, he asked what was wrong. I blurted out right away that I needed to share this passion inside me with others. And then do you know what happened? Stephen smiled and his eyes welled up too. He said he felt the same way, but that he had been keeping it to himself. We fell onto the bed, crying and laughing at the same time, our hearts beating furiously with the excitement of it all.

I'm still amazed the Spirit touched both of our lives separately yet simultaneously. I can hardly bear to think what it would have been like if only one of us had felt such a conviction. For weeks afterward we talked freely and prayed to know when and where we should begin. That's when your letter arrived, speaking about the hospitable folks in Mildmay and your desire for fellowship. It seemed to break a log jam in our minds, and although you didn't intend it so, we took it as a sign, like the call from Macedonia. After pleading for affirmation in our hearts, we are settled that God is calling us to preach the gospel in Mildmay.

So yesterday, right after the Sunday morning meeting, we shared our plans with the church. The feelings of joy were just as powerful as when George and Jack announced their calling. Tomorrow we intend to write to the brothers and tell them too.

Stephen and I wonder if you would consider staying on in Mildmay. We would be thrilled if you could help us in the meetings and in getting acquainted around the village. Sometimes I just don't feel able for it, but I know that if Christ is the power behind our feeble efforts, anything is possible. It will likely be the end of August before Stephen can sell his shop and be free to set out in the work.

My good man has just come in for supper, so I must bid adieu for now. He sends his warmest greetings. Both of us look forward to seeing you at the end of June. Until then, we'll be keeping our eyes peeled for your reply.

Your sister in Christ,

Emily

P.S. Perhaps you could ask if the school might be available!

Laura put down the letter and gazed blankly across Otter Creek, her head swimming as she thought about the sudden change in her own prospects. Could she really stay on in Mildmay and continue teaching the children she had grown fond of? Praying earnestly about Emily's request, Laura wondered if perhaps God had sent her on ahead to water the soil for the coming of the gospel plough. She wrote back three days later, confirming that she would be very happy to stay in Mildmay. After posting the letter to Emily, she stopped to see Mr. Hindley and told him that she was willing to stay on for another year if the trustees were still interested. Dave Hindley bent down to look into the young teacher's earnest eyes.

"Interested!" he exclaimed. "It's the best news I've heard all month."

Blushing, Laura tried to explain the abrupt shift in her outlook. She sincerely hoped he didn't think it was the offer of a larger salary.

"Do you think it would be possible for my friends to use the school in the evenings to preach the gospel?" she asked.

"Absolutely! Any friend of yours is welcome to use it anytime."

When Laura surprised the Brunstedders with the news that she would be staying on, Katrina squealed with elation. "And your friends, Stephen and Emily? Zey vill be needing a bed."

"I'm sure they will, if you want to take on two more boarders."

"Vunderbar," Katrina exclaimed. "If zey are anyzing like you, zey vill be a real shoy."

Laura thought of George as she folded her thin summer dresses, preparing to leave the Brunstedders for July and August. She allowed herself to hope that she would see him again before she returned for the next school term. She recalled with wistfulness the summer gatherings on the lush grass at Wood Creek Farm and the joy and delight of the warm family feeling. Bill and Alice's daughter, Madeleine, would be a baby no longer, but a little girl of four in a tiny Mother Hubbard pinafore. Laura tingled with anticipation at the array of faces she hoped to greet—George's chief among them, if he and Timothy happened to be home for a few days.

George and Jack kept in touch by letter and decided to come together early in July to baptize the Belwood and Elora saints. They would have preferred to have had the baptism when the friends first began to follow Jesus, but the water had been perishingly cold. George found a quiet bend in the Grand River just a few hundred feet upstream from the Gartshore Iron Bridge. This place at the edge of Fergus was about midpoint between the two churches. Under the overhanging branches of a mountain ash, he selected a calm spot that was deep enough and well away from the rocky rapids.

Early that peaceful Sunday morning, the Belwood church gathered at Robert and Amelia's, planning to meet the Elora saints at the river at nine o'clock. George and Timothy, who had cycled from Orangeville the previous evening, borrowed a pile of Amelia's towels and packed them into a wooden apple crate. Robert's team of light horses stood hitched and waiting for the little company. The brothers and sisters on the wagon sang hymns of rejoicing as they rode along the narrow twisting road. Led by Walter Merrick's melodious voice, the songs of Zion rang out through the misty woods which stood like consenting witnesses on either side.

As the Belwood church approached the meeting place, they could see Jack and Eddie lingering with the Elora friends beside the water. But they saw something else. A second crowd was congregating on the Iron Bridge. Someone had learned of the baptism, and word had spread through the town like a summer grass fire before a stiff breeze. Shouts and catcalls erupted from a few of the onlookers as the two churches greeted and embraced each other.

Jack, who had arrived ten minutes earlier with Eddie and the rest of the Elora saints, turned to George. "For some reason we've got extra company," he said motioning toward the bridge. "And they seem to be heated up. Someone threw a couple of rocks, but they didn't hit any of us."

"We got the message all right," Eddie pronounced. "Written in stone."

This hostile presence made the friends uneasy, but they decided to go ahead as planned. Several of them joined hands as they made their way to an exposed sand bar at the shore. Tension ran high as everyone on the bridge pushed and shuffled to get a better view. The noisy crowd yelling from the bridge marked a sharp contrast with the saints quietly preparing to be baptized at the river's edge. The friends sang a hymn just as the Puslinch church had done at Wood Creek Farm two years earlier. As the first notes of the rising melody drifted toward the bridge, the mob quieted down, straining to catch the elusive words.

Rejoicing in the Lord,
We walk His lowly way;
We love His precepts and His word,
And joyfully obey.

Baptized in Jesus' name,
Renouncing self and sin:
To all the world we thus proclaim
The Saviour dwells within.

He leads us by the hand,
Our Master true and kind;
Obedient now, at His command,
We leave the world behind.

Baptized in Jesus' name—
Hushed is the voice of strife—
To all the world we thus proclaim
His Way and Truth and Life.[4]

As the last verse receded across the current, only the pleasant warble of red-winged blackbirds could be heard. George and Jack stood together on a large flat rock almost submerged at the water's edge looking at the saints gathered arm-in-arm in a close semicircle around them.

"The first act before God is to believe, but the first act before men is to be baptized," George said, mindful of the boisterous crowd in the background. "Today we are showing that we have come out of the world and have entered into Christ. It isn't just the ritual of being immersed, it's our declaration that there's no longer a relation between us and the world. Why? Because we now consider ourselves dead to this world. The New Testament meaning of baptism is not only a cleansing; it is also a burial. We believe we are dead, so we ask someone to bury us beneath the waters in baptism. If you don't believe that you are dead, you shouldn't be baptized. No one wants to be buried alive, do they?" Several of the saints smiled and shook their heads at George's disarming logic.

"How do we express our faith in the blood of Christ for the cleansing of our sins? Through baptism. And how do we show that we believe our old self-nature was crucified with Christ upon the cross? Through baptism. Baptism signifies that we are both cleansed and dead. But we aren't left under the water, permanently buried. We're raised, resurrected with Christ. Our old selves have died and His new Spirit is forever alive in us."

When George had finished speaking, the little assembly bowed their heads. Jack's deep voice trembled as he implored God to draw close and overshadow them as each person was baptized.

When Jack finished praying, George, dressed in a woolen shirt and trousers, turned and waded calmly out into the water up to his waist. Again jeers, howls, and whistles from some of the younger men ripped through the tranquility of the morning. Jack took Evelyn Applebee by the hand and helped her along the slippery bottom toward George. A stray rock splashed into the river well short of Mrs. Applebee, who pretended not to notice.

"Go home tramp preachers," a raucous voice bellowed from the bridge. "You're a bunch of heathens!"

Heathens. The word struck Eddie hard; it made him think. He remembered hearing that little companies of Christians had been led to their deaths in the Roman Colosseum to satisfy the pagan observers' thirst for brutality. "Being a genuine Christian has never been for the fainthearted," he whispered to Walter Merrick, who was standing next to him.

When Walter glanced at the bridge again, he suddenly recognized the angular silhouette of Nelson Borthwick, his former steward. His face drained and his throat constricted in nostalgic sorrow as he thought of the kindred judgements he and Nelson had once held. And of the small laughs they had shared about the congregation's foibles. Among the burgeoning mob, he could identify at least five other faces from his final charge, including a couple he had joined in holy matrimony the previous summer amid a garden of roses and pageantry. Hanging his head in incurable sadness, he winced, remembering how the man had slapped him on the back after his breathtaking solo at the reception. It grieved him to think that the very people he loved so much had turned against him now.

As Eddie waited to be baptized, he continued to ponder the scene in the Colosseum. "It's tragic," he said to Timothy, "that we're being troubled today by people who are adamant that they are Christians and we're pagans. The road of history takes some strange hairpin turns." Mrs. Applebee and all the others seemed to Eddie like heroes of the faith as they unselfconsciously wrung the river water from their draggled clothes. The last four lines of the hymn echoed in his mind as the baptism concluded and the saints climbed back onto the wagons.

The friends were barely home before the rumour mills of Elora and Belwood had peddled details of the unusual baptism above the Iron Bridge. Some in the district took to calling them the Dippers. For most it was simply a harmless witticism, but for others the intent was more insidious—to ridicule their scriptural method of baptism. Although only a few would mock them openly, the saints were occasionally shunned by the more starched of the traditional churchgoers. Regardless, the funny names and the jokes didn't deter the believers from pursuing their chosen course.

~

When Stephen and Emily heard how eager the Elora and Belwood friends had been to be baptized, they were spurred on in winding up their affairs. For Laura, the summer months had been filled with the joys of her visit to Wood Creek Farm, but in late August she found herself looking forward to the new school year. She was excited to introduce Stephen and Emily to the village as they began their work toward a spiritual harvest.

The McElderrys arrived shortly after Laura had begun teaching her class in September 1902. Thrilled to have their company, she spent every spare moment helping them get acquainted. It was the first gospel mission for all three of them, and they soon got busy, making invitations and delivering them in Mildmay and the surrounding countryside.

Suddenly, it seemed, the time for their first meeting was at hand. The schoolhouse basked in the evening light as Laura greeted each family warmly at the door and introduced them to Stephen and Emily. As each student surveyed the rearranged room, Laura could almost predict their reaction. Some, after identifying their desk, gave a shy smile in her direction and led their parents to sit next to it. One enthusiastic lad hastily retrieved an opaque jar of grass and fuzzy caterpillars from the windowsill to show his father. Not to be outdone, his sister boosted a stack of readers to display a collection of leaves flattened between sheets of brown paper. Still other students abandoned their parents to the room and asked if they could sit next to Miss Chapelton. Nodding, she pointed each one to the front row near the piano. As the schoolhouse filled, Laura couldn't help but be intrigued to see who had chosen to respond to the invitation.

Among the early arrivals were the three trustees and their wives. After respectful introductions all around, they chose a seat and settled back, eager to hear what Miss Chapelton's friends would have to say. Dave and Sarah Hindley's two daughters, both scholars in the upper readers, led their parents past the art wall blossoming with watercolours and sketches. They twittered self-consciously as they paused to point out their own creations.

When Mrs. Brunstedder bustled in, she kissed Laura lightly on the cheek while Herman laughed and shook hands with Laura and Stephen and Emily, even though all five of them had just eaten supper together an hour before. Pointing to an open window, Mrs. Brunstedder guided her husband to a place where she expected a cool breeze.

Glancing up at the clock, Laura turned to Stephen and Emily, only to discover the young man's normally ruddy face had turned blank and ashen. She quickly assessed the apprehension in his eyes. Other than when he was amongst his friends at Alistair and Priscilla's, he had probably never spoken to more than a handful of people at any one time in his entire life.

"Ready?" she whispered. When Stephen didn't budge, Laura felt a wash of panic. She'd have to take charge. "Just imagine you're talking to a circle of fellows around your forge," she counseled quietly.

When he gave a slight nod, Laura started up the aisle followed by Emily and a diffident Stephen. Sensing the need to help her friends get underway in their first meeting, Laura moved to stand in front of her desk, pointing the couple to the two chairs beside it. As they sat down, she clasped her hands across her waist and smiled at the gathering.

"It's a pleasure," she began, "to have so many of you out to the school this evening." Laura looked down at the beaming youthful faces on the front row. "I'm especially delighted to see so many boys and girls from my class. I want to say how happy I am to introduce my dear friends Stephen and Emily McElderry to all of you." As she stretched a hand in their direction, Laura's face grew intense. "Most of you parents have known me for only a year, but you've entrusted your precious children to my care. Thank you for that confidence." Laura scanned the earnest faces before her. "I can say without reservation that Stephen and Emily are two people I would entrust with *my* life. And I pray you'll receive them."

When Laura glanced at Stephen, a little of his colour had returned. "Stephen, would you like to say a few words before we sing the first hymn?" she coached gently.

Standing up, the young man moved to join Laura, his powerful hands clenching his Bible. His eyes swept back and forth across the room, taking in the whole but, like a startled bird, failing to settle on any one face. His muscular forearm curled as he fingered his heavy blond sideburns with abstraction. "I'm Stephen," he said hesitantly. "I reckon you all can see that I'd be more at home standing at the back of this room than at the front." Stephen's cheek trembled as he struggled to continue. "I had something ready to say from the Bible, but to be honest it's left me for the minute. Maybe it'd be all right if I just told you a bit about myself."

The compassion in the faces of Stephen's listeners told Laura they felt sorry for the young blacksmith. Hardworking country folks themselves, they would have felt the same strain.

"I was born in a cottage on the edge of Hespeler," Stephen began uncertainly. "And I grew up there next to a blacksmith shop. My father died before I was three, and my mother reared me. Life wasn't easy, and she worked her fingers to the bone to make ends meet. Like most boys, I figured schoolwork was for girls and I preferred to play with my friends on the rusty mowers or hay rakes behind the blacksmith shop. Smithy took a liking to me, and, when I got old enough, he asked if I'd like to do some little chores after school—cleaning up after the horses, stoking the forge, straightening nails, and the like. Smithy knew my mother could use the extra pennies." Stephen drew in a deep breath, relaxing slightly. "He was a powerful man with the coarse tongue of a teamster and, at first, I kept a sharp eye on him. But I liked the warmth of his shop and the smell of the horses and the forge when I came in on a frosty day after school. And listening to the stories of the men standing about, waiting to have their animals shod. I reckon horses got into my blood and Smithy saw that."

Stephen shifted his weight to his other foot as he continued. "Helping out around the blacksmith shop changed me. And not just that I grew from a boy to a man. Being there made me feel useful both to Smithy and to my mother. At the end of each month, Smithy would press a few coins into my hand, and I'd hurry home to give them to mother. Her bone-weary face always brightened, and she kissed me on the head as she accepted them. To this day, I can still remember the glow I felt inside."

Oblivious to the crowd, now caught up in Stephen's testimony, Laura slipped from the speaker's side to her chair on the front row.

"When Smithy wanted a little job done, I listened carefully so he wouldn't have to show me twice. I saw that he treated people the way he wanted to be treated. And, except for the day he grabbed a hot poker and chased a cantankerous fellow out the door, things went pretty well. In spite of being a rough man, Smithy was gentle with the horses and always spoke to them while he worked around their feet. You can tell a lot about a man by the way he treats a dumb beast. As I got older, Smithy gave me simple jobs to do on my own and eventually, I became his apprentice. Then, when the old man wanted to sell out, he took a chance on me."

A flicker of light ran across Stephen's face. "And God took a chance on me too. Four years ago, a friend of mine, Alistair Stanhope, came to my shop one morning and said there were a few church things that had him unsettled. Although we talked a lot over several weeks, I couldn't really get hold of what it was that troubled Alistair. I was used to dealing with things you could see and handle. Then one day while I was turning some bars for a fireplace grate, it dawned on me that he was seeking a more spiritual life, a greater sense of God in his daily routine. This path he was drawn into stood outside the familiarity of church as we knew it. Alistair was tired of religion with its stiff rules and traditions—the familiar do's and don't's of life—that tinker with the outward man but leave our souls faint."

Laura leaned back and smiled. From her vantage point beside the piano, she could see the ruddiness returning to Stephen's face and hear the passion edging into his voice. Before her, God was speaking through a fledgling preacher. Now Laura, too, fell captive to Stephen's story.

"The path Alistair was being led into is a little like my early years in the blacksmith shop. Just as the shop shaped and changed the natural side of me, that path began to transform Alistair. But in a deep and a spiritual way. It wasn't that Alistair himself was doing the shaping but rather he was *being* shaped.[5] And in a way he could hardly comprehend. He didn't leave his farm or travel to a far country or go off to study. In fact, to his neighbour looking over the line fence, nothing had changed. And yet, Alistair's inner man was moving from darkness to light."[6] Stephen took a deep breath. "It wasn't long before God touched the hearts of a few of us around Alistair and began to draw us into the same path. That's why I said earlier that God also took a chance on me."

Smiling, Stephen unfolded his arms and looked around. "Perhaps that explains how a blacksmith from Hespeler who's never been more than forty miles from home happens to find himself in Mildmay. You know, I always figured the benefit of being a Christian was for the life hereafter, and that's true. But now I know it actually starts the minute God draws us into His path. Perhaps I should clarify that this path is Jesus.[7] He is the way, and we need to give ourselves to Him. If the path we're following now hasn't changed us in the past ten years, it's likely not the way of Christ. A man who passes a decade without change has wasted ten years of his life. I know; I've done it myself. In the next few evenings we'd like to tell you a little about this path, this way, this man called Jesus."

A startled look crossed Stephen's features as if he had just wakened and found himself in front of a crowd. "I believe we were going to sing a hymn to begin," he faltered. "But I have nothing left to say, so perhaps we'll close with one." Turning, he beckoned to Laura and Emily.

Emily straightened her leg and rose stiffly. With all the graciousness of a young duchess, she limped to Stephen's side as Laura adjusted the piano stool and flattened her hymn book. Although the Wedgewood blue of Emily's flowing dress, finished with a high cameo collar, gave her all the charm of a Victorian figurine, it was her warm eyes and endearing smile that drew a gasp from the audience. In every way she seemed a delicate bluebell springing from the solid rock of her burly husband.

After thanking folks for coming, Stephen trailed Laura and Emily to the door, where they said goodnight to the crowd. Crickets chirped from the damp woodpile as the buggies pulled away from the school fence and disappeared into the night. After blowing out the lamps and dropping the key into her pocket, Laura looked up and saw that the stars had begun their slow journey across the sky.

Next to the road at the school gate, Stephen and Emily stood waiting. In the soft September darkness, pungent fragrance redolent of autumn lingered on the air: wood smoke, burning leaves, boiling jam behind kitchen curtains as a thrifty housewife stirred her last batch of the day.

Stephen raised a hand to his forehead as they stumbled onto the gravel street. "I surely seized up tonight," he offered apologetically. "For days I intended to speak about Nicodemus and the new birth. But when I got up to the front, I drew a complete blank. I was lucky to remember my own name. Why, I even forgot to sing an opening hymn. And to pray."

Emily slipped her puffed sleeve through Stephen's arm. "I think the Spirit was leading you and the evening turned out just as it should have."

The note of misgiving persisted in Stephen's voice. "Thanks," he said glumly, "but some folks are sure to be disgusted. Imagine a farmer rushing through his chores to get here on time, only to have the whole thing over in twenty minutes. I just hope I didn't cut off anyone's ears."[8]

"Don't worry, they'll be back," Laura reassured him. "I could see it in their faces. People want to know a little about an unfamiliar speaker. His rearing often tells more than a lot of fancy words. Besides it's better to quit while they want more than to drone on until they're itching to leave."

Emily looked up into Stephen's chagrined face. "Jesus set an example for short gospel messages," she observed. "Many of them lasted only a few minutes—at least what we have recorded."

The three young people walked arm in arm toward the Brunstedders, absorbed with their own reaction to the first meeting in Mildmay.

The next evening as Laura watched her tall, refined friend moving with her usual limp to the front of the classroom, she felt a rush of admiration for her. Before Stephen shared his message, Emily rose to stand at the front of the classroom, pausing for a moment to close the gap between her and the faces before her. As she smiled, a stillness, like the hush before gentle rain, swept over the room. Every eye connected with hers.

Emily's fragile form swayed slightly before her lips parted and her voice, innocent as a child's petition, came forth. "If you would be willing to listen," she entreated, "I'd like to share my testimony this evening."

"You shust go right ahead, Miss Emily. Ve vant to hear vat ever you have to say." The robust assertion belonged to Katrina Brunstedder and was followed by a few nods from others in the room.

"Thank you, Mrs. Brunstedder," Emily acknowledged. Then, after glancing out the window at the dying embers of the autumn sun, she clasped her hands and fixed her gaze on the crowd. "Even as a child, I wanted to know about God. When I was very young, I asked my mother what He was like. But she had no answers. A few years passed, and I continued to think about God. Finally, when I was about eleven, I asked again. Why don't miracles happen today? Again the same slow shake of the head. No one knew. Only in the book of nature did I see His handiwork."[9]

Emily tightened her eyelids for a fleeting moment. "Life went on in our home as it did in most," she explained, "nothing unusual. I had four brothers and a sister. Although Clara was two years older, we were two peas in a pod and loved each other as only sisters can. When the snow covered the fences, we would walk to school on the only pair of snowshoes our family owned. After Clara strapped her boots into the harness, I'd wrap my arms around her waist and balance on the webbing behind, laughing and counting out loud as we lifted our feet at the same time to walk in tandem. Clara showed me how to cut out my first dress and taught me how to make pie pastry. I loved my sister and rejoiced in our happiness.

"Then in early December of '84, she fell through the ice and caught a chill that turned into a cough. Within a couple days she was gasping for every breath. For the first time in my life, I was truly afraid. My beloved Clara lay sprawled on the kitchen couch with her eyes closed, panting and burning with fever. When the dreaded rattle settled deeper in her chest, mother rubbed on goose grease and sulphur and made up a cot beside the parlour stove. Grimly, father saddled the horse and sent my oldest brother off to town with terse instructions. In those days our doctor alternated two fast horses, and within a couple of hours his cutter pulled up in front of our porch, the long rangy driver lathered and steaming. The doctor barely grunted as he grabbed his black bag and followed mother straight to the parlour to examine Clara. The rest of us huddled in the kitchen. It seemed an eternity before he finally emerged, tight-lipped and sombre, to utter the dreaded word. Pneumonia. I couldn't decipher the low voices as the doctor talked to Father and Mother at the door, but when they came back to the kitchen, Mother was crying and I knew it was bad. The doctor had listened with his stethoscope, she said, and Clara's lungs were filling up with fluid. She wasn't to have anything to drink. Throughout the night, it was pitiful to hear Clara pleading for a drop of water to moisten her mouth and cool the fever, and I must admit I slipped her a little when no one was looking."

Leaning forward, Laura tightened her fingers into the desk's groove that held the pencils, remembering her last visit home to Stratford. Didn't she recall her father saying that in the last couple of years medical opinion had reversed the old wisdom? Some doctors were actually recommending that patients with pneumonia be offered plenty of fluids. But, of course, they hadn't known that at the time Emily's sister had been ill.

Across the room, Dave Hindley's oldest daughter, nearly fourteen herself, hunched forward, her face in her hands, her shoulders shaking in sympathy. All around her the adults looked stern as they tried to conceal their emotion. Each one hung on Emily's words, dreading the story's anticipated outcome. Here and there a soft sniffle could be heard in the otherwise silent room.

Emily hesitated, her graceful face now a pallid mask of pain. "Clara died on Christmas Day," she said quietly. "She was only sixteen." Emily touched her slender fingers to her forehead as if reliving those hours. "Except for the heart-wrenching spells of crying and despair, I have no memory of the next few weeks. The bleakness of that lonesome winter melted into an equally dreary spring, and I wondered if I could go on. Each day blurred into the next, and there seemed no letup from my distress. Without Clara and her laughter, I found it impossible to face school and I never went again. One day in April when I was alone, wandering in a field of slush and mud, I started screaming, 'It's a waste, an appalling waste!' I hated God for taking her from me and bringing me to a place that seemed to have no future, no escape, nothing but desolation. But what right did I have to be angry with a God I wasn't even sure existed? In those trancelike months of misery, a stormy sea of doubt stood before me while melancholy as relentless as Pharaoh's chariots sought to overtake me."[10]

Instinctively, Dave Hindley slipped an arm around his daughter's shoulders before glancing over at his wife. She, too, had her eyes fastened on the young speaker while beyond Sarah, next to the piano, he could see Miss Chapelton edging forward on her seat. She and her friends certainly had an extraordinary fervour and a forthrightness he'd rarely witnessed. The young woman's words drew him back.

"Clara and I always marked her birthday in August by picking berries around the marsh at Puslinch Lake. We'd pack a lunch, and after sharing a piece of johnny cake, we would laugh and swim until dark. But Clara was gone, and for the first time I would have to stay home—or go alone. I could have asked one of my brothers, but there seemed to be a conspiracy of silence at home, and I was determined to remember her seventeenth birthday—if only by myself. Hoping for a breeze off the water, I stuffed a lunch into the berry basket and grabbed my sunhat before striking off in the blistering heat. I hardly know how it happened, but as afternoon wore into evening, I had pushed my way through brambles and thickets until I found myself up against the shoreline of the lake, crying uncontrollably, embroiled in a snarl of despair and terrible agitation. Brought to the end of myself, I flung my body across a sandy hummock at the water's edge and begged God to release me. That first urgent prayer overflowed with unbelief, and although I didn't really expect anything to happen, somehow I got up from my knees feeling that God would part the sea and open a way through the depths.[11] In that moment He planted a mustard seed of faith, and by the time the September harvest had ripened, I was beginning to think straight again. That's when I dusted off the family Bible."

Emily paused reflectively for a second or two. "How amazing it was to find my own story in Psalm 107. And to see that it's God who commands the stormy wind to churn the waves of the sea. Just as He planned that the children of Israel would find themselves squeezed between the Red Sea and the advancing Egyptian chariots, so it was God who had arranged my troubles.[12] Why? So we—myself and the Israelites—would call upon His name, depending on Him as never before. As I read further, I discovered that I wasn't the first person to sink to the depths until my soul melted.[13] Others, too, had reeled to and fro, staggering like drunken men at their wits' end. When I cried to God, He stilled my storm and gave me peace. Since then He has never led me into anything He didn't lead me out of."[14]

Emily looked steadily into the eyes of her listeners. "In another place the psalmist says that God made a way through the sea and paths through the deep waters, but His footprints were not seen."[15] Emily paused. "That's why I'd never seen Him, even though He'd been there all along. Although I had heard about God since childhood, for the first time I saw Him with my own eyes—the eyes of faith."[16]

Clasping her hands, Emily searched the earnest faces. "I sincerely believe that I travel an appointed way and that God orders my steps and seeks my best in every circumstance. Of course I have choice, and choose I must, but God knows in advance what choice I'll make. He knows my words before I utter them, even before I think them.[17] Because the great I Am, the eternally present One, has perfect foreknowledge, He knew each one of us would be gathered here tonight. God simply wouldn't be God if He had to sit on the edge of His chair like the rest of us, waiting to see what folks would do. But does God's knowledge of my future excuse me from having to choose? Not a whit. My part is to choose wisely, give thanks for His unfailing love, and fit into the wonderful path He charts for me."

Emily leaned forward, shifting her weight onto her strong leg. "The following spring I went by myself to a nearby church—Saint Patrick's. There I met my future husband." Glancing sideways at Stephen, Emily offered a loving smile. "And some wonderful friends, the Stanhopes and the Joneses. For eight years or more, all seemed bright and rosy. But after a time, I felt something was still missing, and I began to pray earnestly, aching for something more than I found in religion, something that would bring me closer to the One who cares for me." Emily bowed her head slightly, allowing her lustrous hair to fall across her temples. "And in the process of time, like Stephen told us last night, God touched our lives and drew us into the way of the Spirit, the way of Christ. A day doesn't pass that I don't think of Clara, but now it's with a profound sense of peace in the providence of God, knowing He will unite us again in an even deeper bond than we had before." Emily smiled. "I felt compelled to share my story this evening. Thank you for hearing me out."

When Emily turned to sit down, a sympathetic murmur of approval rose from the room of beaming faces. Nearly everyone's eyes glistened at the sincerity and candour they had felt in the young woman's message. Beside the window Katrina Brunstedder dabbed her eyes and laid her hand on Herman's arm.

The following evenings, Stephen and Emily spoke more about their search for God, His ongoing work in their hearts, and how they had come to trust Him for everything. The Spirit of Christ seemed to be especially near each time Emily spoke. And although the odd person stiffened at the sight of a woman speaking, most were visibly touched by the sincerity in her words. Emily herself seemed to have matured beyond the mere prettiness of a porcelain doll as her very features took on a new intensity and conviction. Stephen, too, seemed to find his voice in front of people much as a young cowbird hatched and learning to sing in a cardinal's nest.

Laura began to search her New Testament carefully for any reference to the question all three of them had been asking: Can a sister share the gospel? Not long into her study, she found a passage in the book of Acts.

There, on the very morning of Pentecost, the apostle Peter spoke publicly about the coming of the Holy Spirit. He had said that Pentecost was the beginning of the time spoken of by the prophet Joel. In the last days, God had said, "I will pour out My Spirit on all people. Your sons *and your daughters* will prophesy...On My menservants and on My *maidservants* I will pour out My Spirit."[18]

Maidservants. The word lodged in Laura's mind. And daughters prophesying.[19] It seemed clear to her that this was what the four single daughters of Philip, the evangelist, were doing when Paul and his companions visited Caesarea and stayed at Philip's home. Following their father's example, these young women were active in telling forth God's mind and will.[20] Clearly, sharing the comfort of the gospel was open to sisters as well as people with families, like Philip.

Later, Laura shared her thoughts with Stephen and Emily. A slow smile spread across Emily's face. "That's a good point," she agreed, her eyes sparkling. "Besides, Mary Magdalene was the first person to meet and proclaim the risen Lord.[21] I'm satisfied that Christ is equally pleased for women today to share the good news of His resurrection."

Stephen agreed and suggested Laura share a few words at the next meeting.

"I don't think I'm ready to do that," she said, declining graciously. "The whole idea still makes me a little uncomfortable. I know it's fine for Emily to speak, but I'm not so sure about me."

Later that day Laura stumbled across the story of Anna, a widow who *spoke* about the child Jesus *to all* who were looking forward to the redemption of Jerusalem.[22] Still, Laura searched for the deeper underlying principles. Eventually, she found what she considered to be Paul's general summation of the subject in Galatians: "There is neither Jew nor Greek, there is neither bond nor free, there is neither male nor female; for ye are all one in Christ Jesus."[23]

The following Saturday morning Stephen went out to deliver some more invitations in the countryside. When he came home, Laura and Emily were boiling bed linens and washing blankets in the summer kitchen. As he opened the door, he found his wife barefoot, up to her ankles in warm water and soap suds. Having gathered her long dress to her knees, Emily was stepping around and around in a circle to wash the blankets. The rank smell of sodden wool rose from the wooden tubs.

"Hello, honey," she said. "Could you help Laura carry these wet blankets out to the clothesline? They're as heavy as stuck pigs."

Stephen rolled up his shirt sleeves and took hold of one end. Outside they twisted the dripping blanket to wring out some of the rinse water. As they tussled with it, Stephen thought about Laura's struggle—still uncertain whether she had the God-given authority to speak publicly.

Stephen heaved the blanket over the line. "Laura, do you remember the time when the disciples were speculating about which of them would have the greatest position in Jesus' kingdom? In effect, they were wondering who would have authority, who would be the boss."

Laura nodded as they walked back inside. "Yes, I recall that."

"Well, I've been reading about Jesus' teaching on greatness and authority. He told his disciples that the rulers of the Gentiles lord it over their people and that their high officials exercise authority over them. 'But it's not to be so with you,' He said. 'Whoever wants to be great among you must become your servant. And whoever wants to be first must be your slave. The Son of Man did not come to be served, but to serve and to give His life as a ransom for many.'"[24]

The autumn sun reflected off Stephen's ruddy face and golden sideburns. "Serving and authority go hand in hand," he said. "I believe that to the extent women are actually *serving others*, they have the authority and the privilege of sharing the gospel. But if any of us, either men or women, ever use that calling as a hierarchical office, a forum, a position of power, we've lost Jesus' leading and we'd better pack up and go home."

For days Laura tumbled these things over. Eventually, it became clear. In the world, the greatest person is the one who manipulates the largest number of people or controls the most possessions. Sometimes he has achieved recognition by his intellectual capacity, or his higher education, or his eminence. And sometimes by his ability to dominate. He is gauged by his achievements or his affluence. But greatness in Jesus' mind is none of these. It is measured by one's servanthood to others: "Bear ye one another's burdens, and so fulfil the law of Christ."[25] *The option of being a servant of God,*[26] Laura concluded, *is open to both men and women, married or unmarried. And that includes me or anyone else called by the Holy Spirit.*

After that revelation, Laura decided to share her testimony at the gospel meeting. The audience was eager to hear what their favourite teacher would have to say. Dave and Sarah Hindley and the Brunstedders sat captivated as they listened to their gentle friend pour out her heart about how Jesus had changed her life.

Over the coming weeks, Mildmay took its teacher and her disarmingly open friends to its heart. Village and farm families invited them for supper, which, it seemed, always ended in an apple dessert—pie, pudding, cobbler, dumplings, or apple sauce. Housewives vied with each other to produce a variation on the apple theme and exchanged their intended recipes over back fences and store counters. Stephen often smiled to himself as he recalled Timothy's delight in bread pudding, and now he—Stephen—found himself confronting bowl after bowl of apple-cinnamon bread wound around a filling of sliced apples and walnuts. Mildmay's hospitality touched the young people to their hearts, but its guarded receptiveness to the gospel drove them to their knees.

The warm summer days of early September gradually chilled into a cool but brilliant autumn. As the leaves fell in splashes of colour from the maple on Herman's front yard, Stephen and Emily gained a bounty of experience, just as George and Jack had done two years earlier in Elora. The mission granted Stephen confidence, and although he did not consider himself a speaker, he became more comfortable in giving account of his faith in a public gathering as the weeks passed.

But despite the earnest supplications of the three young preachers, only a handful, including Herman and Katrina Brunstedder and Sarah and David Hindley, showed more than a passing interest in the gospel meetings. The opposition that others in the ministry had faced elsewhere had been mollified here because of Laura's sterling record as the village teacher. This appreciation for the teacher, however, did not translate into spiritual blessings for the majority of villagers, proving once again that God's work is a gift of grace and not a matter of human influence or persuasion.

Walking home with Stephen and Emily after the last gospel meeting in October, Laura realized with a jolt that sharing the good news of Jesus had given her deeper satisfaction than anything else she had ever done. As the second sister among five in a lively home, she had occasionally felt herself merely one of the crowd—a diminutive version of her elder sister or mother, not to speak of her stout and imposing Grandmother Chapelton, whose word had been as inflexible as that of the Medes and Persians. As Laura sat in her white nightgown by the window that night, listening to the soft nocturnal sounds and hoarse rustle of the wind in Herman Brunstedder's corn stalks, she opened her heart to both reminiscence and expectation. Although darkness had fallen, she knew that beyond the village confines of Mildmay the harvest fields stretched away in a rich and delicate spectrum of yellow, ochre, and gold, interspersed by hardwood forests and stands of evergreens. Somewhere across those miles tonight, George, too, would be preparing for sleep. Her constant love and concern for him had sustained her through the recent changes in their lives. But now her heart, like a swept and garnished chamber, began to entertain a new possibility. Could it be that the still small voice, like the breeze rippling through the cornfields, was calling *her* to enter the work?

An hour later, in the deeper darkness of midnight, Laura was still sitting at the window with her arms folded on the sill. It was marriage and little ones she'd always wanted. Could she ever remember Mother without a gaggle of little girls around her skirts? A happy home meant children.

In the coolness of the autumn night, Laura drew a shawl around her white shoulders and released her chestnut hair from its combs to tumble around her face. No evening prayer shaped itself easily on her lips as she pressed her forehead against her arms. The stars of the October night, cold and distant, looked into her window and passed by on their appointed course. Mrs. Brunstedder found her there when she bustled in at seven o'clock with good-morning smiles and a steaming cup of tea.

December's first soft snowfall whitening over the dark landscape marked the evening when Stephen and Emily extended to the villagers the age-old invitation to express their desire for the life that is divine. It had already been fourteen weeks since the McElderrys stepped off the train at the Mildmay station, but they promised to stay on and celebrate Christmas with their friends before leaving the security of Laura's companionship and the warmth of the Brunstedder household. On hearing their plans, Herman rose from the chimney corner, heaved on his mackintosh and ploughed out to the woodpile intending to bear inside his choicest blocks of beech. And Katrina, fingering her handwritten cookbooks in search of the Weinachten torte, dispatched Laura to the Hindley family with an invitation for Christmas dinner.

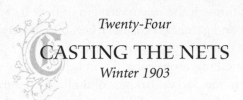

Twenty-Four

CASTING THE NETS
Winter 1903

Early dawn on the first Monday in January 1903 disclosed a damp layer of overnight snow that clung to the south side of every roadside tree and hoary fence post alike. The rising sun, sparkling upon them, created a glistening landscape of ivory and silver and gave promise of blessing as the mail carrier's sleigh pulled up at the Brunstedder's home. Stephen and Emily were departing with him for Neustadt; and Herman and Katrina, cheeks red with cold, bustled about setting the travel bags in place.

Laura's hands rested lightly on Emily's shoulders as she bade a tender farewell to friend and sister. But her throat swelled with a hard lump she couldn't swallow down. The devoted trust and affinity she had witnessed between Stephen and Emily reminded her poignantly of her bond with George. And now she must again bid goodbye to dear ones she might not see for months to come. When Stephen's ruddy face appeared above her, Laura opened her lips, trying to speak, but the words of farewell tightened in her throat. As the sleigh sliced through the soft crust and pulled away, she turned aside, wrapping her muffler around her neck and trying to shake off the tears that assailed her.

In the following weeks, Herman and Katrina and the Hindley family rejoiced in their newfound faith that, for the past several months, had unconsciously been modeled by, indeed embodied in, Laura Chapelton. She, too, felt the exhilaration of new fellowship that had been wanting until the Mildmay mission. Still, at a time when Laura felt she should have been content, a vague uneasiness filled her heart and she ached for news of the missions—George and Timothy's, Stephen and Emily's, Jack and Eddie's. Racing home after school, she scanned the Brunstedder table for the day's mail.

At least once a month, in a pattern long since established, a lengthy epistle flew each way between George and Laura. It was in Laura's first letter after Stephen and Emily had moved on that George again sensed her feelings of isolation. Wistfulness etched his thin face as he reread Laura's careful script, wishing he could look into her eyes and soothe her ache. But that was impossible—seventy-five miles, as the crow flies, stretched in a rolling patchwork of fields and woods between them. Setting Laura's letter aside, George kneeled to pray, seeking God's help.

The weeks came and went and the thaw of early spring had begun to trickle into the creeks before a solution arrived in the form of a letter from Katie Keats, the teacher in Elora. In it, Katie rehearsed the solitariness she felt at times and wondered if God intended to set her in a family.[1] How, she asked, did George deal with being apart from *his* kin? George took Katie's letter as an answer to prayer and before the day was out, he wrote to both young women encouraging them to correspond.

Before long a veritable stream of lively letters flowed between the two sisters, exchanging recipes, patterns for dresses, and musical scores. Over the months their communication deepened in forthrightness, and as she started into the new school year in September of 1903, Laura sought Katie's opinion on her ongoing quandary with the "Hipple tribe." Among other things, Laura, in response to a question from Katie, described the quiet time she spent alone with God each day after school.

In an October letter, Laura articulated the immeasurable satisfaction and quiet euphoria she had felt welling up as she played her part in the Mildmay mission with Stephen and Emily. Such was the warmth and candour of their exchanges that Katie posted a letter in November urging Laura to join her and Mrs. Applebee for the Christmas holidays.

And so it was, that on the evening of December 24, Laura found herself briskly alighting from the Wellington, Grey & Bruce at the Elora station. A festive figure in her green cloak, her arms were laden with violin case, travel bag, and small packages. Feather-soft flakes settled over Elora and blanketed the houses and yards, lending a sense of the ethereal as Laura made her way along the unfamiliar streets. Katie had offered to meet the train but Laura, for reasons she couldn't quite explain, had insisted that she would follow Katie's careful directions. Candles set in the bay window of one cottage reflected a tree decorated with strings of popcorn, Christmas cards, and icicles fashioned from the foil lining of a tea can.

As Laura studied the homes on Victoria Street, she slipped off her kid gloves and withdrew from her pocket Katie's description of a two-storey brick home. After once again matching the inviting wooden veranda and arched Gothic window with the note, Laura unlatched the picket gate. On either side of the freshly-shovelled path, powdery snow mounded on the shrubbery and flower beds and before her, frosty windows glowed with cheer among the giant icicles and snowpuffed roofline. *So this,* she thought, *had been George's first home after leaving Puslinch.*

At the sound of Laura's knock, she heard eager footsteps hastening to greet her. The knob clicked open and in a moment, Mrs. Applebee's rosy face and plump apron-clad figure appeared with outstretched arms.

"Come in, come in, my dear," the motherly figure entreated. "We're so delighted you're here at last."

Behind her in the lamplight, Katie Keat's dark eyes and merry face beamed with enthusiasm while delectable odours floated around them— mincemeat pie, cinnamon bread, hot mulled cider. Through the parlour doors, she could hear the cheerful warbling of a canary.

"What a thrill to have you with us," Katie bubbled as she reached for Laura's snow-clad coat and violin case. "You're just as I pictured you."

"Come to the fire, dear, and warm yourself," Mrs. Applebee called over her shoulder as she bustled off to the sizzling pots on the cookstove.

Laura could feel herself relaxing as the three women tucked into the savoury pot roast with chunks of winter vegetables.

"Lyman and Jessie would like us to go over tomorrow evening and have some music around the organ," Katie offered brightly as she passed Laura the basket of warm bread. "I've started a choir at school and their boys like to sing. Especially, Jimmy—at the top of his lungs."

The evening unfolded with gaiety and stories until, later around the fire, Laura proffered a stationer's box with fountain pen set to Katie. She, in turn, headed to her room and returned with red mittens and muffler she had knit for Laura. Mrs. Applebee unfolded some tissue and held out a dainty apron to each of the teachers—exquisite workmanship of white muslin sewn with rows of lace insertion. In the pocket of each reposed a plump orange. Afterward, the girls presented Mrs. Applebee with their own beribboned packets. How they convulsed with gales of laughter when it became apparent that both Katie and Laura had knit honeycomb shawls!

"Now, I've reason to live to be one hundred," Mrs. Applebee proclaimed as she got up and wrapped both girls in a huge hug. "We Scots like to wear out every last thing before we fly away."

After winding the grandfather clock in the front hall, Evelyn felt a sudden impulse to step out onto her icy porch before turning in. Above her the clouds had shifted and Christmas stars sparkled in the clear heavens. From upstairs she could hear high girlish voices as Katie and Laura prepared for sleep. And on the midnight air like a heraldic flourish she heard the pealing bells of St. John's church. It was Christmas Eve.

Laura snuggled in her flannel nightgown among the hot water bottles that Mrs. Applebee had filled. Unbidden, an old memory rose up before her. She recalled the family pew at church one Sunday, filled as always with her parents, the five sisters, and Grandmother Chapelton enthroned on the aisle seat. Following the opening hymn, the minister's voice had risen with the first verse of the Old Testament reading: "In that day seven women shall take hold of one man…"[2] During the moment of silence that followed, two of her father's cronies—his lawyer and the undertaker—had turned to grin at each other, their heads nodding in the direction of the Chapelton pew near the top of the church. Laura's eyes crinkled in her pillow as she recalled how her father, Dr. Chapelton, who was known to be well and truly henpecked, had blushed to the roots of his hair.

How different Katie's home life must have been, she reflected, mindful of her own family bonds and the closeness among the five lively sisters. In spite of their spirited personalities and inevitable upsets, the Chapelton clan was, nevertheless, encircled by arms of deathless loyalty. Laura drew the double wedding-ring quilt around her slender shoulders. What a contrast her life had been to Katie's, the only daughter, who had been cast out of her widowed mother's home. Laura had thrilled to discover the many common loves she and Katie shared, but this one difference she could barely fathom.

On Christmas Day the frost-encased cedars lining the banks of the Grand River extended their soft branches as the skaters swept past. Stopping at a rustic bench hewn from a giant log, Laura and Katie tightened the keys on their skates. Before them, in the centre of the mill pond, a skirmish of boys flailed wildly at a chunk of frozen horse manure with their tangle of improvised hockey sticks while, hand in hand, strings of girls on skates circulated along the river's edge singing Christmas carols. Interspersed among the uproarious shouts and sweet-voiced singing, a few grown-ups exhilarated in spending the crisp afternoon on the smooth ice. Schoolgirls with sharpened blades cut white arcs into the dark ice as they wheeled to join hands with Miss Keats and her friend. How excited they were to learn that she was another teacher visiting for a fortnight.

"Let's skate up the river a piece," Katie suggested after they had taken several turns around the pond with her pupils. Nodding, Laura followed as Katie broke free from the swirling cloud of skaters. Over their shoulders floated the girls' poignant voices, "Peace on earth, goodwill to men, from heaven's all gracious King." Settling into long graceful strokes, the pair drew invigorating breaths as they glided past the hardwoods and billowy fields on either side. The sweetness of wood smoke from a snowcapped cabin on the north bank wafted through the bracing air.

After a few minutes, Katie motioned toward a large willow that had fallen over the river, the soil beneath its roots eroded. "Let's catch our breath," she called over to Laura. "On that log."

Sitting side by side, their long serge skirts tucked beneath them, the two young women thrilled at the splendour and stillness of the Grand River in all her winter finery. The sheer tranquility of the moment prompted Laura to return to the conversation she and Katie had begun the evening before. "The ministry's been on my heart since Stephen and Emily were in Mildmay this past fall. I got to share in every aspect of the mission from writing invitations to giving my testimony in the gospel meeting."

Katie's dark eyes turned to Laura. "Yes, go on."

"But perhaps the most powerful part was the urgency we all felt in prayer, begging for God's presence to overshadow us. During our day we talked to God privately, but then after supper we would gather in one of our bedrooms for a prayer meeting, pouring out our souls before God and each other. I can hardly explain how this unity of heart and purpose bound us so closely together." Laura raised a red woolen mitt to her face. "I must admit I felt pretty blue when Stephen and Emily moved on to Neustadt."

"Maybe God intended you to stay on until the little church got rooted."

"Yes, Katie. That may be so," Laura responded. "But, for a few days, it felt as if I'd been abandoned. Like a body that had moved on and left its hand behind. Anyway, I'm willing to wait until God gives me clearer direction." A little snap in the underbrush silenced her words.

As the women stared across the frozen river with studied concentration, a white-tailed deer emerged from the scrub to stand alert on the far edge. After what seemed like a long time to Laura but was in fact only moments, the dainty creature started across the snowy plain, each step of its slender legs taken with poise and confidence. Cast in the glow of the setting sun, the doe's sorrel coat contrasted with her milk-white underside and throat patch. Suddenly the deer paused, startled it seemed, by something Laura couldn't detect. The doe's delicate head jerked up, her soft brown eyes scanning the woods, her large sensitive ears searching out the faintest sound. Laura's breath caught in her throat. What an illustration of untaught grace, of moving forward at just the right time, cautiously but with optimism. Satisfied once again, the beautiful creature relaxed, prancing lightly through the low drifts as she angled in front of her audience. And then, as if on springs, the doe leapt straight-legged onto the opposite shore and disappeared on her solitary journey.

When the majesty of the moment had subsided, Laura turned to Katie. "What ability you have to draw back the curtain and present your visitors with the grandeur of Elora," she laughed as they rose from the log.

The steel of Laura and Katie's blades cut into the ice and scattered the topping of white powder as they continued eastward along the river. After rounding a bend, Katie slowed, scanning the high bridge ahead. "We'd better turn around," she cautioned. "We're getting near the linseed mill at Aboyne, and I hear the swift current has thinned the ice."

Laura's full lips stretched into a girlish laugh. "Too cold for a swim today," she chuckled as they circled back towards Elora.

"One of my students fell in and nearly froze before he got home," Katie added. "I worried he might catch pneumonia, but he was fine."

Laura's face clouded. "Did you ever hear about Emily's sister, Clara?"

Katie shook her head. "No. What about her?"

Laura's mind went back to the second evening of the Mildmay mission. Again she pictured Emily's tall slender form limping toward the front and the warmth in her eyes as she drew her audience to her. "Clara fell through the ice and caught pneumonia," she said quietly. "She died. It's a very precious story, and I'd prefer Emily told you about it herself."

Absorbing the tragic news, Katie waited until it became clear that Laura was finished. "I'm sorry," she offered. "A lot of things shape our lives, don't they?"

In that instant, an image of George's face and the picnic at Doyle's Mill flashed across Laura's mind. "They certainly do," she acknowledged. The two young women had just passed a stand of bulrushes penetrating the ice at a bend in the river when Laura glanced sideways at Katie. "Is it all right to ask if you have a special someone in your life?"

Katie laughed and then her voice dropped. "The fact of the matter is I don't know any eligible bachelors who have the same heart for the gospel as I do. And to be yoked with someone who is otherwise would smother me. I must admit I feel as if God has a purpose for my life that I'm not yet experiencing," she paused, "but somehow I don't think it's marriage..."

The light was almost gone as Laura and Katie approached the millpond. They could see the last two boys sliding the blocks of wood they had used for goal posts toward the bank.

"I'm ready for Mrs. Applebee's woodstove and that mug of hot cocoa she promised would be waiting," Laura said as she and Katie unbuckled their blades. "Thanks for a splendid afternoon."

~⊙~

Correspondence flew between the sisters over the next three months. In one letter, Laura confided to Katie her certainty that she was being called into the ministry and was simply waiting for God to open the way. And then one afternoon in April, she came home to find the letter that would change her future. Laura's pulse quickened as she read the main sentence for a second time. "At last I am not only ready, but eager, to join you in sharing the gospel." Katie's message was as clear as her neat round penmanship. The young teachers exchanged two or three letters to clarify the details, and then they both notified the school trustees of their intentions. And this time Dave Hindley, the Mildmay trustee, understood exactly why Laura was leaving.

To the children, for whom Miss Chapelton had become the light of their lives, their teacher's resignation was nothing short of a calamity. When their parents, around the various supper tables, discussed the trustees' reluctance to see Laura resign, many teary-eyed girls sniffled through the meal. Meanwhile, their brothers sat in glum silence or perversely made eyes until their sisters cried. As the days wore on, nothing would suit the girls but that their mothers host a strawberry tea in their teacher's honour, a proposal that dried their tears and precipitated much scurrying about to wash and starch white dresses with sashes of pink or lavender. On the final Saturday of June, Laura sat on the Brunstedders' lawn surrounded by the gaiety of little girls who presented farewell offerings of embroidered hankies, pansy faces pressed onto bookmarks, and even a real cake of Pears soap, purchased in the Walkerton apothecary.

Herman Brunstedder, banned from the party by the simple fact of being a man, leaned on his hoe and gazed across the lawn. "Time vas ven ze teacher resigned to be married," he ruminated. "Our Laura could've been hitched to any of ze finest young men in zis district. But she's heard a different call, one zat's come from above. Noble, I call her…"

When Katrina Brunstedder, balancing a tray laden with empty glasses and her special crystal pitcher, stumped her way past the garden, he hurried over to help. "How is ze party going?" The smooth skin of his square face glistened with sweat as he beamed with anticipation.

"Shust fine, Herman, everybody's having ze time of zere life," the heavyset woman replied. She leaned forward to kiss him on the cheek. "Danke for making ze yard so lovely and for picking ze strawberries."

The sweet violin strains of "The Red River Valley" wafted across the afternoon air as Herman carried the tray into the cool kitchen.

"Zat tune shust makes me feel like bawling," Katrina sniffed behind him. "Now I know vot it's like ven a muzzer says goodbye to her daughter." She wiped her eyes with her apron. "Anyvay, I can't get sappy now, zey need anozer shug of apfel shoos out zere."

Turning, Herman put his hands on her round shoulders and looked into her tender face. Then he drew her into a hug. "Here, here, my lammchen," he comforted her.

When the screen door slammed, Herman Brunstedder slipped upstairs and knelt beside his bed. "Our Fazer, I'm coming before Zee now to ask zat You vill go vis Laura even to ze ends of ze earz. Ve love zis girl like our own. Ven she leaves zis house, I can't stand betveen her and trouble, but You can. Please touch my own heart until I do Zy vill. Also remember Stephen and Emily in zere mission as vell and increase zis family of love. I ask zese zings in ze name of Zy Son. Amen."

When the chalk dust had settled and the Mercator's world map had been rolled up, signaling the end of the school year in 1904, Katie came to Mildmay by train to meet Laura. Flushed with the excitement of their new endeavour, Laura and Katie stayed one more night with the Brunstedders before setting out on the road toward Hepton Bridge.

Laura's final evening in the hospitable yellow brick home found Katrina red-eyed, and even Herman was unusually silent. Their devotion to Laura showed itself in taking her friend Katie to their hearts—literally—while Katrina in her motherly fashion cooked enough *kalbsbraten* and packed sufficient lunch to support a traveling army.

Indeed, something of this idea shone in Katrina's countenance as she raised her head and confronted Herman, who sat polishing four Gravenstein apples. "Vasn't it Bismarck vat said, an army marches on its stomach?"

"*Nein, nein*, Muzzer. It vas Napoleon."

"A Frenchman?" Katrina retorted. "Never!"

Herman eyed his wife's scowl. "Maybe it vas Josephine," he rejoined meekly. "In any case, Muzzer, you have forgotten to butter zis bread…"

Katrina tightened her lips and thrust a butter knife into the crock. "*Dumkopf,*" she muttered darkly. Whether she meant herself, Herman, or Napoleon Bonaparte, no one ever knew.

The sisters had walked about an hour out of Mildmay when Katie glanced over her shoulder to the sound of a horse's hooves on the hard-packed gravel. "There's some sort of boxy rig coming up on our heels," she advised. "Looks a little like a stagecoach." The women moved to the grassy shoulder as the sound drew closer.

"Hullo, there," a hearty voice called out as the rig pulled alongside.

Turning abruptly, Laura and Katie looked up at the black vehicle to read the gold letters on its side: Dr. Farquharson—Traveling Dentist.

A portly gentleman in a silk waistcoat and pinstripe trousers beamed down through a pair of round gold glasses from the driver's seat. "Putting for Hepton Bridge, are you?" he asked affably. When he smiled, his beard, full and gray but neatly trimmed, puffed out like the tail feathers on a turkey gobbler. "How about a ride, ladies? I could use the company."

Laura turned to Katie. "What do you think?"

Katie smiled. "This travel bag says it's ready to ride for a spell."

"Right then," Dr. Farquharson instructed. "One of you can scramble up on the seat with me and the other can sit in my chair inside. It's a little warm in there but the windows are open."

"You take the air," Laura suggested. "I'll be happy to ride inside."

After sliding her travel bag onto the floor of the compartment, Katie joined Dr. Farquharson up front as Laura settled into the black leather chair facing the side window. With a word from the driver, the horse and rig lurched forward. Steadying her sturdy laced oxfords on the foot rest, Laura surveyed the confines of the chamber. Just enough space for the dentist to get around without anything to spare. A bracket table with an extendable arm for his instruments had been fastened to the wall. And above it, a glass-doored cabinet rattled and tinkled with all manner of curiosities—flasks, extraction forceps, cotton napkins, rubber dams, amalgam carvers. On a higher shelf, separated by a metal impression tray, a row of gleaming dentures and plaster casts grinned back at her. Certainly different instruments from those in the doctor's office of her father. Laura's musings were interrupted by the conversation drifting back from the driver's seat.

"You ladies have family in Hepton Bridge?" the dentist was asking.

"No, not really," Katie replied. "We're Christian workers, and we're planning to hold a few gospel meetings there."

"Now that'll be interesting," Dr. Farquharson exclaimed. "They're a strong-minded community to put it politely. I stopped there once to practice my trade, but they're well served by two dentists already—a Catholic and a Presbyterian. That I was told in no uncertain terms. So now I just sail right through on my way to Teeswater." The man stretched his jowls into a wide grin, which fluffed up his beard as he turned to Katie. "Anyway, I can see you two ladies have some considerable charm I don't possess."

An enamel pail, still partly filled with water, sloshed in one corner of Laura's jostling cubicle as the carriage's steel wheels clattered over a pothole. Glancing to the right, Laura's eye traced the cords running down from the drill to the foot-treadle where the apparatus's three-legged stand had been bolted to the linoleum floor. Her nose wriggled in disgust at the brass spittoon with its tiny pipe leading to the ground below.

As the jig jostled westward, Katie's curiosity flared."So what's involved to become a dentist?"

"Not as much as you might think," Dr. Farquharson rejoined. "I apprenticed with an older chap for a year and then I had to take a four-month course at dental school to get my license. Nowadays, they ask for one year of high school, too." He chuckled again. "But mostly you need a strong arm for extractions."

"What's the going rate for an extraction, these days?"

"Seventy-five cents if it's quick and easy. A dollar if I have to fight with the roots."

Katie winced. "Is it hard to get the roots out?"

Dr. Farquharson lifted his bowler hat and wiped the perspiration from his bald pate. "It's a beggar at times. And most folks can't stand the pain."

"So what do you do about that?" Katie asked incredulously.

"Mostly I just snap off the crown at the gum line and let the abscess drain. That gives the patient relief."

"Ouch," Katie grimaced. "Haven't I been reading about some sort of gas to deaden the pain?"

"Nitrous oxide," Dr. Farquharson declared authoritatively. "They use it in the States but so far I'm only equipped with a milder sedative." He gave a slow wink. "It comes in a brown bottle."

Half-turning, Katie exchanged a mirthful glance with Laura, each assured that her own white teeth would receive no attention from their benevolent driver.

For a time all was quiet in front, and Laura gazed out the carriage window, admiring the full-leafed parade of roadside elms and maples in all their stateliness. The grassy dips and hills of Culross Township reminded her of George's old farm. As she mused all the ambience of summer drifted in through her open window: the sweet scents of clover and hidden wildflowers, the bawling of a weaned calf, and the buzz of a bumblebee that made a full circle around the chair before flying back outside.

"Well, Miss Keats," Laura heard the dentist say as the rig ground to a halt. "Parting is such sweet sorrow." Dr. Farquharson stepped heavily to the roadside and helped each of his passengers down.

After thanking the dentist for his graciousness and watching his square rig rattle away in the distance, Katie eyed Laura cheekily. "Could you imagine that crinkly beard tickling your tonsils while Dr. Farquharson wrestles out a wisdom tooth?"

Their resounding laughter ended in Laura's more sober speculation, "I wonder how Hepton Bridge's fixed for places to board..."

Aside from Dr. Farquharson's cryptic review, the sisters were unaware that this particular settlement was notorious for its strong sectarian feelings. It was well-known among the residents that the Alexanders, the Cooks, the MacDougalls, and their families had their names on the Presbyterian roll while the Flahertys, the O'Malleys, and the Cavanaughs worshiped at the Catholic church along with all their relations. Each group had its own butcher, blacksmith, dry goods store, and school. Traditions in the village were time-honoured, decent, and not to be interfered with by two bold young women. Still, everything appeared to go well until the sisters began to hand out invitations and openly share their faith.

Katie had just finished playing the last hymn during their first meeting when a prosperous farmer got up in the third row of desks, lifting a portentous arm and turning to confront the gathering. His collar tightened around his throat as his eyes swept the rows of neighbours. "I cannot believe," he said, breaking the silence in ominous deliberation, "that outsiders have come to our village to upbraid us—we, whose families have been established in Bruce County since 1852. In any case, young women have their place at home in subjection to mother or husband. I cannot countenance any word coming from their assumed authority." With this dismissal he seized his top hat, thumbed a gesture of rejection, and trod heavily to the door.

The door had just slammed closed when a neatly attired old gentleman of distinguished face struggled to his feet. He didn't look like a man who would be easily upset but his eyes seethed. "Mr. Cook is right," he contended, his lips quivering. "Some of us aren't too well served to have you here in our village." His voice was as bitter as nettles. "You ladies make it sound as if we're all sinners. We don't want to hear that kind of talk! We've had two fine churches in this settlement for over fifty years."

Laura could feel her palms growing clammy. "What don't you like about what we're doing, sir?" she asked politely.

"What don't we like?" the old gentleman scoffed. "We don't like your unseemly presumption! We have all the religion needful. Word from Mildmay is that you're against our most sacred traditions. Why is that?"

As Laura reached behind her head, nervously fingering her dark French braid, she suddenly decided to give a very candid reply. "We're not against religion in its purest form, sir.[3] What we are against is the deception that most organized religion offers. It misleads people into thinking that if they go to a particular church and refrain from drink or tobacco, they'll go to heaven. They're given the false impression that they can please God just by tinkering with a few minor aspects of their lives. That's very different from the radical changes seen in the lives of Jesus' true followers."

Her accuser glowered, his eyes scouring Laura's delicate face.

Taking a deep breath, she looked the man straight in the eye and plunged in deeper. "The Holy Spirit influences the hearts of *honest* people, regardless of what religion they belong to, and gives them a desperate yearning for God. As the Spirit stirs their hearts, He tries to reveal Jesus of Nazareth—the Way, the Truth, and the Life[4]—to each and every one of them. Scripture tells us there is no other way, no other truth, no other life."

"We don't want to join whatever you're talking about," a beefy man with a florid face thundered from the back of the room.

"Yeah, and we don't follow women around here." The voice spit out the words with obvious contempt. "Women follow their menfolk."

In spite of the nasty comment, Laura maintained her composure, forcing a strained smile as she struggled to understand. "We're not asking people to join anything," she insisted, her voice soft and even. "You can join a religion, but you can't join God's family. You have to be born into a family. Even if you could join us and did so seventy times over without having the Spirit of Christ in your heart, you'd still go to a lost eternity. But if you give Him a home in your heart, He'll give you a home in heaven."

Hostile words from a thin man near the window sliced through Laura's voice like a knife. "Don't you hear what my neighbour's telling you?" he taunted. "We don't like women preachers. What a woman needs is a husband and a tribe of young ones to run after. Not telling us what to do."

With the firestorm growing before her very eyes, Laura couldn't help but feel frightened. Scanning the room, she saw only stern red-faced glares or blank expressions—even among the few women who had come to the meeting. Laura looked over and saw Katie slowly shaking her head, her face pale and chalky. She, too, could see that there was no point in trying to reason. These people had their minds made up and were getting more brazen as the minutes passed.

The burly man pounded the desk in front of him so vehemently that a battered copy of *Oliver Twist* pitched out of the shelf and slid along the floor on its back. "If you don't depart this village by eight in the morning, there'll be hell to pay." His words hung like a thundercloud. In alarm people got up and pulled on cloaks and wraps as if personally threatened.

"Somebody's going to get lynched," a woman's nasal voice warned.

"Yeah, and it won't be a MacDougall or an Alexander," somebody growled ominously as the crowd pushed out the door. From the school steps could be heard the hapless yelping of a dog that had patiently waited for the meeting to end, and now found its paws trampled.

Katie and Laura blew out the lamps, locked the dark schoolhouse, and hurried briskly into the night. Scrutinizing the shadows, they kept a careful watch over their shoulders. Their hearts pounded at the crunch of hobnail boots on the gravel behind them for a block or two until they arrived breathless at their boarding place.

The people who owned the home where they were staying looked grim, but they seemed determined to help the two young women who were being treated so despicably by their neighbours. Fearing for their safety, the girls pushed the heavy Victorian armoire and wardrobe against the bedroom door before they climbed into bed. They were not accustomed to threats of physical abuse and pleaded with God for direction. Should they leave the village or should they stay? They finally decided, as had the apostle Paul in similar circumstances, that it was more prudent to leave. But how, they wondered? Before daylight they packed up their travel bags, hoping to get away before the powder keg exploded.

⁓

Back in Mildmay, Herman Brunstedder awoke. He stirred restlessly and listened to the clock chiming downstairs. It was only four o'clock in the morning, but for some inexplicable reason he could not get back to sleep. He finally nudged Katrina.

"Vat is it, Herman?" she gasped, sensing Herman's restlessness.

"I've been lying avake for over an hour," he said, "vi' ze strong feeling zat our girls are in trouble. I vonder if I should go to see zem."

"Ya, ya," Katrina urged, her voice full of alarm. "You better go zen."

Herman carried his oil lantern to the horse shed and hitched the bay mare to the buggy. He felt a little foolish as he started out past the darkened homes of his sleeping neighbours, wondering if his fears might all be a mistake. By daylight he was nearing the village where Laura and Katie were staying. He rolled past the schoolhouse where the square-paned windows, glistening in the morning sunlight, revealed no secrets. Finding the address, he glanced at his pocket watch as he approached the house. It was a few minutes before eight. Herman shrank down into his collar as he rapped on the door. *What reason*, he wondered, *can I give for showing up unannounced and so early in the morning?* When the woman of the house opened the door, the retired farmer was startled to look past her and see the sisters packed and ready to leave.

For a split second the sisters gaped in stunned silence. Then Laura reached out and grasped his arm. "Herman, we must leave quickly," she whispered as she threw on her coat. "You're an answer to our prayers."

Without hesitation Herman grabbed a bag in each hand and headed for his rig. After thanking their landlady and relinquishing the school key, the sisters raced out the door and scrambled into the front seat beside him. Only after they were well beyond the village were they able to relax and tell him about the threats. They marveled at the way the Holy Spirit had touched their old friend and brought him at just the right time.

That evening Katrina Brunstedder was still fuming as she gathered the two young women and the Hindley family around her kitchen table. "Vat a miserable bunch," she fussed. "Who in zere right mind would treat young ladies so shamefully? And teachers at zat."

At the sound of Katrina's motherly indignation, Laura's face grew bleak. "It was rejection—outright rejection. I've never experienced anything like it." She wiped her eyes with her hanky. "Nevertheless, it isn't the first time believers have faced persecution. Nor will it be the last."

Twisting her ankle around the chair leg, Katie shifted uncomfortably beside Laura, heart-struck at the remembrance of her own mother standing at the door with an ultimatum on her lips. Lowering her chin, she thought of the appalling night when she had lugged her clothes and books from her childhood bedroom to Mrs. Applebee's home. Katie's eyes smarted as the conversation went on around her. Rejection by strangers stung. But when it came from one's own mother, it seared like hot steel to the heart.

"God's closed one door," she heard Dave offer comfortingly. "The question is, where will He open another?"

Sarah Hindley cut another slice of Katrina's raspberry strudel. "The fishing village where I grew up keeps coming to my mind. Those folks are as gentle as lambs, and I'm certain they'd receive you."

Laura's chestnut hair shone in the lamplight. "And where is that?"

"Not too far from here," Sarah responded. "It's on Lake Huron. The bugbear is you have to get there by boat. There's no road in."

Katie's dark eyebrows arched. "Really. I've never seen the Great Lakes, let alone been in a boat."

Laura smiled. "Father took us on vacation to the beach at Bayfield when we were girls. It would be nice to see Lake Huron again."

That evening, after the friends had sung a few hymns and Dave and Sarah and their girls had gone off home, Laura retired to the familiar corner bedroom. How easy it would be to become discouraged and settle in here for another spell. She knew her teaching position was still unfilled. Giving her head a toss, Laura pushed the distraction from her mind and knelt in prayer.

Staying on with Herman and Katrina for the rest of the week, the two women finally settled on the fishing village of Sarah Hindley's childhood. On Monday morning, the sun shone brightly as they set out once again.

~⌒~

Laura Chapelton set her travel bag down on the cupped planks of the dilapidated wharf. "It's going to be a grand day for your first boat ride, Katie," she assured her as her eyes swept the rocky arc of the shoreline.

Katie stared at a ship, tiny on the horizon. "Yes, but it's a little unnerving just the same. Lake Huron's huge, and I've read that storms can spring up pretty quick." Raising her hand to shield her eyes, she scanned the light chop across the water. Stretched under the dazzling July sunlight, the bay glittered like a sea of shifting diamonds. "But God's brought us this far," she added with conviction. "And He won't abandon us now."

Farther along at the dogleg in the rickety pier, a barefoot boy dangled a hook in front of a big rock bass taking refuge in the wharf's shadows. Beside him, belly down, his friend peered through the clear green water.

"Your worm's drownded," the second boy pontificated as the women passed. "That's why they don't bite. Even if it swipes their gullet."

Laura smiled at the boys' happy chatter as she clutched her dress and attempted a long step over two missing boards. She had not taken twenty paces before the rank odour of fish assailed her nose from the dory lashed to the end of the mooring. Drawing closer, Laura surveyed the clutter of nets and buoys heaped on the bottom of the faded blue boat. Two oars and a barge pole lay along the ribs of the skiff while a coil of knotted rope wound itself like a sea serpent around a battered tin pail. A puddle of water sloshed under the stern seat as the boat bobbed at the end of her tether.

The vessel's owner, a fisherman in baggy brown trousers and rubber boots, grinned as he wiggled a dead fish from among the mound of smelly nets and unceremoniously tossed it overboard. Returning his smile, Laura studied the wizened face pocked from years of sun and wind. The man's rumpled tweed jacket might, years before, have bedecked a Toronto lawyer at a dinner party but, like the boat and her skipper, it had seen better days. *The sea exacts her own toll,* she deduced as she ventured forward.

Laura set her travel bag on the wharf. "You must be Mr. Kittrick."

Without acknowledgement, the man fixed his watery green eyes on his prospective passengers. "Jump aboard," he said, nodding toward the canvas bag in the high bow. "I've got the mail pouch and I'm set to rip." He bent over to swipe a shapeless sleeve of tweed across the centre seat. Beckoning toward the dry spot, he reached up a hand to steady Laura.

As the women lowered themselves into the boat, they felt the strangeness of its gentle rocking beneath them. Taking a seat on the bench, Laura listened to the swells lapping against the pilings and stared down into the translucent water. Pickerel glided among the boulders scattered on the rocky bottom. It all seemed so romantic and wondrous. She watched as the fisherman untied the rope and pushed off with a pole. Rowing a few rods from shore, Mr. Kittrick unfurled the tattered sail from around the mast and yanked it along the boom. Catching its wind, the tired dory surged forward.

Silent until now, Katie extended a hand over the side of the boat to wriggle her fingers in the cool wetness of the coursing waves. "What kind of fish would you catch around here?"

"Just the usual. Lake trout, sturgeon, perch. No sign of any salmon for nigh onto ten years."

"Salmon has a lovely flavour," Katie asserted. "I've had it once or twice. How is it you don't catch them anymore?"

"All fished out, I reckon," the skipper replied as he threaded a rope through the sail's grommets, securing it in place. "So what brings you way out here to this godforsaken place?"

Laura looked up. "We're hoping to have some gospel meetings in Salt House Bay. We've friends from Mildmay by the name of Hindley. The wife lived here as a girl and seemed to think we should come for a few weeks."

The man grunted, his rheumy eyes pondering a ridge of clouds building far off to the west.

As the boat rounded a craggy promontory, the whitecaps caught the wooden hull at an angle, tossing it severely. Laura tightened her cloak around her shoulders and huddled lower on the bench. Even for July the wind off the lake blew fresh and raw. Before long she noticed Katie's usual ruddiness growing pale. "Are you all right?" she asked, tentatively.

A vacuous expression had overtaken Katie's face. "Maybe I'm coming down with a bout of the grippe."

The fisherman grinned. "Kind of grippe a landlubber gets on the sea," he chuckled. "Keep your eye on the shore and sit near the stern. You can hang your head over the back if you need to feed the fish, but we're nearly there. That's Salt House Bay ahead."

Sure enough, when Laura focused her eyes, she could make out a scattering of clapboard cottages clinging to a green rise above the limestone beach. Farther up and drawn around the cluster of weathered dwellings hung a necklace of small green-and-brown patches, one of which appeared to be a pasture for a handful of chestnut dots. No doubt, the brownish corduroy plots were gardens or tilled land encircled by an unbroken stand of dense evergreen forest. As the dory drew closer to its destination, she could see several fish shanties huddled to the north of the jutting pier where hemp nets hung on reels to dry in the sun. To the south, the rock changed abruptly to a sandy shoreline with a smattering of round boulders.

As soon as the dory bumped up against the side of the dock, Mr. Kittrick jumped out, snubbing a rope through a worn hole in the planking. "Let me help you," he offered, taking Laura's hand and steadying her as she stepped up onto the dock. The fisherman, burlap sack in one hand, returned to help Katie stagger out of the boat with her travel bag. "The lady in the store looks after the mail. Would you like me to make you acquainted?"

Laura looked into Katie's blank face. "Thanks, but maybe we'll find a spot for Miss Keats to lie down for a bit. She looks rather peaked."

"A tad green around the gills, I'd say," the man noted in a twist of wry humour. After Laura handed him a shinplaster for the passage, he shook hands. "Well, I best be off while the weather holds. Good luck to you."

Overhead, the sun stood at its zenith, a faithful witness to the coming of the gospel to Salt House Bay and to the unflagging fervour of its two young messengers. "Like to find a place to settle your stomach for a bit?" Laura suggested as she and Katie stumbled along the wharf.

With a dispirited nod, Katie followed her along the sand beach to an overturned skiff. Propping her back against the barque, Laura stretched out her cloak for Katie. "We look quite the pair," she observed. "You reeling and me slumped up against a boat. Folks working on the nets'll wonder what on earth's going on." Her ripple of laughter sounded like a girl's as she opened a sack and laid a piece of shensel cake beside a brown bun and slice of cold beef. "I don't imagine you feel like eating right now?"

Katie wrapped herself in the cloak. "Not now," she mumbled weakly.

After finishing the last of her lunch, Laura watched a trio of fishermen crouched over a net they were patching. *Not much has changed,* she mused, *since James and John mended their nets with Zebedee at the Sea of Galilee.* Opening her Bible, she read about their call to become fishers of men.[5]

For nearly an hour Laura listened to the hoarse cries of the gulls soaring overhead. She sat engrossed with the antics of the sandpipers pursuing each fringe of receding wave to the water's edge only to retreat before the ensuing breaker. A sudden movement arrested her attention.

Katie was sitting up, her colour and good humour fully restored. "I feel right as rain again," she announced. "If there's still some bread I'll take a piece in my hand as we hunt up a boarding place."

Laura smiled. "I'm glad you're on the mend. It's not like you to be the toad under the harrow."

As the afternoon waned, the two sisters moved purposefully from cottage to cottage, knocking on each door. And one by one, the bashful fishing families smiled but declined to take in two strangers. Three wide-eyed faces peeked from behind one mother's skirts after she had answered the light enigmatic knock. Laura glanced beyond the careworn features to see two small rooms opening off the kitchen. Certainly most of these folks hadn't enough room for themselves. How could they possibly take in two travelers?

Turning down a narrow lane that tumbled toward the bay, Laura realized with a start the sun had dropped below the jumble of roof lines. "Our time's run out for today," she declared solemnly. "I'm afraid we'd better hurry back to the beach before we lose the light."

As dusk fell, the young women trudged wearily back to the harbour and began to pick their way along the sandy shoreline, looking for a suitable place to pass the night. In the dim light, Laura saw the outline of a large rock thrusting itself out of the sand. "That boulder might break the wind a bit," she said, pointing into the darkness. "What do you think?"

Katie forced an exhausted smile. "The shadow of a great rock in a weary land," she quoted sagely.[6]

After the two sisters had scooped out a shallow depression in the sand with a piece of driftwood, they covered a little pile with their petticoats to support their heads. This would be the first time for either of them to sleep under the stars. It was an hour past sunset, but gentle warmth still lingered on the beach while, solemn and majestic, the constellations of summer rose overhead. As the waves crashed and foamed on the rocks a few yards from where the young women lay, they talked about Jesus and His great love for them. They were, strangely, thankful to God. Cold and uncomfortable, they both felt a certain awe at their taste of rejection and the cost of discipleship.

Laura tossed aside a stone that was grinding into her hip. "This reminds me of the night George and Jack slept in the haystack."

Katie straightened her back. "I hope our mission here will be as fruitful as the one in Belwood," she murmured.

A woman with weaker convictions might have pined for the cozy home, the dry roof, and the warm bed she had left a month ago. Or about the teaching position she had given up. But to Laura those comforts seemed like the elements of someone else's life. She was happy to be with Katie in this work—and committed to her calling. Laura turned toward her friend.

"The apostle Peter wrote that we should be glad for the chance to share in Christ's sufferings," she said. "We should count this a blessing."[7]

She reached for Katie's hands, already cold and damp from the breeze off Lake Huron, and rubbed them gently. "Katie, you're perishing. Take my other shawl, do." As she turned her back to the lake, trying to shield Katie from the night wind, she whispered, "Remember when the man promised to follow Jesus wherever He went? Jesus told him, 'Foxes have holes and birds of the air have nests, but the Son of Man has nowhere to lay His head.'[8] Look! You don't have much of a pillow either."

Shivering, Katie pressed her back against Laura and drew her cloak over both of them. "Yes, you're right. But at the moment I feel more like Jonah after the fish spit him onto the beach."

"A servant isn't above his master,"[9] Laura said quietly as she huddled against her friend for warmth. "Why should we expect to fare any better than our Lord?" She paused. "Still, I miss Katrina's wood stove and the coziness of my goose-down comforter. Goodnight, Katie."

Towards midnight the sand turned clammy and resistant, and in the distance the sharp barking of fox cubs magnified their sense of isolation. Shifting as she tried to get comfortable once again, Laura lifted up her soul to God and began to sing:

> Apostles, prophets, martyrs,
> A great and noble throng,
> This road that lies before us,
> In ages past have gone.
>
> They marked it with their footprints,
> With tears and pain and blood,
> Yet bravely struggled onward,
> Strong in the strength of God.[10]

Stirred by the assurance in her companion's soft voice, Katie drew her cloak tighter as she hummed the alto notes to the hymn's fervent message.

For a long time, Laura lay listening to the sound of the wind and the breakers. *Could it be,* she wondered, *that somewhere above us in one of the humble cottages we might find a disciple of Jesus?*[11] Beside her she heard deep breathing sounds: Katie seemed to have fallen into a light sleep.

In the gauzy light of early morning, a beautiful rainbow threaded itself through the mist. Although weary from a restless night, Laura and Katie took it as a promise of God's provision, a positive sign that they were to continue in their search for a place to board. Shortly before noon, they came upon a cottage where an old fisherman and his wife invited them to stay. Laura smiled to herself as she recognized their resemblance to a water-colour illustration in her childhood volume of fairy tales.

As the days passed, Laura and Katie became acquainted around the village and soon a few people began to attend their gospel meetings. "I can hardly believe these are the same people who turned us away at the beginning," Laura remarked one day as they passed the beach.

Over the next three months, the shy, reserved people of the fishing village grew to love Laura and Katie and before they said goodbye, fifty-four people, out of the seventy homes in the village, began to follow in Jesus' way. Three separate homes were needed for the Sunday meetings of the church. In a tiny community, it was astonishing that so many embraced the gospel after such an uncertain beginning.

As they waited on the wharf for Mr. Kittrick's mail boat, the sisters moved jubilantly among the small crowd gathered to bid them farewell.

"I'm mighty thankful you didn't take a huff and leave us after that first night," the fishwife declared as she hugged them. Her arms had surprising strength, like a man's, and her calloused knuckles and empurpled palms bore resemblance, as the sun struck them, to fish scales themselves. "This village is a tough shell to pry open, my mam used to say." The rank smell of sturgeon and lake perch hung around her, but her ruinous straw hat, slack jaw, and sun-mottled cheeks did nothing to diminish her dignity or the benevolence she flashed upon Laura and Katie from her gap-toothed smile.

"We're grateful we stayed on too," said Laura as she embraced the older woman. "We'll drop you a line now and then as we move along."

With tears of joy Laura and Katie climbed into the fishing boat and waved goodbye to the little group of friends standing on the beach where they had once slept, huddled against each other in the raw wind.

As the necklace of fields around the weathered cottages shrank in the distance, a smile spread across Katie's round face. "What a contrast with the reception in Hepton Bridge," she marveled. "We definitely weren't casting our nets on the right side of the boat.[12] It'll be interesting to see where God takes us from here."

With shining eyes, Laura turned to Katie. "I do believe we've become fishers of men."

Twenty-Five

FLOWERING OF THE FELLOWSHIP
1904–1905

Although the cycle of the seasons had revolved through two abundant and event-filled years since George and Jack had separated in Belwood, the bright memory of Hunters' Hollow and Robert and Amelia's hospitality remained crisp and clear. The four brothers, each as blithe as Johnny Appleseed, had sustained their early vigour in the planting of churches while working hand in hand with the endeavours of the settled saints. Every soul within this colourful cast of personalities faithfully played the part that God had assigned to them.

After leaving Robert and Amelia's, George and Timothy had moved north, working missions in towns and villages as they went. They had planted a small church in Orangeville before moving on to do the same in Shelburne. Turning north toward the Bruce Peninsula, they had felt prompted to have meetings in a particular village, but were unable to find a place to board. At last they rented an abandoned log cabin that sagged against two shady maples in the corner of a pasture.

One day in June of 1904, George was writing a letter to the Shelburne church while Timothy sat outside reading his Bible in anticipation of the evening meeting. Looking up, he noticed that a curious sheep had ventured onto the narrow porch. In a flash he scooped the ewe up, opened the door and pushed her into the tiny cabin. He could hear her small hooves tapping on the wooden floor as she trotted over to the table where George sat absorbed in his writing. Timothy chuckled as he heard George's chair slide back and then, the inevitable scuffle: George lunging, the sheep bleating and hooves scrabbling on the pine floor. Finally the door burst open and the indignant ewe was successfully evicted. George tried to sound gruff as he stood in the doorway, but there was an unmistakable twinkle in his eye. "My boy," he said, "that's not the kind of lost sheep we're looking for."

~⌒

Meanwhile Jack and Eddie had held meetings in Georgetown, starting a little church there before they continued south to Milton. At the lake shore, they had turned east toward Port Credit and eventually into Toronto where Eddie was still well-known, thanks to his previous business dealings.

"This is all new to me," Jack admitted as he and Eddie coasted down to the sandy flats where the Humber River pushed a muddy current out into Lake Ontario. "I've never been into the big city before."

Eddie cast about for a spot on the bank, and finding a suitable place, the two men coasted their bikes to a stop and ate a small lunch they had purchased that morning. "In a way it's new for me, too," Eddie said as he unwrapped a sandwich and offered it to Jack. "I always caught the train out of Guelph. I never thought of riding a bicycle into Toronto because time was always at such a premium." Lying back on the shore grass, he cocked one leg over the other as he lay watching the clouds piling themselves into cumulus masses. "I was usually in a rip to get back with the orders after I finished with my appointments."

Jack sat upright on the bank, arms wrapped around his knees, staring across the blue sheen of the lake. "So how do you think we should start?"

"There's a lady near the intersection of Queen and Spadina who owns a big house. Her name's Mrs. Partridge. She's the mother of one of my customers, and I'm hoping she might give us lodging—at least for a day or two." Eddie watched the clouds drifting slowly eastward. "Russell invited me to his mother's one evening after his store closed, and the three of us talked about the Bible near on to midnight." Eddie grinned sheepishly. "But I was certainly trumpeting a different tune in those days."

"Spadina, I've heard that name before," Jack mused aloud as he bit into an apple. "Walter Merrick said he and Ida Rose used to live near Spadina and College. His boys still live in that neighbourhood. How close would that be?"

"Not more than a few blocks. Half dozen maybe." Eddie paused. "It won't do any harm to look up somebody who's related to our friends."

Their meal finished, the two men fell silent, listening to the soft rhythmic wash of the waves against the shoreline before climbing back onto their bicycles. As Jack rode along, he thought about the package Amelia had sent a week ago in response to his own rather cryptic letter. He had opened the package at the Port Credit post office to discover a letter and a small sealed envelope, simply inscribed "To Miranda." The bulk of the package, however, consisted of a batch of oatmeal cookies and two pounds of nutty maple fudge. He and Eddie had savoured the sweets ever since, licking the sugar off their fingers after each treat. Although Jack had disclosed the newsy parts of Amelia's letter to Eddie, he withheld the closing paragraphs.

Hunters' Hollow
Belwood, Ontario
July 19, 1904

Our dear Jack,

Many thanks for yours of Sunday last. Robert and I can hardly wait to tear into each envelope from either you or George. I'm sure you know that he and Timothy are having gospel meetings in Tobermory on the Bruce Peninsula. Apparently the limestone cliffs along the Georgian Bay are simply breathtaking. It seems fitting that their rustic cabin sits on a hill overlooking the harbour and the Big Tub lighthouse. I pray the witness of their lives will shine into all of the village and guide some lost soul into the safe harbour of Christ, the light of the world.[1]

We had a lovely meeting this morning and some beautiful but simple thoughts were passed along. Sissy Boggins has not been so well since her weak spell, but she was able to ride out here with Walter and Ida Rose after missing three Sundays. Although we'd been to visit her a number of times at her cottage, we were thrilled to see her gathered with the rest of us around the dinner table. Her usual spunk and droll humour haven't suffered a smidgen in spite of her nasty tumble. I'm amazed at the way Walter and Ida Rose dote over her. But then again, why should I be? You and George were an example to all of us. Robert and I remember the care you men showed us when we were up against it. Archie Hampton and the Stonehouse family are thriving.

The summer's getting on and Robert's in grand fettle again. It seems as if nothing can hold him back now. Yesterday he spent the afternoon up to his waist in the neighbour's pond. The man's sheep needed a second round of dipping. I guess the lice and ticks were driving the poor creatures to distraction.

In your last letter you suggested meeting my former pupil, Miranda Warmington, who Robert spoke to you about back at the sugar camp. What a splendid idea! I'm amazed you even remembered her. Thank you so much. Miranda's definitely not your traditional stodgy kind of woman, but whether she will give ear to the message of our Lord remains to be seen. The last letter I had from her was at Christmastime a year and a half ago.

Her address is: 248 Aspen Ridge Avenue, Toronto.

Please give her my warmest greetings. I have enclosed a small note for her, telling a little of the happenings in West Garafraxa and attesting to our love for you and Eddie and your work.

Love from all here,

Amelia and Robert

Following Eddie's unerring lead through the maze of the city, Jack gazed awestruck at the grand scale of the place as they wheeled past block after block of rail yards, factories, and red brick houses. Pulling up at a decorative Queen Anne house on a narrow street off Spadina Avenue, Eddie leaned his bicycle against the lattice work of the front porch.

Stepping confidently across the impressive veranda, he knocked on the heavy door. When it swung open, Jack could see that Mrs. Partridge, in total contrast with her namesake, was tall, willowy, and ethereal—rather like the heroine of a Jane Austen novel. Her late husband had been a contemporary of Oliver Summers and was well-known in the fabric business for his importing of Priestley's dress goods and English suiting.

"Eddie Summers!" she exclaimed. "What on earth brings you here?"

"I hope we're not imposing by arriving unannounced, Mrs. Partridge."

"Not at all, Eddie. Some folks are nothing but a bad memory, and I don't care if I ever lay eyes on them again. But you're not one of them."

When the introductions were completed and the men's mission outlined, Mrs. Partridge showed the two young men to their rooms.

Later that evening as Jack settled in, he rummaged in the bottom of his travel bag for the worn photo and laid it beside Amelia's letter. Once again, he felt the familiar ache as he studied the dark eyes, the soft curved chin, the smile—vibrant, high-spirited, carefree. Wondering what might have enticed his mother away from the familiarity of home, he moved to the window and looked down, noting the figures of men and women hurrying along the busy thoroughfare. As Jack gazed through the gathering dusk at lights in nearby windows, address still clutched in hand, Miranda seemed so near, so palpable. The warmth of her presence reached out to him.

Still, an unsettling thought niggled in the back of his mind. When he dug around to unearth it, he realized it was Mrs. Partridge's comment. "Some folks are nothing a bad memory," she had declared, "and I don't care if I ever lay eyes on them again."

Although Jack had endlessly imagined what it might be like to meet his mother, the reunion had always been so elusive and tentative that he had never examined the depth of feelings that might arise. The illusion had always been one of a young woman with a smiling face and open arms. But now as the possibility seemed within reach, a sudden, jarring thought occured to Jack. Would *she* want to lay eyes on him again? That disturbing notion left him reeling. He grappled with it, reliving the distress this innocent young girl must have felt when she had learned she was going to have a child out of wedlock.

Retreating from the open window, Jack slumped across his bed, the streetcar wheels screeching in the distance. Penetrating questions, like the squeal of metal on metal, tortured his mind: *Would Miranda have admitted to her husband the shameful blot from her youth? Does she have other children? How would they feel about me? Would she even acknowledge me if I appear on her doorstep unannounced?* "I might be nothing more than a long-forgotten disgrace," Jack muttered. "As welcome as a skunk on the front stoop." The more he thought about it, the more certain he was that she had returned home from that horrible exile in Guelph, never to give voice to it again. Trapped in the certainty that she had been irrevocably tainted, she had banished it from her mind. And now Jack felt convinced that he must too. Face down on the pillow, he groaned with the pain of partial knowledge. His shoulders shook with grief as he suffered the death of a dream he had held close to his heart for more than seventeen years.

One afternoon several days later, a summer downpour danced on the sidewalk as Jack and Eddie hurried toward Mrs. Partridge's after visiting one of Eddie's former customers in the northerly part of the city. As they approached the streetcar stop, Eddie cast about for a dry place to wait. A majestic stone church stood opposite them and immediately beside it, a government-run orphanage. Discovering that their streetcar would not arrive for another twenty minutes, the two men dashed over to the lobby of the church.

To pass the time, the men read the sign on the elegant foyer wall. Topping the list was the minister's name followed by letters showing his credentials. Below this were the names of the men on the church council and the date the church had been founded. Three unlit candles sat on an oak table, flanked by neat stacks of donation envelopes and doctrinal tracts. Down the hall in the church office, a smartly dressed lady sat behind a desk while a janitor stood polishing the brass door handles.

"I see there's a public orphanage next door," Jack commented after a few minutes. "I wouldn't mind taking a gander. I've never been inside one."

"If it's anything like the House of Industry and Refuge on the Fergus road, it'll be pretty eerie and dismal."

Jack raised his eyebrows. "Is that the big limestone building on the brow of the hill between Aboyne and Fergus?"

"That's the spot," Eddie replied. "It's full of the destitute and waifs of every age and shape, either abandoned or unwanted. The day I delivered a bolt of cotton was cold and miserable, but they were all outside on their hands and knees, mostly in rags, grubbing about in the vegetable gardens."

Jack's face registered shock. "You mean the little ones too?"

"Apparently you have to earn your keep there. You can't just pull up to the table like I did as a lad."

Shivers ran down Jack's spine, thinking of his own fate and mindful that his girlish mother had lived only a few miles from the place at the time he was born. "It's great to have parents who love you," he said lamely.

Eddie peered outside. "The rain's letting up a tad," he noted. "Let's hike over and take a look."

Jack pulled down the peak on his cap as he and Eddie sprinted next door. Here, too, a sign was posted on the entrance wall. At the top of the list was the managing director's name followed by the letters of his university degrees. Listed underneath were the names of the board of directors and the date the institution had been established by the Province of Ontario. The parallel leapt into Jack's mind. Sure enough, when he turned around, he saw an information bulletin listing the orphanage's objectives. And through the glass door was a lady scrubbing the terrazzo floor below a red arrow pointing to the business office.

Pushing the door ajar, Jack walked over and squatted down in front of the scrub woman. Her pretty face, almost childlike itself, contrasted sharply with her coarse hands, the colour of weathered burlap. "G'day," he greeted. "Is it possible to talk to some of the children?"

The woman clambered to her feet. "You da papa?"

"No," Jack asserted hastily, meeting her accusative eye with a blush.

"Sorry man. No posseebla without talka to bossa lady."

"That's all right." Jack grinned and slipped a few coins into her hand. "Could you please buy the children a bag of bonbons with this?"

As the young men ran back to the streetcar stop, Jack noticed that both organizations had large impressive signs on the front lawn. No doubt both had a financial budget, a bookkeeper, a bank account, and both were run by hired help. If the income dropped off, both would dramatically cut back on their operations. And if they couldn't keep the wolf away in the event of financial ruin, they would close their doors and leave.

Mindful of a man absorbed in the *Globe* behind him, Jack leaned toward Eddie. "I understood what Jesus meant when He spoke of being the good shepherd," he said quietly. "But what I didn't grasp until today was what he meant about the hireling."

Eddie cocked his head and listened.

"The hired man doesn't own the sheep," Jack continued, "or have a stake in their well-being. That's why he abandons them and runs away when he sees the wolf coming, leaving the flock to be attacked and scattered."

Eddie glanced up to see the streetcar approaching. "In other words, the hired man cares nothing for the sheep."[2]

Jack stepped toward the curb. "Still, there are well-meaning men like Walter Merrick. They possess the heart of a shepherd, but unless they're careful, they can lose sight of the Good Shepherd and His example."

Eddie gave way as the older man behind the *Globe* stepped forward. "Yes," he acknowledged, "a person could be reduced to the status of a hireling without even realizing it."

When the car pulled up, its bell clanging, the two men scrambled up the steep steps. As Jack followed Eddie down the aisle, he looked into the weary faces of factory workers heading home after a long day. Two empty seats remained near the rear door, and the two men slid into them.

Shaking the water droplets off his cap, Jack settled back against his seat and relaxed, studying the people who rose and jostled their way to the exit as the car swayed and shook along Yonge Street. As he watched them scurrying away from the stops, he imagined them gathering their families around a supper table. Then, after trying to visualize the meagre dining hall at the orphanage, his mind returned to the similarity between it and the church. As Jack gazed through the rain streaming over the streetcar window, he wiped the mist off the inside of the pane. It was clear to him that the power of both operations sprang from their income.

Jack turned to Eddie. "Things have changed drastically since our Lord sent out His disciples," he observed. "They were to take nothing for their journey—no bag, no bread, no copper in their money belts."[3]

Eddie reflected for a moment. "When Jesus called them, they *forsook all* and followed Him, didn't they?"[4] He paused, checking the streetcar's progress. "I'm glad my father honoured my decision and let me go without a struggle. At first I worried he might persist with my monthly stipend just because I'm his son, but he didn't. He seemed to understand that would reduce me to a hireling and that I need to go forth in faith, trusting God."

Jack's eyes misted at the clarity of Eddie's revelation. "Yes," he said softly. "It truly is a privilege to be able to forsake *all*. We're blessed to be invited to search for our Master's sheep." Jack rode silently for a few moments, thinking of the ministry. Then he turned to Eddie. "But today where's the sacrifice?"

Eddie shook his head. "I don't know," he replied as he stood up, heading toward the door. "But without it, religion becomes meaningless."

Stepping down from the streetcar, the men threaded their way past the main entrance of the T. Eaton department store as people milled in front of its expansive windows, admiring the new fall fashions. One window dressing offered an array of ladies' Cravenette waterproof cloaks, raglan coats, and squirrel fur-lined capes, while another displayed men's ulsters, reefers, and dressing gowns. Numerous carriages and buggies stood at the curb waiting to receive shoppers with armfuls of merchandise. Turning the corner, the men picked up the pace as they strode west along Queen Street.

Jack admired the orphanage for its excellent work for the poor. The employees genuinely cared for their unfortunate charges, he knew, and no doubt most did their best to make the children as comfortable and happy as possible. But at night, the staff went home to their own families, and the income they had earned cared for their own children. Without a weekly wage, most of them wouldn't, or couldn't, be there. "Orphanages do a marvelous work," Jack declared as they walked past the imposing stone arches of Osgoode Hall, "but they can never take the place of a home or a family. It seems to me that an orphanage is to a family what the denominational system is to a fellowship meeting of the saints."

"That's an intriguing analogy," Eddie replied as his mind flashed back to his last Sunday with the little church at Lyman and Jessie's. "But meeting in a home would be pointless without the love and spirit of a family," he added with discernment.

Eddie recalled how tender and sensitive the friends had been about his leaving. And how deeply that realization had touched his heart. Giving him a surprisingly robust hug, Mrs. Applebee had handed him a parchment writing tablet and, with a twinkle in her eye, had advised him that she would be expecting regular correspondence. At dinner, Jessie had prepared one of his favourites, cornmeal muffins laced with maple syrup, and afterward Gertrude Foster had pressed a box of crystallized figs into his hand. "I buy them by the case," she confided with a wink, "but don't let on to Hugh." One by one, each of the friends had embraced him as they offered their blessing and Godspeed for his mission. Eddie was savouring the memory as he and Jack mounted the steps of Mrs. Partridge's veranda.

That evening, unknown to the other, both men sat down in their rooms to write letters home. Jack thanked his parents for taking him into their lives as an infant and for the love with which they had nurtured him ever since. Eddie wrote to his dad with the name and address of the orphanage, knowing that his father would be interested in sharing his wealth with needy children—the same as Eddie's heavenly Father. And although Eddie couldn't have known it then, five years later would see two of the Toronto orphans established in Oliver Summers' home as apprentices in the clothier trade, lanky lads who were honoured and treated as adopted sons while Oliver's hair and beard took on the frost of winter.

Bright sunshine reflected off the stone walls and brass plate of the stalwart old post office as Jack and Eddie picked up their mail one Monday morning in September. Across the street a teamster ogled a stylish young belle while his horses drank deeply from one of the city's watering troughs. Stopping at a wayside bench along the sidewalk, Jack tore open a letter from Percy Ellington, the brother in Milton who had responded to the message he and Eddie had preached the previous year.

"Percy's planning to leave the stonemason trade," Jack announced after he had read the letter twice. "Says he'd like to join us and wonders if that would be all right with us."

Laying aside his own correspondence, Eddie gazed across Queen Street at two men rolling casks of molasses down a plank from the back of a livery wagon. "It'd be nice to have Percy's company. He's a fine brother and likely kind of lonely out there in Milton by himself. Too bad he was the only one to make a start." Lifting his cap, he touched the centre part in his oiled hair. "How would it work out to have three preachers, though?"

Jack crossed his legs and stretched his right arm along the back of the wood bench. "I reckon there's some Scripture to support three of us working together. Didn't Paul and Barnabas take John Mark with them when they finished their mission in Jerusalem?"[5]

Eddie nodded. "I believe so," he mused aloud.

"Besides, one of us could preach and travel alone for a short spell," Jack added, "or with one of the friends.[6] Last winter, Morgan offered to help out anytime he was needed."

"Good, it's settled then," Eddie concluded. "Tell Percy we can't wait to see his shining face at Union Station."

The week before Percy Ellington was to leave Milton, he went to the railway station. Approaching the wicket, he greeted the station agent cheerfully. "Morning, Horace. It's a lovely day. I'd like to buy a ticket to Toronto." Almost as an afterthought, he added, "One way, please."

Horace peered sharply over his wire-rimmed glasses. He had sold Percy several tickets before. "It's a lot cheaper to buy a round-trip ticket."

"Thanks, Horace, but I'm not coming back."

"You may not be coming back for a while," the crusty stationmaster retorted. "But when you get done with your holiday, you'll be back. This round-trip ticket's good for a whole year."

"I won't be back in a year either." Percy smiled, his high spirits difficult to contain. "As far as I know, I won't ever be back. I'm going to become an itinerant minister."

Horace squinted through the bars. "First I heard of it," he muttered.

"I've kept it kind of close so far, just among my own kith and kin."

Curious, Horace plied Percy with pointed questions. Percy answered carefully and spoke a little of his new life. By the time he had finished, Horace's face had contorted with disgust. "Well," he huffed, peering down his sharp nose, "some people sure twist the Scripture to suit themselves."

Percy, stung by the acrid retort, reflected for just a moment. "Yes, Horace, what you say is often true." He smiled graciously as the stationmaster handed him the ticket. "But you're looking at a man who's twisting himself to suit the Scriptures."

One evening in October soon after Percy had joined Eddie and Jack, the three gathered in Jack's bedroom to make plans. Through the open window, the clip-clop of passing livery horses could be heard on the street.

Eddie's face suddenly alerted as if he were recalling forgotten times. "I'd like to visit Meni Finkelstein one of these days," he suggested. "He owns the factory that we ordered some of our suits from. I doubt he'd come along to our meetings, but it'd be nice to look in on him just the same."

Percy crossed his arms and grinned. "I'm the new man on the watch, so anything sounds interesting to me."

Jack chewed thoughtfully on the end of his toothpick. "Maybe it'd be better for the two of you to go," he mused. "I owe a letter to George, and then I think I'll head out for a long walk."

The following morning after Eddie and Percy had struck out for the Finkelstein factory, Jack sat down at a table under his bedroom window. Outside, a sparrow twittered and hopped from branch to branch, and the first tinges of autumn had rusted the oak leaves that scraped the window.

As he wrote to George about Robert and Amelia, he was suddenly reminded of the photo album at Hunters' Hollow and the dinner he had missed after being unnerved by the picture of his mother. He swallowed, thinking how much he craved to talk over his feelings with someone. One evening he had come perilously close to confiding his past to Eddie. But although he and Eddie were growing closer with the passing months, it was still not the same as being with George.

Jack doodled, wondering if he would find the courage to reveal his dilemma when he saw George next. It was then, as if on impulse, that he jumped up and retrieved the distracting photo from his travel bag. As he studied it again, he suddenly shoved the chair under the table. "Goodness gracious," he muttered, "I'm stuck. And there's only one answer." He turned and grabbed his tweed cap and headed down the stairs.

As Jack turned onto Aspen Ridge Avenue, he surveyed the street with the acuity of an Apache scout. The tree-lined street had a grassy median studded with stately elms that arched over the road on either side. Elegant homes were surrounded by carefully manicured lawns. *A quick pass along the street can't do any harm,* Jack reasoned as he started down one side, his eye searching out the numbers. He could feel his heart hammering and breath coming in short gasps as he strode along one side of the street. He noted numbers 237 and 241 as he angled across the median. His mouth felt oddly dry, and he took deep breaths as he approached the house at 248 Aspen Ridge.

The classic Georgian flaunted a double door with a transom and Palladian window above. On either side of the entrance, tall windows with white muntins and forest green shutters glistened in the sunlight. Jack's mind throbbed like a festering wound as he approached the imposing residence. He supposed Miranda must work for these folks—hiring out as a washerwoman or a dressmaker for a genteel family.

Without breaking stride Jack peered at the small panes, hoping to catch a glimpse of movement inside. The dark glass, however, disclosed nothing more than his own distant reflection. Jack's expression sagged, and a bitter tear ran down his cheek as the house disappeared behind him. At the end of Aspen Ridge Avenue he turned south and headed toward home, his face clouded with pain and disappointment.

Jack had walked for nearly an hour when he abruptly hauled himself up short in the centre of the sidewalk. It suddenly occurred to him that he could just introduce himself simply as Jack, a friend of Amelia Hunter's. There would be no need to say more than that. He could also let her know about the gospel meetings at the empty storefront on Queen Street.

Jack noticed that the sun had shifted, bathing the double oak door in the warm September sunlight that filtered through the elms. His hands were clammy as he paused on the side of the street, steeling himself for the short walk to the front door. Then, taking a deep breath to steady his nerves, he stepped onto the flagstone porch. Wiping his palms on his pant legs, he lifted the brass knocker and rapped twice. Jack heard footsteps followed by the metallic click of the deadbolt. When the door swung open, Jack found himself facing a dark-haired lady in a lavender dress and white apron.

"Good morning," she said with an enquiring smile. "Can I help you?"

As Jack perspired, struggling to determine whether this might be his mother, he looked into the soft eyes. His voice trembled slightly as he spoke. "I'm looking for Miranda Warmington."

The woman's face clouded and she shook her head. "There's no Miranda Warmington here," she replied.

Jack's hand shook as he reached into his pocket and drew out Amelia's letter. He checked the letter and glanced up at the brass numbers beside the door. "I…I was given this address by a good friend of hers," he stuttered.

Wiping her hands on her apron, the woman looked thoughtful. "I'm sorry. There must be some mistake," she sympathized. "I can't help you."

After thanking her, Jack turned and headed down the path as the deadbolt clicked shut. A wave of acid welled up in his belly as he started along the street.

"Excuse me, sir." The voice seemed distant, ringing in his ears above the maelstrom in his head. "Excuse me." Jack wheeled to see the dark-haired woman on the front porch. She began to speak as he retraced his steps. "This family I work for has only been here for six months. Now that I think of it, we used to get mail for a Mrs. Miranda Longstaff. I'll fetch her forwarding address if you can wait a minute."

In a moment the maid returned with a scrap of paper and on it were written the words: Professor Dwight Longstaff, 4803 Stornoway Road, London, Ontario. As Jack studied the address, the woman spoke again. "I understand the professor's teaching at the university in London now. Western, I believe it's called."

Jack thanked the maid a second time and trudged toward the street, his legs moving like lead pipes.

While Jack's quest had drawn him into the maze of his past, Eddie anticipated introducing Percy to Mr. Summers' humourous old business acquaintance. As the King Street car clanged its way toward the textile district, Percy sniffed the pungent city air rushing through the windows: acrid coal smoke and smells of burning grease, yeasty scents from brewery and bakery, and the distant but unmistakable reek from the tanneries and slaughter houses. Soon, the textile district's smoky haze, shoddy brickwork, and faded signs proclaimed their destination. While Eddie chatted to the driver, it was Percy who first spotted the aggressively painted sign on a factory wall: Finkelstein Textiles Ltd.

Inside, the roar and hum of looms and machines almost deafened the visitors as they approached the factory office. The receptionist looked askance, but Meni Finkelstein bowed deferentially to the young men, his hand over his heart. "Velcome, velcome. Sit down a little. You trink a cup of coffee maybe? It's a cold day. Ha, ha, ha." Then he raised his voice, his heavily inflected English nuanced with Yiddish. "Sadie, my girl, bring in t'ree cups coffee mit cream. Ha, ha, ha."

"Meni, this is Percy Ellington, a friend of mine."

"Nice to meet you lad," Meni said, looking Percy up and down. "So what bring you in to shmooze mit an old man? Need more clot'?"

When Eddie told Meni of the change in his life and the purpose for which he and Percy were in Toronto, the old man sighed. "Oy vey, oy vey. You got chutzpah, son. No business, no salary. And your fadder. What he do mit'out you?"

Eddie drained his coffee cup. "He keeps busy still running the business. A little slower, but he likes to work for himself."

"My fadder, may his soul rest in peace, he alvays say, 'T'ears no profit vorking for somebawdy else. You must for yourself go into a good business. Sooo, forty years long since I rent a building and set up my shears and sewing machines. Later I buy some for steam and pressing. And afterward, forty years I sit here mit my original investment and my money, vaiting, still vaiting for the Messiah..." His clouded eyes were full of warmth and a leathery smile showed teeth gleaming with caramel.

Eddie felt struck to the heart. The Christ of God, the Anointed One, the Messiah had already come to His own people, and the rulers among His own people had not received Him. Eddie's usual genial manner and forthright friendliness seemed paralysed as he pondered how to reach out to this old business associate of his father's generation. After some chat about the competition in the haberdashery industry, he finally leaned forward. "We're having some Christian meetings in a storefront on Queen Street. It'd be nice to have you come along some evening."

Mr. Finkelstein's voice cut softly into Eddie's perplexity. "I don't t'ink so, but I have for you t'e deepest regard, son. I hope eberyt'ing is fixed up good for you and Percy here. I vould have hoped, maybe, some vedding bells for you. My son-in-laws who marry my daughters, they vill someday have all vot I have. You should make vot t'ey make. You know about t'e law and t'e profits, no? My modder alvays say, 'Put avay a few shekels. It can't hurt.'" His hands, which so eloquently played along with his words, now searched his suit pockets. "Eben so, take for yourselves a little spare change. For your meals today, here are five dollars. Maybe for that you can get in a deli some nice roasted chicken. Or some smoked herring on rye mit pickles and a cup of tea. Ha, ha, ha." His eyes twinkled at his own wit.

Eddie slid the money back across the table. "You're most generous, Mr. Finkelstein, but we have plenty for the present. How about we come again and have another cup of coffee with you?"

Meni Finkelstein stroked a careworn finger over the hairs that sprouted from his ear. "Any time, lads, you need some change, come by."

As the men rose to leave, Meni's eyes roved over Percy again. "Yellow hair! You kin tell he's not of the tribe of Judah. I em sorry you are not my sons. I have daughters only, to my sorrow."

Percy laughed and shook the kindly old manufacturer's hand as he and Eddie slipped out the door.

When the men arrived home in the afternoon, they found Jack bent over his writing pad. "Must be one long letter," Eddie joked good-naturedly.

Jack turned toward the voice. "I decided to go for my walk and write my letters later. All work and no play makes Jack a dull boy, you know."

"Meet anybody interesting on your constitutional?" Eddie persisted.

Jack's eyes wavered as he slipped Miranda's picture under his Bible. "I certainly got lots of exercise and fresh air," he said offhandedly. "And how did you fellows make out at Mr. Finkelstein's?"

"I don't think we should hold our breath waiting for him to show up at the gospel meeting this evening," Eddie replied as he moved toward the door. "Well, if you fellows'll excuse me, I'd like to scrape off a few whiskers before supper."

"Meet you in the kitchen at six," Jack answered as he dipped his pen in the ink bottle. "I want to finish this epistle to Hugh and Gertrude and pop it in the mail before the post office closes."

"Please add my greetings," Eddie said. "Tell them I remember the first night we all showed up at the Elora schoolhouse to hear the new preachers in town."

Hearing Eddie's door close, Percy rose to leave. "Actually, Jack, Mr. Finkelstein's a fine old gentleman," he said earnestly. "A self-made man. And generous to boot. He offered us the week's wages of a stonemason and treated me as if I was Oliver Summers' son too. All three of us'll have to go along to drink a cup of coffee with him the next time."

～⊙～

Although Jack adapted to sleeping and waking to the incessant rumble of the streetcars, he remained a country boy at heart, and as the seasons came and went, he eagerly read George's letters of the mission work continuing in the villages of rural Ontario. But if at times he longed for the first trills of spring peepers, the scent of fresh-cut alfalfa in summer, or the golden ripple of wind gamboling across autumn grain fields, he made no complaint as he plodded on faithfully among the masses in the province's capital.

Night after night, confronted by the florid faces of boilermen, factory hands, textile weavers, and office workers, Jack responded with a full heart to the openness he sensed in the restless gatherings. On several evenings a pair of bankers or financiers from Bay Street would sit with an amused twinkle in their eyes as they listened to this country bumpkin from Nassagaweya Township. The constraints and boundaries of town and rural life seemed overturned among the fomenting energies of a city still young with roisterous life, and added unto daily by the shiploads of immigrants and travelers docking at the foot of Yonge Street. Nevertheless, a few gentle souls gave ear to the simple message and lent hope to Jack and Eddie's mission.

Meanwhile George and Timothy tore open every letter from Toronto, mesmerized by Jack's description of the city's soaring buildings and bustling waterfront. Freighters laden with goods from around the world lay side by side with the *Primrose* and *Mayflower,* paddle steamers that ferried nine hundred passengers at a time to Toronto Island, the veritable circus of all things curious. In the winter of 1904 Jack had described iceboaters skittering their sailed skiffs around the frozen harbour, while in stark contrast *The Toronto* lay immobilized, icebound until spring.

Nothing, however, brought a sense of reality to the newspaper articles like Jack's eyewitness account of the great fire that had broken out on the windy evening of April the 19th that year. Seeing the furious red glow from Mrs. Partridge's windows, the three young men had set off on the run to see how they could help. For most of the night, they hauled wet blankets, placing them against the window frames of the Queens Hotel in an attempt to thwart the seething furnace immediately to the east. Firemen with lanterns, some from as far as Hamilton, London and Buffalo, frantically lay hoses and pumped water from the bay but by morning the towering inferno had destroyed eighty-six buildings at the heart of the city. Fourteen acres at Bay and Front Streets lay smoking in collapsed rubble and charred ruins. Mercifully, Jack wrote, in answer to prayer, no one had been killed.

A world away, George and Timothy continued to sow the seed among the rural settlements. The winter of 1905 passed, and once again the blossoms of May were bursting into bloom as they struggled to find a boarding place in Owen Sound. As the day wore on, George was beginning to watch for a stopgap place to bed down when they met a farmer on the road.

"Give Caul Hornbeck a try," the man suggested, stubbing a finger toward the east side of the village. "First place on the right, top of the rise."

Thanking the helpful farmer, the men shouldered their bags and set off with renewed spirit. The road over the rise wound around one side of a mossy outcropping, and just beyond it, a steep bank had covered itself with long-stemmed white violets that escaped from a garden fashioned long ago. Craning his neck, Timothy caught sight of a weathered gable rising behind a forest of lilac bushes. A set of rickety board steps led up the embankment to the Hornbeck homestead. Coaxing the wire gate ajar, the travelers squeezed inside and approached the dilapidated structure through a thicket that had overgrown the front yard at least two decades before.

"Cozy-looking place," Timothy quipped as they emerged from the grove in front of a sagging side porch, its splintered and disordered gingerbread hanging askew like the hieroglyphics of an ancient civilization.

When George knocked on the door, a bellow resounded. "C'mon in."

Stepping into the kitchen, the men came face-to-face with a squat man in a soiled woolen undershirt partitioned by leather braces that cut into his barrel shape. George appraised the unruly sheaf of grizzled gray hair that jutted from under the man's cap and the crow's feet stitched around his eyes. The veined skin over his cheekbones appeared thin and shiny. George surmised the man's age to be about eighty.

"What can I do for you chaps?" the man asked as he wiped the grease off his jowls with the back of his hand.

"We're looking for a place to board for a few weeks," George replied, mentally counting out the twelve plates set around the table. "And we wondered if you had any space."

The round chinless face tipped back in a bronchial guffaw. "Space and to burn. Why this place housed seventeen people in her heyday."

As Timothy stood listening, a sullen Persian cat emerged from behind the stove while a striped tabby jumped off the lounge. A soft thump jerked his head to the left to see yet another cat landing from the china dresser.

After hearing the two strangers out, Mr. Hornbeck agreed to take them in. Pushing back his chair, the old bachelor, trailed by five cats, their tails high in the air like flag bearers near the head of a parade, showed George and Timothy to a large bedroom at the top of the staircase. Cobwebs angled across the upper corners and flies, still dopey after winter, buzzed dizzily against the window pane. Here and there a dry curl of fern-patterned wall-paper hung down dejectedly.

From where he stood behind Mr. Hornbeck, Timothy shot George a quizzical smile, and then, a slow nod.

"Looks just fine," George said. "We'll be delighted to take it."

"Land o' Goshen," their host drawled. "Help yourself to the fixin's in the pantry, seein' as how you're stayin'. I ain't any fist of a cook, so you'll have to fend for yourselves. See you when the rooster crows."

As Mr. Hornbeck's lumbering steps retreated down the hall, Timothy shooed the cats out the door, pressing the warped door tightly behind them. A grin spread across his face as he surveyed the room. "Wouldn't Aunt Maggie be horrified at our choice of hotels?"

"I don't reckon Mr. Hornbeck knows a heap about keeping house," George returned wryly. "But we'll bring it to shipshape first thing in the morning. Nothing a little elbow grease won't turn into a castle. Besides, it's a far cry from a haystack."

Evening overshadowed the old house as the pair set about to straighten the rumpled beds and brush the clumps of cat hair off the flattened pillows. While George polished the chimney glass in the lamp with his handkerchief, Timothy slipped off the pillow cases and shook them, taking care to turn each one inside out before he put it back on the bed.

As the sun rose the following morning, Timothy's eyes were still closed and his covers drawn to his chin as George tiptoed out of the room and down the stairs to find their landlord leaning over the cookstove. "Morning, Mr. Hornbeck," he greeted cheerfully.

"Say, lad. Just call me Caul, would you?" the old man grunted as he half-turned at the voice. "Will you have bacon and eggs?"

George was about to reply in the affirmative when he caught sight of the range top. He paused, mid-stride, recoiling as he saw Mr. Hornbeck slap another slab of bacon directly onto the sizzling stove lids. George blinked with incredulity at the grease bubbling over the lifter hole.

"Well, lad. What do you say?"

George opened his mouth and closed it again. "Maybe I'll make some oatmeal, if that's all right," he stammered.

"Suit yourself," the old bachelor said as he moved to dip a pan of water from the reservoir.

Poking around in the cluttered pantry, George glanced out to see Mr. Hornbeck retrieve three speckled eggs and plunge them, unwashed, into the piping water. While he watched, the big Persian jumped off the lounge and sprang onto the table, stalking the length of the oilcloth to sniff at the dirty plate from last night's supper. As deftly as a grizzly catching a salmon, the old man transferred the bacon and eggs onto a fresh plate next to the one he had used at suppertime the previous evening. But before sitting down to breakfast, he reached into a can on the windowsill and trickled a handful of tea leaves into the egg water.

"Tea'll be steeped in two shakes of a lamb's hind leg," he announced with the expansive air of a country squire. "Make yourself at home."

"Thanks," George replied as he scrubbed an enamel pan and let it boil before stirring in enough oatmeal for Timothy and himself.

Caul Hornbeck raised his head from the mountain of bacon and eggs. "Take any plate you fancy," he said. "I move around the table until they're all dirty and then I wash the bunch. Efficiency's the thing, you know."

When the last of the bacon had disappeared, he shoved the rinds off the back of the plate for the long-haired cat who sat eagerly waiting.

Tipping back in his chair, the old bachelor hooked his thumbs under his suspenders as an ominous rumbling in his windpipe erupted in a satisfied belch. "So you're preachers," he mused aloud. "I've no use for those stuffed shirts in the village myself. Guess that's why I'm tickled to have you here. Give them a dose of competition."

George winced as he listened to Mr. Hornbeck's cast-iron opinions. Like his own father, the man abhorred the local clergymen. Perhaps his motives for accepting the two strange preachers had been to rub salt into a wound that should have been healed long ago. George's stomach knotted. He detested the idea of being a pawn in a unpleasant game.

George was busy spooning in his oatmeal by the time Timothy bounded down the stairs.

"Have a cup of tea 'fore it gets too powerful," Mr. Hornbeck bellowed affably.

"That's the best way," Timothy rejoined as he filled a mug. "There's nothing like a good stiff cup to start a fellow's day."

George suppressed a grin as he watched Timothy's eyes suddenly flicker at the floating particles in the cup. He could see no way to catch the young man's attention unobtrusively.

After washing up the breakfast dishes, the brothers struck off to scout out the village and schoolhouse. Bees buzzed among the fragrant blossoms as George and Timothy followed the worn footpath through the lilac veil to the outside world. Pausing at the gate, Timothy drew in a deep breath and stretched in the warm sunshine. In a flash he saw that the rusty top hinge had long since given way and he sprang forward to help George muscle the bottom rail out of the mud.

"Tea have a nice flavour this morning?" George asked deadpan as the pair started toward the village.

"Grand," Timothy replied quickly. "Are you off it?"

When George explained the source of the tea water, Timothy screwed up his face and stuck out his tongue, convulsing with hoots of laughter. "So that explains the bits of straw floating in the pan," he exclaimed when he could catch his breath. "I guess the yoke's on me this time."

Three days later, after arranging for the use of the school, George sat down to write a letter while Timothy did housemaid duties accompanied by hearty snores from Mr. Hornbeck's bedroom.

Owen Sound, Ontario
May 24, 1905

My dearest Laura,

The river valley and the roofs and chimneys of the village stretch before my eyes as I look out the bedroom window on this beautiful Victoria Day. Although a little tired now, this house must have been a grand old dame in her day, sitting as she does at the top of a grassy bluff above the bay, eyeing the activity below.

Our landlord, Mr. Hornbeck, is a charming old gent in his own way. Other than the odd foray around the yard and to his chicken coop, the old bachelor lives between the kitchen and his bedroom. Says he closed the parlour up when his mother was carried out and hasn't set foot inside since. Judging by what I can see through the French doors, everything remains untouched in twenty years except, of course, for the inevitable dust.

Yesterday at supper time we came back from handing out invitations to find a chicken on its back bubbling in large iron pot. Now boiling a chicken is nothing new, but to see the pot lid suspended between the chicken's two legs was. And even more startling was to see the hen's two feet and claws pointing skyward. No doubt, part of the efficiency that Mr. Hornbeck touts.

How wonderful to hear of the interest you and Katie are having in Goderich and that the three little churches in Salt House Bay continue to do well. Most of the churches that have been planted in other areas are also thriving and their spiritual lives have begun to bear fruit which, in turn, contains the seeds of new life. Often within a year or two, they're eager to reach out to others and invite their neighbours to a Thursday evening meeting. It's become clearer to me than ever before that the work of the settled saints and that of the traveling ministry are beautifully united as each of us, in our own way, tries to obey our Lord's instruction to go into all the world.

Now for some exciting news that I'd like you to hear first from me. There are plans in the wind to make up a hymn book, one that focuses on Jesus and the simplicity of His way. You should have seen Timothy's face light up when we first talked about it. He and I discussed the matter every now and then as we went about our work. Finally, I wrote to Alistair and Jack asking for their opinions. Alistair suggested the cover include the words: Come!—Abide!—Go! because these are three fundamental teachings of Jesus: Come unto Me, all you who are weary and heavily burdened, and I will give you rest[7]—Abide in Me, and I in you. No branch can bear fruit by itself, it must abide in the vine,[8] and finally, Go into all the world and preach the gospel to every creature.[9]

In the next week or two, letters will be written to all the believers asking for their suggestions and favourite hymns. A few may even compose their own hymns for the new book. I'm hoping you might consider doing that yourself. I suggested to Alistair that you might, with your ear for music, look over the hymns to be sure they can all be sung easily.

Alistair and Bill will compile the suggestions and take them to Nunan Bookbinding in Guelph for printing. When the order's completed, a copy of the hymn book will be mailed to each of the saints and workers. I'm sure they'll be delighted to have one hundred hymns or more that are familiar to everyone in the home churches.

Hugh Foster wrote two months ago and said that after Eddie Summers left the Elora church, he and Gertrude had many serious talks. Although their son went to school with Eddie, it seems, they, too, have heard God's urgent call to tell the story of Jesus. In his letter, Hugh said he couldn't find a single verse in the Bible that limits the call to younger people. Just that a person's love for Jesus be genuine. And I agree with him wholeheartedly. Besides, their children are grown and they're free to go. Gertrude still has her sense of humour. Says that now she has something so precious to share, she doesn't want to spend the rest of her days crocheting doilies and callousing her elbows on quilting frames.

Last week a second letter came from Hugh and Gertrude saying they've sold their home and store to their son and are preparing to strike out for

Bayfield. I feel choked up when I try to imagine the sacrifice and tremendous change for a couple who expected to live out their days in Elora. Nevertheless, they say that they felt a deep sense of peace as they dispersed their household possessions and packed their bags. Tomorrow they'll kiss their son and daughter-in-law and two grandchildren goodbye and leave the village behind. Please, Laura, join with me in praying that God will sustain them in the days ahead and give an opening for their message.

Susan Green sent me a note that she and Joe are planning to tie the knot sometime in August. It would be nice to be there to witness their new beginning and to celebrate with all our old friends in Puslinch, but we don't feel able to pull away from our mission.

Nevertheless, Timothy suffers from homesickness by times, and I hope it works out for him and me to visit Wood Creek Farm around threshing time for a few days. I expect we'll be ready to leave Owen Sound by late September. Is there a chance you and Katie'll be at the summer wedding?

I can't help but wonder when I'll see you again, Laura, my girl. If only it were granted me to have two lives, one would be spent in this daily journey of faith and the other, in hourly showing my love for you. Meanwhile, words alone must carry this precious message.

Much love,

George

From Victoria Day onward, the southern Ontario summer presented a benevolent face of sunshine and showers. As if an artist were painting the seasonal changes, the fields moved from their annual dance of daisies and pink clover to the richly tinted crops of high summer, when the clacking of hay loaders sounded from one concession to the next. Early apples in the orchards around Owen Sound took on golden cheeks, and baskets of Yellow Transparents began to make their appearance on the train cars bound for Guelph and Toronto. Just as the fields ripened to their harvest, an air of happiness and excitement gathered the friends from Guelph and Puslinch to celebrate the marriage of Joe Purves and Susan Green on the twenty-fifth day of August, 1905.

Joe's devotion to Bella over the decades had not gone unnoticed by the rural settlement. The consensus among older spinsters had been, "That Joe Purves, he's clean wasted as a widower." Married men, viewing Joe's enviable state, complained, "A widower can't set on his own woodpile without the women conniving and scheming. Most of 'em, sooner or later, gets hounded back into marriage." But Joe was not the only subject of wagging tongues. One of Susan's cronies had acknowledged to another, "Some that go through the woods for the second time pick up a crooked stick, but Susan's managed to find a man with a heart of oak."

Because they both were part of the church that met at Morgan's home in Guelph, Joe and Susan had grown to appreciate each other—first as believers and then as friends. Susan had a comfortable manner with Joe and often invited him for dinner. She liked to talk over the events of her day with him and she missed holding a masculine hand. Joe liked Susan's thick Yorkshire accent and her musical laughter that greeted his jokes. He wanted to garden again and share its rewards. As time passed and they each healed from the pain of losing their former mates, they had come to love one another. They looked forward to the warmth and security, tenderness and love, and laughter and joy of marriage again. In considering a partner for the sunset of their lives, they both were conscious of Paul's counsel to avoid being yoked together with an unbeliever. Can people who follow the Lord have anything in common with those who don't? Paul had asked.[10]

After a simple legal ceremony at the City Hall on Carden Street, they arrived at Susan's home to celebrate with their friends and family. Amid Susan's overgrown flowerbeds, the little company gathered in a semicircle on the lush back lawn. Bill shared a short message about God's marvellous plan for marriage that portrays the love and oneness between Christ and His church.[11] Afterward Priscilla, Alice, and the other sisters served a scrumptious wedding dinner in the shade of Susan's walnut trees.

Clusters of friends sat around the yard on press-back kitchen chairs. "Did you read in the *Herald* about the new flying machine in Ohio?" Alistair asked. "Seems a pair of brothers by the name of Wright can stay up in the air for half an hour or so."

Bill frowned. "I heard they were in Kitty Hawk in North Carolina."

"That was a couple years back. December of aught three. Now they're working out of a cow pasture near Dayton."

Alice's round face beamed. "Half an hour 's nothing. I can stay up in the air all morning if somebody gets my goat."

Susan laughed. "T' 'ole ting's foolishness, far's I can make out. If God wanted us to fly, 'e'd 'ave given us wings." She looked over at Joe. "But 'e gave us arms—for 'uggin', ain't that so, Joe?"

Joe nodded, eyes alight. "I been on the lean end of it for too long," he allowed as Susan's warm arms slipped beneath his jacket and wrapped themselves around his waist.

In the far corner of the yard, Phoebe nestled beside Andrew Gillespie on a garden swing. "I just love a wedding, Andrew. They're so much fun. I went to the last one with Laura. Three summers ago, she invited me along to her sister's marriage in Stratford. It was simply splendiferous—lots of flowers, guests, scrumptious food, pretty dresses. I even accompanied the organist on my violin. And Laura was the most gorgeous maid of honour."

As Phoebe chattered gaily along, Andrew sat with legs crossed as if listening to the most ravishing of birdsongs yet fearful of speaking or moving in case the songster might be startled. But this bird had no notion of flitting and as her effervescent prattle became more animated, he noticed that Phoebe's hand often brushed his own.

"What kind of weddings do *you* like, Andrew?" she was asking.

Andrew cleared his throat. "I don't know much about weddings. In fact, I don't even own a tie," he admitted. "Guess I'd have to leave those details up to my better half, if I ever have one."

"So what *do* you know about?" Phoebe persisted playfully.

Misreading her flippancy, Andrew's brow crinkled. "Well, something about running a mill, I s'pose. The owner leaves me in charge now when he's not there, says I'm his right-hand man. If any of the mill machinery breaks down, the teeth in the sprocket or such, he sets me to fixing it."

"Dad says you're good at a lot of things. He likes it when you come and work along with him. I think he misses Timothy—and you're a man."

An unaccustomed blush rose in Andrew's cheeks. "Your father's a good teacher, and I'm as happy as a pig under an apple tree when I'm at Wood Creek Farm," he admitted. "A lot's happened since we talked at the mill and he invited me to the meetings."

"Yes, it has," Phoebe agreed. "Speaking of being happy as a pig, when I was at S.S. #3, I usually cut across the fields on the way home. Well, one afternoon in October I ran across old Jordie's sow under an apple tree in the fence row. She was standing there in the warm sunshine with squarshed apples and juice dripping out of the corners of her mouth. Funny part was, when she saw me she staggered forward and nearly fell on her snout."

Andrew's eyebrows sprang into arches. "Was she sick or something?"

"Or something," Phoebe chortled. "Unless you call a feed of too many fermented apples sick. The ground was littered with them."

A twinkle flickered in the young miller's eyes.

Phoebe look sharply at him, her face suddenly stern. "Getting tipsy's not what you had in mind at Wood Creek Farm, is it?"

"Goodness, no," Andrew blurted out.

Phoebe burst out laughing, "Just fooling," she said as she nudged him in the ribs with her elbow. "Why don't you ask for a day or two off at threshing time?" Then with a nonchalant wink, she added, "I'm sure Dad would like to have you along…"

The banter stalled as Susan approached. "Andrew, wot's t' problem? Y' allus eat more than that. A lanky lad like you needs t' fill out. C'mon and 'ave another 'elpin' o' t' roast beast. We're tryin' to get it used up, so we are."

Torn between two joys, Andrew rose reluctantly, heading to the table. "How 'bout you, Phoebe? You're a growin' girl."

"I think I've grown enough," Phoebe chuckled, patting her hips.

"Then how 'bout givin' us another round of 'Danny Boy' or 'T' Irish Washerwoman'?" Susan suggested, motioning toward the violin case propped against the struts of the swing. "Edmund and ah could do all t' reels and t' jigs when we were lad and lass." She winked at Phoebe. "D' ye reckon Joe'd take a conniption if ah 'iked up me dress and did t' 'ighland fling?" Her head bobbed this way and that until she pinpointed Joe's bent form standing next to the spirea bushes. "Ah see me man's needin' me," she exclaimed as she bustled off.

A few minutes later Joe raised his voice as people emptied their tea cups. "Before you leave, Susan and I would like to have a picture that includes everyone. You're all part of our family," he insisted.

While the photographer was setting up his tripod, Joe crooked an arthritic finger toward Priscilla and Alice. After directing them to stand on either side of him and Susan, he cleared his throat. "Susan and I can never forget the part these two wonderful sisters played in helping to bring us into fellowship with Christ. Eventually that led to this love we share today."

Turning to Susan, the warm afternoon light shining in her silver-gray hair, he tenderly placed his palm on the back of her neck. They looked into each other's eyes as if catching a glimpse of what it was that connected them. Then, in front of all their special friends, he leaned forward and kissed his new bride with the flair of a man half his age.

A few weeks later, after Alistair and Bill had loaded the last chair and heaved the Berlin organ onto the wagon, Joe, for the last time, turned the key in the lock of the cottage where he and Bella had raised their children. Later that evening, Joe dug into his shirt pocket and fingered the wedding ring that had lain on the clock shelf since Bella's death. Tenderly, he wrapped it in a white hanky and tucked it away in a tiny velvet-lined box. Then, he settled back beside Susan into one of the Windsor rockers drawn up to the wood stove.

Autumn had come with cold dew at night, and George and Timothy were home for a few days after the Owen Sound mission. It was threshing time, and Alistair had waited eagerly to see them again after several months' absence. Although the extra hands were appreciated, he found it a thrill to work alongside his son—even if just for three or four days. As Timothy had grown through boyhood, Alistair had often looked forward to the day when he would work with him, man and man. In spite of the initial upheaval at the time Timothy had left the farm, Alistair was overjoyed that his son had chosen to spend his life reaping a more enduring harvest.

On the first morning, a dozen or so of the neighbouring farmers and their teams plodded through the mist of early dawn to the foot of Alistair's gangway. He, in turn, had taken his horses and helped with the threshing at their farms over the last few weeks. Power for threshing was generated by hitching the horses to a *horse power*, which was built rather like a large rotating buggy wheel. Alistair and the men set about hooking up a team to each of the six spokes. George and Timothy connected the spindle and shaft to the threshing machine inside the barn, making sure it turned freely. Horse powers came in different sizes, but the one at Wood Creek Farm could accommodate twelve horses walking around and around at a steady pace.

Bill Jones controlled the horses while the others fed sheaves into the machine, shoveled the grain into the granary, or forked the straw. Timothy wore a wet handkerchief over his nose and mouth as he tramped the straw in the thick swirling chaff. It was a hot, dusty job that no one liked, but in order to pack in the most bedding for the animals, it had to be done.

Alistair stretched out his hand, allowing the stream of grain from the separator pipe to splash off his splayed fingers as the expanding cone covered the floor. "The first bin's full to the top of the fifth board," he shouted above the roar of the threshing machine outside the granary door.

Morgan leaned forward, cupping his hands on each side of his mouth. "So what's the yield, do you figure?" he yelled back.

Alistair pulled a pencil stub from his overalls pocket and scribbled on the back of a granary board. "That's off the six-acre field to the north of the beaver meadow. So about sixty bushel to the acre, I reckon. Pretty fair for a dry year, but then that field's a bit wetter than the others."

After sliding another board into the front of the second bin, Alistair grabbed the scoop shovel and clambered inside to level the flowing grain. "Morgan, a rat's got a hole chewed in here. Would you fetch a hammer and some big-headed nails? And a little chunk of tin? You can ask Timothy where to find a scrap."

Stepping through the granary door, Morgan turned sideways, moving himself gingerly past the howling belts and spinning pulleys on the side of the threshing machine. A flailing arm connected several of the vibrating sieves that separated the kernels from the chaff. Above his head, George and Malachi forked sheaves off the top of a loaded wagon into the throat of the thresher. Particles of dust and straw floated up and down like soaring hawks in a shaft of dazzling sunshine that angled from a knothole in the outside wall. When Morgan crooked a finger in Timothy's direction, the young man scrambled down from the straw mow.

"It's hot up there, right under the barn roof," Timothy exclaimed, yanking the handkerchief off his face. "I need a pair of those newfangled waist overalls. For a sticky job like this, they'd be cooler by a long shot."

Morgan's eyebrows quirked in bewilderment. "What in tarnation are waist overalls?"

"Don't tell me the *Illustrated London News* didn't inform its erudite readership about waist overalls," Timothy baited Morgan.

"Come on, lad. Out with it."

"They're the absolute latest," Timothy teased. "Made of blue denim in the States by a fellow called Levi Strauss. They only come up to your middle and don't have a bib." He spit out a bit of chaff. "You can write to the editor of the *London News* and assure him that even though they look a bit flimsy, the Strauss outfit claims two horses can't pull them in two."

"Maybe a bathing costume would suit you better," Morgan chided wryly as he watched Timothy mopping his neck and forehead. "You're soaking wet." He paused. "Speaking of new things, you look like you've just leaped out of one of those fancy vapour bath cabinets that Eaton's is flogging. But you're not as dainty as the young things I fancy using them."

Timothy's lips twisted into a droll grin. "I thought only proper English gents used contraptions like that."

Morgan mimicked a sword thrust. "Touché!" he acknowledged.

Timothy glanced up at the growing pile of straw. "Now tell me why you came to bother me."

"Oh, I'm looking for another modern invention. A piece of tin to nail over a rat hole."

From daylight until dark, Priscilla, Phoebe, and Alice worked their fingers to the bone, cooking huge platters of food for the hungry men at dinner and supper times. The tired farmers would wipe away the trails of sweat from their foreheads, open a couple of buttons on their damp, dusty shirts, and splash cold water on their faces and hands at the pump. They would then beat the dust out of their pant legs before sitting down to a table laden with hot roast beef, mashed potatoes, gravy, carrots, kohlrabi, and Priscilla's fresh bread and butter. Three kinds of pies and cookies were waiting to be washed down with tea or a cold drink.

The animosity that had once been sparked by the ministers' reactions to the little church at Wood Creek Farm had long since dissipated. In fact, a few of the neighbouring farmers preferred to come to Alistair or Bill if they had any difficulty at home that they needed to discuss confidentially.[12]

The same, however, couldn't be said for the religious establishment in general. As Alistair waited in the granary after dinner for the grain to start coming through the separator, George drew him aside.

"Our little flock has been given a nickname," he offered enigmatically.

Alistair stared into George's face. "What is it?"

"The go-preachers. A sister in the church in Shelburne wrote and told me. Jack heard the same thing from Port Credit. It's inevitable. Clergymen meet at their ministerial conferences and must pass the name around."

Reacting with chagrin, Alistair's face fell. "Why would anyone want to reduce something so precious to a mere label?"

"I'm sure some folks are still trying to discredit us," George responded. "But really, when you think about it, the established churches are unwittingly describing what they've failed to do themselves. In choosing the label that best illustrates what's unfolding so vividly before their eyes, they're quoting Jesus' parting instructions to His disciples to *go* into all the world and *preach* the gospel to every creature."[13]

Alistair's blue eyes brightened. "Didn't the early disciples experience something similar? I think it was in Antioch that the Lord's followers were first called Christians."[14]

"Right," George replied with a quick nod. "And the name stuck. The apostle Peter later used it to refer to true believers." The rush of grain sliding through metal pipes grew and George grinned as he raised his voice above the din. "I'd better get out there and give Malachi a spoke or Priscilla might not set a place for me at the supper table."

Priscilla couldn't say why it happened, but on the second night of the threshing bee, she had a strange dream. Perhaps it took shape because she was exhausted, or maybe it was because her mind was busy, already planning the next day's meals as she fell asleep. Or maybe, as Malachi Jackson said later, "Reckon it was the Lord speakin' to her in a dream."

In her dream Priscilla imagined herself in Saskatchewan during the harvest excursion. Train car loads of men from Ontario had come to help. Instead of twelve men garnering in the wheat, there were seventy. During the long hot days they gathered sheaves and brought them to the barn. In her dream the harvesters stayed for several days, sleeping in sheds and eating breakfast, dinner, and supper at the Saskatchewan homestead.

But then the dream shifted abruptly and Priscilla was back at Wood Creek Farm. The farm labourers became itinerant preachers and saints working together in God's harvest field. They ate together at long tables. Everyone helped with the necessary work, and at night they all slept in the driving shed or in tents. The house and yard buzzed with happy conversation and activity. For four days, they sang hymns and shared in the joys of Christ. Priscilla was deep in a conversation with two friends when, suddenly, she felt a gentle hand on her shoulder and heard Alistair's voice.

"My dear, it's time to get up," he whispered. When she opened her eyes, the sun's rays were already playing on the bedroom wallpaper.

Each morning Priscilla was in the habit of taking a few moments to pray. She found it helpful to read a passage from the Scripture before rushing into the busyness of the day. Like a ruminating sheep, she would turn it over all day long, allowing the Holy Spirit to draw out its essence for her spiritual nutrition. Now her eyes widened and her jaw dropped when she opened her Bible to find Psalm 126 on the page before her:

> When the LORD turned again the captivity of Zion, we were like them that dream. Then was our mouth filled with laughter, and our tongue with singing: then said they among the heathen, The LORD hath done great things for them. The LORD hath done great things for us; whereof we are glad. Turn again our captivity, O LORD, as the streams in the south. They that sow in tears shall reap in joy. He that goeth forth and weepeth, bearing precious seed, shall doubtless come again with rejoicing, bringing his sheaves with him.[15]

Priscilla felt overwhelmed. Coincidences, she knew, did happen, but this was more than that. She felt certain God was trying to speak to her. But because she didn't understand the message, she decided to wait until it was clearer before she told anyone else about her dream.

During the day she sang part of a hymn over and over as she worked:

> Sowing in the sunshine, sowing in the shadows,
> Fearing neither clouds nor winter's chilling breeze;
> By and by the harvest, and the labour ended,
> We shall come, rejoicing, bringing in the sheaves.
>
> Go then, ever weeping, sowing for the Master,
> Tho' the loss sustained our spirit often grieves;
> When our weeping's over, He will bid us welcome,
> We shall come, rejoicing, bringing in the sheaves.[16]

Three weeks passed and the mows of sheaves remaining in the neighbours' barns had all been threshed before Priscilla shared her dream with Alistair. When she finally did mention it, his eyes crinkled with interest. "Do you really think we could manage it?" Priscilla asked as she ironed a pile of shirts, fresh from the clothesline, still stiff and smelling faintly of autumn leaves. "You know, feeding a crowd and finding a corner for them all to bed down."

Alistair folded the *Guelph Daily Herald* and laid it beside the rocker of his chair. Clasping his hands behind his head, he leaned back and closed his eyes. "I can just picture it," he said, smiling broadly. "Folks laughing, talking, having fellowship together. For four days. Think of the beauty of it—a time of inspiration to encourage the scattered friends in their love for Jesus." He straightened up, returning to the question. "I'm sure it could work if everybody helped out like you said."

Priscilla reached toward the trivets on the cookstove. Unhooking the wooden handle from one sad iron, she clipped it onto a hot one. "But there's a lot of details to work out. Like this ironing for example," she said. "How do you press dresses for fifty or sixty sisters?"

Alistair snorted. "Do you think a wrinkle or two would kill a woman? Folks'll just need to rest easy. Besides, things have a way of working out." He leaned forward, lacing up his boots. "The mouldboard on the plough's not going to get fixed with me sitting in this chair."

Priscilla looked up from the collar she was sprinkling. "Are you game to bring it up with Bill and Alice?" she said, drying her hands on her apron.

Pausing at the kitchen door, Alistair caught the intensity in her dark almond eyes. Impulsively, he turned back toward the ironing table. Catching Priscilla's elbows in his palms, he drew her towards him and kissed her soft cheek. "If you are, I reckon I am."

Over the winter the idea gathered momentum until, like an inspired vision, it engaged the whole church. As word of the gathering spread among the believers, anticipation grew and some began to refer to it as a *convention*. When George and Jack came to discuss the plans, the little group decided the best time would be in July or early August when it was warm enough to sleep in unheated buildings. Since many of the friends were farmers, the gathering was scheduled for a time after the haying was done and before the harvesting of the oats and barley began. Meanwhile, the rolling fields and pastures of Puslinch Township bided their time.

Twenty-Six

SETTING GOD'S TABLE
Late Spring 1906

As Percy Ellington cycled up the maple-lined lane of Wood Creek Farm with Timothy, his eyes roved over the setting for the forthcoming convention. The former stonemason paused to admire the fieldstone house which sat on the left, its long veranda facing the laneway. The builder had adorned the steep-pitched roof and gables with scrolls of white gingerbread and carved bargeboards. A flagstone walk to the front door led across a neat yard surrounded by a fence. He noticed a board-and-batten wing on the back housing the summer kitchen and woodshed.

In the orchard beyond the home itself, cherry and pear trees flourished among the Northern Spy and MacIntosh apple trees. A few beehives sat on the grassy floor to pollinate the spring blossoms. Past the house the lane curved to the right before crossing a creek and ending at the barn. Farther along the stream, Percy noticed a pond just beyond the driving shed.

"We built the dam to water livestock and wash sheep," Timothy offered as he followed Percy's gaze. "The trout lie in the cooler water at the bottom. But they're cagey, and you need to be mighty clever to catch them."

Percy grinned. "How many have you been able to catch?"

"Thousands," said Timothy with a straight face.

Teddy trotted over to greet the men, his tail wagging as he licked Timothy's hand. "Teddy goes to the pasture by himself and fetches the cattle for milking," he explained as he leaned over to pat the Scotch collie. "We've also got a Great Pyrenees, Natasha. She lives with the sheep."

After leaning their bicycles against the driving shed, the pair walked along the worn path to the house. Percy noted the efficient tidiness of the place. On one side of the path was the ice house, on the other, a tall wind-mill which straddled the well on its four steel legs. Timothy stepped onto the rough plank lid that covered the well and unhooked a white enamel cup from a bent wire. Grasping the pump handle, he filled the cup with cold water and handed it to Percy.

Timothy's face beamed. He loved the work he had been chosen to do—telling others about the wonderful gospel story. But there was no doubt about it, he loved coming home to his father's farm. Trying to be objec-tive, he studied Percy's face as his fellow worker absorbed the natural tran-quility of Wood Creek Farm. What could he be thinking as he saw it for the first time? After casting a hasty glance around the familiar yard, Timothy closed his eyes, imagining people, lots of people. How would it look to have them meandering along this path between the barn and the house?

As the two men approached, they could see that several others had already arrived to help with the preparations for the convention. Alistair greeted the pair at the door and pulled his son into a rib-crushing bear hug. "You're filling out, my boy," he laughed as he released him. Then he turned and extended a warm welcome to Percy. "While you're here, Percy, con-sider Wood Creek Farm as your own home. If there's anything you need, just let me know." Alistair turned to Timothy again. "I was wondering if Percy could bunk in your room."

Timothy glanced around at the number of people mingling in the kitchen and parlour. "Looks like Percy and I may have other roommates too." From across the room, he acknowledged a wave from George.

Alistair's blue eyes crinkled with mirth. "You could be right. Dave Hindley and Herman Brunstedder are coming from Mildmay next week."

Percy excused himself and hurried over to greet Jack and Eddie, whom he hadn't seen for several months.

As the three friends chatted, Percy saw out of the corner of his eye a pretty cream-complected woman with dark hair reaching out to embrace Timothy.

"Well, look who's here after all these months!" Priscilla exclaimed, kissing her son on the cheek and enfolding him in a warm hug.

The other women were bustling about the kitchen, and before long nearly thirty hungry people were sitting down to a bountiful supper. A bubble of excitement rose as old friends laughed over a good story. The conversations were happy as they shared news of other friends, the churches, and the missions. Priscilla's hand lingered on Timothy's shoulder as she urged her boy and Percy to "eat up and do the cooks justice."

When supper was over and the dishes washed, everybody squeezed into a circle in the big kitchen to discuss the convention project. They tried to estimate the number of people who might come. Emily kept a tally as each of the twenty-one churches was counted and put onto the list. Then she added the two sisters, five brothers, and two couples in the ministry.

"We should allow for about one hundred and eighty-six," Emily announced after adding it twice. "Plus a few visitors."

For weeks Alistair had been wondering how they could get everyone bedded down comfortably. As he had worked in his various farm buildings, he had often interrupted a task to pace off the dimensions of the floor trying to figure out how many people might sleep here or there. Now he leaned forward, hands on knees, in the usual posture of a hardworking man.

"Let's sweep out the upper floor of the barn for the men and boys," he suggested. "And the women and girls could sleep in the driving shed."

Alistair glanced around at the sisters. "Do you think you ladies could organize a bee and sew up some covers for straw ticks?"

"We surely could," Alice offered enthusiastically.

"We could stuff them with fresh straw or swale grass and lay them side by side in rows," Alistair went on. "Maybe everybody can bring their own bedding and a pillow to lay on the ticks." The solution was beautifully simple and practical. With that hurdle out of the way, they moved on.

For meetings, they decided to put up a large canvas tent at the side of the orchard. The area was fenced, and each May Alistair pastured three ewes and their lambs there to keep the grass short and neat. He found it easier to work around the fruit trees if the turf was trimmed. Two tall elm trees against the orchard fence would provide a cool shady spot for the tent.

Finally, they discussed how to feed all these people. "The food should be easy to prepare and serve up," Priscilla asserted. "Alice and I have seen two huge cast-iron kettles at the foundry in town. We could hang them over a wood fire for cooking two hot dishes. We could also serve bread, fresh vegetables, and fruit preserves."

Alice smiled. "Nothing fancy, but it should be filling and tasty."

Before they retired at midnight, each person had volunteered to be part of a specific team—one for sleeping quarters, another to prepare food, a third to set up the meeting tent, and a final team to do construction tasks.

During the month of preparations, the various helpers slept in every nook and cranny and lived together in a marvelous spirit of adventure and cooperation. Although taking time off work was a sacrifice, two or three able-bodied helpers came for a few days from almost every church. Some stayed with Bill and Alice while others bunked with nearby friends.

George, however, returned to the green room in the attic where he had spent his first night in the ministry and which bore such a palpable presence of someone especially dear to him. Amid the excitement and energy devoted to setting God's table, his heart stirred in anticipation of joining her at that table.

Everybody started work at seven o'clock, including the cooks, who soon had a big breakfast on the table. Ten minutes before each meal, someone rang a large brass dinner bell. After washing up in granite basins in the woodshed, everyone sat down at a long table in the main kitchen. The hot oatmeal, bacon and eggs, and lots of toast, jam, and tea satisfied even the hungriest person. Afterward, the kitchen helpers cleared the dishes, washed them in a metal tub, and reset the table for the next meal.

Before the preparations began, Alistair had filled the upper part of the barn with sweet-smelling hay, keeping the centre of the barn floor and the straw mow area clear. He had also turned most of the livestock from the lower stable out to pasture.

After the sleeping area crew moved the implements out of the driving shed and the upper floor of the barn, they attacked the dusty cobwebs with brooms and whitewash brushes. They erected rough lumber benches to support washbasins and set a pail for clean water and a dipper at one end. Small looking glasses were hung on spikes driven into one of the side timbers, making it convenient for the men to shave and the women to fuss with their longer hair.

Finally in mid-June, Laura and Katie stepped lightly out of the mailman's cart at the lane of Wood Creek Farm. After a rapturous reunion with the various personalities in the Stanhope kitchen, Laura hurried to the window. Her blue eyes, searching and wistful, discreetly swept the yard and paddock. *Where,* she wondered, *is George?* Hadn't he written that he'd be the first to greet her?

Late afternoon sunshine flickered over the supper table as Priscilla carried a dish from the stove. "First of the peas," she smiled. "Emily added mint to them. Oh, and by the way, George left word, if you should arrive, to tell you..." Priscilla's voice trailed off, her attention caught momentarily by some good-natured shouts in the woodshed. "George said," she resumed, "…oh, take the hot pad, Phoebe, that fat's dripping…George said he knew you'd like to sleep in the little room for old time's sake, so he took his clothes and Bible out of it yesterday…and is settled into an empty corner of the granary for now."

Laura's eyes glistened. She rose from the table early, ostensibly to wash her face and remove the stains and dust of travel. The evening wore on and a high, overarching sunset still hadn't witnessed George's return. Nothing was mentioned. Outside on the lawn she saw Percy and Katie deepening their acquaintance while the soft sounds of evening mingled on the summer air.

When Katie called goodnight, Laura found herself tarrying under the maples of the lane as the fireflies darted in and out of the ferny under-growth and the stars blossomed overhead. At length she heard the distant clatter of a horse's hooves on the plank bridge in the hollow and after a few moments the rider pulled up alongside her. "Laura, my girl!" The familiar voice reached out through the shadowy darkness as George swung down. "You've taken me by surprise. I figured you'd be along tomorrow at the ear-liest." His words fell silent as he dropped the reins and swept her into his arms, savouring the delicate fragrance that enveloped him. Extending his arm across her shoulders, George sauntered up the lane with Laura to the moonlit yard. After tethering the horse at the narrow gate, they stood under the windmill for a long time, talking and catching up.

"Thank you for giving up the attic room," Laura said softly when at last she turned toward the house. "You're a dear, George. As considerate as always."

～◯

When Oliver Summers from Elora heard of the convention plans, he wondered what he could do to help. Being a wholesaler of dry goods, he thought about the straw tick covers and promptly ordered several large bolts of cotton. Without mentioning his intentions to anyone, he had them shipped to Wood Creek Farm. Although mystified at the source, every-body was delighted at the unexpected arrival of the fabric, and immedi-ately several of the women set up a long table in the front parlour to cut and stitch the striped covers.

Many of the supplies seemed to arrive from nowhere, and the saints were thrilled with God's bounty and people's generosity. This way of anonymous giving took the pressure off those who could not help out financially, and each saint was equally welcome. Nobody wanted another to give if it would create a hardship in any way.

As the meeting team considered various tents in the area, Bill could see that some money was going to be needed. Nobody had mentioned the subject, but that evening he prayed about it. In the morning it was still on his mind as he spoke to Alice. "A fair sum is going to have to change hands for George to get the use of a big tent like the one Jake O'Grady pitches for auctions."

"Yes, I can understand that," she acknowledged. "But why are you in a lather about it?"

"Well, I just don't know if George has enough money."

Alice frowned. "George has got a tongue in his head," she retorted. "He'll speak up if he needs help."

"I doubt it," Bill said, pulling on his boots. "See you at dinnertime."

As Alice swept the kitchen that morning, she continued to stew. "Why does Bill take on someone else's concerns," she fretted aloud, "and worry himself sick about details? He's so conscientious it'll be on his mind all day."

After she blacked the stove, Alice lugged a bucket of ashes out to the garden. Could it be that George really did need money for the tent? Her mind flitted to the egg money she had been putting aside for years. She could picture herself buying one of the new Bell pianos, and now she nearly had the forty-eight dollars she would need. Tightening one hand over her furrowed forehead, she shook her head, remembering how long it had taken her to save that money. But still thoughts of the tent kept coming back each time she went into the pantry. She glanced up at her bank, an old cookie jar on the top shelf.

The day shimmered with humidity as Eddie dug a pit for an extra outhouse. As the spade bit repetitively into the cool damp clay, he had plenty of time to muse about the anonymous way in which provisions were arriving. It appalled him to think that he had often posted the list of offerings from specific families on a display board in his former church. At the time this practice had never bothered him, even though it embarrassed poorer folks. Most churches, he knew, had the habit of listing the donations in a ledger for the *inside people* to see. Jesus' teaching suddenly rang clear to Eddie: When you do a charitable deed, don't let your left hand know what your right hand is doing. Then your gift will be given in secret. And your Father who sees in secret will reward you openly.[1] Eddie wiped the perspiration from his forehead with his shirt sleeve and heaved another shovelful of earth up onto the pile. *Many churches would collapse,* he speculated, *if this simple principle were adopted.*

On Monday evening Alice gathered a basket of fresh eggs for the next morning's breakfast at Wood Creek Farm. Placing them into the buggy, she climbed onto the seat, flicked the lines, and started down the laneway. Halfway down the lane she pulled the horse to one side and sat thoughtfully. No, she just couldn't do it. Even as a girl she had dreamed of taking piano lessons. Long-familiar tunes played in her imagination. It was too much to ask.

Alice sat still for a few minutes, tears running down her cheeks. Then she stirred herself with alarm. What if Bill saw her? Wheeling the horse around, she drove back to the house. As she tethered the horse to the fence post, she spied Bill coming up from the driving shed. She raced into the house and washed her face[2] before grabbing an empty bottle. Quickly she poured the coins from the cookie jar into it and tightened on the zinc sealer ring. Wrapping her treasure carefully in a towel, she placed it in the six-quart basket with the eggs.

"Forget something?" Bill asked as he walked in.

"Yes, I did." Alice hurried past him. "See you in a bit, Bill. Please tuck the children in early tonight."

After she dropped off the eggs in the summer kitchen, Alice went to find George. Hurrying past the ice house, she spotted him in the orchard pacing out the dimensions of the tent and driving pegs into the soft earth.

"A right likely spot for the meetings," she observed as he reached for the blocky wooden mallet.

George nodded. "Yes, I think it will be," he concurred. Suddenly, catching Alice's solemn expression, he paused. "What's ailing you, Alice? You look distressed…"

"I thought you might be able to use this tomorrow." She took the glass bottle out of the towel and handed it to him as if uncovering hidden treasure. A few crumpled shinplasters lay buried among the mixture of silver and copper faces that glimmered in the evening light.

As George surveyed the variety of coins, his eyes registered a deep sensitivity at the sacrifice. "Thank you, Alice, thank you. We certainly can. You know, I was beginning to wonder just how it was going to work out." He paused, letting out a deep breath while his eyes searched her face again. "I couldn't have gone in the morning without it." Involuntarily, George took her wrists in his hands. "I can see you've been collecting these coins for a long, long time." Alice's already florid cheeks showed an even deeper flush as she shrugged and turned to walk back to her waiting horse and buggy.

"Didn't scramble the eggs on the way over, did you?" Bill teased when Alice got home. She shook her head and felt a secret happiness, like a warm egg in her palm. Perhaps Bill would never need to know.

George left early on Tuesday to find a tent large enough for all the friends to assemble. He spent the day searching but finally decided that it would be wiser to make their own. It would cost twice as much as a rented one, but this way they could use it whenever they wanted. At the library, he ferreted out a book with instructions and diagrams. Tucking it under his arm, he set off for Bond Hardware to order the canvas, grommets, ropes, and other items. When the material came in stock, he and Malachi picked it up in Guelph with a team and wagon and hauled it to Bill's driving shed.

Now they could start work in earnest. A few men went to the woods and picked out two straight pines for the main tent poles and a number of slender maples from which to saw the sidewall posts. After trimming and debarking the poles, the men painted them green to match the canvas. The other half of the team worked in Bill's driving shed, sewing and stitching. Joe Purves used his former harness-making skills as he helped the younger men sew heavy straps to the coarse canvas. It seemed a massive undertaking, and at times George wondered if he had made a poor decision.

The men were dripping in the stifling heat of the driving shed as Joe unclamped the last seam. Viewing the completely sewn canvas, Malachi swatted a persistent horsefly that had crawled under his sweaty collar. "Now we're tent makers too," he exulted. "Took more'n a penny or two to pay for the supplies. Somebody help you, George?" His gaze seemed to penetrate George's mind as they loaded the tent onto the wagon.

"A generous woman in our midst," George replied, perusing the older man's face. "She squirreled the money away through many a season, for all she could have spent it on herself."

Suddenly Malachi comprehended and slapped his knee. "That's Priscilla, I don't doubt. She's so durned enterprising she'd slit open a chicken and haul out the corn in its crop. I'll be hornswoggled."

George's eyes twinkled in the penetrating afternoon sun that drove through the open door. "Wrong woman," he allowed. "But the sister did give it to me on the Q.T., so…"

Next, the meeting tent team turned their attention to constructing wooden benches. They would be used in addition to chairs that could be garnered from the friends who lived nearby. The benches were made from a wagon load of maple logs which had been hauled to the sawmill in Hespeler and cut into three-quarter inch thick boards. In addition, Stephen bought a number of rickety old chairs at an estate auction in Guelph for a pittance. After the tent team had repaired and painted the chairs, they began to build a portable speakers' platform about a foot high.

Priscilla and Alice described the two old cast-iron kettles, and Percy Ellington went to purchase them. After the rusty spots had been wire-brushed off, they were to be hung over an open fire. Last fall Alistair had stored extra firewood in the woodshed so they were all set except for the construction of the cooking pit. Percy hooked the horse to the stone boat, and he and Andrew lugged granite stones in from the back fields. With a practiced eye, Percy picked out the ones with a grain suitable for splitting.

"I don't believe you've left a single stone unturned," Timothy quipped as he hurried past Percy with a plank on his shoulder.

Percy grinned wryly. "Don't be rocking the boat of hardworking folks, young man," he shot back.

After piling the rocks nearby, Percy dug and prepared a shallow foundation and low wall just outside the summer kitchen. The stonework would contain the fire and provide maximum heat to the kettles. Percy then fashioned a column at each end of the fire pit, into which he embedded a horizontal bar to support the heavy kettles. He also made a large flat area with an old stove top that he found dumped behind Bill's barn. This would be ideal for heating tea in a copper boiler.

Dave Hindley, the carpenter and school trustee from Mildmay, had also come for a week to lend a hand. Using some leftover maple planks, he built three long workbenches in the summer kitchen. The hardwood gave an ideal surface for cutting meat, chopping vegetables, and slicing bread. He also put up shelves for storing nonperishables—salt, pepper, raisins, and the like. And just in time too. Donations from the friends were arriving in a constant stream. No sooner would Dave finish a shelf than Alistair or Timothy would fill it up with crates of preserves or jams. A hundredweight of white sugar leaned against the back wall beside a barrel of blackstrap molasses and a smaller one of cider vinegar. Golden and amber bottles of honey also appeared, like the very essence of summer in a jar. Each one bore the invisible yet unmistakable imprint of Morgan's generosity and his eager wish to take part in nourishing his adopted family.

A trap door and steep stairs led to the root cellar under the kitchen. For Timothy, the cool darkness of the earthen pit evoked old pictures of the Roman catacombs. Two barrels of apples stood guard near the foot of the steps while sacks of potatoes, bushels of squash, and carrots in boxes of sand lay sleeping on the floor beneath the hanging sides of smoked pork.

Putting their heads together, Alistair and Dave devised a plan to serve the friends. They installed two windows in the side of the summer kitchen so food could be passed to a serving table. This would reduce congestion at the doorway. On the day that Dugan came to help, he and Dave framed a porch roof over the serving area to provide shelter in case of rain.

Dave also built a large wooden chest in the ice house to keep the butter, cheese, eggs, and milk cool. When the chest was finished, Alistair packed ice around the outside of it and set up the butter churn on the side porch. Each day, one of the men milked the cows and brought the pails to the house, where Priscilla and Emily poured them into large flat pans in the cool basement. The following morning the cream was skimmed off and the milk used on the table or fed to the calves that had been penned up. The sisters stirred some of the cream into their baking, and when enough surplus had been collected, Alistair set up the churn on the side porch. Every morning Teddy, their toffee-coloured collie, ran in a treadmill to provide momentum for the churn. Afterward Phoebe rustled up a plate of table scraps for his efforts while Priscilla and Emily worked the lump of butter with a wooden ladle until the buttermilk was completely separated. They then salted the yellow butter and cut it into one-pound pats.

Bill had been raising a pen of six hogs specifically for the convention, and several of the men went over to help with the hog-butchering bee. After killing the pigs, they hung the carcases up by the hind legs to drain the blood. Tubs of water were boiled over an open fire and poured into a wooden barrel. The men dipped each hog in the scalding water to loosen the bristles before scraping the hide and cutting up the meat. Bill and Malachi hung some of the pork to cure in the smokehouse while the other men submerged the remaining slabs in clay crocks of salty brine to preserve them against the heat.

The morning after the hog-butchering bee, Laura was serving tea at breakfast when a gust of wind flung the door open with a bang. Startled, she jumped, spilling tea over the edge of Morgan's cup and onto the table. Morgan thrust his chair backward to avoid the hot liquid.

"I guess that's poetic justice," he laughed as Laura grabbed a cloth.

"Just what's that supposed to mean, Mr. Butterwick?" Timothy hooted.

Morgan leaned back in his chair. "A few weeks ago I met a philosophy student when I was out selling honey. He was a friendly, outgoing young fellow with a long beard. He liked to talk and said he wanted to be more spiritual. One day when I was at home, he stopped by for a chinwag."

Morgan continued the story, recalling the way it had unfolded. For over an hour the student had spoken in eloquent rhetoric about his aspirations. As Morgan listened patiently, he wondered what he could do to truly communicate with this intelligent young man. Then a dramatic idea flashed into his mind. "Would you like a spot of tea?" Morgan had interrupted.

"That would be grand," the scholar had replied, barely missing a beat in his steady monologue.

Morgan went into the kitchen and pumped a cup of water before placing it in front of his visitor. In a minute he returned with the teapot and began to pour tea into the already full cup. It overflowed, soaking the tablecloth and dripping over the edge.

"Hold your horses!" the student exclaimed, aghast at the tea spilling onto the floor. "The cup's already full. It can't take anymore."

"You're absolutely right," Morgan had replied quietly. "Neither can any of us if we're already brimming with our own wisdom. If we truly want to be filled, we must be emptied first. If we want to be reborn to a new way of being, we must die to the old way first."

The budding philosopher look befuddled. Then, stroking his beard, he nodded slowly. "I think I see what you mean," he said. "Death is a metaphor for the letting go of the tangible world and its wisdom, and rebirth, the passage into a spiritual one. I've never considered it like that."

"It surprises some people what they can learn outside of the ivory tower," Morgan had teased him, but with challenge in his voice.

After breakfast, the mishap was still vivid in Laura's mind as she sifted spelt flour in the kitchen. Outside, the wind tore at the cedar shingles with the vigour of a young ram. Across the yard the flag on the pole flapped violently, displaying the Union Jack's brilliant red, white, and blue.

Glancing toward Laura, Katie rolled her eyes upwards as she stirred sugar and baking soda into the dry ingredients. "Do you reckon the roof's ready to take leave of us?"

"It's a powerful force," Laura acknowledged. "The Bible says the Spirit's like the wind. It blows wherever it wants to. Even though you hear the sound, you don't know where it comes from or where it's going."[3]

As Katie looked out the window, she saw that the tail on the windmill had turned the head, causing the steel blades to catch the gale. The connecting rod between the overhead gears and the pump below was oscillating wildly as cold water gushed through a pipe to the watering trough in the barnyard.

"Listen to the chatter of that windmill, Laura," she instructed. "Yesterday it stood idle. Today it's pumping water as if we're on the verge of a seven-year drought."

Consulting the worn recipe, Laura measured out three cups of buttermilk. "What a brilliant illustration," she exclaimed. "Can you see it? The windmill's like us, Katie. Without the invisible power of the wind, it's useless. Although it's perfectly designed, it can't function on its own. The wind is the source of its life."

The analogy struck Katie with force. "I've got it," she responded. "Once the wind touches the windmill, it begins to pump water from the deepest level. It's certainly needful for plants and animals alike."

"And people too," Laura concurred. "We need the power of the Holy Spirit to function according to God's design, to quench the thirst of our souls. Even Jesus said He could do nothing by Himself."[4]

Katie's eyes twinkled with a theological challenge. "But wouldn't you agree that waiting patiently for the Spirit is also fulfilling God's will? Like before you went into the work. You were eager for God to arrange things."

Thoughtfulness crept across Laura's pretty features. "You're right," she conceded. "But when the Spirit stirs us, we'd better make certain the windmill brake isn't locked on." She paused. "When you and I set out again after convention, we need to sense where it is the Spirit wishes to lead us."

"So we don't end up in another Hepton Bridge?" Katie chuckled.

Untying their aprons, the young women took a break from the sweltering kitchen and strolled out to the rail fence around the barnyard. There sat a mossy old watering trough, weathered from years of constant use by a thousand thirsty visitors. Fresh, cold water spilled over its edge and splashed into an expanding pool at the base. From there it trickled into the crevices of the dry cracked ground, providing life for the parched plants and tiny creatures who were neighbours of the old trough.

As Laura regarded the trough, Morgan's story of the empty cup came back. *Only when I'm continually filled by the Holy Spirit,* she discerned, *can my cup truly run over and refresh those around me.*[5] *Whether I was filled yesterday or last Sunday makes no difference if I'm dry now.* When Laura ran her fingers lightly over the surface of the old trough, worn smooth by time and circumstances, she was reminded of a familiar tune:

> God has here on earth a treasure—
> None but He its price may know—
> Deep, unfathomable pleasure:
> Christ revealed in saints below.
>
> Thus, though worn and tried and tempted,
> Glorious calling, saint, is thine;
> Let the Lord but find thee emptied,
> To be filled with love divine.
>
> Oh, to be but emptier, lowlier,
> Meek, unnoticed and unknown,
> And to God a vessel holier,
> Filled with Christ and Christ alone;

> Naught of earth to cloud the glory,
> Naught of self the light to dim,
> Telling forth His wondrous story;
> Emptied—to be filled with Him.[6]

Leaning against the faithful old trough, Katie listened as the wind caught Laura's melodious voice. "Both the words and music were simply sublime," she said when her friend had finished.

"Thanks," Laura acknowledged with a smile. "God's work of emptying me will be a lifelong process. But it isn't by knowing more that we please Him. It's by being emptier, lowlier, meek, unnoticed, and unknown that we become a vessel holier, filled with Christ and Christ alone." Suddenly, she turned toward the summer kitchen. "The loaves'll have burnt crowns if we don't get them out of the oven pretty quick."

As the two sisters hurried back to the kitchen, they noticed Hugh Foster limping slowly across the yard towards the driving shed.

Clamping his cap on his head, Hugh grinned in Laura and Katie's direction. "It's so windy that the birds are walking," he called out. As part of the team doing construction tasks, Hugh did a lot of walking himself as he fetched tools and supplies. Still overweight from years behind the store counter in Elora, he suffered from pain in his feet and ankles. During these days leading up to the convention, George often encouraged him to take a break and soak them in a tub of warm water. One afternoon Hugh decided to ride along and see the doctor while George was in town picking up a few coils of rope to anchor the tent.

The summer darkness was dissolving as George rose from his knees and made his way to the rough window in the granary. Burning a fuzzy hole through the mist that lingered over the beaver meadow, the red ball of fire balanced on the line fence. George pulled on his shirt and trousers and made his way down the darkened barn stairs and across the misty yard. After pocketing the kitchen scissors from the nail where Priscilla hung them, he dipped a basin of water from the reservoir, grabbed an old mug, and tiptoed back outside.

Standing in his undershirt, George leaned forward, scrutinizing his sandy beard in the mirror suspended by a string from a loose knot in the granary boards. It had been a part of him for a long time. Withdrawing the scissors from his pocket, he began to snip methodically, uncovering a swath of pale skin as the sandy clumps floated onto a towel. When he had removed the bulk of his beard, he grinned at the tattered face confronting him. *Ragged as a dog fox in the spring of the year,* he mused.

George rummaged in a brown paper bag and took out the supplies he had bought in Guelph yesterday. He dropped the block of shaving soap into the mug and added a few drops of water before working up a lather with the bristles of his shaving brush. Then after daubing the white foam onto the remnants of his beard, George dowsed the brush in the basin and reached for the straight razor. The cool steel gleamed in the morning light streaming through the little four-pane window. After each pass, George whished the blade in the basin of water until his cheeks glistened. Then splashing off his face, he beamed with triumph into the looking glass. As he entered into the woodshed for the second time, he overheard morning greetings and the scraping of kitchen chairs.

Shock plastered every one of the twenty-two faces as George sauntered up to the table and pulled back his chair. "Morning, everybody," he offered airily.

Recovering after a split second of paralysis, Timothy blurted out, "Excuse me, sir, but have we made your acquaintance before?"

"Reckon so," George laughed. "Perhaps at the supper table last night."

"So what's provoked this about face?" It was Jack's voice laced with irony. "Is this your notion of putting off the old man?"[7]

From the head of the table, Alistair chuckled at Jack's wit.

"I guess I'm not up to snuff," George admitted. "I find it pretty warm working in the heat. Besides, I figured it was time for a change. I don't want to get too stodgy, you know."

From across the table, Laura smiled shyly at George. "I didn't know you had your mother's dimples and a cleft chin like your father."

Phoebe pressed a palm to her lips to suppress a burst of laughter. "But your skin's as white as a fresh-plucked turkey," she giggled.

"Don't worry, George'll brown up before you can say Jack Robinson," Priscilla admonished her daughter. Then she turned to look along the table. "The clean-shaven look suits you, George."

Susan gave a broad wink from her place at Joe's side. "Yer a right 'andsome gent without your beard, George, so you are," she observed. "Lucky for you Joe's got 'old o' me or I'd be flirtin' wi' you meself."

George reddened with all the attention. "I think Alistair's ready to sing the blessing," he said modestly. All eyes turned to Alistair as he led the group in breakfast grace:

> We thank Thee for each token of Thy love
> This table spread and manna from above.
> Thy bounteous hand feeds every living thing
> In gratitude to Thee our hearts we bring.

As they took seats for their meal, the clatter of dishes and discussion of the day's projects supplanted the talk about George's new physiognomy.

When Timothy ladled maple syrup onto a second helping of rhubarb pancakes, he noticed that Hugh's plate was still clean. "Hugh, you're missing the best part of the meal," he teased. "Oatmeal just isn't enough."

Hugh sighed. "When the doctor looked at my feet the other day, he said, 'Mr. Foster, there's just too much of you. That's your problem.'" Hugh roared with laughter. "So eat up, Timothy, you're skin and bones. I'm a downright fleshpot."

Afterward Alister contemplated Hugh's story as he sat on a block in the woodshed lacing up his boots. *When there's too much of us, it affects our spiritual walk too,* he reasoned. Getting up, he followed George out to the orchard. *Why's it so hard to keep small and humble, laying aside our puffed-up minds so Jesus can truly live through us?*

Picking up his pruning saw, Alistair started to cut off a lower branch that would interfere with the tent. Suddenly the weight of the lopsided limb shifted, binding the saw blade. "You rotten thing," he expostulated.

George straightened up from cutting off a sucker. "I beg your pardon."

"Oh, I was just griping to myself," Alistair replied sheepishly. "Would you mind jamming a prop up under this branch to free up the blade?"

When the errant limb was finally sawn off, Alistair turned to George. "Did you ever notice how puffed up the old man gets when things go his way?" he asked.[8] "I soak up anything that makes me sound clever or look confident and prosperous. But if things turn sour, I'm quick to blame the other fellow. Or bellyache about the tool or whatever. It's never me."

George grimaced. "I've fallen into that ditch myself," he admitted. "How different we are from the humble Man of Galilee."[9]

As the date for the convention neared, the preparations sprang forward with vibrant energy. At first Alistair had presumed that some things might have to be left unfinished. But as the days passed, he was surprised at the tremendous changes that hard work had accomplished. He appreciated the spirit of cooperation and harmony among the friends. A remarkable patience and kindness seemed to pervade the place, and the anxious striving or self-preoccupation he sometimes sensed at a threshing or a sheep shearing was absent. Even the fellowship so far had made the undertaking a remarkable success for Alistair. Just as nature was returning the first harvests of early summer—red rhubarb and bright strawberries—so this shared life had already offered up the first fruits of love, joy, and peace.

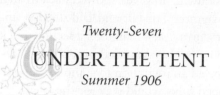

Twenty-Seven

UNDER THE TENT

Summer 1906

Word spread across the country concessions that a large tent had sprouted like a giant mushroom, overnight it seemed, at Wood Creek Farm. Naturally, country folks with their keen sense of rumour surmised one thing or another, whether in the privacy of their pantries or the more open forum of their barnyards.

"'Tain't like Alistair to break out like this," pronounced one farmer. "They say he's going to bring in some ripsnortin' preacher from Philedelphy for this here revival. Him that's always done things the way his pa done 'em. Foolish, I call it."

"Yaas," another drawled, "what with him harbouring old Malarkey Jackson around, the old sot, there's no telling what freak thing he'll break out into next. Though they do say him and Bill Jones between 'em got old Mal dried out some…"

"Pigs may whistle, but they've poor mouths for it," rejoined the first.

"There's people crawling around Alistair's place like ants on a rotten apple core." The man leaned forward, lowering his voice. "There's no telling what goin's on might happen behind his back when y' get a bunch of strangers all hunkerin' together like that. A right bad lot, maybe."

"But did you hear what they say Priscilla's aimin' to do?" The third voice came from behind the smokehouse. "Why, I hadn't hardly hoisted a leg into bed las' night afore my old woman come puffin' up the stairs. She said *she* was told Priscilla sent that hefty Foster fella and Percy what's his name to get two iron cauldrons outta Guelph—from the foundry was it? They dragged them home on the wagon, so they did. They say she's fixin' to invite all that riffraff livin' near the railway tracks out t' stay here fer good. Now that'll be a fine how-do-you-do. Nobody's chicken coop within two miles will be safe. Them types got sticky fingers, y' know."

The Stanhope goodwill, however, showed itself in an ironic twist. Two days before the convention, Alistair and Bill divided up the countryside surrounding Alistair's farm. Each man took a section and kept their drivers and saddle horses busy as they knocked on doors. It was the neighbours themselves who received an invitation to come for supper during the convention. Alistair hoped folks would stay for the evening meeting and for tea and a snack afterwards, enabling them not only to meet the friends and to see what was going on firsthand but also to hear the gospel invitation.

Over the months, weeks, and, finally, days, the convention had become the focus of attention for the saints in all of the scattered churches. Those who needed to had arranged to be off work from Wednesday to Monday. The convention would start Thursday morning, July 12, after everyone had recovered from the excitement of their trip and arrival at the farm.

Early Wednesday, Clarence, the Elora stationmaster, sat in his usual chair not far from the spittoon. He chewed meditatively on the wad of tobacco in his cheek, looking forward to a quiet morning. Although the 7:30 train was due in from Fergus and Belwood in a few minutes, the platform was usually deserted at that hour. So when the Elora saints began to arrive in twos and threes, it took the stationmaster a while to absorb the fact that an unusual number of travelers were purchasing tickets to Guelph. After selling tickets steadily for twenty minutes, he began to cogitate. These were all working folks. Where on earth could they be going at this hour and in the middle of the week?

Finally he could stand it no longer and was just about to ask that young Lyman Liddle what the commotion was all about when the engine on the old Wellington, Grey & Bruce Railway line could be heard whistling at the distant road crossings as it approached the Elora station. Clarence nearly lost his tobacco when the train pulled in with folks reaching out the windows, waving and laughing. "What under the sun…" he gasped. Was this a holiday he hadn't taken note of?

As people scrambled down from the coach, they began hugging and shaking hands everywhere. Introductions and greetings flew back and forth while the Elora and Belwood churches waited for the southbound train to leave for Guelph at 8:05. The Elora passengers shifted their luggage to the edge of the platform and took their children by the hand as they listened for the boarding call. This would be the first train ride for most of the children, and they could hardly stand still.

When the huge engine hissed, releasing a blast of steam from its cylinders, three-year-old Virginia Liddle grasped her mother's long skirt. The conductor descended from the passenger car as the Elora people lined up with their tickets and luggage. Many had brought provisions. A few cases of homemade preserves, two large cans of English tea, three boxes of fresh fruit and bread, small bales of bedding tied with twine, and a hundred-pound sack of potatoes rolled past on a high steel-wheeled wagon to the baggage car.

"All aboard," the conductor called out as he swung up onto the steps of the coach. From the open door, he waved at the stationmaster as the train started to grind forward, belching black coal smoke.

Clarence took off his cap, scratched his head, and squinted at the train rolling into the distance. "Wherever that gang's heading, they sure are cranked up," he muttered as he turned back toward his chair. "So be it."

~⌒~

Every train arriving in Guelph that day was met by a team of horses and a farm wagon with front racks to pile the luggage against. Excitement ran high as people met each other for the first time, having only heard names and pictured faces since they had begun to walk with Jesus. Happy tears were shed when some of the workers greeted old friends they hadn't seen since leaving their community. They had exchanged letters over the months, but these could not hold a candle to a heartfelt embrace.

With all the luggage heaped on the front and centre of the wagon, the ladies and children sat along the sides and back, their dresses and feet hanging over the edge. If there was still room, the boys and men rode also. Otherwise, they walked behind. As they made their way through unfamiliar country, many wondered what Wood Creek Farm would look like.

~⌒~

As a former minister, Walter Merrick had been to many gatherings of church people, but nothing that he had ever witnessed before prepared him for what he saw at Wood Creek Farm. As he walked up the laneway with the men, he met Ida Rose who had jumped off the loaded wagon as it paused at the small gate to the house. The first wagon was greeted with hugs and handshakes by about twenty-five friends who stood eagerly awaiting their arrival. As the day passed, an increasing number of happy saints welcomed each successive wagonload. Old friends and newcomers alike were received with equal enthusiasm by folks they had never laid eyes on before. Then Walter saw George making his way through the crowd.

"Good to see you," George exclaimed as he embraced first Ida Rose and then Walter. Walter ran a handkerchief quickly over his moist eyes, not wanting to betray emotion right now.

Eager helpers swarmed around the yard offering cold drinks to the new arrivals. When the team stopped in front of the driving shed, several pairs of strong arms carried each woman's luggage and bedding to a straw tick of her choosing. Somebody was on hand to help each one make up her bed and punch down the tick to a comfortable shape. The women and girls were left to hang up their clothing on spikes and ropes while the men and boys went on to the upper barn floor.

After spreading his covers on a tick, Walter returned to Ida Rose, and they began to explore the grounds together. Wherever they looked, people laughed and talked and no one could walk more than a few steps without being greeted by some kind soul. Children ran from place to place with their new friends, peering in doors, throwing stones in the pond, feeding a handful of grass to the cows, or trying to catch frogs in the stream. Most of the parents were too distracted to notice the grubby knees and elbows.

Walter and Ida Rose strolled over to the meeting tent and pulled back a flap. In the diffused sunlight pouring through the green canvas, they saw neat rows of chairs and benches arranged in a semi-circle around a small, low platform. The floor was neatly clipped grass, but the wooly four-legged "lawn mowers" had been returned to the main pasture a few days earlier.

When the bell rang, people began making their way toward the porch of the summer kitchen where supper was ready to be served. The brothers and sisters all stood silently in a circle, waiting until the last person had arrived. Then, they bowed their heads and sang a song of thanksgiving.

Bless Thou dear Lord this food
In love so freely given,
May thanks from all our hearts ascend
As incense sweet to heaven.

Under the porch overhang, a long table was laden with stacks of plates and forks, a huge boiler of potatoes and a large pot of savoury stew. Bill

Jones had made the stew by braising pieces of beef with salt and pepper and various spices in the cast-iron kettle. Then he had added chunks of carrots, diced onions, and peas along with water and flour. Just as Priscilla and Alice had suggested, the meal was plentiful, tasty, and easy to serve.

A line formed on each side of the table, and everybody picked up a plate and helped themselves to as much as they could eat. Mothers with smaller children were served supper inside at the kitchen table. The others carried their plates to chairs and benches around the yard. The younger ones sat cross-legged on blankets, picnic style, eating and laughing together. Over a hearty meal, old friends reminisced while new friends exchanged stories, telling how they had first met the friends and workers.

After finishing the first course, each person took his plate to the wash-up area before going back to the serving table for a round of homemade preserves, fresh baked bread, fruit, and pastries. Someone dipped cups of tea from the big copper tub at the end of the table.

Timothy and Percy sat like two Cheshire cats on a bench beside the windmill as the sun began to set, grinning at each other. Nonchalantly, Timothy clutched a brown paper bag in his left hand.

"Phoebe's up for a little job in the women's quarters," he confided.

"She's going to slip it between Katie's bed sheets?"

"Right, down near the bottom where Katie's bare feet'll touch it as she snuggles in," Timothy explained, opening the bag for Percy to take a peek.

"She'll need help down from the rafters," Percy laughed.

Dusk was falling as people began to amble in the direction of their sleeping quarters. Walter and Ida Rose stood in the gathering darkness outside the driving shed where she was to sleep that night.

"Feels like we're courting again," he said, smiling.

Ida Rose laughed. "Well, Mr. Merrick, it's been a wonderful day."

"I hope I shall see you again tomorrow, Miss Thompson."

"I should think so, Mr. Merrick." Ida Rose made as if to shake her husband's hand, but he grabbed her and kissed her gently. Ida Rose giggled and said goodnight. Walter strolled over to the men's quarters, feeling younger and more carefree than he could remember for a long time.

Walking between the rows of ticks, he saw brothers here and there quietly reading their Bibles. Some stretched out face down on their beds in a few moments of silent prayer before they went to sleep. A few exchanged whispered comments, careful not to disturb others. Walter tiptoed to his sleeping place, contented as he realized that never before had he been among such a godly group of brothers.

Lying in the dark barn, he could see the outlines of the heavy timbers overhead. Outside, the moon began to rise, and as it did, silver streams of light crept through the cracks between the barn boards. Here and there a few men snored in the darkness, and high above on a beam a pigeon cooed as its mate changed position. Walter felt welcome here. He felt released and at peace with God. And he might as well admit it, since he had become part of this new church, his understanding with Ida Rose had steadily improved. Now he was more contented and happy in his marriage than he had been for years. With that astonishing realization he drifted off to sleep.

Walter awoke in the early morning to rustling and the sound of whispered voices as men dressed. Although he was warm under the covers, the morning air felt cool on his nose. A low-lying mist hung over the pond just beyond the driving shed. Finding his washcloth and towel, he went to shave at one of the granite basins and was delighted to find that someone had already fetched a bucket of warm water from the kitchen boiler. When he had finished, he glanced out the door at the rising sun, smiled, and stretched. Towel draped around his neck, he whistled a jaunty tune as he sauntered back toward his tick to put on a fresh shirt.

He arrived at the driving shed just as Ida Rose was coming out. "Good morning, my love," he said, presenting her with a single dandelion.

"Walter, it's beautiful!" She cupped the back of his head in her palm and drew his cheek to her lips.

Walter watched as Ida Rose closed her eyes and brushed the yellow velvet flower against her upper lip. "How did you sleep, my dear?" he asked, taking her slender hand as they headed to breakfast.

"Splendid after all the excitement," she laughed. "I'd just fallen asleep when I heard a bloodcurdling scream in the dark. Katie thought she felt a snake in the foot of her covers. Anyway, she and Laura scrambled out of their beds and Laura got a candle lit. After they hustled the tick outside, they found a long thin curl of cucumber skin sticking to the bottom sheet."

Walter's eyes sprang open like clam shells. "Who on earth would pull a prank like that on Katie?"

Ida Rose frowned. "I haven't the foggiest, but Katie's says she going to nail the culprit's hide to the wall when she finds out. Anyway, after a good laugh things settled down, and I slept like a slug in a cabbage leaf."

Walter squeezed her hand. "Cutest little slug I ever met," he chuckled.

Many were helping and others stood visiting as Stephen ladled steaming oatmeal porridge speckled with flax seed out of the cast-iron kettle. Beside him Emily offered a cheerful morning smile as she flooded each bowl with cream. The second course consisted of scrambled eggs, bread, and jam with lots of hot tea.

After breakfast a number of men gathered in the stable. All the animals except a sow and her litter had been turned out to pasture for the summer, and an area had been swept and whitewashed. When Walter stepped through the stable door, he saw two rows of men sitting across from each other on planks supported by blocks of wood.

"Morning, Walter," Jack greeted him. "Come on in and have a seat."

After Walter sat down, someone passed him a sharp knife. Sacks of potatoes lay piled on a layer of fresh straw ready for peeling. Eight men were busy already, and although Walter had never peeled a potato in his life, he took the knife in his hands gingerly and settled in to butcher a few. The men chatted as the mounds of peelings grew on the floor between their feet. The potatoes were rinsed and tossed into a clean tub and then carried to the summer kitchen ready to boil for dinner. In the meantime, another gang of men was occupied cutting beef into chunks for stew.

After the peelings were shoveled into the sow's pen, Walter wandered across the yard. He passed Timothy pumping himself a cold drink at the windmill. "Have you seen Ida Rose?" he asked.

The young man pointed toward the house. "She's in the summer kitchen." Then he grinned. "Watch out you don't get recruited. Those ladies are buzzing around like a bunch of bees in a molasses barrel."

When Walter poked his head through the door, he could see Ida Rose chatting in one corner with Laura as they brushed warm butter onto loaves of freshly baked bread. The rounded crusts glistened in the morning sunlight that sparkled through the vine-hung window. There had to be at least thirty, Walter figured as he savoured a deep breath of the yeasty aroma. The food preparation was being done smoothly and cheerfully, and after only an hour and a half, everything lay in readiness for the next meal.

About half-past nine folks began to file quietly into the tent. Two chairs had been set up on the platform for those who were to guide that particular meeting. This morning George and Alistair took these seats in the silence that pervaded the tent.

Without fanfare George stood up at ten o'clock. Around him the fresh morning wind tugged at the tent, but instead of resisting its soft influence, the canvas billowed outward and inward as though responding to the breath of God. "It's so wonderful to be together in one place," George began. "We've been looking forward to this for some months. I know it wasn't easy for many of you to get time off work and to arrange for someone to care for your farms and businesses while you're away. Several of you are far from home, and I understand the difficulty of traveling with a family. I also want to thank you for sacrificing your time and resources to make this convention possible. And just as importantly, I want to thank each of you for labouring on your knees at home, earnestly praying that God's will would be done. I hope each of us will feel His presence especially close over the next four days. Perhaps we can begin now with a hymn."

As we gather now together,
Show us Thou art here;
Breathe on us Thy Holy Spirit,
Scatter every fear.

As we pray, Lord, pray Thou through us
By the Holy Ghost;
Perfect Thou Thy strength in weakness,
Vanquish Satan's host.[1]

After the hymn had finished, a few of the friends stood up one by one and offered an audible prayer. When fifteen minutes or so of prayer had passed, they sang another hymn and then George gave people an opportunity to share a spiritual thought that had strengthened their own faith. Most testimonies were brief, capsulized in a few sentences.

"The first Scripture I ever learned was the Lord's Prayer," Hugh Foster disclosed as he got to his feet. "I repeated it every morning for the four years I went to school. And since I've come to know our Lord, the first two words of that prayer mean more to me than ever. Our Father.[2] When I meet a neighbour, a stranger, or whoever it might be, the Spirit reminds me of the little word, 'our'. Not just my Father, but *our* Father. Even the most wayward man has been entrusted with a soul by our Father. I'm convinced that a saint becomes a saint not so much by having people see the good in him as by recognizing that potential, by the grace of God, in other folks."

Hugh paused for breath, his thick hands gripping the back of the bench in front of him. "But even more important than the word 'our' is the word 'Father.' I never knew my own pa. Smallpox took him off in '49 before I learned to walk. And I remained fatherless until the day George and Jack brought the gospel to Elora. Then, for the first time, I knew what it felt like to have a father who watched my faltering steps. Even now, when I wander off course, I feel comforted to know that He's still my Father, that He sees and understands. Like the father of the prodigal, watching for his son from afar off, God's boundless love seeks us in every situation. Let me say before I sit down that if I had to summarize my faith in two words, they would be: Our Father." A murmur of assent ran through the tent as Hugh settled down into his seat beside Gertrude.

"I've had the best five years of my life since I became part of this little gathering of saints," Mrs. Applebee declared, her round cheeks flushing with ardour as she gazed into the faces of her adopted family. "And I'm glad that Christ has grown in my heart. I've been reading about our sister Hannah, the mother of Samuel. Each year she and her husband, Elkanah, went to worship and sacrifice at Shiloh. And each year she stitched a new coat for her little boy who lived there with Eli.[3] I'm sure she made it a tad bigger because she would anticipate him growing into it over the coming year. True worship and sacrifice make room for Christ to grow in our hearts during the next year, during the rest of our lives. I hope that each of us go away from this convention with bigger hearts for our Lord."

Hilda MacGladry's face softened as she listened to the emotion in Mrs. Applebee's voice. Instinctively she tightened her arm around her own little Samuel, who sat on the bench between her and Dugan studiously sketching the meeting tent surrounded by sheep grazing and resting in its shade.

Emily's tall willowy figure could be seen outlined against the soft green canvas. "When I was a girl we had a team of Clydesdales. As children we were often in the barn when my mother went out to help with the milking. And we'd be playing around the horses. One horse was as gentle as a lamb, and she'd lift her feet to avoid stepping on us. The gelding was different. He'd kick or bite us if he got a chance. In fact, I've still got this limp to show for his nastiness. The point is this: At the end of the day, and in spite of her lovely temperament, the mare was still a horse."

Raising her hand, Emily swept back a tress of wavy hair caught by a mischievous breeze. "That's true with people too," she continued. "Some have a sweet, generous nature. Others are, let's just say, not so agreeable. But the fact remains that until Jesus comes to live within us, at the end of life's day, we're still just human. Jesus capsulized it best when He said that flesh gives birth to flesh, but the Spirit gives birth to spirit.[4] Men can reproduce human life and to a measure, human goodness, but only the Holy Spirit can give birth to a truly spiritual life. It's my prayer to be more sensitive than ever before to God."

A rich German accent turned the heads of the friends toward the opposite side of the tent. "I vant to say how much I enshoy zis convention." It was Katrina, her motherly face beaming. "Ven Laura came to live vis us, I knew she vas different. Ven she vant to move back to her friends at Vood Creek Farm, I zought zis is very strange. To like your friends so much zat you leave a perfectly good shob. But now I know vy. And I'm so happy to be here vis her and vis all of you." Beside her, Laura smiled, mindful again of the measure of love Mrs. Brunstedder had stirred into the creamy batter of each shensel cake.

Unfolding his arms, Malachi sucked through his missing front tooth and looked around to see if anyone else was getting up. Seeing no one, he stood up, brushed aside a fly trying to land on one of his leathery ears and began. "When I was a lad in Haldimand, there was a tea peddler often stopped at the general store. He'd trained his dog to play dead. The collie was so good at it that you could tug on his tail or his ears or roll him over, and he'd stay perfectly limp. The tea man would make small wagers that you couldn't wake the dog up—without hurtin' him of course. And mostly the peddler won his bet. So one day a few young fellows were gathered around and one them says, 'I'll take up your bet.' Then he went inside the store and came out with a chunk of fresh meat. He took the liver out of the paper and held it near the dog's nose. For a moment or two nothing happened, and then the dog's nose began to twitch and his pink tongue came out. Finally, he opened his brown eyes and rolled onto his stomach.

"I pretend to be dead to my old feelings and instincts. But sure as shootin', when I'm tempted enough, my nose begins to wiggle and my human nature springs to life. I just can't count on it to stay out of trouble. From now on I intend to depend on Jesus, to give His Spirit more control. But when I fall down, I'm thankful that His precious blood puts me right."

From his place beside Alice and the children, Bill scratched his neck thoughtfully. He knew some of the struggles Malachi had faced and the significant victory he had exercised over the bottle in the last few years. He was also mindful of his own struggles and failures as he uttered a quiet "amen" to Malachi's testimony.

Clad in a long-sleeved shirt rolled up to his elbows, Timothy was the last one to rise before George called for the next hymn. His youthful voice, keen and resonant, could be heard easily throughout the tent. "Jesus said it's easier for a camel to go through the eye of a needle than for a rich man to enter the kingdom of God.[5] Ancient cities were often walled with a large gate that was bolted at night to prevent attack. However, next to the main gate was a small low door that a man, if he arrived late, could stoop and enter through. And even his camel, if its load was taken off and it knelt down, could wiggle through on its knees. Apparently that little opening was sometimes referred to as 'the eye of the needle'. Why is it so difficult for a rich man? Likely because he refuses to take off the bulk of his load.

"But I've been thinking of it another way. Imagine the enviroment outside of the city to be like a life focused on self and on the things around us—what the Scripture calls 'the world'. These are wise pursuits in the view of common wisdom. But picture the alternative, life inside the walls, the city of God, the kingdom of heaven to be like a life consecrated and centred in God. The passage between the two worlds is constrictive, not only for the man rich in material goods but for any of us rich in our own opinions and objectives. Self, even in pursuing what it considers to be God's will, is still taken up with itself—not with God. I realize this journey through the needle's eye is impossible—humanly speaking. But Jesus said, 'With God everything is possible.' I'd like to lay down my burdens and get on my knees so that, by God's mercy, He might enable me to pass through the eye of the needle." Several in the tent nodded reflectively at Timothy's discernment as he took his seat beside Morgan again.

During the preparations at Wood Creek Farm, the friends had talked about who would share the longer messages from the platform. Everyone had agreed that there should be an open platform to allow anyone with the gift of teaching to come forward and speak as they felt inspired by the Holy Spirit. The brother guiding the meeting would preach the closing message.

Amelia Hunter from Belwood was quietly enjoying the spirit of thankfulness that ran as a common thread through the prayers and testimonies when she heard George's voice. "After this hymn, anyone who has been given a message by the Holy Spirit can come forward to share it."

During the singing Amelia wondered if she should speak about the things in her heart. Then an unexpected thought jolted her: *What if it's me the Holy Spirit is calling? But surely someone else will have something better to bring for the Lord's people.* She began to fidget, suddenly aware that God was indeed touching her heart. Her pulse raced and her breath quickened. Feeling inadequate and unprepared, she closed her eyes. *Why me, Lord? There are others here who are much more capable than I am.*

Immediately the words of the apostle Paul echoed in her mind: I was with you in weakness, in fear and in much trembling.[6] Amelia knew Paul had said that his weakness enabled the Spirit to demonstrate the power of God through him—far better than any wise and persuasive words of his own. As the melody died away, Amelia raised her head expectantly and looked around to see if anyone was standing to go forward. But no one was. To Amelia, the silence in the tent seemed to go on forever, and yet she sat rooted to her seat. She could almost feel the Holy Spirit nudging her to step forward. Taking a deep breath, Amelia stood up.

The sound of a chair being pushed aside made people turn and look. And what they saw pleased them: a slim, middle-aged lady in a long summer dress quickly making her way toward the front. Amelia brushed her ash-gray hair back over her ears as she stepped onto the low platform.

"Sitting here this morning, I've enjoyed hearing how thankful each one of you is for Jesus. I was thinking about my own life before I met Him." She searched the crowd and met Robert's eyes. "I had a bedridden husband, more farm work than I could do, and plaguing headaches that I woke up with every morning. I prayed without hope back then, without so much as a mustard seed of faith. Never mind moving mountains; some days I could barely move myself. But God heard my cry and answered me. It still takes my breath away when I think about it. And about the way I can laugh and talk now. The way I can pray, and above all, trust Him with my life." Amelia paused for breath and swallowed. Her throat felt dry. "Please excuse me," she said shakily. "I'm quite nervous up here."

Then she heard George's reassuring voice behind her. "You're doing just fine, Amelia, and we're all enjoying what you have to say." Amelia turned slightly and nodded. She could always count on George.

"Jesus performed His first miracle at a wedding in Cana when He learned that the bridegroom was out of wine," she continued. "When He told the servants to fill the water pots with water, they filled them up to the brim. Then He said to them, 'Draw some out now and take it to the master of the feast.'[7] When the man tasted the water that had been turned into wine, he didn't know where it had come from. But the servants did. The master of ceremonies called the bridegroom over and said, 'The best wine is always served first. Then, after the guests have had plenty, the other wine is served. But you have kept the best wine until last.' This first miracle showed Jesus' glory and caused His disciples to put their faith in Him.

"I can imagine how that young bridegroom felt," Amelia said, her eyes glowing with warmth. "He had planned and worked to prepare for the wedding, but then the unexpected happened. More people showed up than he could provide for. He was at his wits' end for lack of wine. Just like him, I had worked hard at being a Christian, but when Robert got hurt and times got tough, I found how empty and unprepared I really was. My struggles and disappointments seemed insurmountable. When George and Jack came into our lives, I had reached the bottom of the barrel in every way." As Amelia looked into the audience, she caught a glint in Jack's eyes before he lowered his head.

"Over the years I had pretty well assumed that the mix of day-to-day emptiness with occasional religious high points was the normal Christian life. I had given up any active search for Christ. Like the wedding host who ran out of wine, I now know that it was necessary for me to come to the end of my own spiritual resources before Jesus could really help me. Life was a burden and I was desperate. Then He sent two strangers into my life, and as I started to listen to Jesus, He transformed my life from water into wine. Before I met Jesus, my life was dull and flat. But now, like a good wine, it has taken on vibrancy, sweetness, and substance. I possess a joy that I once thought was impossible. This was the first real miracle in *my* life.

"Even today men put forth the best they have in the beginning," Amelia asserted. "I've been to revival meetings where people became excited about God. There was lots of emotion and enthusiasm, and the sunny inspirational messages made me feel good for a week or two. I even professed to accept Christ as my Saviour at one of those places. But when the music died away, I was the same old Amelia—no inner change, no transformation. That only comes when we hear and obey Jesus' voice—not the voice of men. But this way of the Spirit keeps getting better and better.

"The kingdom of heaven is like wine; it seems sweeter to me as time passes. And it's limited only by the measure to which I am willing to draw it out and receive it. I hope the transformation in all of our lives will attest to the glory of Christ and encourage others to put their trust in Him. Before I sit down, I want to thank God before you all for this opportunity of sharing Jesus." Amelia closed her Bible and stepped down from the platform. She felt a wave of relief as she made her way back to her chair beside Robert.

As she settled back to listen, he cradled his arm around her narrow shoulders. "Amelia," he whispered, "what you said was laid on your heart by God."

After about an hour of sharing, George asked for someone to select another hymn. He invited the crowd to stand and stretch their legs while they sang. When the music was finished, he remained on his feet. Clearing his throat, George began: "I want to try to speak a little about Christian living. When you read the Sermon on the Mount,[8] you may wonder, 'Can anybody live the Christian life?' Is there anyone in the tent who knows the answer?" A hush swept over the crowd as they waited for George to carry on. Some thought that George, for one, was living such a life.

"The answer is 'No'," he asserted. "No one can live the Christian life except the Son of God. The apostle Paul confirmed this when he said, 'I have been crucified with Christ; it is no longer I who live, *but Christ lives in me.'*"[9] Many leaned forward intrigued by George's line of thought.

"In all of God's dealings with us, He works by taking us out of the way and substituting Christ in our place. Jesus took our place on Calvary's cross and died for our forgiveness, and He takes our place in everyday life and lives to obtain our victory. Paul went on to say that if he could become acceptable to God by his own efforts, then Christ died for nothing.

"In my early life, I thought I could become like Jesus with God's help," George admitted. "I wanted Christ to enhance my own activities. Now I know that's not God's way. Instead, *I must die* so Christ can live. Paul does not say, 'Live *like* Christ', or '*imitate* Christ', or 'take Christ *as your model'*. Paul said, 'For me, to live *is* Christ.'[10] If we are wholly given to our Lord, His Spirit will live again the life which Jesus Himself once lived." As the sun rose, the tent began to heat up. George unbuttoned his shirt collar and rolled up his sleeves.

"In those early years I struggled diligently, trying to produce the Christian life. If only I could remedy certain things in my life, I'd be a good Christian, I thought. And when things were going my way, I did pretty well. But if someone crossed me, my loving exterior broke down and I felt most unloving. I tried to be humble, but often the humble words were spawned by a proud self-righteous attitude. In some situations I smiled and appeared patient, but inside I felt decidedly intolerant. To my dismay, I found that no matter how hard I tried, the Christian life never came spontaneously. Finally God showed me that the virtues He requires of me—love, patience, meekness, kindness, and humility—are beyond my ability to produce. It's not what I do or what I am; rather it's what Christ's Spirit does in me. Trying to act Christlike was nothing more than a pretense. Jesus spoke of *hypocrites,*[11] which in the original Greek language meant *stage actors*. We may appear to have the walk, the talk, the attitude of a child of God, but if *we* are the source of power behind the appearance, it's meaningless. We may abstain from eating this, wearing that, going there, or doing the other and think we're pleasing God. But if intense human effort is needed, then we know that it is not Christ living, it's us.

"One cold day in November about eight years ago, I was walking up and down the field behind the plough when a question came to me." George tucked his Bible under his arm and extended his two hands in front of him as if he were gripping the wooden handles of a single furrow plough. "Some of you know what it's like following the horses back and forth, back and forth. It gives you plenty of time to think." George could see several of the farmers smiling and nodding. "Anyway, the question I asked myself was this: 'Who was it that redeemed my soul from sin? Was it Jesus, or George, or Jesus and George together?' The line of a hymn gave the answer: 'Jesus alone can save me.'"[12] An hour or more went by as I turned over several long furrows of sod. I still remember stopping to give the team a breather. I was weary myself and sat resting on a particularly large rock in the field when another question struck me: 'Who can live the Christian life? Is it Jesus, or George, or Jesus and George together?' The answer—Jesus alone—was like a personal revelation.

"For the first time, I realized that I needed to utterly surrender my will to the Spirit of Christ, take my hands off my life, and let Him control. Surrender is not me promising to do God's will: It is me unconditionally submitting to His dominion and influence.[13] It's only when we're fully surrendered that we can walk *according to the Spirit*.[14] We must believe in His power and trust Him fully with our past *and* our future, our good *and* our bad, our strength *and* our weakness." George was so intent on his message that a wasp landed on his cheek without him noticing. Some in the audience were distracted. Would the wasp sting him if he raised his hand?

"The *old George* wants to live *for Jesus* by making a display of George's goodness," he continued. "But only when I acknowledge that I'm the problem, not the solution, can Jesus truly live *for me*. Just as all of us have been set free from our sins, we need to be set free from ourselves. Perhaps we accepted the atoning blood of Christ for our sinful past, but afterward attempted to live and perfect our own lives. By doing so we have only half a salvation, which is not salvation at all. We'll be miserable knowing what a Christian life should be and yet repeatedly falling short." When the wasp attempted to walk down the side of George's face, he shooed it away with a sweep of his hand.

"So then, how is it possible to have Christ living for us?" George paused to give a moment of reflection. "The answer is contained in Jesus' invitation: 'If anyone wants to be My follower, let him *deny himself,* take up his *cross,* and follow Me.'¹⁵ What is this cross that Jesus spoke about? Certainly not a piece of wood. Rather, it's the burden of my human nature that runs contrary to, or across, the divine nature of Christ. Two natures in one body. Whichever one we feed will increase and become the stronger." George noticed several bewildered faces and decided to share a story.

"When Jack and I were in Elora, a man who had just moved from the city came to our gospel meetings. It didn't take him long to discover that we had been farmers." George saw a grin flicker across Jack's round face.

"One day the man rushed over to see us at Mrs. Applebee's. Out of breath, he told us, 'I bought my first sheep two weeks ago and now it's sick. Could you come over right away?'

"We threw on our coats and hurried over to his shed at the edge of the village. The lamb was lying in the corner of a pen. But it wasn't alone; it shared the pen with a small pig. Jack and I scrambled over the side to check the lamb. We felt for fever, lumps, swelling. We peered into her eyes and opened her mouth, but nothing showed up. Still, she was so weak that she couldn't get to her feet. As I ran my hands over her trembling body, I could feel her ribs.

"'She's pretty thin,' I said to the man. 'How much do you feed her?'

"He motioned toward the pig. 'A gallon of rolled oats between the two,' he said.

"'And do you watch them eat?' I asked.

"The poor fellow looked perplexed at this strange question. 'No,' he said. 'I feed them in the morning before I leave for the factory.'

"We soon discovered the problem: The pig was eating all the feed and the sheep was starving.

"'You'd better separate the two animals,' Jack told the man.

"The poor fellow glanced around the shed. 'But I've only got this one pen,' he answered forlornly."

George leaned forward and looked into the gathering. "That, my friends, is the story of the daily Christian life—one pen, two natures. Our city friend realized he needed to *spend enough time with the lamb* to ensure it got properly nourished.

"The point is simply this: Unless we make time in our hearts and minds for the Lamb of God, His Spirit in us will weaken. We only grow to the extent we die to a life centred on self[16] and nurture one that allows God to *will* and to *do* through us according to His purpose.[17]

"A whole hour is too long to go without breathing. The length of time we spend in formal prayer or in Bible study is not as important as breathing in an awareness of God in every aspect of our daily life. Nevertheless, the self-nature will complain and try to distract us from the Jesus life by crying out, 'Away with Him',[18] as it attempts to dominate every waking hour.

"Unpleasant experiences often expose our self-nature for what it really is. How do we react when a loved one takes our words and twists them? Can we hold our peace when a brother or sister in the church lifts a heel against us?[19] Or when we face rejection in the settlement for our faith? Do we turn the other cheek when someone weighs our grain and measures short? Sometimes God demands a difficult thing: to ask forgiveness of someone we don't care for, to undertake a task most inconvenient, to provide substance to the stranger. At times we may be stripped of much that makes life beautiful or face inner struggles that wean us from self-chosen plans, a critical attitude, a love of praise.

"Most of us resist this cross of Christ, this death to our human nature. Humanly speaking the cross is the end of everything, but spiritually it's the beginning of fruitfulness. Remember, Jesus *consciously* chose the way of the cross; it didn't just happen. It's something that we, too, must *choose*— daily, even hourly. But we must guard against any tendency to fashion a cross of *our* choosing. We need the spirit of the cross of Christ, not just its message, to be truly reconciled to God."[20]

When Priscilla saw George pause to swallow a couple of times, she stood up and slipped through a flap in the sidewall of the tent.

"The book of Romans tells us that our old self-nature *was* crucified on the cross with Jesus, so that sin might lose its power in our lives.[21] For a long time I wondered if *putting off the old man*[22] is a single act or a gradual process. In fact, it's both. The apostle Paul uses a Greek word that's often been translated as 'die' or 'dead'. However, I've been told that in some verses the original text really means *dying off*—a gradual process. In one place the apostle said that he was *dying off* day by day."[23]

George gestured over his shoulder in the direction of the barn. "Think of the wheat in Alistair's granary," he said. "It can remain in storage for years and still retain its identity as a seed. But let's give one of those seeds a personality and presume that it chooses to be planted. At some precise point in time, it must accept death if it's going to germinate and grow.

Nothing physical changes in that split second; yet the seed *suddenly* considers itself dead.[24] There is a resolution—from that moment on—to live as a vivacious growing plant. Day by day, its old life as a seed *gradually* dies away and it emerges in its new form. Before long you would never identify the tender green sprout as the seed from Alistair's granary."

George turned to see Priscilla reaching out to hand him a cup of cold water. Thanking her, he took a long swallow before smiling into the faces of his friends again. He held up his hands as if they were a set of imaginary balance scales. "Christ must increase, but we must decrease,"[25] he said as he raised one hand, lowering the other one at the same time. "But how can we tip the scales in the right direction? Some of us have tried very hard to get rid of this sinful life, but we found it most tenacious. And none of us have had the power to crucify ourselves. So then, how is it accomplished?

"Once again, Jesus is the only answer," George continued. "Hearing His voice produces death in our Adam nature, and at the same time, fills our being with divine life.[26] But because the Lord never forces Himself on anyone, we must hasten to open the door of our heart when He knocks.[27] When we say yes to Him, and no to self, our Beloved enters and begins to share His character with us."

Turning briefly, George laid his Bible on his chair and picked up his hymn book. "Remember when we were children? How hard did we have to try to grow? Not hard at all. It just happened because we were alive. But we had to breathe, to eat, to rest. And that's the key. Moment by moment we must be alive to Christ—drawing in His Spirit, hungering for Him, resting in His work rather than our own."[28]

George thumbed through his hymn book for a minute. "Let us close this meeting by singing an audible prayer together. It's one that conveys many of these thoughts we've been speaking about."

I am now a child of God:
Christ redeemed me by His blood;
For my sins He did atone,
Called me, sealed me as His own;
Henceforth all my life shall be
Consecrated, Lord, to Thee.

Help me, Lord, to daily die,
Self in all its forms deny;
Bid my carnal mind depart;

Reign supreme within my heart;
God of love and purity,
Fix Thy dwelling place in me.

Clothed in true humility,
Let me find my all in Thee;
May Thy life in me increase,
Love of self forever cease;
Finish, Lord, Thy work begun—
Mould and make me like Thy Son.[29]

As people filed slowly out of the tent at noon, they were greeted by the tantalizing aroma of beef stew—evidence of Bill's industry during the morning. The afternoon meeting wouldn't start until half past two, and many took advantage of the break. The tranquil atmosphere of Wood Creek Farm gave respite from the rigour of everyday life. Some took a nap after the noon meal while others relaxed under a shady tree.

During the two-hour interlude between the meetings, Walter meandered along the back lane until he came to the beaver meadow where blue dragonflies hovered among the reeds and tall grasses. Overhead, a red-tailed hawk circled lazily as it rode the heat thermals above a field of oats. He couldn't help but marvel at God's meticulous and creative handiwork as he ambled into the woods. He was watching for wildlife when suddenly he caught a glimpse of Morgan kneeling in prayer behind a large rock. Fearing he might disturb him, Walter tiptoed farther along the path. As a few rays of bright sunlight filtered down through the leafy canopy, he was amazed to discover that George had also come here to be alone with God. Walter was so moved by the sight that he resolved to find a place of solitude himself. He threaded his way into the woods until he came to a mossy bank where he, too, sat down to open his heart to God and to meditate about what he had been hearing and seeing.

The order of the afternoon meeting was the same as the morning. Laura came forward to the platform and spoke before Jack, who had been scheduled as the closing speaker.[30] Laura began by asking the saints to open their Bibles at the letter to the Ephesians. "Paul says that Christ has generously divided out a measure of grace to each of us. And that when He went up to heaven, He gave us gifts. Some to be apostles, or sent ones, and some to be prophets. Others have special gifts in winning people to Christ. Still others have the gift of caring for God's people as a shepherd does his sheep, leading and teaching them in the ways of God. All of these gifts are supplied to equip God's people for works of service, so the church may be built up and become mature, attaining to the fullness of Christ.[31]

"This passage suggests that every person who is born of the Spirit, and therefore alive to God, has been presented with a gift by Christ." Laura paused as a sparrow fluttered around the tent before finding its way back out the flap opening. She scanned the attentive faces. "Do you know what your gift is?" she probed ingenuously.

Laura's pleasant voice reached out to the edges of the tent and drew her listeners to the very essence of her message. "God expects us to use the gift that He, in His eternal wisdom, has selected for us. If you had prepared a costly gift, only to have it ignored, you'd be heartbroken. God is the most magnanimous Giver we'll ever know. The weighty gift of His precious Son was given in love and at a great sacrifice. But humans do not have the capacity to receive this gift of Christ on their own.

"Imagine someone giving a two-year-old a gift weighing fifty pounds. The child wouldn't have the capability or strength to receive it. Only if an adult placed his hands under the child's hands could the child actually accept the gift. The Father presented His Son to mankind, but we are only able to receive Him with the power and help of the Holy Spirit."

As Laura examined the eager faces before her, she closed her Bible, gripping it with both hands. Her voice carried an intensity that few in the tent had ever known of Laura, least of all George, who sat transfixed.

"When we receive Christ, we also receive practical, functional gifts—such as apostleship, or evangelism, or shepherding, or teaching. The phrase 'to prepare God's people for works of service' is vital. It means that each one of us is equipped with a unique and personal gift, enabling us to minister to our fellow man. We need to keep asking ourselves an important question: 'Am I doing all I can to serve my neighbours and to build up my brothers and sisters in Christ?'" Many eyes met Laura's in mutual assent.

"Paul sent a letter to Timothy cautioning him not to neglect the gift that had been given to him.[32] He also wrote to the church at Corinth, telling them that the Spirit had given each of them a special way of serving others.[33] In his letter Paul listed many potential gifts that the Corinthians might have received." Laura tapped her forefinger on the cover of her Bible. "We, too, must be about our Father's business[34] by allowing the Holy Spirit to actively use the tool or gift He has placed in our hands." Laura's face, flushed with intensity, radiated like a candle newly blown upon as she stepped down from the platform and resumed her seat.

The morning and afternoon meetings focused on subjects that spoke particularly to those who were already saints, messages that encouraged them to deepen their relationship with God, to give themselves more fully to His service. However, the friends were also concerned about unbelievers in the surrounding district. But they knew that most of these neighbours would be busy working during the day. Hoping that a few of them might come after supper, Alistair and George and the others had decided that the evening meeting should emphasize the urgency of receiving Christ.

Every evening Alistair waited patiently at the side of the lane to greet any visitor who might have decided to accept the friends' invitation. To his delight several appeared over the course of the convention, including some who had indulged in rash gossip about the fellowship. Each guest was ushered to the eating area and, after meeting a few of the friends, a heaping plate of potatoes and stew was pressed into their hands. Afterward, if they wished to stay for the evening, Bill or Morgan took care to find them a seat in the meeting tent and joined them with a copy of the friends' hymnbook.

On Friday evening, just before the meeting was to begin, a young man and an older woman in a dusty buggy made a tentative turn at the gate. The buggy wheels paused and then rolled toward Alistair and Morgan. The driver pulled up the horse. "I understand there's a meeting here tonight."

The man didn't give his name, and although they looked strangely familiar, Alistair couldn't identify either one. The woman leaned forward, tipping her head so that the brim of her hat shielded her eyes from the sun. Alistair pondered her anxious gestures. Whose mother might she be?

"Yes, there surely is." Alistair smiled. "We're glad you came. Can I tie up your horse for you?"

With a quick nod, the young man jumped down. "That'll be fine."

Alistair extended his right hand. "I'm Alistair, and this is Morgan. He'll help you find a seat."

"Pleased to meet you," the man allowed, returning Alistair's firm grip. Then as if suddenly remembering his companion, he turned with a start.

"Oh, and this is my mother." The dark hat brim bobbed forward and the woman offered a slight smile as her son helped her to the ground.

Still puzzled by the pair's awkward reserve, Alistair took the horse's bridle, heading toward the stable as Morgan ushered them toward the tent.

The benches were almost full and many sat, heads bent, waiting in prayerful reverence for the meeting to begin. Morgan showed the latecomer and his mother to three empty seats near the back and slid in beside them.

Alistair guided the evening meeting, and when it was time for him to speak, he began with a simple utterance: "Nothing matters but salvation in this world or that to come." He paused for a minute, looking at the ground in front of him. Again he emphasized the phrase. He wanted people to be filled with the truth of these words, to really think them through. Surveying the faces before him, he could see the concentration in their eyes.

"I'd like to tell you about a good friend of mine who was a captain for an American shipping line. This company hauled cargo on the Great Lakes from the lake head to southern Ontario. The owners of the ship were eager to load it as heavily as possible to ensure a maximum profit. The captain and crew were paid a bonus based upon the tonnage, and sometimes they overloaded the vessel far beyond its safe capacity.

"On one particular sailing in 1888, the weather was fair and prospects looked extremely favourable as the ship's hold was filled at Port Arthur. My friend and his crew prepared to set sail on what promised to be a routine voyage. The trip south through Lake Superior was uneventful, but about mid-point through Lake Huron, the autumn sky began to darken.

"As the day progressed, the clouds grew blacker and the wind picked up. Every effort was made to batten down the hatches and secure the load. Two hours passed and the freighter began to list dangerously in the mounting waves. Sheets of wind-driven rain lashed the decks and wheelhouse. Within another hour she started to take on water as the high seas crashed over the bow. The situation had shifted from worrisome to desperate, and the sailors decided to lighten the vessel. Barrels of flour and grain were jettisoned, and eventually a few purebred cattle were led up from the hold and pushed overboard as well. Since they were only a few miles from the Michigan shore, the men hoped that the animals might swim to safety. Instead, the abandoned creatures followed the ship pathetically until they were overcome with exhaustion and drowned in the towering waves.

"For the men on the ship, nothing mattered now but making it safely to shore themselves. The dull moan of the storm rose to a high-pitched scream, drowning out the sounds of breaking glass and crashing furniture. Before the gale blew out the lanterns, the sailors could see chairs, tables, china, and cooking equipment sliding back and forth until they smashed. When the last flicker was extinguished, the men struggled on the dark, steeply pitching decks to claw their way into the lifeboat. It was only a question of survival now. No more than ten minutes passed from the moment the lifeboat pushed away until the ship faltered. Then, with an enormous turbulent gasp, she slid into the darkness of her watery grave."

Alistair leaned forward. "This is a picture of human lives," he said, his tone low and serious. The audience strained to catch every word. "Circumstances can change fast. And suddenly, nothing matters but salvation. We start out as young people with the brightest prospects and highest hopes. The voyage looks so inviting. No thought that trouble might cloud the skies ahead. And little provision is made for rough seas.

"As we approach our middle years, we often load up our lives with more and more baggage. My friend and his beleaguered crew escaped to shore, but the ship had sunk, the cargo was gone, the profit lost, the venture in shambles. Only a few poor farm folks along the rocky shores of Lake Huron benefited when the scattered sacks and barrels of flour washed up on Inverhuron Beach. The bags were wet and caked on the outside, but the interior was dry and useable.

"Imagine if the captain had ordered the cargo be thrown overboard while the sailing was smooth. People would have called him crazy, and he would have been criminally liable for wasting the goods committed to his care. But in the tragic last moments of their fateful voyage what, at one time, was unthinkable became the only sensible option."

"Why is it," Alistair asked thoughtfully, "that we hesitate to let go of meaningless things that last only for a brief season when we can take hold of priceless things that last for all eternity?" He shifted his weight uneasily onto his other foot. "My friend was an ambitious man, and twelve years ago he plunged into a partnership that imported tea from Ceylon."

Alistair stared far beyond the coal oil lantern hanging over the platform, its soft light revealing the beads of perspiration that glistened on his furrowed brow. When he spoke again, his voice was filled with deep emotion. "The enterprise became tremendously successful, but nine years ago my old friend contracted galloping consumption. His doctor advised him that he only had a few weeks to live. The storm inside him raged every bit as violently as the one on Lake Huron had done years earlier.

"One winter evening Priscilla and I went to visit him as he lay dying at his sister's. We talked for a bit about old times, about the rapscallion things we had done together as boys." Alistair paused and wiped his brow with his handkerchief. "As long as I live, I'll never forget his last words as I stood by his bedside, his voice hollow and anguished.

" 'Alistair,' he cried. 'I've wasted my life. It's *too late* for me. It's only *now* that I know what's most important—peace with God.' Then he closed his eyes and turned toward the wall as if all his hope was gone. Even in his last moments, my friend seemed unable to repent.[35]

"Had I known what I do today, I would have assured him that it was still not too late. I'd have reminded him how the thief on the cross had accepted Jesus in his dying moments. And how Jesus had given the man a marvelous promise: 'Today you will be with Me in paradise.'[36]

"As I closed the door and struggled out to the cutter behind Priscilla, those sad, haunting words, *It's too late for me,*' stabbed into my heart like a farrier's knife. On that dark road home from the face of death, I begged God to grant my friend the gift of peace." The crowd could hear the melancholy in Alistair's voice and see the bleak, wintry feeling in his eyes. "The next afternoon his sister sent word that he had died a few hours later."

"Why do I share this sad story? Because we need to be reminded that *nothing* matters but salvation. And that we need to lay aside everything that hinders us from setting our eyes on Jesus, the author and perfecter of our faith.[37] So now, before we close, let's sing a hymn composed by a man who dictated these words to his friend during the last few days of his own life."

God gives you the invitation
To a life that is divine;
For this full and free salvation,
Come in His accepted time.

Nothing matters but salvation,
In this world or that to come;
Nothing matters but salvation,
When the race of life is run.[38]

As Alistair sat on the platform listening to the chorus of the hymn, the weathered face of Ben Aberlochy, his old school friend, flashed into his mind again. Although he had been careful not to mention Ben's name during his message, Alistair deeply appreciated this spiritual journey that his friend's death had started him upon. And when he looked up at the tent full of saints, he marveled at the miracle that had sprung forth from the pain and sadness he had felt at Ben's funeral. When Alistair considered all the spiritual life that had flowed from that event, he wanted to believe that God had been able to touch Ben's heart. That he, too, in the moments before he died, had received the gift of eternal life.

After the meeting Morgan escorted the visitors to the serving table for a cup of tea and some cookies. As they stood scanning the crowd in the gathering dusk, they picked out George the moment he slipped out of the tent flap. A moment later he turned in their direction. Halting, he absorbed their outlines in the dim light and then ran to embrace both his mother and brother at the same time. "Oh, Mum, Cyril. I had no idea you were here!" His face softened and his eyes moistened as he struggled to contain his feelings. This was the first time anybody in George's family had bothered to show any interest in the purpose and meaning of his ministry.

Mrs. Farnham's face wrinkled with elation as George released her. "I looked all around the tent," she said, "and couldn't see hide nor hair of you."

"I did too," Cyril added. "But it was pretty dim under the canvas, and you certainly don't look a whit like yourself without the beard."

George offered a jaunty grin. "I guess I was hidden by Hugh's shadow at the far end of the tent."

Happily, he introduced them to each of the friends who drifted past, balancing oatmeal cookies and cups as they offered a hearty handshake. As the three stood talking and drinking tea, Laura caught sight of them and sprinted across the yard.

"Oh, it's so good to see you," she exclaimed as she hugged George's mother. "It's been far too long." George's mother shed a few tears, and even Cyril seemed moved to see Laura again, extending his hand in a gesture half playful, half serious.

"It's been eight years since you left," Mrs. Farnham said pensively, looking at Laura, "and even now when I walk past your bedroom, I often think of you fixing your French braid in the mirror. Sometimes I pretend you're still there, that if I knocked on the door you might greet me from the other side. Those were some of my happiest days."

Laura tightened her grip around the older woman's waist. "Be sure to say hello to Dad Farnham for me. And tell him I missed him here tonight."

"I will, Laura. Hardly a week goes by he doesn't speak of you."

Cyril and his mother seemed to be in no hurry to end the conversation, and it was late before George and Laura walked them to their horse and rig. George smiled as he hugged them goodbye and helped his mother climb in. But the longing in his heart almost made him cry as he watched the lantern on their buggy growing fainter and dimmer in the darkness. He thought of how much he loved his family, of how much he missed them.

"I really hope they heard and felt Jesus here tonight," he said to Laura after the light had disappeared into nothingness.

"I'm sure they were touched by the whole evening," she responded softly. "I could see it in your mother's eyes."

"This is a very special day for me," George said. "To see you happy and fulfilled in your ministry and to have my family at the convention. It's truly an answer to my prayers." He looked up into the distant galaxies, as if imagining the magnitude of God's plans. "All the people whom I once worried that I might have to leave behind were here with me tonight. I'm glad we can trust Jesus to accomplish His perfect work."

George fell silent, his face upturned to the silvery clouds that sailed in majesty past the full moon. Its luminous haze flooded the farmyard and shimmered off the roofs of the many farm buildings, creating the effect of a tiny community caught in a silver trance. A nightjar winging its way past George's shoulder edged him out of his stargazing to a reminder of the woman beside him. "Look, Laura! There's the Big Dipper away in the northwest, so clear tonight. And if your eyes follow the handle to the big star on the end, you'll see Arcturus, mentioned in the book of Job."[39]

Instinctively bending down, he pointed, trying to align his vision with hers. "It's as if the Big Dipper is pouring out a blessing on me tonight." He took Laura's hand and kissed it. Then his voice deepened. "I'm proud of you, Laura. You're still my favourite girl." George knew he must leave unuttered the further words of devotion he longed to add. Yet he bent his thin shoulders and clasped her face tenderly in his hands.

Together they walked to the door of her sleeping quarters, where a few mothers were hushing their still-chattering children. Laura's eyes turned to find George's face in the soft darkness. "George, I want you to know that I'm happier than I ever thought possible," she said. "Everywhere I look I see God's hand in the way our paths are leading." She touched his shoulder lightly. "I'll see you in the morning." Laura smiled to herself as she watched George round the corner of the porch to disappear into the moonlit night, whistling softly as he went.

On the way home, George's mother, pulling her cloak away from the wheel, broke the silence. "Well, I never would have thought it. Imagine a quiet fellow like your brother having so many friends."

"Good friends too," Cyril agreed. "Thick as thieves—the kind you can count on. There's nothing put on. No show about it."

"It's like George is part of another family," his mother said wistfully.

"Some things never change though," Cyril remarked. "He still passes around that horehound candy of his as freely as ever."

"I noticed how the children flocked around him. I had to smile at the way they all said, 'Thank you, Uncle George' when he gave them a piece."

Cyril grunted. "Maybe they think George really *is* their uncle."

As the horse's hooves pounded a cadence on the gravel road, they talked about what they had witnessed and about the significant change they had noticed in George. How he was at peace and how he seemed to have grown into who he was destined to become. Then they fell silent for a mile or two, and Cyril got to thinking about his own life. *Could I dig up two or three people,* he asked himself, *that I could really count on if I were in serious trouble? And here is my own brother, who appears to have a hundred friends.* Silently he asked himself why this should be so, but deep down he knew. He turned to his mother and said, "It's a long piece to go—an hour or more. But I think I'll head back tomorrow night, Mum."

Mrs. Farnham didn't say anything for a while, and Cyril knew she was anticipating his father's reaction. Cyril also wondered what his dad would say. And how he would make them feel. But then, in a soft yet determined voice, she said, "If you're going, Cyril, I'll go too."

On Sunday morning the friends gathered under the translucent canvas for the last meeting of the convention. They had come to Wood Creek Farm hardly knowing what to expect, and God, they felt, had in every way blessed them most abundantly. As they drew together in singing the final hymn, they joined hands along the rows and focused on going forth with Jesus to sow these seeds of love among others:

> No reputation, with Jesus I go,
> Willingly, cheerfully, my life to sow.
> Sow to the Spirit, in faith lay it down;
> Strive for the mastery, hope for the crown.[40]

As their harmonious chorus billowed out of the tent, many found tears of joy upon their cheeks. Yet even as the notes faded across the lawn, they felt a certain twinge of melancholy, knowing that within hours they must part company—at least for another year.

After dinner at noon, most of them began to roll up their bedding and tie the bundles with cords. Mothers poked under the edge of bed ticks for stray stockings while fathers rounded up their errant boys from the pond or beaver meadow. From every corner women and older friends followed young men, arms laden with clothing and baggage, toward the wagons loading for the train station. Oblivious to the well-wishers all around, Alistair and Bill's teams switched their tails under the pouring July sunshine and waited, one hip sagging over a relaxed flank.

As George heaped boxes and luggage against the wagon's front rack, he surveyed the jubilant crowd with deep satisfaction. All over the lane, saints stood chatting in ever-shifting clusters, hesitant to disengage from friendships forged over the four days by saying goodbye. Others meandered among the crowd like roving troubadours, attempting to embrace or shake hands with each soul before the call to climb aboard.

Mrs. Applebee, George mused, *is slightly thinner and whiter than the day she greeted Jack and me so warmly on her front porch*. As he watched, the old woman, her rosy cheeks blooming in a heartfelt smile, threw her arms around Priscilla and squeezed her. "I can't thank you enough for having us all here," he heard Evelyn avow. "These four days of fellowship have been the high-light of the year for all of us."

As she approached him, George positioned a box under the edge of the wagon. "Let me help you to a spot with some support for your back, Mrs. Applebee," he said, assisting her up and onto to the makeshift seat he had fashioned and covered with a blanket.

Over Mrs. Applebee's shoulder, he caught the sun's lustre on Laura's chestnut locks and the animation in her delicate face as she lingered with Herman Brunstedder and two couples from Salt House Bay. This, he could tell from their bright expressions, had been an extraordinary experience for outport folks who rarely ventured far from their boats. George mopped his forehead with his handkerchief. If he had followed his own inclinations and taken Laura as his wife, they'd have missed it all.

Turning toward the sound of Sissy Boggins' uproarious cackle from the end of the driving shed, he saw Malachi doubled over, wheezing and slap-ping his leg as Timothy shared a joke with them and the Purveses.

Susan's musical laughter and Yorkshire accent rose above the vivacious commotion. "Ah'll see you 'ere next year, Sissy," she promised.

George caught sight of Sissy's ostrich feather bobbing as Susan stepped forward to kiss her on the cheek. "Shore 'nuff will," Sissy affirmed as she waddled toward the wagon. "And I'll post ya my butter tart pie recipe soon's I get home. It'll rid yer wrinkles fer ya, don't ya know."

"That'll make me man 'appy," Susan laughed, turning to wink at Joe.

An arc of smiles—Jack Gillan, Ida Rose Merrick, Alice and Bill Jones, Dugan McGladry, Oliver Summers, Lyman and Jessie Liddle—radiated from under the dappled shade of the maple. George watched as the little company ambled toward the wagon. Aside from a slight limp, Robert Hunter seemed to have recovered fully and stepped blithely forward, as though the ablest of them all. About a dozen men and a handful of lads assembled to walk behind the last wagon. Among them, Gilbert Jones, serious as a young judge, said goodbye to his new friend Jimmy Liddle who was already sporting the downy shadow of a beard.

"We'll see you next year," several voices rang out as the last stragglers climbed aboard. Those departing checked their luggage and children one last time, and those who were staying overnight moved to one side as Alistair's black Percherons leaned into their harness. From where they stood at the house gate, the remaining friends shouted goodbye and waved their hats until the wagons crested the first hill and rolled out of sight.

It was a grand send-off, carried out in the spirit of a true and unified family.

Twenty-Eight

STRUGGLE IN ST. MARYS
Autumn 1908

The abundance and fellowship of two more summer conventions rained down upon the believers at Wood Creek Farm. The apple blossoms that canopied Alistair's orchard turned to early fruit as the preparations for the annual gatherings got underway. On both occasions the friends welcomed a fresh slate of faces to the growing family with the same warmth and hospitality as the first. For four days old and new alike united as one to celebrate their simple faith in Christ. And every year, after packing away the tent, the bed ticks, the dishes, and setting the place to rights, the workers struck out again for new districts in which to share the gospel. Although Laura and Katie formed a strong bond, they prayed that other sisters would join them in the harvest field. The single brothers, on the other hand, decided to interchange companions from time to time in order to learn from the strengths of each other.

In the fall of 1908, George and Jack found themselves together again— for the first time since their mission in Belwood. As apostles of the faith, each of them had been careful to plant the simple truth of the gospel and to live it out in a practical way. People in different regions of Ontario had received the Spirit, and as they began to live their lives in this revealed way— this unpretentious way of Christ—George and Jack had witnessed the blossoming of spiritual life. Still, in spite of so much apparent success in the intervening years, the two brothers continued in the same humble manner as they had in the beginning. Although they were older, more seasoned, and had endured the tests of time and the quirks of human nature, their faces still bespoke a strong and youthful faith.

The morning was gray with the cold light of late November as George and Jack passed the stone water tower near the centre of St. Marys. A farmer seated on a wagon piled high with turnips waved as the two men parted near the centre of the village to begin handing out invitations to the gospel meetings.

Jack had just come down the path from a small cottage when a woman pulled her buggy abruptly to one side of the road and scrambled down. Jack watched as the diminutive figure in a beaver cloth cape led the horse ahead a few paces, peering down at its feet. With the eye of a practised horseman, Jack could see that her mare was lame in one front foot, stumbling with each step. "She nearly fell," the woman explained, as Jack approached. "I can't imagine what's wrong. She's a good horse."

"Moves like she twisted her foreleg in a chuckhole," Jack noted as he looked at the chestnut mare, her coat so flecked with gray that she almost appeared to be a roan. She was a tall stylish animal, and he could tell at a glance that she was well cared for, her coat shiny and her tail plaited. Jack took the bridle and urged the horse to take a few more steps, noting how sensitive she was about putting weight on her front right hoof. Jack patted the mare's neck and ran his hand gently over her withers and down her cannon bone to her fetlock.

"Steady, girl," he said as he crouched down, lifting her hoof against his knee. Nothing seemed amiss, but the frog was caked with mud. Reaching into his pocket, he took out his jackknife and began to flick out bits of impacted clay. "Proper hoof pick would be handy," he commented as he worked, "but this'll do the trick just the same." In a minute a sharp stone shot out. "That's the problem," Jack exclaimed rolling the sharp edges between his thumb and fingers, "the caked mud was jamming this rascal up against her frog once you got onto the hard road. Have you come far?"

The woman's concern cleared and she broke into a smile. "Not far, just up the road a piece, second place on the left past the edge of the village. Thank you so much, Mr..."

"Gillan. Jack Gillan," he said, holding out his hand.

"Mrs. Newton," she responded, shaking hands. "I was ever so worried. I've an engagement in London tomorrow, and I was afraid Dolly might be going lame." Thanking Jack profusely, the woman accepted an invitation card to one of the meetings. In return the woman issued her own invitation. "Plan on a cup of tea when you are going past."

The mention of London stirred up old anxieties as Jack continued with his morning's work. Five years had passed since his last attempt to find Miranda had been thwarted. For a while she had remained in his thoughts, but with the passage of time, the death of his dream seemed less grievous. The image of a young mother with open arms had been supplanted with a harsh, aloof woman rebuking him for dredging up her past. Still, he couldn't push her out of his thoughts as he headed to meet George at noon.

"How'd the morning go for you?" George inquired cheerfully.

"Pretty fair. I gave out a handful of invitations along Water Street."

"Any visits?"

Suddenly, Jack felt the same rush of adrenalin he had felt that morning in Toronto when he had set out from Mrs. Partridge's to find his mother. "George, I've got to talk to you," he gasped.

George looked into Jack's ashen face. "Are you sick, Jack?" he urged.

"No…no, I'm not sick." Jack's hands signaled a capitulating gesture. "But let's sit down for a minute."

The two men made their way to a grassy spot near the foot of the limestone water tower. As Jack slumped onto a log, George sat on the grass looking up into his friend's twisting face, his neat tweed cap crumpled to one side. For nearly an hour, Jack sweated, his expression haggard, his voice rising and falling with swells of emotion as he poured out the details of his parents' revelation, Amelia's album and letter, his disheartening search. But most of all he talked about the denigration he anticipated if he were to pursue his quest for his mother.

A prickly sensation ran up George's spine as he listened to the pain of rejection flow from the lips of one of his best friends. At length, when Jack had emptied himself out, George offered his encouragement. "Jack, it's not for me to say, but I feel in my bones that your mother will be delighted to see you. And even if I'm off the mark, at least you'll feel better for having tried. The throb of uncertainty is worse than any reality, good or bad." George plucked a blade of grass and rolled it between his fingers. "That Mrs. Newton who triggered your story. Why don't you march over there after dinner and ask if it's convenient to get a lift into London tomorrow?"

The corners of Jack's mouth betrayed his misgiving. "I'll chew it over."

George jumped to his feet and reached out a hand in good humour. "Up and at it, old man. Let's get moving," he said as he gave Jack a yank.

They had only gone a block or so along Queen Street when George spoke, suddenly solemn. "Jack, what a load you've carried all these years, unknown to me. I'm so sorry." He paused. "I'd be happy to go along with you now if you'd like."

Jack plodded along, head down, forehead furrowed. "Thanks, George. But I need to try this alone. Besides, you've done the most important part. You've given me the boost to shake my fear."

Jack alternated his gaze between the flat rich farmland and the genial face of his driver, Mrs. Newton, who regaled him with her family's gossip. At times, while she gripped the buggy reins in her black kid gloves, he gazed at her as if she held his fate too in her hands. The raw chill of the late autumn day contrasted with the heat that coursed through his limbs and pounded at his heart.

"Dolly's stepping it out right smartly today," Mrs. Newton observed as the sharp breeze caught a few gray wisps around her bonnet. At length she turned, rummaging for a sack behind the seat. "Goodness gracious, time flies when you're into a good conversation. I near forgot the lunch," she exclaimed. "Can you see the jar of tea? It's wrapped in a newspaper and tied with string. There's a package of oatmeal cookies too."

As she watched Jack taking a swig of tea, she smiled. "London's a pretty town in summer—the forest city, they call it. And it's reaching farther along Dundas Street each time I come."

Jack tried to sound offhanded. "Do you have any idea where Stornoway Road might be?"

Startled by the intensity in his voice, Mrs. Newton turned toward Jack. "It crosses Dundas up about a mile or so. There's a shoeing forge and iron-monger on the northeast corner."

Jack moistened his lips. "I'd like to get out there if I could."

Mrs. Newton scanned his face, seeming to sense profound intention in his tone. "I hope your errand goes well," she offered. "I'll be heading back to St. Marys in about four hours if you'd like a lift home."

Around the forge stood a huddle of houses interspersed by a ditch, a livery stable, and across the road, a dilapidated barn sagging against a tow-ering elm. As Mrs. Newton's black rig pulled away, Jack took stock of the intersection. Stornoway Road was much more of rural road than he had anticipated. Looking north and south, he decided to head into the forge and inquire before walking too far.

A man with overalls, his face black with soot, glanced up from his anvil. "G'day," he said straightening up.

"I'm looking for a Professor Longstaff," Jack said tentatively. "Do you know where he lives?"

The man deliberately fingered his rib cage as though checking for vital signs. At length he laid aside his pipe, exhaling a cloud of fumes. "I'm not rightly sure 'bout that, but I reckon it's that odd house with the white cla'board," he coughed, pointing along the road. "Built by some 'merican fella a few years back. 'Bout half a mile up, I'd say. On the west side."

Jack thanked the man and started out along the narrow gravel road, scanning the neighbourhood. Unmasked maples extended their bare limbs toward the sky, a burdened gray, while dry leaves swirled around their stark trunks. In spite of the cold wind driving through his jacket, Jack felt the familiar trickle of sweat down his back. The homes were built on small hold-ings, and he had only passed two before he saw a stately antebellum resi-dence—a style he had seen in pictures of the deep South. Graceful columns supported its Southern plantation porch and a white railing ran across the front and wrapped itself along the near side.

Jack's pulse roared in his ears, and he gulped the sharp air as he drew closer. Like a paradox the unusual house stood aloof yet its gracious porch beckoned, drawing him into its arms as he turned up the short laneway. On either side of the wide steps sprawled flower beds blanketed in straw for the coming winter. Jack paused, one foot on the bottom tread of the wide staircase that led up a half flight to the porch. *What kind of reception will I receive?* he agonized. *Or will this again be the wrong house, too late?* He felt strangely disembodied, like a man in a dream watching tragedy approach but lacking any ability to move. For what seemed like several min-utes, Jack remained paralysed, his hand glued to the smooth handrail. Then, with a childlike moan, he broke free and mounted the steps.

A sickening wave of fear welled up as he raised his hand and knocked on the door. It seemed an eternity before he heard quick footsteps and the door swung open. A dark haired woman with the first threads of gray looked into Jack's face. In a flash, his racing mind absorbed her pleasing appear-ance. The vivacious face and sparkling eyes radiated toward him as if through the photograph in his pocket. Jack noticed her full blue dress with wide sleeves was drawn trimly around her waist by apron strings and her hair cascaded over her ears before being swirled into a fashionable roll on the nape of her neck. But most of all he noticed her face, softened with age but as youthful and fresh as a September rose. "Can I help you?" she offered.

Although Jack had rehearsed this moment a thousand times, nothing prepared him for the emotion he felt now. "I-I'm looking for Mrs. Miranda Longstaff," he choked in a breath-starved voice.

The soft warm eyes seemed to peer deep into his soul. "I'm Miranda Longstaff," she responded.

Hesitating to blurt out his whole story, Jack paused. "My name's Jack Gillan. I'm a friend of Amelia and Robert Hunter from Belwood," he said lamely. "They asked me to look you up when I came to London."

Mrs. Longstaff's lips stretched into a congenial smile. "Well, how nice. Come into the parlour, Mr. Gillan. I haven't heard from Amelia for a long while." She turned and led Jack across the foyer and into an expansive parlour overlooking the front porch. As Jack followed Miranda into the room, his heart pounded. *How drastically*, he wondered, *will her mood shift once my true mission has revealed itself?*

A low mahogany table sat in front of one of the deep windows. On either side, facing each other, were two terra cotta wing chairs to which Miranda pointed. When Jack had slid into one, she settled opposite him.

"Do tell me about Amelia and Robert before I fetch a cup of tea," she insisted graciously.

Jack explained how he and George had met the Hunters a month after Robert had been gored by the bull. He watched Miranda's eyes widen as he told her about George and himself and their reason for being in Belwood. Seeing only intrigue when he described the friends that met at Hunters' Hollow, he went on to tell Miranda about their meetings in St. Marys.

"How lovely you went to all this trouble to look me up," Miranda said when she realized that Jack had come to London specifically to visit her.

She then rose, moving with a measured grace as she glided toward the kitchen. While she prepared a pot of tea, Jack sat looking out the window, his legs trembling beneath the edge of the round table. Hearing a soft meow, he glanced down to see a sleek gray cat stalking along the gleam cast by the window on the polished oak floor. Approaching him, the cat stopped short a yard or so from his boot and sat down, the narrow slits of its green eyes appraising him. When Jack reached out to entice the elegant creature closer, she rose and angled away.

In a few minutes Miranda returned with tea biscuits and blackberry jam and settled back into her chair.

"Lovely cat. What's its name?" Jack asked.

Miranda set a fancy teapot with embossed legs in front of Jack. "Lady Jane Grey. She's a stray and very unpredictable. Sometimes she'll come in and stay a day or two as if she's the queen of the palace. And then just as suddenly, she'll disappear. I'll call and search for her, but nothing. You'd almost imagine she had two homes." Miranda smiled. "She's elusive, doesn't want to be hemmed in. Like some of us women," she added with a quick chuckle. "I suspect she goes mousing at the farm across the road."

As Jack reached for his tea, he realized the time had now come to remove the mask, to bare his soul. He felt the tremor in his hand as he added a spoonful of sugar to his cup and wondered if Miranda had noticed.

"Do you have children, Mrs. Longstaff?" he ventured.

Miranda lowered her teacup. "Two. A son and a daughter," she replied brightly. "They'll both be here for Christmas." She rose and brought a family photograph from the top of the organ, holding it out to him.

Jack studied the features of Miranda's children and although neither of them looked exactly like himself, there was an irrefutable resemblance. Handing the brass frame back to Miranda, he took a deep breath. "Mrs. Longstaff, I haven't been completely honest with you. There's another reason I came here today. I have another question." Jack watched his mother's eyes tense around the edges and her smile lines soften slightly, but she remained cordial.

"Certainly, Mr. Gillan. Go right ahead."

Jack's right hand shook so badly that he could hardly draw the picture out of his trouser pocket. "Do you know this girl?" he choked as he passed it across the table.

Miranda took the photograph and looked at it without speaking, her face stark and expressionless. Then a guarded consciousness suffused her features. "Yes. Yes, that's me. But…where did you get it?"

Shivers ran through Jack's whole body from head to toe. "It was given me on my sixteenth birthday."

Miranda's teacup clattered onto the saucer. Her face drained of colour. With the realization of Jack's identity she gasped, "My son!" Tears seeped from the corners of her eyes, staining her soft complexion. Before Jack could reply, his long lost mother cried, "Can you ever forgive me? I'm so sorry…

giving you up was the hardest thing I've ever done. My mother insisted…"
Then Miranda fell silent, as if recalling the memory.

Jack reached across the table and took his mother's hand in his, connecting for the first time with the warmth of his own stock.

Miranda's lips trembled. "That was such a painful time for me. Mother sent me away to my aunt's and told me not to come home with…with you." Miranda paused a moment and then added, "When I tried to plead, I was threatened and told never to breath a word of it again. I was utterly powerless. I've lived with terrible guilt all these years."

Jack sat stupefied at Miranda's reaction, tears running down his own cheeks. "Please don't feel bad," he implored in a voice he barely recognized as his own. "I didn't come to make you feel awkward. I just wanted to meet you."

For several minutes neither said a word, each coming to grips with the present reality. When the tide of his emotions had ebbed, Jack offered consolation. "You made the best choice. My life's been very good. Ma and Pop Gillan, are wonderful parents, and God's given me His very best."

Pulling a lace hanky out of her sleeve, Miranda sniffled woefully. "It was awful being sent to Guelph, and some days I wished I could've died. My aunt wouldn't let me stick my nose out the door in case somebody might recognize me. I only had one quick look at you before the midwife whisked you away, and I was crying so hard I could hardly see. But the vision of you asleep—so peaceful and beautiful—has stayed in my memory all these years. Signing you away was the most wretched moment of my life."

Miranda poured herself another cup of strong tea. "Sometimes my mother's voice could cut glass. When I got home she said, 'Put it out of your mind. It never happened, you hear?' That statement cut me like a knife, and although the ordeal made me a stronger person in some ways, when I got into my bed at night, I would break down and cry myself to sleep. All the energy I used to hold my head up during the day had drained out of me. I wanted to hold you so badly my arms ached."

Jack tried to smile as he wiped a tear with the back of his hand. "How long did you feel that way?" he asked.

"For years," Miranda said quickly. "Eventually it eased a little, but still I thought of you every day. And every May eleventh I celebrated your birthday in my heart. I knew somewhere you were having a birthday cake, and I wanted so much to be part of it." She looked reminiscent. "One time when I tried to tell an older cousin named Mildred how much I ached for you, she scolded me and said that you were just a mistake, and a bad mistake at that. I cried all the way home from her place in Elora. But after that it came so clear that you were beautiful, a gift from God."

Jack looked into the face of the woman who had brought him into the world under a black pall of sorrow and condemnation. "Life is never an accident," he said with conviction. "God's the giver of all life, and He loves each one of His children. The brightest and the best. The weakest and the most unwanted." He grinned wryly. "And I'm thankful that He sustains the ones who seem to come along by accident."

As Jack tightened his knuckles his face clouded. "Did you ever try to find me?" he asked quietly.

Miranda's voice came as if from afar. "Once when I was eighteen I traveled to Guelph on the train and talked to the midwife, but she wouldn't say a peep—just that you had a good home. Then a few years later, I tried to get ahold of her again, but she'd moved. Nobody seemed to know where." Miranda sat, clearly admiring her son. "Sorry if I seem to be staring. For so long I've imagined what you might look like. I can't take my eyes off you."

Jack smiled and studied her eyes. "I understand perfectly." They sat in silence, holding hands across the table, each drinking in the miracle and warmth of the other.

"Does your family know about me?" Jack inquired apprehensively.

"My husband does," Miranda said. "He's very understanding. Dwight will be delighted to meet you. The children, I've never told. I figured it would be soon enough if I ever found you." She hesitated, a wistful look crossing her face. "As I said, they're all coming for Christmas Day." Her face suddenly brightened. "Could you join us too?"

Jack sighed. "I'll be in St. Marys with George, my fellow worker."

"Bring him along too. There'll be a table full of food. Besides, it sounds as if he's important to you, so he should know your family."

Jack's eyes shone with gratitude. "That's most considerate. Thank you." Suddenly, he thought of Mrs. Newton and hauled out his pocket watch. "I need to be going now," he apologized as he got up.

Miranda accompanied Jack to the door. "Can I give you a hug, Jack?"

"Nothing I'd like better," he responded as he put his arms around the woman who had given birth to him. For a long time they held each other close, both crying softly.

"I've been waiting for this wonderful moment for forty-three years," she murmured as she wiped her eyes. "Now don't forget—Christmas Day."

Jack strode down the laneway feeling spent but bubbling over with happiness. At the end of the lane he turned to see Miranda still leaning over the porch railing, her hand waving in farewell. Waving back, he hurried down the road to meet Mrs. Newton at the shoeing forge.

As London fell away in the distance, the fiery sunset reflected the tumultuous passions in Jack's soul. He had just settled back, his toes still working in his boots when Mrs. Newton's pleasant chatter broke into his thoughts. "I hope your day worked out as profitably as mine." The unadorned statement carried an edge of curiosity.

Startled, her reticent passenger tried to gather his scattered thoughts. "Yes. Yes, fine," he responded lamely before once again falling silent.

"After the Women's Institute tea, I had time to visit the shops," she continued, nodding toward the bulky brown package behind the seat. "And I found a lovely blue fox boa for winter..." She paused as if giving Jack time to respond to her fashion choice, but his mind had already drifted back to his mother's face.

The sun threw Jack's solemn shadow far ahead of the horse as the farms of Middlesex County inched past. He felt a vague sense of guilt as he struggled to reciprocate amicably to Mrs. Newton's incessant prattle. She had, after all, been most hospitable. And indeed, instrumental in motivating him to push forward with the search for his mother.

Resisting the urge to draw out his pocket watch for the third time, Jack looked up with relief to see the water tower of St. Marys in the distance. The dome of the stone structure was catching the sun's last rays as they entered the village. "Thank you very much for the ride," he said as Mrs. Newton pulled over to let him out. "And for your generosity."

George was waiting on the front step, bundled in his heavy coat when Jack turned in from the street. Even in the darkness he noted Jack's jaunty step. "How'd you fare?" he asked eagerly.

At first the words caught in Jack's throat. "Just spectacular, George," he replied. "You were absolutely right about my mother's reaction. I had no idea how much she loved me."

George's face glowed as he listened to the unravelings of the day.

"She's been itching to see me as much as I've wanted to find her," Jack exulted. "And I had to reassure her several times that I'd keep in touch. In fact, you and I are invited to spend Christmas with her and my brother and sister. And her husband, Dwight, of course."

"Sounds dandy to me," George smiled as he stood up. "Now let's get upstairs before you freeze in that light jacket. The weather's certainly taken a turn. I smell snow in the air."

At his bedroom door, Jack lifted the lamp. "It's been a full day and I'm simply bushed, George, but thanks for supporting me like a brother."

George gave a perceptive nod. "See you at breakfast, Jack. Rest well."

One blustery evening in early December, George preached a particularly compelling message about opening oneself to the reality of the Spirit. "God's so close that we can almost reach out and feel Him," he asserted. "It's in Him that we live and move and have our being.[1] But unless our minds are receptive to that wisdom, we can't even begin to comprehend His marvelous kingdom."

Before him, a slim English-looking gentleman with a strong jaw and a wool cardigan leaned forward, listening intently. The man, George noted, flipped with careful deliberation to each of the references in his large Bible. After the closing hymn, he hurried forward and thrust out his hand.

"Evening, sir," he boomed. "Ireton Woods."

George smiled at the gravelly voice issuing from such a modest frame. "Glad to have you with us, Mr. Woods," he replied affably. "I'm George Farnham." As George released the hand, he noted its softness. *Must be a shopkeeper or office man*, he mused.

"I've a doctrinal question for you." The man somehow managed to sound both religious and adversarial. George listened attentively, expecting a debate. "Do you mean to say that if I don't go in for this teaching that I'll have no salvation and will go to hell?"

George had heard a variety of questions over the years and, as always, he breathed an instant prayer for wisdom. Apparently, the man had some relatives in Puslinch and had heard rumours of this strange fellowship that had rejected the traditional edifice and met in homes.

George's voice was gentle but authoritative. "Let's be absolutely clear. It makes no difference what I say or what my companion says. But what Jesus says does matter. It matters very much." Mr. Woods nodded reluctantly as George continued. "Jesus told Nicodemus, a religious man and a leader of the Jews, that unless one is born again, he cannot *see* the kingdom of God.[2] So what we're saying is that until a person receives the seed of His precious life, he's not spiritually alive."

"Are you then telling me that I'm not saved?" the man persisted, his voice raised angrily so everyone in the room could hear. Others who were leaving edged warily past the disputer. Although George was no stranger to confrontation, he felt embarrassed at the prospect of a nasty scene that seemed ready to boil over at any second. Across the room he could see Jack smiling and shaking hands as people filed out the door.

"I wouldn't even dare to entertain that question," George attested quietly. "Salvation belongs to the Lord.[3] It would be totally wrong for me to judge someone else's relationship with God. He will be as hard on any person making that kind of judgement as that person is on the one he's judging. The Bible says that the measurement we use will be measured back to us.[4] I'd be afraid to apply a measurement of *limited grace* to anybody, because that would limit God's grace to me. And I can't exist for one minute without it."

"Let me ask you this," Mr. Woods retorted, his words sharp, his lips pinched and tight. "Should I presume then, that a person can't have spiritual life unless he worships in one of these so-called fellowship homes?"

"Absolutely not," George replied. "We'd be limiting God's power if we insisted that He can only save souls through our ministry. Nobody's big enough to put a fence around God and stand at the gate. However, true Christians worship in spirit and in truth.[5] They eat His flesh and drink His blood.[6] That means they imbibe the Spirit of Christ, which compels them to live as He did. It's hard for Jack and me to picture true believers who wouldn't want to live and experience fellowship in the same way as Jesus and the New Testament saints. In the original way."

"I don't think that spiritual life has a thing to do with where we worship," Mr. Woods blustered, shifting his big Bible to his other hand. "I've been to home meetings that were as dead as a doornail, and I've met fine Christians in several churches."

"You're absolutely right on both scores," George agreed. "But still, humble people meet in humble ways, and the spiritual man finds little to attract him to a physical edifice. Rather the Christ child in him leaps for joy in anticipation of sweet fellowship with another saint—wherever they meet.[7] They yearn for frequent times to commune and converse. Like the Scripture says: Deep calls unto deep.[8] On the other hand, hypocrites, Jesus taught, are those who draw near to God with their mouths and honour Him with their lips. But their hearts are stony and far from Him…"⁹

The man cut George off. "Are you suggesting that I'm a hypocrite?" he snapped.

"Not at all, sir," George said politely. "I'm just trying to describe two very different kinds of people: One type who is not willing to repent, to make real changes, and yet feels obliged to worship. And the other who's living each day in the reality of the Spirit. It's up to you to decide which group you fit into." Ireton Woods glared at the response and waved George's words away with his Bible.

"Every child of God has an invisible yet real connection with Him," George continued as Jack came to stand beside him. "In experiencing this reality, he receives life—for life and reality are joined together. Even if he never meets another true believer, he's still part of God's spiritual family."

"Sounds like balderdash," the man snorted. Trembling with anger, he turned on his heel and stormed out of the house, slamming the door behind him.

The brothers were still puzzling over the confrontation as they walked toward their boarding place. "Do you suppose a lot of folks have the same opinion as that fellow?" Jack asked. "That we're saying join our church and you'll have spiritual life?"

"I really don't know. But being part of any visible group, including ours, will never produce spiritual life. Only an invisible connection with the Father can do that. One thing is for sure, though. Anyone who is alive to the Spirit will never be content in a body that is spiritually dead—whether that group calls themselves a church or not."

An involuntary grin spread across Jack's face. "Exactly right," he replied. "I never saw a living hand on a dead body."

The next evening while Jack was preaching, a rock crashed through the parlour window. As shards of glass tinkled to the floor, people jerked their heads around to see what had happened. When the man of the home went to the door, he recognized the voices of two youths in the darkness. Although the rock had thudded harmlessly against the wall behind Jack, it was a harsh reminder of several such incidents that had occurred.

"I feel sorry for these troublemakers," George said later as he offered to pay for the shattered window. "Jesus' harshest criticism was leveled at self-righteous people—templegoers who were absolutely sure they were right. They lived by their own set of man-made rules."

Violence designed to drive out the traveling preachers had increased. Often these disturbances were directed by men who should have known better but who felt their positions were being threatened by those preaching in the pattern of the early apostles. The religious establishment worried that these new preachers would lead away their parishioners. Nobody objected to folks talking about Jesus in a general way. But, ironically, some became very angry when they saw the itinerants actually attempting to live like Jesus—and encouraging others to do the same.

"I guess the lads who threw the rock through the window last week have cronies up in Bruce County," George said solemnly after breakfast one morning. "Laura and Katie have run into a rough patch too. Here, let me read you a few paragraphs from a letter I got yesterday."

Jack's eyebrows shot up. "What kind of trouble?" he said, instantly concerned. Sitting beside the cookstove, he crossed his legs and stared out the window at the wind pummeling snow into a thick spruce.

Burgoyne, Ontario
December 16, 1908

My dearest George,

Thanks for yours of the fifth instant. I surely was glad to hear that the rock didn't hurt anyone. If you'd been sitting on the other side of Jack you might've been injured. I couldn't bear to have anyone hurt you, George. Please be careful!

Katie and I've been stirring the dander of certain local people too. At least our gospel meetings seem to have. Even though some folks support our work with enthusiasm, the opposition is severe. Last evening as I stood speaking to a crowded schoolhouse, I noticed that a few of the listeners had dozed off in the heat. As you know it's a cooker if you're sitting close to the stove. Besides, I feel sorry for men who work a long day in the cold and still attend our meetings at night. You can sympathize with that young man Eutychus who sank into a deep sleep in Paul's meeting and tumbled out the third floor window. Likely, he was trying to get a little cool air to stay awake with all the heat from the lamps.[10]

Coming back to the Burgoyne schoolhouse. I was just finishing when suddenly a sharp explosion like the sound of a shotgun rattled the building. The metal straps that held the stove together snapped and the firebox split apart at the top. As Katie raced down the aisle, two burly men seized blocks of wood and jammed the two halves back together so the red-hot coals and flames wouldn't spill onto the floor. Although the snoozers' eyes flew open, it's not exactly the wake-up call I had intended. I whispered to Katie to see if she wanted to wind it up for the evening. But she's a real brick and carried on as if nothing had happened. She acted as if the incident had been little more than a schoolboy's prank in Elora.

Afterward we discovered that someone had drilled holes in a few blocks of the firewood and poured in gun powder. A wooden plug had been inserted to camouflage the devious act and then the pieces placed back on the pile. I guess we're unsuspecting and a bit naive to boot. Fortunately, no one was hurt and the hooligans haven't caused any further trouble. Still, it's worrisome, and you can bet your boots we'll be checking the wood before each meeting…

George glanced up from the letter. "What kind of dolt would harm two well-meaning women?" he chafed. "That really gets *my* dander up." He paused, his face softening. "But it's all part of trusting God, isn't it?"

"I've come through fire myself," Jack responded thoughtfully. "But now I can see that God's hand was at work—even in the furnace." Getting up from the rocking chair, he sauntered to the window and propped his elbows on the meeting rail. "The psalmist certainly knew God was in control when he wrote, 'Fire and hail; snow and vapours; stormy wind fulfilling His word.'"[11] Jack pondered the whiteness swirling outside. "Even the elements do His bidding."

George nodded. "The weather's hardly fit for giving out invitations this morning," he declared as he put the kettle on the cookstove. "I don't think the landlady'll mind if we brew another pot of tea."

⌐◦

While all of southern Ontario shivered under the unusually cold spell accompanying the days leading up to Christmas, Jack's mood varied between quiet introspection and confident good spirits. The discovery of a mother, a brother, and a sister of his own flesh and blood gave him an invigorated energy, yet at the same time George found his friend strangely absentminded. He smiled to himself when, more than once, he caught Jack checking the December calendar. Long before daylight on the morning of the twenty-fifth, he awakened to see Jack at the window already dressed and squinting out into the uncertain darkness.

An hour later the brakes of the Grand Trunk engine screeched as the train thundered into the London station and black smoke billowed into the frigid blue sky.

"What a beautiful Christmas Day," Jack remarked. "Pristine and white everywhere. The roofs look like Alpine gingerbread cottages laden with a foot of white frosting." The fresh snowfall blanketed the yards and streets and stood like bakers' caps on fence posts and telegraph poles. No sign of life emanated from quiet shop windows, closed for Christmas Day, but among the nestled homes reflections of light winked cheerfully at the two strangers hurrying east along Dundas Street.

"This is a big day for you," George remarked as they plodded out from the railway station toward Stornoway Road. "Are you up to it?"

"Fine as frog's hair," Jack exulted. "My mother wrote to say the family is looking forward to meeting us. And Ma and Pop wrote from Eden Mills to wish me all the best and said some sweets are in the mail." He bounded through the heavy snow with such vigour that George had to hurry to keep up. "What a lucky fellow I am to have two mothers looking after me."

As George and Jack turned in at the Longstaff lane, they could see fresh cutter tracks leading to the horse stable. The white clapboard gleamed in the sunlight and, to Jack, the house offered a gracious charm he had missed on the first visit. Even from the lane, he could see the front steps and veranda had been swept clean and a wreath resplendent with green holly and a bright red ribbon had been mounted on the door. But most of all, his eyes focused on the banner strung between the two central columns bearing the bold words: "Welcome home, Jack and George."

"Looks like we're expected," George observed with dry humour.

The men were still approaching the steps when the door flew open and Miranda bustled onto the veranda, a red apron tied over her long flared skirt and white ruffled bodice. "I'm so thrilled to see you," she squealed, giving Jack a warm motherly hug. Turning, she smiled and extended her hand to George. "Jack's told me what a wonderful friend you are. I'm delighted you can join us. Now come on in and meet the family."

The tantalizing aroma of roasting goose and sage dressing wafted from the kitchen as the two men stepped into the foyer. The burnished oak floor shone and through an arch Jack caught a glimpse of a tall patrician-looking man with round spectacles approaching along the hall. Beside him trotted Lady Jane Grey, her tail raised high in a plume of greeting.

Miranda beamed. "Dwight, I'd like you to meet Jack." The professor's thin clipped moustache curved up at the ends to match his happiness.

"The elusive lad I've heard about for forty years," Jack's host exclaimed, reaching out his hand. "How splendid to meet you at last." His other palm found its way onto Jack's shoulder while his eyes seemed to penetrate the younger man's soul. Introducing George to his mother and Dwight, Jack remembered that, in part at least, he owed this reunion to his companion's practical insistence.

Feeling suddenly vulnerable, Jack shifted to see a round-faced man with oarsman's shoulders, in his mid-thirties, staring back from one of the terracotta wing chairs in the parlour. At his feet, a young woman in a flounced green skirt balanced on a hassock. Stone-faced, the man in the adjoining room appraised the newcomer with cool reserve. Jack turned away and swallowed. Could he bridge the wariness he felt from the man he presumed to be his only brother? Before his eyes, all the illusions he had entertained of a genial reunion melted as certainly as snow on a May morning.

Meanwhile Miranda's shoes danced like sunbeams on the gleaming hardwood. "Come along into the parlour," she urged, beckoning to the men. "I'll introduce you to Lawrence and Eliza."

Led by Lady Jane Grey, the men followed Miranda through the French doors and into the parlour, where a fire crackled in the grate. They waited as Lawrence rose, reluctantly it seemed, to stand beside his beaming wife.

Miranda touched her younger son's elbow. "Jack, I'd like you to meet Lawrence and Eliza."

"How do you do?" Jack shook hands with each of them, searching his brother's face like a sleuth gathering clues. Lawrence, he noted, had the same cheekbones and chin as himself, and the same eyebrows. But it was the eyes that held him at bay. Clearly, his brother was far from welcoming him into the Longstaff family.

Regarding the two men critically, Lawrence gave a terse nod. "Hello," he managed to say. In spite of the obvious stiffness, Miranda's warm brown eyes flitted from face to face as she reveled in the moment, affixing it permanently into the album of her memory.

With all the graciousness of an intercessor, Eliza smiled at the two strangers as her husband dropped back into the wingback chair. "This is a most special Christmas," she acknowledged.

"Thank you for saying so," Jack responded. "I feel the same."

"Now, do make yourselves comfortable," Miranda ordered cheerfully, "while I run upstairs and tell Lucy you've arrived."

Following Dwight's lead, George and Jack each settled into a velour chair near one end of the hearth. In the centre facing the fireplace, Eliza took a place on the davenport sofa while across the room Lawrence buried his face in a copy of yesterday's *London Free Press*.

George glanced around the spacious parlour, taking in the high ceiling framed with an ornate cornice and Corinthian dentils. Several oil portraits, no doubt some of Jack's own kin, gazed sternly from their gold frames. A leather box of Robert Browning's poetical works sat on an oak library table beside a copy of Sir Walter Raleigh's *The British Dominion of the West*.

After heaving a few more pieces of maple into the grate, Dwight drew up an armchair and crossed his long legs. "You have no idea how much this means to Miranda," he confided, slipping his fingers into his vest pockets. "To have all of her children gathered around one table at last."

For a few minutes, the four sat in silence watching the orange-and-blue flames curl along the rough bark, each absorbed in the moment. Jack, a distant look in his eyes, reflected on the evening, shortly after his sixteenth birthday, when, long after his parents had gone to bed, he had stared through the cookstove door wondering about his mother. At the time she had seemed as elusive and ephemeral as the flickering shadows on the roughcast wall behind him. When the logs had collapsed out of sight in the firebox and the embers turned to cinders, he had fallen asleep confused.

The French doors opened and Miranda entered, her arm wrapped around a young woman with square shoulders and the same erect posture as Dwight. "Jack," Miranda said, "I'd like you to meet Lucy, your sister." Dark tresses fell across the young woman's milky complexion and a tiny Limoges watch gleamed from her ivory bodice. She smiled self-consciously and took a few steps forward.

When Jack stood, he could see Lucy's brown eyes welling up as she extended her hand. "Sorry, I'm getting weepy," she choked. "I truly *am* happy to meet you."

Brother and sister stood in front of the glowing fire shyly taking in the subtle similarity in the other's face. An awkward pause intervened until Lucy broke the silence. "I can't imagine not knowing my own mother," she ventured. "It must have been awful."

"I'm just glad I know her now," Jack responded with fervour.

After Dwight had pulled up two more chairs, he beamed proudly at his gathered family. "Jack, would you be willing to tell us a little about your growing up years?" he instigated. "We're all terribly interested."

The reflection of the dancing flames in the professor's eyeglasses offered Jack assurance that this indeed was home and hearth. "I guess I could do that," he responded with the shy smile of a lad.

Fidgeting on the far side of the parlour, Lawrence laid aside his newspaper and moved to join Eliza on the davenport. Behind the young couple's shoulders, Miranda caught her husband's eye, nodding almost imperceptibly as they exchanged a smile.

Eden Mills and the home farm seemed far removed as Jack closed his eyes, allowing his boyhood memories to come forward. When he looked up, Miranda had edged forward and Eliza had drawn her velvet slippers beneath her while Lucy settled onto the hearth rug. In the manner of a gypsy princess, her dark hair tumbled over her ears and the hem of her red dress spread around her in an informal hoop. Their frank, open faces above their silk blouses and colourful skirts warmed Jack's heart and eased the narration. Choosing his words carefully, he told of his first days at school and the collie puppy his parents had gotten him for a playmate. He recounted how he had held the lantern for Pop Gillan to milk the cows, read Henty books, and fished along the Eramosa River. Lastly, he divulged his bewilderment at receiving Miranda's photograph on his sixteenth birthday.

The ice broken, Lucy exchanged stories with Jack about her girlhood. Questions and answers fell fast upon each other as the siblings sought to capture a fuller picture. George sat listening with great interest to the various anecdotes. An anguished smile interpreted Miranda's response as Jack spoke with affection of his adoptive parents, and she wiped away a tiny tear when he reiterated how well he had been cared for.

"How did you meet my mother?" Jack asked the professor.

"It all happened most innocently," Dwight chuckled. "Miranda always pursued an interest in history, and I taught her at the University of Toronto. It was my first time to teach, and she took advantage of my inexperience." He smiled at Miranda. "Let's just say, I fell into the fowler's net."

"Enough of that," Miranda blustered in mock exasperation. "The goose wants carving. Lucy and I'll set things on the table. Eliza, would you be good enough to light the candles?"

When they were all gathered around the dining room table, Dwight looked at Jack. "Miranda tells me that you are a minister. Would you please ask the blessing for us?"

As everyone bowed their heads, Jack began. "Our dear Father, thank You for caring for me as a little boy, for bringing me home to my mother, for gathering us around this table as a family. Most of all Father, we ask that each of us will be brought home safely to You, uniting us in a tie that can never be broken. A place where every kind of human prejudice and pain is banished, where tears are forever wiped away. We appreciate this food that You have so graciously provided as a token of Your continuing care. Please guide our conversation and enrich our love for each other. All we ask is in the name of Jesus. Amen."

When George glanced up, he saw Miranda wiping her eyes with her linen napkin and even Dwight seemed to be touched by the tenderness of the prayer. As he and Jack joined with the others in the bounty of roast goose, cranberry sauce, mashed potatoes and gravy, and an array of autumn vegetables, Dwight asked about their ministry. George left his companion to share most of the details, but he saw Jack smile when Miranda said, "You and George have chosen to spend your lives in a most worthwhile way."

"Will the two of you be together for a number of years?" Lawrence's question carried a distant yet warming curiosity about the men as he passed them the plate of baked squash.

"No," Jack explained. "George and I started out together in Elora, but now we interchange with other brothers as well. In fact, after our summer convention, I'm going to travel with Timothy Stanhope for several months and a man by the name of Percy Ellington will join George."

"Pass George some butter for his parsnips and turnip," Miranda instructed from her place at one end of the table.

As Lucy reached for the butter dish, she asked another question. "I don't suppose there are women missionaries?"

"Actually, two sisters are having meetings in Burgoyne," George said with a smile. "Our fellowship doesn't place any limitation on who the Holy Spirit can work through. In fact, if I might be so bold, one of those sisters looks a lot like you, Lucy."

"Must be very pretty to resemble Lucy," her sister-in-law teased.

"All joking aside," George said seriously, "I've been sitting here thinking about the resemblance ever since dinner started." He turned to his right. "Don't you think so, Jack?"

Jack looked across the table and studied his sister's features. "Yes, you're right," he allowed. "I've been so busy talking that I missed it."

"Where's she from?" Lucy inquired.

George buttered his parsnips. "From Elora."

"Elora?" Lucy's dark eyes widened. "Mother grew up in that area, but I've never been there."

Miranda tucked a stray hair over her ears. "Once I left Belwood and Elora, I never wanted to go back. They held too many painful memories. I threw myself into my studies to avoid them." Her voice dropped. "Lawrence and Lucy never knew why until Jack showed up in November." She took a sip of mulled cider. "Anyway, what's the woman's name?"

"Katie Keats," George replied.

Miranda gave a start. "Katie Keats!" she exclaimed. "That's likely my cousin Mildred's daughter."

Jack sat bolt upright, staring at Miranda. "You mean Katie Keats could be my second cousin?"

Miranda's soft brown eyes reached out to Jack. "Yes, that would be right. Or first cousin once removed, however you look at it. Mildred is on my mother's side. Our mothers were the two Bonnetfield sisters."

Jack remained mystified, still sorting out the details in his mind. "So did they grow up around Belwood?" he questioned. "Or in Elora?"

"The old people farmed in Nichol Township. Pioneered there, in fact."

Jack nodded, eager to hear more about his heritage. "What were your grandparents like?" he asked.

"Grandma Bonnetfield was a sweetheart with a tremendous sense of humour. I think she needed it to put up with Grandpa. The old geezer was as cantankerous as an owl in a rain barrel. And, sad to say, I think both my mother and Mildred got a generous dose of his disposition."

"What you say makes sense. She put Katie out of the house when she became part of our fellowship. She cut off all contact," Jack revealed.

Over a bowl of rich plum pudding smothered with hot brandy sauce, Jack learned that his Grandpa Warmington had played not only the fiddle, but also the guitar, and he had loved to sing. Little by little, Jack traced some of the characteristics that made him the man he was.

George was just finishing his dessert when he crunched down on something hard in his pudding. "My goodness," he mumbled as he extracted a shiny silver coin with his fingers. "This is a first."

Miranda laughed as the family raised their glasses in a toast. "That's an age-old Warmington tradition, brought from Lincolnshire. Whoever finds the coin gets an extra helping of wealth, health, and happiness."

George glanced around at the beaming faces. "I'm already about as wealthy as I can stand," he said with ironic humour, "but to know that my happiness and health are assured into the New Year is marvelous news."

Jack, equally surprised by the coin, nudged George with his elbow. "If the apostle Peter could find a coin in a fish's mouth," he chuckled, "there's no reason you can't find one in a plum pudding."[12]

Miranda winked at George. "Just be glad you didn't discover a ring. That means the finder is going to be married within the year."

George smiled, his face an enigma. "I must admit that certainly would have floored me," he conceded graciously. And although he didn't belabour the subject, he did wonder just where in Burgoyne Laura and Katie might be eating their Christmas dinner.

When the dinner was over, Dwight rose and invited the men to return to the fireside in the parlour. Pleasant conversation interspersed with mugs of hot coffee filled up the afternoon while Lady Jane Grey purred on the hearth, her stomach full of goose trimmings.

After tidying the table and leaving the kitchen and larder in order, Lucy and Eliza bustled into the parlour. "How about a tune on the phonograph?" Lucy suggested brightly. Jack and George watched her crank the handle on the new oak cabinet standing on graceful legs against the far wall. As the lilting sounds of the "Poet and Peasant Overture" emanated from the horn, they looked at each other and grinned broadly.

After an couple of hours in front of the parlour fire, Jack noticed the dwindling daylight. "Well, George, if we're going to catch the seven o'clock train, we need to get a hustle on."

George smiled and rose to his feet. "Thanks for a most delightful day," he said to Miranda as Jack made his way around the family, offering each of them a hug in turn.

"The pleasure's all mine," Miranda said, looking into his pale blue eyes. "The little boy I missed through all the years has been brought back to me with the understanding of a man." She stepped forward to give George a parting embrace. "Jack told me it was your encouragement that helped to get him here. I'm indebted to you."

"It's what anyone would do for his best friend," George said modestly.

Behind him, Lucy gripped Jack in a jocular embrace. "When Mother first told me you were coming for Christmas," she admitted, "I wasn't at all sure I wanted to meet you. Now I can't tear myself away. You must have a slice of that old Warmington charm," she ribbed him, grinning in the same broad way that Jack himself did. "I'm a bit of a nut, but I *am* your sister, so you're stuck with me now."

"It sounds as if we're going to be separated by a few miles," Dwight declared as he shook hands heartily with Jack and George. "But don't forget to come back. Next time plan to stay with us for a few days."

Jack's wistful eyes locked with those of the father bidding him goodbye. At first his words of gratitude would not come. All the fear and frustration wrung from him throughout his long wait for the unknown mother rose up before him and misted his eyes. Then he opened his lips. "Thank you," he said. "It's as if—as if you've brought forth the ring and the robe for the prodigal son..."[13]

"And don't forget the fatted goose," Lawrence interposed wryly.

Saving his final embrace for his mother, Jack looked into her warm, sensitive eyes. "In you, I see myself," he murmured. "The piece of me that was lost has now been found."

"I couldn't have put it better." Drawing him close, Miranda kissed him on the cheek. "The ragged hole in my own heart has finally been healed."

Twenty-Nine

THE SHOOTING
Summer 1911

As the early years of the new century passed, the fellowship flourished. Churches were planted in various parts of the province. Many single brothers and sisters and married couples felt called to forsake all and go forth to preach the gospel by faith. They had been farmers, businessmen, school-teachers, nurses, engineers, harness makers, policemen, lawyers, blacksmiths, seamstresses, maids, soldiers, carpenters, and fishermen. They followed the pattern of Jesus' disciples and God blessed their efforts. Here and there a few were inspired to see faith in action and joined hands in fellowship with them.

Elders—or bishops as they were sometimes called—were appointed as each small church became established. The need to *appoint elders in every city*[1] became more evident as the itinerant preachers spread farther apart. A mature saint, settled in his faith, was vital to shepherd and guide new believers as they were added to each church by the Spirit. Some cities, like Guelph, eventually had several meeting places and several elders.[2]

Lyman Liddle was the elder in the Elora church which met in his and Jessie's home. In Belwood, Walter Merrick was the appointed bishop, even though the friends continued to meet at Robert and Amelia's. The various men chosen for this work were kind and gentle, like fathers, and were of good reputation, self-controlled, and sensible. They were friendly to strangers and able to teach the new believers.[3] They watched tenderly over each of the new saints and tried to give them solid guidance. Like the full-time workers, each elder gave freely of his time in caring for the souls of others. Any love of money would have been a hindrance. Their regular work provided their everyday needs, but their adoration for Christ prompted them to pour out a *labour of love* on His church. The Spirit worked through such devout men, causing the little churches to prosper.

~⊘

Typical of many dedicated elders, Lyman lived a quiet unassuming life. Nevertheless, he was always able to speak comfortably and openly about his faith.[4] Such men enabled the work to carry on as George and Jack and the other itinerants scattered farther afield. The meetings at Lyman and Jessie's home had become well-known throughout Elora.

One afternoon, Frederick, a fellow employee at the Mundell Furniture factory, joined Lyman as they left work. Not one to mince words, Frederick jumped to the point with a question. "Lyman, the Scripture says we need only to believe in Jesus in order to have eternal life. Do you agree?"

Lyman thought for a moment. "Yes, Frederick, I agree with that. But there's one catch: that belief must be real and truly come from the heart."

The two men walked in silence for a few minutes. Finally Lyman spoke again. "Do you recall that high-wire walker who came to Elora a few years ago? He tied a heavy cable around an elm tree on one side of the gorge and pulled it across to a big oak on the other side."

Frederick nodded as he thought back to the lonely cable stretching high over the limestone chasm and the river far below. Many in the village had gathered around the elm tree to witness this folly.

"Do you remember the question that the man asked the crowd before he stepped onto the high wire with his soft shoes?" Lyman asked.

"He asked them if they believed that he could walk across the cable."

"As I recall only a few of the people watching him nodded," Lyman said. "And even those folks didn't seem very sure."

Frederick glanced sideways at his workmate. "I still remember how confident the man seemed when he took his balancing pole and started across the gorge," he said. "Just looking at him made my stomach feel queasy, and by the time he got to the other side and back I had the jitters."

Lyman raised his eyebrows. "I still felt like that on the second attempt when the fellow asked if anyone believed that he could carry that pot of red geraniums across. But almost everybody else seemed convinced. In fact,

I wasn't persuaded until the third crossing when he said, '*Do you believe* I can cross with this wheel barrow?' If the aerialist had asked me directly, I would have said, 'Yes, sir. I believe you can.'"

Frederick recalled standing in the crowd and shouting enthusiastically with the others, "Yes! Yes, you can." Then the high-wire expert had made a fabulous offer. "I'll pay the first person who gets into this wheel barrow twenty dollars." Although twenty dollars was a lot of money—nearly a month's wages for most of them—neither Frederick nor anyone else in the crowd had taken up the offer.

Skirting a pothole, Lyman glanced over at his friend. "Do you remember that when the man said, 'Who believes that I can take *you* across?' everyone seemed to melt away from the elm tree? Not one person had enough faith to trust the tightrope specialist with his life."

"But that's different," Frederick stammered as Lyman's example struck home. "I'm sure many of those people did believe. It's just that they were afraid they might fall and be killed."

"That's the point," Lyman said. "Almost every person I know claims to believe in Jesus to some degree. But do they truly believe in their hearts that He can keep them from falling and take them safely across the river of death? And even if they do, are they willing to step into the simple vehicle of salvation He provides?"

Lyman's fellow employee fell silent as they walked to the next intersection. Before turning down the side street to his home Frederick stopped. "That's a stunning illustration, Lyman. You've certainly given my faith a jab in the ribs."

Walking home to supper that balmy May evening, Lyman considered his own faith. What a call to higher ground it had received when George and Jack had first come to Elora. The fragrant profusion of lilac and grape blossoms reaching over the low stone walls along the street reminded him of the growth in the little body of believers that met in his and Jessie's home.[5] Soon they would all be packing up to make their annual pilgrimage to Wood Creek Farm. To him and Jessie, the convention never became old. Indeed, after three years the pull was more compelling than ever.

During the summer of 1911, George was busy again setting up tables and benches in the dining tent at Wood Creek Farm. Out of the corner of his eye, he noticed a lady making her way through the tent.

"Good day, my name's George." He held out his hand cordially.

"I'd be Mrs. Alec Delaney from Guelph. I just be stopping by to drop off some loaves of soda bread." The woman's voice was surprisingly rich, her brogue lilting. "I be following Jesus of late and gathering at the Butterwick home." Looking into the woman's eyes, George felt unsettled. Her face lingered in his memory. But from where?

Saturday evening after the meeting was over, Mrs. Delaney sat visiting with Priscilla and Ida Rose on the side porch. George and Walter drifted up the steps to join them, relaxing after the events of the day. They were all tired, but it was a happy kind of weariness, and they intended to go to bed soon. The haunting calls of a mourning dove from the peak of the driving shed were soothing after the busy day.

Mrs. Delaney was telling about her life, and how she had come to accept the gospel invitation. She and her husband, Alec, owned a prosperous shop on Wyndham Street that tailored custom-made suits and stylish gowns for wealthy patrons.

When her son had to repeat his third class at Central School, she had inquired among her acquaintances for a tutor. Ashleigh Duffield, the teacher from Puslinch, was recommended and soon she began coming twice a week. Sometimes the Delaneys would invite her to stay for supper.

Gradually, Mrs. Delaney began to see that Ashleigh radiated a remarkable outlook, one that was refreshing in its uniqueness and almost everpresent joy. "It must be wonderful to be having such a relaxed and peaceful nature," she had said one day after noticing the consistent patience Ashleigh accorded her new student.

"Actually, by nature I'm fairly tense and high-strung," Ashleigh had replied, "but I try to let Jesus express His love through me. It brings me peace; I don't know how else to describe it." Ashleigh had gone on to speak about Jesus in the way one speaks about her closest, most intimate friend. She spoke too of the weekly gatherings where she had come to know Jesus. After a few similar conversations, Mrs. Delaney wanted to learn more and eventually asked if she could go along one Thursday evening.

"Before I began to be following Jesus, nary a thing really brought me much satisfaction," Lena Delaney confessed to her new friends. "I'd always be having some faraway goal that I hoped would cheer my soul. But it never did. 'Tis the moments of solitude I now share with Jesus bring me that true peace and satisfaction, so they do." She adjusted her hair pin. "The verse o' the hymn that begins: 'Had I wealth and love in fullest measure,' really touched me heart at that time. It still means a lot to me."

Priscilla balanced her empty mug on the porch railing. "We could sing it now if you'd like."

Lena smiled. "Yes, I'd be liking that very much." Looking off across the dusky meadows, she began to sing softly and the others joined in.

If all things were mine, but not the Saviour,
Were my life worth living for a day?
Could my yearning heart find rest and comfort
In the things that soon must pass away?

Had I wealth and love in fullest measure
And a name revered both far and near,
Yet no hope beyond, no harbour waiting,
Where my storm tossed vessel I could steer.

If I have but Jesus, only Jesus,
Nothing else in all the world beside,
Oh, then, everything is mine in Jesus:
For my needs and more He will provide![6]

The voices died away and the cricket chorus resumed. "There's a matter I've never breathed a word o' with any o' the friends," Mrs. Delaney confided. "But for some queer reason, it seems I should be doing that now."

George listened to her soft Irish lilt amid the night sounds, wondering just what she was going to say next. She paused in the deepening darkness and drew in a breath of summer air, heavy with fragrance.

"It takes me breath away," she began quietly, "to see how God's been at work in me life, always leading me closer to Him. When me son was just a baby, we were in terrible trouble. Me first husband had been killed in a mishap with dynamite and I had nothing. No money, no food. I was so close to freezing and starving that I barely existed from day to day. I would be begging God to help me and I promised to give Him me life in return.

"When I thought I couldn't go on one more day, a total stranger came to our pathetic shack. I know it be sounding unbelievable, but he just turned up, knocked on our door, and offered to help. Can you imagine? He wasn't a big talker, but he was set on helping us. I knew then God had answered me prayer. The young man bought me a sewing machine and fabric so I could be working. Before leaving, he gave me money to feed meself and me baby, and he paid the rent in a warm building 'til spring. When I asked him why he was doing this, he got an odd look on his face. All he said was, 'I hardly know meself. I'm just beginning to follow Jesus.'"

A chill ran up George's backbone as he listened. Despite the lingering heat of the evening, goose bumps stood out on his arms and neck. Would Mrs. Delaney recognize him? Back when he had met her, he had still worn a full beard. But having shaved it off the previous year, and having aged ten years had certainly changed his looks—but was it enough to conceal his identity? George hazarded a glance in the darkness at the sister and felt a sense of awe at the mysterious way God had worked.

So this, he mused, *was Lena.* Those imploring eyes had seemed so familiar. And the soft lilting voice, surely he'd heard it before. Instinctively, George raised a hand to obscure his own sharp features. But her married name, that's what had fooled him. And her face, it had grown fuller, more highly coloured. He had often thought about Lena, but he had never felt the Spirit leading him to visit her again. And now he knew why. God in His wisdom had chosen Ashleigh to water where he had planted.[7]

Lena Delaney continued with her story. "I thought I'd be seeing him again, but I never did. His gift gave me a fresh start, and I worked day and night. For a while I thought about me promise to God, but eventually it faded away, almost entirely. At first me work would be taking the attention, overshadowing me thoughts o' God, and then I met me husband. We would be falling in love and marrying a year later. After a time, we'd saved a down payment to buy our store and apartment from the landlord. I had a family and measure o' prosperity and love, but still I wasn't happy.

"Nary a week went by that I didn't be thinking about the kindness o' that obscure stranger. And then Ashleigh came along. For some reason her gentle spirit reminded me o' him even though I had long forgotten the details o' his face. I still be praying that someday I'll meet that man again. After I met Ashleigh, I felt troubled until I renewed me promise to God."

The listeners sat spellbound by the dramatic account. Although the darkness obscured their faces, George leaned back into the cedar at the edge of the porch. He didn't want anybody to see his tears of happiness. He had sold his farm and gone blindly, blundering, he felt, into other people's lives as he tried to obey God. George had never told anyone the details of how he had dispersed his money. God knew and that was enough. He felt honoured that God had drawn them together on this tranquil evening to give him a glimpse of the fruit of his stumbling obedience. George felt a sense of his Lord's delight and his eyes brimmed with joy.

During the preparations, Bill and Alice had been talking with Stephen and Emily about the fellowship, sharing their thoughts about its direction and the need to remain fresh and sensitive to the Spirit's leading.

The following morning, Bill spoke last from the platform. "Years ago before Alice and I were married, I went to every barn dance I heard about. A friend of mine told me about one a mile or two south of Corwhin. So that evening I tossed my fiddle case behind the seat and we started out for a night's entertainment. We were late leaving, and when we got there we saw dozens of horses and rigs tied up to every rail fence around the barn.

"Once inside, I found a seat on a rough plank beside a young fellow wearing a red plaid shirt. He barely noticed me when I sat down, and he kept on clapping his hands and keeping time with his feet. The fiddler was a seasoned old veteran, and he played 'Turkey in the Straw' while his partner called off for the square dancers swinging around the barn floor.

"A couple of times I tried to shout over the lively beat of the music to the young farmer beside me, but he seemed to ignore me. Finally a woman leaned forward from behind and shouted in my ear. 'That fellow beside you is as deaf as Old Dick!' she said. 'He can't hear a sound.'

"I was dumbfounded. I could hardly believe her as I watched him clapping and swaying in time with the dancing couples on the threshing floor. You see, he was watching the other spectators and carefully imitating them. I'm sure he felt the vibrations coming through the floor and enjoyed a little of the rhythm. But in spite of the appearance of being engrossed, he wasn't able to fully appreciate the vivacious life in the music. He could never truly comprehend what he was missing because he had never experienced more. Since then I've often admired the courage that young fellow had to go out and enjoy his evening. However, spiritual life is entirely different—we each make a conscious choice about hearing."

Bill paused as he rolled up his shirt sleeves. "Today I want to stress that if we're only doing what others are doing and don't really hear the music for ourselves, we're missing the best part. If we find it hard to be Christians and hard to continue, it could be that we're not hearing the symphony of heaven. We must guard against this. Not only for ourselves but for our children growing up in this simple way of Jesus. Tradition could make our religion outward instead of inward. Slavish loyalty to any form of worship, no matter how scriptural, will smother a burning love for Jesus—like the church at Ephesus.[8] The candlestick could be removed and we might not even know it's gone. The next generation could practise the external form of our fellowship, defending it as the only correct way to worship. They may do things in the *right way*, say the *right words*, believe the *right doctrines*. But over-emphasis of any doctrine is apt to make a person hard and sour or exclusive toward those who don't agree with him."

Bill noticed some confused faces as he paused to mop beads of sweat off his forehead. "I'm not minimizing the necessity of sound doctrine," he asserted, "but being a Christian is essentially loving a Person, not believing this or that doctrine or obeying this or that commandment. Instead, our children need to hear the sweet voice of Jesus for themselves, allowing Him to compose the daily melody in their lives."

Bill peered through his thick lenses into the attentive faces. "One of the great weaknesses in some circles is that they talk so much about their church and what the people in the church are doing instead of about the Lord Jesus and what He is doing. This tendency can easily creep in among us as well. If we narrow our outlook, and our main focus is on the activities of the friends and the workers instead of on Jesus, we'll begin to lose His power and life. In reality these two things are only received by hearing His voice, the powerful voice that spoke our universe into existence, the life-giving voice that raised the dead. Most of us can remember feeling that power and experiencing that life when we first began to hear Jesus. But the minute we turn a deaf ear, we'll start to die spiritually. Remember, in every age God's children have mingled with mere professors of Christianity. Instead, may I encourage you to be a possessor in the coming year."

Over lunch Lyman and Jessie talked with Alice about her husband's message. "Bill made some important points," Lyman remarked. "Particularly for those of us with young families."

"I appreciated his warning about using *the right words*," Jessie said. "If we become so casual with our expressions of faith that we use them without meaning them, they'll eventually destroy us."

"Could you give me an example, Jessie?" Alice asked.

Jessie paused, smoothing her wavy blonde hair back over her ears. "Well, we might talk about trusting Jesus when in fact we're frantically trying to solve our problems without Him. What good does it do to extol the virtues of separation from the world if we're busy grabbing everything we can get our hands on? Or to speak eloquently on Sundays about hearing God's voice if in reality we never listen for Him? Sooner or later empty words themselves could become the essence of our spiritual activity. And that meaningless practice will harm our souls and damage our inner life."

"Having a vocabulary of pious expressions may make us feel comfortable and accepted," Lyman concluded. "But it's worthless if we're only parroting a set of lifeless sounds."

"Yes," Alice agreed. "Insincere words could be disastrous for children. We must say what we mean and mean what we say."

Jessie reflected for a minute as she stacked up the empty plates within reach. "Our children could practise all the *right* things that Bill was talking about together with a certain sentimental and emotional feeling in the meetings and be deceived into believing they have spiritual life."

Alice glanced around the yard. "Speaking of children," she said as she stood up from the table, "I'd better check on my youngest and see if she's staying out of mischief."

Lyman's cheeks creased in a playful grin. "There's a heap of tomfoolery afoot." He leaned forward and lowered his voice. "You know Joe and Herman and Hugh all wear false teeth, don't you?"

Alice nodded, her eyebrows crinkling with curiosity.

"After they scrub their teeth with baking soda at night, they soak them in three cups that sit in different places on a board above the washbasins." Lyman took a breath. "Well, last year Hugh got up in the morning before daylight. When he slipped his teeth back in his mouth he certainly made some strange noises. Same thing with Herman."

Alice's eyes widened. "Don't tell me."

"That's right," Lyman insisted. "Some lad must've switched the teeth in the cups after the lights were blown out."

"Doesn't that beat all," Alice exclaimed indignantly. Then, her face darkened. "Surely it wasn't one of mine, was it?"

"No," Lyman said, "I don't think so. I suspected Jimmy too, but he looked me square in the eye and said nope."

"I'd wring their necks if I caught them at a stunt like that," Alice declared as she jumped to her feet. "You just can't be up to all the antics. If I'd have pulled something like that when I was a girl, my father would have given me such a trimming that I wouldn't be able to sit down for a month of Sundays." Alice's face turned red with annoyance. "So what did Hugh say?" she asked.

Lyman smiled. "Oh, you know Hugh. He just laughed and said Joe's teeth fit a lot better than a pair he got from Harold MacQuarrie one time."

"Is that the dentist in Elora?"

Jessie beamed at the joke. "No. The undertaker."

Alice hunched her shoulders and winced. "Thank goodness he wasn't upset," she shuddered, surveying the yard furtively. "I better get a wiggle on and see where that daughter of mine is."

⁓

The conventions at Wood Creek Farm had become an annual celebration of the work of Christ. Each year at preparations, the helpers had made improvements to accommodate the growing crowd. A dining tent was added with long tables so everyone could eat inside, and the summer kitchen was replaced by a primitive cookhouse. The meeting tent, expanded by adding sections to the centre, now seated four hundred people.

George rested his boot on the rail fence as he and Alistair watched the crowd spilling out of the meeting tent into the cool evening air. "We were packed in like sardines tonight," he observed. "What do you think about finding an additional place for a convention in eastern Ontario?"

The golden rays of the sunset revealed concern on Alistair's weathered face. "It might be better to have conventions here over two weekends," he replied. "Friends could choose which one would meet their needs. Besides, that would avoid the time needed to keep another set of tents in shape."

"True," George agreed. "Extra preparations would draw both friends and workers away from their foremost mission—reaching out to others."

"As long as everybody can get here comfortably in less than a day's journey, I think it'll be fine." Alistair paused and leaned back against the gate. "The whole thing needs to remain simple and practical, though."

George hauled out a paper bag. "Nothing elaborate," he concurred as he offered Alistair a sweet. "After all, it's only for four days each year."

⁓

After the 1911 convention, the men took down the big meeting tent and fastened the two end sections together to make a smaller tent. Jack and Timothy had decided to pitch it in settlements where nobody would afford them the use of the school, a hall, or a home for gospel meetings. Whenever they arrived in such a community, they would find a vacant lot and obtain permission from the owner to erect their tent. The brothers moved it from place to place on a wagon rented from a local farmer.

Inside, a canvas curtain divided the tent into two sections. In the main section, wooden benches from the convention were set up for the meetings. Behind the canvas partition, the brothers slept on two cots and stored a few provisions for camping. During the day, one of them always stayed near the tent to guard against pranksters.

One night, Jack and Timothy had undressed and were sound asleep when some young men stole noiselessly to the side walls of the tent. With lightning speed they cut the taut ropes that held the side posts in place and the entire tent collapsed. Startled, the brothers jumped up, only to find their faces swathed in canvas. In the darkness it was unnerving, to say the least. When their confusion subsided and they were able to crawl out to the edge of the canvas, they found nothing but an empty field of footprints.

But this incident was mild compared to the trouble in Gooseberry Hill, where malicious vandals poured kerosene all around the tent before igniting it with a match. Fortunately, Jack awoke to the pungent smell of smoke and saw the brightness as a ring of flames leapt up the canvas walls. He sprang out of bed and shook Timothy awake before dashing out through a gap in the fire. Running to a nearby ditch, he brought back a pail of water to douse the flames. When the neighbours saw the blaze, they sounded the alarm and soon a bucket brigade formed in the darkness. It was only a few minutes before the fire around the smouldering tent was extinguished.

As Jack and Timothy stood staring at the damage, a handful of people gathered around them. "That's the meanest trick I've seen in Gooseberry Hill for a dog's age." Turning at the sound of the indignant voice, the brothers recognized the man as the shoemaker in the settlement.

"It's the devil's own work," another man pronounced solemnly. Suddenly realizing that Jack and Timothy had no place to spend the night, he conferred with his wife. "You men are welcome to stay with us tonight."

"And I've got a little shop you can use for your meetings," the shoemaker offered generously.

In the morning Jack and Timothy saw that one side of the blackened tent had been burned beyond repair. They packed up the rest of the canvas and the benches and stored them in a nearby shed. Still, as they continued their gospel meetings in the cobbler's tiny shop, they soon discovered that their misfortune was drawing many people from the surrounding countryside to hear them. God turned what had appeared to be a calamity into something for His glory. Before the brothers left the village several weeks later, a fledgling church was taking its first steps of faith in the home of the shoemaker and his wife. Over the winter and early spring Jack and Timothy worked missions in a circle of nearby villages, traveling back and forth to the shoemaker's home each Sunday.

Meanwhile in March of 1912, George and Percy were conducting gospel meetings about sixty miles away from the sisters. Many attended, including one cordial woman whose face paid tribute to the courage life demanded of her. Each evening she listened intently, a teenage daughter on either side. Her husband, Red Cafferty, was furious that she would consider leaving their present denomination. He took it as a rejection of himself. One evening after he arrived home hot and dirty from his work at the railway yards, he headed straight to the cabinet where he kept a supply of Little Brown Jug. As the hard rye began to permeate his brain, he growled threateningly, "If you go to that meeting tonight, I'm going to come over to the school and beat that preacher to a pulp."

This was not the first time Mrs. Cafferty had seen her husband this way. She had gotten into the habit of remaining silent when his words began to slur, when his eyes turned hollow and he stared at her as if she were a stranger. But this time it was different.

Mrs. Cafferty drew in a deep breath and straightened her back. "I've never gone against you before," she began, "but this is very important to me and the girls. There's nothing wrong with these meetings. I make you a tasty supper every day before I go. For twenty years straight, it's always been hot and on the table precisely at six o'clock. And I've had the bruises to show for the odd occasion when it wasn't." Her voice trembled as she confronted her husband's icy stare. "The girls and I would be so happy if you came along with us, Red. But if you won't, we're going anyway."

Red clenched his fists and sprang forward as if to strike out, his eyes blazing. Then, as his terrified daughters stared, he slammed down his glass on the table, spilling his drink. Face livid, he wheeled and headed for the door. The sickening sound of a dog yelping could be heard through the closed window. Red's wife had never stood up to him before, especially in front of his daughters.

After his wife had left with the girls, Red slunk into the house and drained the bottle, his fury growing until he shook with rage. He slammed the cupboard door so hard that it broke the antique china plate which had been an heirloom handed down from his wife's grandmother. Red took out his revolver and started to clean the barrel, but after a few minutes he put it away again and buttoned on his wool jerkin.

It was a short walk to the schoolhouse, and he arrived at five minutes to eight. When Percy greeted him at the door, Red stood rubbing his bared knuckles. "Send the preacher man out," he demanded. "Let's see what kind of stuff he's made of."

Recoiling from the heavy smell of liquor on Red's breath and his obvious agitation, Percy hurried back inside. George stroked his narrow face and chin as he mulled over the possibilities. The meeting was almost ready to begin. After a couple of minutes, George sent word that he would be willing to meet Red Cafferty at any other place and time. This strategy, George hoped, would give the man time to cool off.

"Tell him to be at the Globe Hotel tomorrow at twelve o'clock sharp!" Red hissed at Percy. "And tell him to come by himself."

"Yes, sir. That'll be acceptable."

After the meeting Mrs. Cafferty took George and Percy aside. "Please be careful," she warned as she and the girls walked out the door. "He's got a white-hot temper, like a match dropped in a tin of kerosene."

The next day the noon bell tolled slowly as George and Percy stepped into the plush red and gold opulence of the Globe Hotel. "You'd better wait here, Percy," George cautioned, "until I see how the visit goes."

"Let me go in with you, back you up."

"No," George insisted. "I promised to meet him alone. And I intend to keep my word."

Startled at the unyielding tone, Percy sank reluctantly onto a sofa, watching George approach the front desk.

"I've come to meet a man by the name of Red Cafferty."

The clerk looked sharply into the earnest blue eyes of the soft-spoken stranger. *Why on earth,* he wondered, *would somebody like this want to meet that hot-tempered Red Cafferty?* He remembered a fight that Red had instigated in the hotel's bar two years earlier.

"Yes, sir," he replied uneasily, pointing to the rear of the hotel. "Mr. Cafferty's waiting in our private dining room."

George stepped into the elegant room and closed the heavy door softly behind him. In one corner a wiry rawboned man, taller than George, stood sideways, one hand clasping the knotted sinews in his neck. When he wrenched around, his body appeared as taut as a coiled spring, and his bony face crimped into a scowl. The room had the look and feel of premeditated confrontation. Forcing a smile, George looked directly into Red Cafferty's cold, mean eyes. He had just opened his mouth when Red cut him off.

"Are you two fixing to dunk my wife?" he demanded angrily.

George, although taken aback at the obvious rage in the husband's spider-veined face and hardened jaw, replied in a low steady voice, "That's entirely between her and God. But if she asks us to do so, we will."

George's quiet confidence caused something to snap in Red's brain. Distorted notions flashed through his mind like lightning. "What's mine is mine, and no preacher's going to fill my wife's head with nonsense!" he yelled. "Neither you nor anybody else is going to prevent me from being boss in my own house. There ought to be a law against fools like you!"

Stepping back to appraise his opponent, Red's lips curled with disgust. "I could break you in two, you skinny runt," he bellowed. Vile invective poured out of his mouth as he stalked the length of the dining room like a wild beast eyeing the vulnerability of its prey.

Outside, Percy paced in the lobby, struggling to honour George's request but fearful to leave him alone with the embittered man, whose cursing could be heard through the oak doors of the dining room.

The desk clerk assessed Percy apprehensively. "Reckon we should interfere?" he asked. "Red Cafferty's a bad one. Bit a piece clean out of another man's ear during a scuffle one time."

"My friend asked to be alone," Percy protested with regret. "Let's give them another few minutes." Perspiration clung to Percy's forehead and patches of sweat broke out under his heavy coat. One call for help, one sound of despair from George, and he would break the door down with his bare hands. The former stonemason had been no stranger to tavern brawls in his younger days. But this, he decided, was the most frenzied yelling he'd ever heard. He glanced up at the gold hands of the lobby clock. George, he noted, had remained silent, listening to the relentless diatribe for nearly ten minutes. Raking his fingers through his blond hair, he resolved to force an end to George's ordeal. At a quarter after the hour, he would go into the room whether his companion liked it or not.

George's mind scrambled for a way to defuse Red's anger. But even in the instant the thought registered, he caught the fire in the seething eyes and Red's forward lunge, his right fist balled into an iron knot. A moment later Red's hardened knuckles slammed into George's nose with the sickening crunch of cartilage and bone. Raising an arm to ward off the second punishing blow, George stumbled backward, his mind suddenly black and disoriented. Blood spouted from his nostrils and bile rushed into his throat.

"Are you *still* planning to baptize my wife?" Red mocked.

Choking, George opened his mouth, trying to speak.

"Shut up!" Red Cafferty screamed as he jerked a loaded revolver from his pocket. He fired swiftly, spattering blood on the gold ceiling medallion as George's head pitched backward and his body slumped to the floor.

Both Percy and the front desk clerk heard the short flat crack of the shot and raced toward the private dining room. For a split second they hesitated at the door, paralysed at the abject sight of George's body, crumpled like an ambushed soldier. His right arm, a twisted rag, lay wrenched in an ungainly angle beneath his back. A growing pool of blood soaked the white carpet at the base of his head while another oozed over his waxen face and into his eye. George's mouth was open as if to cry, and from it Percy detected short anguished spurts of breath in his windpipe. The acrid smell of gunpowder lingered in the air, but Red Cafferty had disappeared—the back door swinging eerily on its hinges.

"George! George!" Percy cried as he hurled himself at his friend's side, clawing blindly for the napkins, the tablecloth, anything to staunch the bleeding. "Get the doctor," he gasped as he cradled George's head in his trembling hands. The clerk ran shouting, his face white from the sight of blood.

"George, I'm so sorry," Percy moaned as he looked at George's stricken face and drooping eyelids. "Why, why did I ever let you come in here alone?" But George's head only jerked convulsively.

The town's physician came running from his office and ordered the manager and the clerk to help Percy hoist George onto the long table. With a sweep of his stocky arm, the doctor sent the silverware and fine bone china into a clatter at one end. Then he stripped off his coat and vest and rolled his sleeves up to his armbands. His hands were as thick and powerful as a bear cub's, but he moved with dexterity and assurance. When he had examined George, he found that the bullet had penetrated his forehead before exiting through the back of his skull.

"Get me a pan of boiling water," he bawled, crumpling the linen table-cloth into a pad and beginning to cut away a patch of George's hair. When the wound was swabbed and clean, he rummaged in his black bag until he found some antiseptic and smelling salts.

"Blast that Red Cafferty," he swore as he dressed George's wounds. "He's mean as a rattlesnake, but this beats all. He'll get his dues when they string him up from the highest tree." When he had checked George's pulse and blood pressure once again, he shook his head doubtfully and beckoned Percy into a nearby room. "I'm sorry," he said, "but I don't believe there's any hope your friend will survive more than a few hours, at most."

Percy returned tearfully to his companion's side. George lay with his eyes closed, his once gentle face now ashen and slack. Percy gripped George's hand as his friend slipped into deeper unconsciousness. The doctor gave hurried instructions to transport George to the nearby hospital on a makeshift stretcher.

Evening came, and night, and noon again without Percy deserting his post. For two days he hovered at George's side as if Percy himself could hang onto life for George. He barely slept, and when he did it was only to catch a few winks in a chair beside the bed.

The grim news was urgently relayed to each of the churches, and the believers gathered in isolated homes to pray.[9] Even when God wants to aid His children, they knew, He often waits for them to ask before He acts.[10]

Laura and Katie were preparing for a gospel meeting in the afternoon when Alistair arrived, flinging the reins of his horse over the gate post. The instant Laura came to the door and saw Alistair's austere face she knew something was desperately wrong. Looking past him, she could see his dapple gray mare lathered with sweat, its sides heaving.

The blood drained from Laura's face. "Alistair, what is it?"

"Bad news..." he choked. "I'm sorry."

"It's Papa," Laura cried, her face crumpling.

For a moment Alistair stood as if clutching the terrible event to himself. At last overcoming huge resistance, he quietly said, "No, not your papa, Laura. It's George. He's been shot."

Swaying, Laura braced herself against the door frame. "Oh, Alistair, what happened?" she cried. "Is he going to be all right?"

"He's not good, Laura. We just don't know..." His eyes filled with tears and his heart with empathy as he watched Laura struggling to absorb the tragic news. Like a father, Alistair extended his arms to her, afraid she might collapse. Upstairs, Katie heard the familiar voice and hurried down to find Laura weeping softly in Alistair's arms.

"Could we sit down in the parlour?" he suggested. When he had drawn three chairs into a tight circle, he explained how the calamity had happened. When Alistair reached out to each of the dazed sisters, the three friends joined hands and bowed their heads. "Our loving Father," Alistair pleaded. "You know we love George with all our hearts and dearly want to see him restored to health. Please spare his precious life. Nevertheless, we pray that Your will might truly be done. Strengthen each of us in these dire straits and give us the peace that comes by trusting fully in Your great power. We plead in Jesus' name. Amen."

Grasping the presence of tragedy in her home, the landlady, after rapping on the door, bustled in with cold cloths and restorative cups of tea for the little knot of three distressed souls in her parlour.

Neither of the women slept much that night, and before morning they decided to close their mission for the time being. Shortly after daybreak Katie confided their intentions to the landlady, who promised to speak to the teacher and make a sign for the school door. After forcing down a hasty breakfast, the sisters set out immediately to go to George. Never for a moment did Katie question Laura's desperation to see him one last time.

Laura was among the first to arrive at George's bedside, and Katie took her arm as they entered the quiet room that reeked of camphor salts and rubbing alcohol. The sight of his thin frame, expressionless face, and bandaged head tore Laura apart. His skin bore the ivory pallor of a dying man. As she listened to his shallow irregular breathing, she struggled to contain her emotions for George's sake. Taking his limp hand, she squeezed it as she closed her eyes and prayed once again. Silently, she stood by his bed, and before she finished speaking to God, a response seemed to come through the lines of a hymn:

> Dear Jesus, as Thou wilt:
> Tho' seen through many a tear,
> Let not my brightest star of hope
> Grow dim or disappear,
>
> Since Thou on earth hast wept
> And sorrowed oft alone,
> If I must also weep with Thee,
> "My Lord, Thy will be done."[11]

As the days passed, Laura kept constant vigil at George's bedside, alternate tears and smiles playing over her pretty face. "I remember the first time I laid eyes on you in your mother's kitchen," she spoke softly. "You sat opposite me at the table, sneaking glances when you thought I wasn't looking. George, you were a shy and awkward farm boy in those days, but that only added to your charm. So different from my family in Stratford. I loved Mother and Grandma Chapelton, but they had titanic personalities, and I needed to get away for a breath of fresh air. What a treat to find myself your special belle without any expectations. For the first time in my life, I could just be me. You spoiled me at every turn, taking me everywhere. Church picnics, fall fairs, barn raisings, auction sales. And then, to meet Alistair and Priscilla." Laura dabbed her eyes. "And when I came home from Mildmay that first summer, you met me at the station with the white horse and we ate my apple together, laughing and giggling in the meadow.

"Remember when your mother and Cyril came to the convention?" she whispered. "Afterward, as we stood under the Big Dipper, you said you felt grateful that you didn't have to leave me and your family behind. As it turns out, you just had to wait for us to catch up, according to God's timing. If He is calling you to be with Him now, George, you can go knowing that you're not leaving us behind. You're just going ahead. We'll catch up later." She leaned forward and kissed him on the cheek.

George showed no signs that he heard, but Laura knew in her heart that he understood. As she sat through endless hours, his hand clasped in hers, Laura marveled at the way God had woven the strands of their lives into such a tight and magnificent tapestry.

For days George's life hung in the balance, but as the first crocuses pushed up through the melting snow, he miraculously began to gain some strength. The lead bullet had ploughed a clean shaft between the lobes of his brain. A hair's breadth either way and George would have died instantly.

One uncommonly muggy day in April, George lay on the hospital bed, perspiration dripping off his forehead as Laura read aloud from the stack of letters accumulated over the weeks of his affliction. Among the pile of inspiring letters from distant friends and workers were numerous envelopes from Mrs. Applebee, encouraging and cajoling this adopted nephew of hers in the fight for his life. George smiled as he listened, mindful of Mrs. Applebee's unflagging love for the gospel. And for him…

After a time Laura laid aside the mail and began to reminisce. "George, do you remember the hot day in 1900 when you broke the news to me that we'd never be married, you and I? It was at Doyle's Mill and the August wildflowers were all around us, so lavish and beautiful."

A weak smile flickered across George's pallid face as he nodded.

"I can still recall my first flush of anger," Laura continued. "But even more clearly, I remember the anguish I felt when I realized that you were suffering so much more than I. Even as a young woman, I recognized the nobility in your dedication to God's work and that saved me from being bitter, then or any time afterward."

George's tousled head twisted on the damp pillow as his eyes sought out Laura's face. Shaping his words slowly and breathlessly, he simply sighed, "Thank you, my girl."

Beautiful clear eyes sparkled in Laura's sensitive features as she eased her fingers under George's neck and slipped a fresh towel into place. "I must confess that sometimes when I hear the laughter of a child or look on the sweet face of a sleeping infant, I feel a pang for the life any woman hopes for. There have even been times when I've overheard a husband and wife whispering or showing their affection for each other that I felt a momentary ache for the life we might have had."

George's pale blue eyes misted as they rested on the long-loved face before him. "I've felt exactly the same feelings," he whispered hoarsely as he squeezed her slender hand.

"But George, at no time did I ever consider leaving the harvest field. Although a single life dedicated to God's service would never have been my first choice, I'm thankful that God has blessed me with a life fuller and more abundant than any course I could have charted on my own. You've given me a gift far greater than marriage."

When Laura bent forward to give him a kiss, his feeble arms found their way around her neck and drew her ear to his lips. "I love you," he murmured as he kissed her. "I'll always be yours no matter where I am."

For the next two months, George lay in the cottage hospital and recuperated in what often seemed to be an altered state of reality. The various experiences that had befallen him and his fellow workers tumbled in his memory, reminding him of Paul's words:

> But in all things approving ourselves as the ministers of God, in much patience, in afflictions, in necessities, in distresses, in stripes, in imprisonments, in tumults, in labours, in watchings, in fastings; by pureness, by knowledge, by longsuffering, by

kindness, by the Holy Ghost, by love unfeigned, by the word
of truth, by the power of God, by the armour of righteousness
on the right hand and on the left, by honour and dishonour,
by evil report and good report: as deceivers, and yet true; as
unknown, and yet well known; as dying, and, behold, we live;
as chastened, and not killed; as sorrowful, yet alway rejoicing;
as poor, yet making many rich; as having nothing, and yet possessing all things.[12]

Lying there and thinking of these words, George knew that he and the
others were following in Paul's footsteps—through both glory and dishonour.
Although he, too, had suffered a beating, he had, nevertheless, not been
killed, and now his body, like an able soldier, was reconstituting itself. *The
only lingering remnants of my ordeal are occasional memory lapses and*, he thought
wryly, *a nose as crooked as a dog's hind leg.*

At the trial that followed, Red Cafferty was convicted of attempted
murder and sentenced to prison for twelve years. For a long time George
felt distressed about Red, wondering if he could have handled the situation differently. Perhaps he might have saved the man from trickling his
life away behind bars. George often prayed for Red, and when he was fully
recovered, even traveled a considerable distance to visit him in the federal
penitentiary. But Red refused to leave his cell and come to the visitor's room.
Eventually, George could do no more and he relinquished the matter to
Jesus' hands.

Thirty

FAREWELL TO A MOTHER IN ISRAEL
Summer 1912

After such an eventful year, Laura and Katie were relieved and delighted to return to Wood Creek Farm to help prepare for the convention in 1912. One afternoon Katie rode into town with Alistair to meet George and Percy's train. She was thrilled to see Percy after all this time of exchanging letters. He had written almost every other week—details of George's recovery, their missions, poems, anecdotes, weather predictions—all of which he infused with his own particular humour and kindness.

When George stepped out onto the platform alone, her smile dropped. Wasn't Percy coming too? Then a minute later Percy's blond head and strapping frame came bounding down the steps of the train car. He flashed her a radiant smile as he shouldered his travel bag. Katie's heart pounded so loudly that she could almost imagine Alistair noticing it too. If he had asked for an explanation, she would have put it down to overexertion; same with the flushed cheeks. It would have been a good answer and covered everything except the brightness of her eyes.

But Alistair, like a man in a trance, stood motionless in the swirling cloud of steam. At the sight of George's sallow face he leaped forward with the breathless emotion that breaks a man. "George, you've surely come along since your ordeal," he exclaimed as he planted his hands on George's shoulders. He glanced at George's crooked nose and at the purplish scar beneath the peak of his tweed cap. "When Priscilla and I saw you right after the mishap, I wondered if you'd ever come right. It's a downright miracle to have you back safe and sound." Then he threw his arms around George before turning to greet Percy.

George smiled while Percy hugged both Alistair and Katie before heading back to the democrat. "You don't mind if I ride in the front with Alistair, do you?" George asked, his face perfectly straight. All of the mail between Percy and Katie over the past year had not gone unnoticed by the recovering patient.

"Oh, I reckon that would be all right," Percy assented with mock disappointment. "You're the oldest, after all." He winked at Katie as he offered to help her into the rear seat. Then he took his place beside her. "Is it all right if we travel together, Katie?" The sparkle in her eyes was her only answer, but in that brief exchange something lifelong was settled.

When Alistair reached around to show George a box of new tent pegs sitting on the floor, he saw that Percy and Katie were holding hands. He caught himself staring, and a grin spread across his face. "Oh, excuse me," he chuckled. "I'm always the last to catch on."

Over the next few days, Percy and Katie seemed to find themselves often with Stephen and Emily. What was it like, they wanted to know, to be married and be traveling? Nothing they learned dissuaded them from wanting to marry and yet continue preaching the gospel. Of course they wished to raise a family, but the call to labour in the Master's harvest field was uppermost in their hearts.

One evening after the hammers and saws were put away and the dishes washed, the couples wandered over to the benches under the apple blossoms. "I'm sure I've read what Paul wrote to the church in Corinth a dozen times," Percy asserted. "But would you hear me out one more time?"

Stephen leaned back, muscular elbows on the back of the bench, legs crossed. "Go ahead," he encouraged.

Thumbing through his Bible until he found his spot, Percy began: "Well, Paul maintains here that he has the right to take along a believing wife, just as the other apostles, the brothers of the Lord, and Peter were doing."[1] He glanced up at Katie. "That begs the question. Why *did* Paul prefer to remain single?"

Stephen pouted out his lips, deep in thought. "Perhaps it was because of the rugged conditions he encountered as a pioneer of the gospel. Maybe he felt that he could travel faster and endure more difficult circumstances with another brother. But by stressing that he, too, had the right to take along a believing wife, Paul confirmed that this is a personal preference."

"There are some minor disadvantages," Emily added, "but as the number of churches grows and the pioneering becomes less oppressive, we can see that there will be some real advantages for a few of the workers to be married. We can understand and talk to married couples about certain problems that single brothers or sisters haven't experienced firsthand. We can actually demonstrate the oneness between Christ and His bride."

The next morning, as Percy and Jack were painting some benches for the meeting tent, they thrashed out the topic of marriage. "History tells us that seven or eight of the original eleven apostles were married," Jack offered. "I'm very glad that you and Katie are not thinking of leaving the work—the harvest is great and the workers are few."

When Katie appeared with three cups of tea and some muffins on a tray, Jack laid his paint brush across the top of the can and settled back on an unpainted bench. "Take a load off your feet, old man," he invited. "The work'll wait for a few minutes."

As the three sat laughing and talking, Jack winked at his painting partner. "You're a lucky man, Percy. This lass comes from a long line of fine stock. Imported from Elora."

"Yep," Percy chuckled. "But there's a black sheep cousin in every family, isn't there?"

Katie made a mock gesture of defiance as she placed the empty cups on her tray. "I could spend all afternoon out here, but there's a mountain of washing to do up before dinner. So now that I've got the two men of my life fed and watered, I'd better quit killing time."

Jack's eyes twinkled as he pried open another can of green paint. "Malachi says the best way to kill time is to work it to death."

After supper that evening as they walked hand in hand along the back lane, Percy and Katie agreed there was no reason they could not marry and still continue in the ministry—providing they were led by the Spirit in both.

About two weeks later, Timothy was sitting across the breakfast table from Percy and Katie. "Well, weddings are in the air, so when is it going to happen?" he joked. But even Timothy was surprised at Percy's answer.

"Today, if I had my way," Percy announced solemnly. He heard Katie give a startled gasp beside him. "Or perhaps next week," he added with a smirk. Then he put his arm around his bride-to-be and gave her a kiss that echoed all along the table and reddened her already ruddy cheeks.

On the third Saturday of June, their marriage was celebrated with the friends at Wood Creek Farm. At Percy's request the dining tables were set up in the orchard where the meeting tent would soon be pitched. When the women had spread the lace and linen tablecloths, pulled up a variety of wicker chairs, and laid out all manner of delicacies, the scene resembled a Renoir painting. Under the arching boughs, summer sunshine flickered across the lawns, sparkling on the china and silver and lighting up the bouquets of wild pink roses the children had gathered in the hedgerows.

As Percy gazed around at the lovingly prepared feast and listened to the heartfelt tributes to his bride, he drew Katie toward him, his eyes misting over. "I'm overwhelmed with everyone's generosity," he confessed. "I want to thank each of you, workers and friends alike, for pulling together and arranging such a special day for Katie and me."

Katie turned to look up into Percy's glowing face. "This morning when Laura and George went with us," she said, "the justice of the peace asked if our family was throwing a wedding dinner for us." Katie dissolved into gleeful laughter. "The poor man had no idea just how far this family can throw a dinner."

As the couple, now man and wife, trailed across the lawn to their borrowed buggy, a white cloud of cabbage butterflies rose from the young wheat beside the lane and appeared to follow them like a hovering benediction. Passing among the well-wishers gathered around the buggy, Katie held out her arms and embraced Laura. "I'm very fortunate," she acknowledged. "In you I've gained a sister and a soul mate, and in Percy, a…"

As Katie struggled to choose the right words, Susan cut in. "Better give it a little time, dearie. Me awd mother always said, 'You never really knows a man 'til you've lived a spell with 'im,' so she did." Unlinking her arm from Joe's, Susan winked at Percy. "Sayin's true o' livin' wi' a woman, too, I 'spect."

When she turned to glance at Joe, he reached out and took her hand. "Susan's as sweet as a bushel of sugar plums," he said mildly.

When Joe fingered a brass key out of his pocket, Susan stepped forward to hand it to Percy. "Now you two have t' time o' yer life in our 'umble nest. Joe and ah are fancyin' a couple nights 'ere at Priscilla's."

~⌒~

During the convention that year, George often sensed Lena Delaney's gaze following him as he helped people to their seats or carried water to the kitchen. She seemed to be struggling to stitch some elusive memory into place with the intense concentration she used when finishing the seams of a gentleman's suit.

George liked to see Patrick's enthusiasm as the boy laughed and talked with the other young people or helped around the kitchen. The thirteen-year-old showed the robust handsomeness that his childhood face had promised. The black hair in a curling mop over his ears and the eyes, blue as Galway Bay, showed his physical inheritance from his long-dead father. It gave George a good feeling to know that he had played a small part in shaping the lad's life. And yet he was still a little concerned that his good deed might be exposed here among his friends.

On Saturday evening just before bedtime, George was spreading jam on toast at a long table in the dining tent when Lena approached and sat opposite him. "It's truly enjoying the convention this year, I am," she said. "And I'm mercifully glad that Patrick has been choosing to follow Jesus." But even as she talked about her family and her faith, George felt her eyes searching his face. Lena glanced around, and then suddenly she leaned forward and lowered her voice. "'Twas *you*, wasn't it, George?"

George tingled with the same feeling he'd had as a child when he snitched hot oatmeal cookies that his mother had left to cool on the windowsill. He blushed and looked down at his toast, half expecting to see the ill-gotten treats. But this time it wasn't guilt he felt: It was his deep sense of humility.

"Yes, Lena, it was me," he conceded quietly. "But, you know, in a way it wasn't me. It was the Spirit of Christ finally able to work…"

Lena accepted his answer with a smile.

"George, you'll be havin' no idea at all how you changed me life. Without you, I might have swept up me hearth and died with me boy. Every day I had been praying desperately, 'God, help me.' Although it wasn't much of a prayer, it brought quite an answer. What you did would renew me faith in God. And even though I didn't be responding to His call for years, I had taken your measure and was never forgetting you. Now, I know it was Jesus I saw in you." When George looked up into Lena's face, her eyes were glistening.

"Then, when the time was right, God brought Ashleigh Duffield. Not only to be teaching me son, but me as well," she continued. "In her, I saw you and I saw Him. I can't thank you enough, but I know God will be rewarding you far beyond anything I could ever do." Lena took his hand in both of hers and wouldn't let go. "You wouldn't be telling me if I hadn't figured it out meself, would you?"

George shrugged with an awkward grin. "Likely not."

Before Lena walked away through the night to her sleeping quarters, she promised to keep their secret. George felt odd, pleased in a way that she had found out, and yet strangely self-conscious to be caught in an act of goodness. But mostly he thanked God for using him to make a difference in somebody's destiny. It was both humbling and deeply satisfying. That death of self, of giving away his money, had, in an unexpected way, given him back himself—a better man than he could have ever hoped for.

But there were times when the converse was true, when George felt unable to provide what it was that people sought from him. In a way this, too, was a small death of self. In the spring of 1913, he received a letter from Wilbur and Florence Stonehouse, the couple in Belwood who had heard the gospel through his and Jack's ministry. They were locked in a disagreement over their oldest son, who was carousing with the village lads and getting into scrapes with the Belwood constabulary. Wilbur wanted to put the wayward son out until he learned to honour the rules of their home, while Florence argued for going the second mile, showing him love and compassion. In writing to George, they once again outlined the painful issue festering between them. "We'll take your decision in the matter as being God's will for us—the final verdict, whatever it is."

The letter burned in George's heart as he prayed and turned the question over. Others in the itinerant ministry had also had requests for decisions in certain matters: marriage troubles, money problems, family squabbles, and inheritance disputes, to name a few.[2] The principle behind providing answers to such questions was of utmost concern to George.

One evening he invited Jack to his room. "I received a letter a few days ago from Wilbur and Florence. Charlie, their eldest, is kicking up his heels again—drinking with the local rascals and dragging in during the wee hours. The folks are between a rock and hard place."

"Is Florence still wanting to give Charlie a little grace?" Jack asked.

"She is," George acknowledged. "She's afraid he'll fall in with a worse crowd if he's away from home. Wilbur, on the other hand, says that a God-fearing home has rules that need to be obeyed. Especially since Charlie has younger brothers who are watching him. Wilbur feels the lad needs to toe the line or get out." George flexed his fingers. "The problem is that they want *me* to decide for them. And I just can't do that."

Jack's brown eyes tensed. "Don't you think it's good to guide them?"

"Guidance, yes. Every saint or worker, settled in home life or itinerant, has a responsibility to offer safe counsel to his brother or sister."

Jack looked puzzled. "So what's the problem then?"

"Advice is one thing," George said. "But making a firm decision for someone else is another thing entirely. Most of us in this simple way of Christ have come from traditional churches. There, religious leaders are sometimes willing to make the type of decision they're expecting of me."

"Decisions!" Jack whistled sharply. "Over the centuries, some leaders not only made *definite* decisions; they exercised absolute control. The horrors of the Inquisition are a testimony to that!"

"Saints can't help but appreciate that workers have laid aside the natural burdens of life in order to follow God's leading into the harvest field. But that doesn't make us leaders or decision makers. Just because we've forfeited position and status, or because we accept no salary, or because we possess no formal religious education isn't enough to prevent a worker from developing the authoritarian perspective of the high priest."[3]

"So you're saying," Jack concluded, "that if those of us in the ministry ever think we're able to make better choices for others or even that we have the ultimate responsibility for managing the church, we've become modern day high priests."

George nodded. "It unnerves me to think just how easy it would be to usurp the place in the body belonging to Christ, and to Christ alone."

Jack's eyes developed a faraway look. "Remember when we first sat around Alistair's table and marveled at being an equal brotherhood of believers?[4] We boasted that we'd put hierarchy and control out the front door forever. And now if we aren't careful, it'll slip in the back door in the form of ourselves. If an attitude of loving guidance shifts to one of control, it must be banished from the life of a servant of God."

"But it can happen so innocently," George cautioned. "Folks like Wilbur and Florence ask you to make a decision, and then with the most noble of intentions you're drawn in, sincerely believing you're doing good. But it's just the thin edge of the wedge. Power is dangerous, Jack."

"So how are you going to respond to Wilbur and Florence?"

George got up and looked out his bedroom window. "I'll write and assure them that we love them deeply and that I'll visit on my way to convention preparations in a couple of weeks."

~

The Belwood station seemed sweetly nostalgic as George stepped down from the train and looked across the Grand River, its ripples twinkling in the May sunshine. *It's too bad*, he thought, *that I won't have time to spend a night with the Merricks and the Hunters this time.* But preparations at Wood Creek Farm were waiting, and he would see them all in a month's time. Picking up his travel bag, he headed for the Stonehouse farm south of the village.

That evening over beef stew and biscuits, George looked into the bright faces of the six young people around the table and prayed, at least for their sake, that he could offer a spirit of reconciliation that might help their parents draw together again. Even Charlie looked freshly scrubbed and chatted easily with George, seemingly oblivious of the reason for his visit. After a vigorous game of baseball with two of the lads, George said goodnight to them and moved into the parlour to visit with their parents.

Undercurrents of dissension melted into softer lines as the three talked late into the evening. The wedge their son had driven between them eased a little, and Florence and Wilbur were able to speak more civilly to each other and to hear what the other had to say.

Looking into the two tired faces, George explained tactfully why he couldn't make a decision for them. "In this way of love, you'll grow strongest by learning to depend on the Father for every decision, not on the ministry. He knows each of our futures—including Charlie's." He turned to Wilbur. "How's the lad's work around the farm?"

Wilbur scowled. "Oh, that part's fine. He's a good worker, all right."

"And up in time in the morning for chores?"

"Well, no hitch there." Wilbur pursed his lips. "He cut four acres of hay before dinner today."

George leaned forward. "You've a cabin down on the second place, if I recall. Have you considered giving him a little space so he doesn't upset things here? But still work at home and pull up at Florence's table."

Florence caught her husband's eye. "I'd be willing to spruce it up a bit," she offered, her voice tentative.

"Might work out," Wilbur allowed reluctantly.

"A lot of young fellows make mistakes when they're just lads," George reminded him. "But they mostly turn out all right. Someday, Charlie'll be one of those."

Wilbur looked sheepish. "Reckon, I was a bit of a roustabout in my day too," he admitted. "The apple don't fall far from the tree."

George's face reflected the lamp light. "In the meantime, God will give you strength to get through it. I'd urge you to pray earnestly. Ask for answers and they will definitely be given—but in His time.[5] After all, revelation from God is the final court of appeal for all His children."

For several minutes the three sat quietly, each in their own thoughts. "Speaking of leaning on the ministry," George went on, "I visited one little church and discovered that a workmate of one of the saints had asked about our fellowship. It saddened me that our friend couldn't give even a simple account of his faith and felt that only workers are empowered to share the gospel. I worry when friends depend on workers in questions of doctrine instead of trusting the Spirit and delving into God's Word for themselves."

Wilbur clasped his rough hands. "Yes, I can see the need of being exercised in these things of the heart." Before blowing out the light he turned to George. "Thank you for coming," he said solemnly. "I know we'll need to work this out between ourselves and God. But you've lifted my eyes to a brighter, grander view. Maybe Charlie'll come right after all."

George grinned. "He might even be in the work with me someday."

Florence wiped away a tear and reached out to join hands with her husband and George as they bowed their heads. Pausing for a minute, George offered a short prayer thanking God for the restorative peace that only He could give.

After spending another day with Wilbur and Florence, George stopped to visit Mrs. Applebee. Although she still radiated her usual warmth, the old widow looked thinner and more frail than George had ever seen her, and she seemed less steady on her feet as he helped her in the kitchen. The pair spent the evening reminiscing about the early days of their friendship and the work that the friends and workers had seen God accomplish since then.

As George took his lamp and started up the stairs, Mrs. Applebee's voice, thin and poignant, followed him. "We're farther along on the road to Emmaus than we were that first evening you and Jack put your feet under my table."

George's footsteps halted and he leaned over the bannister. "Yes, Mrs. Applebee, I feel that in my heart too. Goodnight now." As he lay in the familiar bedroom, George's mind went back, as if often did, to the beginning of his ministry in Elora. *What*, he wondered, *would have happened if Jack and I had been shut out of the village in our first mission?* But they hadn't. God had provided for His fledgling messengers beyond their most optimistic expectations.

Not much had changed, George noticed the next morning, in the sumptuous spread Mrs. Applebee laid out for him at breakfast. "I'll see you with the others in July," she promised cheerily as she embraced him at the picket gate. "There's not another place on earth I'd rather be."

An hour later, settling back in the train coach, George watched the unending stream of fields and full-leafed woods scroll past his window. He smiled to himself, looking forward to times of hearty fellowship with the brothers and sisters in their common goal. As the Guelph station drew near, he began to scan the platform for Alistair's tall lean frame.

And although Mrs. Applebee arrived as she had predicted with the rest of the Elora church in July 1913, her face was not among them the following year. The absence of her cheerful voice and smiling face produced a deep melancholy among the friends who had grown to love her so much. Two weeks before the convention, Evelyn had caught a chill working in her garden during a damp spell. Trying to shake it, she inhaled steam steeped with eucalyptus oil and took a balsam of liverwort tonic, but when she suffered a turn for the worse, the doctor ordered strict bed rest. All the resources of her body could not prevail against the pneumonia that was setting in. The friends in Elora responded like the family she never had.

In recent years Evelyn had kept herself busy, always dropping off a hot meal if someone in Elora was sick, knitting socks or mittens for a child's birthday, or offering a kind word in a difficult situation. Like Dorcas of long ago,[6] anyone who needed warm clothing could count on Evelyn's practical love. She kept in touch with the traveling ministers, especially George and Jack to whom she wrote weekly. Anytime she heard about a saint with a special need, she posted a short note of encouragement and a small gift to help them. She received letters too—a whole box of them—from friends and workers, sharing news of missions and activities of the little churches.

And her generosity didn't stop with those who were part of the *household of faith*.[7] Evelyn reached out in the same kind way to her neighbours or anyone else who crossed her path.[8]

When the convention time arrived, Harriet Chambers stayed behind to be with Evelyn. Late Friday evening after the meeting, George, Jack, and Herb brought Katie and Jessie back to Elora to nurse Mrs. Applebee. Lyman and the young people in their family were to follow later on the Sunday evening train. George and his companions had driven all Friday evening with Alistair's fast dapple gray and arrived in the small hours of the morning. When the tired horse finally trotted up Evelyn's darkened street, a lonely candle was burning in the familiar Gothic window as Harriet sat at the bedside of her worsening patient. Mrs. Applebee lay pale and inert under the thin Dresden-plate quilt she had made as a bride.

In the morning Herb and Harriet returned to Wood Creek Farm, but George and Jack could not bear to leave the first old saint who, thirteen years earlier, had so graciously welcomed two complete strangers into her home. George bent over Mrs. Applebee with tender solicitude. How had their capable, bustling hostess shrunk into this shadow of an old lady whose wedding ring sparkled on her thin blue-veined hand?

On Saturday afternoon, George and Jack took turns sitting at Mrs. Applebee's bedside. "I'm so thankful you boys brought the gospel to Elora," she whispered to Jack in a feeble voice. "Just knowing Jesus loves me and is waiting for me means everything now. The joy of living for Him as part of this church has made these last years the best ones of my life."

Jack reached out and squeezed her wrinkled hand. "You've been a mother in Israel[9] to all of us," he replied in a husky voice.

No matter Evelyn's lack of relatives, her friends were adamant that she would not die alone. They loved her as much as they loved their own families, and they intended to save her from the solitary death that some endure when family and friends are unable to confront suffering or to accept death themselves.

Saturday dragged on into Sunday, and Mrs. Applebee weakened. The Elora friends hurried home from the convention, and one by one, they came to take turns sitting with her and holding her hand. She had made it clear that she didn't want the doctor to try to extend her natural life even by a few days. Mrs. Applebee had a serenity about her as she approached death, and she did not hesitate to speak openly about it. "Why should I try to hang on to an old body that's impossible to keep," she asked Jessie one evening, "when I can go forward to a new one that's impossible to lose?"

As Evelyn's clarity and wisdom broke through, Jessie bent over and kissed the old lady's hand. "I admire your faith, Evelyn," she whispered.

People quietly came and went from Mrs. Applebee's, doing what they could to make her comfortable. The neighbours watched the comings and goings and learned firsthand of the love that existed among the little church. What had at one time seemed to some as nothing more than a peculiar religion now took on a definable shape, a particular beauty.

Swishing her lace curtains to and fro at the arrival and departure of each visitor, Mrs. Quinn, the widow across the street, pondered her own life and inevitable death. *Who do I have*, she brooded, *as loves me like these folks loves Evelyn?* But she couldn't bear the answer.

Although many of Evelyn's visitors shed hidden tears as her health diminished, Evelyn herself remained positive and at peace. Early Tuesday, in the lonely hours of the morning, she whispered to George, "I'm looking forward to seeing my Lord face-to-face." A soft smile crossed her face. "I can't imagine what life would have been without Jesus. And this family has been so wonderful, every one of you.

"I've been thinking of Harold MacQuarrie too. When you and Lyman go to arrange my funeral, please tell him that I lost a little boy long before Harold was born. He was the image of Wilson. Tell him it wounded me more than anything else in my life. And that I agonized with God. And he can too. Even though Harold's been unpredictable at times, George, I know God is still trying to soften his heart. His journey isn't over yet, and when it is…" Evelyn's voice struggled with the words. "Remind him, there'll be his children waiting for him too…"

George's heart ached for the secret grief that Mrs. Applebee had borne alone since her husband's death.

That Wednesday after supper was over, a little group assembled in Mrs. Applebee's bedroom. The evening gathered in, serene and still, as the sun cast long shadows across the faded quilt. As Katie sat soothing Evelyn's hair away from her forehead, George watched the progress of an ant struggling to cross the wide cracks in the plank floor. *Life might hold valleys of intense struggle and unavoidable trials*, he thought to himself. *It might be long and difficult. But it's also very purposeful—an eternal reason and power behind its beginning and its end.*

Only the mantel clock punctuated the stillness, ticking from its place on Mrs. Applebee's bureau. Evelyn lay looking out the window at the orange glow of the setting sun as Jack recited the Twenty-third Psalm. When he came to the final line, "And I will dwell in the house of the LORD forever," his tone deepened, warm with affirmation. As stillness fell over the room, he heard Evelyn's voice from the pillow, "Would you sing that hymn for me?"

"Which hymn, Mrs. Applebee?" he asked softly.

The response came in a whisper. "Katie knows the one I want."

Katie began to sing and the others joined in. Evelyn had been told that this hymn had been written during the final week of the composer's life:

> Abide with me, fast falls the eventide;
> The darkness deepens—Lord, with me abide;
> When other helpers fail and comforts flee,
> Help of the helpless, O abide with me!
>
> Swift to its close ebbs out life's little day;
> Earth's joys grow dim, its glories pass away;
> Change and decay in all around I see;
> O Thou, who changest not, abide with me!
>
> I fear no foe with Thee at hand to bless;
> Ills have no weight and tears no bitterness;
> Where is death's sting? where, grave, thy victory?
> I triumph still if Thou abide with me![10]

George watched Mrs. Applebee's lips as they faintly formed the shape of each word. She had no strength to sing, but every phrase carried special meaning to her now. Just as they finished singing the last words, they heard the grandfather clock strike nine times in the downstairs hall.

Evelyn's aged body could not withstand the disease that attacked her lungs. The loss of her cough reflex prevented her from clearing the phlegm rattling in her windpipe with every breath. Although she drifted in and out of consciousness and grew steadily weaker, she remained serene and calm.

A few minutes after midnight on Thursday, she murmured hoarsely to Jessie, her eyelids closed, "I'm ready to go now." Her hope did not come because she expected any relief from her present distress, but because she looked forward to being with God. After that, Evelyn became quiet and tranquil, comatose most of the next day. By late afternoon, she had not spoken but George and Harriet believed she could still hear their voices.

Harriet was speaking softly, telling her how much her life had meant to them when all at once Evelyn's face broke into a wide, glowing smile. It was as if, through closed eyes, she suddenly witnessed some glorious sight. "Whatever she saw must have been beautiful," Harriet would say later. "Death draws away a curtain that hides infinite wonders."[11]

A moment later Evelyn was gone. Like a captive dove released from its confining cage, her spirit flew free to her Lord and home. "Go, Evelyn," George whispered softly. "Your Father is waiting for His child."

Years later each of the believers could still recall the exact place where they had been when they first heard of Evelyn Applebee's death. Malachi was cutting burdocks with a scythe when Bill came to the field to break the news. The tenderhearted old bachelor broke down and wept, his tears washing streaks down his hot dusty face. "The young may die, but the old must," he groaned, trying to comfort himself as he pulled out his handkerchief and blew his nose.

A few of Mr. Applebee's surviving acquaintances and former legal clients attended the funeral. Word had spread quickly of the family who had stayed around the clock with his old widow. Friends and workers who could travel the distance came to pay their last respects and to support the Elora friends in their grief.

The mourners were gathering in Mrs. Applebee's own parlour as the two o'clock sunshine filtered in and illuminated the peaceful old face. Just before the hour, her old neighbour Mrs. Quinn tottered forward to the coffin and stood uncertainly before it, clasping and unclasping the crook of her cane. As she reached out a trembling hand and touched Mrs. Applebee's cheek, the funeral gathering fell silent, deferring to this final confabulation between old neighbours. Then in the tenuous silence, Mrs. Quinn's voice rose intoning the old Irish bidding prayer: "May you be forty days in heaven afore the devil knows you're dead." When, suddenly, her bony shoulders slumped and a low wail escaped her lips, Harriet hurried forward, wrapped an arm around Mrs. Quinn and led her to a seat beside a spray of blue delphiniums.

Aside from Mrs. Applebee's nephew, those who felt the loss most keenly were her brothers and sisters in Christ. Fittingly, the simple service was open for anyone to share, and many in the Elora church reiterated the truth of Mrs. Applebee's magnanimous spirit and how her life had influenced their own. Central in that outpouring of gratitude was the transformation she accorded in its entirety to Jesus, her Lord and Saviour. Honouring one of her last requests, those who spoke emphasized God's great love for each of her friends and neighbours.

Lyman stood and said, "I read something once in one of Henry Van Dyke's books." His hands quaked slightly as he took out a sheet of paper and said, "I wrote down the story as best I could remember it. It went something like this."

I recall standing at the side of a lonely harbour in a foreign land after saying goodbye to my dearest friend. She was weary of traveling and now she was going home to her family. We embraced and held each other close as long as we could. But eventually the time to separate could be delayed no longer.

After she climbed the gangway and stood at the rail, we waved and waved as long as we could see each other. I will never forget her radiant smile as she lingered for a few seconds before disappearing inside the cabin door. In my mind she and the ship had become one. All I could do was to watch helplessly as she sailed out of the harbour. I have to admit my faith faltered and doubts flooded into my heart. "Will I ever see her again?" I questioned. Like a dam, suddenly broken, a torrent of tears burst out.

What an object of beauty and strength as her sails caught the stiffening breeze. She was free at last. I watched until she was only a tiny light in the evening sky, vanishing at length between the horizon and the deepening orange-tinted clouds. Then, someone at my side whispered, "She's gone!"

Gone where? Gone from my sight, that's all. She is just as large in dimension and magnitude as she was when she was here. Just as able to bear that special life contained within her to the place of her destination. Her diminished size is found only in the limits of my human perception, not in reality.

And just at that moment when someone cries, "She's gone," the splendour of a bright new day is dawning in her distant homeland. There, other eyes are eagerly watching for her arrival, other arms waiting

to embrace her, other voices taking up the glad shout, "Here she comes!
Oh, how wonderful, she's safely here."

Lyman Liddle paused to look over the funeral gathering. Inspired faces—
some of village stalwarts, others, like that of Malachi Jackson, who had made
the dusty journey to reverence the passing of an old friend—gazed back
into his, caught up in the vision of a sublime voyage, a welcoming harbour.
A tear rolled down Lyman's cheek as he smiled and said, "And that, my
dear friends, is dying in Christ!"

At the edge of the village, the Elora Cemetery overlooked the Irvine
River running through the limestone gorge far below. After the funeral
service, the mourners threaded their way through the village streets, three
or four abreast, behind the black horse-drawn hearse. Harold MacQuarrie
customarily draped his matching team with black lace nets, but Mrs.
Applebee had requested a more modest service.

Beneath two tall maples, a fresh pile of earth stood beside her husband's
headstone. Chiseled into the side of the granite monument was the inscrip-
tion: David Jonathon Applebee 1852–1856 Our Beloved Son.

The pallbearers took a firm hold on the three thick straps and carefully
lowered the oak coffin into the open grave. Mrs. Applebee had gone ahead

to rest in paradise, but her body would have to wait here until Christ's return on the day of resurrection.[12] Once the coffin was safely settled into its resting place, the little company gathered close around the sides of the grave. Many wept as they joined hands and sang.

> When life is ended and I must travel
> Through death's dark chambers, I need not fear:
> If I have Jesus to guard and guide me,
> I walk securely with One so dear.

> Though dark the valley that lies before me,
> A light far brighter than noonday sun
> Shines o'er my pathway, and hope eternal
> I see in Jesus; earth's day is done.

> Oh, glorious dawning, blest resurrection!
> When I with Jesus come forth again,
> I shall adore Him, my wondrous Saviour:
> He freed my soul from sin's curse and stain.[13]

As George moved abstractedly out of the cemetery, the finality of Evelyn's parting took hold of him and tears ran freely down his narrow face—he had lost a loyal friend. Never again would she bustle out to greet him on her front porch. Or rattle the stove lids as she cooked breakfast, talking to him all the while of the things dear to both their hearts. For the last time he had heard Evelyn's comfortable words over the supper table and her cheerful goodnight calling up the stairs afterward. She had sent her last weekly letter in the spidery hand he had quickly come to recognize and, most of all, she had offered her final prayer on his behalf.

George was trudging along Victoria Street when a Scripture suddenly arrived to comfort him. Precious in the sight of the Lord is the death of His saints.[14] A smile flickered across his face at the thought that even now God had already received His child.

George reached into his pocket and touched the edge of the envelope that Mrs. Applebee had mailed to him at Wood Creek Farm. She had written it, not knowing whether she would ever see him again. At the time he had not realized that this would be her last letter to him. George had read and reread the letter several times and didn't have to pull it out now to know what it said.

Elora, Ontario
June 24, 1914

Dear George,

This may be my last letter to you. I'm not feeling as good as I once did, and I don't have the energy to concentrate the way I used to. When I look out the window and see the morning dew, I'd like to take my stick and walk around the garden to pick a handful of flowers, but I'm just not up to it anymore.

I feel the gentle Spirit of Christ calling me home, and I don't want to resist when the time comes. But before that happens, I want to tell you again what a difference God has made in my life. I can't honestly say that I've allowed Him to guide absolutely every word or action or thought, but I have a peace now that would never have been possible if He hadn't come to live within my heart. And I thank Him every day.

I want to thank you too, George, because it was you and Jack who came to my door and showed me through your words and actions that Jesus is the way, the only way, to salvation. The Scriptures say it is a beautiful sight to see the feet—the walk and the life—of someone coming to preach the gospel of peace, the good news of life ahead.[15] I could never understand the meaning of that verse until I met you.

People are hungry for this simple, practical gospel. They're hungry for His love, for His promise of an eternal life with Him. Indeed, this hunger is unlimited. I hope that you and others like you will reach far beyond these few counties, going into all the world and preaching the good news to all who will listen.[16] If I were young again, I'd want to help in doing just that—like you and Jack.

May God bless you in your efforts. Goodbye, George.

Your ever-faithful friend,

Evelyn Applebee

Pushing open the little picket gate, George stepped into Mrs. Applebee's quiet yard. The hollyhocks and peonies bloomed with the same vibrant colours and the purple glory of the lupins exuded the same spicy fragrance as they had on his first evening there. But the soul of the place had departed. Mrs. Applebee's warm spirit had lent an air to her home that nothing could ever restore.

George meandered among the blossoms before sitting heavily on the edge of the porch. A tear ran down his cheek as he admired Mrs. Applebee's yard in all its splendour and summer freshness. Bowing his head, he thanked God for all that Evelyn had meant to him and for her faithful life. It was then that he was reminded of a coming day when God will wipe away every tear from the eyes of His people, for there shall be no more death nor sorrow or crying, neither shall there be any more pain: for the former things are passed away...[17]

Birds had been twittering in the shrubbery for some time when George heard the approaching sound of horses' hooves and steel-rimmed wheels. Looking up he saw Alistair and Priscilla, pulling up in the black buggy after the funeral tea at Lyman and Jessie's. He rose to retrieve his travel bag from his bedroom in Mrs. Applebee's upstairs.

Stopping for a moment in front of Jenny L.'s gilded cage, he pressed his finger between the bars. Silent now, the bird seemed older, more hunched as she clung to her hanging perch. "Goodbye, Jenny," he said softly. "We'll both miss her laughter." Looking back, the canary blinked slowly. George doffed his cap and tucked it under his arm before picking up his travel bag.

He was winding his way down Mrs. Applebee's front path for the last time, when suddenly, over his shoulder, he heard the most brilliant burst of Jenny Lind's sweet melody. As if to lift his spirits, the eloquent song followed him to the buggy step.

"Thanks for giving me a little time to be alone," he murmured as he climbed up onto the front seat beside Priscilla.

"Don't mention it," Alistair grunted as he clicked his tongue to the horse. "In Mrs. Applebee you had a loyal friend. We all did." The dapple gray mare broke into a stiff trot after the buggy rounded the corner onto Geddes Street and headed past Foster's General Store, past the new post office and down the steep hill. On the west side of the bowstring bridge over the Grand River, the millpond reflected the dazzling sheen of the four o'clock sun. For a time each of the travelers rode immersed in their own memories of their faithful old sister. On either side of the maple-lined gravel road, golden fields of grain stood ripening for the harvest as the buggy rattled south towards Guelph.

"Maybe we'll overtake the others," Priscilla speculated at length. "Jack and Timothy left just ahead of us. They're with Bill and Alice and Malachi in the democrat. Mind you, old Nell's not as fast as she used to be—rising nineteen this year."

George's eyes twinkled. "Like the rest of us," he added wryly.

They had just passed Joe and Bella's old home place on the south side of Guelph when, without a word of explanation, Alistair reined in the driver and turned west along a concession road mottled with shade. Neither of his passengers questioned the sudden departure from the familiar homeward route as they tipped their hats and squinted into the setting sun. Pulling up abruptly at the narrow gate to the old burying ground, Alistair thrust the lines into Priscilla's lap as he sprang down from the buggy and strode toward Ben Aberlochy's grave. After tying the mare to the iron fence, George extended a hand to Priscilla and together they approached Alistair, his head cast forward and shoulders bowed under his funeral blacks. He stood before the mossy headstone, drawn within himself by earnest contemplation.

"Last night I dug out my old packet of letters from Ben," Alistair remarked at last. "Postmarked from Southampton, Gibraltar, Bombay, and suchlike. Ben was a carefree soul and roamed the seven seas. But he could have had no notion of the remarkable passage he would embark me on." Alistair's sunburned lips moved in wordless gratitude.

Nodding thoughtfully, George glanced sideways. The intervening years had eroded their share of creases into his friend's lean face and a cast of gray had tinged Alistair's temples since that first encounter in the Berlin sale barn. But the profound peace now radiating from those blue eyes had been missing in the early days. The old restlessness had been supplanted by a settled faith in his older friend's spirit.

Alistair's gaze roved over the lilies in the fence row to the slumbering summer fields beyond. "What a contrast to that stormy day in January when we said goodbye to Ben," he mused aloud as the three friends ambled back to the buggy. "My heart seemed frozen then in a sort of spiritual winter, but God, in His mercy, has blessed me abundantly above all that I could ask or imagine. The past sixteen years have been the richest of my life."

George's own cheeks shone in the sun's evening glow as he turned over the words. Alistair's assertion of God's bountiful blessing, he recognized, had been *his* lot as well. This testament of two funerals stood like milestones on the journey of the little church. Through eyes misted with joy, George offered a silent prayer of thanksgiving as the buggy bounced over ragged potholes. "Dear God," he prayed, after a few days' respite at Wood Creek Farm, "please grant me a double portion of the Spirit of Christ as I set out once again into Your great harvest field."

EPILOGUE

As the seasons passed, leaving their largesse in George's heart, he often took Mrs. Applebee's tattered letter out of his pocket. The dear saint proved to be right in her prediction of the hunger for the gospel. And eventually that message of life was far reaching indeed. The stirring in Alistair Stanhope's heart to know God after the death of his friend, Ben Aberlochy, had been instrumental in drawing many into a new and simple faith in Jesus.

Over the years the Holy Spirit continued to move and speak through the ministry of the friends and workers. The simple way of Jesus grew and eventually spread across Canada, England, Ireland, Scotland, and the United States. All this was accomplished without a hierarchy, a head office, or a human leader as each person kept in touch with Christ, the head of His church.

Because the believers within the fellowship were primarily English speaking, the itinerant preachers scattered from Canada to Great Britain to the far reaches of the globe coloured in British Empire red. Some of the saints, who were not free to travel, sold their most treasured possessions—furniture, heirlooms, pianos, property—to pay for others' ocean passages. Just as Laura's students in Mildmay, during her lessons on Mercator's map, had traced the parallels of latitude and the meridians of longitude, so the itinerants followed the navigational routes to the four corners of the earth.

The first to leave Ontario was Morgan Butterwick. Even as he marveled at the blossoming of the fellowship throughout the counties of southern

Ontario, he continued to invest his days hauling his honey cart from door to door and preaching on the street corners. But often when people would remark on his Liverpudlian accent, his thoughts would skim the trackless swells of the Atlantic to his aunt's cottage on the Welsh seashore. What, he wondered, was *his* responsibility to his own family and to other folks he had known as a youth? Would he be willing to wrench himself away from this adopted family of his at Wood Creek Farm and return to the land of his birth so that seeds of a richer life might reach his kith and kin?

And so it was that five years after Mrs. Applebee's death, the Spirit had laid upon Morgan's heart the conviction to return to England, the converging point of the world's shipping lanes. When Eddie Summers learned of Morgan's intentions, he offered to sail with him, and together the pair booked a crossing in steerage on a White Star liner bound for Liverpool.

Upon landing they soon had a mission underway and found an eager response to their simple message. The hunger for the gospel in the war-weary towns and cities soon led others to join them in the harvest field. Before long a scattering of little home churches girded the rolling downs and the quaint thatched villages from Derbyshire to Dorset and from Cornwall to Kent.

Only a few years later, a light sea breeze stirred the Union Jack as the first workers prepared to leave for the southern hemisphere. In the bustling port of London, England, a merchant ship stood ready to sail down the Thames and into the open sea. Amid the excitement and commotion, a little farewell party had gathered on the wharf. Twelve brave men and women hugged their friends and family goodbye. Tears flowed abundantly as the twelve friends walked up the gangway to board the vessel. Although they had no assurance that they would ever see these familiar faces of home again, a burning desire within their hearts compelled them to share the invitation of Jesus with hungry souls.

In the ensuing weeks, the ship docked at several ports of call below the equator. In South Africa, the first two brothers got off in Capetown and two sisters did the same in Durban. Another pair of brothers said goodbye in India to their friends remaining on board. Two more waved farewell as the boat steamed out of the harbour in Adelaide, Australia. The last four hugged each other tightly before two more young women disembarked in eastern Australia. Then the vessel sailed on to Wellington, New Zealand. Far from home and family, these six pairs of traveling preachers began to hold gospel meetings and to sow their lives as seed.

At times the hundreds of men and women who had become itinerants faced severe hardship and difficulties. Occasionally they were hungry, living for days on berries or a raw turnip found in a ditch or eating from roadside fruit trees.[1] They slept under the stars, in haystacks, in barns, in empty stores, in schools—with neither bed nor covering.[2] Some waded through the snow in the bitter cold of northern climates while others endured the searing heat or malaria-infested tropics of Africa. A few were flogged and imprisoned for their faith and many were victims of malicious and false accusations.[3] Although they were tramps because of their tramping, they never begged nor took a collection for their work. These itinerants considered it a privilege to spend their lives living and preaching like their Master.

Mrs. Applebee's correspondence, long after her death, called out to the hearts of the friends who had loved her. In 1926, using Evelyn's old box of letters and several eyewitness anecdotes, Ashleigh Duffield, Phoebe's former schoolteacher, pieced together the beginnings of the little church. At first the saints hoped the written record of their early days might assist others in comprehending the beauty of a simple faith. But after much deliberation, they concluded that preaching was the preferable way to reach out as long as people continued to attend gospel meetings. After only a handful of copies had been printed, Ashleigh's account of the glorious work of Christ in the hearts of ordinary men and women was laid aside for the time being, but the life that welled up in their hearts could never be forgotten.

After the horrors of World War I, the delirium of the roaring twenties crumbled under the weight of the Great Depression. Each of the early friends knew of some fresh-faced lad who had failed to return from the dank, rat-infested trenches of Vimy Ridge, Passchendaele, or Hill 70. And in the thirties no one could remain insulated from the plummeting prices of livestock and crops, the escalating loss of jobs and the knowledge of lengthening breadlines in the cities. But in spite of being troubled on every side and perplexed at the meaning of such unsettling events, the believers' faith enabled them to escape much of the distress and despair felt by their neighbours.

As the decades passed, the early friends in the fellowship grew older and one by one God began to call them into eternity. Here and there, one was taken and another left—first Oliver Summers, then Joe Purves, Katrina Brunstedder, Malachi Jackson—as they went home to their Father.

One mild day in April 1937, after being housebound for over a month, Alistair retrieved his walking stick from the woodshed and picked his way carefully along the path to the barn. He needed some fresh air, he told himself, and this was a fine morning to look over the new stanchions his son-in-law, Andrew Gillespie, had built in the stable. On the way back past the milk house he failed to notice a slick patch of melting ice and landed hard on his back, the wind knocked out of him, his spectacles broken. It was Phoebe who found him a half hour later, his bruised face a pallid mask of pain, his hip hopelessly fractured. A rattled Andrew dashed to the barn for his sons, Seth and Caleb, and together they got Alistair onto a plank and hoisted his sparse frame into the bed in the room off the kitchen. A hasty telephone call to Central brought the white-walled tires of Dr. Moore's new Packard bouncing up the lane, but after a rigorous examination the doctor concluded that little could be done for the ailing eighty-five-year-old Alistair.

For over a fortnight, he lay immobile, unresistant to the kindly ministrations offered him. As the days passed his swollen upper leg blackened and he grew lightheaded, drifting in and out of restless sleep. One evening just as darkness fell, a clot traveled to his heart, releasing him from the tenuous existence on which he balanced. Dr. Moore, his benevolent white-whiskered face filled with compassion, made small talk with Priscilla over a cup of tea until the undertaker could arrive.

For the first time, Alistair lay like a guest in his own home, rough hands clasped and slightly steepled on his chest, features relaxed in the utter repose of his final sleep. A quiet nobility had always distinguished the man, a nobility enhanced by the symbols of his labours—the three-pronged fork and the scythe that his eldest grandson had brought from the barn and leaned in a kind of dignified grace against the foot of the coffin. A cluster of snowdrops—the only blooms the chilly spring sunshine had called forth—lay wrapped in green cedar fronds upon the casket. Priscilla and Phoebe, the two women he had loved most, stood before it, their arms encircling each other's waists. Phoebe stooped and kissed her father's cheek, then raised herself and turned with a pensive smile to her mother. "He shall doubtless come again with rejoicing," she quoted softly, "bringing his sheaves with him."

In the hushed hour before nightfall, Priscilla hurried to the barn—a man's domain almost exclusively—to retrieve from a barn beam a folded paper stained by dust and the rising breath of cattle over the years. It was a letter, hidden away with deliberate intention years before, a letter in large and painstaking script. It exuded the faintly yeasty scent of summer fields as though the paper had absorbed into its very fibres the sweet-scented hay the barn had sheltered. Slipping back into the darkened house, she found

Phoebe in the kitchen, her face sad as she bent over the oil lamp and struck a match, touching it to the wick. When the soft circle of light glowed and shone reflected in the windows, the darkness seemed to retreat.

"It won't do to leave Dad without a light in the parlour," she murmured. "George and Jack are in there with Timothy now, and Andrew said he'd be in as soon as the milking's done."

Priscilla drew close to her daughter, her face portentous. "Phoebe, now the lamp's lit, sit down and read this letter."

In mystified silence, Phoebe found herself reading lines in her father's own hand—a letter as lyrical as the constraints of his upbringing had been limiting.

> Lot 13, Concession 5
> Township of Puslinch
> County of Wellington
> Ontario, Canada
> March 14, 1927

> My dearest Phoebe,

> Twenty-five years ago this morning I waved Timothy off in the stage-coach as he set out to join George and Jack in the work. And to this day he retains his first love in that calling. In the meantime, you and Andrew have formed a steadfast union, and I'm proud of you both. It's been a delight to live under the same roof, admiring the way the pair of you are rearing three outstanding children—Seth, Caleb, and Mamie. Watching the lads grow up into responsible young men and keen herdsmen has brought me immense pleasure, and my only granddaughter—gentle like you and your mother—is my third singing bird.

> I have directed your mother to give this letter to you after my death and when that hour comes—and it must—don't grieve unduly. Somewhere in my vision I see a future of purpose and joy for you and Andrew and my grandchildren. Having once been a miller's apprentice and now a farmer, Andrew has witnessed God's plenty in the many golden sheaves ground into flour at the mill. Both you and he shoulder with grace the responsibilities you share in God's harvest of souls.

> Phoebe, my daughter, on my death Wood Creek Farm is yours and Andrew's. Take care of your mother, giving daily thought to her comfort and remember her blessed influence in all our lives. May you continue to grace a hospitable home for many years where Timothy and the other

brothers and sisters in the work will always find welcome and refuge under the old ridge pole. And when it comes your turn to think of passing the home place along, remember my wish that Wood Creek Farm fall into the hands of someone who will honour God's decision to place the convention in our family's care. My dear Phoebe, be assured I love you dearly until we're united again on the far shore.

Your loving father,

Alistair Stanhope

Phoebe's hand shook as she tenderly folded the letter and pressed the comfortable words to her lips. That hour conferred on Phoebe her father's affirmation of a woman's worth.

In the dim light of the funeral morning, Priscilla stood haggard before the mirror, pinning into a bun at the back of her head her thinning strands of grey hair. The stillness of death pervaded the house, and an unusual formality took possession of the muted rooms of Wood Creek Farm. All night long through the broken sleep of sorrow, Priscilla had resisted an urgent final gesture. But now the integrity of her nature won out as she searched for and found the faded packet of letters from Ben Aberlochy. In the silent parlour, she slipped the little bundle into Alistair's coffin.

Well before the appointed hour, horses and buggies and black cars of every vintage from Model A Fords to Packard coupes began to stream up the lane of Wood Creek Farm. A line of sombre men and women, some with children in hand, filed through the parlour to pay their last respects and to say goodbye to this man they loved so dearly.

Many broke down and, in spite of the rigid custom of the day, wept openly, embracing Priscilla, Phoebe, and Timothy and the others standing at the end of the oak casket. Then, blinking and red-eyed, handkerchiefs in hand, they wended their way through the well-known kitchen and back outside to the welcome April sunshine. Hasty improvisations were made as Jack and Stephen directed men to haul dusty convention benches out of the driving shed and set them up on the grass. Although Alistair had requested that his funeral be small and modest, no amount of suggestion had been able to dissuade the believers from far and wide who packed the yard at Wood Creek Farm. His simple quest for spiritual reality had affected many of their lives in a profound way.

George, in his late sixties, stood on the side porch and looked over the swell of familiar faces as he opened his lips to express his final sentiments to those assembled. He spoke as one to whom the words had been given. "The measure of a man," he began, "lies in his willingness to listen to the voice of God and to act upon it. Our friend, Alistair, was one of those men. A faithful brother upon whom I could always depend for sound spiritual counsel. I recall the summer evening, thirty-seven years ago, when he and I sat in his stable, thrashing over my notion of starting out as a homeless preacher. As we looked over a young heifer struggling to give birth, he looked into my eyes and said, 'George, I'm behind you one hundred percent.' And since that day, Alistair has never wavered or made the least shadow of turning from that commitment to me. Wherever I went, whatever circumstances befell me, I knew there was a brother at Wood Creek Farm who loved and supported me to the utmost. A man can't have a better friend than that."

George drew his handkerchief out of his back pocket and pressed it to his eyes. "I can barely express my appreciation for the gospel of Christ and for the call that Alistair heard in the beginning days of this humble fellowship.

"Alistair once told me that as a boy, he often struggled to open the farm gates for his dad. And I give thanks that he searched diligently for and nudged ajar the gate of our heavenly Father, the gate that many of us have stepped through since then, the gate leading to a life guided by the Spirit. Kneeling beside the gate post, this youthful herdsman witnessed his father coaxing open a stubborn bolt or bar and directing the sheep into virgin pastures. As we well know, Alistair in that humble way of his played a faithful role in enabling God's earthly flock to be fed and shepherded. Through the years, his life moved from season to season by the fastening and unfastening of a gate, and today Alistair rejoices in the finest season he has ever known. He has stepped through the final gate that leads to our Father's house."

After the service the crowd slowly returned to their vehicles and a procession nearly a mile long wended its way north through Puslinch Township. Although clay-coloured banks of snow lingered in the lee of the woods, a soft wind from the south blew over the waiting fields. Patches of sunshine burst through scudding clouds, illuminating the landscape where the ploughed furrows gave back the glint of sun as from the ploughshare itself. When the procession reached Guelph, the old civic buildings looked on with faces of stone while men along the funeral route removed their hats and stood silent for a moment, hands clasped.

When the hearse drew up under the budding trees of Woodlawn Cemetery, the six pallbearers—brothers chosen from the church that met in Alistair's home—eased his coffin out and brought it to rest under the spreading branches of a red oak. The friends and neighbours gathered around the grave, some with arms linked as they sought comfort from each other and sang one of Alistair's favourite hymns:

> Lead me through this vale of shadows;
> Bear me o'er life's fitful sea;
> Then the gate of life eternal,
> May I enter, Lord, with Thee.
> Close to Thee, close to Thee;
> Close to Thee, close to Thee. [4]

After the prayer of committal and the heart-searching silence that followed, a tartan-kilted figure, standing a short distance apart, raised his bagpipes to his lips. As the plaintive, yet compelling strains of "Amazing Grace" rose and fell on the afternoon air, touching the hearts of the company, Priscilla stepped forward and laid a single red rose on the casket. With the help of Timothy's strong arm, she moved back between him and Phoebe to receive folks who came to offer their condolences.

When Alistair's family pulled away, one by one the dispersing crowd followed them out of the cemetery gates. As if reluctant to forsake his friend, George hesitated beside the grave before walking slowly across the faintly greening lawn to where Gilbert Jones stood waiting, one foot on the running board of his old Gray-Dort. The same bittersweet conflict of grief and hope flooded over George that he had felt when Mrs. Applebee had died more than twenty years earlier.

Four years later, George and Jack again stood beside Timothy and Phoebe at their mother's graveside. After the funeral service for Priscilla, Phoebe's husband, Andrew Gillespie, led his eldest son to the nearby grave of Alistair's little brother, Cory. Andrew spoke about the tragic hay loader accident in which the little boy had died. As the pair stood looking at Cory's weathered headstone, Andrew laid his arm across his son's shoulders. "Your grandfather shared that story with me when I was still working at the feed mill," he said softly. "It changed my life in so many ways. That's how your mother and I first met."

Jack Gillan had always maintained the illusion of a youthful scholar with his satchel of history books in hand and a collie running along behind him. A new energy, even exuberance, filled his life as he cherished his newfound family, and as the years ensued, he reveled in the joys of small nephews and nieces. Each Christmas if Jack were close enough to London, he would board the train and squeeze in a day or two with Miranda and Dwight and his siblings, a gift he never would have savoured had he not forsaken his former life and set out in the traveling ministry. And after the convention each year at Wood Creek Farm, he always found a few days to go home to Ma and Pop Gillan, showering them with love and appreciation and regaling them with stories of his life in the work.

Laura's role in the fellowship drew inspiration from a different well. In the years after Katie's marriage to Percy, she united with other sisters in the work, sisters who were also part of the bride of Christ on earth. Touched by a divine influence, Laura was able to tread the earth lightly, retaining always the sweet and trustful spirit that had endeared her so long ago to the church at Wood Creek Farm.

George continued happily in his ministry until he was in his nineties. He and Timothy were together again for the third time, staying with a family in a remote district in northern Ontario. In the days since they had arrived in the bush settlement west of Cochrane, George's eyes had shown an otherworldly light and his gestures and demeanour had become evermore thoughtful. One evening while watching the amethyst clouds of autumn gather around the sun, he had remarked to Timothy, "The early dusk swallows up the forest in a hurry, but on a frosty night you can always pick out the candle taper of a star. When my evening hour comes and night falls, I hope it'll fall quick and not linger." George paused in the pale light, his face upturned and wistful. As the two old pilgrims sat on the porch reminiscing the autumn sky flowered with stars.

Resting his elbow on the arm of his chair, George turned to Timothy with a heartfelt appeal. "When my time comes, Timothy, please arrange a simple burial wherever I am. We're a long piece down the road from Puslinch, but I'd be happy resting right here among the rocks and stars of the northern shield. I reckon God Himself will be waiting to greet me at the final gate."

One Sunday morning shortly thereafter, a tightness in his chest prevented George from going to the morning meeting a few miles away. With the customary twinkle in his gentle blue eyes, he reassured Timothy and his friends. "You go along without me. Besides, I'll be with you in spirit," he promised. "I'll be with you in prayer."

When Timothy arrived home shortly after noon, he tapped lightly on George's door. Hearing no sound, he eased the knob and peeked inside. The room was empty. They searched the house and yard without finding a trace of him. Finally, they assumed he must have ventured for a walk through the thick grove of maple and elm that lay behind the house. A white picket gate, partly screened by the autumn foliage, stood ajar, beckoning the searchers. The narrow path beyond threaded its way among tall trunks supporting their golden canopy. Shafts of light splashed across the forest floor as the terrain steepened and the trail looped up to a secluded clearing on higher ground.

When, years ago, George had pondered his ministry, the early bloodroot were unfolding in the southern Ontario woods. Now, at the close of his ministry, a profusion of crimson berries gleamed in the late September sunshine that penetrated this tranquil glade in the northern forest. There, on a thick bed of autumn leaves, they found George lying at rest. In the filtered sunlight, his face, even in what men would term old age, appeared as youthful and unchiseled as a boy's. He had slipped away as gently as he had lived, leaving the creases along his smile lines relaxed and soft like his wrinkled hands. Catching the sun's eye, a single scarlet cardinal flower lay clutched to his chest. The serenity on his face registered the peace he must have felt at the moment His Lord had called him home.

Tenderly, the men carried George's body back to the house. As they placed him upon his bed, a folded piece of paper dislodged itself from his shirt pocket and floated to the floor. Unfolding it, Timothy discovered it was a recent letter in Laura's spidery yet firm hand.

Puslinch, Ontario
September 1, 1962

My dearest George,

This afternoon finds me once again at Wood Creek Farm for a few days. Looking around at this loved and familiar home, I'm reminded of you, George, and your warm influence among our friends. We're not spring chickens anymore, and I was thankful to hear that you're still as fit as a fiddle. I remember when you could toss sheaves from daylight 'til dark and still have energy to burn. Speaking of getting older, isn't it a corker to imagine Timothy turning seventy-nine this year? He was just a ruddy-cheeked lad out of school when I first stayed here in the green attic room. Over the years, he's been a faithful brother, and I'm glad you two are together again.

My young companion, Summer-Lynn, comes to pick me up on Monday, and we'll get started with a few gospel meetings in Niagara Falls—a lot farther south than you and Timothy. Over the years, you and I've stumped up and down this province from one end to the other, from Ailsa Craig to Vankleek Hill. Isn't it wonderful to be able to offer the evening sacrifice of our lives traveling and sharing the good news of God's abundance with hungry souls?

Even though Phoebe and Andrew have to doctor a bit, they, too, do well for their age. Phoebe watches her blood pressure and Andrew's arthritis kicks up now and then, so their son and grandson are the farmers now. Alistair would be pleased to think of five generations and the convention continuing on the home place.

I must say, George, that at times I feel a little lonely for our good friends who have gone ahead to their reward. I still remember the boisterous comradery around the long table as we prepared for that first convention in June 1906. And the marvelous times we shared as hand in hand we set out on our journey of faith. They were all there—Katie, Percy, Malachi, Alice, Bill, Stephen, Emily, Eddie, Morgan, and all the others. And I look forward to joining them all on the other shore.

And someday, don't forget, we'll both put our heads down on the same pillow, wrapped in the same arms of earth. And in that unknown hour, when I join you at last, you'll know I'm still your girl. Somehow, George, I've been remembering that time you collected me from the train and we rode behind the white horse from Guelph to Arkell. It was a June morning and the green landscape around us looked like the fields of Eden. I loved you then, or thought I did. But through the years, since our lives have been dedicated to God's family, I've loved you immeasurably more.

I hear Phoebe calling for supper, so I'll sign off for now. This evening we're going to dust off our violins and gather around Priscilla's piano for old times' sake.

I look forward to hearing from you soon.

Much love as always,

Laura

Timothy tucked the letter back into George's shirt pocket and patted it flat, knowing that he would want it forever close to his heart. Then he went to the telephone, took down the receiver, and put a call through to Wood Creek Farm. Laura must be the first to know.

Honouring his old friend's earnest plea, Timothy made no effort to return George's body to Puslinch Township. Instead, he was laid to rest in a plot owned by someone else. Only a single row of towering pines and a rusty page-wire fence separated the peaceful family burying ground from the woods, the birds, and the wildflowers George had so much loved.

NOTES

Chapter One: Spiritual Winter
1. Psalm 107:6-14,19-20
2. John 10:27
3. John 3:3-6

Chapter Two: Troubling Questions
1. Luke 18:9-14,39

Chapter Three: Encounter in Berlin
1. Acts 9:2; 18:25-26; 19:9,23; 22:4; 24:14,22
2. John 14:6
3. Genesis 18:1-8; Acts 3:1-11
4. 2 Timothy 2:26; 1 Timothy 3:7
5. Luke 22:61
6. John 12:27; 13:1; 16:32-33
7. "Was It for Me?" J.M. Whyte (19th Century)
8. 1 Peter 2:22-24
9. Romans 5:6-10
10. Colossians 2:14
11. 1 Corinthians 1:30; 2 Corinthians 5:21
12. 1 Corinthians 1:8
13. Romans 5:10

Chapter Four: First Sunday in May
1. Ephesians 2:14
2. Matthew 26:41

3. "Lord, We Are Met Together," Edward Cooney (1867–1960)
4. 1 Corinthians 14:26,31
5. 1 Corinthians 14:3
6. John 1:41-45
7. "Satisfied," Clara T. Williams (1858–1937)
8. Matthew 26:26-28,30
9. "Calvary," Sam Jones (1877–1946)
10. John 8:32
11. 2 Corinthians 3:17

Chapter Five: Frustrations and Firestorms
1. Hebrews 11:32-38
2. Deuteronomy 11:18-21
3. John 18:15-27
4. Luke 10:31
5. Matthew 23:27-28
6. Revelation 17:5-6
7. Revelation 18:4
8. Luke 23:34; 1 Peter 1:22-24
9. Acts 8:1-8
10. 2 Corinthians 8:16-17,23-24

Chapter Six: Reaching Out in Love
1. Genesis 3:23
2. Jeremiah 18:2-6

3. Romans 9:21

4. Matthew 6:28-29

5. This concept was suggested to me by a section (Chapter 5, "Things in Their Identity") in Thomas Merton's classic book, *New Seeds of Contemplation.*

6. Mark 4:26-32

7. John 5:19

8. James 2:26

9. 1 Corinthians 14:23-25

10. Acts 8:4-8

11. Acts 21:8-9; 8:26-40

12. Romans 1:7; 8:27; 12:13; 15:25,26,31; Ephesians 1:1,15,18; 2:19; 3:8; 4:12; 5:3; 6:18

13. 1 Timothy 5:17

14. Acts 11:19-21

15. Acts 18:24-28

16. Luke 2:49

17. Matthew 16:16-18

18. John 1:12-13

19. Colossians 1:27

20. Galatians 5:22-23

Chapter Seven: Dropping Pebbles

1. John 15:13-14

2. Luke 2:7

3. 2 Kings 4:8-37

4. "Have You Any Room For Jesus?" Daniel Whittle (1840–1901)

5. John 13:34-35

6. Matthew 22:2-14; Luke 14:15-24

7. John 10:10

8. "Now None but Christ Can Satisfy," Author Unknown

9. Luke 12:16-21

10. Matthew 5:45

11. Mark 3:31-35

12. 1 Corinthians 3:16-17; 2 Corinthians 5:1-2

13. Matthew 16:13-19; John 3:2-7; 2 Corinthians 4:7; Galatians 2:20-21

14. Psalm 133:1-3

15. Ephesians 4:3

16. Isaiah 40:12-15

17. 1 Corinthians 1:30-31

18. Colossians 1:27-28

19. Ecclesiastes 3:20

20. "Life at Best Is Very Brief," William Kirkpatrick (1838–1921)

21. "I Must Have the Saviour with Me," Lizzie Edwards

22. Luke 6:43-45

Chapter Eight: The Epiphany

1. Isaiah 9:6

2. Genesis 3:16; 25:21-28

3. John 6:44

4. Ephesians 4:14-15; 1 Peter 2:2

5. Matthew 5:8

6. John 3:1-8

7. 1 Peter 1:23

8. 2 Thessalonians 2:11

9. Philippians 4:7

10. Luke 19:40

11. Daniel 6:10

12. 2 Corinthians 12:10-11

13. Daniel 1:11-15

14. Mark 16:15

15. 1 John 3:18-19

16. "Not What These Hands Have Done," Horatio Bonar (1808–1889)

17. Acts 2:47

18. Mark 2:19-20; John 3:28-30; Revelation 19:6-9; 21:9-10

19. Revelation 2:4-5

20. Luke 10:27

21. John 3:6; Exodus 32:1-10

22. Matthew 18:3-4

23. Mark 6:6-12

24. Luke 10:1-10
25. Matthew 10:8

Chapter Nine: The Baptism
1. Ephesians 4:13
2. Acts 8:35-39
3. Matthew 3:15
4. Acts 8:37
5. Matthew 3:2-8
6. Matthew 3:8
7. John 3:22
8. John 4:2-3
9. Matthew 28:18-20
10. Acts 9:17-18
11. Matthew 3:16
12. John 3:23
13. "Moment by Moment," Daniel W. Whittle (1840–1901)
14. Romans 6:3-6

Chapter Ten: Tear-Shaped Beads of Dew
1. Mark 10:21
2. Mark 10:29-30
3. Luke 9:58
4. Isaiah 50:7; Matthew 4:19; 8:22; 9:9; 16:24; 19:21
5. Romans 10:11-17
6. Acts 15:7
7. Luke 19:20
8. John 12:24-26
9. 1 Corinthians 9:27; Hebrews 6:4-6
10. Revelation 3:3-5
11. "There Is No Gain," C. Booth-Clibborn (1858–1955)
12. Mark 3:13-14
13. Matthew 17:14-21
14. Matthew 19:11-12
15. Matthew 10:34-39

Chapter Eleven: Giving Everything to the Poor
1. Titus 1:1; James 1:1

2. Matthew 19:27-29
3. Mark 10:21-24
4. Matthew 6:1-4
5. Ecclesiastes 5:16; Psalm 144:4
6. Hebrews 11:13
7. Hebrews 11:26-27
8. John 9:3
9. Ecclesiastes 7:14
10. Isaiah 30:20
11. 1 Timothy 6:9-10
12. 1 Timothy 6:6-8
13. Matthew 15:5-6
14. Matthew 26:8-10

Chapter Twelve: The Inaudible Voice
1. Matthew 8:21-22; Luke 9:59-60
2. Mark 5:1-20; Luke 8:26-39
3. Acts 13:2-4
4. Matthew 9:36-38
5. Matthew 25:35
6. Luke 24:13-36; Matthew 14:19
7. Acts 19:9
8. Philippians 4:23
9. Romans 1:1
10. Mark 9:40; Luke 9:50
11. Acts 4:12
12. John 17:21-23
13. 1 Corinthians 1:10-18
14. Ephesians 3:14-15
15. Philippians 2:9-11
16. Matthew 5:44

Chapter Thirteen: Sowing the Seed
1. "Tell Me the Story of Jesus," Fanny J. Crosby (1820–1915)
2. John 1:35-39
3. John 21:9-14
4. 1 Kings 19:9-14
5. Matthew 11:28-30
6. John 10:1-28

7. Luke 17:21

8. Mark 6:34

9. Hebrews 13:20

10. "Why I Love Jesus!" Author Unknown

11. "Jesus, I My Cross Have Taken," Henry F. Lyte (1793–1847)

12. Matthew 8:27

Chapter Fourteen: Beholding the Glory

1. 1 Kings 17:1-9

2. Genesis 18:25

3. Genesis 2:17

4. Genesis 3:1-19

5. "Live for Others Every Day," R. MacNaughton

6. 1 John 4:1

7. 2 Corinthians 11:3-4

8. 2 Corinthians 3:18

9. John 1:14

10. John 1:1; 8:56-58; 20:28; Philippians 2:5-8; Hebrews 1:8; 1 John 5:7

11. Hebrews 1:1-3

12. Jeremiah 18:2-6; Ephesians 2:10

13. Mark 10:17-22; Matthew 19:16-22; Luke 18:18-23

14. Psalm 119:103

15. John 4:23

16. John 14:1-3

17. Matthew 28:20

18. John 8:11

19. Acts 9:2; 18:25-26; 19:9,23; 22:4; 24:14,22

20. Hebrews 11:6

21. Matthew 7:13-14

Chapter Fifteen: Locked Out

1. Acts 2:37

2. Mark 12:37

3. Acts 4:13

4. Acts 17:6

5. Acts 5:39

6. Luke 23:34

7. John 15:18-25

8. Matthew 10:34-38

9. "The Waves Rolled High," Sandy Scott

10. Acts 18:6-8; 19:8-10

11. Jude 3

12. Mark 7:8; Colossians 2:8

13. Luke 6:29

14. Matthew 6:14-15

15. Luke 5:37-38

16. Luke 5:36

17. Isaiah 64:6

18. Matthew 22:10-13

19. Luke 5:39

20. "There Is a Way, a Narrow Way," Sam Jones (1877–1946)

21. Mark 10:18

22. Romans 3:23-25

23. Matthew 5:10-12

24. Psalm 122:7; Luke 4:21

Chapter Sixteen: Render unto Caesar

1. 2 Corinthians 5:17

2. 1 Thessalonians 4:16-17

3. Matthew 6:31-34

4. John 14:16; 17:15; 17:20-22

5. Philippians 1:9-10; 2 Corinthians 13:7

6. James 4:3

7. John 2:23-24

8. John 6:26-27

9. John 6:66-68

10. John 6:53-60

11. 2 Peter 1:19

12. John 8:12; 9:5

13. Matthew 6:25-34

14. Job 2:7

15. 2 Corinthians 12:7-10

16. Romans 8:18; Hebrews 12:2
17. Genesis 50:20
18. Romans 8:28
19. Hebrews 5:8-9
20. Luke 14:26-33
21. Acts 18:3-4
22. 2 Thessalonians 3:8-9
23. Acts 20:33-35
24. Luke 21:1-4
25. Philippians 4:15-17
26. 1 Corinthians 3:11-15; 2 John 8
27. 3 John 7-8
28. 3 John 6
29. 1 Corinthians 9:18
30. 2 Timothy 2:15
31. Hebrews 9:16-18; 10:19-25
32. John 4:23-24

Chapter Seventeen: Ancient Affirmation
1. Matthew 19:21
2. Luke 10:1-4
3. Hebrews 11:32-40
4. John 7:15; Acts 4:13
5. Matthew 10:18; 26:58; Mark 13:9-11; 14:54
6. Matthew 11:8
7. John 10:16,27
8. Much of the historical information for this chapter came from: *The Pilgrim Church* by E. Hamer Broadbent (1861–1945) Gospel Folio Press, Port Colbourne, Ontario, www.gospelfolio.com

Chapter Eighteen: Just As I Am
1. Matthew 6:24
2. "I Hear Him Call," Sam Jones (1877–1946)
3. Matthew 26:18-30
4. Matthew 27:32-56
5. Exodus 12:4

6. Matthew 26:26-30
7. Exodus 12:9-11,14
8. Exodus 12:30-34
9. Hebrews 11:24-28
10. Exodus 3:8,17; Deuteronomy 8:6-9
11. Ephesians 2:8-10
12. James 2:14-18
13. "Just As I Am," Charlotte Elliott (1789–1871)
14. 1 Corinthians 3:16-17; 2 Corinthians 6:16
15. Matthew 12:6; Luke 21:5-8;
16. John 4:21-24
17. Acts 12:12
18. 1 Corinthians 16:19
19. Romans 16:3-5
20. Colossians 4:15
21. Philemon 1-2
22. John 14:6
23. Luke 14:33
24. 1 Peter 4:10-11
25. Hebrews 2:3
26. James 2:10

Chapter Nineteen: Second Harvest
1. Romans 15:12; Revelation 5:5; 22:16
2. Galatians 5:22-23
3. Hebrews 10:22
4. "Let Us Draw Near To God," Sam Jones (1877–1946)
5. Luke 18:9-14
6. "Teach Me To Pray, Lord," Albert Reitz (1843-1919)
7. 1 Corinthians 14:3,26,31
8. Hebrews 10:19-25
9. 1 Corinthians 12:12-26
10. Matthew 16:24
11. John 13:34-35
12. Galatians 6:2
13. Romans 12:4-5

14. Matthew 26:26-30
15. 1 Corinthians 11:23-30
16. 1 Corinthians 10:16-17
17. John 6:53-54
18. "Calvary," Sam Jones (1877–1946)
19. Genesis 46:29

Chapter Twenty: Conscientious Ploughmen

1. Luke 9:62
2. Luke 9:57-59
3. Mark 11:11-12; John 12:1-2
4. 2 Corinthians 11:23-28
5. Romans 8:26-27
6. Hebrews 10:25
7. "I Am Waiting for the Dawning," Trevor Francis (1834–1925)
8. Hebrews 13:2
9. Luke 10:25-37
10. Matthew 22:37-40; Luke 10:27
11. Numbers 22:21-35
12. Acts 2:41; 8:12-13; 8:36-38; 9:18
13. Matthew 9:36-38
14. Matthew 13:5-6; 13:20-21
15. Matthew 11:25
16. This diary contains excerpts taken from J. Pattison's letter of 1925.

Chapter Twenty-One: The Home Visit

1. 1 Corinthians 11:21-22
2. Job 2:11; 8:1
3. John 15:13-17
4. Matthew 23:12
5. Matthew 23:8-12
6. John 5:39-40
7. Matthew 18:3
8. Proverbs 4:18
9. Matthew 16:13-19
10. Psalm 19:1-5; Romans 1:19-20
11. John 6:66-69
12. Romans 10:10

13. Acts 5:34-39; 22:3
14. Galatians 1:11-19
15. Genesis 1:12
16. Mark 14:36
17. "Dear Jesus, As Thou Wilt," Benjamin Schmolck (1672–1737)

Chapter Twenty-Two: Settlement of Belwood

1. Matthew 9:22, 15:28; Mark 10:52; Luke 17:19
2. John 8:32
3. James 2:8-11
4. John 21:15-17
5. Luke 8:39; 1 Timothy 5:17
6. Romans 8:22
7. John 20:20-22
8. 1 John 4:10-12
9. John 3:16
10. Luke 19:42-44
11. Ruth 1:7-8
12. Ruth 1:16-17
13. Acts 17:6
14. "Come, Follow Me!" George Watson (1816–1898)
15. 1 Thessalonians 5:19
16. 2 Corinthians 6:8-10
17. This letter contains excerpts taken from J. Pattison's letter of 1925.
18. Matthew 23:2-11
19. Romans 16:1
20. Genesis 22:1-18
21. Romans 8:35-39
22. Matthew 13:3-9,18-23
23. "What Shall the Harvest Be?" Emily S. Oakey (1828–1883)

Chapter Twenty-Three: Laura's Dilemma

1. "Alone with God," Johnson Oatman Jr. (1856–1930)
2. John 17:23

3. Matthew 16:26

4. "Rejoicing in the Lord," Sam Jones (1877–1946)

5. Isaiah 29:16; 45:9; 64:8; Jeremiah 18:4-6; Romans 9:21

6. Proverbs 4:18

7. John 14:6

8. Luke 22:50-51; John 18:10

9. Psalm 19:1-3

10. Exodus 14:1-9

11. Exodus 14:21-22

12. Exodus 14:2-3

13. Psalm 107:25-31

14. 1 Corinthians 10:13

15. Psalm 77:19-20

16. Job 42:5

17. Psalm 139:3-6

18. Acts 2:14-18

19. 1 Corinthians 14:3

20. Acts 21:8-9

21. Matthew 28:1-10; Mark 16:1-11; Luke 24:1-12; John 20:1-18

22. Luke 2:36-38

23. Galatians 3:28

24. Matthew 20:25-28

25. Galatians 6:2

26. Romans 16:1-2

Chapter Twenty-Four: Casting the Nets

1. Psalm 68:6

2. Isaiah 4:1

3. James 1:26-27

4. John 14:6

5. Matthew 4:19-21; Mark 1:17-20

6. Isaiah 32:2

7. 1 Peter 4:13-14

8. Matthew 8:20; Luke 9:57-59

9. Matthew 10:24-25

10. "Come, Let Us Follow Jesus," Robert Skerritt (1875–?)

11. Acts 9:10,19,25,36,38; 11:29; 20:1,7; 21:4,16

12. John 21:6

Chapter Twenty-Five: Flowering of the Fellowship

1. Matthew 5:14-16

2. John 10:11-13

3. Mark 6:7-12

4. Luke 5:10-11; Matthew 19:27-29

5. Acts 12:25

6. Acts 10:23-48; 11:12-22; 17:15-16; 18:5; 19:1

7. Matthew 11:28

8. John 15:4

9. Mark 16:15; Matthew 10:7; 28:19

10. 2 Corinthians 6:14

11. Mark 2:19-20; John 3:29; 17:22-23; Revelation 19:6-9; 21:2,9-10

12. 1 Timothy 3:7

13. Mark 16:15; Matthew 10:7; 28:19

14. Acts 11:26

15. Psalm 126:1-6

16. "Bringing in the Sheaves," Knowles Shaw (1834–1878)

Chapter Twenty-Six: Setting God's Table

1. Matthew 6:1-4

2. Matthew 6:17-18

3. John 3:8

4. John 5:19,30

5. Psalm 23:5

6. "God in Heaven," Paulus Gerhardt (1607–1676)

7. Ephesians 4:22; Colossians 3:9

8. 1 Corinthians 4:6,18,19; 5:2; 13:4; Colossians 2:18

9. John 17:4

Chapter Twenty-Seven: Under the Tent

1. "As We Gather Now Together," Edward Cooney (1867–1960)

2. Matthew 6:9; Luke 11:2

3. 1 Samuel 1:1-28; 2:19

4. John 3:6

5. Matthew 19:23-26; Mark 10:23-27

6. 2 Corinthians 2:3-4

7. John 2:1-11

8. Matthew, chapters 5–7

9. Galatians 2:20-21

10. Philippians 1:21

11. Matthew 6:2,5,16

12. "Jesus Alone Can Save Me," Kate Ulmer

13. James 4:7-8

14. Romans 8:1-4; Galatians 5:25

15. Mark 8:34; 10:21

16. Galatians 5:24

17. Philippians 2:13

18. John 19:15; Acts 21:36; 22:22

19. Psalm 41:9

20. Ephesians 2:16-18

21. Romans 6:6; Romans 6:2; Galatians 2:19-20; Colossians 3:3

22. Colossians 3:9; Ephesians 4:22

23. 1 Corinthians 15:31

24. Romans 6:11

25. John 3:30

26. John 5:25-29; John 6:63

27. Revelation 3:20; Song of Solomon 5:2

28. Hebrews 4:11

29. "I Am Now a Child of God," Sam Jones (1877–1946)

30. Acts 14:12

31. Ephesians 4:7-13

32. 1 Timothy 4:14

33. 1 Corinthians 7:7; 2 Corinthians 12:1-31

34. Luke 2:49

35. Hebrews 12:17

36. Luke 23:39-43

37. Hebrews 12:1-2

38. "Nothing Matters But Salvation," John Martin (1876–1956)

39. Job 9:9

40. "No Reputation," Sam Jones (1877–1946)

Chapter Twenty-Eight: Struggle in St. Marys

1. Acts 17:27-28

2. John 3:1-8

3. Psalm 3:8

4. Matthew 7:1-3

5. John 4:23-24

6. John 6:53-58

7. Luke 1:41,44

8. Psalm 42:7

9. Matthew 15:7-9; Ezekiel 36:26

10. Acts 20:7-10

11. Psalm 148:8

12. Matthew 17:27

13. Luke 15:22-24

Chapter Twenty-Nine: The Shooting

1. Titus 1:5-9

2. Acts 11:30; 20:17

3. 1 Timothy 3:1-12

4. 1 Peter 3:15

5. Genesis 49:22

6. "If All Things Were Mine," Anna Olander (1861–1935)

7. 1 Corinthians 3:5-7

8. Revelation 2:4-5

9. Acts 12:5,12

10. Matthew 7:7-11; 18:19; 21:22

11. "Dear Jesus, As Thou Wilt," Benjamin Schmolck (1672–1737)

12. 2 Corinthians 6:4-10

Chapter Thirty: Farewell to a Mother in Israel

1. 1 Corinthians 9:5; Matthew 8:14

2. Luke 12:13-15

3. Matthew 26:51-65

4. Matthew 23:8-12

5. Matthew 7:7

6. Acts 9:36-42

7. Galatians 6:9-10

8. Matthew 5:46-48

9. Judges 5:7; 2 Samuel 20:19

10. "Abide with Me," Henry F. Lyte
    (1793–1847)

11. From a letter written by Jeanne
    Guyon (1648–1717)

12. 1 Corinthians 15:20-26,43-44,52-55;
    1 Thessalonians 4:16-18; Acts 1:9-11

13. "When Life Is Ended," James Jardine
    (1884–1969)

14. Psalm 116:15

15. Romans 10:15

16. Mark 16:15

17. Revelation 21:4

Epilogue

1. Matthew 12:1; Mark 11:12-14

2. Luke 9:57-59

3. 2 Corinthians 11:23-28

4. "Close to Thee," Fanny J. Crosby
    (1820-1915)

GLOSSARY OF HISTORICAL AND IDIOMATIC TERMS

Adze—a hand tool with a heavy steel blade attached at right angles to a wooden handle, used to dress timber.

Antimacassar—a cloth covering the back of chairs to prevent soiling. Macassar oil, used on hair during the 19th century, often stained the fabric.

Apothecary shop—an archaic word for drug store or pharmacy.

Apple peeler—a mechanical cast iron device with an oscillating blade. The peeler clamped onto a table and was patented around 1863.

Bairn—a Scottish idiom for a child.

Battleship linoleum—a tough heavy gauge linoleum used in kitchens after first being designed for use on ships.

Bed tick—a strong cotton fabric, often striped, used as a mattress cover.

Berlin, Ontario—settled by people of German origin. In 1916, torn apart by the tensions of World War I, this peaceful city changed its name to Kitchener. Many wished to distance themselves from the stigma attached to the name of the German capital, while others remained silent for fear of being accused of enemy sympathies.

Bertha—a wide deep collar, often of lace, usually to cover a low neckline.

Blind staggers—a symptom of several horse diseases in which the animal staggers and appears blind. Caused by inflamation of the brain or eating noxious weeds infected with fungus.

Boa—a woman's long thin scarf made of feathers or fur; common at the end of the 19th century. Sometimes included the animal's head and tail.

Bob sleigh—a sleigh with a moveable front bob or steering mechanism that enables the rider to turn it. Also described larger horse-drawn sleighs.

Bolster—a long narrow pillow or cushion.

Bootjack—a wedge-shaped device that grips the heel of a boot to enable the foot to be withdrawn easily.

Breeching—the part of a harness that passes behind a horse's haunches to prevent a wagon or buggy from rolling against the horse's hind legs.

Cannon bone—a bone in the legs of horses; an elongated fused metatarsal.

Carbolic soap—a rough soap made with a disinfectant ingredient.

Charlady—a British term for a woman hired to clean a house.

Chop—roughly ground oats or barley used as animal feed.

Cistern pump—a hand pump in the kitchen used to pump water from a cistern in the cellar. Rainwater from the roof filled this concrete reservoir.

Clincher—a blacksmith's tool used to bend the protruding points of the nails against the side of a horse's hoof.

Colporteur—a church employee who distributes Scriptures and other religious materials, often door to door.

Copper flashing—a thin metal sheet used to weatherproof the adjoining slopes of a roof or a chimney.

Concession—a land subdivision of a township survey; another name for the road that runs between concessions, usually one and a quarter miles apart.

Cooper—a person skilled in making or repairing barrels or casks.

Corduroy road—made by laying logs side by side; placed crossways over swampy areas of the road bed and covered with gravel.

Corker—old-fashioned slang (1891) for something or somebody striking or outstanding; an irrefutable remark that puts an end to discussion.

Corn mash liquor—is made from fermented corn mash distilled in a cooker using cornmeal, sugar, water, yeast, and sometimes bran.

Crazy quilt—a quilt made of random pieces of rich, colourful fabric and blanket stitched.

Curry—to brush or groom a horse.

Cutter—a type of sleigh with curved runners instead of wheels, pulled by a single horse over the snow.

Democrat—a style of buggy that had two or three parallel bench seats.

Doll's eyes—a plant of the buttercup family that grows in moist woods. Its white flowers turn to white berries, each with a single black spot.

Draper—a common 19th century term for a dealer in fabrics and materials.

Dresden-plate quilt—a quilt sewn in the design of elaborate fluted circles.

Driver—a light driving horse kept for pulling a buggy or cutter on the road, in contrast with the ponderous draught breeds used for heavy farm work.

Drugget—a coarse fabric.

Dump rake—a steel two-wheeled rake drawn by horses. A foot mechanism allowed the operator to lift the tines, releasing the hay into windrows.

Eaton Beauty doll—an elegant doll with head and hands of fine porcelain and outfitted in a velvet and silk dress; offered in Eaton's 1901 catalogue.

Face cord—a pile of cut and stacked firewood 16 inches deep by 4 feet high and 8 feet long; one-third of a standard 128 cubic foot bush cord.

Fanning mill—a hand-cranked implement that blew the chaff from the grain and screened the kernels according to size.

Farrier—a person who shoes horses or another name for a veterinary surgeon.

Fiddleheads—a young, edible, tightly coiled fern frond that resembles the spiral end of a violin (fiddle).

Fortnight—a period of fourteen consecutive nights; two weeks.

Flannels—bed sheets made of a soft light wool fabric.

Galloping consumption—a rapid wasting away of the bodily tissues; especially in tuberculosis of the lungs.

Gangway—the sloped mound of earth allowing access to the upper floor of a bank barn.

Gargling oil—a medicinal liquid used to reduce infection and inflamation of the throat.

German shensel cake—made from flour, sugar, butter, and peeled apples, cut in thin wedges. Normally served warm with whipping cream on top.

Gilt—a young female pig, especially one that has never given birth.

Grain cradle—a framework of several wooden fingers attached to a scythe to gather grain into bunches as it is cut.

Greengrocer—retail trader in fruit and vegetables.

Grippe—an archaic term for influenza or other stomach disorder.

Grog—diluted spirit, usually rum, as an alcoholic drink.

Guelph—the principal city in the County of Wellington boasting a population of 11,496 in the 1901 census; founded in 1827 by John Galt. The name is pronounced: "gwelf."

Hame strap—the strap connected to the two curved bars holding the traces of the harness and attached to the collar of a draught animal.

Hand—a unit of length equaling four inches used for measuring the height of a horse at its withers (taken from a man's standard handbreadth).

Hod—an open wooden box attached to a pole for carrying bricks or mortar.

Hoof stand—a stand used by a blacksmith to hold the horse's foot at the right height for working on.

Horehound—a bitter herb of the mint family with small white flowers that contain a bitter juice formerly used as cough syrup or flavouring; sometimes used in the making of a hard candy.

Ironmonger—a British word for a dealer of metal utensils, hardware, etc.

Jerkin—a sleeveless short jacket worn by men or women.

Johnny Appleseed (1774–1845)—A gentle itinerant who dreamed of a land without hunger, John Chapman spent forty-nine years planting apple seeds in the American wilderness.

Joiner—a person skilled in making finished cabinets, stairs, caskets.

Kneeler—a bench, hinged to the pew in front, on which a worshipper knelt during portions of the church service.

Kohlrabi—a variety of cabbage whose thickened stem is eaten as a vegetable; common during pioneer times.

Lectionary—a book containing appointed readings to be used in church services throughout the year.

Leghorn hat—ladies' hat style popular in the summer of 1902. A concoction of lace, velvet, and chiffon with silk flowers and foliage trimmed with feathers, priced from $4.50 to $10.00.

Leg-of-mutton—a sleeve or sail, tapering sharply.

Lemon balm—a perennial mint with white or yellowish flowers and aromatic leaves; used in flavouring food, liqueur, tea, and medicines.

Lightning rods—a metal cable terminating in sharp points, attached to the peak of a building to provide a safe path to earth for lightning strikes.

Lind, Jenny (1820–1887)—born in Sweden, she became one of the most popular opera singers of the 19th century, performing widely in both Europe and North America.

Mangling laundry—the process of squeezing the wash water out of the clothes by passing them between two heavy rollers.

McCormick harvester and binder—first machine controlled by one man and pulled by three horses which cut and bound grain in a single operation. McCormick sold 50,000 binders between 1877 and 1885.

Mensch—a Yiddish term meaning an honourable and ethical man.

Mercator's map—a map commonly used in classrooms of 1904, named after the Flemish cartographer and mathematician Gerardus Mercator. (1512–1594)

Merino—a particularly fine wool from a breed of sheep originating in Spain.

Monarch of the Glen—a commonly reproduced oil painting of a stag by Sir Edwin Henry Landseer. (1802–1873)

Mouldboard—the curved metal portion of a walking plough that rolls and inverts the soil.

Mow—the upper part of a barn where hay or straw is stored; the term can also refer to a pile of hay or straw.

Muntins—slender wood members in a window sash that divide it into panes.

Murther—an archaic or obsolete variation of the word "murder."

Nightjar—any of a family of nocturnal birds which have large eyes and feed on insects.

Northern Spy apples—an antique variety known for its tart flavour and yellow flesh; excellent for baking in pies or apple sauce.

Osgoode Hall—erected in 1829 by the Law Society of Upper Canada and named after William Osgoode, the province's first chief justice.

Pacer—a horse trained to move his legs in a particular gait.

Paling fence—a wooden fence made of upright boards.

Pie safe—a wooden cabinet with shelves and screen doors for the purpose of cooling and storing pies.

Pin money—money saved or earned by women for incidental purchases, often in coins or small denominations of paper currency.

Pinafore—an apronlike garment, usually with a bib, buttoned or tied at the back and worn over a dress.

Pitch holes—soft holes in the built-up layers of hard-packed snow, often appearing during a thaw. Caused by horses' shoes and sleigh runners, they were dangerous if sharp and deep enough to make a horse stumble.

Pocketbook—a leather pocket purse formerly used by men.

Pomade—perfumed oil to dress men's hair, making it smooth and shiny.

Prior—the head of a priory or other religious house; in an abbey, the person next below the abbot.

Purlin—the horizontal beam providing support for the rafters in a barn roof.

Quoined corners—the alternating squared stones or raised brick panels set in the external corner of a building for decorative effect.

Rag-and-bone man—a man who buys and sells discarded clothing and other household items.

Ragtag and bobtail—a derogatory term for common people.

Rainwater leader—the metal pipe used to carry rainwater from the eave trough to the ground or rain barrel.

Rasp—a coarse metal file with rows of raised teeth.

Redcoat—a British soldier.

Reefer—a man's short double-breasted jacket of sturdy wool; also called a reefing jacket.

Rod—a unit of length equal to 16½ feet. Most 100 acre pioneer farms measured 80 rods by 200 rods.

Rubbers—a rubberized waterproof overshoe.

S.S. #3—a common abbreviation for School Section No. #3.

Sad iron—a detachable wooden handle for pressing irons. Patented in 1871 by Mrs. Mary Potts, it permitted the user to heat a number of iron bodies on a stove, attach the handle to one of them and iron until it cooled. Priced in 1900 at 89 cents.

Sailor king—a common epithet used of King William the Fourth well-known for his love of the high seas. (1765–1837)

Sally Lunn cake—a flat round cake made from a sweet yeast dough, said to be named after an 18th century English baker who invented it.

Sarsaparilla—taken from the dried aromatic roots of tropical American prickly climbing plants having heart-shaped leaves. Promoted in the 19th century as a blood purifier or tonic.

Scours—prolonged diarrhea in young pigs or cattle.

Scuffling—a colloquial term for cultivating a crop or a garden.

Separator—the common term for threshing machine; also referred to the hand-cranked device invented circa 1870 and used to separate cream from milk by centrifugal force.

Shakedown—a pioneer term for a bed, particularly a makeshift one.

Shanks' pony—one's own legs as a means of transportation.

Sharp shoe—a horseshoe with raised metal cleats on the toe and heel of the shoe that cut into the ice or snow to give the horse stable footing in winter.

Sheaves—the plural of sheaf which is a bundle of reaped but unthreshed grain tied with one or two bands.

Shinplaster—paper money of small face value, usually twenty-five cents; printed in 1870, 1900, and 1923.

Shivers—something that is broken into fragments or small pieces.

Shoofly pie—a Pennsylvania Dutch recipe containing flour, brown sugar, and shortening covered with molasses, eggs, soda, and hot water.

Sir John A.—an abbreviation for Sir John A. Macdonald, the first prime minister of Canada. (1815–1891) Born in Glasgow Scotland, this colourful statesman was one of the Fathers of Confederation.

Slash—littered brush and wood chips that remain after felling trees.

Slate—an economical writing tablet of the same material as the blackboard used by 19th century schoolchildren. These wood-framed slates measured 8 inches by 11 inches or larger.

Slippery elm—a folk cure for skin disorders.

Smock—a loose protective garment made of blue denim and worn by farm workers. Priced in 1900 at 50 cents, heavy duty 75 cents.

Soffits—the underside of an overhanging eave on a building.

Spelt—a species of wheat, common in the 19th century, that has been used to develop cultivated varieties.

Spiles—a spout or rigid tube for tapping sap from the sugar maple tree; inserted into a hole that has been drilled in the trunk of the tree.

Spool bed—a bed with a wooden headboard and footboard made of turned spindles.

Spooner—a glass spoon holder usually kept in the centre of the table.

Sprigged—a pattern depicting small floral clusters common in 1901.

Stile—a set of steps over a fence to allow people to pass, but not animals.

Stooking—the work of setting clusters of sheaves upright in a field to dry the heads of grain.

Stone boat—a low solidly-built wooden sledge used to gather stones from the fields; drawn by horses.

Stone pig—a corked container made of crockery and filled with hot water to provide warmth under blankets.

Stuck pig—an expression describing a hog that has been killed by sticking a knife into its heart during butchering.

Sweating like a hen drawing rails—a humorous rural idiom describing extreme perspiration. Normally a team of horses would have been used to pull or draw fence rails.

Swill—wet feed, especially for pigs. Made by soaking ground oats and barley in a wooden barrel and often included kitchen waste or skim milk.

Taking a turn—a rural idiom meaning to experience a sharp change in health, usually a deterioration.

Tintype—an early process in which a positive photograph was taken directly on a thin plate of black-enamelled iron coated with a sensitized emulsion.

Toadflax—a perennial plant having narrow leaves and spurred two-lipped yellow-orange flowers. Also called butter-and-eggs.

Toad-in-the-hole—a British dish made of sausages baked in a batter.

Traveling a stallion—an expression referring to the business of leading a well-bred stallion behind a buggy from farm to farm to breed mares.

Trumpeter swan—a large North American swan having white plumage and black bill. Now extinct in Ontario, its former range included the Great Lakes region during the 19th century.

Ulster—a heavy double-breasted overcoat with belt or half belt.

Valenciennes lace—a flat bobbin lace typically having scroll and floral designs and originally made of linen; first made in Valenciennes, a town in northern France.

Vapour bath cabinet—a rubber-lined cabinet 30 inches square and 42 inches tall with alcohol heater and lamp. An opening in the top allowed the user's head to remain outside the steam.

Waist—a girl's or woman's blouse often with long sleeves and hooked or buttoned in the back.

Walker's Kilmarnock whiskey—in 1880 Alexander Walker opened a store in London, England, from which to sell this brand all over the British Empire; renamed 'Johnnie Walker' about 1900.

Wedding-ring quilt—a hand-pieced quilt sewn in the pattern of entwined wedding rings.

Wheat smut—a fungal disease of grain in which black sooty masses of spores cover the affected parts.

Whist—a card game for four players, common in the 19th century, that was the forerunner of bridge.

Wicket—a small opening, especially one fitted with a glass or grate; often used at train stations to sell tickets.

Widow's weeds—a dark mourning dress worn by a woman after her husband's death.

Wincey—a flimsy inexpensive fabric made of cotton or flannel, used in clothing during pioneer times.

Windrow—a long row of hay raked into a low ridge to achieve the best conditions for drying or curing.

Winterhalter, Franz Xavier (1805–1873)—a famous German portrait painter of European royalty who did at least 120 works for Queen Victoria and Prince Albert and their family.

ABOUT THE AUTHOR

Raymond Reid has lived his entire fifty-six years in the area of Guelph, Ontario, the core and focus of the novel's events. After graduation from school, he designed and built custom homes and later developed subdivisions, specializing in affordable homes. His building career extended over twenty-five years until the early 1990s, but he felt restless for something beyond the having and the getting. After struggling with one of the most difficult decisions he had ever made, he wound up his business and traveled extensively with his wife, Gretchen, and their son and daughter, Darren and Andrea.

In his travels he visited home churches and itinerant preachers in many parts of Europe and climbed high into the Italian Alps searching out the remote valleys where the primitive Waldensians took refuge prior to the Reformation. But still he needed something more, something that was eventually satisfied by the writing of *The Gate Seldom Found*.

Throughout the first three years of working on the novel, the author regularly invited input from the public at large and took the innovative approach of advertising in local newspapers and delivering flyers door to door to find readers with whom to share the manuscript. Hundreds of men and women from ages sixteen to eighty-six and from all walks of life read the work-in-progress and shared their feelings. The result is a book that truly reflects the yearnings in the hearts of many ordinary men and women.

The author greatly appreciates the friendships
that have come as a result of writing this book
and welcomes your candid comments.
Please send any correspondence to the postal
address below or e-mail him directly at:
woodcreekfarm@sympatico.ca.

Raymond Reid
R.R. #6, Guelph, Ontario
CANADA
N1H 6J3